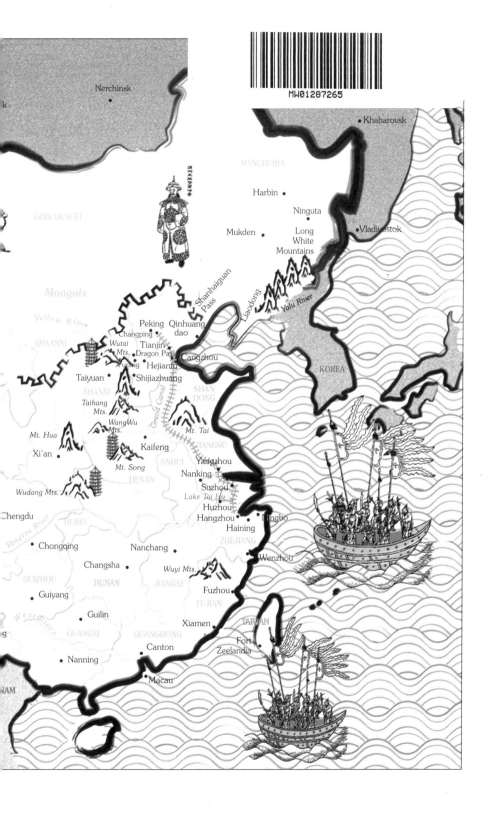

THE DEER AND THE CAULDRON

The Second Book

THE DEER AND THE CAULDRON

The Second Book

A Martial Arts novel
by
Louis Cha

Translated and edited
by
John Minford

OXFORD
UNIVERSITY PRESS

OXFORD
UNIVERSITY PRESS

Oxford University Press is a department of the University of Oxford.
It furthers the University's objective of excellence in research, scholarship,
and education by publishing worldwide in

Oxford New York

Athens Auckland Bangkok Bogotá Buenos Aires Cape Town
Chennai Dar es Salaam Delhi Florence Hong Kong Istanbul Karachi
Kolkata Kuala Lumpur Madrid Melbourne Mexico City Mumbai Nairobi
Paris São Paulo Shanghai Singapore Taipei Tokyo Toronto Warsaw

with associated companies in Berlin Ibadan

Oxford is a registered trade mark of Oxford University Press

Published in the United States by Oxford University Press Inc., New York

© Oxford University Press 1999

First edition 1999
This impression (lowest digit)
5 7 9 10 8 6 4

British Library Cataloguing in Publication Data
available

Library of Congress Cataloging-in-Publication-Data
Chin, Yung, 1924–
[Lu ting chi. English]
The deer and the cauldron: a martial arts novel / by Louis Cha;
translated and edited by John Minford,
v. <1 > cm.

ISBN 0-19-590325-0
Translations into English. I. Minford,
John. II. Title.
PL2848.Y8L7913 1997
895.1'352—dc21
97–36366
CIP

Printed in Hong Kong
Published by Oxford University Press (China) Ltd
18th Floor, Warwick House East, Taikoo Place, 979 King's Road, Quarry Bay
Hong Kong

For Tonto

CONTENTS

TRANSLATOR'S NOTE

Tamardy! Trinket is back! This Second Book continues the Adventures of that Incorrigible Turtle. I had once planned to call the three books of the translation 'Trinket in Trouble', 'The Trials of Trinket', and 'Trinket Triumphant'. These trilling (if not thrilling) subtitles were considered (no doubt justifiably) a trifle too trivial for the trilogy, and were abandoned, but I still feel they capture something of the romping spirit of Trinketian Trumpery that is this novel's True Life Force.

These ten chapters represent twenty chapters of the Chinese original. There has been quite a bit of condensation, but I (we) have tried to lose nothing significant from the plot. My unheralded collaborator David Hawkes has (once again) been far cleverer than I have at this business.

My students and colleagues at the Hong Kong Polytechnic (avid Cha-readers all!) have taught me a lot over the past four years. In particular, Agnes Chan and Joanne Tsui provided me with several valuable suggestions during the final stages of revising this volume.

And once again, all thanks and praise to my gifted editor Rachel May, whose superb literary kungfu skills and miraculous patience have salvaged many a careless blunder.

Hong Kong, November 1998

Important Dates in the Historical Background

1559 Birth in the North-Eastern Long White Mountains of Nurhachi, the Exalted Founder of the Manchu Imperial House of Gioro, descended from a noble family of the Jurched Tartars (rulers of China in the twelfth and thirteenth centuries, during the Jin or Golden dynasty).

1592 Birth of Abahai, eighth son of Nurhachi.

1572–1620 Reign of the Ming Emperor Wan Li; beginnings of the decline of the Ming (Bright) dynasty.

1616 Nurhachi declares himself Khan or First Emperor of the Later Jin (Golden) dynasty and presides over a growing Manchu state in the North-East.

1626 Death of Nurhachi, who is succeeded by Abahai, the Illustrious Ancestor.

1628 Accession of Chong Zhen, grandson of Wan Li, and last Emperor of the native (Han) Ming dynasty.

1636 Rise of rebel movements in northern and central China, including that led by Li Zicheng (General Bash-em); Abahai proclaims himself Emperor of the Qing (Pure) dynasty, in the Manchu capital Mukden (present-day Shenyang).

1638 Birth of Fulin (later to be the Emperor Shun Zhi), fourth son of Abahai.

1644 Rebel leader Li Zicheng enters Peking; the Emperor Chong Zhen commits suicide; the Manchu army enters Peking, aided by the turncoat Satrap Wu and his force of Chinese troops; beginning of the Manchu Qing dynasty proper in China and of the reign of Shun Zhi.

1646–1647 Manchu conquerors try to consolidate their hold over central and southern China; Ming Princes (Pretenders) establish short-lived refugee courts in the South.

1654 Birth of Xuanye (later to be Emperor Kang Xi), second son of the Emperor Shun Zhi.

1659 Coxinga, leader of the anti-Manchu resistance, tries to take Nanking but fails.

1661 Death of Empress Donggo, the Emperor Shun Zhi's favourite consort; also supposed death of Emperor Shun Zhi.

1662 Accession of Kang Xi. Ming Pretender Prince Gui taken prisoner in Burma and strangled in Kunming, with the connivance of Satrap Wu (acting on the orders of Oboi the Regent). Coxinga moves his base to Taiwan. Death of Coxinga. Formation, under Coxinga's General, Helmsman Chen Jinnan, of the Triad Secret Society, committed to the overthrow of the Manchus and the restoration of the Ming Imperial House.

1662–1663 Inquisition surrounding the *Ming History*.

1663–1664 Dutch fleet helps Manchus drive Coxinga's son from Taiwan; Manchu rule is established throughout mainland China.

1667 Kang Xi, aged thirteen, dismisses his Regents.

1669 Death of Oboi, formerly Chief Regent.

1673 Rebellion of Satrap Wu (Yunnan and Guizhou Provinces), Shang Zhixin (Guangdong Province), and Geng Jingzhong (Fujian Province)—the Three Feudatories.

1678 The Dzungar Prince Galdan invades Eastern Turkestan, taking Kashgar and Yarkand, then (1679) Hami and Turfan.

1681 Three Feudatories are finally put down.

1682 Death of Fifth Dalai Lama. The Grand Lama Sangge seizes power, and supports Galdan's territorial expansion.

1683 Manchus finally conquer Taiwan.

1686 Kang Xi calls unsuccessful conference of Mongols and Tibetans.

1689 Treaty of Nerchinsk between Manchus and Russia, defining their border.

1690 War finally breaks out between Galdan and the Manchus.

1696 Galdan is finally defeated by Kang Xi's army at the battle of Jao Modo.

For an excellent, readable account of the historical background to *The Deer and the Cauldron*, see the first three chapters of Jonathan Spence's book, *The Search for Modern China* (New York: Norton, 1990).

GLOSSARY OF PEOPLE AND PLACES

Dates given are historical ones; the novel does not always interpret history literally

AH KI *see* Blue Girl

AH KOR *see* Green Girl

AO BIAO The Blue Tiger. One of the Mu Family retainers, the much tattooed disciple of Shaker Wu.

AUREOLE, Father Abbot of Pure Coolness Monastery on the Wutai Mountains.

BAG-OF-BONES *see* Fat Dhuta

BASH-EM, General Li Zicheng (1605–1645), rebel leader who drove the last of the Ming Emperors from Peking in 1644, only to be ejected in his turn by Satrap Wu and the Manchus. His subsequent fate is unknown. One legend says that he did not die in 1645, but escaped to a monastery.

BAYEN, Brother Elderly Tibetan fighting lama from one of the great lamaseries of Lhasa.

BIG BEAVER Guan Anji, bearded Triad.

BLACK DRAGON MARSHAL Zhang Danyue, senior member of the Mystic Dragon Sect.

BLOSSOM One of the Empress Dowager's maids-in-waiting; Trinket's first girl-friend.

BLUE DRAGON MARSHAL Xu Xueting; elder of Mystic Dragon Sect.

BLUE GIRL Wang Ah Ki, twenty-year-old disciple of the White Nun.

BO HANFENG, Maple Mu retainer, descended from one of the original Paladins of the Ming dynasty; surviving younger brother of Bo Hansong (Pine).

BRIDGE OF HEAVEN (*Tianqiao*) District of Peking famous for its storytellers, acrobats and other street-performers.

BUBBLING SPRING, Temple (*Yongquan si*) The easternmost temple on the Wutai Mountains.

BUDDHA LIGHT, Monastery (*Foguang si*) One of the more eminent religious establishments on Wutai.

CHALJU, Colonel Commander of the Plain Yellow Banner; Colonel of the Valiants.

CHANG, Princess *see* White Nun

CHONG ZHEN, Emperor (1611–1644) Zhu Youjian, last Emperor of the Ming dynasty, who hanged himself on Coal Hill when the rebel leader Li Zicheng entered Peking.

CLARITY, Brother Shaolin Monk attached to the Vinaya Hall.

CORDIAL, Brother One of the Eighteen Lohans of Shaolin.

COXINGA (1624–1662) This was the Western name (sometimes written Koxinga, based on a title Guo-xing-ye given him by the Ming Court) for the naval warrior Zheng Chenggong, Marshal Zheng, Prince of Yanping, leader until his death of the anti-Manchu resistance, cryptically referred to as Dragon Brother by the Triads. His father was a Fukienese pirate and adventurer, his mother Japanese; the remnants of his army are supposed to have formed the first Triad Lodges.

CRYSTAL, Father Fat, twittering Abbot of Buddha Light Monastery on Wutai.

DENG BINGCHUN Member of the Mystic Dragon Sect, and lover of Mao Dongzhu, the false Empress Dowager, who dresses up in woman's clothes and poses as a lady-in-waiting. Father of Princess Ning.

DOLONG Colonel and Chief Intendant of the Palace Guards, a member of the Plain White Banner.

DONGGO, Empress (1639–1661) The 'fox-woman', favourite consort of the Emperor Shun Zhi, and mother of Prince Rong.

DORGON (1612–1650) Fourteenth son of Nurhachi, regent during the early years of Shun Zhi's reign.

DOUBLET Pretty young orphaned maid given to Trinket by Widow Zhuang, as a reward for having killed Oboi. A superb fighter, she becomes Trinket's devoted companion.

DUAN JIN *see* Yellow Dragon Marshal

EIGHTEEN LOHANS Elite Corps of Shaolin Fighting Monks.

EMPRESS DOWAGER Wife of Shun Zhi, daughter of the Mongol Prince Korcin, of the Borjigit clan; referred to by Trinket as the Old Whore. It transpires during the course of the Second Book that the 'Old Whore' is not in fact the real Empress, but an impostor, a woman named Mao Dongzhu, the daughter of Mao Wenlong, a Ming general who had fought against the Manchus on the frontier for several years.

FAN, Brother Fan Gang, Triad with bass voice.

FANG YI Mu Family retainer; beautiful sister-in-arms of the Little Countess, much admired by Trinket.

FAT DHUTA Also known as Bag-of-Bones. Originally a very fat disciple of the Mystic Dragon Sect; becomes excessively thin and tall after taking the Leopard Embryo Pill. Tries to ambush Trinket and take him to Snake Island. Brother-in-arms of Thin Dhuta (Lump-of-Flesh).

FEMALE REPOSE, Gate of (*Kun'ning men*) One of the northern gates within the Forbidden City, leading from the Hall of Female Repose to the Imperial Flower Garden.

FEMALE REPOSE, Hall of (*Kun'ning gong*) Residence of Empress, north of the Hall of Heavenly Purity.

FENG, Brother Feng Jizhong, Triad with superb kungfu skills.

FENG THE BLOODLESS SWORD Feng Xifan; general in service of Zheng Jing; evil mentor (and father-in-law) of Zheng Keshuang; supreme master of the Kunlun School of kungfu.

FUDENG Son of head of the Plain Blue Manchu Banner.

GALDAN (?1644–1697) Mongol prince, Bushktu Khan of the Dzungars (a tribe of the Eleuths or Western Mongols), with ambitions to rule over Chinese Turkestan. Finally defeated by Kang Xi's armies in 1696.

GAO YANCHAO Young Triad, member of the Green Wood Lodge. Trinket's contact man.

GENG JINGZHONG (died 1682) Chinese Bannerman, Satrap of Fujian Province, later involved in the Rebellion of the Three Feudatories against Manchu rule.

GOLDEN PAVILION, Monastery of the Pure Land Buddhist establishment north of the Monastery of the Holy Precinct on Wutai.

GOODLY AUSPICES, Temple of the Local temple in Fuping County town, east of the hills leading to Wutai.

GREEN GIRL Chen Ah Kor, beautiful sixteen-year-old disciple of the White Nun, much admired by Trinket, but infatuated with the 'cad', Zheng Keshuang.

GU YANWU (1613–1682) Renowned Loyalist scholar and philosopher.

HAI DAFU Hai Goong-goong, Old Hai; an elderly eunuch, and formidable Martial Arts adept, loyal to the Emperor Shun Zhi; referred to by Trinket as the Old Devil, or Old Turtle. Dead by the beginning of the Second Book (killed by Trinket, during a confrontation with the Old Whore).

HATIEMO Mongol envoy sent by Galdan to Yunnan.

HEADLONG, Brother Religious name taken by Manchu ex-soldier Hebacha, who accompanies the Hermit Emperor, Shun Zhi (Brother Wayward), and guards him on Wutai.

HEAVENLY PURITY, Palace of (*Qianqing gong*) Central compound of the Forbidden City, used as an audience chamber by the Manchu monarchs.

HEBACHA *see* Brother Headlong

HOCHABO Head of the Bordered Red Manchu Banner, owner of one copy of the Sutra. Colonel Rui steals the Sutra from him (on the Empress Dowager's orders) and murders him.

HOLY PRECINCT, Monastery (*Lingjing si*) One of the oldest religious establishments on Wutai.

HONG, Leader Hong Antong, elderly Leader of the Mystic Dragon Sect.

HONG, Madame Su Quan, beautiful young Consort of Hong Antong, Leader of the Mystic Dragon Sect.

HUANGFU, Mr Civil Chinese official from the Western Marches, between the province of Sichuan, and Tibet.

HUBAYIN Tibetan Lama, acting under the orders of the Grand Lama Sangge.

IRON DRAGON *see* Liu Dahong

KANG, Empress (1640–1663) Deceased mother of the Emperor Kang Xi.

KANG, Prince (1645–1697) Giyešu, great-grandson of Nurhachi.

KANG XI, the boy Emperor (1654–1722) This was the reign title of the second Manchu Emperor; his personal name was Xuanye (which means, roughly speaking, Dark Effulgence—he calls himself Misty, for Trinket's benefit). He was the third son of the Emperor Shun Zhi, whom he succeeded at the age of eight. By the beginning of the Second Book he has got rid of the overweening Regent Oboi, and assumed the reins of power.

LAUREL ('Laurie Goong-goong') Junior eunuch in attendance on Old Hai, murdered and subsequently impersonated by Trinket.

LI, Brother Li Lishi, tall thin Triad.

LITTLE COUNTESS Mu Jianping, younger sister of Mu Jiansheng, descended from old Duke Mu. At the beginning of the Second Book, she has been 'kidnapped' by Trinket.

LITTLE FLOWER Galumphing peasant woman, impersonated by a Mu Family retainer in order to incriminate Sir Zheng.

LIU DAHONG Shifu of Mu Family; a ruddy-faced, vigorous old man with wispy white whiskers and piercing eyes, known on River and Lake as the Iron Dragon.

LIU YAN *see* Sister Swallow

LIU YIZHOU Member of Mu Family, of pale complexion and questionable courage; in love with Fang Yi.

LU, Doctor Senior member of Mystic Dragon Sect; a man of wide reading and culture, and a connoisseur of calligraphy and painting.

LU YIFENG Churlish official in the service of Satrap Wu; he ill-treats Xu Tianchuan, and is punished (at Trinket's request) by the Satrap's son; subsequently he is made Governor of the Black Hole, a prison in Kunming.

LUMP-OF-FLESH *see* Thin Dhuta

MANJUSRI Monastery A lamaist establishment on Wutai.

MAPLE *see* Bo Hanfeng

MA BAO Brigadier on staff of Satrap Wu.

MADAME HONG *see* Hong, Madame

MAO DONGZHU *see* Empress Dowager

MAO WENLONG Ming general, father of Mao Dongzhu.

MATERNAL TRANQUILLITY, Hall of (*Cining gong*) Empress Dowager's residence, in the north-west corner of the Forbidden City.

MILITARY PROCLAMATION, Gate of (*Xuanwu men*) The south-west gate of the Tartar City.

MU FAMILY This was the common appellation for the powerful faction surrounding the descendants of Old Duke Mu, who had made the South-Western Province of Yunnan their personal fief throughout the Ming dynasty, and were loyal to the Ming Pretender, Prince Gui. They were implacably opposed to Satrap Wu, who after the arrival of the Manchus supplanted them in the South-West. The Family had its own distinctive style of kungfu.

MU JIANSHENG The Young Count.

MU JIANPING The Little Countess.

MU, Old Duke (1345–1392) Mu Ying, one of the foremost generals, and adopted son, of the founder of the Ming dynasty, Zhu Yuanzhang. He was the founder of the Mu Family, and was much spoken of in *The Heroes of the Ming*, from which Trinket loves to tell stories.

MU, Young Duke (died 1661) Mu Tianbo, descendant of Old Duke Mu, loyal supporter of the Ming Pretender, Prince Gui.

MYSTIC DRAGON This fanatical sect, with its powerful mantra-based kungfu, is based on Snake Island. Details of the sect emerge in the Second Book. It is divided into Five Branches, each having its own colour, and its own Dragon Marshal. Among other things, there has been a purge of the Sect's 'elders', in favour of the young, and more fanatical, 'acolytes'. And it is explained that one of the ways in which the Leader, Hong Antong, maintains control over the members of his Sect is by giving them the powerful Leopard Embryo Pill, which then makes them dependent on regular doses of the antidote.

NING, Princess The Emperor Kang Xi's fifteen- or sixteen-year-old tomboyish 'half-sister'; in actuality, the daughter of Mao Dongzhu and a Han-Chinese father, Deng Bingchun.

NURHACHI (1559–1626) The Grand Progenitor, founder of the Manchu (Qing) dynasty.

NURTURING NATURE, Hall of (*Yangxing dian*) Hall in the north-east corner of the Forbidden City.

NURTURING THE MIND, Hall of (*Yangxin dian*) Hall in northwest section of the Forbidden City, between the Hall of Maternal Tranquillity and the Hall of Heavenly Purity.

OBOI, Lord (died 1669) This Imperial Guardian and Former Regent was one of Dorgon's trusted men. He was elevated to the rank of Duke in 1656 and at the death of the Emperor Shun Zhi (1661) he was one of the Four Regents for the boy Emperor Kang Xi (with Soni, father of Songgotu; Ebilun; and Suksaha). He is arrested and put to death in the First Book.

OBSCURUS, Father Xuanzhen Daoren, Taoist Triad. Orphaned son of a frontier fur-trader shot dead by the Russians.

OSHOKHA Head of the Bordered Blue Manchu Banner.

PALADINS, the Four These were the four original aides of Old Duke Mu, whose surnames were Bo, Fang, Liu, and Su, and whose descendants continued to be loyal retainers of the Mu lineage.

PERCEPTION, Father Monk at the Shaolin Monastery; Master of Discipline.

PRAJNA HALL One of the compounds of the Shaolin Monastery.

PURE COOLNESS, Monastery The establishment on Wutai to which the Old Emperor, Brother Wayward, has retreated.

QIAN, Butcher Triad, pork-butcher to the Palace.

RADIANT, Brother Shaolin monk who knows a great deal about poisons.

RAT-TRAP CONGRESS Gathering of various sectors of the anti-Manchu Resistance held at Hejianfu, to co-ordinate efforts for a Ming Restoration and plan the demise of Satrap Wu.

ROOTLESS, the Taoist Red Dragon Marshal; senior member of the Mystic Dragon Sect.

RUI, Lieutenant-Colonel Rui Dong, of the Palace Guards, known as the Invincible Iron Palm.

SANGGE Chinese name for sDe-srid Sangs-rgyas-rgya-mtsho, Tibetan Grand Lama, formidable amd somewhat sinister exponent of Tantric kungfu. Historically, Sangge was the Tepa, or Temporal Ruler, of Tibet, and seized absolute power after the death of the Fifth Dalai Lama in 1682, allying himself with Galdan.

SHANG KEXI (died 1676) Satrap of Guangdong Province, later involved in the Rebellion of the Three Feudatories against Manchu rule.

SHI LANG (1621–1696) An officer in Coxinga's army, who surrendered to the Manchus. One of the teachers of Zheng Keshuang.

SHUN ZHI, Emperor (1638–1661?) The Hermit Emperor, often referred to as the 'Old Emperor' (even though he is, in fact, barely forty years old), and sometimes the ex-Emperor. Shun Zhi was the reign title (the words mean literally 'obedience and rule') of Fulin, first Emperor of the Manchu dynasty, the ninth son of Abahai. He was known to have been deeply interested in Zen Buddhism, and it was widely believed that after the death of his favourite consort, the beautiful Empress Donggo, in the autumn of 1661, the young Emperor, 'pining for his lost mistress and weary of the dull routine of statecraft, voluntarily handed over the government to four of his Ministers and retired to the contemplative life.' As one contemporary poet wrote, 'He threw away the Empire as one who casts away a worn-out shoe. Following the example of the Lord Buddha, he preferred to seek the mystic solitudes.' This is the legend that lies behind the plot of *Deer*. The more conventional version of Shun Zhi's death is that he died of smallpox.

In the Second Book, he appears in the guise of Brother Wayward, in retreat in the hermitage behind the Pure Coolness Monastery. His Zen Master is the Venerable Yulin.

SIMPLE, Brother Elderly white-bearded monk at the Shaolin Monastery, in charge of the Prajna Hall; pedantic kungfu scholar, with an encyclopaedic knowledge of martial arts.

SITU BOLEI Officer in Wu Sangui's army, who in disgust at Wu's collaboration with the Manchus, withdrew with some 30,000 of his men to the Wang Wu Mountains (on the borders of Henan and southern Shanxi Provinces) and formed the resistance band, with its own distinctive style of kungfu, known as the Wang Wu Clan. His son, Situ He, commanded the Wang Wu detachment that ran into Colonel Wishy-Washy's regiment en route to Shaolin.

SNAKE ISLAND Snake-infested island in the Gulf of Bohai, lair of the Mystic Dragon Sect.

SONGGOTU (died 1703) This powerful Manchu statesman of the Heseri clan, third son of the elderly Regent Soni, becomes Trinket's 'adopted brother'.

SU GANG Known as the Magic Hand, a distinguished member of the Mu establishment.

SU QUAN *see* Madame Hong

SWALLOW, Sister Liu Yan, the Sow, plump member of Mystic Dragon Sect, posing as a lady-in-waiting in the Palace, and working for the Empress Dowager. Comes to a sticky end.

TAO, Aunt Tao Hongying, once a maid serving the Princess Chang (see the White Nun), the Princess Royal, daughter of the last Ming Emperor. She has sworn vengeance on the Tartars. Adopts Trinket as her 'real' nephew.

THIN DHUTA Alias Lump-of-Flesh; originally a thin disciple of Mystic Dragon Sect, becomes fat as a pumpkin after taking the Leopard Embryo Pill. One of the False Empress Dowager's lovers.

TREASURE, Father Trinket's *nom de réligion*, given him by the Abbot of Shaolin.

TRIBULATION *see* White Nun

TRINKET Wei Xiaobao, the novel's principal character. He is an incorrigible scamp born to Spring Fragrance in the Yangzhou whorehouse, Vernal Delights. He is an egregious impostor, knave, and poltroon, and a young man of many identities. In the course of his (never very convincing) attempts to learn kungfu from Whiskers Mao he acquires the *nom de guerre* Little White Dragon. In the Imperial Palace he kills, and takes the identity of, the eunuch Laurel. He meets and befriends the young Manchu monarch Kang Xi, whom he knows as Misty, and who calls him by the affectionate nickname Laurie. Subsequently in his encounter with the Triads he is made Master of the Green Wood Lodge. During his eventful visit to Snake Island, he is appointed White Dragon Marshal of the Mystic Dragon Sect. In order to enable him to travel to the Wutai Mountains, the Emperor appoints him Lieutenant Trinket Wei of the Imperial Guard. He is subsequently promoted to Lieutenant-Colonel and adopts the Manchu-style sobriquet Wishy-Washy. As a monk, he takes the *nom de réligion* Father Treasure. Kang Xi subsequently makes him a Viscount (Lord Wei).

TSERENG, Brother Tsereng-bLo-do, Tibetan Grand Lama of Manjusri Monastery, on Wutai.

UNIVERSAL SALVATION, Monastery of Buddhist establishment on the summit of Brocade Peak, on Wutai.

VERNAL DELIGHTS One of Yangzhou's more up-market pleasure-houses, home of Trinket's mother.

WANG WU CLAN *see* Situ Bolei

WARTHEAD Character invented by Trinket, to explain his own presence in the Forbidden City.

WAYWARD, Brother Emperor Shun Zhi's Buddhist name, taken when he retreated to his hermitage on the Wutai Mountains.

WHISKERS Mao Eighteen, notorious brigand, who escapes from prison, befriends Trinket, and takes him to Peking. Does not feature in the Second Book.

WHITE DRAGON MARSHAL Zhong Zhiling. Executed for failing to accomplish a Palace mission, and replaced by Trinket.

WHITE NUN One-armed Shifu of Green Girl; also called Tribulation; once upon a time Princess Chang, the Princess Royal, daughter of last Ming Emperor Chong Zhen. A refined and beautiful woman, practitioner of the Buddhist style of kungfu known as Iron Sword.

WIDOW ZHUANG Her husband and many other Zhuang menfolk were executed at Oboi's orders, as part of the Ming History Inquisition (see Prologue to First Book). She and other Zhuang womenfolk escape on their way to penal servitude in the north-east, and take up residence in a 'haunted house', where they set up shrines to the victims of the purge.

WISDOM, Father Abbot of Shaolin Monastery.

WU, Satrap (1612–1678) Wu Sangui, the Big Traitor, was a turn-coat Ming general who joined forces with the Manchu commander Dorgon to drive the Chinese rebel Li Zicheng (General Bash-em) out of Peking. He subsequently established his own fiefdom in the south-west, in Yunnan Province.

WU, Shaker Wu Lishen, the Shaker Lion, retainer of the Mu Family, Martial Arts veteran and brother-in-arms of Iron Dragon Liu.

WURTLE Yu Ba; servant provided to escort Trinket on his journey to the Pure Coolness Monastery by the Abbot of the local temple in the county town, Fuping.

WUTAI, Mountains (literally Mountains of the Five Terraces, from the five pagoda-crowned peaks of the range) This was a sacred range or massif on the eastern borders of Shanxi Province (said to have been the location of an apparition of the Bodhisattva Manjusri), with a long-standing link to the Imperial houses of China. Of its 150 monasteries, some 24 were Lamaist. 'It remains to this day an important place of pilgrimage. . . . On those days when the air is bright and sunny the range's grey and silver outline can be seen from afar, and when the sun sets behind it, the holy hill glows like a purple pyramid. Then it speaks of peace and per-fection, of remoteness from the worries and futilities of earth, of another life, better and nobler than ours. This life the pilgrims, toiling slowly upwards, hope to attain through patience and perse-verance' (Bredon and Mitrophanow, *The Moon Year*, 1927.) The Manchus regarded their great Founder Nurhachi as a re-incarnation of Manjusri,' and according to some, the name Manchu itself derives from this.

WU YINGXIONG (died 1674) The Little Traitor, eldest son and heir of Satrap Wu.

XU TIANCHUAN The Eight-Armed Ape, Triad plaster-seller.

XU XUETING *see* Blue Dragon

YANG YIZHI One of the Little Traitor's entourage, a big man befriended by Trinket.

YELLOW DRAGON MARSHAL Duan Jin; Mystic Dragon elder of shifting loyalties.

YOUNG COUNT Mu Jiansheng, brother of the Little Countess; head of the Mu Family; a tall, thin young man of twenty-five or six, with a vigorous, manly air.

YULIN, Venerable Elderly Zen Buddhist monk, inscrutable Shifu of Brother Wayward.

ZENG ROU Fifteen-year-old female member of Wang Wu Clan, daughter of one of Situ Bolei's officers.

ZHANG KANGNIAN Palace Guard, friend of Trinket.

ZHANG, Old Elderly peasant who helps the Riders of the Mystic Dragon find shelter from the storm.

ZHAO QIXIAN Palace Guard, friend of Trinket.

ZHENG JING, Prince (died 1681) Eldest son of Coxinga, and present Prince of Yanping. In 1664 he organized the government of Taiwan, and in 1674 went to the aid of Geng Jingzhong, Satrap of Fujian, in his revolt against Manchu rule.

ZHENG KESHUANG (?1670–1707) Sir Zheng; second son of Prince Zheng Jing; a dashing (and insufferable) young man of twenty-three or so. He took over nominal control of Taiwan on the death of his father in 1681, finally surrendering to the Manchus in 1683. His father-in-law was Feng Xifan.

ZHENG KEZANG (died 1681) Eldest (illegitimate) son of Zheng Jing; son-in-law of Chen Jinnan, the Helmsman. He took charge of Taiwan in 1679.

ZHONG ZHILING *see* White Dragon Marshal

GENERAL GLOSSARY OF TERMS
relating to kungfu, Chinese culture, history, and society

BALD PATE Common appellation for any male member of a Buddhist monastic order (they had to shave their heads); but it also carries connotations, especially in Chinese fiction, of a more ordinary sort of male member.

BEILEH Manchu prince of the Blood of the third degree.

BONZE A word used since the sixteenth century to designate Chinese and Japanese Buddhist priests.

BROTHER-IN-ARMS (Chinese *shixiong, shidi*) Term used by fellow disciples of the same martial arts Shifu.

CAMERARIUS Monk charged with accomodating visitors.

CINNABAR FIELD (Chinese *dantian*) The Inner Cinnabar is the alchemic elixir which the Taoist and Martial Arts adept distils. Cinnabar Field is the name given in Taoist, alchemical and Martial Arts terminology to the area in the lower abdomen, where all energy is stored. 'It is the root of the human being. Here men keep their semen and women their menstrual blood. It houses the gate of harmonious union of yin and yang. It is also called the Palace that keeps the Essence.' (The Book of the Centre, in Schipper, *The Taoist Body*, 1993.)

DHARMA The Buddhist law, or doctrine.

DHUTA Buddhist recluse, one who follows ascetic practices and precepts in order to purify body and mind.

DRAGON The dragon is one of the supreme symbols of Chinese culture. Unlike the Western dragon, which is so often the primordial enemy, and combat with which is the ultimate test of virtue, the Chinese dragon is essentially an auspicious and spiritual beast, embodying cosmic energy, and representing the Yang principle. It is also a symbol of power, and associated with the Emperor.

DRAGON GATE (Chinese *longmen*) This term is used for the Five Branches into which the Mystic Dragon Sect is divided.

DRAGON LINES (Chinese *longmo*) Sometimes translated as

Dragon Veins. According to *fengshui*, the system of Chinese geomancy (the traditional science of harmonising human habitations with the earth's natural environment), it is extremely hazardous to interfere with or cut across features of the landscape that the geomancer declares to be parts of the Terrestrial Dragon's body, especially the Dragon Lines or Veins, through which flows the vital energy (*qi*) of the earth.

DZUNGARS Western nomadic Mongol tribe, who dominated large areas of Central Asia, including Tibet, in the late seventeenth century. Galdan was their leader.

EIGHTEEN FIGHTING LOHANS OF SHAOLIN Traditionally there were Eighteen Buddhist Arhats or Lohans (Chinese *luohan*), sixteen of them Indian, the other two Chinese. In Shaolin kungfu lore, there have been various groupings of eminent fighting monks. The group of Eighteen in *Deer* includes Father Aureole, formerly of the Shaolin Temple, subsequently Abbot of Pure Coolness Monastery on Wutai, and Brother Cordial of the Dharma Hall of Shaolin.

FENGSHUI *see* Dragon Lines

FIVE DRAGON DISC Talismanic symbol of authority in the Mystic Dragon Sect.

FOX-SPIRITS (Chinese *hulijing*) These were-vixen are one of the favourite archetypes of feminine beauty in Chinese literature. These beautiful, sensual, irresistible creatures could be destructive and heartless, ruthless and vindictive (sucking out the essence of their lovers), but could also be tender and vulnerable, and capable of deep love and loyalty. They were an expression of the deeply ambivalent attitude of the Chinese literati towards women. The power of feminine beauty and sexuality, as personified by the fox-spirit, inspired them, and simultaneously incapacitated them, with a mixture of infatuation, fascination, and terror. This fear (of which Trinket, being still only a boy, was still innocent) was at the root of the sexual vampirism conducted under the guise of the so-called Taoist techniques of the bedchamber.

GOLDEN GATE School of Martial Arts based in Liaoning Province.

GOONG-GOONG Term of address for a Palace Eunuch.

IMMORTAL (Chinese *xian*) An eternally youthful being, the supreme Taoist adept, one who through occult practice has mastered supernatural and magical skills, and attained physical and spiritual immortality.

INTERNAL FORCE (Chinese *neiqi*) The vital energy stored within the body, which the Martial Arts practitioner strives to conserve and strengthen through various exercices.

KARMA The law of cause and effect, by which actions and thoughts in one life create a necessary response and due retribution in a sub-sequent life. Human destiny is determined by acts done in an earlier existence.

LEOPARD EMBRYO PILLS A potent drug (with steroidal, or hormonal, properties?) used by the Leader of the Mystic Dragon Sect to induce dependency among his followers. Its administration necessitates doses of an antidote. Among those affected by Leopard Embryo dependence are the fake-Empress Dowager and Doctor Lu. The scrawny Fat Dhuta (aka Bag-of-Bones), and his counterpart, the corpulent Thin Dhuta (aka Lump-of-Flesh), were transformed from their original shapes as a consequence of not taking the antidote.

MANJUSRI (Chinese *Wenshu*, or *Manshu* in Southern dialects) A bodhisattva who symbolises the wisdom aspect of mind, and is greatly revered in Lamaist Buddhism as the Enlightener of the World. He often appears in iconography as the left-assistant of Shakyamuni Buddha, seated on a lion, with a sword in his right hand and a book resting on a flower in his left. He is the presiding genius of the Wutai Mountains, and is said to 'appear at the mountain retreat from time to time, sanctifying its misty peak so often veiled in clouds'. (Bredon and Mitrophanow, *The Moon Year*, 1927.)

MANTRA A mystic syllable, word, or verse recited to still the mind and harness certain energies.

PRAJNA The fundamental wisdom inherent in all men.

PURE LAND Sect of Buddhism, founded in China by Master Huiyuan (died 417), its adherents teaching salvation through faith in Amitabha Buddha (the Buddha of the Pure Land or Western Paradise), aided by single-minded recitation of mantras and visualisation techniques. Widespread in China and Japan.

REALGAR ELIXIR Realgar (Arabic *rehj al-ghar*, 'Powder of the Cave', Chinese *xionghuang*, 'Male Yellow', the mineral disulphide of arsenic) was a substance much used in traditional Chinese and Indian medicine.

SHANZAI! Exclamation expressing admiration and approval.

SISTER-IN-ARMS *see* Brother-in-arms (term used by female disciples)

STELE An inscribed stone tablet, often erected to commemorate a person or an event.

TIBET An independent state during the Ming dynasty (1368–1644), it came under Dzungar domination (1635–1713), and was invaded by Kang Xi in 1720.

TURTLE (*wugui*) Creature symbolising both immortality (often supporting inscribed stone tablets, as in chapter 14) and immorality (metaphor for the penis). Turtle-head is a common term of abuse (a reference to the glans penis).

VINAYA The vinaya, or discipline, texts of Buddhism constitute one of the Three Baskets (Tripitaka) of scripture. The Vinaya Hall was the disciplinary centre of the Shaolin Monastery complex.

ZEN Japanese pronunciation of Chinese word *chan*, from the Sanskrit Dhyana, contemplation or meditation. The mission of the legendary founder of the Zen School of Buddhism, the Indian monk Bodhidharma (fl. 470–516), was to point directly to the Mind as a path to enlightenment.

NOTE ON PRONUNCIATION

In this book, Chinese names and place-names are in general spelled according to the Chinese system known as *Hanyu Pinyin*, which is now internationally accepted. (Occasional exceptions to this rule include well-established geographical names such as the Yangtze River, and the cities of Peking, Nanking and Canton.) The following short list may help readers with some of the more difficult sounds used in the Pinyin system:

Letter	Pronunciation
c	*ts*
q	*ch*
x	*sh*
z	*dz*
zh	*j*

The following very rough equivalents may also be of help to readers.

Word	Pronunciation
Bo	*Boar* (wild pig)
Cai	*Ts'eye* ('It's eye', without the first vowel)
Cang	*Ts'arng*
Chen	*Churn*
Cheng	*Churng*
Chong	*Choong* (as in 'book')
Chuan	*Chwan*
Dang	*Darng* or *Dung* (as in 'cow dung')
Dong	*Doong* (as in 'book')
Emei	*Er-may*
Feng	*Ferng*
Gui	*Gway*
Guo	*Gwore*
Jia	*Jeeyar*
Jiang	*Jeeyung*
Kong	*Koong* (as in 'book')
Lii	*Lee*

Long	*Loong* (as in 'book')
Lü	*Lew* (as in French 'tu')
Qi	*Chee*
Qian	*Chee-yenne*
Qing	*Ching*
Rong	*Roong* (as in 'book')
Shi	*Shhh!*
Si	*Szzz!*
Song	*Soong* (as in 'book')
Shun	*Shoon* (as in 'should')
Wen	as in 'forgot*ten*'
Xi	*Shee*
Xiao	*Shee-ow* (as in 'shee-cow' without the 'c')
Xing	*Shing*
Xiong	*Sheeoong*
Xu	*Shyeu* (as in French 'tu')
Yan	*Yen*
Yi	*Yee*
You	*Yo*-heave-ho
Yu	*Yew* tree (as in French 'tu')
Yuan	*You, Anne!*
Zha	*Jar*
Zhe	*Jerrr!*
Zhen	*Jurn*
Zhi	*Jirrr!*
Zhou	*Joe*
Zhu	*Jew*
Zhuang	*Jwarng*
Zi	*Dzzz!*
Zong	*Dzoong* (as in 'book')
Zuo	*Dzore*

CHAPTER 10

*In which Trinket acquires a
Second and most Delectable
Companion, and learns what it
means to be Jealous; an
Attempt is made on his Life;
the Emperor plays at Detective
and offers Trinket another
Opportunity to enrich Himself*

A Summons from the King of Hell

The Little Countess giggled, threw back the bedspread and climbed
out of bed. She laughed.

'*My* Vital Points opened a long time ago. Why are you back
so late? I've been sitting here waiting for you for ages.'

'Who opened them?' asked Trinket in some surprise.

'You just have to leave them for six or seven hours, and they
open themselves,' she explained. 'Come on, let me help you into
bed. I have to go now.'

'Oh no you don't!' cried Trinket agitatedly. 'You can't! The
cuts on your face haven't healed properly yet! They need some
more of my ointment.'

The Little Countess laughed.

'You're so naughty, always fibbing, and trying to scare me to death. You never carved anything on my face, did you?'

'How do you know?' asked Trinket.

'Because I got out of bed and looked at my face in the mirror, that's how! And there was nothing the matter with it!'

Trinket looked at her face. It was clean, and positively glowing and smooth. Every last bit of his bean-fudge and lotus-seed mash 'New-Skin Ointment' was gone.

'What an idiot I am not to have noticed!' he thought to himself.

'Of course there's nothing the matter with your face *now*,' he said promptly. 'It's thanks to my special ointment. That's why I went to so much trouble to get you these extra pearls. I had to hunt everywhere! *And* I've bought you a pair of lovely little knick-knacks.'

'Show me!' cried the Little Countess.

'Open *my* points first,' said Trinket.

'That's easy!'

As the Little Countess reached out her hand, she glanced at Trinket. He was rolling his eyes histrionically. She stopped and smiled.

'I almost fell for it again! If I open your points, you'll never let me go.'

'I promise I will!' said Trinket. 'By my plight and troth!'

The Little Countess hesitated.

'Well, don't you want to know about the knick-knacks?' asked Trinket. 'They're very cute. One's a boy, one's a girl . . .'

The Little Countess could not help being curious.

'Are they rabbits?'

Trinket shook his head.

'No, ten times cuter than rabbits.'

'Goldfish?'

Trinket shook his head even more vigorously.

'*Much* cuter than goldfish!'

The Little Countess made several more guesses, none of which was correct.

'Well, what *are* they?' she cried impatiently. 'Show me!'

'Open my points first,' insisted Trinket.

'No,' said the Little Countess. 'I've got to leave straight away. My brother must be terribly worried about me by now.'

Trinket frowned, and gave a sudden grimace of pain.

'What's the matter?' cried the Little Countess. 'Are you hurt?'

'I was rushing around so much trying to find your stupid pearls, I tripped and hit my chest on a rock. It suddenly got worse again. All because you . . . you . . . you closed my points, and now you won't open them. I . . . I . . . can't . . . t . . . brea . . . the . . .' moaned Trinket, his voice trailing very touchingly into silence.

Suddenly he rolled his eyes like a fainting man, and held his breath. The Little Countess put her hand to his nostrils. There was no trace of breath. She gave a scream and started trembling with terror.

'What's the matter with you?'

'You . . . closed . . . closed the wrong points,' stammered Trinket. 'You . . . you closed . . . a fatal . . . one!'

'No! No, that's impossible,' said the Little Countess in some agitation. 'I *couldn't* have done. My Shifu taught me how to do it, and I couldn't have got it wrong. I closed the Wasteland and the Walkway, and then the Pool of Heaven. I'm sure that's right.'

'You . . . you were probably so frightened, you went and clos . . . closed the wrong ones,' said Trinket. 'Oh! Oh! I can feel the blood pounding in my veins! It's like a raging torrent! I can feel my whole Inner Force flowing backwards! My whole body's gone topsy-turvy! I think I must be possessed . . .'

'By what? A devil?'

'Yes, yes, that's it, a devil! You've killed me! Closing points is *very* advanced kungfu, much too advanced for you! You've been fooling around with me, and now look what you've done! It wasn't the Wasteland or the Walkway—you've gone and opened the Gate of Death! Deeeeeeeaaaaaath!' wailed Trinket. He would have come up with the names of one or two genuinely fatal points, but unfortunately didn't know any.

There was one thing he was right about, however. Opening and closing Vital Points *is* a highly advanced branch of kungfu. There are hundreds of such points dotted all over the body, some of them situated just a few centimetres from one another. The Little Countess was young and far from expert in this art, so it was quite plausible that in the heat of the moment she might have closed the wrong points. (In actual fact, she had done nothing of the kind. She had closed the three correct points with great accuracy, though with a certain lack of force in her fingers.)

Trinket's display of agony was so convincing that she now began to doubt herself.

'Maybe I opened your Middle Chest point by mistake?' she said anxiously.

'Yes, yes, that's it!' replied Trinket. 'But don't worry, I . . . I know you didn't do it on purpose. I won't blame you when I'm dead. When the King of Hell asks me how I died, I swear I won't tell. I'll say I did it myself. I'll say it was all my own fault!'

The Little Countess felt her heart welling with gratitude and remorse.

'Don't say any more, let's...let's open your points first. Maybe there's still a chance!'

She quickly began massaging him on his chest and beneath his armpits, and because she had not closed the points very forcefully in the first place, a little rubbing and squeezing soon did the trick. Trinket was able to move again.

'It's no good!' he groaned. 'It's the Gate of Death! I'm done for!'

'Maybe there's something else I can do,' cried the Little Countess, now quite distraught. 'I . . . I'm really so sorry, it's all my fault!'

'I know how good you are really,' said Trinket. 'That's why when I die, I promise my ghost will stay with you day and night.'

The Little Countess let out an ear-piercing scream.

'Your *ghost*!'

'Yes, my ghost has to stay with whoever killed me. But don't be afraid. It won't hurt you.'

'But . . . but I didn't mean to kill you,' said the Little Countess, more terrified than ever.

Trinket sighed.

'I promise I'll never scare you. I'll just look after you. During the daytime, when you're sitting down, my ghost will shoo off the flies; when you're asleep at night, it'll keep away the mosquitoes. And it'll come to you in your dreams and tell you lots of wonderful stories.'

'Why are you being so nice to me all of a sudden?' sighed the Little Countess sadly. 'Oh dear! I just wish this tragedy had never happened. I wish you weren't going to die.'

'I'll only have one regret when I die,' said Trinket. 'That you promised me something during my lifetime, and never kept your word.'

'What was it? What did I promise?'

'You promised to call me "my darling" three times. Remember? Oh, if I could just hear those precious words on your lips before I died, then I think I could go peacefully!'

The Little Countess had grown up far away in the deep South, on the Mu Family estates in Yunnan, protected and loved by her parents, by her brother, and by a host of officials, generals, maids, servants, and other family retainers. She had never been lied to or intimidated in her entire life. She was used to hearing the plain truth, and at first she had seen no reason to doubt Trinket. But then he had started hopelessly overdoing it: the more he spoke, the more carried away he became, and by the time he got to the three 'my darlings' even she could detect a sly twinkle in his eyes. She was naive, but she was not stupid. It finally dawned on her that he was teasing her.

'Liar!' she cried, drawing back from him. 'You're not dying at all, are you?'

He laughed.

'If I don't die now, I'll die in a couple of days.'

'No, you won't.'

'Well, *sometime* or other I'm bound to. And if you don't call me "my darling" three times, when I do die my ghost is bound to follow you wherever you go. It will be forever crying "My . . . sweetheart . . . my . . . sweet . . ."'

Trinket managed a long drawn-out growling sort of noise. It sounded extremely gruesome. Then he stuck out his tongue, and looked just like the ghost of a hanged man. The Little Countess was absolutely terrified again and ran to the door.

Seeing her pull out the wooden door-bar, Trinket dashed forward and quickly seized her by the waist.

'You can't go. There are too many fierce ghosts lurking outside.'

'Hands off!' protested the Little Countess. 'I'm going home!'

'You can't!' insisted Trinket.

The Little Countess raised her right hand, and brought it down with a sharp chopping motion on Trinket's right wrist. Trinket turned his own palms upward, intending to seize her forearm, but she drew her elbow back quickly, and at the same time clenched her left fist, striking at the top of his head. Trinket ducked backwards, neatly escaping her blow, and wrapped his arms around her legs. She replied to this with a move known as the Tiger's Leap, bringing her left hand sweeping down at him. This time Trinket was unable to dodge, and took a sharp crack on the shoulder. He tugged at the Countess with all his might, and they both went tumbling to the ground, her on top of him.

Trinket immediately leapt up and grappled with her. She aimed a quick Ring Chain Double Kick at his face. He dodged out of the way, at the same time twisting back her left forearm. The Little Countess had obviously been taught these moves by an excellent Shifu, and she was a far better fighter than Trinket. In serious combat, he would not have stood a chance. But he was not too bad at this kind of close scrapping. The Little Countess managed to give him two hard blows to the chest, but then he succeeded in seizing her right arm and twisting it back. He laughed.

'Surrender?'

'No!' she cried.

Trinket knelt on her back, pinning her to the ground.

'Now?'

'No! Never!' she cried.

Trinket applied extra force, and raising her twisted arm, yanked it towards him. The Little Countess screamed with pain.

In the past, when Trinket and Kang Xi were fighting, neither of them would ever give up, far less cry out, however much pain they were in. Not until one side had conclusively gained the upper hand, and victory was assured. Then the other side would call out 'I surrender!', and the next round would begin at once. Trinket was therefore shocked to see the Little Countess burst into tears at her first setback.

'Useless girl!'

He gave a snort of contempt and let her go.

Ghost or Whore?

At that very moment, there was a knocking on the window-frame.

'Listen!' said Trinket in a barely audible whisper. 'It's a *ghost!*'

The Little Countess turned around in abject terror, and hugged him tightly.

There was another knock on the window-frame, followed by a series of creaks as the window was pushed open. This time even Trinket was frightened.

'It *is* a ghost!' His voice was shaking.

The Little Countess threw herself onto the bed and crept trembling under the covers.

The window was pushed slowly open, and an eerie, high-pitched voice drifted into the room:

'Laurel . . . Laurel . . .'

At first Trinket thought it was the old eunuch Hai Dafu's ghost come to get him. But then he realized it was a female voice.

'It's a woman ghost!' he cried in terror, staggering backwards, until his legs gave way beneath him completely and he collapsed onto the bed.

A sudden gust of wind blew out the candles. Now Trinket and the Little Countess could see nothing. But they could sense the presence of a third person in the room.

'Laurel . . . Laurel! The King of Hell has summoned you. He says you killed Old Hai Goong-goong!'

The woman's voice sounded cold as ice.

'I didn't kill him!' was what Trinket *meant* to say in reply. But he was so terrified, that all he could do was open his mouth and gawp.

'The King of Hell has ordered me to arrest you and take you for punishment. You are to climb the Mountain of Knives, and be dropped into the Wok of Boiling Oil! Laurel, this time there is no escape!'

Trinket suddenly realized who it was: this woman was no ghost, it was the Empress Dowager! But this did nothing to allay his fears.

'A real ghost would have been better than *her*!' he thought in panic. 'I might have been able to get away from a ghost. But I don't stand a chance against the Old Whore. She wants me dead. I know too much. She wants to shut me up for good.'

Ever since he had overheard her talking that night with Old Hai, and had discovered a part of her secret, he had known that his life was in peril. One day she would certainly come for him and kill him. But then the days went by, and still she made no move, and after some time the danger began to fade from his mind. He began to assume that she must have believed him when he said that he had heard nothing of her conversation with Old Hai. Or else she was giving him a chance, reckoning that he would never dare to expose her, that he was too indebted to her for her earlier kindness in promoting him to eunuch-in-charge of the Imperial Catering Department.

Such were the speculations that raced through Trinket's mind. But the *real* reason for the Empress Dowager's delay in coming to get Trinket (or 'Laurel', as she knew him) was a great deal simpler. She herself had been badly injured in the fight with Old Hai. Seeing 'Laurel' survive the older eunuch's devastating kick, she had assumed he must be a young fighter of great Inner Force, and deemed it dangerous to take any further risks with him for the time being. She had decided to wait, until such time as her own injuries were healed and *her* Inner Force fully recovered. Then, when the moment was right, she would strike. She could trust no one but herself to do this dark deed. Some hired assassin might learn too much from 'Laurel', even in the last minutes before the little eunuch died. The Empress Dowager was a woman of unstoppable determination, prepared to snuff out anyone who stood in her way, whether that person was an Imperial consort, a prince, a general, or an important official. Disposing of a little eunuch was a mere bagatelle.

So she bided her time. Even tonight she was still not fully recovered, but she had decided she could wait no longer. She must act. She had hidden outside Trinket's apartment, and then his mentioning of the word 'ghost' just as she was opening the window had been her inspiration. She climbed into the room, still unaware of the Little Countess's presence, slowly concentrated her strength, and raising her right hand, began striding towards the bed.

Trinket had no intention of putting up a fight, and wriggled under the bedspread. The Empress Dowager brought down the edge of her open palm. The blow struck both Trinket and the Little Countess at the same time. Fortunately the quilting was thick enough to absorb a certain amount of the impact.

She raised her hand for a second strike, and brought it down more powerfully than the first time. As her palm made contact with the bedspread, it was pierced by something extremely sharp. She was wounded! The pain was excruciating! She gave a great cry, and leapt clear of the bed. At that very moment voices could be heard from outside the window.

'Assassins! Assassins in the Palace!'

The Empress Dowager started, thinking for a moment that somehow her plan to kill the little eunuch had been discovered. But how? She had told no one. Meanwhile the pain in the palm of her hand was growing more intense with every second. She retreated, and clambered out through the window, without even bothering to find out if Trinket was dead or not.

As she landed on the ground, two men attacked her from behind. She whipped round and swept her fists through the air in the countermove known as the Double Rear Guard, delivering two well-aimed blows to the chest, which sent both men crashing to the ground.

Even as they fell, the clanging of gongs could be heard echoing throughout the Palace, and a voice in the distance shouted: 'Platoon One and Platoon Two to protect His Majesty! Platoon Three to protect Her Majesty!'

'They're over here!' yelled another voice behind a rockery, closer at hand.

The Empress Dowager could tell it was one of the Palace Guards, and immediately hid herself behind the bushes. The throbbing wound on her palm was growing more and more difficult to endure. She could now make out the shapes of several clusters of men fighting fiercely, and the clashing of their weapons reached her ears across the darkened grounds of the Palace.

'So there *are* intruders in the Palace! But who?' she wondered. 'Friends of Old Hai? Supporters of Oboi?'

From far away drifted sounds of more orders, as yet more Palace Guards were dispatched, while closer at hand torches and lanterns began to gather from every direction, forming a circle of light. Sensing that this might be her last opportunity to escape, the Empress Dowager crouched down, then jumped from behind the bushes out into the open, and ran in the direction of the Hall of Maternal Tranquillity.

She had only covered a short distance, when she encountered a man hurrying towards her.

'Halt!' he shouted, thrusting a pair of vicious-looking fighting clubs into her face. It was another guard.

She dodged slightly to one side, then feinting with her wounded right hand, she struck at the man's shoulder with her left palm. The man lowered his shoulder to evade the blow, then spun round and brought the club in his left hand swinging upwards. The Empress Dowager dodged again to the left and hit back, this time with her right palm. They exchanged quite a few such moves in quick succession.

'It's a woman!' shouted the man.

The Empress Dowager needed to finish him off quickly, before reinforcements arrived.

'I am Her Majesty the Empress Dowager!' she blurted out.

The guard was momentarily stunned. In that precious moment of hesitation, she struck him a double-handed blow on the chest, sending him to an instant death. She herself gasped for breath, then leapt into the bushes.

A Password

The Empress Dowager's first blow had caught Trinket in the small of his back, and knocked the wind out of him. In a desperate last attempt to save himself, he had pulled out his dagger, and held it point upwards beneath the quilt. With her second blow, she had impaled her hand on the dagger.

Trinket waited until she had jumped out of the window, then lifted one corner of the quilt. He could hear a confused hubbub of voices outside—no doubt the Empress Dowager's men coming to get him. Quickly he threw back the quilt and leapt out of bed, saying to the Little Countess, 'Come, let's go!'

'It hurts . . .' sobbed the girl.

The Empress Dowager's first blow had caught the Little Countess with more force than Trinket, and fractured her left leg.

'What's up with you?' asked Trinket, grabbing her by her collar, and hauling her out of bed. 'Just run for it! Hurry!'

The Little Countess tried stepping on the ground with her right foot, but immediately felt an agonizing pain in her left leg, lost her balance, and went tumbling onto the floor.

'My leg . . . It's broken!' she cried, bursting into tears.

Trinket was in much too much of a panic to be sympathetic.

'Great timing! You would have to choose *now* to go and break a leg . . .'

His one thought was survival. She could break four legs, or eight . . . She could leave a dozen bits of leg lying around the room, for all he cared . . .

He hurried to the window, and looked out, hoping that there would be no one outside, and he could spring out into the garden. He got there just in time to see the shadowy outline of the Empress Dowager executing her Double Rear Guard. One of the two men flew through the air and crashed hard onto the ground right under the window. Even in the dark, Trinket was able to make out that he was wearing a Palace Guard's uniform. He was curious why the Empress Dowager should want to kill a Palace Guard. Then he saw her go skulking off into the bushes. Several yards away from her, six or seven men were engaged in fierce combat.

'Catch the assassins! Get them!' shouted a voice in the distance.

'So they haven't come for me after all!' thought Trinket, with mixed feelings of joy, fear, and confusion.

Peering into the distance, he saw the Empress Dowager fighting another guard. The guard's metal clubs glimmered in the shadows. The struggle lasted for a while, and then she finished him off and disappeared into the dark once more.

Trinket turned around. The Little Countess was sitting on the floor, groaning with pain. Now that he was in no immediate danger, he was a little more disposed to be nice to her.

'Does it hurt a lot?' he whispered. 'Sh! There's someone out there who wants to catch you, so you'd better keep very quiet!'

The terrified Little Countess complied at once.

A voice outside the window shouted:

'The Black-Legs are too many for us! To the Mountains!'

'That's our men!' exclaimed the Little Countess in utter astonishment.

'Your men? How do you know?' asked Trinket.

' "To the Mountains!" is a Mu password. Just . . . just help me up. I want to have a look.'

'They've come to the Palace to rescue you, haven't they?' said Trinket.

'I don't know,' said the Little Countess. Then suddenly: 'Is this the Palace?'

Trinket did not answer her question.

'They mustn't find out that she's in my room,' he was thinking to himself.

He clamped a hand over her mouth and whispered in his most frightening voice:

'Don't make a sound! If the guards find you, they'll break your other leg. And then I'd really be upset!'

There was a loud scream outside, followed by a cheer.

'Two down!'

'They're heading east! After them!'

Gradually the hullabaloo died away, and Trinket loosened his hand.

'Your friends seem to have gone for good.'

'No, they haven't,' replied the Little Countess. 'It's just a temporary retreat. That's what "To the Mountains" means.'

'And who are the Black-Legs?' asked Trinket.

'The Tartar guards.'

The Girl beneath the Window

Suddenly they heard groans of pain coming from outside the window. It was a female voice, evidently not a Palace Guard.

'That must be one of the assassins!' cried Trinket. 'I'll finish her off with my dagger!'

'No . . . Don't kill her! She's probably one of our people,' said the Little Countess, supporting herself on Trinket's shoulder, and hopping to the window on her right foot. She could see two figures down below.

'Southern Skies and Northern Lands . . .' she began whispering through the window, when Trinket reached out his hand, and clamped it tightly over her mouth.

'Beneath the Throne of the Peacock King,' returned the female voice from beneath the window. 'Is that . . . the Little Countess?'

If this woman discovered the whereabouts of the Little Countess, thought Trinket, it could mean big trouble for him. He quickly raised his dagger and was about to hurl it at her through the window, when the Little Countess seized his wrist, and he felt a sharp pain under his armpit, which obliged him to loosen the hand that had silenced her.

'Sister, is that you?' asked the Little Countess.

'Yes! What are you doing here?' replied the voice.

'What the hell are *you* doing here?' cried Trinket.

'Please . . . please don't be hard on her! She's my sister-in-arms.' The Little Countess turned from one of them to the other as she spoke. 'Sister, are you hurt?' To Trinket: 'Please save her! Please! She's always been so good to me!'

'I don't need any help from *him*!' said the voice with a groan. 'And anyway, *he* couldn't save anyone's life even if he wanted to.'

Trinket struggled hard to free himself, and the Little Countess finally let go.

'Smelly little tart!' he cried to the owner of the voice. 'Who the hell does she think she is? I'm not taking that from a third-rate little kungfu slut like her! Tamardy! I can save lives! I could save twenty or thirty girls like her without batting an eyelid! Seventy, eighty...a hundred!'

At that moment, more shouts could be heard in the distance.

'Get them all! Don't let a single one of them escape!'

The Little Countess was desperate. She begged Trinket to help.

'Please save my sister! I . . . I'll call you *it* . . . three times. My darling, my darling, *my darling*! There!'

Finally she had done it! Trinket was ecstatic.

'Sweetheart! What would you like me to do for you?'

The Little Countess blushed.

'Save my sister!' she whispered.

'Don't!' protested the voice outside fiercely. 'He can't even save himself.'

Trinket snorted contemptuously.

'For the sake of my *dear sweetheart* the Countess, I *will* save your life! My dear, the two of us must never break our word. *I'll* save your sister, and then *you'll* call me "my darling" for ever and ever.'

'Yes!' replied the Little Countess. 'Whatever you want! My darling, my darling brother, my darling uncle, my darling grandpa if you like!'

As she said this she gave Trinket a gentle push, and he vaulted through the window. He found himself in front of a female form in black, lying huddled up on the ground just below.

'Come on. Up you get. Or the guards'll mince you into little pieces and use you to stuff dumplings . . .'

'I don't mind! One day someone will avenge me.'

'Stubborn little tart, aren't you!' said Trinket. 'Anyway, they won't kill you straight away. First they'll strip all your clothes off and . . . rape you.'

'Then finish me off now!' spat the voice furiously.

Trinket smiled.

'I've got a much better idea. Why don't *I* strip your clothes off, and rape you myself.'

As he said this, he bent down and made as if to put his arms around the girl. She tried to slap him angrily on the face, but was too badly wounded to manage more than a feeble sort of tap. Trinket laughed. He lifted her up in his arms and helped her through the window and into the room. The Little Countess limped forward, and staggered with her to the bed. Trinket was about to climb back into the room himself, when suddenly he heard another barely audible voice coming from near his feet.

'Lau . . . Laurel Goong-goong, that girl . . . that girl . . . you . . . you mustn't . . .'

It was the guard who had been sent flying by the Empress Dowager. He was still alive, though badly wounded and incapable of movement.

'I suppose he's right really,' thought Trinket to himself. 'I ought to hand the girl in. But then what about the Little Countess? They might find out about *her*!'

The decision was quickly taken. He pulled out his dagger, and stabbed the guard in the chest.

'Sorry about that,' said Trinket, to the unfortunate corpse. 'Forgive me. If only you'd kept your mouth shut, I wouldn't have had to kill you.'

He searched every inch of the nearby garden for any further survivors, but only found five more corpses, three of them Palace Guards, two intruders. He heaved the body of one of the intruders up onto the window-sill, its head protruding into the room, its feet hanging outside into the garden. Then he stabbed it a few times in the back with his dagger for good measure.

'He . . . he's one of our people,' said the Little Countess in a frightened voice. 'He was dead already. What did you need to do that for?'

Trinket humphed.

'I had to. If you want me to save that smelly tart of a sister of yours.'

'*You're* the smelly one, not me!' protested the girl, from where she lay on the bed.

'How would you know?' asked Trinket.

'Your whole room stinks!'

'It smelled nice enough, till you arrived.'

The Little Countess interrupted them.

'Would the two of you please stop? You don't even know each other! Sister, what are you doing here? Did you come . . . to rescue me?'

'No, we didn't even know you were here. When we found out that you'd disappeared, we searched everywhere, but it was hopeless . . .'

She was already out of breath.

'Why don't you just shut up!' said Trinket.

'And if I *don't* shut up? What are you going to do to me then?'

'Nothing,' replied Trinket. 'You'll wear yourself out sooner or later. Oh dear! The Little Countess is such a nice, gentle girl; but you're—'

'No, no, you don't understand,' the Little Countess hurriedly interposed. 'She's really very nice.'

She went on:

'Sister, are you badly hurt?'

'Of course she is,' said Trinket. 'I told you, she's a third-rate little kungfu slut, and she obviously can't fight for peanuts. I shouldn't think she'll live more than three hours. She'll probably die before dawn.'

'No! She mustn't! My . . . my *darling* . . . You must save her, *please!*'

'I would rather die!' growled the girl. 'I don't need any favours from him! Little Countess, why do you keep calling him . . . calling him *that*?

'Calling me what?' asked Trinket.

The girl didn't fall for it.

'Little *ape*! That's what *I'll* call you!'

'Well, in that case, we can be Mr and Mrs Ape!'

Trinket was an old hand at this kind of whore-house repartee. He had heard no end of it at Vernal Delights as a small boy. The girl tried to ignore him, and lay there panting in pain.

Trinket took a candlestick from the table, and proposed that he should examine her wounds.

'Don't you *dare* look at me! *Don't!*' she cried.

'Stop screaming like that! Do you want the guards to come running in here and rape you?'

Trinket approached her with the candlestick in his hand. Through the blood smeared all over her face he could make out that she was a young woman of extraordinary beauty, about seventeen or eighteen years old.

'So, the smelly little tart turns out to be quite a babe!'

'Don't be so rude about my sister!' protested the Little Countess. 'She . . . she *is* beautiful.'

'All the more reason for me to marry her!' said Trinket.

The girl protested vehemently, and struggled to sit up and hit him. But the pain was so great that she could only gasp, and collapse onto the bed again.

As far as matters sexual and matrimonial were concerned,

theoretically Trinket knew it all. As a child he had heard such things endlessly discussed in the whore-house—by other people. But he had never taken them seriously himself. Even now he didn't actually *mean* to marry the girl, or have sex with her, not in any real sense; he was just having a bit of fun at her expense, baiting her, enjoying her reaction.

'Be patient!' he said mischievously. 'You'll have to wait until we're properly wed! This isn't a whore-house, you know! Aiyo! You're bleeding all over the bed.'

The girl was indeed seriously injured, and the blood was still seeping from under her clothes.

Just at that moment a group of people came hurrying up outside.

'Laurel Goong-goong, Laurel Goong-goong!' shouted one of them loudly from the garden. 'Are you all right?'

Now that the intruders had been driven off, a number of Palace Guards had been dispatched to ensure the safety of the Emperor, the Empress Dowager, and a couple of high-ranking consorts, while others had received orders to protect senior officials and some of the more important eunuchs.

'Get onto the bed,' he whispered to the Little Countess.

He covered both the girls with the bedspread, and closed the bed-curtains.

'Come on in, I've got one of them here in my room!' shouted Trinket.

A shudder passed through the body of the girl, but she was too weak even to sit up.

'Don't do it!' the Little Countess pleaded with Trinket, *sotto voce*. 'Don't hand her over to the guards!'

'She wouldn't be my wife,' Trinket whispered back. 'Why should I do anything for her?'

As they were talking, a dozen guards came up to the window.

'Here he is!' one of them shouted. 'Here's the man!'

'Yes, that's him!' said Trinket casually. 'He tried to climb into my apartment, so I went for him with my dagger.'

The guard held up his lamp, and examined the corpse. It had several wounds in the back, and blood was running down the clothes, over the window-sill, and onto the floor.

'I think you should run along,' said Trinket to the guards. 'You never know, you may find another one hiding in some dark corner. If you do, give him a good beating; if it's a woman, take off her clothes and . . . you know, have a bit of fun with her!'

The guards burst out laughing. Trinket asked them to remove the corpse from the window, and they left.

Ointment and a Splint

Trinket closed the window, turned around, and lifted the quilt.

'You're so naughty!' said the Little Countess with a smile. 'You had us really scared . . . Aiyo!'

Her hand had touched a large patch of blood on the mattress. The other girl's face had now turned an ashen white, and she was breathing very faintly.

'You must find out where she's been hurt,' said Trinket, 'and try to stop the blood.'

'Go...go away!' said the girl. 'Little Countess, the wound's here, on my chest.'

She had lost a great deal of blood, and Trinket was now genuinely afraid that she might die at any moment.

'Little Countess, have you got any ointment you could use?'

'No.'

Trinket heard a ripping sound as the Little Countess tore off the girl's blouse.

'Aiyo!' she screamed. 'What's this?'

Trinket could see a two-inch-long wound right below her right breast. Blood was pouring from it.

'She mustn't die!' moaned the Little Countess helplessly.

The girl was overwhelmed with a mixture of fear and shame. Her voice was trembling.

'Don't . . . don't let him see!'

'Come on,' said Trinket. 'It's no big deal.'

But even he began to panic when he saw how much blood was still flowing from her wound. He looked around the room for some strips of cloth to bandage her with, and spotted the little mortar containing his bean-fudge and lotus-seed mash.

'This magical mixture of mine is *very* effective,' he announced proudly.

He scooped some out and smeared it on her wound. The texture of the ointment was very gluey, and it did in fact succeed quite well in clogging up the wound and staunching the flow of blood. Trinket's fingers were now very sticky, and the sight of the girl's trembling little breast inspired him with an irresistibly mischievous notion. Very casually, as if it was the most natural and thoughtless thing in the world, he began rubbing the leftover mixture into the breast itself.

This time it was not fear that mingled with the girl's shame, it was fury!

'Little Countess!' she screamed. 'Kill him!'

'Sister, he's only trying to help!' said the Little Countess, rather feebly.

The girl almost fainted with rage. She was much too weak to do anything.

'You must close her points at once,' ordered Trinket. 'If she talks or moves around too much, she'll only lose more blood. She might die.'

'All right!' replied the Little Countess, and proceeded to close the points on the girl's stomach, armpits, and legs.

As the Little Countess begged her friend not to move, she suddenly became aware again of the pain in her own broken leg, and tears welled up in her eyes.

'I think you'd better lie down,' said Trinket.

He remembered as a child in Yangzhou watching the bone-setters mend the broken arms of his street-urchin friends, how they used to set the break with a splint made of two pieces of wood, then apply a herbal liniment of some kind. He pulled out his dagger, sliced two legs from a chair, and fashioned from them a rough splint, which he bound tightly to the Little Countess's broken leg. But he still needed the ingredients for the liniment. An idea occurred to him at once. He turned to the Little Countess:

'You two stay in bed, and keep quiet.'

He closed the bed-curtains, blew out the candle, and unbarred the door.

'Where . . . where are you going?' asked the Little Countess.

'To find some medicine for your broken leg,' said Trinket.

'You will come back as quickly as you can, won't you?' she said.

'I will.'

Something about her pathetic tone of voice gave Trinket a little thrill. He rejoiced at the prospect of being her saviour. He barred the door from the inside, and jumped out through the window, closing it behind him. Now no one in the Palace would dare to try entering his apartment, with the possible exception of the Empress Dowager, or the Emperor himself.

Medical Supplies

He had only taken a few steps, when he felt an ache in the small of his back, where the Empress Dowager had hit him.

'If the Old Whore wants me dead, I must get out of here as soon as possible!'

He walked towards some lights. A couple of guards on patrol dashed forward to greet him as soon as they saw him.

'How many of your men have been injured?' asked Trinket.

'Goong-goong, seven or eight guards are badly hurt, fourteen or fifteen lightly.'

'Where are they?' said Trinket. 'Show me.'

'Certainly, Goong-goong! We really appreciate your concern,' said the guards, and led the way. There were some twenty wounded men lying in the Palace Guards' mess-room, and four Imperial Physicians were in attendance, working hard to treat their injuries.

Trinket went up to the men and made a great show of expressing his concern, commending them for their loyalty and bravery, and asking their names one by one. But all the while he was paying the most careful attention to the way the Imperial Physicians were treating the various knife wounds, internal bruises, broken bones, and other injuries.

'I think I'd better have a supply of different types of medicine myself,' said Trinket casually. 'Just in case. Then if one of the guards gets hurt, I'll be able to give him first aid myself before the doctor arrives. You never know when those intruders might be back.'

'A very wise precaution, Laurel Goong-goong,' said the guards.

'In fact, just a moment ago, three of them tried to kill me,' Trinket went on. 'I dealt with one, but the other two got away. One of them hit me hard in the small of the back. It still hurts.'

'After all,' he was thinking to himself, 'it's true, the Old Whore *did* try to kill me!'

The four physicians, hearing that Laurel Goong-goong was hurt, left their patients at once, and came over to examine him together. They removed his gown, applied some medicine to the large bruise on his back, and gave him a herbal decoction to take internally. Trinket asked them to wrap up quantities of different types of drugs for him, which he put carefully away in his inside pocket, having first ascertained exactly how to use each one. Then he asked for two splints. Before he left, he showered the guards with more compliments and expressions of his undying concern. His attempts at courtly language were still far from perfect, and were interlarded with many a tamardy-this and a tamardy-that, but what did the guards care? They were so overwhelmed to have received all this attention from the Emperor's favourite (and from one who had himself also received wounds in defending His Majesty's person), that they themselves would gladly have gone out and been wounded again twice over.

Trinket the Physician

When Trinket reached his apartment, he pressed his ear to the window, and listened. There was absolute silence within.

'Little Countess, it's me,' he whispered.

He was afraid that if he climbed in unannounced, the girl might mistake him for an intruder, and welcome him with a well-aimed sword-point—in which case he would be needing all of his medical supplies for himself.

'We've been waiting for you for ages,' said the Little Countess, glad to see him return.

Trinket clambered in, closed the window, lit a candle, and drew apart the bed-curtains. The injured girl and the Little Countess were lying side by side. When the girl caught sight of Trinket, she closed her eyes immediately. The Little Countess beamed at him with gratitude.

'Little Countess, let me put some medicine on your wound for you,' said Trinket.

'No, I'd like to treat my sister first,' she replied. 'Would you please hand me the medicine. I'll put it on for her.'

'Why do you keep saying "you" and "I"?' asked Trinket. 'Have you forgotten our deal?'

'What *is* your real name?' said the Little Countess, smiling evasively. 'The others seem to call you Laurel Goong-goong all the time.'

'*They* can call me that, but *you can't*. Come on now: what are you supposed to call me?'

She lowered her eyelids slowly, and said in a hardly audible voice:

'In my heart . . . in my heart I can call you . . . my darling, but I don't think . . . I should say it out loud all the time.'

'All right, I'll make things easier for you. If there's someone else in the room, you can call me "brother Laurel"; but if we're alone, you're to call me "my darling".'

The girl did not wait for the Little Countess to reply:

'That's disgusting!' she cried, casting an angry glance at Trinket. 'Don't listen to him, he's harassing you.'

Trinket gave a little snort.

'I wasn't talking to you, so mind your own business! Even if *you* wanted to call me that, I wouldn't want to hear it!'

'Then what *do* you want her to call you?' asked the Little Countess.

'Simply "dearest husband", or "darling husband"!'

The girl blushed, and gave him a scornful glance.

'*You*, my husband? Huh! Don't even *think* about it! Ever!'

'All right, all right,' said the Little Countess. 'The two of you can't seem to stop quarrelling! Obviously you were deadly enemies in a previous life. Brother Laurel, please give me the medicine.'

'No, I'll put it on for you,' insisted Trinket, lifting the quilt.

He rolled up her trouser leg, removed the home-made chair-leg splint, then applied some ointment to her broken leg, and bound it tight in a new double splint. The Little Countess thanked him profusely.

'Tell me,' he asked her. 'What's my wife's name?'

She looked at him in amazement.

'Your wife?'

Trinket shot his lips out in the direction of the girl. The Little Countess smiled.

'There you go again! My sister's surname is Fang, and her name is . . .'

'Don't tell him!' the girl cried.

Trinket laughed. He passed the medicine to the Little Countess, and bent down to breathe into her ear:

'Go on, my dear, tell me her name! Whisper it to me!'

Trinket had lowered his voice until it was scarcely audible, but the girl was lying right next to the Little Countess, and could hear his every word.

'Don't tell him!' she protested agitatedly.

Trinket chuckled to himself.

'It's entirely up to you. Either you tell me your name, or else you let me kiss you: first on the left cheek, then on the right, and then on the lips. Which do you prefer? I can only presume you prefer to be kissed.'

By the flickering light of the candle, Trinket gazed at the delicately sculpted beauty of the girl's face. He detected a faint feminine fragrance emanating from beneath her flimsy clothes. He was enraptured.

'Delicious!' he murmured, breathing in her perfume.

The immobilized girl was seething with rage. She reminded herself that this loathsome urchin was only a child, and (more importantly) a eunuch. When he moved closer and threatened to kiss her, however, she decided to compromise.

'Oh all right then, tell him.'

The Little Countess gave a peal of laughter.

'My sister's name is Fang Yi.'

'That sounds like a pretty average sort of name to me,' said Trinket. 'And what's your name, Little Countess?'

'I'm Mu Jianping.'

'Better. But still not the best.'

'Well, I suppose *yours* is bound to be the *best* name,' said Fang Yi. 'May we have the honour of knowing what it is?'

Trinket ignored her question, and spoke to the Little Countess instead.

'You'd better put the ointment on straight away, my dear, or the pain will kill her. She's the only wife I've got. If she dies, I'll never be able to afford another one.'

The Little Countess closed the bed-curtains, lifted the quilt, and began applying the ointment to Fang Yi's wound.

'Brother, what should I do with the ointment you've already put on her wound?' she asked.

'Does it seem to be doing any good?'

'Yes, it does.'

One of the main ingredients in Trinket's bogus ointment had been honey, and because of its sticky texture honey *is* in fact rather an effective substance for staunching the flow of blood. It had clogged up the bleeding in her wound entirely. The other fudge-like ingredients, although they had no healing properties, had also helped.

Trinket was delighted.

'You see, my special medicine is far better than any magic potion! All those crushed pearls are working wonders. By the time she's fully recovered, she'll have the most beautiful breasts! What a pity that my son will be the only person lucky enough to get a good look at them—apart from me, of course!'

The Little Countess giggled.

'You are peculiar. I don't understand what you mean at all . . .'

'When she's breast-feeding the little boy, obviously.'

The Fang girl gave a snort of disgust.

The Little Countess stared at Trinket in wide-eyed bewilderment. She still didn't understand.

'You'd better gently wipe off my special ointment first,' said Trinket, 'and then apply some of the new stuff.'

Colonel Rui, the Invincible Iron Palm

Suddenly, in the midst of these medical ministrations, they heard the tramp of boots outside the door. Then a booming voice called out:

'Laurel Goong-goong, are you asleep?'

'Yes, I was as a matter of fact,' replied Trinket. 'Who are you, and what do you want? Can't it wait till the morning?'

'Lieutenant-Colonel Rui Dong,' replied the man.

'Oh! Colonel Rui! What's the matter?'

From his daily conversations with the guards, Trinket knew something about this Lieutenant-Colonel Rui Dong. He was a highly praised and widely respected officer, and something of a Martial Arts pundit. Among the guards, he was second only in popularity to Dolong, the Chief Intendant. In recent years, he had been posted outside the Palace, and this was Trinket's first encounter with him.

'I'm here on an extremely urgent matter, Goong-goong. I do apologize for waking you from your dreams.'

Trinket was indeed deeply engrossed, not in dreams, but in urgent thought:

'What's *he* doing here in the middle of the night? I expect he knows I've got two of the intruders hidden here and has come to search for them. What next? If I don't open the door, he'll probably break it down. I'd better play it by ear . . .'

Colonel Rui spoke again.

'Goong-goong, this really is very important, otherwise I would never have presumed to wake you.'

'That's fine. Just coming,' said Trinket, as he did so popping his head through the bed-curtains, and whispering to the girls to be silent.

He walked out into the ante-chamber, closing the bedroom door behind him, then somewhat hesitantly opened the main door. Outside stood a strongly built man, a good head taller than himself.

'Goong-goong, I'm sorry to disturb you,' said the Colonel yet again, pumping his hands apologetically.

'Not at all, not at all.'

Trinket was still totally in the dark. He scanned the Colonel's face, but could detect no expression of any kind on it, neither the faintest smile nor the slightest sign of anger.

'What's so urgent?' he asked. He pointedly did not invite the Colonel inside his apartment.

'Her Majesty is most concerned about this unpleasant disturbance in the Palace tonight. She has ordered me to carry out a full investigation, and to begin by asking you a few questions.'

The two words 'Her Majesty' were enough to put the wind up Trinket.

'Yes . . . As a matter of fact, *I've* got a few questions to ask *you* about that,' he improvised. 'I've just come back from seeing *His* Majesty, who didn't seem *at all* pleased. "What a nerve that fellow Rui has!" he said when I saw him. "Causing trouble the minute he gets posted back to the Palace . . . "'

Trinket was just bluffing, playing for time while he figured out how to make his getaway. But Colonel Rui clearly believed his every word.

'What else did His Majesty say?' he asked in great alarm.

'He said that I should get started immediately after dawn and question all of the guards. We've got to find out who's behind this plot of yours, what you were aiming to do, and how many accomplices you had. That's what he said.'

This sent Colonel Rui reeling.

'His . . . His Majesty said that!' he stammered. 'I've been set up! I'm innocent! This . . . this is the most terrible injustice!'

'His Majesty asked me to keep *my* investigation top secret,' Trinket babbled on. 'Otherwise he was afraid you might try to kill *me*. I said that you would never dare to raise your hand against me inside the Palace. But His Majesty was not so sure about that. "If the villain's prepared to kill his own Emperor," he said, "he's clearly a man who'll stop at nothing!" '

'That's . . . all lies! I was never part of any plot!' cried Colonel Rui. 'His Majesty . . . His Majesty would never put the blame on a good man without solid evidence. Why, this very night I killed three of the intruders myself. Several of the guards witnessed it. His Majesty can question them.'

His veins were bulging blue on his forehead, and both his fists were tightly clenched.

Trinket thought quickly:

'I've got to seriously scare him. I've got to make him panic. Otherwise I'll never survive till morning. I'll never make my getaway. The girls'll just have to take pot luck. I've got to get out of this place. Once I'm out, I'll give it all up. Imagine! I'll never have to dress up as a eunuch again! I'll give up being a Triad Lodge Master too! I'll just spend my half million, and have some fun! I'll go back to Yangzhou and set up a whole chain of whore-houses!'

He brought his day-dream to an abrupt close and turned to Colonel Rui.

'So you mean to say, those intruders had nothing to do with you?'

'Of course not,' insisted the Colonel. 'In fact Her Majesty herself told me that *you* were the one who let them in. She gave me orders to kill you, and not to waste time listening to your stories.'

'Well, it looks as if we've both been framed, doesn't it? But don't you worry, Colonel. I'll go to His Majesty myself, and speak up for you. His Majesty is young, but he's very smart, and trusts me absolutely. I'm sure he'll get to the bottom of this.'

'I should be most obliged to you,' said Colonel Rui. 'But right now, I must still insist that you come with me to see Her Majesty.'

'In the middle of the night? Whatever for? No, I really think I'd better go and see His Majesty straight away. I'm afraid he may have already sent someone to arrest you. Let me give you a word of advice, Colonel. If they come, whatever you do, don't put up a fight. It will only make it look worse.'

Colonel Rui's face twitched.

'Her Majesty was quite right to warn me about you!' he declared angrily. 'She said you were fond of telling lies, and she was right! I've done nothing wrong, why should I want to put up a fight? Now you come along with me!'

Trinket leant to one side, and whispered in Colonel Rui's ear: 'Look, they're coming to get you now!'

The colour drained from Rui's face, and he swivelled round to look behind him. As he did so, Trinket dashed back into his room. Rui immediately realized that he had been fooled and ran after him in hot pursuit.

Trinket had planned to make a desperate leap through the window and then to hide somewhere in the dense bushes and rockeries of the garden. The Colonel would never find him in the dark. He took a flying leap up onto the window-sill, and was about to jump out into the garden when Colonel Rui came racing up behind him and struck him a fearsome blow on the back with the palm of his right hand. Trinket's legs gave way, and he fell from the window into the room. Rui Dong now lunged with his left hand, and tried to grip him by the small of his back, but Trinket whirled round and counter-attacked with a Catch-Can technique he knew, blocking him with both palms. The move upset his balance, and he toppled with a great splash into the vat of water that stood by the window—the vat in which Old Hai had been accustomed to cool himself during his bouts of fever, and which Trinket had not removed since the old eunuch's death.

Colonel Rui gave a triumphant laugh. He plunged his hands into the water and made a grab for Trinket. But the boy had curled up into a ball at the very bottom of the vat. Rui made a second attempt, and was able to get hold of the back of Trinket's collar, and drag him dripping out. Trinket spat a mouthful of water in Rui's face and threw himself forward, butting the Colonel in the chest and wrapping his left arm around his neck.

Colonel Rui let out a loud shout, shook himself several times, and gradually loosened his grip on Trinket's collar. His entire face was drenched with water. Then his eyes opened wide, and a terrible expression of fear and bewilderment came over him. A few nasty groans issued from deep inside his throat, vain efforts to say something. Then suddenly there was a ghastly ripping sound, and the Colonel saw a dagger slicing its way neatly down from his upper chest to his lower belly. He stared at the blade. He failed to understand where it could have come from. His blood just kept spurting from the wound, and then all of a sudden he fell heavily to the floor. Even as he breathed his last he was still trying to puzzle out how Trinket had managed to kill him.

It was now Trinket's turn to give a triumphant cry. With his left hand he drew the dagger out of the Colonel's belly, and brought his right hand out from beneath his long robe. When he had fallen into the water, he had curled himself up tightly into a ball, meanwhile drawing out his dagger, and hiding it under his long robe, its tip pointing outward. Spitting the water in Rui's face had served to blind him momentarily, and then, in that precious instant, Trinket had thrown himself forward, grappling his opponent by the neck, and simultaneously plunging his trusty dagger, with the blade that could slice its way through metal, into the Colonel's heart and then down. This was the desperate Trinketian ruse that had saved his own life, and taken that of his great burly opponent. If they had engaged in real combat, ten Trinkets would have been no match for one Colonel Rui.

Peeping through the bed-curtains, the Fang girl and the Little Countess had watched all of this with their own eyes. But they too were still trying to puzzle out how Trinket had done the killing.

'I . . . I . . . This . . . this . . .' stammered Trinket huskily.

He had wanted to boast in front of the girls, but he found himself frightened out of his wits by his narrow encounter with death, and incapable of putting two sensible words together.

'Thanks be to Heaven that you . . . you've killed the Tartar!' cried the Little Countess.

'I know that man,' said the Fang girl. 'He was called the Invincible Iron Palm. He killed three of our people tonight. You've taken revenge for us!'

Two Sutras, a Sword, and a Soaking Waistcoat

Trinket searched through Rui Dong's clothes and found a little notebook the pages of which were densely covered with small writing, along with a bundle of official documents. He couldn't decipher a single word of either, so he put them casually aside.

As his hands continued to rummage around, they encountered a package concealed in the back of Rui's gown. Trinket cut open the gown with his dagger, to reveal an oilskin packet, tied with a silken strip. He cut the silk and unwrapped the packet. To his amazement it contained yet another copy of the *Sutra in Forty-Two*

Sections. It looked exactly the same as the others he had already seen, except that this one was bound in a different colour.

Trinket let out a loud cry, and immediately produced the copy from inside his own gown, the one that had been hidden under the tiles by the thief at Prince Kang's. Luckily, Colonel Rui had lost no time in pulling him out of the vat, and Trinket's Sutra had sustained no severe damage. The water had penetrated no further than the silken binding. Putting the two copies on the table, Trinket could see that they were indeed identical, apart from the colour of the silk: the one from Prince Kang's was bound in plain red, the one in the Colonel's package was bound in red with a white border. He had now seen four Sutras altogether: two were in the Empress Dowager's hands, and two in his own. There must be something very special written in these books, he thought to himself, if only he were capable of reading them! He could hardly ask the girls to read them for him; he would lose too much face. He opened a drawer, and put them both away.

He continued to muse on his predicament:

'First the Empress Dowager comes and tries to kill me herself, so she can keep my mouth shut, and stop me giving away her secret. Then, when that fails, she sends this Colonel Rui to finish the job off. Now, when Rui doesn't show up, she'll send someone else after me. I've got to keep one step ahead of her! I'd better go and see His Majesty. I have to survive till tomorrow morning! Then I'll run away from this Palace, and never come back!'

He turned to the Fang girl.

'I've got to start a rumour in the Palace. I've got to pretend that Colonel Rui was in the plot with you and the Mu Family. Dearest . . . I mean, Miss Fang, tell me, what *were* you doing here tonight? Did you come here to kill the Emperor? Why didn't you bump off that Old Whore the Empress Dowager instead? She really *is* a monster.'

(Originally Trinket had meant to call Fang Yi his 'dearest wife', but in the heat of the moment he had been too overwhelmed by the seriousness of his situation, and had ended up letting a golden opportunity pass him by.)

'I suppose you have the right to know what's going on,' replied the Fang girl. 'We disguised ourselves as guards working for Wu Yingxiong, the Satrap's son, and pretended to be on a mission to assassinate the Emperor. Of course, we would have been more than happy to kill the Emperor ourselves. But the main point was to give the Emperor a good reason for killing Satrap Wu.'

Trinket gave an astonished sigh.

'Wow! What a brilliant plan! But how were you going to make it look like a plot by the Satrap?'

She explained how they had marked their weapons and their clothes with the Satrap's insignia. They were all sworn to say nothing if they were caught. They were to allow the Palace Guards to torture them, and only then were they to confess that they had been sent by the Satrap. It would be more convincing that way. As she spoke of their plans, her breathing quickened and a flush of excitement stole across her cheeks.

'Have you got a weapon with one of the Satrap's marks with you?' asked Trinket.

She produced a sword from beneath the quilt, but barely had the strength to lift it.

'It's a good thing I wasn't lying next to you,' said Trinket, with a big grin. 'You'd probably have murdered *me*!'

She glared at him.

Trinket took the sword and laid it next to the Colonel's corpse.

'See, perfect evidence! I'll tell the Emperor that Colonel Rui was in league with the intruders.'

Fang Yi explained to him why this was not a good idea: the mark on the sword was the one used by Satrap Wu's Chinese soldiers years earlier when they had fought *against* the Manchus, before the conquest. It would have been quite impossible for a Manchu guard such as Colonel Rui to be in possession of such a sword.

'Oh well, what *can* I use?'

After a moment's thought, Trinket decided to stuff the Colonel's gown with some of the presents given him at the party by the Little Traitor, Wu's son: these included pearl necklaces, a jade cock and hen (the 'cute little knick-knacks' he had been about to show the Little Countess), and wads of banknotes. Such things could quite easily be traced back to Wu, and would thus be very incriminating.

He heaved up the Colonel's corpse, thinking he would move it out into the garden. But just then he heard someone outside the door of his apartment, and gently lowered the body again.

'His Majesty demands Laurel Goong-goong's presence!' cried a voice outside.

'Just coming!' Trinket called out, delighted to have received this timely summons. 'I have to change, but I'll be ready right away.'

He slid the Colonel under his bed, and gestured to the Little

Countess and Fang Yi to stay lying quietly on the bed. Then he took off his wet clothes, and changed into something dry. But, even though it was soaked through, he decided to keep on his black waistcoat.

Just as he was preparing to leave, it occurred to him that he could not entirely trust the Fang girl. Quickly grabbing the two copies of the *Sutra in Forty-Two Sections* and a handful of banknotes, he stuffed them into his inside pocket, then blew out the candle and set off.

Eunuchs and Guards

Of the four eunuchs waiting outside the door, Trinket was unable to recognize a single one.

'Laurel Goong-goong,' announced the eunuch who seemed to be in charge of the delegation, 'His Majesty has been asking for you since midnight. You'd best hurry along. And where is Colonel Rui? He's wanted too.'

Trinket felt a chill run down his spine.

'Is the Colonel back in the Palace?' he asked innocently. 'I haven't set eyes on him.'

'Really?' replied the eunuch. 'Then we'd better just hurry along without him.'

He turned around and set off.

'Why's he asking about Colonel Rui?' Trinket puzzled to himself. 'And anyway,' his thoughts ran on, 'what's he doing striding on ahead of me? I'm supposed to be a much more senior eunuch than he is. He ought to know the Palace rules by now!'

'Hey, Goong-goong,' he asked, 'what's your name? I don't remember ever setting eyes on you before.'

'Oh, we're just odd-job eunuchs,' came the reply. 'You wouldn't have had any occasion to meet us.'

'His Majesty wouldn't send any old odd-job eunuch to fetch me,' mused Trinket out loud. He also noticed that they were heading west, whereas the Emperor's bedchamber was definitely to the east.

'Are you by any chance lost?' he asked.

'No, His Majesty is at present in attendance on Her Majesty. He was concerned that she might have been unsettled by the recent break-in. We're on our way to the Hall of Maternal Tranquillity.'

Trinket froze to a halt. As he did so, two of the eunuchs following him broke ranks and took up positions one on each side of him. He was surrounded, and outnumbered four to one.

'Of course it's not the Emperor—it's the Old Whore! She sent them to bring me in!' thought Trinket frantically. His heart was thumping wildly.

'So we're going to Her Majesty's quarters,' he said, trying to affect an unconcerned little simper. 'How nice! Every time I see her, Her Majesty always insists on giving me money or sweets or cakes or something delicious! She really spoils me!'

The eunuchs were relieved to see him walking on, and fell back into their previous formation.

'Last time I saw Her Majesty, I remember she gave me five thousand taels of gold and twenty thousand taels of silver. She wanted to reward me for dealing with Oboi. I hardly had the strength to carry it all away. She told me to come and collect it a bit at a time. She asked what I was planning to do with it,' he babbled on, all the time trying to think of an escape plan, 'and I told her that what I liked best was sharing money with my friends. There's nothing I like more than sharing!'

'She couldn't have given you *that* much money!' said one of the eunuchs behind him.

'You don't believe me? Take a look, my friend!'

So saying, Trinket reached into his inside pocket and extracted a wad of notes, some for five hundred, some for a thousand taels, some for as much as two thousand.

This brought the eunuchs to a halt. They could see by the light of their lamps that this was genuine money all right. They gazed at it, and held their breath in utter amazement. Before they could take another pace, Trinket extracted four notes, held them out, and said with his most charming smile:

'Their Majesties are always loading me with money! I couldn't ever spend it all! Here, have one each. It's your lucky day.'

The eunuchs simply couldn't believe their luck. They were too stunned even to reach out their hands to take the money.

'Honestly,' Trinket went on, 'with all this money, and no way of spending it all, I really do get quite depressed. And in a minute or two they'll be giving me more . . .'

'Laurel Goong-goong,' ventured one of the eunuchs, 'I think you're just having us on . . .'

'Why should I want to do that? The other goong-goongs in the Catering Department are always getting money from me. Come on, don't be silly, take what you're offered!'

The eunuch gave a little laugh:

'I'll take mine.'

'Hold on,' said Trinket. 'Let's shed some proper light on this.'

He held the notes out directly under a lamp, and the eunuchs could now see beyond a doubt that they were notes of seriously large denominations—thousands upon thousands of taels. They gulped. Denied the normal joys of marriage and family, and disqualified from public service or a career in the armed forces, eunuchs had few genuine pleasures in life. The one thing they did value was money.

Trinket raised his hand and rustled the notes in the breeze.

'Go on then!' he cried to the eunuch who had expressed interest.

The eunuch reached for one of the notes, but as he was about to touch it, Trinket let go of them all and they fluttered away on the breeze.

'Clumsy me!' cried Trinket. 'Quick now! Go for it! Finders keepers!'

The four eunuchs scrambled after the notes.

'Don't let them get away!'

As he uttered this last cry, Trinket ducked down, and, in a well prepared dash, disappeared through an opening in one of the rockeries. He knew these Palace rockeries. Once he was behind one of the artificial mountains and inside the carefully contrived miniature landscapes, which grew out of each other in an endless maze, he would never be discovered.

The eunuchs were too busy chasing banknotes to notice that he had gone. Two caught one note each, one caught two, and one was left empty-handed. During the ensuing squabble, the one holding two notes insisted (correctly) that Laurel Goong-goong had said 'Finders keepers!', and that therefore both notes were his. The one with nothing protested that there should be one note each. 'I'll be happy with the one thousand-tael note!' he cried. 'What one thousand-tael note!' said the first. 'You're not getting anything!' And so it proceeded to fisticuffs, and finally to cries of, 'Why don't we get Laurel Goong-goong to decide!'

But when they turned round to find him, Laurel Goong-goong was nowhere to be seen. They searched for him desperately, the empty-handed eunuch still grabbing the other by the collar and demanding his note.

Trinket was by this time yards away in the depths of a miniature mountain range.

'We're in serious trouble now!' he heard one of them say. 'Her Majesty said it was very important to bring in Laurel Goong-goong and Colonel Rui. Where can he have got to?'

'He must be somewhere in the Palace,' said another. 'He can't have got very far. But whatever you do, don't mention the money.'

Just then Trinket heard footsteps coming from the west, and shortly afterwards a voice:

'That break-in last night is going to mean trouble for all of us in the morning.'

They were clearly Palace Guards.

Trinket stole out of the rockery and whispered to them not to make a sound. They recognized him at once.

The first two were carrying lanterns, and Trinket could now make out that there were about fifteen or sixteen of them altogether. It must be the same platoon that had come a little earlier to his own room. He knew one or two of them and hailed them by name.

'See those four eunuchs over there?' he whispered craftily. 'They plotted with the intruders. Let's grab them. I'm sure we'll be well rewarded.'

The guards thought nothing of rounding up a few eunuchs. They blew out their lanterns, and lay in wait. Two of the eunuchs were searching for Trinket in the rockery, the other two were still engrossed in their argument over the notes. One of the guards gave a low signal, and they closed in. There were four guards for each eunuch, and they soon had all four eunuchs pinned to the ground. By dint of much grappling and punching the guards succeeded in silencing and immobilizing the eunuchs, who were utterly perplexed by this new turn of events.

'Take them in there and question them!' ordered Trinket, pointing to a room off to the side. The guards dragged them in, and one of them lit a lantern. Trinket sat down, and the guards ordered the eunuchs to kneel, which they did after a lot more kicking and punching.

'What were the four of you plotting and scheming just now?' began Trinket. 'What was all that I heard about one of you getting a thousand taels, and another two thousand taels? And how the filthy Palace Guard dogs had killed quite a few of your friends from outside? Who *are* these "outside friends", then? And why would you call the guards filthy dogs?'

The (now gravely insulted) guards had not missed the chance to put the boot in again a few more times.

'If they let in the assassins, then they deserve to be executed!' put in one of the guards. 'Let's search them, and see what they have on them!'

And so, needless to say, the four notes were discovered. When the guards saw what huge sums of money were involved, they let out a cry of astonishment. The average eunuch earned no more than five or six taels a month. After the guards had delivered a few more well-placed kicks, Trinket insisted on a proper interrogation.

'Who put you up to this?' he demanded. 'Whose orders were you following?'

'We've done nothing wrong!' one of the eunuchs managed to get out. 'It was the Empress Dowager who told us to—'

Trinket slammed his left hand across the eunuch's mouth and reduced him to silence again.

'Rubbish! Expect us to believe that? Another word and we'll kill you!'

With his right hand Trinket extracted his dagger and began tormenting the eunuch with it, running the blade several times threateningly close to his scalp. The terrified creature passed out on the floor.

'He says they were under orders from the Empress Dowager,' said Trinket to the guards. 'That . . . that could have very serious implications!'

'You don't mean to suggest that Her Majesty could have let the assassins in herself?' stammered one of the guards, pale-faced at the thought of such an outrage. They all knew that the Emperor was not her son, and that she was a woman of great cunning and determination. Could the Emperor have offended her in some way? This might be one of those sinister Palace intrigues, that could drag innocent bystanders like themselves down with it.

'Were you really sent by Her Majesty? This is very important, so be sure to tell the truth.'

The wretched eunuch to whom Trinket addressed these remarks was still incapable of speech, and could only nod his head in desperation.

'And did Her Majesty give you these notes?' continued Trinket.

The three other eunuchs, who still had their wits about them, shook their heads.

'Let's get a few things straight. You came here on someone else's orders, right?'

They nodded.

'Now: do you want to die, or do you want to stay alive?'

This was a hard one to answer by nodding. One eunuch nodded, one shook his head, the third began by nodding, then shook his head, and finally ended up by giving his head a vigorous nod.

Trinket tried again:

'Do you want to die?'

Three shaking heads.

Trinket took two of the guards by the arm, and led them outside.

'This is a tricky one,' he whispered.

'What do you mean?'

'If we let them go, and word gets to Her Majesty, I'm afraid that every one of us will be sliced into pieces . . .'

The two guards shivered. Then one of them raised his right hand, and made a swift stabbing movement through the air. The other guard nodded silently, and added in a whisper:

'And what about the banknotes?'

'You can share the money amongst yourselves,' said Trinket. 'I don't mind telling you I'm scared by all this. I just want the whole thing settled, and me kept out of it. I'm not interested in the money.'

That clinched it. The guards returned, and gave four of their comrades a few whispered instructions. They took the eunuchs aside, and made a pretence of being about to escort them back to the Empress Dowager's quarters. The eunuchs set off with them. The next thing they knew, Trinket and the others heard screams of pain coming from a little way off, and confused voices shouting:

'Assassins! Intruders!'

'Help! They've killed four eunuchs!'

Presently the four guards returned, and reported nonchalantly to Trinket:

'Laurel Goong-goong, there's been another raid. Four eunuchs have been killed.'

'I'm so sorry to hear that!' said Trinket, affecting a sigh. 'Did the intruders get away?'

'They disappeared without trace.'

'Then I suppose there's nothing we can do about it. You'd better report the incident to Chief Intendant Dolong.'

'Yes, Laurel Goong-goong!' cried the guards, barely stifling a laugh. Trinket himself burst out laughing, and eventually they joined him.

'Well done, my friends!' said Trinket.

Trinket and the Old Whore

Trinket hurried back to his quarters. He was almost there, when he heard a voice in the shrubbery:

'So, Laurel Goong-goong, and how are you?'

He would have recognized that chilling tone of voice any-where. It was the Empress Dowager again. He turned to flee in terror. He had barely taken a few paces, when he felt a hand on his left shoulder, and his whole body went numb. It was as if a hundred-pound boulder had descended on him. He was rooted to the spot. He bent down to draw out his trusty dagger, but no sooner did he feel the hilt in his hand than another crushing weight descended onto his right upper arm. He yelped with pain. The Empress Dowager spoke. She sounded grim:

'Laurel Goong-goong, you're a clever lad, for one so young . . . So, you got rid of four of my eunuchs, and even had the nerve to suggest that I'd done something wrong . . .'

'Your Majesty,' stammered the terrified Trinket, desperately seeking for some means to stall her, 'kill me now, and you'll regret it . . .'

'What do you mean, regret it?' sneered the Empress Dowager.

'You think that by killing me you can keep your secret. But you see, the guards already know all about—'

'You mean that story of yours about my plotting to let in the assassins?' said the Empress darkly. 'And why on earth would I want to do a thing like that?'

'How should I know? But His Majesty might know.'

Trinket decided to gamble all on one last desperate throw.

'There's a lot of strength in these hands of mine,' muttered the Empress Dowager angrily. 'I'm going to throttle the life out of you, you worthless scum!'

'Go ahead. They *are* strong hands, I'll give you that. Throttle me, and then when you've done it, everyone in the Palace can start gossiping about *why* Your Majesty needed to do it; they'll wonder why you had to shut my mouth, what your secret was, your very special, very dirty secret . . .'

The Empress Dowager's hand was trembling with fury as she squeezed Trinket's shoulder. She took a deep breath.

'Why, even if those guards *do* know a thing or two, I'll simply tell Colonel Rui to execute the lot of them. I've got nothing to fear.'

Trinket laughed. The Empress Dowager was surprised.

'How can you laugh, with death staring you in the face?'

'It's just that Colonel Rui isn't likely to execute anyone, under the circs . . . Ha ha ha!'

'What do you mean?'

'I've already . . .'

He had been meaning to say 'put a knife through his heart', but then had a brainwave.

'I've already had a word with him.' He laughed again. 'He's done some thinking. From now on he's going to listen to what *I* tell him, not *you*.'

'As if you could persuade him to do a thing like that, you little whippersnapper!' snarled the Empress Dowager.

'I may only be a eunuch, I know. But it's not *me* he's afraid of, it's someone else.'

The Empress shuddered.

'You mean the Emperor?'

'Don't we all fear His Majesty?'

'What did you say to Colonel Rui?'

'Everything.'

'Everything?' repeated the Empress to herself mechanically. After a moment's reflection she asked:

'And where is he now?'

'Oh, a long way away. A very long way away. And he won't be coming back either. It *might* be a very good idea for you to go and see him, Your Majesty, but then again, I'm afraid it *might* be rather difficult.'

She seemed thoroughly taken aback by this.

'You mean he's left the Palace?'

Trinket was in full swing.

'That's right. He said that things were getting on top of him, and he had to leave the world and all its bears behind—'

'Snares,' the Empress corrected him. She humphed.

'So where's he gone then?'

'He said . . .' Trinket had another brainwave. 'Something about some mountains, Tutai, Butai, Mutai, I can't exactly recall . . .'

'The Wutai Mountains?' snapped the Empress.

'Yes, that's it! The Wutai Mountains! Your Majesty, you seem to be very well informed!'

'What else did he say?'

'Nothing much really. He just gave me his word of honour, that whatever danger came his way, he'd do everything I'd asked him to do.'

'And what exactly *did* you ask him to do?'

'Oh, nothing much. Then he said he might be away for quite some time, and he'd be a bit short of cash. So I gave him notes for twenty thousand taels.'

'What did he agree to do?'

'I'd rather not say, Majesty.'

'You'd better.'

She tightened the pressure on his shoulder. Trinket gave a little 'Ouch!' and she loosened her grip.

'Come on, out with it!'

Trinket sighed.

'He promised me that if ever anything happened to me here in the Palace, he would tell the whole story—everything I told him—to His Majesty. He'd have it all written down, and keep it in his pocket at all times, just in case. And we agreed that every two months, I'm to . . .'

He paused.

'Well?' The Empress Dowager's voice was trembling.

'Every two months I'm to go to the Bridge of Heaven . . . and find the old man who sells toffee-apples. I'm to say to him: "Have you got any Turquoise Toffee-Apples today, sir?" And he's supposed to reply: "Yes, a hundred taels a stick." Then I'm to say: "That's a bit expensive, isn't it! Would you sell me one for two hundred." Then he says: "Certainly not! You still alive?" And I say: "Yes, tell the old man." And then he reports back to Colonel Rui.'

The Empress Dowager humphed again.

'Colonel Rui must have taught you all that. A little urchin like you wouldn't know any of those underworld passwords.'

Trinket could still feel the Old Whore's hand trembling on his shoulder. After a long silence, she asked him:

'And supposing you *don't* turn up at the Bridge of Heaven, what then?'

'Colonel Rui said he'd wait ten more days, and then he'd *know* I was . . . well, dead. So he'd find a way to report everything to His Majesty. That way, even with me dead, at least his Majesty would be warned. Then he could think about vengeance.'

'Vengeance . . .' muttered the Empress Dowager.

'All this time,' Trinket went on, 'I've never breathed a word to His Majesty of the things I know. So long as I was alive, I didn't think I needed to trouble him.'

A sigh of relief escaped the Empress Dowager's lips.

'You've been a very good boy!'

'His Majesty has always been so good to me, and so have you, Your Majesty. All I ever wanted was for you to appreciate my loyalty, and reward me with a few taels now and then. That way, I thought everybody would be happy!'

The Empress gave a sinister chuckle.

'Still scrounging for tips, you shameless little urchin!'

But she seemed hugely relieved by what she had heard. Trinket saw that his little improvisation was working.

'Oh come on, Your Majesty, I'm not really greedy. I just want everyone to live happily ever after, me included! That's why tomorrow I'll be off to the Bridge of Heaven and give my message as arranged. Then Colonel Rui'll keep his mouth shut. And while I'm about it, I think I should . . . give the toffee-apple-seller another three thousand taels for the Colonel, and say it's from you, Your Majesty . . .'

The Empress Dowager humphed.

'*That* incompetent deserter! Give him *my* money! He's lucky I don't chop his head off!'

She released his shoulder, and said slowly:

'Laurel, are you loyal to me?'

Trinket fell to his knees, and performed an impressive series of kowtows. Even as he was protesting his undying loyalty, she bent down and struck him three times on the back, each time muttering something to herself. Trinket felt an instant faintness, and an intense desire to vomit. He made loud retching noises.

'Laurel,' the Empress Dowager began, 'do you remember that evening I was talking with the old eunuch Hai Dafu? Do you remember us mentioning something called Soft Crush karate? A single blow of Soft Crush, well executed, can destroy a man's body.

It is very hard to learn, and I'm certainly no expert. But I feel like having a little try on you . . .'

Trinket could feel the blood pumping through his head. And then out it came, blood, water, vomited forth in great spurts.

'So all that time the filthy Old Whore never really believed a word I was saying!' he thought to himself, in between the gushings of vomit. 'And now she's going to do me in once and for all!'

'Don't worry. I'm not going to kill you. After all, if you were dead, who would go to the Bridge of Heaven? I just wanted to hurt you a little, make you a little less quick on your feet . . .'

'Most obliged, Majesty,' muttered Trinket.

He stood up slowly, then tottered back into a sitting position on the ground, and began vomiting all over again. The Empress Dowager laughed coldly, and disappeared into the shrubbery.

Trinket dragged himself to his feet, and staggered towards his room. He reached the window, and slumped panting over the window-sill. Then he began clambering in.

More Decomposing Powder

'Is that you, Laurel?' whispered the Little Countess.

Trinket was not in the most cheerful of moods.

'Mother's! Of course it's not me!'

'She was only being friendly!' protested Fang Yi.

Trinket's body was by now half over the window-sill.

'I . . .'

That was as much as he could get out. The next he knew, he fell with a thud to the ground, and lay there incapable of movement.

'Aiyo!' the two girls cried. 'What's the matter? Are you hurt?'

The unmistakable note of concern in the two girls' voices seemed to have a miraculous effect on Trinket's spirits. He even managed a little laugh, which was followed quickly by another fit of panting.

'Who knows,' he thought to himself, 'perhaps the Old Whore never learned that Soft Crush stuff properly. Chin up, Trink!'

'My dear young ladies,' he finally said, 'dear sister, dearest wife, you are the ones who were really hurt. I had to get a little bit hurt too. After all, we're supposed to share everything, in sickness and in health, till death us do part . . .'

'Laurel,' said the Little Countess, 'be serious. Where are you hurt? Is it bad?'

'It's very kind of you to ask, dear sister. To tell the truth, I *was* in a lot of pain, but the sound of your voice has made it all go away! It's a miracle!'

'There you go again!' cried the Little Countess.

Trinket got hold of a table and hauled himself upright.

'If the Old Whore finds Colonel Rui's corpse,' he was thinking to himself, 'I'm done for!'

He staggered to Old Hai's medicine chest, and found the familiar bottle containing the yellow Decomposing Powder, which he had already used to such good effect on the 'real' Laurel. Then he dragged the Colonel's body out from under the bed, and relieved it of any remaining money and valuables.

'It's been so scary,' said the Little Countess, 'having that thing under the bed all the time you've been away.'

'I'm now going to perform a little trick,' announced Trinket. 'Do you want to watch?'

'No thank you,' said Fang Yi.

'Then close your eyes.'

She did, and the Little Countess followed her example, though from time to time she couldn't resist peeping.

Trinket took a little silver spoon from the medicine chest, and removed the stopper from the phial of Decomposing Powder. He tipped a small amount of the powder onto the Colonel's wound. In a matter of seconds the wound began to smoulder, then it gave off a disgusting stench, and a few seconds later a foul yellow liquid began to ooze from it. The wound spread as it gradually decomposed. The Little Countess let out an involuntary 'ugh!', and Fang Yi was so overcome with curiosity that she too opened her eyes. What she saw rendered her quite incapable of closing them again.

As the yellow liquid spread, everything it came into contact with became soft and putrid. The more it spread, the faster the whole corpse decomposed.

Trinket could see how appalled the two girls were by what they saw.

'If you ever disobey me, I shall sprinkle some of this magic powder of mine on your faces!'

'You're . . . you're just trying to scare us!' gasped the Little Countess.

Fang Yi glared at him, but could not mask her terror. Trinket walked up to her with a chuckle, and dangled the phial in front of her face, before putting it in his pocket.

Soon the Colonel's corpse had dissolved into two distinct halves. Trinket used the legs of a chair to push the two halves together, and within an hour the whole mush was no more than a yellow puddle.

'The Old Whore can take a whole army to Wutai,' thought Trinket to himself. 'She'll never find her Colonel now!'

He fetched some water from the vat and began washing the floor but was soon overcome with a sense of weariness, and flung himself exhausted onto the bed.

When he awoke, it was already broad daylight. He had fallen asleep fully clothed at the two girls' feet. He jumped up.

'I've got to go to the Emperor's at once! The two of you must stay where you are. Don't move!'

He thought of climbing out through the window, but his back was still too sore. So he went out through the door instead, locking it after him.

Kang Xi, Imperial Detective

Trinket waited an hour in the Upper Library, until finally Kang Xi returned from his morning audience.

'Laurel!' he exclaimed as he came in. 'Well done! I hear you killed one of the intruders last night!'

Trinket paid his loyal respects, and wished his Sovereign a long and healthy life.

'What was the man's kungfu like? Tell me all about it.'

Trinket invented a whole sequence of moves, using what he could remember of the fight between the Bo brothers and Xu the Eight-Armed Ape, which had been so vividly reconstructed by Father Obscurus and Brother Feng that day at Willow Lane. He described the Two Way Sweep, the Tiger's Leap, and the Cataract. Kang Xi clapped his hands.

'Excellent! Excellent kungfu! The very thing!'

Trinket looked at the Emperor in amazement.

'Your Majesty, I had no idea you knew those moves!'

'Of course. And what did you counter with?'

Trinket proceeded to flatter Kang Xi by claiming to have overcome the assassin using a number of moves the Emperor had taught him during their practice bouts, including such manoeuvres as Stork Preening Feathers, Breaking the Branch of the Plum Tree, and Purple Clouds. Kang Xi entered totally into the spirit of the thing, and even taught him one or two new, and more deadly, moves.

'You see, you should have got him here!' he cried, grasping Trinket by a Vital Point on his wrist, in between the two acupuncture points known as the Assembly and the Outer Pass. Trinket was instantly incapacitated.

'If only I'd known!'

'But seriously, Laurie,' said Kang Xi, 'who *were* these assassins?'

'I don't know. If you could recognize their style of kungfu, that should be a clue.'

'I am beginning to. It seems to point in one direction.'

He clapped his hands, and sent one of the eunuchs to summon Songgotu and Dolong, the Chief Intendant of the Palace Guards. They were already waiting outside the Library, and hurried in to perform their kowtow.

Dolong was a member of the Plain White Banner, a soldier of great Martial Arts prowess, who had served faithfully during the campaigns before the Manchus had finally entered the Pass. But Oboi had always kept him down. It was only after Oboi's fall that he had been promoted by Kang Xi to his present position, in charge of the Gate of Heavenly Purity, the Hall of Middle Harmony, the Hall of Supreme Harmony, and other central parts of the Forbidden City. There were six Intendants of the Guards, two each from the Plain Yellow, Plain White, and Bordered Yellow Banners. But Dolong was the one with the most power—and the most responsibility. He had been up all night, concerned that Their Majesties would hold him responsible for the unpardonable breach of security that had occurred. When he came in, Kang Xi could see that his eyes were red from exhaustion.

'Well, have they questioned the intruders?' he asked.

'Majesty, three of them were captured alive. At first they refused to speak. But then we tortured them. In the end they confessed . . . that their orders came from Satrap Wu!'

Kang Xi nodded, and humphed.

'We found the Satrap's mark on their weapons and on their clothes,' Dolong continued. 'Even if he did not send them himself, he must somehow have been involved.'

Songgotu confirmed his account. Kang Xi demanded to

see the weapons and the clothes for himself. Dolong had already anticipated this request, and one of his guards was standing outside the Library with a bundle of the items. Dolong deposited them on the table, and withdrew a few steps. Manchu warriors were accustomed to battle and the sight of weapons. But there was the strictest possible taboo on the wearing of weapons in the presence of the Emperor, and Dolong was more than a little apprehensive about the danger to himself inherent in the present situation.

Kang Xi examined the swords. Sure enough, their handles had engraved upon them the full title of the army commanded by Wu Sangui when he had served the Ming dynasty, more than two decades earlier. But that in itself was enough to arouse the Emperor's suspicions.

'Satrap Wu is a clever man,' he commented to Songgotu. 'Too clever to make a silly mistake like that. He would have known that one of these swords might easily fall into our hands.'

'Indeed, Your Majesty,' replied Songgotu. 'You are most perceptive.'

Kang Xi turned to Trinket.

'Laurie, that intruder you killed, what kind of moves did he use?'

'The Two Way Sweep, and the Cataract.'

Kang Xi addressed his next question to Dolong.

'And what school of kungfu do those moves belong to?'

Dolong knew enough about Martial Arts to be able to answer without hesitation.

'Why, Your Majesty, those moves are part of the fighting style of the Mu Family, who used to rule Yunnan during the former dynasty.'

Kang Xi clapped his hands.

'Excellent! Excellent! My congratulations, Dolong!'

Dolong received this compliment with a barely visible smile, fell to his knees, and kowtowed.

'Now, if the Satrap wanted to break into the Palace,' Kang Xi went on, 'he would hardly have chosen to do it while his own son was in the Capital. That is my first doubt. Then, the Satrap is an experienced commander of men and a seasoned planner of campaigns. He would never have sent such incompetent fighters, or so few of them. That is my second. And what good would it do him to try and kill me anyway? Unless he were planning a rebellion. In which case, why hand me his son on a plate? That is my third doubt.'

Trinket was most impressed by his Imperial friend's powers of detection. It seemed that the Mu Family plot was a flawed one, and that Fang Yi had been wrong to be so confident in its success.

'Let's carry this one step further,' continued Kang Xi. 'Suppose the intruders were not the Satrap's men; but suppose they deliberately brought weapons with the Satrap's name on them into the Palace; what was their intention? Clearly they were trying to get *him* into trouble. Now the Satrap has done the Manchu Throne a great service. He has quelled uprisings throughout the South-West. In so doing, he has undoubtedly made many enemies. We must find out exactly who those enemies are, and who is behind this.'

Dolong and Songgotu applauded the Emperor's great wisdom, and seeing that he had no further orders for them, withdrew from the Library.

'Laurie,' said Kang Xi once the other two had left, 'do you want to be rich?'

Now there was a word to brighten Trinket's day.

'If you were to give the order, Your Majesty, I would have to obey . . .'

Kang Xi laughed.

'Well, I do! I order it! I want you to take these swords, and the intruders' clothes, and their confessions, and show them to a certain person . . . *Then* you'll be rich.'

Suddenly Trinket understood what he was driving at.

'You mean, the Satrap's son?'

'Clever lad! Now off you go. What are you going to say to him?'

'I shall say: "Hey you! Wu! His Majesty has been very kind to you. But remember, His Majesty knows everything that goes on, in the furthest part of his Empire. So if you and your dad are thinking of stirring up any tamardy trouble, forget it! Just behave yourselves and be good!"'

'Oh Laurie, you really are priceless!' said Kang Xi with a laugh. '"Stirring up any tamardy trouble!" You took the words right out of my mouth, and added a little sauce of your own!'

Trinket gathered up the pile of things on the table, left the Library in the highest of spirits, and set off back to his own room.

Pangs of Jealousy

As Trinket was unlocking the door, he felt a sharp pain shooting up his back, and experienced a renewed desire to vomit. He dragged himself into the room, and sat down panting on a chair.

'What's the matter? Does it hurt again?' asked the Little Countess.

'The sight of your flowerlike face has made me feel better already,' returned the irrepressible Trinket.

'It's my sister-in-arms who has the flowerlike face,' protested the Little Countess playfully. 'If you remember, *my* face has a turtle carved on it, and is ugly as anything!'

It raised Trinket's spirits to hear her joking like this.

'How are we going to get out of here?' asked Fang Yi after a moment's silence. 'You must think of a way.'

But Trinket was beginning to enjoy having the two girls to come home to. Life had been rather lonely without them. He was in no hurry to see them go.

'We'll have to take things one at a time,' was his reply. 'You're both wounded, and if you try to escape now, it will be easy for them to catch you.'

Fang Yi gave a little sigh.

'I wonder how many of our men lost their lives last night? Do you know any of their names?'

Trinket shook his head.

'I could find out for you, though, if you want me to.'

'Thank you,' said Fang Yi very quietly. 'I would.'

Trinket had never heard her speak so nicely to him before. He found it somewhat puzzling.

'Yes,' added the Little Countess. 'She'd specially like you to find out if a man by the name of Liu managed to get away.'

'Liu?' said Trinket. 'Who's he?'

'He's our brother-in-arms. We all studied under the same Shifu. His name is Yizhou. Fang's . . . she's in love with him. So you must . . .'

Suddenly she burst out laughing. Fang Yi was squeezing her under the arm, in an attempt to stop her from saying any more.

Trinket let out a little cry.

'Oh dear! I know who you mean. I'm afraid *he's* in serious trouble.'

'What do you mean?' Fang Yi burst out.

'Well, if we're talking about a tall, good-looking young man, a little over twenty, excellent at kungfu . . .'

'Yes, that's him!' cried the Little Countess. (In fact Trinket had not the faintest idea who this Liu was. But anyone Fang Yi was in love with was bound to be tall and good-looking; and any brother-in-arms of the Little Countess had to be excellent at kungfu. So he couldn't go far wrong.) 'Sister Fang said she saw him being knocked down last night by three guards, and then they took him away. What's become of him?'

Trinket shook his head and sighed.

'Dearest brother Laurel!' said Fang Yi, her face a picture of misery. 'Tell us!'

'You little bitch!' thought Trinket to himself. 'Never a nice word for me till now, and suddenly, when this boyfriend of yours is involved, I'm your dearest brother! I think you've got a little fright coming your way . . .'

He sighed again and shook his head tragically.

'Such a sad story!'

'What do you mean?' cried a distraught Fang Yi. 'Is he wounded? He's not . . . dead, is he?'

Trinket burst out laughing.

'How the hell should I know? I've never set eyes on this Liu or Pooh or whatever his smelly fart of a name is! How would I know if he's dead or alive? But I'll tell you what. Call me "darling husband" three times, and I might try and find out for you.'

Fang Yi had thought for a moment that her lover was dead, and her anger at Trinket was tempered with relief.

'Can't you *ever* be serious!'

'If I was to get hold of this Liu,' continued Trinket, regardless, 'I'd tie him up and beat him till his bum was black and blue. I'd make him tell me how he managed to worm his way into my "wife's" affections! Then I'd lift my sword high into the air and bring it down with a great whoosh on his—'

'You've killed him, haven't you?' cried the Little Countess.

'No!' teased Trinket. 'I just chopped his balls off, and turned him into a eunuch!'

The Little Countess had no idea what he was talking about. Fang Yi did, and blushed to the roots of her hair.

'You rotten liar!'

'Seriously now,' said Trinket, 'that pretty boy of yours has almost certainly been captured. If I *did* tell them to make a eunuch of him, I'm sure they would. So, my dear, do you want me to do something for you?'

Fang Yi's face was still flushed, and she was unable to form a reply. It was the Little Countess who spoke.

'Brother Laurel, surely you don't need to wait to be asked. Do this for us! Do the right thing, if you are a person of honour and courage!'

'No!' cried Trinket, with a wave of his hand. 'That's where you're wrong. I *do* need to be asked. The more a certain someone calls me "dearest husband" and "darling husband", the more inspired I'll be to do the right thing!'

After much hesitation, Fang Yi finally came out with:

'Dear Laurel, dearest brother Laurel, please do this for me.'

Trinket's face was unmoved.

'It's got to be "husband" . . .'

'This is very wrong of you!' protested the Little Countess. 'My sister-in-arms is betrothed to Liu. *He's* going to be her husband. So how can she call *you* husband?'

'In that case I'm very jealous,' was Trinket's reply. 'Most terribly jealous.'

'My brother-in-arms Liu is a fine young man,' went on the Little Countess.

'I don't care how fine he is! The finer he is, the more jealous I'll be! Woe is me! I shall die of jealousy! Ha ha ha!'

And laughing hysterically, he picked up the bundle he had carried with him from the Library and walked out of the room, locking the door after himself again.

He mounted his horse, and set off with four junior eunuchs to Young Wu's residence in Chang'an Street West.

As he rode along, he kept waving his right hand in the air, and giving excited whoops of joy. Understandably, his escort could not imagine what it was he was so excited about. Little did they know that Laurel Goong-goong had received an Imperial order to make himself rich, and was about to lower his bamboo bucket deep into the Satrap's well!

Negotiating with the Little Traitor

When he heard that an Imperial Edict was on its way, Wu Yingxiong, the Little Traitor, hurried out to greet Trinket. He performed the requisite number of kowtows, and welcomed him into the main hall of his residence.

'His Majesty has asked me to show you one or two things,' said Trinket. 'Tell me, sir, are you feeling brave today?'

'Not very. In fact the slightest shock might be too much for me!'

'The slightest shock?'

Trinket stared hard at Wu and then smiled.

'But you seem brave enough when it comes to planning something big . . .'

'I'm afraid I don't know what you mean, Goong-goong. I do most humbly beg you to enlighten me.'

His tone of voice was positively obsequious.

'Just how many men did you send on that mission to the Palace yesterday evening? His Majesty wants to know.'

Wu had heard of the assassination attempt, but this direct accusation came as a bolt from the blue. He fell trembling to his knees, and began kowtowing frantically out towards the courtyard (in the direction of the Imperial Palace).

'His Majesty has been so extraordinarily good to both my father and myself. We would do *anything* to repay his Majesty's great kindness. We would happily be his cattle or his horses! We would willingly give our lives, if that was needed.'

'Come on, get up, man!' said Trinket gallantly. 'You can keep the kowtows for later. First I want you to take a look at these things.'

He opened his bundle and spread its contents on the table.

Wu stood up. When he saw what was on the table, he began to shake uncontrollably.

'These . . . these . . .'

He picked up the confessions and read them through. They stated quite categorically that the assassins had entered the Palace at the express orders of his father the Satrap, with the clear intention of murdering the Manchu Emperor, and setting the Satrap on the throne. Wu was a young man of the world, and had already dealt with more than one crisis in his life, but this quite unmanned him. He fell to his knees again, in utter terror. This time he was kneeling directly in front of Trinket.

'Laurel . . . Goong-goong . . . this isn't true! We have been framed! Please . . . please, Goong-goong, you must put in a word for us with His Majesty!'

'These weapons were brought into the Palace by rebels plotting to murder the Emperor! And they have your father's mark on them!'

'My father and I have many enemies,' pleaded Wu. 'One of them must have plotted this.'

'There may be a grain of truth in what you say,' said Trinket gravely. 'But will His Majesty believe it?'

'You *must* put in a word for us, Goong-goong! Our lives are in your hands!'

'Get up off the ground, man!' said Trinket. 'I suppose those presents you gave me last night were to soften me up for this . . .'

Wu had in fact been in the process of standing up, but when he heard this latest accusation, he sank once more to his knees.

'Goong-goong, just a few words from you, and I'm sure His Majesty will see that we are innocent.'

'I'm afraid the whole thing has already got as far as Minister Songgotu and Dolong, Intendant of the Palace Guards. They've been to see His Majesty, and reported the assassins' statements. It will be very hard to stop things now. There could be a way . . . But it might mean rather a lot of trouble for you . . .'

'Anything!' stammered Wu. 'I'll do anything, if you'll save me!'

'Well, first of all, stand up properly and talk like a man!'

Wu finally managed to stand up, but continued to do a lot of bowing and scraping.

'First, are you absolutely sure that these assassins were not your men?'

'Absolutely! How could I ever dare to even think of doing such a terrible, terrible, *terrible* thing!'

'All right, all right. We're friends, and this time I'll give you the benefit of the doubt. But if it ever comes to light that they *were* your men, and I get buried alive for sticking up for you, I shall make sure that every single member of your family has his head chopped off! Understand?'

'I swear I'm telling the truth, Goong-goong, I swear it!'

'So, in your view, who did it? Who sent the assassins in?'

'As I said, we have many enemies. It is really hard to tell.'

'If you want me to put your case to His Majesty, and you want him to believe it, you'll have to come up with a suspect.'

'Yes, I understand . . . In restoring peace to the Empire my

father offended several factions. There's General Li, Bash-em Li;
then there are the Ming Pretenders and their followers; and the Mu
Family in Yunnan . . .'

Trinket nodded.

'All these various groups—what sort of kungfu do they use?
Can you show me any of their moves? That way I could say to His
Majesty that I recognized the style of fighting of the assassins, and
your case would be that much stronger.'

'Yes, that's an excellent idea. My own knowledge of kungfu
is, I'm afraid, very limited. I shall have to ask one of my men.'

With a quick bow, Wu hurried off.

A short while later he returned with one of his bodyguards.
It turned out to be Yang Yizhi, the very man Trinket had befriended
at the gambling table the previous evening. Yang bowed to Trinket.
There was a sombre expression on his face.

'Friend Yang,' said Trinket, 'set your mind at ease. We were
all at Prince Kang's together yesterday, and watched your fine
display of kungfu. We can all testify that *you* were not one of the
assassins.'

'Thank you for saying so, Goong-goong. But others might
claim that what we did was by way of a diversion, to draw attention away from the intruders . . .'

'Hm. Yes, I suppose they could.'

'My master says you are willing to put in a word for us,
Goong-goong. We would be eternally indebted to you. As for our
enemies, they are many, and they have many different styles of
fighting. The only ones with an easily recognizable style of their
own are the Mu Family.'

'Pity we can't find one of them to demonstrate it for us,' commented Trinket.

'The Mu style of boxing and swordplay is well-known
throughout Yunnan. I can remember some of it, and can show you
how it goes. Since the assassins were armed with swords, I suggest
I start by demonstrating the Mu Family sword technique known as
the Whirlwind.'

'I'd rather you stuck to boxing,' said Trinket. 'I'm quite out of
my depth when it comes to swordplay.'

'Very well,' said Yang. 'But you must correct me if I go wrong.
After all, you are the famous fighter that brought down Oboi the
Manchu Champion!'

He proceeded to give a demonstration of the Mu Family style of boxing. This style had been handed down from the original Duke Mu, through several generations, over a period of three hundred years. It was very distinctive. Although Yang was by no means an expert in it, he was quite capable of doing the basic moves.

When he came to the Two Way Sweep, and the Cataract, Trinket gave a little cry of appreciation.

'Excellent kungfu!'

He proceeded to imitate Yang's performance, and asked Yang if his own versions were recognizable.

'You have caught them exactly!' replied Yang.

'When I return to the Palace,' said Trinket, 'I can demonstrate them myself for His Majesty's guards.'

'Goong-goong, our whole family depends on you!' exclaimed Wu, bowing profoundly.

'Yes,' Trinket was thinking to himself, 'I know. And you're going to pay for it!'

He returned Wu's salutation.

'Please, no more of this bowing and scraping. We're friends, and I'll do what I can.'

Trinket picked up his bundle and made ready to leave. Then a thought occurred to him. He turned to Wu once more:

'Tell me, is there a man of yours here in the Capital by the name of Lu Yifeng?'

'Why, yes, now you come to mention it, there is.'

Wu was rather taken aback by Trinket's question. He knew that Lu had managed to procure an appointment from his father the Satrap, by paying a bribe of some forty thousand taels (of which he, Wu Yingxiong, had received a cut of three thousand). But Lu was small fry; what could Laurel Goong-goong want with him? (He knew nothing, of course, about the confrontation between Lu and Xu the Eight-Armed Ape, which had had such terrible consequences for the elder Bo brother, Pine.)

'Your Mr Lu doesn't know how to behave himself, so I've heard. I'd like you to teach him a lesson.'

'Why, yes, of course. We'll look into it right away.'

Wu turned to Yang and gave orders for Lu to be brought in and given fifty strokes of the rattan.

As Trinket took his leave, Wu produced a large packet from his inside pocket, and presented it to him.

'How can we ever manage to repay you, Laurel Goong-

goong? This is just a little token, which I hope you will distribute for us to Minister Songgotu, Captain Dolong, and the other guards.'

They saw him out. As soon as Trinket had climbed into his sedan chair, he opened the package. It contained a hundred thousand taels.

'Hot momma's!' whistled Trinket. 'Time for a little division and subtraction here, I'd say.'

He helped himself to fifty thousand and stuffed it in his pocket.

Multiple Largesse

Trinket returned to the Upper Library and reported the success of his mission to Kang Xi. Young Wu had been overwhelmed with gratitude, he said, at the Emperor's wisdom and clemency, and so on and so forth.

'Good,' commented Kang Xi drily. 'Gave him a bit of a fright, did we, eh?'

'Made him piss in his pants, more like!' quipped Trinket. 'I told him he'd better tell that Rat Trap of a parent of his to smarten up his act a bit in future.'

Kang Xi nodded.

'Then I told him how brilliantly clever and all-knowing you were, and how you spotted the Mu Family kungfu a mile off. He was absolutely flabbergasted!'

Kang Xi laughed.

'He came up with a tael or two,' Trinket went on. 'Fifty thousand, actually. He told me to keep ten thousand, and the rest was for the guards, for doing such a good job. Nice little stash . . .'

He produced the thick wad of notes: a hundred notes in denominations of five hundred taels.

'How could a young lad like you ever find a way to spend all that money?' asked Kang Xi.

'Little does he know!' thought Trinket to himself. Then he cleverly proposed to donate his share to the guards as well.

'We'd better say it's a reward from Your Majesty,' he went on. 'We don't want them thinking that the Little Traitor can buy them over.'

Kang Xi agreed to this 'generous' proposal, and the money

was duly distributed to the appreciative guards and their Chief Intendant.

Dolong took Trinket to one side.

'The men would like to show their appreciation,' he said, handing Trinket ten thousand taels, which Trinket made a great show of refusing.

'I'd like you to do something for me instead, though,' Trinket said. 'See if one of the captured men is someone by the name of Liu Yizhou.'

Butcher Qian, Again

When Trinket reached the entrance to his own rooms, he saw a junior eunuch from the Imperial Catering Department waiting for him.

'Laurel Goong-goong, that Butcher Qian is here. He wants to present you with another pig. This one is called a Swallow's-nest Ginseng pig.'

Trinket frowned.

'That China-root pig caused me enough trouble . . . Is he trying to turn the Palace into a pig-sty?'

But he thought he had better see what the man wanted.

When he reached the Catering Department, there was Butcher Qian, wreathed in smiles.

'Why, Laurel Goong-goong, that China-root pig of mine's done you a power of good! What a wonderfully ruddy complexion you've got today! I've brought you another.'

He pointed to an animal beside him. This time it was a live pig. A beautiful little white porker, wriggling around in a cage made of bamboo splints. Trinket had no idea what this was all about, but just nodded. The next thing he knew, Butcher Qian had taken him by the hand and was busy taking his pulse.

'My oh my! You really are blooming! My word, what a healthy beat!'

Trinket felt him slipping a scrap of paper into his hand. He said nothing.

'Now this little pig here needs *very* special feeding,' went on Butcher Qian. 'He needs to be given the best lees of wine for ten days. Then I'll come and take a look and see how he's getting on.'

After a few more pleasantries, the butcher took his leave.

Trinket knew that he would be unable to read whatever was written on the paper. He could still at very best only decipher one or two characters—and they had to be written very large. He told the Catering Department staff to feed the pig, and made his way back to his rooms.

'Laurel . . . dear Laurel . . . did you . . .'

It was Fang Yi.

'Yes, I did,' said Trinket. 'So far there's no news of anyone called Liu having been caught.'

'Thank you for asking. Perhaps he's been killed! Anyway, if he was caught, he wouldn't give his real name.'

Trinket handed the note to the Little Countess.

'Would you mind reading this for me?'

She took it and read:

' "Storytelling at the Ascension Tea-house: *Heroes of the Ming*." What does that mean?'

Trinket knew it was a message from the Triads.

'Surely you know the *Heroes of the Ming*? You're one of the Mu Family yourself.'

'Of course I know the stories about the founding of the Ming.'

'There's one part called "How Duke Mu shot three arrows and brought peace to Yunnan"—everyone knows that one; and then there's another called "How Laurel Goong-goong put his arms round two beautiful women." Do you know that one?'

Before they could even reply, Trinket had somersaulted onto the bed with his shoes on, and had wriggled under the covers between them. He put his left arm round Fang Yi's neck and gave her a good cuddle, and his right arm round the little Countess's waist and squeezed her.

'You see!' he crowed. 'It's true!'

They both gave a coy cry of alarm, but he had them held fast. The Little Countess tried to push him away. Trinket spun round, and planted a smacking kiss on Fang Yi's lips.

'Hm! Delicious!' he cried ecstatically.

Fang Yi struggled, but this only succeeded in bringing back the old pain in her ribs. She managed to get her right hand free and give him a quick box on the ear.

Trinket then sprung out of the covers, and this time threw

his arms well and truly round the Little Countess, and kissed her
too.

'Likewise delicious!'

He scrambled laughing across the room, grabbed his clothes
and ran out, locking the door behind him.

CHAPTER 11

*In which Lodge Master Wei offers to settle
a Score with the Mu Family; successfully
organizes an Escape; has a Narrow
Scrape with the Fat Sow; uses a Pair of
Trotters in a Novel Fashion; and meets
Auntie Tao*

Bean Sprout Lane South: a Life for a Life

Trinket's rooms were situated to the side of the Imperial Catering
Department, west of the Gate of Heavenly Purity. Trinket, after
winding his way north past Nurturing Nature Hall, then west
through Longevity Gate, then north again past Longevity Hall and
the Hall of Heroic Splendour, finally emerged at the Shenwu Gate,
the 'Gate of the Divine Warrior', left the Palace, and made straight
for the Ascension Tea-house.

He sat down, and the proprietor served him tea. It was not long before Gao Yanchao, his Triad contact man, came sidling up to him, and gave him a meaningful wink. Trinket waited, and then, seeing Gao leave the tea-house, he took a few sips of tea, left his money on the table, and sauntered towards the door, muttering casually as he left:

'I'm afraid today's story doesn't really do much for me . . .'

There was Gao outside, waiting at the street corner, with two sedan chairs. He showed Trinket into one of the chairs, and followed him a little distance on foot, making sure no one was following them, then climbed into the other chair himself.

The bearers set off at quite a pace, and after half an hour or so came to a halt outside a small courtyard house. Trinket and Gao went in through the main gate, and were greeted by a whole assembly of Triad members. There were many familiar faces, including Big Beaver, Brother Li, and Tertius (back from Lodge meetings in Tianjin and Baoding), Brothers Fan and Feng, Father Obscurus the Taoist, and Butcher Qian.

They showed him into the inner hall, and Trinket—the Master of the Green Wood Lodge—was seated. Obscurus spoke first. He seemed rather agitated.

'Look at this, Master,' he said, handing Trinket a red visiting-card, decorated with a gold splash, and inscribed with several columns of characters in thick black ink.

'The words . . . seem to know me . . .' Trinket faltered, 'but I'm afraid I don't really . . .'

'Master,' put in Butcher Qian helpfully, 'it's an invitation. To a meal.'

'That sounds fun,' commented Trinket. 'Who's treating us?'

'The name on the card is Mu Jiansheng,' said the butcher.

Trinket pulled a face.

'Mu Jiansheng?' (He knew that Mu Jian*ping* was the Little Countess.)

'He's the Young Count of the Mu Family.'

Trinket nodded.

'You mean the China-root pig's big brother?'

'Exactly!' replied the butcher.

'Are we all invited?'

'The invitation is very politely worded: "The presence of Lodge Master Wei of the Green Wood Lodge, and all brave Triad members of the Lodge, is requested at a banquet to be held this evening at Bean Sprout Lane South, within the Sun-Facing Gate."'

'Not Willow Lane this time?'

'No. They seem to think it safer to keep changing venues.'

'What do you think they'll do this time? Put something in the wine?'

It was Brother Li who replied:

'The Young Count is an important figure in the Mu Family. He has the same rank as our Helmsman. I hardly think someone like that would stoop to such underhand tactics. But we should be careful all the same.'

'Well, should we go or not?' Trinket wondered aloud. 'Hm, I like the idea of a slice or two of Yunnan ham, and some Yunnan stewed chicken . . .'

The others exchanged silent glances. After a long pause, Big Beaver spoke:

'We would like you to decide, Master.'

'Why don't I invite you all out instead! We could have a nice feed in a restaurant, then dice, pretty girls . . . Of course, if you want to save me money, we could just accept the Mu invitation . . .'

Trinket had managed to sound generous, and had at the same time avoided the responsibility of taking the decision.

'It's very kind of you to invite us out,' said Big Beaver. 'But I'm afraid if the Triads turn down the Mu invitation, it won't look too good.'

'So you think we should go then?' said Trinket.

He glanced round at the others. There seemed to be a general, if slow, nodding of heads.

'Then if you all say so, let's go! Nothing ventured nothing gained!'

'We should take certain precautions,' said Brother Li. 'Some of us should drink wine, some of us tea, some nothing at all. Some should avoid the meat, some the fish. That way, if they *are* trying to poison us, we won't all fall into their net at once.'

They continued to discuss their plans for the evening. By the evening watch, Trinket had changed out of his eunuch's costume into something more dignified and Lodge Master-like, and, climbing into a sedan chair, off he set, with the others crowding round him.

It was less than a mile to Bean Sprout Lane. When they arrived, they heard festive music coming from inside rather a grand gateway, where a dozen or so men were lined up to receive them. Foremost among these was a young man of twenty-five or six, a tall, thin fellow, with a vigorous, manly air, who now stepped forward and introduced himself as Mu Jiansheng.

'I am honoured to welcome Lodge Master Wei.'

By now Trinket was quite used to highfalutin compliments and was able to pull off this kind of encounter rather convincingly. After all, the Young Count was certainly no grander than either Prince Kang or Little Traitor Wu. He brought his hands smarmily together and bowed.

'You pay me too great a compliment, sir!'

Meanwhile, he was sizing up his host. The young man had a slightly swarthy complexion, but otherwise there was certainly a visible resemblance between him and his sister. Mu Jiansheng for his part had been briefed on Trinket by the trusty Mu retainer Maple Bo, who had painted a none too flattering picture of the young Lodge Master, describing him as a foul-mouthed, jumped-up little urchin, who knew no kungfu, and owed his position entirely to the Helmsman's favouritism. Seeing Trinket now, however, the Young Count could not help being impressed by the young fellow's calm, self-assured manner.

He led the way on into the inner hall. Here the chairs were spread with red damask covers and brocade cushions. As they took their seats, the Triads noticed that among the dozen or so Mu Family retainers lined up behind the Young Count were Su Gang (the Magic Hand), and Maple (the sole surviving Bo brother). Introductions were made, and Big Beaver and the others could see that the Young Count was making a big effort to be friendly.

Scented tea was served, and the musicians struck up again. In the middle of a rather solemn ceremonial piece, the Young Count announced, 'Let the banquet begin!', and led them on into another inner room. His retainers closed the doors behind them.

A large octagonal Eight Immortals table had been set in the middle of the room, with two smaller tables on each side. The tables were spread with elaborately embroidered cloths, and laid with tableware not quite as grand as at Prince Kang's, but stylish enough. The Young Count made a slight bow, asked Trinket to be seated, and introduced a ruddy-faced, vigorous old man with wispy white whiskers and piercing eyes, by the name of Liu Dahong. This, he explained, was his Shifu.

'The Triads have been making quite a name for themselves recently . . .' said the old man.

When he spoke, he boomed. It was the sort of voice ordinary men could only emulate by shouting.

'And as for Lodge Master Wei,' the old man went on, 'clearly we have among us an up-and-coming young hero, a veritable prodigy in the Martial Arts fraternity!'

'I'm afraid I'm more of a clumsy clot!' quipped Trinket. 'I certainly made a fool of myself the other day, when Maple Shifu twisted my arm. I just about tamardied myself in my up-and-coming pants! What a little wimp I must have looked! Ha ha ha!'

The others listened in appalled silence to this exhibition of Trinketian argot, and Maple looked decidedly ill at ease. But old Shifu Liu erupted in a loud bellow of laughter.

'Frankly spoken, sir! Now that's what I call a hero, a man of parts! You've already earned a third part of my respect!'

'I'd be happy with a tenth!' cried Trinket. 'Just so long as you think me better than a beggar, or a clown, or a monkey!'

'I see Lodge Master Wei likes to joke!' replied the old man.

Father Obscurus had already recognized Shifu Liu as the renowned Iron Dragon, the kungfu Master who had done so much to save the Mu Family when they were on the run from the Manchu troops. He knew that this old man ranked second only to the Young Count in the Mu Family. He bowed to him and said:

'It is indeed a great honour for us today to meet one of the true heroes of our age!'

'Father Obscurus pays me too great a compliment,' returned old Liu, unable to conceal his pleasure.

The Mu Family knew the names of their guests, Obscurus observed. They had clearly done their homework.

They took their seats, and noticed that there was still one seat empty at the high table. Just as the Triads were wondering which famous kungfu Master they were going to be presented with next, the Young Count announced:

'Tell them to bring in Mr Xu. I should like our friends to see him, so that they can set their minds at ease.'

Su Gang went into the next room and returned leading an elderly man, with bent back and unsure step. Big Beaver and the others recognized the man at once.

'Brother Xu!' they cried out in astonishment.

It was indeed Xu Tianchuan, the Eight-Armed Ape, the Triad Brother they had all but given up for lost. His complexion was extremely sallow, his wounds were still not completely healed, but none the less it was Xu, and he was obviously out of mortal danger. They crowded round him excitedly, plying him with questions.

The Young Count showed Xu to the seat 'above' his own. As he sat down, Xu made a bow in the direction of Trinket.

'Greetings, Lodge Master.'

'Greetings, Brother Xu,' returned Trinket, clasping his palms together. 'I don't suppose the medicated plaster business has been too busy of late?'

Xu sighed.

'No business to speak of at all, I'm afraid. The Satrap's dogs got their teeth into me. I'd be a dead man now, if Count Mu and Liu Shifu hadn't saved me!'

The Triads listened to this aghast.

'So it was the Satrap's men who did it?' said Brother Fan.

'That's right. They broke into my medicine shop and carried me off. That filthy cur Lu Yifeng began abusing me, and stuck one my own plasters over my mouth. He said he hoped I starved to death!'

The Triad Brothers expressed their profoundest apologies to the Mu Family, who it now turned out, so far from having been old Xu's kidnappers, had in fact been his saviours.

'Say no more,' said Su the Magic Hand gruffly. 'We were acting on Count Mu's orders. Any enemy of the Satrap is a friend of ours.'

Trinket meanwhile was musing to himself along somewhat different lines:

'Smart fellow, this Count! He knows I've got his sister under lock and key; so now he's gone and "saved" our Brother Xu. Soon he'll be asking for his sister back! I'd better pretend I haven't spotted his little game . . .'

He asked Xu how his wounds were healing.

'Slowly but nicely, thank you.'

Maple scowled at Trinket. Trinket pretended not to notice.

Generous helpings of food and wine were served. The Triads, who had by now put aside all of their earlier suspicions, ate with a hearty appetite, and filled their cups enthusiastically.

Old Iron Dragon Liu tossed back three cups, and gave his whiskers a little twirl:

'Gentlemen, which of you is in charge of the metropolitan district?'

Brother Li replied that Lodge Master Wei was in charge.

Liu nodded.

'Good, good . . .'

He drank another cup, and continued:

'But can he accept the responsibility in a serious matter such as this?'

'Uncle,' said Trinket, 'whatever it is, just say it. Cut the crap. I'm only a junior, I know. But I think I can shoulder the odd little load. Just don't dump too much on me all at once, or I'll end up looking like Lodge Master Squash-me-all-flat . . .'

Triads and Mu Family alike frowned at this latest instance of urchin-talk, and looked at each other in horror. Old Liu laughed darkly as he replied:

'This matter concerns the death of Brother Pine. As we all know, he died at Xu Tianchuan's hands . . . I think we may need to ask your Helmsman to advise us how to resolve this matter once and for all.'

Xu leapt to his feet.

'Count Mu, Liu Shifu,' he declared bravely, 'it was you who delivered me from the hands of the Satrap's men, it was you who saved me from a fate worse than death. My gratitude knows no bounds. Pine's death *was* my doing, though I never meant to kill him. I will gladly repay his death with my own!'

He turned to Brother Fan, and held out his right hand:

'Lend me your dagger!'

Everyone knew what he had in mind. To 'settle the matter' there and then, by slitting his own throat.

'Wait!' cried Trinket. 'Hold on a minute, Brother Xu. Sit down, and calm down. You're too old to let yourself get carried away like this! Now, tell me, am I or am I not Lodge Master Wei of the Green Wood Lodge?'

Disobeying a Lodge Master was a very serious offence for a Triad. Xu bowed to Trinket.

'Your word is my command, Master.'

Trinket nodded.

'That's more like it. Pine is dead and gone, and nothing will bring him back, not even your death. It'd simply be chucking good money after bad . . .'

They all looked at him aghast, wondering what appalling thing he was going to say next. Trinket continued unabashed, addressing himself to the Young Count:

'Tell me, Count Mu, when you came up from Yunnan to the Capital, surely you brought a few more people with you? There seem to be one or two men missing, somehow . . .'

'What are you driving at, Lodge Master Wei?'

'Oh, nothing in particular. I just thought a big shot like you would have one or two more people around, you know, just in case. You never know what these Tartars might try and do to you . . .'

Iron Dragon Liu cast a glance in his direction.

'My young friend,' he said to Trinket, 'you seem to be hinting at some mystery. Please be so good as to enlighten us.'

'You flatter me! I'm more *hys*terical than *mys*terical. Most particularly hysterical and unheroical . . .'

'To be precise, my young friend,' said the Young Count, 'you seem to be implying that one of our men may have been taken prisoner by the Tartars. Is that it?'

'Oh, not really. It must be the wine. A little goes a very long way with me. I get a bit woozy, boozy, mysterical, hysterical, whatever. Put it down to the wine. I'm probably just drunk and talking a lot of tamardy twaddle!'

'Young friend,' said old Iron Dragon Liu, 'if indeed you *are* a friend, will you *please* stop beating about the bush and say whatever it is you have to say!'

'Bush? What bush?' protested Trinket. 'I'm talking about Peking! It's such a tricky, sticky sort of place, and if you don't know your way around it, you never know—people *do* have a way of disappearing in the middle of the night . . .'

Old Iron Dragon shot a glance at the Young Count again.

'So?'

'So,' Trinket replied, 'I've heard that the Forbidden City is one big maze! Gateway after gateway, hallway after hallway—if you just go crashing in, and don't happen to have an Emperor or an Empress handy to guide you around, before you know where you are, you're lost! Stuck for life! Up to your ears in Tartar sauce . . . The trouble is, I'm not sure if Their Imperial Majesties are available for daytime guided tours. Or night-time ones either, for that matter.

But you could always try your luck. After all, Count, you're a bit of a big shot, aren't you? Why not try and see what happens? You'll probably scare the Emperor to death, *and* that Old Whore the Empress Dowager!'

The assembled company had never in their lives heard the Empress Dowager referred to as an Old Whore. Big Beaver, Tertius, and the others found it all rather novel, and could barely suppress a smile.

'As a matter of fact,' Trinket continued, 'I've got a friend who works in the Palace. He's attached to the Guards. Does a fair bit of gambling, actually. He told me there was a break-in last night. Some people tried to kill the Emperor, apparently. They were caught, and they confessed. They said they were working for you . . .'

'What?' cried the Young Count.

His right hand trembled, and he dropped his wine-cup on the floor, where it smashed into pieces.

'I'd already guessed as much, mind you,' continued Trinket. 'After all, you Mu Family *were* very big under the Ming dynasty, you'd be just the people to do something heroic like try to bump off the Tartar Emperor!'

'It's more likely to have been the Satrap's men,' said Iron Dragon Liu. 'His son is in town, and I wouldn't put it past him—'

'What a shame!' Trinket interrupted. 'In that case, I'd better get word to that friend of mine, make sure those men are given a hard time. Tamardy! Anyone who works for *that* traitor deserves it!'

'My dear fellow,' put in Iron Dragon Liu quickly, 'can you give me the name of your friend in the Palace? Where exactly did you say he works?'

'Oh, he just cleans the floors for the Guards, makes tea, pours water, that kind of thing. He's nobody important, I'm afraid. People usually call him Warthead. Nobody bothers with his real name—if he's even got one! When I heard the assassins were tied up, I asked him to smuggle them in a snack or two. But now I know they're the Satrap's men, I'll get him to slice them up a bit!'

'That was only a guess of mine,' said Iron Dragon Liu, rather feebly. 'You never know. Whoever the intruders were, they must have been brave men to break into the Palace at all. Perhaps you ought to ask that friend of yours to help them out a bit anyway. That might be rather a River and Lake sort of thing to do, don't you think?'

'Warthead would do anything for me,' boasted Trinket. 'Whenever he loses at cards, I always lend him money. So whatever it is you want, I'm sure he'll do it—for me.'

Iron Dragon breathed a sigh of relief.

'Thank goodness for that. I wonder how many men were caught, and what their names are? You can't help admiring them. Perhaps your friend could find out how they are faring? I should be most obliged, Lodge Master, dear friend.'

Trinket slapped his own chest.

'Easiest thing in the world! It's just a shame that these are the Satrap's men. If they were *your* men, Count, I'd go one further. I'd try and get one of them out for you—that way, we could settle scores, you know, a life for a life . . . It could even solve Brother Xu's little problem . . .'

Iron Dragon cast the Young Count another glance, and nodded slowly.

'We don't know for sure who these men are,' said the Young Count, 'but one thing is certain: they showed great courage in trying to kill the Tartar Emperor, and they clearly stand on our side! I think I can say, Lodge Master Wei, that if you were able to find a way to rescue them, I should be eternally indebted to you, and this whole unfortunate matter with your Brother Xu would be forgotten.'

Trinket turned and looked at Maple.

'But Sir Maple here may not forget so easily. Next time we meet, for all I know he'll grab me by the arm again and squeeze the living daylights out of me! He'll have me bawling my poor little tamardy heart out again! *Not* my idea of fun . . .'

Maple leapt to his feet.

'Lodge Master Wei! Rescue our . . . our . . . those poor brave men trapped in there, and I will take a solemn oath: if this hand of mine should ever offend you again, may it be cut off at the wrist and presented to you as my personal punishment!'

'Please, please!' cried Trinket. 'There's really no need for that! What would I do with your hand anyway, even if you did chop it off? And besides, I'm not even sure if my friend Warthead *can* pull this rescue job off. These men are in serious trouble, they're probably in shackles and leg-irons, with hundreds of men guarding them.'

'Whether your friend succeeds or not,' cried the Young Count, 'we will still be eternally indebted to you both for trying!'

After a short pause, he continued.

'There is one other matter. A day or two ago, my own younger sister went missing. I'm very worried about her. You Triads are very well-connected here in the Capital. If you get wind of anything, or see any chance of rescuing her from whatever predicament she is in, I should also be eternally grateful!'

'No problem at all,' said Trinket. 'Set your mind completely at rest. Come, I think we've drunk enough of this wine. I'd better go and find my old friend Warthead. Tamardy, it's about time he and I threw the dice together again!'

He produced a set of four dice from his inside pocket and rolled them on the table. Four Fours, four lots of four winking little red dots. Trinket clapped his hands.

'Crimson House! Our luck's in! Let's just hope *their* house isn't crimson with *too* much blood already!'

Everyone shuddered at this somewhat macabre remark.

Trinket bowed.

'I must be going. I'd like Brother Xu to come with me, if that's all right?'

'Of course!' said the Young Count. 'And we insist on seeing all of you on your way. That's the least we can do.'

So Trinket, Xu the Eight-Armed Ape, Big Beaver, Brother Li, and all the other Triads walked out of the door, and the Young Count, Iron Dragon Liu, and the other members of the Mu Family, having seen them off, and Trinket into his sedan chair, went back inside.

Settling the Score

The Triads returned together to their 'safe' courtyard house. As usual Big Beaver was the most agitated about the recent news.

'Lodge Master Wei,' he said, 'this certainly looks like a Mu Family break-in.'

'I'm sure it was,' said Trinket. 'Did you notice *they* didn't seem a bit surprised when I told them about it. But no one outside the Palace knows about it. It's been kept top secret.'

'Well I think they deserve our admiration for trying,' said Father Obscurus. 'It must have taken a lot of courage to get in. And getting out will be even harder. Lodge Master, do you really think we can do it?'

Trinket had already been contemplating this very problem.

There seemed small chance of getting the main band of assassins out; but he had a couple of Mu Family girls stowed away in his own bedroom. It might be feasible to get *them* out. In answer to Father Obscurus's gloomy prognostication, he smiled and said:

'We won't be able to get many of them out, but we might be able to manage one or two. Even one would be enough to settle the score, and get Brother Xu off. And then there's that young lady Butcher Qian smuggled in. Brother Qian, I want you to come to the Catering Department first thing tomorrow morning with two more pig carcasses. Big ones. We'll take them to my rooms and stuff them with you know what ... Then I'll make a big fuss in the kitchen, and complain that the meat's gone off, and you can take them away again.'

The Butcher clapped his hands.

'Sounds like a brilliant plan, Lodge Master!'

Trinket said a few comforting words to Xu Tianchuan.

The Emperor's Plan

Trinket arrived back at the Palace, and entered by the northern Gate of the Divine Warrior. Two eunuchs came out to welcome him.

'Quickly, Laurel Goong-goong! His Majesty has sent for you!'

'What's the matter?'

'It must be something important. He keeps asking for you. He's in the Upper Library.'

Trinket went directly to the Library and found Kang Xi pacing up and down. The Emperor looked happy to see him.

'Tamardy, Laurie, where the devil have you been all day?'

'Majesty, I've been so worried about the assassins! You said we should track down the masterminds behind the plot, and deal with them quickly, or we're sure to have more trouble on our hands. So I've been doing a little plain-clothes detective work in town.'

'Well done! And did you discover anything?'

'I've been out there most of the day, but I'm afraid I still didn't spot anyone suspicious. I'll try again tomorrow.'

'It may get us nowhere, you rushing around town,' replied the Emperor. 'Besides, I have another idea. Just now Colonel Dolong was here, and he tells me they've been interrogating the three prisoners all day, and no amount of torture can get a word out of them. They still swear blind that they're the Satrap's men. I was thinking, rather than go on torturing them, which probably won't get us anywhere, why not just set them free.'

'Let them go? Just . . . just like that?'

'They were clearly acting on orders. The important thing is to catch the people who *gave* the orders, and round *them* up. Otherwise, mark my words, this thing will not end here.' He smiled. 'So: we'll set the little wolf-cubs free, and they will lead us to Mother Wolf . . .'

Trinket clapped his hands in delight.

'Brilliant! A stroke of genius!'

'Don't overdo it!' said Kang Xi, laughing. 'The difficult part will be to follow them without being seen ourselves. That's where you come in, Laurie. I'm going to put you in charge of that. I want you to pretend to be their saviour. You rescue them, and they'll take you straight to their leader.'

Trinket thought this over for a second or two.

'I'm not sure . . .'

'I know it's all rather dangerous,' said Kang Xi. 'You mustn't let them suspect you even for a moment, or they'll kill you in cold blood. If only I wasn't Emperor, dammit, I'd do it myself! It all sounds so tamardy exciting!'

'If those are your orders, Majesty, then I'll do it. Nothing frightens me.'

Kang Xi patted him on the shoulder.

'I always knew what a smart, brave fellow you were, Laurie . . . You look so young, I'm sure they'll never suspect you. I'd thought of choosing a couple of guards and sending them along, but they'd have been spotted straight away. This plan of mine will only have one chance of working. We've got to get it right first time, Laurie! Having *you* do it is going to be almost like doing it myself!'

As he grew up, the young Emperor had come to feel more and more frustrated at not being able to 'do things himself', at having to preserve his 'Imperial person' from danger. Through Trinket he could at least experience vicariously some of the excitement of this hazardous escapade.

'You must be as convincing as possible,' Kang Xi continued. 'It mightn't even be a bad idea to kill a couple of guards, just to prove your credentials. I'll put Dolong in the picture, and give him special instructions to let you pass out of the Palace.'

Kang Xi was rubbing his hands together in his excitement.

'Laurie, pull this off, and I'll give you anything you want!'

'I just want to please you, Majesty! That's all I want. And to be sent on your next dangerous errand!'

'Excellent! Good man!' exclaimed the delighted Kang Xi. 'Oh Laurie, if only you weren't a eunuch! Then I could make you one of my Great Ministers or something!'

Trinket reflected on this possibility for a moment.

'Thanks for the thought, Your Majesty,' he said. But secretly he was thinking to himself: 'You may be wonderfully *pleased* with me *now*. But wait till you find out who I really am! Wait till you know that I'm *not* a eunuch after all! You'll be wonderfully *angry* with me *then*!'

'Majesty, I've got one favour to ask you.'

'What is it? *Do* you want to be a Minister?'

'Oh no! It's just . . . Well, I'm going to do my very best, and I'll always be your most loyal and brave servant, but just supposing something went terribly wrong . . . Would you forgive me? Would you spare my life?'

'Just be loyal to me,' said Kang Xi, 'and you'll never have any cause to worry. I'll make sure that head of yours stays firmly attached to your neck!'

The Emperor had a good laugh.

Curly-Beard, Pale-Face, and Tattoo-Chest

As Trinket left the Library, he pondered this unexpected turn of events.

'Now the Emperor has ordered me to set free the prisoners, so I can take my time with the Little Countess and Fang Yi. As for them taking me straight to their leader, why, I've just *been* with their leader, having a few drinks . . . I wonder if I should have told the Emperor the truth? Should I just hand over the Mu Family, including that turtle the Count and his old Shifu, and have the lot of them arrested? No, I don't think so. If I did, *my* Shifu the Helmsman would never forgive me. A Triad Lodge Master betraying one of the Mu Family . . . Tamardy! This is all getting too complicated and difficult! What do I want to go on being a Triad Lodge Master for? Why don't I just quit?'

After all, life wasn't so bad in the Palace, he reflected. It was rather pleasant being the Emperor's favourite and having everyone sucking up to him. In fact there wasn't even really too much wrong with the idea of being a (theoretical) eunuch for the rest of his life. But then he remembered the Empress Dowager, and gave an involuntary shudder.

'The Old Whore will stop at nothing till she's done me in. I'd never last long in the Palace.'

As he was thinking these thoughts, he had reached the Guardroom next to the Hall of Heavenly Purity. It so happened that his old friend Zhao Qixian was on duty that day. The previous day Zhao had been distributing money for Trinket, and today he had received another reward from Colonel Dolong, which he understood had come his way because Trinket had been saying good things about him to the Emperor. When he saw Trinket coming, he jumped up to greet him.

'Laurel Goong-goong, what good wind blows you here?'

'I've come to have a look at those rogues you've got locked up,' said Trinket with an affable smile. Then he put his mouth close to Zhao's ear and whispered:

'His Majesty wants me to help with the interrogation, and see if I can't worm out of them who was behind their little plot.'

Zhao nodded, and whispered back:

'None of the three will say a word. We've broken two whips on them already, and they still stick by their story that the Satrap sent them.' 'Let me have a go,' said Trinket.

He went in to find three big fellows strapped to the pillars of the room, their naked bodies bleeding and bruised. One of them was a man with a large curly beard, the other two were younger men, one pale-skinned, the other tattooed all over his body. (On his chest he had a tattoo of a ferocious-looking tiger's head.)

'I wonder which one of these two is Fang Yi's young man?' thought Trinket to himself. He turned to Zhao.

'I have a sneaking feeling you may have arrested the wrong men. Leave us alone for a moment.'

Zhao went out, closing the door behind him.

'Now,' began Trinket, 'tell me your names.'

Curly-Beard glowered at him.

'Think we'd give our names to a dirty little pup of a eunuch like you?'

Trinket lowered his voice to a whisper:

'I'm here to help a friend by the name of Liu Yizhou get out of here . . .'

He observed the three men looking at one another in utter astonishment.

'Who sent you?' asked Curly-Beard.

'Is one of you Liu Yizhou or not? If so, then I might have something more to say. If not, you can forget it.'

They looked at one another again. They were obviously wary of falling into some kind of trap.

'Who are you?' asked Curly-Beard.

'I've been sent by two friends. One of them is called Count Mu, the other is Iron Dragon. Do you know them?'

'Everyone in Yunnan and Sichuan has heard of the Iron Dragon!' cried Curly-Beard. 'As for Count Mu, he is the son of the Young Duke, and since his father's death has been wandering on River and Lake. Nobody even knows if he is still alive.'

He shook his head sadly.

'Well, if none of you know the Count or Iron Dragon personally, that means you can't be their friends. And I suppose you don't recognize this either?'

Trinket proceeded to execute a passable version of the Two Way Sweep and the Cataract.

The young man with the tiger tattooed on his chest could not help letting out a gasp of astonishment.

Trinket halted his little routine.

'Well?'

'Nothing.'

'Who taught you those moves?' asked Curly-Beard.

'My woman did.'

Curly-Beard gave a snort of contempt.

'What kind of a woman would a eunuch like you have?'

It appeared that Curly-Beard might be beginning to have second thoughts about Trinket. He had at least stopped calling him 'a dirty little pup'.

'Why shouldn't a eunuch have a woman? If the woman wants to be had, what business is it of yours? I'll tell you her name. It's Fang. Fang Yi . . .'

The pale-faced younger man suddenly let out a great bellow: 'That's a lie!'

Trinket could see the man's veins bulging on his neck, and his eyes breathing fire. That must be Liu, he thought to himself. Not a bad-looking fellow, but a trifle daunting in his present overwrought state.

'What do you mean a lie?' he went on. 'I told you, her name is Fang, she's descended from one of the Four Paladins that fought with Old Duke Mu. One of our matchmakers was a gentleman by the name of Su Gang, they call him the Magic Hand. Another one was one of the Bo brothers, Maple. His Elder Brother Pine was killed recently, and Maple was a bit short of cash for the funeral, so he took on a few odd jobs like matchmaking.'

Pale-Face was looking as if he was about to spontaneously combust.

'You . . . you . . . you . . .'

'Quieten down, Brother!' said Curly-Beard. Then turning to Trinket he continued:

'You certainly seem to know a thing or two about the Mu Family.'

'Well I ought to, seeing I'm getting married into it!' replied Trinket. 'Mind you, my woman—that's the one who used to be Miss Fang—she wouldn't marry me at first, said she was betrothed to some Liu fellow. Then she heard how Liu had turned out bad, and gone to fight for that traitor the Satrap, and got caught breaking into the Palace. So she decided to dump him for me . . .'

Pale-Face was getting more and more agitated.

'I . . . I . . . I . . .'

Curly-Beard shook his head.

'And what about *you*? It's hardly the most glorious thing in the world to be a eunuch working for the Tartars!'

'You're right there,' agreed Trinket. 'Be that as it may, my woman asked me to find out if this Liu fellow is alive or dead. If he's dead, she'd like to burn some paper money for him. But it seems that none of you is Liu, so I'd better be on my way. Our wedding's this evening . . .'

He turned to go.

Pale-Face opened his mouth.

'I'm—'

'Don't fall for it! It's a trap!' shouted Curly-Beard.

Pale-Face was struggling to contain himself. He was foaming at the mouth, and spat in Trinket's face.

Trinket ducked, and as he made for the door, made a mental note of what had been used to tie the three prisoners to the pillars: strong lengths of ox sinew. They'd have some trouble getting free from those.

'Pale-Face is obviously Liu,' he thought to himself. 'He was about to say so, only old Curly-Beard stopped him.'

Another moment's reflection, and he had hatched a plan.

'Wait for me here,' he said to the three men. 'I've got to report back to my woman.'

Zhao Qixian was waiting for him in the outer room.

'I think I'm getting somewhere with those three,' said Trinket. 'Don't torture them any more for the time being. I'll be back shortly.'

A Libation

Trinket thought the girls must be getting hungry. On his way back, he dropped in at the Catering Department and gave orders for a big spread to be served in his rooms. He said he wanted to celebrate with some of the guards. They would be discussing confidential matters, he added, and should not be disturbed.

He unlocked the outer door, and tiptoed into the inner room. He heard the Little Countess give a tiny cry and sit up.

'Why have you been so dreadfully long?' she asked in a whisper.

'I've got good news!' announced a gleeful Trinket.

'*What* good news?' asked Fang Yi, lifting her head from the pillow.

Trinket lit a candle on the table. He could see that Fang Yi's eyes were red from crying.

'Good news for you!' he said, heaving a sigh. 'Lousy news for me! Goodbye to a lovely wife, when I just about had her in the bag! That Liu of yours is alive and kicking, I'm afraid to say.'

Fang Yi let out a little cry of joy.

The Little Countess also seemed delighted:

'Is Brother Liu unharmed?'

'Well, let's just say he's alive. I can tell you, he's lucky to be that. Ever since the guards caught him, he's insisted on sticking to his Satrap story. It's a shame, really. He'll be executed anyway, but this way he'll die with his reputation ruined! Everyone on River and Lake will despise him as a traitor.'

Fang Yi propped herself up in bed.

'We'd thought of that beforehand. We just wanted to strike a blow against the Satrap, and to revenge Duke Mu and the true Ming

Emperor. Our own lives and reputations seemed of little importance.'

Trinket stuck his thumb up in the air.

'Bravo! Shows guts! Now listen here, Miss Fang, we've got some very important business to discuss. Supposing I *do* manage to get your Liu fellow out—what then?'

There was a momentary gleam of hope in Fang Yi's eyes, and her face grew flushed.

'If you really can save him, I'll do anything, *anything*, to show my gratitude!'

There was something wonderfully plucky about the way she said this.

'Very well then,' said Trinket, 'let's make a deal. And I'd like the Little Countess to witness it for us. If I save your friend Liu, and deliver him safely to Count Mu and Iron Dragon—'

'You mean you know about *them*?' interrupted the Little Countess.

'Of course I do! Everyone does!'

'I know you're a good person!' cried the Little Countess. 'I know you'll save Brother Liu for us!'

Trinket shook his head.

'No, I'm not a good person. I'm just making a deal. This Liu friend of yours is not a petty thief, you know. He tried to kill the Emperor! Rescuing him is going to be a *very* dangerous assignment. If I get caught, do you have any idea what'll happen to me? Do you have any idea what'll happen to all my family—my grandpa, my grandma, my mum and dad, my three brothers, my four sisters, my aunties and uncles and cousins? Off with their heads, that's what! Every one of them! And do you have any idea what'll happen to all my worldly goods—my gold, my silver, my estates, my wok, my trousers, my socks, my shoes—what do you think will happen to them? Confiscated, the lot of them! Taken! Gone!'

The Little Countess accompanied this tragic recital by nodding her head every time he asked her if she had 'any idea', and muttering sympathetically, 'Yes, I know.'

'You're right,' said Fang Yi. 'It really *isn't* fair to ask you to do something so dangerous. But . . . if Brother Liu dies, I won't want to go on living! I suppose we'll just have to let fate take its course!'

Tears were coursing down her cheeks.

'Don't do that!' cried Trinket. 'Don't go upsetting your dear little self! Don't cry! It breaks my heart, to see those pearly tears running down your flowerlike face! Oh Miss Fang, I'd do anything for you! I promise I'll save him for you. Let's swear an oath. If I fail, I'll be your ox or your horse for the rest of *my* days! And if I succeed, you'll be my wife for the rest of *your* days! There! My word is my troth!'

Fang Yi stared at him wide-eyed, and the colour drained from her cheeks. Her face was almost white.

'Brother Laurel,' she began, 'if you can save Brother Liu, I'll do anything . . . Bring him back to me alive, and for the rest of my days I'll . . . I'll serve you, I'll obey you in everything! But I can't . . . I can't . . .'

They heard footsteps outside the door.

'Laurel Goong-goong, the meal you ordered is here!'

'Very good!' said Trinket, and went to the outer door. Four junior eunuchs deposited everything—twelve dishes, including one particularly delicious-looking steamed Yunnan chicken, wine, plates, bowls, and chopsticks—in the outer room, gladly accepted their tip of one tael each, and took their leave.

Trinket carried the food into the bedroom himself, and drew a table up to the bed. He filled three cups with wine, and three bowls with rice.

'Miss Fang, just now you were saying something . . . ?'

With some help from the Little Countess, Fang Yi had managed to sit up. The flush had returned to her cheeks, and she sat there with head bowed. Finally she said, in a scarcely audible voice:

'What I meant was, I can't see what someone like you would *want* to get married for—I mean, with all your duties in the Palace . . . But anyway, if you *can* save my friend's life, for the rest of my days I'll be . . . your companion.'

Trinket looked at her. In the warm glow cast by the red candle, her face was positively radiant, like a piece of lustrous jade. She seemed in that moment indescribably lovely. Trinket was only a boy, but he couldn't help being quite transported by her beauty. He smiled.

'What you meant was, you can't see why a eunuch should want to get married. Well, I think that's something for the eunuch to worry about, not you. Let me ask you again: will you or won't you be my wife for the rest of your days?'

A little frown crossed Fang Yi's brow, and a momentary flash of anger lit up her face. This was followed by a long silence, during which she seemed to be struggling to reach some kind of decision. Finally she spoke.

'All right! I'll do anything! I wouldn't even have to be your wife! Have your way with me if you want to, and sell me off to a whore-house! I'd gladly do whatever you say!'

Anyone else would probably have taken offence at this. But Trinket, having been born and raised in a whore-house, didn't see anything very unusual about her proposal. He laughed.

'Very well then, let's all drink to it! The three of us! Come! Sister! Wife!'

Fang Yi had learned over the past day that she had under-estimated this eunuch. Watching him rip open the Colonel and dissolve his corpse with the powder, and witnessing how respectfully the other eunuchs all treated him, she was beginning to realize that he was something a little out of the ordinary. It had broken her heart to watch Liu being captured, unable to go to his aid because of her own wounds. The two of them, though not yet actually married, were deeply in love and had already sworn themselves to each other. If this eunuch could bring her true love back from the jaws of death, she would gladly endure any suffering! And besides, the chances were that he only wanted to have her as an ornament, to show her off, perhaps steal the occasional kiss and lick the lipstick off her lips. So why not go along with it? She raised the wine-cup.

'Very well, I'll drink this cup with you. But I warn you, if you *don't* save my Brother Liu, I'll have your head!'

Trinket loved the way her face dimpled when she smiled. He raised his cup.

'This is a solemn oath. There's no going back on it. If I rescue Liu, and you betray me . . .'

Fang Yi's face became serious.

'I swear by Heaven and Earth,' she declared solemnly, 'that if Laurel Goong-goong can save Liu Yizhou and bring him safe out of danger, I, Fang Yi, will marry Laurel Goong-goong, and be true to him. Even if he can never be a proper husband to me, I will serve him faithfully all my days as his wife. If I betray him, may I be hacked to pieces and never born again.'

She poured a libation of wine from her cup onto the floor.

'And may you, Little Countess, be my witness.'

Trinket was ecstatic. He turned to the Little Countess:

'Do *you* have a true love I could rescue for you?'

'No! Certainly not!'

'What a pity!'

Trinket went on to describe to the Countess the two other assassins taken prisoner. Curly-Beard was, it transpired, a distinguished retainer of the Mu Family called Wu Lishen, a kungfu Master, known to the Martial Arts community as the Shaker Lion. (Trinket had already observed that he did a great deal of head-shaking.) The younger man with the tiger on his chest was called Ao Biao. He was known as the Blue Tiger, and was one of Wu's disciples. The Little Countess pleaded with Trinket to rescue the two others while he was about it.

'Do they have pretty women waiting for *them*?' asked the incorrigible Trinket. 'This is starting to sound like a lot of fun!'

Suddenly something came whizzing towards him through the air, crashed into his forehead, and fell to the ground, where it smashed to smithereens. It was Fang Yi's wine-cup. Blood and wine trickled from his forehead down his face.

'Come here and let me have a look at that cut,' said the Little Countess, alarmed.

'I'm not coming anywhere near you two!' cried Trinket. 'My own wife just tried to murder me!'

'I'd have been angry myself,' said the Little Countess, 'after the things you said.'

'Oh, I see!' said Trinket, laughing loudly. 'Now both of my womenfolk are starting to get jealous!'

The Little Countess raised her cup in the air and threatened to follow Fang Yi's example. Trinket wiped his eyes with the sleeve of his jacket. The sight of the Little Countess trying to be cross, with a little smile still playing on her face, combined with the charming spectacle of Fang Yi looking almost repentant, more than compensated for the ache he felt on his forehead.

'Go on, throw!'

'All right then, I will!'

She raised her hand in the air, but instead of throwing it she emptied the contents of her cup all over Trinket's face. He made no effort to avoid it, but just stood there letting the wine run all over his face, then stuck his tongue out and began licking the mixture of wine and blood that came trickling down.

'Hmm! *Dee*licious! Blood courtesy of wife number one; wine courtesy of wife number two; what a yummy combination!'

The two girls both burst out laughing, first the Little

Countess, then Fang Yi, who took out a handkerchief and, after examining his wound, cleaned it up for him.

They were hungry now, and between them did justice to the excellent food before them.

After dinner, Trinket yawned.

'Which of my two wives should I sleep with tonight?'

Fang Yi pulled a face.

'For goodness' sake be serious! If you so much as try getting into bed with me, I'll . . . I'll kill you with my sword!'

Trinket stuck out his tongue.

'One of these days you probably *will* kill me!'

He carried the leftover food into the outer room. Then he came back in, spread a mat on the ground, and lay down on it fully clothed. He was exhausted, and within minutes had fallen fast asleep.

Plotting the Escape

Trinket awoke early the next morning feeling surprisingly warm and cosy. He opened his eyes, to find that someone had thrown a padded quilt over him, and placed a pillow under his head. He sat up, and could just make out, through the bed-curtains, the figures of the Little Countess and Fang Yi, lying fast asleep side by side.

He stood up and stole across to the bedstead. Drawing the curtains, he beheld a sight of the most soul-bewitching beauty. The two girls complemented each other wonderfully: Fang Yi was enchantingly seductive, in an almost coquettish way; the Little Countess, though in fact the younger of the two, possessed a graver and more sedate beauty. The two of them together were like pearl and jade, a perfect combination. Trinket felt an irresistible desire to kiss them both, but was afraid of waking them.

'Tamardy!' he mused to himself ecstatically. 'If I had these two as my wives, I'd really live happily ever after! They never had girls as pretty as this at Vernal Delights!'

He crept over to the door. As he opened it, it creaked very slightly. Fang Yi awoke at once.

'Laurel . . . Good morning!'

'Don't you mean husband?'

'You haven't rescued him yet . . .'

'Don't you worry: I will.'

The Little Countess also awoke.

'What are you two chattering about so early in the morning?' she asked sleepily.

'We couldn't get to sleep,' said Trinket. 'We've been awake all night, talking.'

He yawned, and patted his mouth somewhat affectedly.

'I'm so tired! It's been a long night! I'd better try and get some sleep.'

He gave a good stretch.

Fang Yi flushed.

'Silly boy! As if I could bear to talk to you for more than a few minutes . . .'

Trinket ignored this remark and asked Fang to write him a little note to give to Liu. It would help him to win the prisoners' trust, he said.

'That sounds like a good idea. But what should I write?'

'Oh you know, anything really. How you're going to marry me, what a wonderful person I am, how brave and good, and how I'm going to rescue him for your sake, because you asked me to.'

He found Old Hai's writing implements, spread a sheet of paper on a little table, and pushed it towards the bed.

Fang Yi sat up in bed, and took the brush in her hand. Suddenly she burst into tears.

'I don't want to write that!'

Trinket felt sorry for her, and relented.

'Oh well, write whatever you like. I can't read anyway. Perhaps on second thoughts it's better if you don't tell him you're marrying me. It's bound to make him mad.'

'I bet you *can* read,' said Fang Yi. 'You're tricking me.'

'If I can read, I'm a rotten turtle, not your husband!'

Fang Yi tried again, but broke down in tears a second time.

'Oh all right!' said Trinket, in a sudden fit of magnanimity. 'I'll rescue him, and then you can marry him! I'm buggered if I'm going to spend my life competing with him! Even if you did marry me, you'd only be mooning for him all the time. You'd end up sleeping with him anyway. You'd might as well get on with it, marry him, and live happily ever after. Tamardy! Put down whatever you like. I don't care.'

Fang Yi looked at him out of big, tear-filled eyes. A happy little wraith of a smile crossed her face, mingled with real gratitude. She wrote a few lines, and folded the paper.

'There. Please would you give him this.'

'I like that!' Trinket thought to himself. 'I've been downgraded to plain old *you* already! She didn't lose much time dumping me!'

But he decided not to make a fuss. He took the message, put it in his inside pocket, and walked out of the room, without even looking back. If he was going to play the part of the hero, he might as well do it properly.

The officer on duty in the Guardroom now was Trinket's other friend, Zhang Kangnian. Zhang had already been briefed the previous evening by Dolong about Trinket's secret mission. He greeted Trinket with a knowing wink, and drew him aside to a secluded spot by a large rock.

'How are you going to manage this "escape", Laurel Goong-goong?' he asked.

Trinket took one look at Zhang's friendly face and realized he could not possibly kill him just to establish his own credibility with the prisoners (as the Emperor had suggested). Luckily he now had Fang Yi's message, which should do the trick just as well.

'First I'll go in and interrogate those three turtles,' he said in reply to Zhang's question. 'After that I don't know; I'll play it by ear.'

He made his way into the room where the three prisoners were being held. They looked weak and dispirited. The effects of two days without food or water were beginning to tell. There were seven or eight junior guards keeping watch over them.

'His Majesty has decided to have these three executed at once,' Trinket said to the guards. 'Go and fetch something for them to eat and drink. They must die on full stomachs, or we'll have three hungry ghosts on our hands.'

Several of the guards went to do his bidding.

'At least we'll die glorious deaths!' bellowed the curly-bearded Shaker Wu. 'Faithful to our master the Satrap! Not filthy Tartar lackeys!'

One of the guards gave him a few lashes with a whip, and cursed the name of the Satrap.

Throughout this Liu Yizhou was staring frantically at the ceiling, mumbling something inaudible.

The guards came back with the food and drink.

'Don't give them too much to drink!' said Trinket. 'They mustn't die drunk, or they won't feel the pain!'

Shaker Wu ate and drank his fill. Ao Biao, his much-tattooed disciple, ate his food, and with every mouthful uttered some foul execration. Liu Yizhou grew paler in the face than ever. He was unable to swallow his wine, and after eating half a bowl of rice, shook his head and ate no more.

'I want to be left alone now with the prisoners,' ordered Trinket. 'His Majesty has ordered me to ask them one or two last questions.'

Zhang took the hint and led his men off.

The minute the guards were out of earshot, Trinket gave a little cough, and turned to face the three prisoners. A conspiratorial smile spread across his face.

'Damn you, you dirty little gelding! What's so funny?'

It was Shaker Wu who spoke.

'None of your business,' replied Trinket. 'Just a little private joke of my own.'

Suddenly Liu Yizhou spoke up:

'Goong-goong . . . I'm the one! It's me! I'm . . . I'm Liu Yizhou!'

Trinket stared at him in silence.

'Hold your stupid tongue!' cried both Wu and Ao Biao together.

'Goong-goong!' continued Liu undeterred. 'I beg you, save me . . . Save us!'

'Coward!' cried Wu. 'Aren't you ashamed of yourself?'

'He said he'd been sent by our people to save us!'

'And you believed him?'

Wu shook his head.

Trinket laughed.

'Sir Wu,' he said, 'the Shaker Lion, if I'm not mistaken? Would you do me a favour, and try not to shake your head at me quite so often!'

Wu started.

'How do you . . .'

Trinket laughed again.

'And you, Brother Ao Biao, the Blue Tiger, isn't it? The Lion's favourite disciple? Honoured to meet you!'

Both Wu and Ao stared at him in disbelief.

Trinket took the folded message from his inside pocket and held it out in front of Liu Yizhou.

'Whose is this writing?'

Liu read the message, and as he did so an expression of hope and joy spread across his face.

'This is from my sister-in-arms, Fang Yi! She says Goong-goong has come to rescue us and we are to do whatever he tells us!'

'Let me see it!' muttered Wu.

Trinket handed him the paper, thinking to himself that it most probably contained all manner of extravagant declarations of love. Wu read it aloud:

'"Dear Brother Liu: The bearer of this letter, Laurel Goong-goong, is one of us. He is a brave and honourable friend, and has come to save you from certain death! You must do whatever he says. Your sister, Fang Yi." Hm, she has even written our secret Mu Family mark. It must be genuine.'

'Of course it's genuine,' said Trinket.

'Goong-goong, where is she?' asked Liu Yizhou.

'In a very safe place,' replied Trinket (thinking to himself, 'Yes—safely tucked up in my bed!'). 'When I have rescued you,' he went on aloud, 'I'll rescue her, and the two of you will be reunited.'

For all his earlier blustering, when it came to the crunch, Liu had been undone by his terror of death. It was fear that had driven him to reveal his identity. He now started blubbing like a baby, sobbing his heart out, and swearing his undying gratitude to Trinket. Shaker Wu, whose courage had not faltered for a moment, was still in need of convincing.

'Would you please tell us your name?' he asked. 'And why you are doing this for us?'

'In the circumstances, I think I ought to tell you,' replied Trinket. 'My friends all call me Warthead. That's because I used to be covered in warts. I have a very good friend called Trinket, who is Lodge Master of the Triad Green Wood Lodge. He told me that a Triad by the name of Xu, the Eight-Armed Ape I think he's known as, got into an argument with one of your men about Prince Somebody-or-other, and ended up killing him. Your man's name was Pine Somebody-or-other. Anyway, your Mu people were very upset about it. You can't bring back the dead, so my friend Trinket asked me if I could rescue you. He said that might help to settle the score.'

Shaker Wu knew about the scrap with the Triads, and all this accurate inside information finally convinced him of the genuineness of Trinket's mission. He kept shaking his head and nodding by turns, and ended up apologizing for his earlier rudeness.

'Forget it!' said Trinket gallantly. 'What we've got to do now is think of a way out of here!'

'You just tell us your plan,' said Liu Yizhou. 'We'll do whatever you say, Goong-goong.'

'That's the whole trouble,' thought Trinket to himself. 'I haven't got a plan.'

'What do *you* think?' he asked, turning to Shaker Wu.

'With all these pesky guards around, we don't stand much of a chance during daylight,' replied Wu. 'It had better be tonight. If you can manage to cut us free, we can try to get out under cover of darkness.'

'Good thinking,' said Trinket. 'But it still won't be easy.'

He walked up and down the room, deep in thought.

'Let's just make a dash for it!' said Ao Biao. 'The worst they can do is kill us!'

'Be quiet, Brother Ao,' said Liu Yizhou. 'You're disturbing Goong-goong's concentration.'

Ao Biao scowled angrily at Liu.

Trinket's Cunning Plan

What was going through Trinket's mind was this: if he could drug the guards, then the prisoners could escape without his having to kill anyone. He went out into the ante-chamber and asked his friend Zhang Kangnian if he could lay his hands on any opiate. It turned out that Zhang had a supply ready mixed. It had been prepared for them to use on a secret mission. Colonel Rui Dong, acting on the Empress Dowager's orders, had sent them to apprehend a man who was something of a fighter, and they had thought it prudent to use the drug rather than rely on their own kungfu skills. The man had been none other than Hochabo, the Head Bannerman of the Bordered Red Banner. The Empress Dowager, so Zhang explained, had wanted to get hold of a copy of some Sutra or other that he possessed. Colonel Rui had duly extracted the Sutra from him, and then afterwards suffocated him, by sticking mulberry-bark adhesive paper over his mouth and his nose.

'So the Old Whore was after that Sutra again!' thought Trinket to himself. 'That must be the copy I found on the Colonel's body. I wonder why he didn't give it straight to the Empress

Dowager? Perhaps she sent him off after me again in too much of a hurry?'

Zhang went to get the drug, and Trinket gave orders for the kitchens to prepare a meal for him and his friends the guards.

Presently Zhang returned with a large packet—it must have weighed at least half a catty.

'This should be enough to put several hundred people to sleep!' he whispered to Trinket. 'For one person, you only need to tip a tiny bit, this much,' (he held out a fingernail), 'into a cup of tea or wine.'

Zhang told the guards to set a couple of tables, as Laurel Goong-goong was going to treat them to a big meal.

'Set the tables in the room right in front of the prisoners,' said Trinket. 'I'd like to watch them drool while we stuff ourselves!'

Presently senior and junior eunuchs and serving-boys from the Imperial Catering Department brought in the food.

'You just stand there and watch us while we eat!' cried Trinket, addressing the three prisoners with a hearty laugh. 'If it's really too much for you and you start yelping like dogs, who knows, I might even toss you a scrap!'

The guards joined in his laughter.

'*You're* the dogs!' cried Shaker Wu. 'Damn the lot of you! When the Satrap raises arms in Yunnan, and storms the Capital, you'll all be killed and thrown into the river to feed the turtles!'

Trinket meanwhile had walked over and was standing right in front of Wu. He reached inside his jacket with his right hand and took out a large pinch of the powder, then picked up the wine jug in his left hand. He raised the jug high in the air and cried:

'Well, you treacherous scum, any of you fancy a drink of wine?'

Shaker Wu was still in the dark as to Trinket's intentions.

'Who gives a damn if we drink or not?' he bellowed. 'Once the Satrap gets here, you are all dead men!'

'Oh yeah?' cried Trinket.

He raised the jug high in the air and poured a little into his own mouth.

'Good wine!'

Then, in such a way that only Shaker Wu could see what he was doing, he tipped open the lid of the jug and used his finger to flick the powder from his right hand into the wine. Closing the lid he raised the jug high in the air again and gave it a good shake, thereby ensuring that the drug was properly dissolved in the wine.

Shaker Wu now had the picture.

'A proper man dies proud! He doesn't beg for mercy!' he cried. 'Go on, I'll drink! I'll drink the whole damn jug!'

'So you *would* like a drink!' laughed Trinket. 'Well, I'm not giving you one! Ha ha ha!'

And he went over and began pouring wine for the guards, making sure they each had a full cup. They all raised their cups and were about to drink when there was a loud cry from the door.

'Her Majesty has summoned Laurel Goong-goong! Laurel Goong-goong!'

'The Old Whore's after me again!' thought Trinket, putting his wine-cup down with a jolt. He went out to find four eunuchs waiting for him, their leader a big, nasty-looking fellow with a large protruding belly and puffed-out chest. Trinket fell to his knees:

'At Her Majesty's service!'

'Her Majesty wishes to see you at once on urgent business!'

'Of course! Of course!'

Trinket did some very quick thinking. His strongest weapon was inside the room, dissolved in the wine.

'Come in here a moment,' he said to the eunuchs. 'There's something that will interest you greatly.'

He ushered all four eunuchs into the room where he and the guards had been about to tuck in to their banquet. The big eunuch made some disapproving remark or other about wasting Catering Department resources.

'But His Majesty specially asked me to reward these guards for having caught the assassins! Come on, join us! At least have a drink with us!'

The big eunuch refused, and insisted that the Empress Dowager was urgently awaiting Laurel Goong-goong's presence.

With a little support from Zhang Kangnian, Trinket succeeded in wearing down the eunuch's resistance, and eventually had him drinking a cup, and then the other three eunuchs and all of the guards followed suit. Trinket raised his own cup, as he did so screening it with his left sleeve and tipping the contents down the inside of his gown. Fearful that one cup would not be enough to put them out, he urged them all to drink another, and went round again with the jug.

The big eunuch protested strongly that they should be on

their way, and that anyway he was not much of a drinker. As he spoke, Trinket noticed that he was beginning to sway from side to side, and deduced that the drug was beginning to take effect. Suddenly Trinket himself doubled up as if he was in pain.

'Aiyo! My stomach!'

The guards were by this time beginning to feel dizzy. One of them cried out:

'What's going on here? Has someone put something in the wine?'

'It's you, isn't it?' Trinket shouted angrily at the big eunuch. 'The Empress Dowager sent you here to poison us, didn't she!'

The eunuch denied this vigorously, but Trinket called on the guards to seize him.

The guards themselves were starting to sway from side to side, and incapable of taking action of any sort. There was a series of thuds as two eunuchs crashed to the floor unconscious, to be followed shortly by the other two and the entire company of guards, including Zhang Kangnian. As they fell to the ground and collapsed in a heap, they brought down the tables and chairs with them. Trinket leapt on top of the big eunuch and gave him a kick for good measure. He groaned and lay there, his hands and feet twitching, his eyes staring helplessly in front of him.

Trinket ran to the door and closed it, then he drew out his trusty dagger and proceeded to stab all four eunuchs in the chest. Liu Yizhou gasped in astonishment. Next Trinket used the dagger to cut free the three prisoners. The blade sliced through the lengths of tough ox sinew as if they had been strips of the softest noodle.

The three men had been tortured and bound, but their injuries were only superficial. They were now impatient to get away.

'Laurel Goong-goong,' asked Liu Yizhou, 'how do we . . . get out of here?'

Trinket ordered Shaker Wu and Ao Biao to change into guards' uniforms, and Liu to put on the clothes of the big eunuch. They obeyed without hesitation.

'Come with me,' said Trinket. 'Whatever anyone says to you, act dumb! Say nothing!'

From his inside pocket he produced a packet of Decomposing Powder. He dragged the big eunuch's body over to a corner of the room, stabbed it a few more times, and then sprinkled the powder directly into the wounds. That would hasten the decomposition process. Then he opened the door, and led the three out.

He closed the door behind them, and they all set off towards the Imperial Catering Department.

The Escape

The Catering Department was situated to the east of the Hall of Heavenly Purity, not far from the Guardroom. They reached it quickly, and found Butcher Qian waiting for them. He had brought two of his assistants, who were carrying two large, carefully prepared pig carcasses.

'What the devil are you playing at!' cried Trinket, a convincing scowl on his face. 'I asked for a couple of decent hogs, not these worn-out lanky sows that look like they've had seventeen or eighteen litters of piglets! Tamardy! I hope you realize your job's on the line!'

Butcher Qian stooped low and made a convincingly abject apology.

The other Catering Department eunuchs assumed that the problem lay in the lack of accompanying 'presents' (since the pigs seemed plump enough) and joined in with a chorus of:

'Take these foul-looking animals away! They're fit for nothing but fertilizer!'

Trinket waved to his companions (Shaker and Ao Biao dressed as guards, Liu as a eunuch) and ordered them to see the butcher to the door, and make sure he never came back.

Butcher Qian was not in on this latest twist in Trinket's plot, and gave a perplexed frown:

'Please forgive me this once, Goong-goong, I'll . . . I'll come back with some really big fat porkers next time, I promise! And I'll make sure I bring the right presents . . . Please forgive me!'

'If I want any more pork from you, I'll let you know!' snapped Trinket. 'Now, get going!'

Butcher Qian hurried out, the three ex-prisoners following behind him, and Trinket bringing up the rear. When they reached the covered walkway and there was no one in earshot, he whispered:

'Brother Qian, these three men are from the Mu Family! I want you to take them to Count Mu's place, and tell your Triad

Lodge Master Wei that Warthead has done the favour he asked for. Once they've escaped, there will be a big hunt on for them, and you'd better not come anywhere the Palace.'

The five of them hurried to the northern Gate of the Divine Warrior. The guards on duty at the gate recognized Trinket and let the party through. When they were a little way from the Palace, Trinket took his leave of the others and returned.

As he passed back through the gate, he explained to the guards that the Empress Dowager had personally asked him to escort these men out of the Palace. They were bearing secret instructions from Her Majesty. The guards believed Laurel Goong-goong implicitly.

Mission Accomplished

When Trinket returned to the Guardroom, he found them all still lying unconscious on the ground. He splashed some cold water on Zhang Kangnian's face, and slowly succeeded in reviving his friend.

'Laurel Goong-goong,' said Zhang, with a perplexed smile, 'I don't understand how I can have got drunk so quickly.'

He looked around him, and saw to his astonishment that the prisoners had all gone.

'It was the Empress Dowager,' explained Trinket. 'She sent that eunuch to drug our wine, and rescue the prisoners.'

Zhang had himself provided Trinket with the drug. But although this fact was still fresh in his memory, and although he found Trinket's story highly incredible, his brain was too befuddled for him to be able to say anything very articulate.

Trinket reminded Zhang that it was his superior officer, Colonel Dolong, who had instructed him to cooperate in the release of the prisoners. Dolong had said that it was a secret plan of the Emperor's, to track down the true perpetrators of the crime. But there were no written instructions from Dolong to that effect, and the guards would still be held officially responsible for the prisoners' escape. And besides, said Trinket, had anyone seen a written Edict from the Emperor to Dolong?

'You mean Colonel Dolong may have made the whole thing up?' asked a shocked Zhang, his teeth chattering with fear.

'I'm not saying that,' said Trinket. 'Just that when it comes to the crunch, Dolong may try to put the blame for this on your shoulders. And if things go wrong, and the prisoners don't lead them to the true ringleaders, His Majesty may want to kill a few people, just to make the escape look plausible.'

This was in a way partly true: Kang Xi had instructed Trinket to do away with a few guards, to enhance the credibility of the operation.

Poor Zhang was now terrified, and fell to his knees, kow-towing and crying:

'Save me, Goong-goong!'

Trinket helped him to his feet.

'It's quite easy: we'll just lay the blame on these four eunuchs. We'll say the Empress Dowager sent them. His Majesty will be happy to leave it at that. He will probably even want to reward you.'

Zhang thanked Trinket profusely for saving his life.

They splashed water on the faces of the other guards and woke them all up. The guards were filled with indignant rage when they were informed that the Empress Dowager's big eunuch had drugged them, killed his fellow eunuchs, and made off with the prisoners. Privately they wondered why the Empress Dowager should have wanted to set the prisoners free. Unless of course she herself had sent them on their assassination mission in the first place . . . But such a suspicion was one that no one dared voice openly.

Needless to say, thanks to the Decomposition Powder, there was no actual trace of the big eunuch, and everyone assumed that he had escaped with the prisoners.

Crazy about a Coward

'Brother Laurel, what's the news?' the Little Countess asked Trinket as soon as he returned.

'Brother Laurel has no news,' replied Trinket. 'Your darling might have though!'

After a little more of this teasing banter, Trinket finally com-municated to the girls that Liu Yizhou was out of danger.

'I said I'd do it,' declared Trinket, 'and I have. My word is my bond.'

Fang Yi seemed overjoyed at the news. She uttered a brief prayer of thanksgiving to Heaven and Earth. Her reaction caused Trinket pangs of jealousy. But he said nothing.

'What did he say when you saw him?' asked Fang Yi.

'Oh nothing much. He just begged me to get him out.'

Fang Yi pouted.

'Did he ask how I was?'

Trinket put his head to one side and pondered.

'No. I told him you were somewhere safe, and that he needn't worry. I said I'd be sending you to see him soon.'

'Yes!' said Fang Yi, with a significant nod of the head. Suddenly two fat tears rolled down her cheeks.

'What are you crying for?' asked the Little Countess.

'I'm just so happy!' sobbed Fang Yi.

'Tamardy!' thought Trinket to himself. 'I can't understand how you can be so crazy about that big coward!'

Then he remembered that he had better at least appear to be searching for the prisoners' ringleaders, and left the Palace once more, this time heading for the Bridge of Heaven district.

United Front

The area of Peking by the Bridge of Heaven is home to a motley assortment of pedlars, acrobats, street performers of every imaginable kind, and all sorts of other denizens of the River and Lake world. As Trinket approached he saw a platoon of twenty policemen with two constables at their head, pushing their way through the crowd. They were dragging after them five ragged pedlars in chains, and were holding seven or eight sticks of small red candied crab-apples, which they had clearly impounded from the pedlars.

Trinket suddenly realized what was going on. The Empress Dowager was rounding up every pedlar in town in an attempt to get hold of his 'contact' with Colonel Rui. He ducked into a side-alley. As he did so he heard a bystander mutter with a sigh:

'Nowadays even selling toffee-apples is a crime!'

Trinket was about to question the speaker when he heard a cough, and saw another man come sidling up to him. It was a stooped, white-haired old man, who on closer inspection turned out to be none other than Xu the Eight-Armed Ape. Xu gave Trinket a meaningful wink, turned around, and set off. Trinket followed him.

When they came to a more secluded place, Xu stopped and spoke:

'Lodge Master Wei,' he began. 'Wonderful news!'

'So he's already heard of the rescue!' thought Trinket to himself with a smile.

'It was nothing!' he replied, with becoming modesty.

'Nothing!' exclaimed Xu. 'I'm talking about the Helmsman! He's here in the Capital!'

Trinket was completely thrown by this.

'My Shifu . . . in Peking?'

'Yes. He arrived yesterday evening. He asked me to arrange an immediate meeting with you, Lodge Master.'

'Of course!'

It was over six months since Trinket had last seen his Shifu, Helmsman Chen Jinnan, and in that time he had done absolutely no kungfu practice whatsoever. His Shifu was not going to be pleased. He decided to play for time:

'Right now I'm on an errand for His Majesty. I'll have to report back to the Palace first, then I'll be able to go and see the Helmsman.'

'He says he can't stay long in Peking. He says you must see him at once.'

Trinket could see he had no option but to go with Xu directly to the place where the Triads had gathered to welcome their chief.

'If I'd known he was going to turn up like this, I'd have done better to stay put in the Palace, out of his reach . . . ' he thought to himself.

They reached the alley, to find numbers of Triads posted at the entrance and along the street as sentries. There were more of them guarding each doorway as they entered the house.

The Helmsman was sitting in the rear hall, holding council with a group of senior Lodge members which included Brothers Li and Fan, Big Beaver, Father Obscurus, and Tertius. Trinket hurried in and fell to his knees.

'Shifu! I deserve to die at your hands!'

Chen Jinnan laughed.

'You're a good lad! Everyone has been singing your praises!'

Trinket stood up, saw the friendly expression on the Helmsman's face, and breathed a sigh of relief.

'Are you well, Shifu?'

Chen Jinnan smiled.

'Very well, thank you. How's your kungfu coming on? Is there anything you don't understand?'

All the way there Trinket had been wondering how he was going to deal with this exact question. The Helmsman was too smart to fool around with. He would have to adopt a more subtle approach.

'Well yes, there are *lots* of things I can't quite figure out. Luckily you're here now, Shifu, and I can ask you to explain them for me!'

'Excellent!' exclaimed the Helmsman. 'I want to spend a bit more time with you during this stay of mine, and give you a few lessons.'

As he was saying this, a Triad Brother guarding the door came hurrying in to announce the arrival of Count Mu Jiansheng and Liu Dahong, the Shifu of the Mu Family. The Helmsman seemed very pleased.

'Come,' he said, rising to his feet, 'we must go out to greet them.'

'I can't meet them in these clothes,' said Trinket, who had never before encountered the Mu Family in his guise as Palace eunuch. The Helmsman told him to wait in the back room.

Trinket eavesdropped as the Triads received the Mu Family delegation, hearing the booming voice of old Liu Dahong expressing his great joy at finally meeting the famed Helmsman, and Chen Jinnan's self-effacing reply. Liu went on to say how much he wished to thank Lodge Master Wei for the great favour he had done the Mu Family in asking his friend in the Palace to rescue their men. The Helmsman apparently still knew nothing of all this. Next it was Shaker Wu's turn to sing the praises of Warthead. Finally Butcher Qian, who had accompanied the Mu delegation, gave the Helmsman a brief account of the whole episode.

The Helmsman was greatly pleased to hear of these exploits, and decided that since the Triads and the Mu Family were allies in the struggle against the Tartars, he ought to put them fully in the picture.

'Gentlemen,' he said, 'I cannot bring myself to deceive you in this matter. The truth is that this Warthead, the Palace Eunuch who saved you, is in fact my own disciple, Lodge Master Trinket Wei!'

He called out:

'You'd better come out and say hello to these gentlemen, Trinket!'

Trinket came out of his hiding-place at once. The astonishment among the members of the Mu Family can be imagined, as the Young Count and old Shifu Liu, on the one hand, and the released prisoners on the other, saw for themselves that Lodge Master Wei and Palace Eunuch Warthead were one and the same person.

Trinket apologized to the three ex-prisoners for having used a false identity, but Shaker Wu was most insistent that he had done the right thing.

'Dangerous measures for dangerous times! Acted like a true hero! Ha ha ha!'

He seemed to find the whole idea quite exhilarating, stuck his thumb up in the air, and started wagging his head interminably and making a series of exclamations of admiration.

Shaker Wu and Liu Dahong had studied with the same kungfu Master, and Shaker had quite a reputation on River and Lake. The Helmsman was needless to say delighted to hear his young disciple being so highly praised by a Martial Arts veteran. He was also pleased to see in this new development a hope for improved relations between their two factions of the Resistance. One of his principal reasons for hurrying to the Capital from Henan had been precisely to try to heal the rift between his Triad organization and the Mu forces in Yunnan.

Just as the Helmsman was contemplating the potential of a united front, old Liu made a remark which threw everything into disarray:

'Helmsman,' he said, intending to pay Chen the highest compliment he could think of, 'when Prince Gui's heir is proclaimed Emperor of a restored Ming dynasty, you will surely be the man chosen to be his Chief Minister!'

The Helmsman mumbled a polite reply, but Tertius immediately leapt into the fray, insisting that in the event of a Restoration it was in fact the heir of Prince Tang, currently in Taiwan, who had the right to be proclaimed Emperor. And so on and so forth, until the two factions, so far from being united, were at each others' throats again, arguing over the very issue that had led to the earlier fatal altercation between Pine and Xu Tianchuan.

The Helmsman tried to make the peace, knowing that the Manchus would be the only ones to benefit from this divisive squabbling, but old Liu was not to be stopped. He delivered a booming and impassioned plea on behalf of the descendants of Prince Gui, who had so tragically given his life after his wretched days of exile in Burma. The old man was in tears, and emotions were running high. Chen Jinnan tried one last argument to restore the peace:

'My friends, let us not allow ourselves to be divided like this before we have even achieved our shared goal! Let us first drive the Tartars from our land! And before we do that, let us first kill that traitor Satrap Wu, and avenge the deaths not only of Emperor Yong Li, but also of Duke Mu, who died with him!'

It was a clever move on his part. Not only had he referred to Prince Gui by his Imperial title, he had also alluded to the Young Count's father, Duke Mu Tianbo, who had been put to death defending his Emperor's final stand in Burma. And he had focused on the Satrap, a man loathed if anything more ferociously by the Mu Family than by the Triads, since it was the Satrap who had personally ordered the execution of the Gui Pretender and of his devoted Duke. The Young Count and his retainers responded by crying enthusiastically 'Yes! Death to the Traitor!'. Some wept openly, others shook with visible excitement at this prospect of revenge.

'We can debate the rights and wrongs of the successsion at a later date,' added the Helmsman. 'For the present, let us agree on one thing: whoever kills the Satrap will command our allegiance!'

'Agreed!' cried the Young Count. He and the Helmsman exchanged a solemn oath to this effect.

The Mu Family delegation drank a few cups of wine and took its leave. As they went, Trinket gave them some parting words of advice:

'Count Mu, I think it would be wise if you were to move from Bean Sprout Lane. The Tartars may track you down . . .'

The advice was gratefully received.

When they had gone, the Helmsman took Trinket aside into a private room, and asked him how his kungfu had been progressing. Trinket tried to avoid answering, instead reminding his Shifu that he was expected back in the Palace at any moment, and adding a few carefully chosen words of flattery. The Helmsman was used to the blunt ways of River and Lake, and tended to believe that people meant what they said. He was genuinely touched by his young friend's words. He had little understanding of Trinket's nature, which had always been crafty, moulded by years spent first in a whore-house, then in the Palace—both places where deceit and duplicity flourished.

Trinket went on to criticize the Young Count's tactics—the

much too obvious attempt to lay the blame on the Satrap, the use of marked weapons and clothes, the way their kungfu moves were so easily recognized, and so on. So impressed was the Helmsman by his young disciple's precocious mastery of strategy (when in fact all Trinket was doing was repeating word for word what the Emperor had said to him a day or two earlier), that he began to think it might no longer be so important for him to be proficient at kungfu—which was exactly what Trinket had hoped to achieve. After all, there were enough good fighters among the Triads already. In fact, the Helmsman was altogether so impressed by Trinket's courage and intelligence, that he even began to reconsider his original plan, which had been to replace him as soon as possible as Master of the Green Wood Lodge. He had only nominated the boy in the first place as a ploy to avoid further dissension between rival factions within the Lodge. Now Chen was beginning to think that the boy was turning out to be surprisingly promising. A few more years, and he might be more than a match for the other Lodge Masters.

'Off you go then!' he said. 'You'd better report back to the Palace. Come and see me again tomorrow, and I'll teach you some kungfu.'

Trinket beat a hasty retreat.

The Great Sage Onion

He found Kang Xi in the Upper Library reading state documents.

'Well,' said the Emperor, when he saw Trinket come into the room, 'did you find anything out?'

'Your Majesty,' replied Trinket, 'your suspicions were correct. The people behind the plot were the Mu Family from Yunnan.'

Trinket's version of events was that he had drugged the guards, and then, when the Empress Dowager had sent four eunuchs to 'kill the prisoners', he had taken it upon himself to kill the eunuchs in front of the prisoners' own eyes (in accordance with Kang Xi's earlier plan). Then he had escaped with the prisoners.

'I wondered what was going on!' exclaimed Kang Xi with a laugh. 'Just now Colonel Dolong reported that it was one of Her Majesty's eunuchs who had let them out. But it was you all along!'

'You mustn't tell Her Majesty that I killed those eunuchs of hers,' said Trinket. 'Or my life will be in danger. She already holds it against me that I respect you more than her—which doesn't make sense to me! Anyway, what right does she have to send her eunuchs in there without your permission?'

Kang Xi reassured him that he would not mention it to the Empress Dowager. Trinket told him the names of the three prisoners, and of the Young Count and his retainers, and their address in Bean Sprout Lane. He went on to explain that they had planned all along to cause trouble for Satrap Wu, and thereby avenge the deaths of Prince Gui and Duke Mu. They had never intended to harm Kang Xi, whom his Chinese subjects considered an exceptionally wise young ruler.

'Come come!' said Kang Xi, secretly pleased by Trinket's flattery. 'You're making that all up.'

'No, honestly, that's what they said. The people hated Oboi. They thought he was a heartless monster, and they praise Your Majesty for having put him to death! They all say you're as great and wise as the Great Sage Onion . . . I'm not sure what that means, but I think it's supposed to be a compliment!'

Kang Xi burst out laughing.

'Tamardy, Laurel! You really do manage to get things tied round your neck! The Great Sages Yao and Sun! They were two of the Great Emperors of Ancient Time, famous for their virtue and wisdom!'

Whoever they were, Trinket was pleased to have brought a complacent smile to the young Emperor's face.

'But all the same, we can't let those Mu folk get away with it,' said Kang Xi. 'Send for Dolong.'

Trinket went off to fetch him, and Kang Xi gave Dolong orders to go out and arrest the members of the Mu Family. Trinket was then told to brief him, and Dolong was shocked to learn the true identity of the three men he had been holding prisoner. He set off to do his duty.

'Laurel,' said Kang Xi, 'I want you to come with me now to visit Her Majesty.'

Trinket looked very nervous at the thought of seeing the Empress Dowager.

'Don't be scared!' said Kang Xi. 'I'll be there to protect you.'

'Yes, Majesty!'

An Unexpected Change of Employment

They reached the Hall of Maternal Tranquillity, and Kang Xi went in to pay his respects to the Empress Dowager. He reported the true identity of the intruders, and that he had expressly ordered Laurel to let them go, with a view to acquiring this information.

The Empress Dowager smiled.

'Laurel, you're a very capable little fellow!'

Trinket fell to his knees and kowtowed several times.

'It was all His Majesty's idea! All I did was follow his orders.'

The Empress Dowager studied him for a moment, then gave a little humph.

'I dare say you've been gadding about all over Peking . . . I wonder, have you been to the Bridge of Heaven by any chance, to see the acrobats? Did you buy any toffee-apples?'

Trinket knew that she'd had every toffee-apple-seller within a mile of the Bridge of Heaven rounded up, and all their heads chopped off, just to be sure that none of them went to the Wutai Mountains and passed a message on to Colonel Rui. The thought of how ruthless she was made him shudder with fear.

'I said, did you buy any toffee-apples?' she repeated with a sinister smile.

'Well, as a matter of fact, Your Majesty, there's been a bit of trouble down at the Bridge of Heaven these last few days, and all the toffee-apple-sellers seem to have been rounded up. There must have been some criminals among them, I suppose. Quite a few of the old sellers have changed to selling peanuts, or cakes, or something else. I recognized some of them. Then there was this one queer-looking fellow who said he was off to some mountain or other to sell vegetarian buns to the monks . . .'

The Empress Dowager got Trinket's point, and snarled back at him:

'You *are* a clever little fellow!' She turned to Kang Xi. 'I've been thinking. I'd like to keep this clever little eunuch here with me . . . What do you say to it?'

This request took Kang Xi completely by surprise. The last thing he wanted to do at this moment was to part with Laurel. But, although the Empress Dowager was not his natural mother, he had grown up under her care and regarded her with great filial respect. He did not dare go against her wishes.

'Laurel, didn't you hear?' he said. 'Her Majesty wants to do you a favour. Aren't you going to thank her?'

'Yes Majesty, of course Majesty!' cried Trinket, who had almost died when he heard what the Empress Dowager was proposing. His one and only thought, now more than before, was of escape. And of never returning to the Palace ever again in his entire life. He fell to his knees yet again, and began kowtowing.

'Your Majesties, I thank you both for your great kindness!'

'Don't you *want* to serve me?' asked the Empress Dowager, with a chilling laugh. 'Do you only ever want to serve the Emperor?'

'I am devoted to both Your Majesties!'

'That's fine then. From now on, you don't need to bother with the Imperial Catering Department. You're just to stay here with me.'

'Yes, Your Majesty. Much obliged, Your Majesty.'

Kang Xi himself was thoroughly unhappy about this arrangement. He made a few perfunctory remarks, and took his leave. Trinket followed him out.

'Laurel, come back!' cried the Empress Dowager. 'The others can perfectly well look after the Emperor. I need you for something here.'

'Yes Majesty!'

Trinket watched Kang Xi disappear out of sight, thinking to himself:

'Now that you're gone, I'm done for! I'll probably never see you again!'

He felt himself about to burst into tears.

Sister Swallow

The Empress Dowager sipped her tea, and studied Trinket. She could tell he was terrified.

'So,' she said at last, 'when is that man coming back from Wutai—the vegetarian-bun-seller?'

'I don't know, Your Majesty.'

'When are you planning to see him again?'

'I arranged to see him in a month's time,' Trinket improvised. 'But not at the Bridge of Heaven.'

'Where?'

'He said he'd find a way of letting me know nearer the time.'

The Empress Dowager nodded her head.

'Then you'd better stay here with me until you hear from him.'

She clapped her hands together softly, and one of her maids-in-waiting appeared from an inner chamber.

This maid-in-waiting was an exceedingly plump woman of

thirty-five or so, but quite sprightly on her feet. She had a big round face like a full moon, small eyes and a large mouth. She giggled as she came in, and curtseyed to her mistress.

The Empress Dowager introduced Trinket to her.

'This is the eunuch Laurel. He is a cheeky little fellow, and very mischievous, but I've taken a liking to him.'

'Yes, Ma'am! He seems very smart. Hey, little boy, my name's Liu, Swallow Liu. But you can just call me Big Sis Swallow.'

'Fat Tamardy Sow more like!' Trinket thought to himself.

'Yes, Sis Swallow!' he said. 'That's a good name for you, you're like a pretty little bird on the wing!'

None of the Empress Dowager's servants had ever spoken like that before. But what did Trinket care? He had a premonition that he was done for anyway.

Swallow gave a little giggle.

'What a cute way of talking he has!'

'And an even cuter way of running wild!' snapped the Empress Dowager. 'What do you think, Swallow, how are we going to keep him under control?'

'Give him to me, Your Majesty. I'll think of a way.'

'No.' The Empress shook her head. 'He's much too slippery a customer for you. I sent Colonel Rui after him, but he managed to scare the Colonel off. I sent four of my eunuchs, and he had them all killed by the guards, every one of them. I sent another four, and he killed them too, goodness only knows how!'

Swallow clicked her tongue.

'My oh my! He really *is* a naughty boy! Your Majesty, I think we'd better chop his legs off . . . Then he won't be able to get up to so much mischief!'

The Empress sighed.

'I think you may be right.'

Trinket bolted for the door.

His left foot had no sooner reached the threshold, when he felt a tug on his pigtail, and his head was jerked upwards. He somersaulted backwards, then landed on the ground. A foot planted itself heavily on his chest . . . a fat foot, in a red satin shoe embroidered with gold thread. Sister Swallow was standing over him.

'Take your smelly foot off me, you dirty old slut!' cried Trinket in the heat of the moment.

By way of reply, Sister Swallow pressed her foot down even

harder, and Trinket felt his ribs go crunch and the breath go out of him.

'I've taken rather a fancy to the smell of *your* feet, little boy!' laughed the Fat Sow. 'I think I'll chop them off and have a good sniff!'

Trinket knew that the Old Whore hated him enough to give the order for this dreadful thing to happen! Then she would have him carried, foot-less, to his rendezvous and secretly send an assassin with him to Wutai to bump off Colonel Rui. He must not panic. He had to think very fast.

'Your Majesty,' he said with a sly smile, 'you're welcome to chop off any bits of me you like, I'm sure a few Laurel-amputations wouldn't matter much to anyone. But there is just one little thing: the *Sutra in Forty-Two Sections* . . . Tee-hee!'

He gave a series of strange little squeaks. As he had anticipated, the Empress Dowager reacted smartly to the mention of the Sutra, and rose to her feet.

'What are you trying to say?'

'Just that it would be such a pity to lose those copies of the Sutra . . .'

The Empress turned to Sister Swallow.

'Get off him!' she commanded.

The fat maid-in-waiting removed her left foot from Trinket's chest, inserted it under his back, and flicked him over. Then she gripped him by the nape of the neck with her left hand, lifted him up into the air, and dropped him with a great thud to the ground. Trinket was like a helpless child in her hands. He was now even too scared to utter the words 'filthy slut' that kept forming themselves on his lips.

'Who have you heard talking about the Sutra?' asked the Empress Dowager.

'Why should I tell you anything,' replied Trinket, 'when you're about to chop off my feet?'

'If you're a smart boy you'll answer Her Majesty nicely!' said the fat maid.

'Why should I, when I'm going to die anyway? Torture me. I'm not scared.'

The Fat Sow took hold of his left hand and gave a sinister laugh.

'Little boy, you've got such pretty, long fingers . . .'

'Go ahead, cut them off! What do I care!'

This was followed by an ear-piercing scream of pain as the Sow took hold of his index finger, and squeezed it so viciously that she almost snapped the bone. All the while she was inflicting this excruciating pain, tightening her vice-like grip on Trinket's finger, she had a big beaming smile on her face.

Trinket was weeping with pain.

'Your Majesty,' he gasped, 'kill me and get it over with! Forget about the Sutra!'

'You tell me what you know about the Sutra,' replied the Empress Dowager, 'and I will spare you!'

'I won't! I don't care if you kill me!'

The Empress Dowager frowned. This little brat was a real thorn in her side.

'Swallow,' she said slowly, after a long pause, 'if he won't talk, gouge out both of his eyes.'

'Certainly, Your Majesty,' said Swallow with another of her beaming smiles. 'I'll do this one first. Oh my poor little boy, what a pretty, clever little eyeball, so bright and shiny, like a little ball, so lovely the way it moves round! I'm afraid when I've taken it out, it won't be such a pretty sight any more!'

She put her thumb against his right eyelid, and started softly pressing.

Trinket felt a shooting pain in his eye, and changed his tune.

'I surrender! Don't hurt my eyes! I'll talk!'

The Sow took away her thumb and gave another of her hideous smiles.

'There's a good boy! You talk nicely to Her Majesty now. She loves you.'

Trinket rubbed his right eye, blinked it a few times, then closed his other eye and squinted with the right one at the Sow, shaking his head and muttering:

'No, she doesn't!'

'Of course she does! Stop playing games, and talk to her nicely.'

'Look what you've gone and done! You've ruined my eye!' moaned Trinket. 'Everything looks different. Your body looks almost human, but on top you've got a head like a big fat pig!'

The Sow reacted to this by giggling.

'What fun! I'd better do the same to the other eye . . .'

Trinket shrank away from her.

'I'd rather you didn't! Thanks all the same!'

He closed his right eye, squinted at the Empress Dowager with his left, and shook his head.

She scowled at him angrily, wondering to herself what gargoyle the little brat was going to compare *her* with.

'Go on, Swallow, poke that other eye out, before he starts seeing something else!'

'But if I can't see, how am I to fetch the Sutra for you?'

'Have you got one?' cried the Empress Dowager eagerly. 'Where did you get it from?'

'Colonel Rui gave it to me. He told me to keep it in a very safe place. Whatever happened to me, I was never to let anyone see it. It was bound in red silk with a white border.'

The Empress Dowager was not sure whether to believe Trinket. It was true that she had sent Colonel Rui to kill Hochabo, the Head Bannerman of the Bordered Red Banner, and to steal his copy of the Sutra. On his return, she had been in so much of a hurry to send him off again to murder Trinket that she had forgotten to ask him for the Sutra. If what Trinket said was true, she had cause to be both pleased and angry: pleased that she now had a clue as to the Sutra's whereabouts, angry that the Colonel should have given it to Trinket.

'In that case,' she said to Trinket, 'I want you to go with Swallow and find that book for me. If it is what you say it is, we'll spare your life, and you can go back to the Emperor and never set foot here again! The sight of you only makes me angry.'

Swallow took hold of Trinket's right hand.

'Come on, little boy, let's be going!'

Trinket tried to shake her hand off.

'Let go of me! I'm a man, you're a woman! Stop trying to feel me up!'

She had used virtually no force, and yet her hand stuck to his like a limpet and Trinket was unable to free himself.

'You're just a eunuch,' she said, with one of her appalling grins. 'You're not a man! And even if you were, you're hardly even old enough to be my son.'

They set off together. When they reached the covered walkway, Trinket's heart was thumping. He was desperately trying to think of a way of escaping from the clutches of the Sow.

'It's no good trying to get out my dagger—she'll notice the slightest move, and I don't stand a chance against her. She obviously knows a thing or two about fighting. She can't have been around when the Old Whore fought with the Old Turtle, or she'd have joined in. She must be new in the Palace. She probably arrived in the last few days, or the Old Whore would have sent her to kill me, and not come herself.'

As these thoughts were running through his head, a sort of a plan began to form itself in his mind. He made an easterly turn and started leading her towards the Upper Library, beside the Hall of Heavenly Purity. He would appeal to the Emperor to save him! It was his only hope! He was counting on the fact that she was new in the Palace and wouldn't know where they were going.

With his second step, he felt her hands close around his neck.

'And where do you think we are going to now, dear boy?'

She accompanied this with one of her pig-like snuffling giggles.

'To my room, to get the Sutra,' replied Trinket.

'So what are we doing heading towards the Upper Library? You weren't thinking of sneaking off to the Emperor by any chance?'

Trinket couldn't restrain himself.

'You fat pig!' he cried. 'You *would* have to know your way around!'

'I know *this* part of the Palace.'

She seized Trinket by the neck and yanked him round into a westerly direction.

'There, off we go! Careful now, dear boy, we don't want to damage the flowers!'

She was all smiles, but her grip was devastating, and Trinket yelped with pain. He thought his neck was going to snap in two.

There were two eunuchs further down the walkway, and when they heard this they turned around.

'Her Majesty's orders,' whispered the Sow to Trinket, 'were that if you tried to escape, or made a noise, I was to kill you!'

Trinket decided it would be no use to call out for the Emperor, since Kang Xi would be unlikely to defy the Empress Dowager anyway. His only hope was to bump into a couple of guards and get them to help him dispose of the Sow.

Suddenly he felt an elbow digging into his ribs.

'What are we plotting now?'

Trinket walked on reluctantly towards his room. He was worried about the two girls. They were still weak from their wounds, and he feared that the Sow might take their lives too if she became aware of their presence.

When he reached the door, he unlocked it clumsily, deliberately making a lot of noise with the key, and exclaiming loudly:

'Slut! Fat Sow! One day I'll get even!'

He pushed the door open as noisily as possible.

'Whether I give you the Sutra or not, I know she'll kill me. I'm not that stupid!'

'If she said she'll spare you, she probably will. She might just gouge your eyes out though, and chop off your legs . . .'

'And what about you, you big fat pig! Do you think she'll let *you* live? Once you've killed me, she'll kill you. You'll know too much to stay alive.'

Sister Swallow paused for a moment, as if seriously contemplating Trinket's remark, but then shoved him forward. He stumbled into the room.

'Hurry up!' she said. 'Get the book!'

She shoved him again, and followed him as he stumbled on into the inner room. Trinket quickly scanned the interior. The first thing to greet his eyes was two pairs of ladies' slippers neatly arranged by the bed. It was evening, and there were no lamps lit. The Sow had still not spotted the slippers.

'Drat!' thought Trinket to himself, and at the same moment hurled himself forward and on to the ground, to push the slippers under the bed. Then on a sudden impulse he wriggled under the bed himself. Perhaps he could deal with the Fat Sow somewhat as he had dealt with Colonel Rui. He was just pulling in his right leg, in order to extract the dagger from the side of his boot, when he felt the Sow's hands close around his ankle.

'What are you up to now?'

'I'm getting the book. It's under the bed.'

She let him go, thinking that he could hardly get away from her under the bed. Trinket curled up in a ball and took the dagger from his boot.

'Come on! Give it here!'

'Oh no!' came a muffled cry. 'It looks as if mice have been down here! Aiyo! They've chewed the book into little pieces!'

'Come out of there! Stop fooling about with me!'

The Sow reached under the bed, but could feel nothing. Trinket was curled up against the wall. She began crawling under the bed herself. Trinket now had the dagger in his hand. He stabbed at her. As the blade made contact with the back of her hand, the

Sow reacted with the speed of lightning, seizing Trinket by the wrist and squeezing it so tightly that his hand went limp and he dropped the dagger on the floor.

'Trying to kill me, were you? Very well then. Out with one of your eyes!'

She gripped his throat with her right hand and began to throttle him, at the same time attacking one of his eyes with her left hand.

'A snake!' yelled Trinket.

'What?' gasped the Sow.

Then she gave a great scream, and the hand on Trinket's throat loosened its grip. The Sow's body writhed, and she lay still.

Trinket scrambled out from under the bed, surprised and delighted by this sudden turn of events. He heard the Little Countess's voice:

'Are you all right?'

He drew apart the bed-curtains, and there was Fang Yi sitting on the bed, holding the handle of her sword in both hands and panting. She had driven the long blade of the sword down through the bolster and the rope bed-support, right up to its hilt. It had gone straight into the Sow's back and out through her heart. Her fat buttocks were still protruding from under the bed. Trinket gave them a kick, and they did not budge.

'Dear . . . dear sister, you've saved my life!' he exclaimed joyfully. Then he clambered onto the bed and stabbed the Sow twice more through the bolster with his dagger, for good measure.

'Who *was* that horrible woman?' asked the Little Countess. 'She said she was going to gouge your eyes out!'

'She works for that Old Whore the Empress Dowager,' replied Trinket.

He turned to Fang Yi.

'Is your wound hurting you?'

She frowned.

'I'll be all right.'

In fact the effort she had made had opened her wound again. She was faint with pain, and beads of sweat stood out on her brow.

A Pair of Feet in a Pair of Shoes

'We don't have much time,' said Trinket. 'It won't be long before the Old Whore sends someone else after me. We must think of an escape plan quickly. The two of you had better dress up as eunuchs, and we'll all try and sneak out.'

He turned to Fang Yi.

'Do you think you can manage to walk?'

'I'll try.'

Trinket produced two sets of clothes and told them to put them on.

He dragged the Sow's body out from under the bed, and sprinkled Decomposing Powder on it. Then he put away his dagger, made a bundle containing banknotes, gold and silver ingots, two copies of the *Sutra in Forty-Two Sections*, his kungfu primer, the sleeping potion, and of course the remains of the powder.

The Little Countess was dressed first, and climbed down from the bed.

'You make a very handsome eunuch!' said Trinket. 'Here, let me do your pigtail for you.'

He braided her hair, and the Little Countess then did the same for Fang Yi. Soon both girls were ready. Fang Yi was taller than Trinket, and his clothes were rather a tight fit on her. When she looked at herself in the mirror, she couldn't help laughing.

'We won't be able to get out of the Palace tonight,' said Trinket. 'But we must find a place to hide. The Old Whore will be after me.'

After a moment's thought, he decided to take them to the room where he and Kang Xi had held their sparring matches—the 'cake-room'. The Little Countess hobbled along, using a door-bar as a crutch. Fang Yi had to be helped by Trinket, who put an arm round her, and half-supported, half-hugged her. Luckily it was growing dark already, and they only ran into one or two junior eunuchs on their way. When they reached the room, they breathed a sigh of relief. Trinket barred the door and helped Fang Yi into a chair.

'We'd better not talk here,' he whispered. 'It's not like my room. There's a passage-way outside.'

Gradually it grew darker and darker, until they could hardly see each other any more. Fang Yi started fiddling with her hair, and suddenly gave a little sigh.

'What's the matter?' whispered Trinket.

'Nothing, I seem to have lost a hairpin.'

'Oh dear!' whispered the Little Countess. 'It's my fault. I took it out when I undid your hair, and left it on the table. It's the silver one Liu gave you, isn't it?'

'It really doesn't matter. It's only a hairpin.'

Trinket detected the note of sadness in her voice, and his mind was already made up. Chivalry must be observed through to the bitter end.

'We'll be dreadfully hungry by morning,' he said. 'I'll go and find us something to eat.'

'Don't be long!' whispered the Little Countess.

Trinket slipped out. He was afraid the Empress Dowager might have already sent someone to his room, so he hid outside and listened for any noise, before climbing in through a window. He could see the silver hairpin lying on the table, shining in the moonlight. It was a cheap little thing, and he mentally berated Liu Yizhou for giving such a beautiful lady such a worthless present. Then he put it in his pocket, stuffed some cakes into a little cardboard box, and put that inside his gown.

He was about to climb back out of the window, when his eye was caught by something on the ground by the bed. It was a pair of crimson satin shoes embroidered with gold thread. And in each of the shoes was a foot.

Trinket nearly jumped out of his skin with fright. It was certainly a terrifying sight to see in the pale moonlight, a pair of amputated feet in bright red shoes! Trinket quickly figured out what had happened. The ground sloped down towards the bed, and when the Fat Sow's body had decomposed, the pus had obviously trickled down under the bed, and left her feet—the Sow's trotters!—stranded high and dry. He thought of kicking them into the ooze, but it had already dried out. The remaining powder was in the other room, in his bundle.

Suddenly an impish idea entered his head.

'Tamardy! Once I get out of here, I may never see the Old Whore again! Why not play one last trick on her! One that will give her a real fright!'

He found one of his gowns and wrapped it round both of the amputated feet, in their shoes. Then he climbed out of the window and stole towards the Hall of Maternal Tranquillity.

Green and Grey

As he approached the Empress Dowager's compound, he thought it safer to make a detour and go through the shrubbery. He was both carried away by the sheer impudence of what he was planning, and at the same time terrified of the possible consequences if he should get caught. Step by step he drew nearer to the Empress Dowager's bedroom. His hands were sweating with fear.

'I'll just leave the trotters outside the door,' he thought to himself. 'She'll find them there tomorrow. It's too dangerous to go inside.'

As he crept forwards, he suddenly heard a man's voice:

'What on earth can Swallow be up to? She's been away too long.'

'A man?' thought Trinket in the greatest surprise. 'In the Old Whore's bedroom? And he doesn't sound like a eunuch either. Has she got a boyfriend? Ha ha! Old Trink's about to catch the Whore in the arms of her lover!'

Actually he was far too scared to catch her doing any such thing. But his curiosity was aroused. He couldn't just leave the trotters and go.

He crawled forwards stealthily on all fours to where he had heard the voice coming from. The man coughed.

'I'm afraid things may have gone wrong. That boy's a crafty devil, I'm surprised you let Swallow go with him on her own.'

'Swallow's kungfu is ten times better than his,' replied the Empress Dowager. 'And she's very cautious. They probably had to go a long way to find the Sutra, that's all.'

'Let's just hope they get it! If they don't . . .'

The man's tone was extremely gruff, almost threatening. Trinket was more puzzled than ever.

'Who on earth would speak to her like that? Surely it can't be the Old Emperor, come back from Wutai?'

That seemed highly unlikely.

'I did everything I could,' the Empress Dowager continued. 'I could hardly go wandering off with a little eunuch myself. All my maids and eunuchs would have insisted on trailing after me.'

'Couldn't you have waited till after dark? Couldn't you have sent for me?'

'I didn't want to risk revealing your presence here.'

The man gave a hollow laugh.

'In a matter as important as this? I hardly think so. You were probably afraid I would take the credit for it.'

Trinket could control his curiosity no longer. He stole up to the window, and peeped through a crack. This was the kind of thing he'd done plenty of times as a child at the whore-house. Then it had been to peep on a customer jumping on his mum; now he was spying on the Empress Dowager with her lover!

He had a side-on view of her sitting in her chair, and he could see a maid walking up and down the room, with her hands behind her back. There did not seem to be anyone else present.

'Where's the man got to?' wondered Trinket.

Then the maid turned round.

'I can't wait any longer,' she said. 'I'm going to look for myself.'

The very first syllable gave Trinket a violent shock. It was a man's voice. The man's voice that he had been listening to. He was still unable to see the speaker's face.

'I'll go with you,' said the Empress Dowager.

'Still don't trust me, do you!'

'Of course I trust you! But Swallow can be a tricky customer, and I think it would be safer if there were two of us.'

'You may be right. Let's go then.'

The Empress Dowager nodded, and went towards the bed. She lifted up the mattress and removed a wooden panel from underneath it. Something flashed in the lamplight, and then Trinket saw her holding a short-sword. She slipped it into a sheath and put it away in a large inside pocket.

'So, she has a secret compartment in her bed!' thought Trinket. 'And keeps a sword there, ready for murderous occasions like this!'

He watched the two of them as they stole out into the night, leaving the door ajar. The lamps were still burning inside the room.

'I know,' thought Trinket with glee. 'I'll put the Fat Sow's trotters in the Old Whore's secret compartment! When she comes back to put her sword away, she'll find them there and die of fright!'

It struck him as a brilliant plan. He crept into the room, and lifted up the mattress. Under it he found the wooden panel, a foot wide and two feet long, with a brass ring in it. He put his finger in the ring and lifted it, to reveal a rectangular compartment, within which he saw to his absolute amazement no less than three copies of the (by now familiar) *Sutra in Forty-Two Sections*. Two of these were the ones he had acquired from the division of Oboi's property, though they no longer had their jade cases. The third was bound in white silk, bordered with red. This must be the copy

Trinket had heard the Old Whore talking about to Hai Dafu, the one the Old Emperor Shun Zhi had given to his favourite Lady Donggo, and which the Empress Dowager had stolen from Lady Donggo when she murdered her.

Trinket was absolutely delighted.

'Whatever it is that's so tamardy special about these Sutras, for some reason people seem to think they're worth their weight in gold! Time for old Trink to help himself to one or two, I'd say, and give the Old Whore a bit more of a scare!'

He removed the three Sutras and put them inside his jacket, then took the trotters out of the gown he had wrapped them in and placed them in the compartment, carefully replacing the wooden panel. He spread the bedding out on top of the panel, and kicked the gown under the bed. He was about to leave the room when he heard the sound of a door creaking and somebody entering.

They had returned far sooner than he had thought possible! Trinket had no time to think. He ducked terrified under the bed. He was hoping against hope that the Old Whore had come back to fetch something she had forgotten, and would leave again as soon as she had found whatever it was, to go away in search of her *bête noire*—himself! And he was hoping and praying that the forgotten item was not one she normally kept in her secret compartment.

The footsteps sounded light and fast, as though only one person was coming into the room. That one person seemed to be a woman, judging from the pale green slippers and silken trousers which now came into view. It was probably a maid-in-waiting. The feet approached the bed. Trinket pulled out his dagger, ready to take her life if necessary.

Then to his surprise she walked away from the bed and he heard her rummaging in drawers, opening a wardrobe door, searching for something. There was a ripping sound as she broke open a couple of boxes with some sharp implement.

'This can't be one of the regular maids,' thought Trinket to himself in some alarm. 'Whoever she is, she seems to have come here to steal something. Perhaps the Sutras? She's obviously got some kind of a knife. I'd better be careful.'

He heard her rummaging in some boxes, then breaking open several more. Her searching became more and more frantic. Trinket had more or less decided to abandon his hiding-place, and chuck the Sutras out from under the bed for her, when he heard more footsteps outside the room, and the Empress Dowager's voice muttering:

'I'll bet that slut Swallow has gone off with the Sutra herself!'

The intruder heard the voice too. It was too late for her to escape. Trinket heard her open a wardrobe and jump inside, pulling the door closed after her.

'I'm beginning to wonder if you ever sent Swallow to get the Sutra . . .'

It was the maid-with-a-man's-voice who spoke. 'How am I to know you're not making it up?'

'What are you trying to say? What else would I have sent her to do?'

'I've no idea what you were up to. Perhaps you just wanted to get rid of her . . .'

The Empress Dowager gave an angry snort.

'Trust you, my own brother-in-arms, to say something as stupid as that! Swallow is my own sister-in-arms, how could I even *think* of doing such a thing?'

'You?' sneered the man's voice. 'You're a vicious scheming bitch, that's what you are! You'd stop at nothing!'

They were speaking in hushed tones, but it was the dead of night and Trinket could hear every word they said. All this talk of brothers- and sisters-in-arms had him more puzzled than ever. When the two of them entered the room, and discovered the chaos of upturned boxes and ransacked drawers, they both let out a shocked cry.

'Someone's been to steal the Sutras!' cried the Empress Dowager.

She rushed to the bed, lifted the bedding, and removed the panel. When she saw that the Sutras were gone, she let out another cry. Then she saw the trotters.

'What's this?' she gasped, horrified.

The maid-with-a-man's-voice reached into the compartment.

'This,' he said, 'is a pair of women's feet.'

'They're Swallow's feet!' cried the Empress Dowager. 'She's been killed!'

'So, I was right after all,' sneered the man's voice.

'What do you mean?' cried the Empress Dowager, both shocked and angry.

'*You* are the only person who knew where the Sutras were hidden. *You* killed her and *you* put her feet in here!'

'Stop talking such utter rubbish! The thief can't be far away.

We must go after him.'

She turned and looked around the room. The wardrobe seemed to catch her eye, and she began walking slowly towards it.

By now, Trinket's heart was thumping so hard he thought it would burst out of his chest. The flickering candlelight was reflected from the Empress Dowager's sword. He knew that when she reached the wardrobe, she would open it, she would use her sword, and the woman inside would have nowhere to escape.

The Empress Dowager was by now only two feet from the wardrobe. Suddenly there was a great crash, and the entire wardrobe came toppling down on top of her. She leapt backwards, and clothes of every colour came flying out of the wardrobe after her, winding themselves around her head. As she tried to extricate herself from the various garments, another great bundle came hurtling towards her, and Trinket heard her utter a piercing cry. In the midst of the bundle he could see a dripping sword. The woman hiding in the wardrobe had tipped it over, thrown dress after dress at the Empress Dowager, and then finally had pounced on her and struck.

The maid-with-a-man's-voice at first stood riveted to the spot. Then when she heard the cry, she went into the attack. Trinket saw the maid in green tumble out of the bundle of clothes, and emerge still clutching her sword dripping with blood. She threw herself now at the man-maid, and the two were soon embroiled in close combat.

From under the bed Trinket watched the progress of the fight, grey trousers and black satin shoes versus green trousers and shoes. The green shoes darted in and out with lightning speed, the black shoes advanced and retreated more heavily. It was an intense struggle, but without any sound of weapons clashing. The Empress Dowager meanwhile was lying motionless on the ground, apparently dead.

One of the candles went out, and the room grew darker still.

'In a minute the other two candles will go out,' thought Trinket, 'and I'll be able to make a dash for it.'

The two were still locked in a hushed and deadly conflict. They both seemed to be afraid of arousing the Empress Dowager's maids and eunuchs. Another candle went out.

Trinket could hear bits of table and chair flying round the room. Then he saw a flash as the maid in green's sword went hurtling upwards and impaled itself in one of the beams of the roof. The two combatants were now grappling with each other hand to hand on the floor. Trinket could see them more clearly. They were fighting within a small space, going for each other's eyes, chest, throat, Vital Points, wrists. Trinket prayed for the last candle to go out. Even if he had made a dash for it now, the other two would probably have been too stunned to stop him. But he did not have the courage.

For a second or two the last candle guttered. The woman uttered a low cry. Then the light flared up again, and Trinket could see the 'maid' in grey trousers astride the one in green, 'her' right forearm pressed down against the other's throat. Green's left arm was also pinned to the floor and out of action, and all she could do was jab wildly with her right, each time meeting with a block from her opponent. Slowly but surely she was being throttled. Her right hand grew weaker and weaker, and she kicked out with her feet, but it was only a matter of time before it would all be over.

'Once Grey Trousers has killed her,' thought Trinket to himself, 'I'll be the next to go!'

This one thought galvanized him into action. He scuttled out from under the bed, and drove his dagger straight into Grey Trousers' back. He ripped the deadly blade upwards, opened up a large gaping wound, then leapt clear.

Grey Trousers let out a great cry, jumped in the air and lunged, grabbing Trinket's head with both 'her' hands. Trinket's tongue popped out of his mouth, and for a moment everything went black before his eyes. The maid in green came flying through the air and brought the edge of her right palm slicing down on the left side of Grey Trousers' neck. Then with her left hand she seized hold of her opponent's hair and tugged at it with all her might. The whole head of hair came away in her hand, revealing a shining bald pate. It was a wig. Grey Trousers' hands went limp, Trinket was free, and with a few convulsions Grey Trousers sank in a heap to the ground, blood gushing from the wound in 'her' back. 'She' was evidently dead.

'Thank you, Goong-goong,' panted the maid in green. 'You saved my life!'

Trinket nodded, and scratched his own neck in utter perplexity. He touched the bald pate.

'So . . . she . . .'

'She was a man dressed up as a woman,' replied the maid in green. 'Up to no good.'

A voice could be heard outside calling for help. This time it was neither a man's nor a woman's, but that mixture of both that characterized the voice of a eunuch.

The maid in green put her right arm round Trinket's waist, and with her left broke a pane in the window and leapt through the opening. She took aim, and threw something out into the night. There was a nasty thud and a cry, and the eunuch fell to the ground, struck by a deadly dart.

The maid slung Trinket over her shoulder, and set off at a great pace in a northerly direction. She ran through the Gate for Nurturing Splendour. Trinket was quite a weight, and she was only slightly built herself, but she carried him as effortlessly as if he was an infant. She ran past the Rain Flower Pavilion, past the Hall of Precious Splendour, to the edge of the burning-ground by the Palace of Established Happiness. There she put him down.

The Burning-Ground

This burning-ground, just inside the Western Iron Gate, was where the Palace refuse was incinerated. At this hour of the evening it was deserted.

'Goong-goong,' said the maid in green, 'tell me your name.'

'Laurel.'

The maid let out a little gasp.

'So you're the one who caught Oboi! You're the Emperor's favourite.'

Trinket smiled modestly. He had hardly had a chance to study this maid until now. He reckoned she must be about forty years old.

'And what is your name?' he asked.

She hesitated.

'Fate has brought us together. Why should I deceive you? My name is Tao. In the Palace they call me Tao Gong-e. Tell me, what were you doing under the Empress Dowager's bed?'

'His Majesty sent me to catch Her Majesty with her lover!'

Trinket was never short of answers.

Tao gave a surprised smile.

'Did His Majesty know that the maid was a man?'

'He knew something was going on, but not the whole story.'

'Well, I've killed her now,' said Tao. 'When they find out, all hell will break loose. They'll close the Palace gates and launch a big search. I must try to get away while I can. Goong-goong, we will meet again some day.'

Even as she said this, they could hear the beginnings of a hue and cry, with drums and gongs sounding throughout the Palace.

'It's too late to escape. You go and pretend to join the search. I'll return to my room and go to bed.'

So saying, she picked Trinket up again and flew with him through the Palace grounds, turning past the Hall of Heroic Splendour, and westwards. Then she put him down.

'Take care!'

She set off again and was soon lost to sight.

The drums and gongs grew louder and louder, and voices could be heard shouting from all over the Palace. Trinket feared for the safety of the Little Countess and Fang Yi, and hurried back to the room where he had left them hiding.

'It's me!' he called out from the door. The two girls were scared out of their wits.

'What's happening? Have they come to get us?' whimpered the Little Countess.

'No,' replied Trinket. 'The Old Whore is dead! It's a madhouse out there! I'll be glad to get back safe and sound to my own room!'

'To your own room? But . . . we've killed two people there!' cried the Little Countess.

'Don't be afraid. Nobody knows anything about that. Let's go!'

He lifted Fang Yi onto his back, took his bundle in his left hand, and set off. They went stumbling along, and soon ran into a group of guards. Their leader held up his torch, and cried out:

'Who goes there?'

'It's me! Laurel Goong-goong!' called out Trinket. 'You'd better hurry to the Emperor's room. What's happened?'

The guard recognized Trinket and, handing the torch to one of his comrades, fell humbly to his knees.

'Laurel Goong-goong, there's been some trouble in the Empress Dowager's Palace.'

'You'd better be off then. I'll be along later.'

The guard bowed and hurried away with his men.

Luckily the girls were dressed as eunuchs, and no one had paid them any attention even though Fang Yi was slung over Trinket's shoulder.

'You two stay hidden here,' said Trinket, when they finally

reached his apartment. 'Whatever you do, don't change out of those clothes.'

He put his bundle away in a chest, and hurried out, locking the door behind him. He then made his way towards the Emperor's sleeping quarters, in the Hall of Heavenly Purity.

CHAPTER 12

*In which Trinket confides in
Kang Xi, and is sent on
a Mission to the Wutai
Mountains; a Lady Warrior
tells him her Story, expounding
the Significance of the Sutras,
and warning him of Dangers
Ahead; and his Party is
waylaid in a Strange Place by
Ten Riders of the Mystic
Dragon*

Trinket comes Clean

Hearing the hue and cry, Kang Xi had thrown on some clothes and
risen from his bed, to receive a somewhat garbled report of the
night's events from one of the guards. The first thing he said when
he saw Trinket enter the room was:

'Is Her Majesty safe and sound? Tell me what has happened.'

'Her Majesty sent me back to my own room for the night,
and told me to report for duty in the morning,' lied Trinket. 'I've
only just heard about it. I was on my way to find out more . . .'

'I must call on Her Majesty myself,' said Kang Xi. 'You'd better come along with me.'

Kang Xi quickly changed into a formal robe. As they hurried out together he asked Trinket why he had not gone straight to the Empress Dowager's apartment, since he was now in her service.

'I heard the gongs and all the noise and the first thing I thought was that another group of assassins had broken in and that you might be in danger!'

Kang Xi glanced at Trinket's dishevelled appearance, and was touched by this evidence of his friend's devotion—not for one moment guessing that it was the result of the time he had spent squashed under the Empress Dowager's bed.

They continued on their way through the Palace grounds, with an escort of eunuchs fore and aft carrying lamps, and in a little while ran into a guard who delivered a breathless report:

'Assassins have broken into the Hall of Maternal Tranquillity! A eunuch and a maid have been killed!'

'And has any harm been done to Her Majesty?' enquired Kang Xi anxiously.

'Her Majesty is safe! Colonel Dolong has her apartment surrounded with guards!'

Kang Xi breathed a sigh of relief.

'Dolong can bring in as many guards as he likes,' thought Trinket to himself. 'I'm afraid it's too late.'

It was not far to the Empress Dowager's. Their route took them past the Hall of Nurturing the Mind, and the Hall of the Supreme Ultimate. When they arrived, the place was bright as day with the light of lanterns and torches. Nothing, not even a mouse, would have been able to force its way through the phalanx of guards that surrounded it. Seeing the Emperor approach, the guards all fell to their knees. Kang Xi waved to them to rise and walked on in.

Trinket lifted the *portière*, and Kang Xi stepped inside to a scene of devastation. Broken boxes and furniture littered the room, and two corpses lay in pools of blood on the ground. He was visibly shaken.

'What about Her Majesty?' he gasped, his voice trembling with terror.

A faint voice came from the bed:

'Is that the Emperor? Don't worry, I am unharmed.'

'That's the Old Whore's voice all right!' thought Trinket in utter disbelief. 'She's still alive, dammit! What an idiot I am! I should have stabbed her a few times myself to make sure! If *she's* alive, *I'm* dead meat!'

Once more his thoughts turned to escape. But he knew he'd never succeed in getting past that phalanx of guards. He stood there, his knees turning to jelly, his head swimming. He could feel himself on the verge of toppling over.

Kang Xi meanwhile had approached the bed.

'Your Majesty, I have failed in my duty! And those worthless guards deserve to be severely punished!'

'It was . . . nothing . . .' panted the Empress Dowager. 'Just a eunuch and a maid fighting . . . They ended up killing each other. It had nothing to do with the guards.'

'Are you really all right, Your Majesty?' asked Kang Xi.

'There's nothing the matter with me,' she replied. 'I'm just sick of the sight of these worthless servants of mine . . . You don't need to stay.'

Kang Xi sent for an Imperial Physician to take her pulse. All this while Trinket had been skulking behind Kang Xi, terrified in case the Empress Dowager should spot his presence or recognize his voice.

'There's no need for a doctor,' she said. 'All I need is a good sleep. Leave the two . . . corpses . . . where they are. I don't want people making a racket in here. You can go now, and tell the others to leave me alone.'

Her voice sounded very feeble. She seemed hardly able to breathe. She had clearly been seriously wounded.

Kang Xi had been about to order a full investigation into the disturbance, and into the identity of the two corpses. But he dared not go against the Empress Dowager's wishes, and withdrew meekly from her apartment, the terrified Trinket trailing behind him, sidling along close to the wall.

Most of the way back, Kang Xi had his head bowed in thought, but eventually he looked up and saw Trinket following close behind him.

'What are you doing here? Why aren't you with Her Majesty? You work for her now.'

'I thought I ought to leave her in peace. She didn't seem to want people hanging around.'

When they reached Kang Xi's apartment, the Emperor dismissed all his other eunuchs, then told Trinket to stay behind. He paced up and down the room, back and forth, and from one side to the other. Finally he spoke.

'Laurel, why do you think those two would have been fighting?'

'I haven't got the slightest idea,' replied Trinket. 'Palace eunuchs and maids are like that, they're a bad-tempered lot, always fighting and arguing. *You* wouldn't know, they always do it behind your back.'

'Well you'd better let everyone know that this ugly business is not to be talked about. We don't want to upset Her Majesty.'

Trinket took his leave, thinking to himself, 'This time I may really never see you again.' As he left the room, he turned, to see Kang Xi smiling at him.

'Come here, Laurel.'

Kang Xi opened a golden casket at the head of his bed and took out two little cakes.

'Here, you must be hungry after everything that's happened!'

Trinket looked at him. To think that one day his friend the Emperor might himself be in grave danger! The Old Whore was a ruthless enemy, and there was definitely a diabolical plot of some kind afoot in the Palace. She had kept a man hidden in her room, disguised as a woman! One day she might try to kill the Emperor himself. And concerning all of this, the Emperor—his friend the Emperor—was utterly in the dark. Suppose he himself, Trinket, were to die at the Old Whore's hands? Then there would be no one left to warn the Emperor. He had a duty to tell him everything he knew! He had visions of Kang Xi's body lying dead on the ground, his bones all broken. He suddenly burst into tears.

'What's the matter?'

There was a concerned smile on the Emperor's face. He patted Trinket on the shoulder.

'You want to stay with me, don't you? Don't worry, that can be arranged. In a few days' time, when she's better, I'll have a word with her. To tell the truth, I really miss you too!'

Trinket put the cakes on the table and took hold of both of Kang Xi's hands. His voice trembled:

'Misty—can I call you that again?'

Kang Xi laughed.

'Of course you can! I always said that when there was no one else around we should drop the formalities. I know what it is: you want to fight, don't you? Come! On guard!'

As he said this, he turned his hands around, and adopted an upside-down grip.

'It's not that,' said Trinket. 'Fighting can wait. It's something else, something very important. Something I need to tell my dear friend Misty. Something I could never talk about to His Majesty . . . His Majesty would certainly chop my head off.'

Kang Xi found all this highly intriguing. He put his hands on Trinket's shoulders and guided him to the edge of the bed, where they sat down together side by side.

'Come on then, speak up!'

'Promise you'll be Misty, not Majesty?'

'Promise. At this moment I'm your good friend Misty, I'm *no one's* Majesty! I can tell you, being a Majesty all day long, without a single real friend in the world, can be very tiresome.'

'All right then,' said Trinket, 'I'll tell you. And even if you want to chop my head off, you won't be able to.'

Kang Xi smiled.

'Why ever should I want to chop your head off? Why should one friend want to kill another?'

Trinket heaved a long sigh, and began:

'Well, here goes. First of all, I'm not really Laurel. I'm not really a eunuch at all. The real Laurel is dead. I killed him.'

'*What?*'

Kang Xi looked utterly flabbergasted.

Trinket proceeded to give him a brief account of his life to date: where he had been born, how he had been captured and brought into the Palace, how he had blinded Old Hai Dafu, how he had impersonated, and then killed, Laurel, and how Old Hai had taught him kungfu.

Kang Xi's first reaction was hysterical laughter.

'Tamardy! Come on then! Undo your trousers and let's have a look!'

He needed more than his friend's word. Trinket did as he was told. He untied his trousers and let them fall to the ground.

Kang Xi was now able to see with his own eyes that Trinket was decidedly overqualified for the role of eunuch . . . He roared with laughter, and made light of the whole thing.

'This *is* a rum state of affairs! Well well well! I think we can let bygones be bygones—after all, killing a junior eunuch isn't *that* serious an offence! But what about the future? We obviously can't have *you*, in your current state, running around the Palace like a eunuch any more, that's for sure! I shall have to see about making you an Intendant of the Palace Guards or something. Dolong's been pretty incompetent anyway.'

Trinket did his trousers up again.

'That's very kind of you,' he said, 'but I'm afraid I'd be no use at all as a guard. And there's something *else* very important I have to tell you. It's to do with Her Majesty.'

'Her Majesty? What do you mean?'

Even as he asked, Kang Xi sensed that there was worse to come.

Trinket braced himself, and launched into an account of what he had heard Old Hai and the Empress Dowager talking about, that fateful night in the garden outside the Hall of Maternal Tranquillity.

When Kang Xi learned that his own father, the Old Emperor Shun Zhi, was still alive, and that he was living as a Buddhist monk in the Pure Coolness Monastery on the Wutai Mountains, his shocked surprise and ecstatic delight can be imagined. His whole body began to tremble. He seized Trinket by both hands and asked in a shaking voice:

'Are you . . . sure all this is true? My father . . . the Old Emperor . . . still alive?'

'That's what I heard them saying.'

Kang Xi rose to his feet.

'Why, this is the most wonderful news!' he declared in a loud voice. 'Wonderful, wonderful news! Laurel, at first light, we must go! You and I will set off for Wutai to see him! We will kneel before him, and beg him to return to the Palace!'

It had always been Kang Xi's great regret (in an otherwise pampered life) that his parents had both died when he was so young. Often he would lie awake at night weeping as he thought of them. This was the most unbelievably happy news—if he could only bring himself to believe it!

'I don't think Her Majesty would approve of such an expedition,' said Trinket. 'There must be some very important reason why she's been keeping you in the dark for so long.'

'What do you think it could be?'

With every second, fresh doubts were rising in his mind, and they began to cloud the unmitigated joy he had at first felt.

'I don't understand Palace affairs,' said Trinket. 'All I can do is repeat the rest of what I heard the two of them say that night.'

'Then do so! At once!'

Trinket went on to describe in lurid detail how the two Empresses, Shun Zhi's favourite Empress Donggo, and the Empress Kang, had met with their deaths. Kang Xi jumped to his feet and cried:

'You're saying . . . the Empress Kang was murdered?'

Trinket observed the change in the Emperor's expression. His eyes were blazing with rage, his cheeks were twitching uncontrollably.

'I . . . I don't know for sure,' he said, somewhat shakily. 'That's just what Old Hai and Her Majesty said.'

'What *exactly* did they say? Go over it again.'

Trinket had an excellent memory for detail, and was a brilliant mimic. He reproduced the content and tone of the conversation to perfection.

He paused for a moment, but Kang Xi was silent. Finally he spoke.

'My own mother! Murdered!'

'Was the Empress Kang your mother?' gasped Trinket.

Kang Xi nodded.

'Go on,' he said. 'Don't leave anything out.'

There were tears streaming down his cheeks.

Trinket went on to describe the Soft Crush karate technique used to murder not only Empress Donggo, her little boy Prince Rong, and her sister the Lady Zhen, but also Empress Kang. He told how Old Hai had extracted the information from the undertaker, and had then sent the undertaker to Wutai to inform the Old Emperor; how the Old Emperor had ordered Old Hai to track down the killer; how Old Hai and the Empress Dowager had fought through the night. He did not dare admit that it was he himself who had delivered the *coup de grâce*, but said instead that the blind old eunuch had been no match for the Empress, and that she had finally killed him.

Kang Xi struggled to compose himself. He cross-questioned Trinket again and again about that evening, and finally convinced himself that the boy was telling the truth. He looked up thoughtfully.

'Why have you kept this a secret from me until now?'

'I was too scared,' replied Trinket. 'But just now I made up my mind: tomorrow I'm going to run away, and never come back. And then I thought of you all on your own here and I knew I had to tell you.'

'Why are you going to run away? Are you afraid of her?'

'There's something else I have to tell you. That maid who's lying dead in her room, the one who was killed last night . . . that's not her maid at all, it's a man! She called him her brother-in-arms!'

After all that Kang Xi had learned during the past few minutes, he was not even especially shocked to learn that this maid was a man. After all, the eunuch in front of him was not a eunuch.

'And how do you know that?' he asked.

'It's all part of the plot,' replied Trinket. 'For some time now, the Empress Dowager has being trying to have me killed.'

He went on to tell Kang Xi how Colonel Rui, Sister Swallow (the Fat Sow), and the four eunuchs had one after another been sent to do away with him; how he'd overheard the man's voice arguing with the Empress Dowager that evening, and how they'd ended up fighting. It was the Empress who had killed him, Trinket said, herself suffering serious wounds in the process. His story was, needless to say, larded with inventions and riddled with omissions. There was no mention, for instance, of Tao Hongying (Green Slippers), or of the fact that it was he, Trinket, who had killed Colonel Rui and the Sow, and stolen the Sutras.

Kang Xi pondered all of this.

'So, this man was some sort of brother-in-arms of Her Majesty's? It sounds as if she was acting on someone else's orders. I wonder who that person could be? Perhaps whoever it was got wind of the fact that she had this man in her bedroom . . .'

Trinket could see which direction the Emperor's thoughts were heading. In the circumstances he did not feel like engaging in any speculations as to the Old Whore's sex life. He shook his head, indicating that he had no idea who was behind it all.

'Send for Colonel Dolong,' said Kang Xi.

Trinket wondered if the Emperor was about to issue orders for the Old Whore's arrest and execution. If so, should he run for it, or stay and help his friend?

When Dolong received the Emperor's summons, he was beside himself with anxiety. Everything seemed to be going wrong at the same time. Even if he managed to survive this latest crisis with his head still connected to his shoulders, it was beginning to look extremely unlikely that he would emerge with the same hat sitting on that head, or the same button of rank sitting on that hat . . . He hurried post-haste to the Hall of Heavenly Purity.

'Things have calmed down at the Hall of Maternal Tranquillity,' Kang Xi informed him. 'You can dismiss your men. Her Majesty says it disturbs her to have so many guards on duty outside her apartment.'

Dolong was hugely relieved to have escaped the Emperor's wrath. He could not help noticing a strange expression on Kang Xi's face, but for the time being at least he, Dolong, had survived unscathed. He hurried off to carry out his orders.

Kang Xi still had a large number of unresolved doubts, and continued to ply Trinket with questions about the previous night's affair. Eventually word came that the guards had been dismissed.

'Come,' he said to Trinket, 'we must go back to the Hall of Maternal Tranquillity under cover of darkness. I want you to come with me on a secret mission!'

In the first place, Kang Xi felt the need to see things for himself before rushing to form a judgement. He should not condemn the woman who had reared him merely on the evidence of this eunuch who had turned out not to be a eunuch at all. Secondly, this offered him a rare opportunity for adventure, something he had long felt the lack of in the confines of the Forbidden City.

'But she has already killed her brother-in-arms,' protested Trinket. 'She's probably just sleeping and regaining her strength. There won't be anything much to see.'

'We must at least *look*. Otherwise, how will we know there's nothing to *see*?'

Kang Xi slipped into some less formal attire, and put on some thin-soled cloth boots. Now he was dressed as he had been in the old days, when he and Laurel had fought. He took a short-sword from the head of the bed, and slung it from his waist. As they left by the side gate outside the Hall of Heavenly Purity, the host of guards and eunuchs on duty outside fell to their knees.

'I want all of you to stay exactly where you are! No one is to move!' ordered the Emperor.

All two hundred of them stood obediently to attention and remained rooted to the spot.

Night Mission

All was quiet in the garden outside the Empress Dowager's apartment. Kang Xi crept to the window and listened. He heard the Empress Dowager coughing. Confused emotions surged through his breast. Part of him wanted to rush in and fling his arms around her and sob his heart out; part of him wanted to throttle her and squeeze the truth out of her . . . about his father's death, his mother's death . . . Part of him prayed that Trinket's story was false; part of him hoped that it was true. He was shaking uncontrollably, chilled to the bone, his flesh shivering.

There was still a candle burning inside, and a flickering light showed through the paper panes of the window. Kang Xi could hear a maid's voice:

'Your Majesty, I've finished the stitching.'

The Empress Dowager cleared her throat.

'Wrap the maid's body . . . in the roll of bedding . . .'

'What about the eunuch's body, Your Majesty?'

'I said the maid!' snapped the Empress Dowager. 'I never said anything about the eunuch!'

'Yes Ma'am!' replied the terrified maid.

This was followed by the sound of a body being dragged across the floor.

Kang Xi could contain his curiosity no longer. He tried to peep through a crack in the wooden casement, but found that every single crack had been sealed with putty. Remembering the age-old River and Lake trick, first told him by Trinket (who had learned it from Whiskers Mao on their way to Peking from Yangzhou), he moistened his finger with spittle and gently (and silently) rubbed a small hole in the paper window-pane.

Through his peep-hole he could now see the Empress Dowager sitting in bed behind a partly closed embroidered bed-curtain, while a young maid was trying her best to stuff a body into a large cloth sack. The body was dressed in maid's clothes, but the head was shiny and bald. The maid finally succeeded in pushing the bald pate into the sack, then after a moment's hesitation picked up the wig and threw it in too.

'Your Majesty, I've wrapped up the . . . body . . .'

'Have all the guards outside gone away? I thought I could hear someone . . .'

The maid went to the door and looked outside.

'There's nobody there, Ma'am.'

'Well then, you're to drag the sack to the Lotus Pond, put four large stones inside it, and then . . . tie it up . . .' she coughed, 'tie it up with rope and then . . .' more coughing, 'push it in the pond.'

'Yes, Ma'am.'

The maid's voice trembled with fear.

'When you've pushed it into the pond, dig up some earth and throw it into the water, so that no one can see the body.'

'Yes, Ma'am.'

The maid with difficulty dragged the sack out of the room and set off into the garden.

'It seems Trinket was right about this maid being a man,' thought Kang Xi to himself. 'There's obviously something very shady going on, or why would she want to throw the body into a pond?'

He reached out and held Trinket's hand in his own. They could each feel how cold and clammy the other's palm was.

There was an audible splash as the body slid into the pond, followed by the sound of earth being thrown into the water. Minutes later the maid returned. Trinket had recognized her voice from the very first. It was his old flame Blossom, she of the honey-cakes.

'Did you manage it all right?' asked the Empress Dowager.

'Yes, Ma'am.'

'What will you say tomorrow if they ask you what happened to the other corpse?'

'I . . . I don't know anything about it . . .'

'Of course you must know something about it: you work here, you're my maid!'

'Yes! Yes, Ma'am!'

'What do you mean, "Yes!"?'

The Empress Dowager sounded angry.

'I saw the one wearing maid's clothes stand up . . . She wasn't dead, she was only wounded.' Blossom's voice trembled. 'You were asleep, Your Majesty, and I didn't want to wake you. The wounded maid just got up and walked out . . . I don't know where she went . . .'

The Empress Dowager gave a sigh.

'Yes! That's what happened! Buddha be praised! She didn't die after all, she just walked out of the room! Heaven be praised!'

'Yes, Ma'am, Heaven be praised!' repeated the unfortunate maid. 'Earth be praised! She didn't die after all!'

A Secret Assignment

Kang Xi and Trinket stood there waiting for a while. There was no further sound. It seemed that the Empress Dowager must have gone back to sleep. They crept away silently, back to the Hall of Heavenly Purity. The contingent of two hundred guards and eunuchs was still there, standing stiffly to attention. They had taken the Emperor's orders extremely literally.

'At ease!' said Kang Xi with a laugh. But his laughing command had a bitter ring to it.

He walked into his bedroom and stared deeply into Trinket's face. A tear stole down his cheek.

'So that's what she . . . she . . .'

Trinket could think of nothing to say.

Kang Xi brooded silently for a while. Then he clapped his hands. Two guards appeared in the bedroom doorway.

'I have a confidential mission for the two of you,' said Kang Xi. 'You are not to breathe a word of this to a soul, understand? I want you to go to the Lotus Pond in the garden of the Hall of Maternal Tranquillity. You'll find a large sack in the pond. I want you to drag it out. Her Majesty is sleeping. Don't make a sound, don't wake her up, or I'll chop off your heads!'

The two guards bowed low and went to do his bidding. Kang Xi sat on the bed deep in thought.

Presently the guards returned, dragging a large, dripping sack. They waited with it outside the bedroom door.

'Did you wake Her Majesty?' asked Kang Xi.

'No, Your Majesty!' chorused the guards.

Kang Xi nodded.

'Bring it in!'

They deposited the sack inside the room, and were dismissed.

Trinket waited until they had gone, then closed and bolted the door. He untied the sack and dragged the body out. The face was beardless, but beginning to show unmistakable signs of stubble. From this, from the protruding Adam's apple, from the flat chest, there was not the slightest doubt that this was a man, a strong, heavily-built man, a man who, judging from his bulging knuckles, had spent much time boxing. Such a person could only have succeeded in masquerading as a maid for a very short period. Even as a male, he was an ugly hulk.

Kang Xi bared his short-sword, and slashed open the man's trousers. What he saw there filled him with rage. He began angrily hacking at the man's thighs and genitals, leaving them a bloody pulp.

'Her Majesty . . .' began Trinket.

'What Majesty?' cried Kang Xi indignantly. 'That slut drove out my father, murdered my mother, defiled the Palace with her filthy behaviour, slept with this vile creature, and you call her Majesty? I should hack *her* into a thousand pieces, execute her entire clan, and confiscate every penny they possess!'

Trinket let out a long breath.

'Phew!' he thought to himself. 'Maybe I'm saved from the clutches of the Old Whore after all!'

Kang Xi stabbed the body a few more times, but this was still not enough to vent his rage. He was on the point of sending his guards to arrest the Empress Dowager for questioning, but thought better of it. It would be very rash to betray the fact that he knew his father was in retreat on Wutai.

He turned impulsively to Trinket.

'Laurel, tomorrow you and I will go to the Wutai Mountains!'

'Yes, Your Majesty!'

Trinket was delighted at the idea of going on a trip with Kang Xi, and at the thought of getting out of the confines of the Forbidden City.

But Kang Xi's impulse was short-lived. He was by now sufficiently grown-up and wise to know that an Imperial Expedition of any kind would inevitably be a cumbersome affair, involving months of planning and an escort of hundreds of guards. Besides, there was always the danger that the Empress Dowager (if she was plotting something) might take advantage of his absence from Peking to usurp power. And finally, just supposing his father was not still alive, or was alive but not in the Wutai Mountains, he would make a laughing-stock of himself by going there now.

'Perhaps not,' he said, shaking his head. 'I don't think I can go. I can't leave the Capital. Laurie, you'll have to go for me.'

'Me? All on my own?'

Trinket sounded very disappointed.

'You must go. I want you to find out the truth. I want to know for sure that my father is there. Then I'll deal with that slut, and afterwards we can both go to Wutai without putting him in any danger.'

Trinket could see that this was a more sensible plan, and reluctantly he agreed to go.

'Court eunuchs are not normally allowed to leave Peking,' said Kang Xi, 'unless they are accompanying the Emperor. I think I'll have to make you a Palace Guard, Laurie. It'll look a bit odd, though, if you suddenly stop being a eunuch, without any explanation. I'll have to make an announcement and say that you were only pretending to be a eunuch on my orders, so as to catch that scoundrel Oboi. Now that he's out of the way, there's no need for you to pretend any more. Come to think of it, Laurie, since you're *not* a eunuch any more, if you studied a bit, one day I really *could* make you one of my Great Ministers!'

'Excellent!' cried Trinket. 'There's only one snag. The sight of a book gives me a terrible headache. Perhaps I could be one of your Little Ministers?'

Kang Xi sat down at a table and began writing a letter to his father. In it he begged forgiveness for not having known until now that his father was still alive, and communicated his intention of visiting him in the mountains and escorting him back to Peking, where he could once more rule over his devoted subjects.

He had reached this point in the letter, when it suddenly occurred to him that if his emissary Laurel did get captured and this letter were to fall into the wrong hands, disaster could ensue. He took the sheet of paper, lit it in the flame of a candle, and burnt it to ash. He began again. This time it was a straightforward Imperial Edict requesting all concerned to give aid to Lieutenant-Colonel Trinket Wei of the Palace Guards, by Imperial Command wearer of the Yellow Jacket, proceeding on an Imperial Commission to the Wutai Mountains.

Having written the Edict, he affixed the Imperial Seal to it, and handed it with a smile to Trinket.

'There. I've given you your first official appointment. Have a look.'

Trinket blinked at the Edict. Apart from his own name there was a grand total of three characters he recognized.

'Sorry, I can't read it, Majesty. But if you gave me the appointment, it must be a good one!'

Kang Xi read the Edict aloud for his benefit. Trinket stuck his tongue out in astonishment.

'Wow! A Lieutenant-Colonel! And wearing the Yellow Jacket! Not bad for a start!'

The Getaway

As Trinket took his leave of Kang Xi and made his way back to his own apartment, first light was dappling the eastern sky. He opened the door quietly.

Fang Yi had been awake since Trinket left them, and greeted him gladly on his return. The Little Countess awoke and sleepily informed him how worried they had both been for his safety.

'All is well!' announced Trinket. 'Now we really will be able to make our getaway at last!'

The morning bells could be heard, as the gates of the Palace were opened and courtiers began to troop in for early audience. Trinket lit a candle and inspected the two girls' disguise. It still seemed quite convincing.

'The trouble is, you're both too pretty!' he quipped. 'Better rub a bit of dirt on your faces!'

The Little Countess was reluctant to do this, but Fang Yi agreed to go through the motions. Then Trinket wrapped up the three Sutras he had taken from the Empress Dowager's room, and handed Fang Yi her silver hairpin.

'I believe this is yours . . .'

She blushed and held out her hand.

'You mean you went through all that danger to get this for me . . .'

She sounded moved, and looked positively moist-eyed. She turned away in embarrassment.

'It wasn't that dangerous,' said Trinket, reflecting to himself that if he *hadn't* gone to get her the hairpin, none of the other things would have happened, including his entitlement to wear the Yellow Jacket!

He set off with the two of them, leaving the Forbidden City once more through the northern gate, the Gate of the Divine Warrior. In the still dim early morning light, the guards on the gate paid scant attention to the two young eunuchs accompanying the familiar figure of Laurel Goong-goong.

Once they were out in the street, Trinket hired three small sedan chairs, and told the bearers to take them to Chang'an Street West. They got out there, and Trinket hired another chair. This carried them to within two alleyways of the Triad headquarters, and here they dismounted.

The girls told Trinket they should be making their way south to join a friend in the city of Shijiazhuang, in Hebei Province. They invited him to accompany them. Trinket (tempted though he was by the thought of roaming around the countryside with these two delectable young ladies) had other more pressing affairs to attend to. He persuaded them to come in with him for a moment, to rest and eat, and then think about their future plans.

The guard at the entrance to the Triad house let them through, and Brother Gao ushered the three of them in, looking somewhat bemused by the two new little eunuch companions that the Lodge Master had in tow. Trinket explained who they really were, and Gao promptly showed them to a seat and served them tea. He took Trinket aside.

'The Helmsman has had to leave Peking early. He went last night.'

This was a huge load off Trinket's mind. He had been dreading the thought of having to face another kungfu inquisition from his Shifu; and he had been unable to resolve in his own mind his latest dilemma, whether or not to inform the Helmsman of the new (and very important) mission on which he was being sent by the Emperor. He still managed an excellent display of disappointment, and stamped his foot on the ground in mock frustration.

'Why did he have to leave in such a hurry?'

'Urgent news from Taiwan,' replied Gao. 'He was obliged to return there at once. He said that you were to be very cautious. It might be necessary for you to leave the Palace and lie low for a while.'

Trinket was touched by this concern on the part of the Helmsman.

'What's happened in Taiwan?'

'There seems to be some friction within the Marshal's family. The Helmsman is needed there to restore the peace. Some of the Brothers have gone with him—Big Beaver, Brother Li, Father Obscurus. Brother Xu and I and some of the others have stayed behind here to wait for your orders.'

Trinket nodded his head.

'Ask Brother Xu to come in.'

The Eight-Armed Ape might be just the person to escort the

two girls to Shijiazhuang, thought Trinket: he was an excellent fighter, and old enough to be their father.

Meanwhile he and the girls had a light meal of noodles. The Little Countess picked at her food.

'Are you sure you can't come with us to Shijiazhuang?' she asked.

Trinket looked at Fang Yi, who had put down her chopsticks and was staring at him with a beseeching expression. He was very tempted. He even thought of suggesting that the two of them went with him to the Wutai Mountains. But a moment's reflection sufficed to tell him that would be a crazy idea. They were both wounded, and their presence would be bound to attract attention. He sighed.

'I must finish my errand first, and then I'll come and find you. Where does your friend live in Shijiazhuang? What's his name?'

Fang Yi picked up her chopsticks and toyed with her noodles.

'He runs a donkey stable,' she said softly. 'His name is Song San, people call him Mr Gallop.'

Trinket gave a mischievous little smile.

'I'll be there, never fear. I'm always game for a gallop, or a canter, or even a trot, so long as I've got one of my women up in the saddle with me . . .'

He received an immediate scolding from the Little Countess for being so flippant at a time like this.

'If you're our friend,' said Fang Yi in an earnest tone of voice, 'you'll always be welcome to come and see us wherever we are. But if all you want to do is make silly remarks like that, then you might as well stay away.'

Trinket was beginning to find their constant priggishness depressing.

'If *that's* how you feel,' he said somewhat petulantly, 'I might as well keep my mouth shut and say nothing at all.'

Fang Yi insisted that there was nothing wrong with occasionally joking and having a little fun. But one should know where to draw the line.

'So please don't be cross with us!' The way she said this was so endearing, Trinket's spirits immediately soared again.

'How could I be cross with you?' protested Trinket. 'But what about you? Are *you* cross with *me*?'

'No one could ever really be cross with you!'

Fang Yi's face was still smudged with dirt, but to Trinket she seemed as lovely as ever, and the sight of her gave him a warm, tingling sensation. He sat there, gazing at her, and silently drinking his noodle broth.

Presently Xu Tianchuan came in, and Trinket introduced him to the two girls. It was only now (on observing Xu's attitude of reverence, and on hearing him address Trinket as Lodge Master Wei) that they became aware of Trinket's Triad identity. Xu informed Trinket that he had escorted the Mu Family out of the city, and that they had headed south. When Fang Yi heard that the group included her beloved Liu Yizhou, her face flushed and she hung her head bashfully.

'Look how happy she is, the minute she hears that her lover is alive and well!' thought Trinket moodily.

But the thoughts running through Fang Yi's mind were somewhat different.

'If Liu *is* saved, then I've given my word, and I'm married to a eunuch! What kind of marriage can that ever be?'

Xu Tianchuan agreed to escort the girls to Shijiazhuang. He was delighted to have this opportunity to show his goodwill towards the Mu Family, and vowed that he would gladly go with them all the way to Yunnan Province if need be, to show his gratitude to Lodge Master Wei.

The Little Countess at first turned her nose up at the idea of being escorted by this old man, but he was so insistent that in the end she consented. He pointed out that while they had little need of protection (given their undoubted kungfu prowess), he could still make himself useful by performing all sorts of necessary services for them, such as hiring carts, booking rooms at inns, procuring refreshments, dealing with grooms, and so on. And it would be such a pleasure, he repeated, to be able to repay Lodge Master Wei for what he'd done for him.

Xu explained to the girls how he had been savagely beaten up by the Satrap's official Lu Yifeng, and how Trinket had had a word with the Satrap's son, as a result of which Lu had had both his legs broken personally by Wu Yingxiong.

Meanwhile Brother Gao had ordered three large carts, and was waiting outside. Trinket had been wondering what to do with the five copies of the Sutra that were now in his possession: the three he had taken from the secret compartment in the Empress Dowager's bed, and the two he had previously acquired. He took Gao aside.

'Brother Gao, a friend of mine in the Palace has been killed by the guards, and I want to bury his ashes. I'd be grateful if you could purchase a coffin for me.'

Gao assumed that the Lodge Master's friend must be a hero who had died in the cause of the Resistance, and he went out and bought the very best coffin available, made of wood from Liuzhou in the deep South. By the time he had also bought the urn, paper money, spirit tablet, spirit banner and other funeral paraphernalia, ordinary men's attire for the ladies to change into, and an assortment of snacks for them to take with them on their journey, he had spent almost all of the three hundred taels given him by Trinket. The few remaining taels went towards hiring the services of a coroner to officiate at the funeral ceremony, and a carpenter. He returned a few hours later, to find Trinket and the girls still taking a nap.

When Trinket awoke, he took the five copies of the Sutra, and the little kungfu manual given him by the Helmsman (when was he going to have time to practise, after all, on this new mission?), and wrapped them carefully in several layers of oil-cloth. Then he took a handful of ash from under the kitchen stove, and put it inside a burial urn. He rubbed some water in his eyes, and, sobbing most convincingly, made his way to the outhouse where the coffin had been placed. There, he knelt solemnly and placed the package and the urn in the coffin. Brothers Xu and Gao, and the two girls, also fell to their knees and bowed their heads, not for a moment questioning the sincerity of Trinket's grief for this departed friend of his. Finally, when the coroner had placed a layer of soft paper and lime on the contents of the coffin, and the carpenter had nailed it up and added a coat of varnish, the 'mourners' departed and the coffin was left standing on its own in the outhouse.

Departure from Peking

After another short rest, Trinket said he would accompany them some of the way, an offer gladly accepted by the two girls. They climbed into one cart, while Trinket and Xu each boarded one of the others. They left Peking by one of the eastern gates, and after travelling in an easterly direction for a while, turned south and travelled another two or three miles, when they came to a small country town. Here Brother Xu ordered the drivers to stop, and suggested that they should drink some tea in a small tea-house, and that the Lodge Master might wish to take his leave. The waiter poured tea,

while the drivers sat at a separate table. Xu himself wandered out
to admire the view, thinking that the Lodge Master might wish to
make his farewell undisturbed.

The Little Countess spoke first.

'Brother Laurel,' she began. 'Now we know that your real
name is Wei. Lodge Master Wei—what does that mean?'

'The time has come to tell you the truth,' announced Trinket
with a smile. 'Yes, my real name is Trinket Wei, and I am Lodge
Master of the Green Wood Triad Lodge.'

The Little Countess let out a soft sigh.

'Then how did you let yourself become . . . a . . . Palace
Eunuch? It seems such a terrible . . .'

Fang Yi knew what she meant: such a terrible shame, such a
waste, to be castrated.

'It was worth it!' she put in fiercely. 'He let himself be muti-
lated for the Great Cause! He's a brave boy!'

If it had been as she imagined—if Trinket really had allowed
himself to be castrated in order to work as a Triad spy—he would
have been brave indeed!

Trinket gave a wry smile.

'Shall I tell them, or not?' he was wondering.

Even as this thought was passing through his mind, he heard
a cry from the next table. Xu Tianchuan had hurled himself at one
of the drivers, and brought the edge of his right palm down sharply
on the man's shoulder. The driver darted to one side. As Xu's right
cut through thin air, he drove his left fist into the driver's side. But
the man caught the incoming fist and turned it back on itself. Xu
now brought his right elbow down on the back of the man's neck,
whereupon the man swept his right hand through the air and
feinted at the crown of Xu's head. Xu saw the danger he was in,
and leapt backwards. Each one of his moves had met with a smart
riposte.

By now Xu was both angry and alarmed. This driver had
clearly been planted to do some mischief. Xu gestured to Trinket,
indicating that the three of them should escape while they still
could. But escape was not at all what they had in mind. Fang Yi
was still too weak to fight, but the Little Countess and Trinket
immediately drew their swords and joined the fray.

The driver turned around.

'Allow me to congratulate the Eight-Armed Ape on having
such keen eyesight!'

It was a high-pitched voice. The driver had a sallow, puffy face, and was dressed in dirty rags. It was hard to tell what age he was. Xu was greatly taken aback to hear himself being called by his *nom de guerre*.

'May I know your name?' he asked, cupping his hands in a polite gesture. 'And why you choose to disguise yourself as a driver, and play tricks on me?'

The driver laughed.

'I can assure you, it is no trick. I am a good friend of Lodge Master Wei's, and thought I should accompany him out of Peking.'

Trinket scratched his head.

'But . . . I don't even know who you are!' he exclaimed.

'Only last night the two of us were fighting together! How could you have forgotten me so soon!'

The truth suddenly dawned on Trinket.

'You must be Tao!'

He slipped his dagger back in his boot, and hurried over to grasp the 'driver' by the hand. It was the maid Tao Hongying, dressed as a man. She had smeared so much grease and powder on her face, that it was hard to tell what expression she wore. But there was a glint of pleasure in her eyes.

'I was concerned that the Tartars might try to intercept you. I never expected anyone to see through my disguise! Tell me, Brother Xu, what was it that gave me away?'

'It was something about the way you handled the whip,' said Xu. 'You managed to control it without ever moving your wrist or your elbow. I knew you were no ordinary driver the minute we left Peking.'

Trinket introduced Tao as a close friend of his, and Xu begged Tao's forgiveness.

'I must be leaving you all,' said Tao. She bowed, and jumped up onto the driver's seat of one of the three carts.

'Where are you going?' asked Trinket.

'Back to where I came from,' she replied enigmatically.

Trinket nodded.

'Until we meet again!'

Tao drove the cart off into the distance.

The Little Countess turned to Xu.

'Was that man's kungfu really so extraordinary?'

'I should say so,' replied Xu. 'Especially for a woman!'

'A woman? Why do you say that?'

'Didn't you see the way she jumped up onto the cart? Did you ever see a man with a wiggle like that?'

Trinket meanwhile had fallen silent. He knew the time had come for him to leave, and he was beginning to think with some trepidation of the dangers that lay ahead of him on the road to the Wutai Mountains. On his original journey to Peking from Yangzhou he had been accompanied by the seasoned River and Lake veteran Whiskers Mao. Since then, in the Palace, whenever danger threatened, which was often, somehow he had always managed to pull something out of the bag. This time he would be travelling alone and across unfamiliar terrain. Suddenly he felt like a scared little boy. For a moment he contemplated going back to Peking and asking Brother Gao to accompany him. But that would entail betraying the Emperor's confidence. No, there was nothing for it; he had to do it alone.

'It's getting late, Master,' said old Xu, who still supposed that Trinket would be returning to the Capital. 'You'd best be heading back, or you'll find the city gates closed.'

'Come and visit us in Shijiazhuang when your mission is accomplished,' said the girls.

Trinket nodded. He could not bring himself to say anything, torn between the sweetness of being with them, and the bitterness of having to say goodbye.

Xu bade the girls climb into their cart, and himself sat down beside the driver. Trinket watched them as they set off towards the south. They leaned out and waved goodbye, then their cart made a turn, was obscured by a row of willow trees, and they disappeared from view.

Trinket acquires an Aunt

Trinket mounted the last cart. He instructed the driver not to return to Peking, but to head directly west. The driver's reluctance soon evaporated at the sight of the twelve taels in Trinket's hand.

'Will this be enough for three days?'

'Yes, sir! At your service, sir!'

That night they stopped in a little market town some seven or eight miles south-west of Peking, and found lodgings at an inn. Trinket had a quick wash, and fell asleep on the heated brick bed without even bothering to eat.

He awoke early the next morning with a splitting headache.

His eyes were so heavy that he could barely open them. His entire
body was in great pain, and he could scarcely move. It was like
waking into a nightmare. He tried to open his mouth and speak,
but could not utter a single sound. Finally, when he was able to
see, he made out the bodies of three men lying on the ground by
the bed. He stared at this sight in horror, then succeeded in com-
posing himself and struggled into a sitting position, only to become
aware of another figure standing before him, looking at him and
chuckling quietly. Trinket let out a little cry.

'Awake at last!' said the figure, which Trinket was enormously
relieved to recognize as Tao Hongying.

'Sister . . . er, Miss Tao, what's going on?'

'Who are those three?' she asked him, by way of reply.

Trinket tried to climb down onto the floor, but promptly collapsed and had to prop himself up against the side of the bed. He
could see that the three bodies were dead, but failed to recognize
a single one of them.

'I don't know. Auntie Tao, it looks as if you've saved my life!'
She laughed.

'Well make up your mind! Am I to be Sister, Miss, or Auntie?'

'Auntie,' decided Trinket.

Auntie Tao proceeded to tell him what had happened. She
had returned to the Palace from their last encounter at the tea-
house, only to find that the Empress Dowager was still alive.
(Trinket pretended to be surprised by this piece of information.
Secretly he regretted not having told her the previous evening.) The
Palace, she had concluded, was now altogether too dangerous a
place for her. She had decided to leave immediately, disguising
herself as one of the menials working in the Imperial Kitchens. It
was then that she had spotted three suspicious-looking guards
setting off on a mission from the Empress Dowager's apartment.
She had ended up following them, and they had led her straight to
this inn and to Trinket. The guards had first overpowered the
innkeeper, his wife, and the tea-boy, and had then put a sleeping
potion in Trinket's tea. She would have intervened, but could
see that Trinket was washing and didn't want to disturb him.
(Trinket recalled that the previous evening, while he was washing,
he had been idly dreaming of how nice it would be if Fang Yi were
his wife and had her arms around him. He vaguely remembered
being aroused, and blushed to think what Auntie Tao must have
seen.)

'So, what did you do then?' asked Trinket.

'I heard them whispering in the kitchen. Their orders were to bring you back alive if possible. But come what may, they were to get hold of something you had on you. One of them said what a cocky little fellow you must be to have stolen Her Majesty's Sutra, the one she uses every day to pray from . . . Tell me, my young friend, is it true that you took her Sutra? Your Helmsman told you to, didn't he?'

Tao was gazing deep into Trinket's eyes.

It suddenly dawned on Trinket that what Auntie Tao must have been searching for in the Dowager Empress's bedroom was a Sutra, or several copies of the Sutra. He feigned an expression of innocent incomprehension.

'What Sutra? The Helmsman isn't even a Buddhist. I've never seen him read a single Buddhist Sutra in his life.'

Auntie Tao was taken in. She was a fine fighter, but in terms of worldly guile, Trinket was far and away her superior. He had grown accustomed to dealing with treacherous Palace intrigue, while she had spent her life in the inner apartments secluded with other maids-in-waiting, and would often speak no more than a couple of sentences in the course of a whole day.

'I saw the three of them searching your belongings,' she said. 'They found a lot of valuables and a large sum of money. They were talking about stealing it. That put me in a rage, and I went straight in and dealt with them.'

'Damn that Old Whore!' cursed Trinket. 'She was after my money! That's why they laid a trap for me here. They would have killed me for it!'

'I don't think so,' said Tao. 'The Empress Dowager wanted the Sutras, not the valuables. Those Sutras are *very* important. My next thought was that maybe you'd given them to Xu Tianchuan for safe keeping, and that he and those two young ladies had taken them to Shijiazhuang. So I followed them south and tried to search their cart outside the inn where they were staying. But that Eight-Armed Ape spotted me before I'd even started. I had to fight with him again, and close their Vital Points, I'm afraid. I went through all their things, I even broke into the cart, but I couldn't find anything. So I came hurrying back here. Tell me, did the Emperor ever talk to you about the Sutras?'

'He did mention them,' replied Trinket. 'To be honest, I can't see what all the fuss is about. Even if the Old Whore spends the rest of her life chanting Sutras, it still won't save her from all the wicked things she's done . . .'

'What exactly did the Emperor say?'

Auntie Tao pressed Trinket for an answer.

'The first time was when I went with Songgotu to look through Oboi's things. He wanted me to keep an eye open for two copies of a Sutra. Something with a Four and a Two in it . . .'

'Yes! That's it! The *Sutra in Forty-Two Sections*! Did you find them?'

'No, *I* didn't. I can't even read. It was Songgotu who found them. Afterwards I handed them over to the Empress Dowager. She gave me some stupid cakes as a reward! If I'd known what a disgusting Old Whore she was, I'd have chucked the Sutras in the kitchen stove and burned them . . .'

'That would have been a tragedy!' cried Auntie Tao.

'I suppose so,' replied Trinket. 'Anyway, now the Old Whore has got four copies of the thing.'

'Four? How do you know?'

'I heard her talking about it with that man-maid of hers the other evening. There's the one she had in the first place; the two I gave her; and a fourth one which Colonel Rui stole for her from some Bannerman or other.'

'Who knows,' muttered Tao, 'she may even have others.'

She paced up and down the room.

'Those Sutras are of the greatest importance. I am counting on you, my young friend, to help me steal them from her.'

'But she may die,' said Trinket in a low voice, 'and then she'll take them with her to her grave.'

'That's very unlikely,' said Tao. 'What I fear is that the Leader of the Mystic Dragon Sect will move first. If *he* should lay his hands on them, that would be a disaster of the greatest magnitude!'

This was the first time Trinket had heard tell of this leader or his sect.

'Who's *he*?' he asked.

Tao made no reply, but continued pacing round the room. First light was beginning to glimmer through the window.

'We had better not talk any more here. These walls have ears!'

They dragged the corpses out and lifted them onto the cart. Tao had killed them with her naked hands, and there was no trace of blood on the bodies.

'They tied up the innkeeper and your driver. We had best leave them to sort themselves out.'

So saying she leapt onto the driver's seat, and the two of them drove the cart off in a westerly direction.

Two or three miles further on, Tao dumped the corpses in an abandoned grave by the roadside, and weighed them down with a few heavy rocks.

'We can carry on talking as we travel,' she said to Trinket, as they continued on their way.

The road broadened into a highway, on both sides of which stretched a wide expanse of uncultivated countryside.

'You have saved my life, and I have saved yours,' said Tao. 'We are bound by a strong tie. What do you say to the idea of calling me your real Aunt? Will you let me adopt you as my nephew?'

Trinket pondered this briefly. He could not see how he could lose from the deal.

'That's a wonderful idea!' he cried. 'But Auntie, before we go any further, there's one confession I have to make.'

'What's that?'

'If you're going to be my Aunt, there are things I think you ought to know about me. I don't have a real father. And my mother was a whore . . .'

Tao was momentarily taken aback by this, but then a smile of pleasure stole across her face.

'My dear boy, that needn't be an obstacle. Why, the greatest heroes have had the humblest origins: take our Founding Emperor—he was once a monk and a beggar, and that never stood in his way. I'm glad that you have been so honest with me. It shows that you really do think of me as your Aunt!'

Trinket jumped down from the cart and knocked his head on the ground.

'Nephew Trinket Wei does homage to his very own Aunt!'

Tao had been shut up all these years in the Palace, and these were the first words of affection she had heard in a very long time. She was strangely moved. She too clambered down from the cart.

'Dear nephew,' she said, a happy smile on her face, 'from this day, I have family in the world . . .'

Tears sprang to her eyes.

'See what a happy occasion this is? Look at me! I'm crying!'

The Eight Sutras, the Dragon Line, and the Mystic Dragons

They continued slowly on their way in the cart, Auntie Tao holding the reins in her right hand, and Trinket's hand in her left.

'Dear boy,' she began, 'let me tell you something of my story. I entered Palace service when I was twelve years old. The very next year I began working for Her Highness the Princess—'

'Princess?'

'Yes. Princess Chang. The daughter of the Emperor Chong Zhen of the Ming.'

'So you served in the Palace under the Ming dynasty!'

'That's right. When the Emperor Chong Zhen had to leave the Palace, he cut off the Princess's arm with his sword. When I heard what was going on, I ran to save her, but I tripped and hit my head on the steps and fainted. When I came to, His Majesty and the Princess were nowhere to be seen. The Palace was all topsy-turvy. No one bothered with me. Not long after that General Bash-em and his troops broke into the Palace. Then the Tartars chased them out and took it over themselves. But that was years ago . . .'

'But why did the Emperor want to cut off his own daughter's arm?'

Auntie Tao heaved a deep sigh.

'She was his favourite child, and he loved her dearly. He knew that the rebels were in Peking, and had already decided to take his own life. He was afraid for what they might do to her, so he thought to kill her.'

'That must have been a pretty difficult thing to do. And then later he hung himself on Coal Hill, right?'

'That's what I heard from others. The Tartars were led into Peking by Wu Sangui. Most of the Palace eunuchs and maids were dismissed as untrustworthy. I was so young, and I'd been tucked up in bed ever since my fall, so no one noticed my existence. It was only three years later that I met my Shifu.'

'Your Shifu must really be someone, to have a disciple that can fight like you!' said Trinket.

'My Shifu was also a Palace maid,' replied Auntie Tao. 'She entered the Palace on the instructions of my Grand-Shifu.'

As she said this, Auntie Tao cracked the whip loudly in the air.

'And the reason my Shifu entered the Palace was to lay hands on the Eight Sutras.'

'Eight?'

'That's right. One for each of the Banners. The Chief of each Banner—Plain White, Yellow, Red, and Blue; Bordered White, Yellow, Red, and Blue—has his own copy.'

'That makes sense,' said Trinket. 'The two I saw at Oboi's were different colours. One was yellow with a red border, one was plain white.'

'Yes. The Sutras match the colours of the Banners.'

Trinket was thinking to himself:

'I've got five of them. That means there are still three more knocking around somewhere. But I still don't know what's so special about these Sutras. I'm sure Auntie Tao knows. I must try and get it out of her somehow.'

He acted stupid again.

'So I suppose your Shifu's Shifu—your Grand-Shifu—must have been a very devout Buddhist. These Sutras must be very valuable. The writing's probably done in gold or something.'

'No, that's not it,' said Auntie Tao. 'Dear boy, what I'm going to tell you today must never go any further than you. I want you to swear.'

Swearing was something that came easily to Trinket. He could swear his head off about something in the morning, and have forgotten all about it by afternoon. And besides, why should he want to go telling anyone else about the Sutras, when his aim was to collect the remaining three for himself?

'If I, Trinket Wei,' he began, 'should ever betray the secret of the Eight Sutras to another living soul, may I be struck dead, and die a horrible death, just like that foul turtle the Old Whore kept in her bedroom dressed up as a maid . . .'

'Come what may, one thing's for sure,' he thought to himself. 'I'll never be like *that* creature! No one'll catch me dressing up as a woman and getting into bed with the Old Whore!'

Somehow, to Trinket's way of thinking, that thought let him off the hook . . . .

'That's a strange kind of oath to swear,' said Auntie Tao with an amused smile. 'Well, listen while I explain this thing to you. When the Manchus came in through the Great Pass, they never thought they would end up ruling China. There were so few of them. They thought they would do a bit of marauding and then head back to the North-East. So they just grabbed whatever treasure they could lay their hands on. There was a huge amount of it. The person in command of all the Manchu forces at that time was the Regent Dorgon, uncle of the Emperor Shun Zhi. But the Banners were powerful, and each Manchu Banner had its own Head. The Banners held a Council, and at the Council they drew a map of the place where they would bury their Manchu treasure. Each of the Eight Banner Heads was to keep a map—'

Trinket leapt to his feet excitedly and cried out:

'I've got it!'

The cart wobbled and he sat down again promptly.

'Each of the Eight Sutras has a map hidden in it!'

'Almost, but not quite. Who knows?' said Auntie Tao. 'Only the Eight Banner Heads who were present at the Council meeting know the exact secret. Even Princes and Great Ministers don't know. My Shifu told me that the hill where the treasure is buried lies on one of the Dragon Lines that controls the destiny of the Manchu people. This Dragon Line has enabled them to set one of their own kind on the throne and rule China.'

'What's a Dragon Line?' asked Trinket.

'It's a line of power in the earth,' replied Tao. 'The Manchu ancestors were buried in this hill. Their sons and grandsons have prospered, and have conquered China. My Shifu told me, if only we can find that hill, and break the Dragon Line, not only can we throw the Tartars off the throne of China, but we can send them back for ever to their homeland, to die there. My Shifu, and my Grand-Shifu before her, gave their lives in the quest for this knowledge. That's how important it is. And somehow or other the secret lies hidden in those Eight Sutras.'

'How did your Grand-Shifu come to know all this about the Manchus?' asked Trinket.

'It's a long story. She was the daughter of a Chinese father living in the North-East. She was taken into captivity by the Head of the Bordered Blue Manchu Banner. She said that when the Manchus took Peking, there was a lot of argument among the Banner Heads. Some of them wanted to conquer the whole of China. Others thought that such a conquest would be too great an undertaking, and that it would be safer to take whatever they could carry and go back to the North-East. In the end it was Prince Dorgon who decided: they would stay and establish their dynasty, but at the same time they would carry off a huge treasure and bury it somewhere beyond the Pass. Then if the day ever came when they were forced to retreat, they would have something to fall back on.'

'So you mean they were *afraid* of us Chinese?'

'Of course they were! They still are. It's just that we won't stand up against them together. Dear boy, you are the Emperor's favourite. If with your help we can find out where the Sutras are hidden, and get our hands on that treasure, we will be able to strike a double blow! We will have broken the Manchu Dragon Line, and with the treasure we will be able to pay for the soldiers and the weapons we need. Then we'll soon have them on the run!'

None of this patriotic fervour found much of an echo in Trinket's opportunist heart. But the thought of all that treasure lying somewhere ready for the taking . . . That was a different matter.

'Auntie,' he asked breathlessly, 'are you saying that the Sutras tell where the treasure is hidden?'

'My Shifu heard it from her Shifu,' replied Tao. 'She heard the Head of the Bordered Blue Banner one day, in a fit of drunkenness, tell his junior Princess that he would leave her something special after his death, a copy of a Sutra. He called it the very Life Blood of the Eight Banners. That was why both my Shifu and my Grand-Shifu spent their lives in search of it. My Grand-Shifu tried in vain to steal it, but there was a highly skilled fighter in the service of the Bordered Blue Banner who prevented her. When she was dying she told my Shifu to get into service in the Palace and find a way to get hold of another copy. But my Shifu discovered how difficult it was to accomplish her mission in the Palace. Then she met me, and since I had been a servant of Princess Chang, she took me as a disciple.'

'No wonder the Old Whore was so desperate to get her hands on the Sutras!' said Trinket. 'She must have been after the treasure! You'd think she had enough money of her own!'

His thoughts ran on silently:

'What about Old Hai? Why was *he* always asking me to get the Sutras from the Upper Library for him? Perhaps he was just using it as a way of finding out who I was working for? Or finding out who killed Princess Donggo? He probably thought they were one and the same person. I'll never know now, anyway . . .'

'There may be something else in the hill,' continued Tao, 'something my Grand-Shifu didn't know about. My own Shifu fell ill and died in the Palace. Her parting words to me were to find the Sutras. She knew it would be too hard for me to achieve this single-handed, so I had to find a reliable disciple in the Palace, someone I could trust with the secret. It mustn't die with me.'

'Absolutely,' thought Trinket. 'We certainly wouldn't want all that treasure to fall into the wrong hands . . .'

Trinket was not much of a patriot, and he was too young to have any feelings about the terrible excesses committed by the Manchus during their conquest: the rape and pillage, and the massacres of innocent women and children. These were things he had heard of from his elders, but never witnessed for himself. In fact, in all his time as a Palace Eunuch, he had received little but kindness from the Manchus—with the exception of Old Hai (though, when all was said and done, Trinket had probably done more harm to the old eunuch than Hai had succeeded in doing to him).

'None of the Palace maids were possible disciples,' continued Auntie Tao. 'They all seemed either stupid, or flirtatious. How could I trust one of them with my secret? But now I have been lucky enough to meet you. I feel so much easier in my mind, so much happier, now that I've shared the secret with you.'

'I feel so much happier too,' said Trinket. 'But not because of all that stuff about the Sutras . . .'

'Then why?'

'Because now I've got a real Auntie! We're family!'

He had a way of saying this that brought a flush of pleasure to Tao's cheeks.

'Yes, and I've got a nephew! So I'm happy too!'

But then, quite suddenly, her expression changed. Her face began to twitch, and a look of terror came into her eyes. She gazed into empty space, and when Trinket asked her what the matter was, it was as if she had heard nothing. He asked again, and she seemed to shudder.

'It's . . . nothing . . .'

Suddenly the whip fell from her hand and landed with a thud on the ground. Trinket jumped down from the cart, picked it up, and leapt back up again. Tao seemed very ill at ease. She pointed to a large tree by the roadside.

'Let's go and rest there for a while, and let the donkey eat some grass.'

The two of them descended from the cart and sat side by side in the shade of the tree.

Tao stared abstractedly in front of her.

'Did he say anything?' she said all of a sudden. Trinket looked at her, at a loss as to what she meant.

After a long silence, she asked again:

'Did you hear him say anything? Did his lips move?'

Trinket was beginning to find her a bit scary. He wondered if she might be possessed.

'Who, Auntie?' he asked, in a trembling voice. 'Where? When?'

Auntie Tao seemed to wake from a dream.

'The man we killed, the man dressed as a woman. That evening in the Palace. Did you hear him say anything?'

Trinket heaved a sigh of relief. At least she wasn't seeing ghosts.

'You mean him! No, I didn't hear him say anything.'

Tao fell silent again. She shook her head.

'I was too weak for him, that's why. He didn't need to use any of their spells.'

Trinket had no idea what she was talking about.

'Forget about him, Auntie. He's dead and gone.'

'Yes,' she repeated, 'dead and gone.'

Somehow this seemed to make her all the more frightened.

'Even his ghost is nothing to be frightened of,' said Trinket.

'It's not that. What worries me is that he may have been a disciple of the Leader of the Mystic Dragon Sect. But the Dowager Empress kept calling him her brother-in-arms . . . So he can't have been. Surely . . .'

She was partly talking to herself, partly calling upon Trinket to reassure her, and her voice was still trembling.

'Don't you worry, Auntie, he never said a word. Who is this Mystic Dragon Leader character anyway?'

'Leader Hong is a man of extraordinary power. You must never speak of him with disrespect. He gets to hear things. He has followers everywhere. Say a single disrespectful thing about him and . . . you're done for!'

Even as she said this she was looking furtively in every direction, as if she feared the presence of some Mystic Dragon informer.

'How can these Mystic Dragons be so powerful? Are they more powerful than the Emperor?'

'No, they are not. But you can hide from the Emperor. You can't hide from the Dragons. They will find you wherever you go.'

'Then they must be a bit like the Triads?'

Tao shook her head.

'They're not the same. The Triads are fighting for a cause. They can hold their heads up high, and everyone on River and Lake respects them. The Dragons are different.'

'You mean everyone on River and Lake is afraid of the Dragons?'

Tao pondered this briefly.

'I don't know much about River and Lake. Only what my Shifu told me. She was an outstanding fighter, and she died at the hands of one of the Dragon Sect.'

'Tamardy!' burst out Trinket. 'Then they are our sworn enemies! We must fight them, not fear them!'

Tao shook her head again, and said slowly:

'If only it were as easy as that! My Shifu told me that their kungfu is like a chameleon, constantly changing, full of surprises. That's part of its strength. And they chant spells which boost their own courage and strike fear into the hearts of their opponents. My Grand-Shifu was up against them when she tried to get hold of the Sutra belonging to the Bordered Blue Banner. She had the upper hand, and then one of them started chanting and all her strength and courage just drained away. My Shifu was there. She saw it happen. She ran to her Shifu's aid, but no sooner did she hear the chanting than her own resolve faltered, she fell to her knees and surrendered. That is the kind of power they have!'

Trinket was privately thinking to himself:

'That's because your Shifu was a woman.'

'What was it they chanted?' he asked. 'Have you ever heard one of their spells yourself?'

'No, I never have. I suspected that man-maid of being one of them, that's why I asked you if you'd heard him say anything.'

'I didn't hear anything like that,' said Trinket.

'The strange thing,' said Tao, 'is that when I fought against him, I felt all my courage and strength draining away too . . .'

'How many people have you fought, Auntie?' asked Trinket. 'How many people have you killed in your life?'

Tao shook her head.

'I've never fought before.'

'There you are. That's why. You must fight more, kill more people. Then you won't be scared.'

'You may be right. But I don't want to fight, I don't want to kill. I just want to get hold of those Sutras, as peacefully as I possibly can. Then we'll be able to break the Manchu Dragon Line. Then I'll be happy. But that Sutra from the Bordered Blue Banner is almost certainly in the hands of the Mystic Dragons, and how will we ever get it back from them?'

Her face was heavily made up, and it was hard to read her expression. But fear was visible in her eyes.

'Auntie, why don't you join the Triads?' said Trinket.

He was thinking that while she might be easily scared, the Triads would surely be more than a match for the Mystic Dragons.

Auntie Tao seemed a little taken aback by this.

'Why should I?'

'Because the Triad cause is the same cause as your Shifu's—to bring down the Manchus and restore the Ming!'

'There may be something in that. Let's talk about it some other time. I must hurry back to the Palace. Which direction are you going in?'

'Aren't you afraid of what the Old Whore might do to you?' asked Trinket in some surprise.

Tao sighed.

'I've been in the Palace since I was a girl. It may not be very safe, but it's probably the only place where I can survive. I don't know my way around out here, in the outside world. I was afraid of my secret dying with me, but now I've found you and passed it on, so even if the Empress Dowager kills me, there is nothing left to fear! The Palace is big enough. I'll find somewhere to hide.'

'I'll come looking for you one of these days,' said Trinket. 'But first I have to complete my mission, the one given me by my Shifu.'

Auntie Tao assumed this to be Triad business, and was too discreet to enquire further.

'Where shall we meet?'

'When I come back,' said Trinket, 'I'll go to the burning-ground and make a heap of stones. In the middle of the heap of stones I'll stick a piece of wood, and on the wood I'll draw a sparrow. That will mean that I'm back, and we'll meet there that very evening.'

Auntie Tao nodded.

'Good. Be careful, my boy. River and Lake is full of danger.'

Trinket nodded.

'And you be careful too, Auntie. That Old Whore is a vicious monster. Don't fall into any of her traps.'

They drove their cart on to the next country town, and there they parted ways, Tao turning back east towards the Capital, Trinket hiring another cart and continuing on his way westward in the direction of the Wutai Mountains. He could see her looking back after him as her cart disappeared into the distance.

'She may not be my real Auntie,' he thought to himself, 'but she certainly seems to be fond of me!'

Close Blade

Trinket dozed off as the cart rumbled along. Evening was drawing on, when he heard the sound of galloping hooves, and a horse pulled up alongside him. He heard a voice hailing the driver:

'Hey, you there! Have you got a boy in your cart?'

Trinket recognized the voice as Liu Yizhou's. He poked his head out of the cart.

'Brother Liu!' he cried amiably. 'Are you looking for me?'

He could see that Liu's face was streaked with sweat and dirt.

'I've found you at last!' cried Liu, and wheeled his horse round in front of the cart. 'Get down here at once!' he shouted, in a tone that was far from friendly.

'Brother Liu,' returned Trinket, greatly taken aback, 'what have I done wrong? Why are you angry with me?'

Liu cracked his whip violently across the head of the mule pulling Trinket's cart. The creature let out a cry of pain, and reared on its hind legs. The cart tipped backwards and the driver, who was almost thrown to the ground, cried irately:

'What are you doing that for?'

'Because I want to!' cried Liu hysterically.

He cracked his whip again, and this time coiled it around the driver's whip and hauled him onto the ground.

'Because I feel like it!'

The driver scrambled to his feet, screaming and yelping. Liu's whip had drawn blood.

Trinket reacted quickly to the danger presented by this maniac, who had no quarrel with the driver and would doubtless turn on him in a moment or two—even more viciously. He pulled his dagger from his boot and gave the mule a quick stab in the rump. The animal responded by bolting down the road, dragging the cart along with it. Liu abandoned the driver and galloped after the cart.

'Stay and fight, you little brat—if you've got the guts!'

Trinket poked his head out of the cart:

'Stop chasing me, *you* little brat—if *you've* got the guts!'

Liu whipped his horse on, and was soon close behind the mule and cart. Trinket thought of hurling his dagger at Liu, but was afraid of missing and of losing his precious weapon. He urged the mule on for all he was worth. The next moment, he felt a sudden sting on his cheek. It was Liu's whip. He ducked back inside the cart. From between the curtains he could see Liu's horse pulling closer and closer. Another moment and Liu would be able to jump onto the cart. In the heat of the moment Trinket reached inside his gown and took out a lump of silver, which he hurled at Liu's horse, catching it on the left eye.

The beast was blinded instantly, and went careering off down the slope at the side, blood pouring from its wounded eye. Liu pulled hard on the reins, but his horse responded by bucking savagely and throwing him to the ground. Liu scrambled to his feet. By the time he started whistling and calling, the horse had vanished into the trees. Trinket burst out laughing.

'Brother Liu, not much of a rider, are you! Try riding a turtle instead!'

Liu ran huffing and puffing after the cart.

Trinket urged his mule on. Looking back, he saw that although Liu was now on foot, he was still drawing closer. It would be hard to throw him off. He prodded the mule again with his dagger, but this time it failed to have the desired effect. Instead the beast stamped its hooves once or twice, turned about, and began heading straight for Liu.

'No! No!' yelled Trinket. 'Wrong way!'

But the more he pulled on the reins, the more the mule hurtled towards Liu. Finally, in despair, Trinket bailed out, and ran for cover in the trees. In a matter of seconds Liu was after him, and had him pinned to the ground. Trinket had his dagger in his right hand, and Liu lost no time in seizing him by the wrist and twisting his arm round (Wandering Clouds and Flowing Water) so that the edge of Trinket's dagger was pressed against his throat. Trinket knew how sharp the dagger was. It would slice through his neck as if it were the softest bean curd.

'Dear friend,' he pleaded, with his most fetching smile, 'please tell me what all this is about! Surely there's no need to be so rough! After all, we're almost brothers!'

Liu spat in his face.

'You, my brother? You . . . you sordid little brat! All that sweet-talking you did in the Palace, with *my* girl! And then you got into bed with her . . . I'll kill you!'

His brow was working with rage, his eyes were blazing, his left fist was clenched and aimed at Trinket's forehead.

So he'd found out all about Fang Yi, Trinket thought to himself. But how? However it had happened, Liu was in an extremely dangerous mood, and he was holding that dagger far too close for comfort. The slightest pressure and there would be a nasty hole in Trinket's throat.

'Can't you see that you're the one Miss Fang loves,' he said, trying to smile without moving his face any more than was absolutely necessary. 'I wouldn't have dreamed of doing anything like that to her. She wouldn't stop talking about you day and night!'

At these words Liu's rage visibly abated.

'How do you know?'

Trinket felt the knife-edge move an inch or so away from his throat.

'She begged me to rescue you, and when I managed to get you out, she was overjoyed. You should have seen her!'

Suddenly Liu flared up again.

'I don't owe you anything, you little runt! Why did you cheat my sister-in-arms into . . . agreeing to marry you?'

'I don't know what you're talking about! Who told you that? A beautiful babe like her could only marry someone handsome and brave like you . . .'

Again Liu's rage abated, again the blade moved an inch or two away.

'But do you deny it? Did she agree to marry you or didn't she?'

Trinket gave a little laugh.

'What's so funny?'

'Brother Liu,' said Trinket, 'just think for a moment: a eunuch, with a wife?'

Liu had come chasing after Trinket in a mad fit of rage. He

had not even stopped to consider the matter calmly. Trinket's logic seemed to brighten him up no end. He laughed, but still held tightly onto Trinket's wrist.

'So why did you make her agree to it then?' he asked.

'Who told you I did?'

'I heard them talking about it together, her and the Little Countess.'

Something Wrong with the Biscuits

It transpired that on their way south to Shijiazhuang, old Xu and the two girls had run into Shaker Wu, his disciple Ao Biao (the Blue Tiger), and (Pale-Face) Liu. The three men were planning to rest awhile and recover from the beatings and torture they had suffered during their detention in the Palace. They were delighted to see the Little Countess and Fang Yi. But Liu soon noticed a change in the way Fang behaved towards him. She hardly even looked at him, and seemed strangely cold. Whenever he tried to draw her aside, so that they could have a moment together, she seemed to cling to the Little Countess. Liu was greatly put out by this. He questioned her about it, and finally she said:

'From this day forth, we are obliged to treat each other as brother- and sister-in-arms. It must go no further than that.'

Her words had a devastating effect on Liu.

'What do you mean? Why?'

'There isn't a reason,' she said coldly.

Liu took hold of her hand and pleaded with her:

'Sister-in-arms, you . . .'

She pushed him away and cried:

'Show me a little respect, please!'

Poor Liu retired to his room in the inn that night in a state of utter desolation. He tossed and turned, but he was much too distraught to sleep. Finally he got up and went outside. He happened to find himself outside the window of the room where Fang Yi and the Little Countess were staying. They were talking. This was what he heard:

'Why are you doing this to your brother-in-arms? You'll break his heart!'

'The sooner it breaks, the sooner he'll get over me and feel no pain.'

'You're not really thinking of marrying that . . . young Trinket, are you?'

'Why, do you fancy him for yourself?'

'Of course not!'

Fang Yi sighed.

'I swore an oath, by Heaven and Earth, and you were my witness.'

'I know, but I never thought he was being serious!'

'Whether he was serious or not, when a girl promises herself to a man . . . And besides . . .'

'Besides what?'

'Well, both of us have slept with him in the same bed, under the same covers . . .'

The Little Countess stifled a laugh.

'He certainly is a mischievous little imp, isn't he! He put his arms round you, and even kissed you . . .'

Fang Yi said nothing, and only sighed. Outside the window, Liu Yizhou was fit to burst. It was all he could do to remain standing upright.

'He may be young,' Fang Yi went on, 'but he has such a funny way with him! And he *was* good to us!'

The Little Countess laughed.

'Why, I do believe you miss him!'

'So, what if I do!'

At this point Liu keeled over and came crashing down on the window-frame.

'What was that?' cried the two girls.

Liu now had one thought only, to catch up with Trinket on his journey west and kill him! He found a horse outside the inn and galloped off, asking every cart-driver he passed if he had seen a boy on the road.

Trinket heard all this from Liu's own lips. He succeeded, by dint of various references to how much Fang Yi adored Liu, and by fabricating an account of the untold dangers *she* had encountered to retrieve the hairpin given her by her beloved, in inducing the gullible Liu to loosen his grip; and what with one thing and another, a few minutes later the two of them were sitting down side by side beneath a large tree by the roadside, Trinket's wrists very blue and swollen.

'You Mu folk certainly know how to squeeze!' commented Trinket wryly. 'That younger Bo brother, Maple, did exactly the same thing to me once. So, how come you were outside their window last night and heard what they were saying? What were you doing?'

'Actually, I just went outside to have a pee,' confessed Liu.

'That's a bit low, isn't it? Stinking out the fair maids' dwelling like that, when you had the whole world to choose from!'

'Tell me some more about Miss Fang,' begged Liu.

'I'm starving,' protested Trinket. 'Go and get me something to eat, something nice, then I might have the strength to tell you some more of Sister Fang's soppy, sickening, sweet-nothings kind of talk . . .'

Trinket was, needless to say, plotting his getaway.

'What do you mean, soppy and sickening? She never talks like that.'

'Oh really? What about stuff like this then: "My darling brother-in-arms Liu, my sweetest, dearest, most adorable, most handsome brother-in-arms . . ." Maybe *you* don't find that kind of thing sickening, but it makes me want to puke! Tamardy! I'd be dead embarrassed if I ever caught myself talking like that!'

Liu was, of course, ecstatic. Trinket repeated his demands for food.

'If you won't go and get some, I will!' he announced.

'No,' cried Liu, anxious to hear more recitals of Fang Yi's adoration. 'I've got some biscuits with me. Have some of these for now, and later when we get to town I'll treat you to a proper meal.'

He handed Trinket a biscuit. Trinket complained that it tasted peculiar, and rummaged around in Liu's bag for another one. He broke off a piece.

'Tamardy, I'm dying for a piss!'

Trinket went behind a tree, opened his trousers, and began peeing on the ground.

When he came back, he rummaged around again among the biscuits. By now Liu was feeling hungry himself, and started munching biscuits too.

'You know,' Trinket said to Liu, 'that Fang girl is a real good-looker. If I wasn't a eunuch, I wouldn't mind marrying her myself. Anyway, I'm afraid *you* never will.'

'What do you mean?' cried Liu.

'Calm down. Have another biscuit.'

'Tamardy! You're . . .'

As he spoke, Liu suddenly began to feel faint.

'What's the matter?' asked Trinket. 'Aren't you feeling well? Something wrong with the biscuits?'

Liu rose to his feet, wobbled, and came crashing to the ground.

Trinket burst out laughing, and gave him a good kick on the buttocks.

'Seems your biscuits had a little something in them, my friend!'

Liu gasped, and then lost consciousness.

Trinket gave him a couple more kicks, but Liu just lay there motionless. Trinket undid his own belt and used it to tie up Liu's legs and hands. There was a large boulder by the tree. Trinket managed to heave this away, and excavated a hollow underneath it, until he had a hole about four feet deep. Into this he dragged Liu's body.

'Buried alive by old Trink!'

He propped him upright in the hole, and filled it with earth and rubble, so that only Liu's shoulders and head were showing.

Feeling very pleased with himself, Trinket went to a nearby stream, took off his gown and dipped it in the water. He returned, and squeezed the cold water over Liu's face.

Liu came round slowly. He saw Trinket sitting in front of him, hugging his knees and staring at him and chuckling mischievously. He struggled to move, but to no avail.

'Don't play games with me!' he pleaded.

'Games!' cried Trinket. 'Arse-hole! Think I've got time to play games with a shit like you!'

He gave Liu a hefty kick in the face. Blood came pouring from his right cheek.

'Miss Fang's *mine*! She's my wife, do you hear me? You shit, twisting my arm, boxing me on the ears, whipping me. Well, now it's Trink's turn! First I'm going to slice off your ears, then your nose, then cook you up in little bits . . .'

He pulled out his dagger, stooped over Liu, and ran the edge of the blade twice across his face.

Liu was terrified out of his wits.

'Dear . . . friend . . . Lodge Master . . . For the Mu Family's sake, put away your knife . . .'

'I rescued you from the Palace, but what did you do? You turned on me and wanted to kill me! It's a bit late to start talking about the Mu Family now!'

'I did wrong!' gasped Liu. 'Forgive me!'

'Not till I've had three hundred and sixty slices at your tamardy rat-face!'

He took hold of Liu's pigtail and sliced it clean off. Then he used the blade as a razor, and shaved Liu's scalp clean.

'Filthy bald arse-hole of a monk! Just the sight of a monk like you makes me want to kill!'

Liu sniggered nervously.

'But Lodge Master, I'm not a monk . . .'

'Then why shave your tamardy head, arse-hole!'

Liu was in no position to argue.

'I did wrong! Forgive me, Lodge Master, forgive me . . .'

'Then answer this question,' said Trinket. 'Whose wife is Miss Fang?'

'I . . . I . . .'

'Speak up!' shouted Trinket. He waved the dagger in front of Liu's face. Liu decided that in the circumstances prudence was definitely the best course of action. This was not the moment for heroics. The boy was only a eunuch after all. He might as well give him the semblance of a victory. He wanted to come out of this with his ears and nose intact.

'Of course she is your wife, Lodge Master Wei.'

Trinket laughed.

'She? Come on, I want a name. I can't hear your monkish mumblings.'

'Miss Fang Yi, Miss Fang, my sister-in-arms, is Lodge Master Wei's Lady Wife . . .'

'Let's get things straight,' Trinket continued. 'Are you my friend?'

Liu thought he saw light at the end of the tunnel.

'Why, yes!' he declared joyfully. 'I mean, I would never have dared to suggest such a thing, but if you are willing to call me your friend, Lodge Master, I consider it a great honour!'

'I am calling you my friend,' said Trinket. 'Now: on River and Lake, friends are bound by honour—am I right?'

'Oh yes, absolutely,' agreed Liu eagerly. 'Why, friendship *means* honour!'

'And honour means a man *never* meddles with his friend's wife, right? So in future, you're to stop messing around with mine. There's to be no more nonsense. I want you to swear it.'

Liu had walked straight into it. He inwardly cursed himself for being such a fool. He hesitated a moment. But then he saw Trinket's dagger glinting in front of his eyes.

'I swear! I will never harbour intentions towards Lodge Master Wei's wife!'

'If you should so much as look at her or speak to her in an improper way, what will become of you?'

'May Heaven and Earth punish me!'

'And turn you into a turtle!'

'Yes! Yes!'

'Yes what? Turn you into a what?'

'Into a turtle!'

Trinket gave a big laugh.

'That's better. Maybe I'll let you off. But I think I'd better piss on your head first . . .'

He slipped the dagger back down the side of his boot, and undid his trousers.

Suddenly a girl's voice was heard crying from the nearby trees: 'No! That's going too far!'

The Storm

To Trinket's surprise and delight, it was Fang Yi. A moment later, she, the Little Countess, and Xu Tianchuan came out of the trees, followed by Shaker Wu and Ao Biao.

The five of them had heard Liu Yizhou's sudden departure during the night, and had followed him. They had been hiding in the trees nearby for quite some time and had heard the entire conversation.

Trinket smiled.

'Out of respect for Mr Wu, I will spare you the humiliation of being pissed on!'

Old Xu hurried over and excavated Liu from his hole. He hauled him out, and untied the belt which bound him. Liu was overcome with shame and remorse, and hung his head, unable to look any of them in the face.

Shaker Wu gave Liu an angry dressing-down, in the course of which he disclosed to all present Liu's cowardly behaviour in the Palace, when he had been frightened by the threat of death into betraying his own name. Shaker declared that he was only refraining from punishing Liu out of respect for their mutual Shifu, Iron

Dragon. This made Liu all the more ashamed and crestfallen, and he stood there ashen-faced and silent.

Trinket stepped in and pleaded with Shaker to let bygones be bygones.

'You see!' said Shaker Wu. 'See what a magnanimous person Lodge Master Wei is!'

'Come over here,' said Fang Yi. It was Trinket she was speaking to. 'There's something I want to say to you.'

Liu observed this public display of intimacy with uncontrollable jealousy. His hand went to his sword.

The next thing he heard was a resounding slap. Trinket jumped back and held his hand to his face.

'What did you do that for?'

'I heard the things you said! How could you!'

Tears of anger and distress were rolling down her cheeks.

Xu Tianchuan tried to steer them away from this personal tiff, his main concern being to preserve the harmony between the Triads and the Mu Family.

'Look,' he said, 'I think we can consider Lodge Master Wei and Brother Liu's matter settled. I don't know about anyone else, but I'm hungry! Let's find somewhere we can have a good meal.'

A wind had blown up from the north-east, and big drops of rain began falling from the sky. Xu looked up into the heavens. He could see great thunder clouds rolling in.

'Looks like a storm brewing. Come, we'd better find shelter.'

Shelter

The seven of them set off on foot down the highway, in a westerly direction. The two girls had still not fully recovered their strength, and made slow progress. The rain fell ever more heavily, and there was not a dwelling in sight—not a farm, nor even so much as a simple roadside shelter. They were soon soaked to the skin.

Presently they heard the sound of rushing water, and came to a river. A few hundred yards upstream stood a small building. They hurried thankfully towards it. As they drew near, they saw that it was a small, and utterly dilapidated, temple. But it was better than nothing. At least it would afford them shelter from the rain. The door had long ago rotted away, and as they entered, a pervading smell of mould and decay assailed their nostrils.

The walk had exhausted Fang Yi, and she was gritting her teeth to endure the pain from her wound. Old Xu smashed up a few broken pieces of furniture and lit a fire, bidding them all to dry their clothes. It was growing darker and darker, and the rain was now a deluge. Xu produced some dry wheat-cakes from his bag and handed them round.

Liu Yizhou stuffed the remains of his pigtail into his hat, and Trinket gave him a scornful look.

Night was falling. The seven of them sat on the ground around the fire. The roof of the ruined temple let in the rain and there were few patches of dry ground left. Trinket felt water dripping on him, and shifted to the left. It was just as wet there. Fang Yi told him to come over and sit next to her.

'Don't worry,' she said, 'I won't hit you!'

Trinket gave a little laugh, and sat down beside her.

Fang Yi leant and whispered something to the Little Countess, who gave a splutter of laughter, nodded, and in turn whispered to Trinket:

'Sister Fang says that now she is yours, you mustn't take it amiss if she hits you or tries to tell you what to do, like asking you to be nice to Brother Liu. Do you understand?'

'No!' whispered Trinket back. 'What does she mean by being "mine", for a start?'

The Little Countess transmitted this to Fang Yi, who gave Trinket a supercilious look and whispered to the Little Countess:

'I swore an oath. Nothing can change that. Tell him to set his mind at ease.'

Once again, the message was transmitted.

'If *she's* mine,' whispered Trinket to the Little Countess, 'what about you?'

She blushed, gave a disapproving little click of her tongue, and reached out to slap him. Trinket laughed and dodged the blow, all the while nodding meaningfully towards Fang Yi, who was looking at him with a mixture of laughter and anger, her eyes flashing. She looked quite bewitching, and absolutely adorable. Trinket caught a whiff of the two girls' scent, and breathed it in with ecstasy.

Liu Yizhou had been watching all this from a distance with mounting jealousy and rage. Unable to contain himself, he rose to his feet. He leant against one of the pillars of the temple, and there was a sudden series of crashes as several tiles fell from the roof.

The rain and wind seemed to have dealt a final blow to the already precarious temple. Old Xu cried out:

'The whole temple is going to collapse! We must get out of here!'

The seven of them hurried out. They had no sooner gained open ground than they heard a great rumbling, and the entire roof of the temple caved in, together with half of the main wall.

A Haunted House

In the same instant, through the torrential rain, they heard the clattering of horses' hooves. A dozen or so horses were galloping towards them from the south-east. It was too dark to catch more than a fleeting glimpse of them.

'Aiyo!' cried one of the riders, by the sound of it an elderly man. 'This temple could have given us shelter, if it were still standing!'

'Hey, Old Zhang,' asked one of the other riders, addressing an old peasant who had accompanied them, 'isn't there anywhere else to shelter round these parts? A cave or something?'

Old Zhang replied:

'Well, in a manner of speaking there is . . .'

'Cut the crap, will you!' swore yet another of the company. 'Is there or isn't there?'

'A little way to the north-west,' replied Old Zhang, 'right on the col, there's a house. It's haunted though. No one dares go inside it . . .'

The men laughed.

'We're not afraid of ghosts! Let's go!'

'I strongly advise you gentlemen not to,' said Old Zhang. 'If we continue another ten miles or so north, we'll come to a small town.'

'Ten more miles in this rain? You must be joking! Come on, there are plenty of us. We don't have to be afraid of ghosts!'

'Very well. You must go on towards the north-west, then turn, and follow the road up to the col. You can't miss it . . .'

They did not even wait for him to finish his sentence, but spurred their horses on. Old Zhang hesitated for a moment, then turned his own horse around and headed back towards the south-east.

'Brother Wu,' said Old Xu, 'Lodge Master, what should we do?'

'As I see it . . .' began Shaker Wu, then paused. 'I think Lodge Master Wei should be the one to decide.'

'The trouble is,' replied Trinket, 'there are some ghosts you can't see. And by the time you can, it's too late!'

This was the nearest he could get to saying 'I'm scared of ghosts!'.

'Ghosts don't frighten me!' cried the valiant Liu Yizhou. 'If we stay in this pouring rain much longer we'll all catch our death of cold anyway!'

Trinket could see that the Little Countess was shivering, and he certainly didn't want to be upstaged by Liu.

'All right, let's go then.'

So off they went in the direction indicated by Old Zhang, up towards the col. But soon they had lost the road, and all they could see was a great torrent of water pouring down the mountainside, through a rain-shrouded expanse of trees.

'That's must be a ghost wall!' said Trinket nervously.

'That,' said Old Xu, 'is simply the water rushing down the road.'

'Yes!' cried Shaker Wu, and began clambering up the course of the torrent. The others followed him.

They could hear horses neighing, and knew that the riders must be in the trees off to the side.

'I wonder what those men are up to?' brooded Xu silently to himself. But between them he thought he and Shaker Wu should be a match for any opposition, and put his best foot firmly forward, up the course of the stream and into the trees.

Presently they heard the sound of a loud knocking on a door close by. That must be the haunted house ahead of them, in among the trees. Trinket was both relieved and frightened. Suddenly he felt a soft hand reach out and take hold of his. Then a gentle voice spoke in his ear.

'Don't be afraid!'

It was Fang Yi.

The knocking continued, but there seemed to be no answer. The seven of them moved forward, until finally the outline of a large mansion loomed out of the mist. They could hear the riders crying:

'Open up! Open up! We're in need of shelter!'

Their cries went unanswered.

'There's no one here,' said one of them.

'Of course not! Old Zhang said it was haunted. No one would be foolish enough to come and live here. Let's climb in!'

There was a flash as two of them drew their swords and leapt in through a hole in the outer wall. They opened up the main door of the house from the inside, and the rest of their party surged in.

'These men look like common outlaws,' thought Xu Tianchuan to himself. 'They certainly don't give the impression of being very good fighters.'

The seven of them followed the others into the house. Inside the main door lay a sizeable courtyard, and beyond that a large hall.

One of the riders had kindled a flame, and seeing candles on a table, proceeded to light them. As the hall lit up, they could all see that it was furnished with quality rosewood furniture. It seemed to be the home of a family of some style.

'There's not a speck of dust on the furniture,' muttered old Xu quietly to himself. 'And the floor has been swept. And yet there's nobody here!'

One of the riders exclaimed:

'This place is so neat and tidy. There *must* be someone living here.'

'Is there anyone there? Is there anyone at home?' cried another.

His voice echoed in the great hall.

When the echo died away, there was no sound apart from that of the pelting rain. They all looked at one another apprehensively.

One of the riders, a white-haired old man, had noticed Xu Tianchuan:

'Would you all be friends of River and Lake?'

'My name is Xu,' he replied. 'These are relatives of mine. We were travelling to Shanxi to visit cousins of ours, when we ran into this storm. May I ask your name?'

The old man merely nodded. The party of seven seemed to match Xu's description (old men and young men, women, a child). But he did not reply to Xu's question and give his name. Instead he muttered:

'This place seems a bit weird.'

'Is there anyone there?' called out another of the riders. 'Is everyone dead?'

Still no sound.

The old man sat down in one of the chairs and gestured to six of his men.

'You lot go into the back and have a look around!'

The six drew their swords and went to do his bidding, making their way cautiously into the depths of the house, stooping and walking slowly. From the hall the rest of them could hear the sound of doors being kicked open, and questions being shouted out. Nothing untoward seemed to happen, and gradually the sounds became fainter as the men penetrated deeper and deeper into the mansion.

The old man now gave orders to four others to find some wood, make torches, and follow the first six inside. They too obeyed his commands.

Trinket and his six companions sat down on the ledge of a long window, none of them daring to say a word. Altogether ten of the riding party had now departed into the inner recesses of the house, leaving eight in the hall. They wore plain cloth gowns, and to Old Xu's experienced eyes seemed like members of some underground fraternity or other. They could have been members of a security escort, if it were not for the fact that they did not seem to have anything to escort. He could not quite make them out.

At that moment, the advance party of six riders returned, looking extremely spooked.

'There's no one there. But the place is all neat and tidy. There's bedding on the beds, and shoes on the floor—women's shoes. And the wardrobes are full of women's clothes. Not a single thing for men!'

'Female ghosts!' cried Liu loudly. 'The house is haunted by the ghosts of dead women!'

They all turned simultaneously and looked at him. No one breathed a word.

Suddenly they heard cries coming from the second search party. The old man leapt to his feet, and the four came running back into the hall. Their torches were all extinguished.

'Spooks! Dead men everywhere!' they cried.

There was terror written on their faces.

The old man scowled.

'Stop panicking! I thought for a moment you had run into a real enemy! There's nothing to fear from a dead man!'

'But they're . . . spooky!'

'What do you mean, spooky?'

'One of the rooms on the right is full of . . . hundreds of shrines to the dead!'

'Are there any bodies or coffins?' asked the old man.

Two of the men exchanged glances.

'We couldn't see too clearly,' they both replied at the same time. 'We don't think so.'

'Light some more torches, and we will all go in together. It's probably just something perfectly ordinary, like an ancestral shrine.'

The old man tried to sound casual, but there was a note of uncertainty in his voice.

His men set about breaking up chairs and tables, and soon they had all set off into the back of the house with blazing torches.

'I'll go with them and have a look,' said Xu Tianchuan. 'You stay here and wait for me.'

He followed after the men.

Ao Biao turned to Shaker Wu.

'Shifu, what kind of men do you think these riders are?'

Shaker Wu shook his head.

'From their accents, I'd say they were from Shandong or from just north of the Pass. Probably smugglers, though I can't see what they're smuggling.'

'*They're* nothing to be afraid of. It's the women ghosts you should be worried about . . .'

Liu Yizhou stuck his tongue out at Trinket as he said this. Trinket shuddered, and held Fang Yi's hand tightly. His own palms were clammy with fear.

'Brother Liu,' said the Little Countess, in a shaky voice, 'will you please stop trying to scare us!'

'You've got nothing to be scared of, Countess,' replied Liu. 'Those nasty ghosts wouldn't come anywhere near a young lady of noble blood like yourself. No, the people they hate the most are the ones who are neither fish nor fowl, neither man nor woman— eunuchs, for instance . . .'

Fang Yi frowned angrily and wanted to say something, but restrained herself.

After a while they heard footsteps again and the search party returned. Trinket breathed a sigh of relief. Xu reported back to his friends in hushed tones.

'There are seven or eight rooms, and each one is filled with shrines to the departed. Each shrine contains the spirit tablets of between five and eight people. They would seem to be family shrines.'

'Ha ha!' chuckled Liu Yizhou. 'So we're talking about a couple of hundred nasty ghosts haunting the place!'

Xu shook his head gravely.

'I don't know. The strangest thing of all,' he continued, 'is that in front of each shrine there are candles burning.'

Trinket and the two girls simultaneously let out a cry of terror.

'When we went in just now,' put in one of the original advance party, 'there weren't any candles lit.'

'Are you sure you are remembering correctly?' asked the old man.

Four of the men exchanged doubtful glances, and shook their heads.

'These aren't ghosts,' said the old man. 'This is some sort of wizard! To light more than thirty candles in a matter of seconds! What do you make of this, Mr Xu?'

Xu adopted an expression of utter bewilderment.

'Perhaps we have disturbed the master of the house in some way . . . Maybe we should kowtow at the shrines!'

Just then, clearly audible above the driving rain, they heard a sound coming from the eastern wing of the house. It was the sound of women's voices wailing. It was a desolate, piercing sound.

Trinket stood there with his mouth gaping, his face paralysed with fear.

They all looked at one another in terror. Seconds later another sound reached them, this time from the western wing. It was the sound of another group of women weeping and sobbing. Liu Yizhou, Ao Biao, and two of the riders cried with one voice:

'Ghosts!'

The old man said something to try and calm them down. Then he turned to Xu Tianchuan.

'Tell me,' he said, 'if you are all from one family, how is it that some of you speak with a Peking accent, some with a Yunnan accent?'

Xu concocted a plausible enough story about the family's

origins and how they were on their way to Shanxi to seek out his younger sister-in-law's family.

'Tell me,' continued the old man, 'on your way here, did you come across a fourteen- or fifteen-year-old eunuch?'

Xu's face betrayed nothing. His companions, when they heard this, registered visible shock, but luckily no one was looking at them.

'There are so many eunuchs in Peking,' replied Xu. 'We must have encountered quite a few of them on our way out of the city.'

'I said on your way *here*,' insisted the old man, 'not in Peking.'

'My dear sir,' said Xu, 'you must surely know that eunuchs are not allowed out of the Capital, on pain of death.'

'Perhaps this one was in disguise,' said the old man, with a humph.

Xu shook his head. He was thinking to himself that these people were most probably after Lodge Master Wei, and that it was his duty to ferret out of them who exactly they were.

'There is one Palace Eunuch who has become very famous,' he ventured. 'The one who succeeded in killing that monster Oboi.'

The old man stared at Xu wide-eyed.

'You mean Laurel Goong-goong?'

'Of course!' replied Xu. 'What courage! What kungfu!'

'What does he look like? Have you ever seen him?'

'He's always gadding about the Capital. Just about everyone in Peking has seen him. Fat, swarthy little fellow. Looks almost twenty. You'd never take him for a fifteen-year-old.'

Fang Yi gripped Trinket's hand tightly. The Little Countess nudged him in the small of the back with her elbow. They were both silently chuckling to themselves. Trinket was so frightened to hear himself talked about like this, he had almost forgotten to be afraid of ghosts.

'Really?' returned the old man. 'I'd heard quite differently. I'd heard he looked about thirteen or fourteen. A shifty little brat—a bit like this nephew of yours, in fact!'

He was alluding to (and looking at) Trinket.

'I've heard that Laurel Goong-goong is a low-down little brat too,' piped up Liu Yizhou, 'forever putting drugs in people's drinks. In fact, that's how he managed to kill Oboi. He'd never have done it otherwise—he's such a pathetic little coward!'

Liu turned to Trinket with a giggle.

'Don't you agree, *cousin*?'

Shaker Wu flew into a rage at Liu's continued provocation of Trinket, and he lashed out at him, using a move known in the Mu Family as Emerald Cockerel Spreads Feathers. Liu darted out of the way, responding with another classic Mu Family move, Gold Horse Neighs in the Wind. Between them, the two men were blatantly betraying their Mu Family origins.

The old man leapt to his feet. His followers followed his example.

'Not a single one of them is to escape!' cried the old man.

Shaker Wu drew a short-sword from inside his jacket, and with a shake of the head to the left, had soon hacked down one of the riders. Then as he shook to the right, another rider received Wu's sword in the throat and crashed to the ground.

The old man now produced a pair of fighting-clubs, and clanged them together menacingly. He swung them through the air, narrowly missing Shaker's throat with the left, and grazing Xu Tianchuan's chest with the right. Xu darted to one side, and as he did so poked at one of the men's eyes with his left hand. The man ducked. Xu seized hold of the man's short-sword and turned it back on him. The man lurched forwards with the blade in his belly. Ao Biao was also engaged in close combat, while Liu Yizhou was busy cracking his whip.

A moment later, the old man leapt back with a crash of his clubs, and all of his men instantly fell into formation behind him. The speed and discipline with which they did this showed it to be a well-drilled manoeuvre. Xu Tianchuan and Shaker Wu gave a start and withdrew a few paces, but Ao Biao rushed impetuously forward. Four blades protruded from the phalanx, while longer pikes protected their flanks. Ao Biao went down with wounds to both of his shoulders, shouting with pain.

'Retreat!' cried Shaker Wu, and Ao Biao scrambled out of danger.

Xu Tianchuan was standing protectively in front of Trinket and the girls, watching how the enemy formation would deploy itself next. Things seemed to be taking a nasty turn. At this point the old man brandished his clubs in the air and gave a mighty cry:

'Long Life to Our Great Leader Hong! Blessings be on Him!'

'Long Life to Our Great Leader Hong! Blessings be on Him!' came back the thundering chorus from his men.

Xu stared at them aghast. But at the words 'the Leader',

Trinket suddenly remembered his conversation with Auntie Tao, and her terror-stricken face.

'They're from the Sect of the Mystic Dragon!' he cried. 'They're Dragons!'

The old rider with the clubs paled.

'How do you know that name?'

He raised his right hand and chanted:

'All Hail to Our Supreme and All-Powerful Leader Hong! Victory is Ours!'

The chanting was succeeding in unnerving his opponents.

'That's part of their technique!' cried Trinket. 'That's what they do! They chant spells! Don't fall for it! Don't give up! Fight back!'

But now it was the entire phalanx chanting with one voice in one great crescendo, louder and louder, faster and faster.

'Our Great Leader Hong will protect us! Our Courage will Multiply! We know no fear! One of us will defeat a hundred of the enemy, a hundred of us will defeat ten thousand! Our Leader Hong's eyes are as the Lightning in the Heavens! They shine upon the Four Corners of the Earth! Willingly we die for Our Leader! He will take us all to Heaven!'

And then in one climactic burst of sound they surged forward.

Shaker Wu, Xu Tianchuan, and the others stood their ground courageously. But the chanting had given the Dragons an added ferocity and power. In a matter of minutes Ao Biao and Liu Yizhou had been hacked down, and Trinket and the two girls were also knocked to the ground. Fang Yi received a wound in the leg, the Little Countess in the arm, and Trinket a pike in the back. The blow was strong enough to send him toppling, though he was protected from serious injury by his trusty magic waistcoat. Next Xu and Shaker were wounded, and the old man leading the Mystic Dragons closed their points and immobilized them.

'Our Great Leader Hong is All-Powerful! Long Life to Our Great Leader Hong!'

The chant rang out once more. Then, in another perfectly coordinated movement, the men all sat down. Sweat was pouring from their brows, and they were panting fiercely. They had obviously drained themselves in the intensity of the onslaught. The whole battle had been decided in no more than the length of time it would take a man to drink a cup of tea. But they looked like warriors who had been fighting for several hours.

'No wonder Auntie Tao was so scared of them!' thought Trinket to himself. 'They're using black magic! They really are All-Powerful!'

The old man sat down on a chair and composed himself. After a while he stood up again, wiped the sweat from his brow, and began pacing up and down the hall. Gradually his men also rose to their feet.

The old man addressed Xu Tianchuan:

'Repeat after me: Our Great Leader Hong is All-Powerful! Long Life to our Leader!'

'Me, chant that mumbo-jumbo of yours!' cried Xu. 'You must be dreaming!'

The old man swung one of his clubs and struck Xu full on the forehead. Blood gushed down his face.

'Bastard!' yelled Xu. 'Sorcerer!'

The old man turned next to Shaker Wu.

'Repeat after me . . .'

Shaker was already wagging his head in defiance. The old man swung his club again, and left Shaker's forehead a bloody mess. He turned next to Ao Biao.

'Fuck your mother!' cried the ever impetuous Ao Biao. 'And a dog's life to your prick of a leader!'

This sent the old man into a rage. He brought his club down with a mighty crash, and Ao Biao fell unconscious to the ground.

'Bravely done, Biao!' yelled Shaker. 'As for you, you pack of arse-lickers, if you've any real courage, why not kill the lot of us!'

The old man raised his club again and turned to Liu Yizhou.

'Repeat after me: Long Life to Our Leader Hong!'

'Long . . . Long . . .'

The old man brought his club up to Liu's forehead and gave him a little thump.

'Come on!' he yelled.

'I am! Long . . . Long Life to Our Leader Hong!'

The old man laughed.

'I'm glad to see that at least *one* of you has some sense! No need to brain this one!'

He advanced on Trinket.

'Say after me . . .'

'There's no need for you to say it,' replied Trinket.

'Heh? Being cheeky?'

The old man raised his club.

'Long Life to Our Great Leader Wei!' Trinket shouted, and promptly rattled off a whole lot more. 'Our Great Leader will protect us! Our Leader Wei's eyes are as the Lightning in the Heavens! They shine upon the Four Corners of the Earth! Willingly we die for Our Leader! He will take us all to Heaven!'

Each time he somehow managed to mumble the 'Wei' part so that it came out as a sort of nasal grunt that was indistinguishable from 'Hong'. The old man looked pleased.

'Good boy!'

He walked up to Fang Yi and put his hand to her chin.

'Not a bad looker! Say it for us, there's a good girl!'

She twisted her face away and cried:

'I won't!'

'Let me do it for her!' cried Trinket.

'Who asked you to say anything?'

The old man threatened to smash Fang Yi in the face, but in the end contented himself with hitting her on the shoulder. She gave a cry of pain.

One of the men called out:

'If she won't say it, let's strip her clothes off!'

'Yes!' bawled the others. 'Strip her!'

'Leave the girl alone!' cried Liu. 'It's the eunuch you really want. I'll tell you where he is!'

'So you know, do you?' snapped the old man. 'Hurry up then, tell us!'

'Only if you promise to leave the girl alone,' said Liu.

'Brother Liu,' said Fang Yi sharply, 'I don't need your help!'

The old man laughed.

'Very well then, I give you my word. We won't touch the girl.'

'Can I trust you?' asked Liu.

'Can you trust me!' growled the old man. 'Come on now. We're after the eunuch who killed Oboi. The Emperor's favourite. His name is Laurel Goong-goong. Where is he?'

'He's here . . .' said Liu, 'and then again he's not . . .'

The old man jumped up. He pointed at Trinket.

'It's him, isn't it!'

He was beginning to be quite overwrought.

'How could someone like him have killed Oboi?' said Fang Yi. 'Don't take any notice of that man—he's just talking nonsense!'

'You're right,' said Liu. 'I am. He could never have done it—without using drugs!'

'*Did* you kill Oboi?' the old man asked Trinket, torn between doubt and belief.

'So what if I did?' replied Trinket. 'And so what if I didn't?'

'Damn you!' cried the old man. 'I thought from the start there was something queer about you. Search him!'

Two of his men came up and untied Trinket's bag, spreading the contents out on the table. The bag disgorged a quantity of precious stones and other valuable items, and then bundles of notes, big denominations, hundreds of thousands of taels' worth. The old man stared at them in amazement.

'Just the sort of thing I'd expect to find on a Palace Eunuch! So you're young Laurel Goong-goong then! Take him next door for questioning!'

'Don't . . .'

It was Fang Yi who spoke.

'Don't be hard on him!'

The Little Countess also let out a pained cry, and started sobbing.

One of the men now seized Trinket by the scruff of the neck, two others gathered up his belongings, and another carried a candle. They hauled him off through the back courtyard, and into a side-room. The old man followed them into the room, and then dismissed everyone except Trinket.

The Inquisition

When they were alone, the old man began walking up and down the room, rubbing his hands together in gleeful anticipation.

'So, we meet at last!'

'Yes, we do! At long, *long* last!' returned Trinket.

'Eh?'

The old man could not understand what was behind this puzzling retort of Trinket's. Little did he know that Trinket was (as usual in such a crisis) doing no more than playing for time.

'Tell me,' the old man continued, 'would you happen to be on your way to the Wutai Mountains?'

'Damn it!' thought Trinket. 'He seems to know everything! This is going to be harder than I thought.'

'I was most impressed,' said Trinket out loud, 'by that display

of Mystic Dragon chanting just now! Most impressed! I'd heard *of*
it, of course, but this is the first time I've actually *heard* it with my
own ears! Most impressive!'

'Where had you heard of the Mystic Dragon Sect, if I may
ask?' countered the old man.

Trinket improvised without a moment's hesitation:

'It was the Satrap's son, Wu Yingxiong, who told me about
it. His father sent him to Peking with several top fighters trained in
the Golden Gate School from Liaodong. Their mission was to exterminate the Mystic Dragons. I remember them talking about the
Great Leader Hong, the All-Powerful, and all the Sect members
under his command. One of the Sect worked for the Head of the
Bordered Blue Banner, and managed to get hold of a copy of the
Sutra in Forty-Two Sections. Excellent kungfu!'

Trinket was a veteran Grand Master of the Liars' Lodge. In
order to deceive effectively, he knew that it was necessary to season
every spoonful of falsehood with the odd grain of carefully selected
truth.

The old man was thinking to himself:

'How can he know so much! Why, even I only got wind of
the Bordered Blue Banner job a month ago. And that was by accident! It was supposed to be a top secret operation!'

'But the Satrap has no cause to exterminate the Mystic
Dragons,' he said to Trinket. 'Why should he attempt anything so
foolish?'

'Of course he has nothing against the Mystic Dragons themselves,' Trinket hastened to explain. 'In fact, Wu's men said all sorts
of very complimentary things about the Great Leader. No, it's the
Sutra they're after. That's the great prize. By the way, I also seem
to remember you have a woman member working in the Palace? A
fat woman by the name of Swallow Liu?'

The old man seemed genuinely taken aback by this.

'How could you possibly know that?'

Trinket was merely snatching at even the smallest detail in
order to construct some credentials, some sort of connection,
however tenuous, between himself and the Sect. He swiftly
pursued this promising tack.

'Oh, Sister Swallow and I were especially close. Once, when
she'd offended the Empress Dowager, I even saved her life. I hid
her under a bed. The Empress Dowager searched everywhere
but couldn't find her. Sister Swallow was so grateful. In fact, she

wanted me to join the Mystic Dragons myself. She said the Great
Leader could do with a young person like me. He'd be sure to
reward me.'

The old man humphed. He was almost beginning to find the
boy plausible.

'But why would Her Majesty want to kill Sister Swallow?
Weren't they . . . partners, in a sense?'

'Why yes,' said Trinket, 'in a sense they were. At the beginning anyhow. So why did Her Majesty want to kill her? You may
well ask. Trouble is, that's absolutely top secret. She made me
promise not to tell another living soul. So I really can't tell you. I'm
awfully sorry. Then there's that *other* person who popped up in
Maternal Tranquillity recently: a man dressed up as a woman, a *bald*
man . . .'

'Are you talking about Deng Bingchun?' gasped the old man.
'Do you mean to say you know about Comrade Deng's secret
mission too!'

Trinket had no idea what the cross-dressing maid's
name was, but nothing ruffled his all-knowing expression. He
smiled.

'Top secret! Not a word of it to *anyone*. Otherwise, you might
be in grave trouble with the Great Leader yourself . . .'

Trinket had worked in the Forbidden City long enough to
know that betraying a secret was a misdemeanour punishable at
the worst with death, at the least with dishonour. That was why
everyone carried on so sneakily in the Palace. No one wanted to
run the risk of betraying anyone else. People acted as if they knew
everything, while at the same time divulging nothing. This was the
basic ploy he was now trying on the old man, and it seemed to be
working a treat. When it came down to it, most of the same techniques worked in the Palace as on River and Lake. It was just
that in the Palace people were a bit more refined about being
underhand.

The old man had been quite thrown by Trinket's display of
inside Mystic Dragon knowledge. He was not sure how to proceed.
He laughed nervously.

'And what did you say to Comrade Deng?'

'I'm not allowed to tell anyone,' replied Trinket. 'Of course,
I'll be making a full report of what I said to him, and of the message
he gave me, when I see the Great Leader in person . . .'

'Of course!' the old man hastily replied. He could not make out who on earth this boy really was. He tried a placatory smile, before venturing:

'I suppose you're on your way to the Wutai Mountains to see Colonel Rui . . .'

'Hm,' thought Trinket. 'So he knows about Wutai and Colonel Rui. The Old Whore must have told him. She and that bald-headed Deng character are obviously mixed up with the Mystic Dragons. Watch it, old Trink! Let that lot get their hands on you, and you're history!'

He feigned surprise.

'My goodness, you are well informed! You even know about Colonel Rui!'

The old man smiled.

'And I know about someone else,' he said. 'Someone much, much more important than Colonel Rui . . .'

'Drat!' Trinket cursed silently. 'The Old Whore has told him *everything*! He obviously means the Old Emperor!'

'Tell me,' said the old man, beginning to sound positively ingratiating, 'were you ordered to go to Wutai, or are you going on your own accord?'

'What do you take me for?' exclaimed Trinket. 'Since when have Palace Eunuchs gone cruising off on out-of-town jaunts? Since when have they done anything but take orders?'

'So it was His Majesty who sent you?'

Trinket looked his most perplexed.

'His Majesty? Ha ha! I'm afraid this time your information leaves a lot to be desired. How would *he* know about Wutai?'

'Then who was it?'

'Guess.'

'You don't mean . . . It can't be . . . *Her* Majesty?'

Trinket laughed.

'You *are* a clever chap! Right first time! Only two living souls know about Wutai—and one ghost.'

'And who are they?'

'In the world of the living, Her Majesty and yours truly,' replied Trinket. 'In the world of the dead, a certain Hai Goong-goong. He's the ghost. Her Majesty used Soft Crush karate to bump him off.'

The old man's fleshy jowls twitched.

'Soft Crush, Soft Crush,' he murmured to himself, almost mesmerized by the words. 'So it *was* Her Majesty that sent you. But why?'

Trinket gave a canny smile.

'Seeing you and Her Majesty are so close, why not go and ask her yourself?'

If Trinket had said that to him when they had first entered the room, the old man would most probably have given him a good box on the ears. But by now he was too confused to know what to do or say.

'Sent by Her Majesty . . .' he muttered to himself.

'She told me that she's already sent word to the Great Leader,' Trinket went on, 'and that he is extremely pleased with the way things are going. Once the mission is successfully accomplished, the Great Leader is sure to reward me highly!'

He could tell that the old man was absolutely petrified by the slightest mention of the Great Leader, and was exploiting this to its fullest.

'And those six people outside are under your command?' asked the old man.

'They're all from the Palace,' replied Trinket. 'The two girls work for Her Majesty, the four men are all guards. Her Majesty sent them with me. But they don't know anything about the Mystic Dragons. Her Majesty has never mentioned it to them . . .'

Trinket saw a sly smile creep across the old man's face.

'What's the matter? Don't you believe me?' He had clearly put his foot in it.

'The Mu Family fight for the Ming cause,' sneered the old man. 'They would *never* work as guards for the Emperor! You're lying!'

Trinket gave a loud laugh.

'What's so funny?'

The old man did not know that this was another of Trinket's standard ploys. When caught out with a monster fib, he laughed, thereby buying precious time. He laughed again.

'What you obviously don't know is that the Mu Family's real enemy, the person they really hate, is not the Empress Dowager at all—'

'Of course I know that!' snapped the old man. 'The person they hate the most is Satrap Wu.'

'Well done!' cried Trinket, feigning the utmost surprise. 'I *am* impressed! You see, the Mu Family don't mind working for Her Majesty if it means they can wipe out the Satrap and his entire camp, down to the last chicken and the last dog! Why, they even have their men planted in the Satrap's headquarters! But you must promise me not to tell a soul!'

The old man nodded. But his confidence in Trinket's story had been seriously dented. He decided to go out and cross-question the others.

'Wait a minute!' cried Trinket, as the old man turned to go. 'Where are you off to? This house is haunted . . . You're not going to leave me here all on my own, are you? I can't even move.'

'I'll be back in a minute.'

The old man barred the door after him, and hurried to the front hall.

Trinket's hands were clammy with terror. The wavering light of the candles threw dancing shadows on the walls. Each shadow seemed to be a ghost. There was a deathly hush in the room. Then all of a sudden the silence was broken by a great cry from outside.

'Where *are* you all?'

It was the old man's voice. It was shaking with fear, and Trinket nearly fainted.

'Have . . . have . . . they disappeared?' he asked.

'Where *are* you?' the old man repeated. 'Where have you *gone*?'

Silence. Followed by the sound of running, and door after door being kicked closed, then more running, a hurried fumbling with the door-bar, and someone burst into the room. Trinket let out a shriek. It was the old man, terrified out of his wits, his face drained of colour, his eyes bulging out of their sockets.

'They've . . . they've all vanished! Every one of them!'

'Then they've been carried away by . . . ghosts!' cried Trinket. 'Quick, help me, let's run for it!'

The old man slumped across the table, and the table started shaking. Then he rose and made for the doorway again, still crying:

'Where *are* you? Where have you *gone*?'

He stood still and listened. A faint sound of sobbing could be heard, carried on the night air. Women sobbing. The old man hesitated a moment, then retreated back into the room, barring the door again, from the inside. He looked at Trinket. The boy's eyes were popping out of his head with sheer terror. Trinket stared back at the old man, who was grinding his teeth, his face whiter than ever.

The rain, which had let up for a while, now began falling heavily on the roof again. Suddenly, through the rain, they heard a woman's voice from the outer hall—quiet, but distinct:

'Come out here, old man!'

It was not the voice of an old crone; but it wasn't a girlish voice either. It was definitely neither Fang Yi nor the Little Countess. There was something horribly chilling about the sound.

'A woman ghost!' whispered Trinket hoarsely.

'Who is calling for me?' stammered the old man.

There was no reply. The only sound was the rain drumming on the roof. Trinket and the old man stared at one another, both shivering with terror.

A few minutes passed. Then they heard the same voice again.

'Come out here, old man!'

The old man finally plucked up his courage and kicked at the door. It was still held fast by the bar. He brought down his right palm with a chopping motion, and split the bar in two. Then he shot out through the doorway.

'Don't go!' Trinket cried after him.

But the old man was already running full pelt out towards the hall.

A Ghost?

There was no sound of fighting. Trinket could hear no footsteps. A cold wind came curling in from the courtyard, blowing the rain in with it. Trinket shivered, and was about to cry out, but thought better of it. The wind blew the door shut, then blew it open again.

So there he was, still incapable of movement, and all alone in a haunted room—alone, that is, apart from the multitude of horrors lurking outside, the horde of vicious ghosts waiting to burst in on him and take his life. But minutes went by, and still there was no onslaught. Trinket comforted himself with the thought that they probably only ate grown-ups, and must have eaten their fill already by now. If only the dawn would come!

Suddenly a gust of wind blew out the last remaining candles and Trinket was plunged in total darkness. He let out a great cry. Now he could feel it, without any doubt. There *was* a ghost in the room. It was standing there right in front of him. He couldn't actually see anything. But he was positive it was there.

'Don't hurt me!' he babbled. 'I'm a ghost too! We're two of a kind! We're all ghosts! Why would you want to harm me!'

The ghost spoke, calmly, with a woman's voice.

'There's no need to be afraid,' it said. 'I'm not going to hurt you.'

Her words put fresh spirit into Trinket.

'Don't worry,' the voice went on. 'I'm not a ghost. Tell me, are you truly the one who killed Oboi, the great Manchu minister?'

'Are you sure you're not a ghost?' stammered Trinket. 'Are you Oboi's friend, or his enemy?'

His question received no reply. Trinket could not make up his mind whether it would be safer to admit to killing Oboi, or to deny all responsibility for it. It depended. In the end, his gambler's instinct took over.

'Tamardy!' he cried. 'Yes, *I* did it! *I* killed Oboi! I stuck my knife in his back! Well? What are you going to do to me now?'

'Why did you do it?'

The same quiet woman's voice.

Once again, Trinket decided to venture all. If this was Oboi's friend, even if Trinket laid the ultimate responsibility for Oboi's death at the Emperor's door (which was the truth), it would not save him.

'Oboi did terrible things to the common people, he treated them cruelly, he took their lives. When he offended the Emperor, I saw my chance and killed him. I wanted to avenge all the innocent people he had wronged!'

He vaguely remembered what the Triads had said about Oboi. In actual fact, it had been entirely the Emperor's idea to kill Oboi. But so what!

The woman before him stood there in silence. Trinket's heart was thumping. He had no idea if his gamble was going to pay off.

He felt a faint breeze, and the woman—or was she really a ghost after all?—flitted out of the room, leaving Trinket standing there, rooted to the spot, his clammy shirt sticking to his body. His points were still closed. He was incapable of movement. The door blew open and flapped noisily. Trinket shivered in the cold gusts of wind.

CHAPTER 13

*In which Trinket acquires a
Devoted Companion; deals with
a Succession of Lamas and
Bonzes; and makes his Way,
with Several Adventures,
to the Wutai Mountains
and Back*

Doublet

Suddenly a glow of light appeared some way off across the room.
It seemed to be coming slowly closer.

'Ghost fire!' thought the panic-stricken Trinket. 'Spooks!'

But as the light came closer still, he was able to distinguish it
more clearly as a lantern. And carrying the lantern was a woman—
another ghost, no doubt—dressed in white from head to foot.
Trinket instantly closed his eyes. Light footsteps pattered towards
him, and came to a halt right in front of him.

He was trembling with fear. Any moment he would choke.

'Why are you closing your eyes?'

It was a girl's voice. The sound was gentle, almost touching.

'Don't try scaring me!' gasped Trinket. 'I don't dare look at you . . .'

The ghost gave a little laugh.

'I suppose you think I've got blood oozing out of my eyes and ears, and my tongue is sticking out of my head. Go on, why not take one little look at me?'

'I'm not falling for that,' stammered Trinket. 'You're just a horrible spook with tangled hair and blood all over your face, I know you are!'

The ghost laughed again, louder this time, and blew gently on Trinket's face.

Her breath was gentle and warm, and carried with it a delicate fragrance. Trinket opened his left eye a crack. He thought he could make out a pale face, curving eyebrows, a small delicate mouth, dimpled cheeks. Then he opened both eyes properly. He found himself looking into the face of a remarkably pretty girl, fourteen or fifteen years old, her tresses neatly plaited at both temples. She was gazing at him with a beaming smile. Greatly reassured by what he saw, Trinket asked her:

'Are you sure you're not a ghost?'

The girl smiled.

'I *am* a ghost. The ghost of someone who died by hanging.'

Trinket started. She laughed.

'You were brave enough when it came to killing that great big brute Oboi. How come you're so scared of a hanged ghost?'

Trinket drew in a sharp breath.

'Living people don't scare me. Only ghosts.'

The girl gave another little laugh.

'Which of your Vital Points have been closed?'

'How should I know?'

She put the lantern down on the table and started rubbing his shoulders, and pummelling his back. Gradually the movement returned to his hands and he waved his arms a couple of times above his head.

'Brilliant!'

'I've only just learned how to do it,' she said. 'That was my first try.'

More rubbing and pummelling under his armpits and round his waist, and Trinket was soon wanting to walk.

'Stop!' he cried. 'That's enough! I'm very ticklish!'

No sooner was he mobile again than he was on the offensive.

'Now I'll give you some of your own medicine!'

He took a step towards her, reaching out his hands to tickle her.

She instantly stuck out her tongue and pulled a ghoulish face. But try as she might to scare him, there was still something very endearing about her. It was not in the least frightening. Trinket tried to pinch her tongue, but she ducked out of the way, with a peal of laughter.

'Aren't you afraid of hanged ghosts any more?'

'I can see your shadow,' replied Trinket. 'And you're warm. You're alive! You're not a ghost at all!'

She fixed him with both eyes.

'You're quite right,' she declared solemnly. 'I'm not a ghost. *I'm a corpse!*'

Trinket started for a second. But by the light of the lantern he could see the colour in her face.

'No you're not! Corpses are stiff, and they don't talk!'

'Then I'm a *fox-spirit!*'

'I'm not scared of *them*!' returned Trinket, secretly wondering if she really could be one. If so, perhaps she would seduce him and suck the life out of him. He walked round behind her and looked her up and down.

'I'm a thousand-year-old fox!' she said. 'My magical powers are highly advanced. That's why I no longer have a tail.'

'I wouldn't mind being bewitched by a pretty little fox like you!'

The girl blushed. She stretched out a hand and scratched him playfully on the face.

'You should be ashamed of yourself! Just now you were scared to death, and now here you are taking advantage of a poor defenceless girl.'

The fact of the matter was, on Trinket's list of things to be feared, corpses came first, ghosts second, and fox-spirits didn't feature at all. Besides, this girl seemed such a darling! She was even more adorable than Fang Yi and the Little Countess. And she had one very important thing in her favour: she spoke with a decidedly southern accent. It was so much softer on the ear than the outlandish Yunnanese spoken by the other two girls.

'Tell me, miss, what's your name?'

He was starting to sound almost polite.

'My name's Doublet,' was her reply. She went on:

'Laurel Goong-goong, you're soaked to the skin! Why don't you go next door and change into something dry? But I'm afraid you'll find that all the clothes here are women's.'

Trinket's heart missed a beat.

'Yes,' he thought to himself, 'I know. That's because all the ghosts here are women!'

'Follow me,' said the girl called Doublet, picking up her lantern from the table. Trinket hesitated. She walked to the doorway, and turned back expectantly.

'I know,' she said with a smile. 'You're probably afraid that wearing women's clothes will bring you bad luck. Why not get straight into bed and give me your wet things? I'll iron them dry for you.'

It was impossible to say no to this girl. She was so sweet, so kind and thoughtful. Trinket followed her meekly out of the room.

'Where have all my companions gone?' he asked.

'My Lady says I'm not to say anything about that.'

Doublet had fallen in by his side.

'You're to eat something first, and then My Lady will come and explain things to you herself.'

Trinket was extremely hungry, and the mere mention of food cheered him up no end.

Doublet led the way down a pitch-black corridor, until they came to a room, where a candle burned on a table. The only other piece of furniture was a bed, simply made up with a padded quilt. Doublet drew back the quilt and let down the bed-curtains.

'Laurel Goong-goong,' she said, 'why don't you get into bed now, and pass out your wet things to me?'

Trinket climbed obediently into bed, stripped himself naked behind the curtains, and burrowed under the quilt, throwing the clothes out to Doublet.

'I'll fetch you some nice hot dumplings,' she called from the doorway. 'Do you fancy something sweet or savoury?'

'I'm so hungry I'd eat a dumpling stuffed with sand!' was Trinket's muffled reply from beneath the bedclothes.

Doublet laughed and went on her way. When she returned a few minutes later, Trinket caught a whiff of something delicious! She parted the bed-curtains and Trinket saw that she was carrying a tray. And on the tray were four large steamed dumplings of the sort called *zongzi*, made with sticky rice wrapped in bamboo leaves. She had already unwrapped them. Trinket was famished. He would have devoured whatever had been put in front of him, even dumplings stuffed with slugs and snails and caterpillars. . . . He picked up the chopsticks and tucked in. The first dumpling he attacked tasted indescribably delicious.

'Doublet,' he managed to say between mouthfuls, 'this tastes wonderful! Just like a real Huzhou *zongzi*!'

Huzhou, in the southern province of Zhejiang, in addition to the silk and writing-brushes for which it was justly renowned, was famous for its sticky rice dumplings, spiced with all sorts of delicious flavours. There was even a Huzhou dumpling shop in Yangzhou, and the customers at Vernal Delights had been in the habit of constantly sending little Trinket off to fetch some. Then, the bamboo-leaf wrappers had made it hard for him to nibble any of the actual filling, but he'd always managed to squeeze a little bit out through one of the corners. This was the first time he had tasted one since journeying north.

'How clever of you to know what they are!' exclaimed Doublet, with a smile of admiration.

Trinket smacked his lips.

'Yum!' he purred. 'How on earth did you get hold of real Huzhou *zongzi* in a godforsaken place like this?'

'We didn't get hold of them. We . . . conjured them up by fox magic!'

She giggled.

'Excellent magic! Excellent kungfu!' exclaimed Trinket.

Suddenly remembering his recent brush with the old man and the Mystic Dragons, he added for good measure:

'Long Life and Great Blessings to the Fox Leader!'

Doublet laughed.

'You eat up! I'm going to iron your clothes now.'

She began to walk to the door, then halted:

'Are you still afraid?'

Trinket's fears had mostly evaporated by now, but none the less he begged her to return as quickly as possible.

A few minutes later she was back with an iron filled with glowing embers. She proceeded to spread Trinket's wet things on the table and iron them, thereby keeping him company at the same time.

Trinket finished three of the four dumplings.

'They really are delicious. Did you make them yourself?'

'My Lady mixed the ingredients together. I helped her to wrap them.'

That lilting southern accent was music to Trinket's ears.

'Are you all from Huzhou, then?' he asked.

Doublet did not reply.

'Your clothes will soon be dry. When you see My Lady, she'll answer your questions for you.'

She chose her words carefully. She seemed such a gentle, thoughtful girl. Trinket wrapped himself in the quilt and sat up, lifting the bed-curtain, and peeping mischievously out at her as she finished the ironing. She looked up at him and smiled.

'Careful you don't catch cold. You've got nothing on.'

Trinket bared his chest.

'I think I'll get out and jump around a bit. That'll keep me warm . . .'

Doublet gave a start. But instead of jumping out of bed, Trinket burrowed back under the covers until not even his head was visible. A muffled chuckling could be heard from the depths of the bed.

A quarter of an hour or so later, Doublet passed the now neatly ironed and dry clothes through the bed-curtains. When Trinket had dressed himself, he climbed down from the bed. Doublet helped him do up his buttons, and, producing a little wooden comb, tidied his hair for him and plaited his pigtail. Trinket breathed in the subtle scent that emanated from her young body. He was in ecstasy.

'I never knew fox-spirits were such nice people!'

Doublet pulled a face.

'Stop all that horrid nonsense! Of course I'm not a fox-spirit!'

'Oh, I know,' quipped Trinket, 'you're a fairy!'

Doublet laughed.

'No I'm not! I'm just an ordinary maidservant.'

'Well, I'm just an ordinary eunuch, so that makes two of us. We both wait on other people, so we are two of a kind!'

'But you wait on the Emperor,' said Doublet. 'That makes you as far above me as the sky is above the ground!'

She finished plaiting his pigtail. He tossed it over his shoulder and admired her handiwork.

'My Lady says that if you like, you can go and see her now.'

'And where's your master?' inquired Trinket. 'Isn't he at home?'

'He's dead!' whispered Doublet.

Trinket shuddered as he remembered that he was in a haunted house, full of strange shrines to the dead. He followed Doublet through the back quarters of the house until they came to a little reception room. There he sat down, and she fetched him a cup of hot tea. He was feeling very nervous, and had lost his appetite for chattering and joking.

Widow Zhuang

Several minutes later he heard the sound of light footsteps, and from behind a wooden partition wall there emerged a young lady dressed in the plain white of mourning.

'You must have had an exhausting journey, Laurel Goong-goong.'

She spoke very politely. Trinket hastened to rise to his feet and return her courtesies.

He judged her to be a woman in her late twenties. Her pale face bore no trace of make-up or rouge, and her eyes were red, evidently from recent weeping. The lantern cast its light on her, and he could see that she had an unmistakable shadow. There was certainly something eerie about her appearance, but she was no more of a ghost than Doublet had been—much to Trinket's relief.

She told him to be seated and he perched on the edge of his chair.

'Thank you very much, ma'am, for the delicious Huzhou *zongzi*!'

'My late husband's name was Zhuang,' replied the woman. 'You can just call me Widow Zhuang. Tell me, Laurel Goong-goong, how many years have you been in service in the Palace?'

She went on to ask Trinket for an account of how the 'villain' Oboi had met with his death. Realizing to his enormous relief that his luck was in and that he was in the hands of Oboi's enemies (which accounted no doubt for the delicious dumplings), Trinket proceeded to give her a blow-by-blow account of the death of Oboi, from the very beginning to the very end, including how he had used the ashes to blind him, then smashed him on the head with the brazier, and trussed him up. He did not give Kang Xi any credit for the stabbing.

The Widow Zhuang listened to all of this recital in complete silence. At the climax (ashes and brazier) she heaved a deep sigh. Trinket was a seasoned storyteller. He knew exactly when to pause for effect, and when to let himself get carried away. And in this case, it was something he had lived through himself, so it was easy to make his story even more dramatic than the real thing.

'So that's how it happened!' exclaimed Widow Zhuang. 'It'squite different from what I thought. The way people always tell it, they make you out to be a great kungfu master!'

'I'm afraid not. In a straight fight, *one* of him would have beaten a hundred of *me*!' said Trinket, with unusual honesty.

He decided to go on and tell her the rest of the story as truthfully as possible, including the final killing of Oboi in his cell, and his own subsequent encounter with the Triads.

'The Triads were Oboi's deadly enemies. So of course they hailed me like a hero. They said I'd avenged them.'

The lady nodded.

'And that is how you came to be the Helmsman's disciple, and Master of the Green Wood Lodge.'

'Wow!' Trinket muttered silently to himself. 'She knows the whole lot! I wonder why she even bothers asking questions!'

'I'm not a real Lodge Master,' he protested, deciding to hedge his bets. He had no way of knowing if this lady was for or against the Triads. 'I'm afraid I'm just a fake.'

She pondered this for a moment.

'Can you show me how you finally killed Oboi in his cell? What kungfu moves did you use?'

There was a strange gleam in her eye as she said this. Trinket decided it might be dangerous to fool around with her. Best stick to the truth. He stood up.

'Kungfu moves, my arse!'

He waved his hands around in the air.

'I was scared shitless! I just thrashed around like this, and—'

Widow Zhuang nodded.

'Please be seated, Laurel Goong-goong.'

She now rose to her feet.

'Doublet, bring some of our laurel-flavoured candy for Laurel Goong-goong.'

She bowed deeply to Trinket, and retired to one of the inner apartments.

Trinket was a little uneasy. What was going on? This lady

might not be quite what she seemed. Or perhaps his bad language had offended her?

Doublet came in with a blue-and-white plate piled high with candy of various kinds.

'Help yourself, Laurel Goong-goong,' she said, depositing the plate on the table and then taking her leave.

Trinket sat there, crunching candy and waiting for the dawn.

After what seemed like an age, he heard the rustling of silk, and became aware of many pairs of eyes peeping at him from all sides. He had the feeling they were women's eyes, but whether they were the eyes of living beings or of ghosts, he could not tell. His heart trembled.

An elderly woman's voice finally spoke through the window.

'Laurel Goong-goong, by killing that wicked villain Oboi, you have avenged a great wrong for us! How can we ever repay the great debt of gratitude that we owe you!'

Through the longest of the windows in the reception room, Trinket could now make out the figures of some twenty or thirty women, all dressed in white, and all bowing deeply towards him. Taken aback, he bowed to them in response. Then all of a sudden the window closed, and a sound of loud ululation began.

The wailing sent a shiver down Trinket's spine. Gradually the sound died away, and he could hear the throng of women dispersing. He wondered if he had been dreaming, or seeing things. Were these women alive, or were they ghosts?

After another pause, Widow Zhuang emerged again from an inner room.

'Laurel Goong-goong, please set your mind at ease. These are all of them women whose menfolk, husbands or fathers, died at the hands of Oboi. They all feel a deep gratitude to you for having taken vengeance for them.'

'Was your husband one of the men killed by Oboi?' asked Trinket.

She lowered her head.

'He was. I too am deeply in your debt.'

'Please,' insisted Trinket, with uncharacteristic modesty. 'It was nothing. I just got lucky. But I would like to know one thing. Where have all my companions gone?'

Widow Zhuang pondered this question for a moment.

'Since they were your friends, we have done our utmost to protect them from harm. You will see them again soon.'

Trinket could tell there was nothing to be gained by pressing her any further. He glanced out of the window.

'Why is it still so dark?' he wondered to himself. Widow Zhuang seemed to read his thoughts.

'Where are you planning to set off to when it's light?' she asked.

Trinket could see it was futile to try hoodwinking this all-knowing lady. She had probably overheard everything anyway.

'I'm travelling to the Wutai Mountains.'

'That's a long way from here,' replied Widow Zhuang. 'The journey could be a hard one. We should like to give you something to take with you. I hope you will accept it.'

'I never refuse presents,' quipped Trinket.

'The present we have in mind is my maidservant Doublet,' continued Widow Zhuang. 'She has served me for several years, and is a thoroughly trustworthy girl. We would like her to wait on you.'

Trinket was both surprised and delighted by this generous offer. Doublet certainly seemed a helpful and resourceful girl, and she was extraordinarily pretty into the bargain. It would be fun having her by his side. But then again, the journey might prove dangerous, and require some speedy responses. She might cramp his style.

'It's very kind of you, Widow Zhuang,' he began, 'but I wonder if . . .'

Then he had second thoughts. It seemed churlish to refuse such a gift. And Doublet was so sweet. . . . There she was, her head lowered, glancing at him out of the corner of her eye. When his glance met hers, she turned coyly away, and a flush stole across her face.

'I'm just afraid that this trip of mine to Wutai may be a bit dangerous for a girl.'

'You needn't worry on her behalf. She is a very capable girl. I don't think she will be a burden on you.'

Trinket glanced again at Doublet. There was such entreaty written on her face, such a pleading look darting from her jet-black eyes.

'Well Doublet,' he said, 'what about you? Do you want to go with me?'

She bowed her head.

'If My Lady says so,' she replied. 'I'll do whatever My Lady says.'

'That's not what I asked,' said Trinket. 'What about *you*? Do *you* want to go? It may be dangerous.'

'I'm not afraid.'

'You still haven't answered my first question. Do you want to go?'

'My Lady has always been good to me. You are My Lady's benefactor. If My Lady wants to give me to you, that is my fate! For better or for worse!'

Trinket gave a little laugh.

'I promise it'll be for better!'

The faintest shadow of a smile crossed Doublet's face.

'There, that's settled then!' said Widow Zhuang. 'You're Laurel Goong-goong's now!'

Doublet's eyes reddened and she fell sobbing to the ground and knelt before Widow Zhuang, who stroked her head.

'Laurel Goong-goong is a brave young hero,' she said gently. 'Serve him well, and he will be sure to treat you kindly.'

'Yes, ma'am.'

Doublet turned and bowed to her new master. Trinket rummaged in his bag and brought out a string of pearls.

'Take these,' he said. 'They're yours. Our First Meeting present.'

'These pearls cost me three or four thousand taels of silver!' he mused to himself. 'Enough to buy twenty or thirty maids! But none as sweet as you!'

'Thank you very much,' said Doublet, taking the necklace and putting it round her neck. The pearls added a charming touch to her pretty face.

Widow Zhuang warned Trinket of the dangers that might lie ahead on the Wutai Mountains, and of the strange characters he might encounter lurking in some of the temples dotted around on the various slopes. She strictly enjoined Doublet to serve her new master well, and then took her leave.

At last the dawn came, and light glimmered through the window. Doublet went in to fetch her own bag, and threw it together with Trinket's over her shoulder.

'Let's go then!' said Trinket.

'Yes, let's go!'

Doublet took one last lingering look behind her. Her eyes were red. She had been crying again.

Secrets Exchanged

When Trinket and Doublet stepped out of the house, the torrential rain had stopped, but the hillside was still awash with water. They walked twenty or thirty yards, and Trinket turned and looked back. The haunted house was already swathed in mist. Another thirty yards and there was nothing to be seen but a white expanse.

'Last night all seems like a dream,' said Trinket with a sigh. He turned to Doublet.

'Can you tell me what happened to my friends?'

Doublet began:

'We saved them, and we captured the others. But then some more fierce Mystic Dragon people arrived, and made off with them all. My Lady said we were not to put up a fight, so we let them go.'

Trinket nodded. He was most concerned, needless to say, about Fang Yi and the Little Countess.

'My Lady made the leader of the Mystic Dragons promise not to harm your friends.'

'Not that *their* promise is worth a donkey's fart,' commented Trinket with a sigh. 'Tell me, is your mistress a good fighter?'

'The best!' replied Doublet proudly.

Trinket shook his head in disbelief.

'Such a delicate looking lady? If she's so good at kungfu, how come she wasn't able to save her own husband from death?'

'At that time, none of the Zhuang womenfolk knew anything about the Martial Arts,' replied Doublet. 'That came later. The men were arrested on Oboi's orders and taken to Peking to be executed, and the women were all exiled to the far north, to Ninguta. They would have ended up as slaves working for the soldiers on the frontier—but they were rescued on the way, and settled down here. The person who saved them also taught them Martial Arts.'

By now the sun had risen in a clear blue sky, and was shining down on a verdant landscape, fresh and brilliant after the previous night's heavy rain. The bright weather helped to disperse Trinket's doubts and fears, and he felt confident now that the house had indeed been inhabited by widows and bereaved mothers, not haunted by ghosts.

'So all those shrines were in memory of their dead husbands and sons, killed by Oboi?'

'Yes. We lived apart from the world. If people ever became curious and poked their noses into our affairs, we would pretend to be ghosts and frighten them away. That's why everyone thinks the house is haunted. For a year now no one has come near the place. Not till you came along. And since you turned out to be the one who avenged their deaths, we felt bound to tell you the truth.'

'And I must do likewise,' declared Trinket, feeling a fit of honesty coming on. 'My real name isn't Laurel Goong-goong at all. It's Trinket. Trinket Wei.'

'You can trust me,' replied Doublet. 'I won't tell a soul.' She seemed thrilled to have had such an important secret confided in her.

She told Trinket that Widow Zhuang had been watching and listening during the fight with the Mystic Dragons. It was Widow Zhuang's women who had put out the candles, and caught the Dragons in a fishing-net.

'Clever move!' cried Trinket.

'You see, the Zhuang family used to live near Lake Tai Hu in the old days. They rented out their boats to the local fishermen, and often watched them at work with their nets.'

'Oh well, if you're all from Huzhou, no wonder the *zongzi* were so delicious! But tell me, why did your master get into such trouble with Oboi in the first place?'

Doublet explained to Trinket how young Master Zhuang had gone blind, and then told him the whole story of the *Ming History* and the terrible punishment inflicted on the entire Zhuang family. In the ensuing purge, many renowned scholars connected with the Zhuang family (and even innocent booksellers and book-buyers) had lost their lives as well. And it had all been because of a number of disrespectful references in the text to the Manchu rulers.*

*** Note to Reader:**
For details of the Ming History Inquisition, the reader is directed to the Prologue of the First Book.

Lamas

After a few miles they came to a small country town and went into an inn for a meal. Trinket sat down at the table, and Doublet stood attentively at his side.

'Come on!' he said. 'Don't be so formal! Sit down and let's have a bite to eat!'

'I couldn't possibly eat with you. That would never do.'

'Tamardy!' cried an exasperated Trinket. 'If I say it'll do, then hot-poppin' momma it'll do! Think of the amount of time we'll waste if you have to stand around waiting till I've finished every time, before tucking in yourself!'

'You just eat, and then we'll leave,' insisted Doublet. 'I'll buy some steamed bread and eat it on the way.'

'You don't seem to realize. I'm funny that way. If I eat on my own, I get a bellyache.'

Doublet let out a little peal of laughter and pulled a bench up to the table.

Trinket had hardly eaten more than two or three mouthfuls of noodles, when he saw three Tibetan lamas walk into the inn. They sat down at a table near the door and began yelling, in broken Chinese, for noodles. One of them looked suspiciously at Doublet's necklace, and nudged his companions. Soon they were all ogling the pearls.

Trinket took them for common thieves. He quickly finished his noodles, hired a cart, and set off again at once, ordering the driver to head west and make good speed. They had only progressed a mile or so when they heard the sound of galloping horses behind them. It was the three lamas from the inn.

'They're after your pearls!' Trinket cried to Doublet. 'Why don't we just hand them over? I can easily get you some more.'

'Of course!' agreed Doublet. 'But there's no need to get me any more.'

'Stop cart!' yelled one of the lamas. The driver reined in his mule.

The lamas urged their horses forward, and barred the way in front of the cart.

'Out of cart, baby!' cried another lama.

Doublet untied her string of pearls and made to throw it down on the ground, crying:

'My master says you can have the pearls!'

One of the lamas, a big fat fellow, reached out—but it was not the pearls he was reaching for, it was Doublet's wrist. He yanked her down from the cart.

'Don't be rough with her!' cried Trinket. 'I've got plenty more money if that's what you want.'

Even as he was saying this, he saw a flash of yellow go whizzing past him. It was the fat lama hurtling through the air.

'Excellent kungfu!' Trinket muttered to himself.

The lama landed with a sickening thump, his feet pointing upwards, his big head in the soft mud. He sank in right up to his chest, and began thrashing his legs wildly in the air.

Trinket found all this most bewildering, and not a little exciting. What weird style of kungfu was this lama into?

The other two lamas were now shouting and tugging noisily at their companion's legs, in an effort to extract him from the ground. When he finally emerged, his face was entirely covered in mud. He looked a dreadful sight. Luckily for him the ground had been greatly softened by the previous night's rain, and he had not been unduly hurt by the fall.

Trinket laughed aloud and ordered the driver to drive on without any further delay. Doublet still had the pearls in her hand.

'Master, should I give them my necklace or not?'

Before Trinket could reply, the lamas charged towards them with daggers drawn, but quick as a flash Doublet seized the driver's whip and flicked it at one of them, coiling the tip around his dagger and bringing it spinning back into her left hand. She then repeated the process on a second lama. The third stopped dead in his tracks, muttering to himself in amazement.

Doublet flicked the whip again. This time she coiled it round the third man's neck and hauled him up close to the cart, where she relieved him of his dagger. The whip was still wound tightly around his neck. The whites of his eyes were showing and his tongue had shot out. Every drop of blood seemed to drain from his face. The two other lamas closed in on Doublet from both sides, with a view to rescuing their companion; but Doublet then leapt down and, placing her left foot on the cartwheel, lashed out with her right, kicking the two advancing lamas deftly on the head and closing their Vital Points. They fell to the ground in an instant swoon. She loosened the whip and the third lama collapsed unconscious before her.

Trinket was ecstatic.

'Doublet!' he cried. 'I never dreamt your kungfu was so brilliant! Excellent!'

Doublet smiled.

'That was nothing. These stupid creatures were useless.'

Trinket gave one of the lamas a good kick and asked him:

'What were you playing at?'

The lama said nothing. He was still unconscious.

Doublet kicked him once in the small of the back, and he came to with a groan.

'My master asked you a question!'

'You . . . fairy?' groaned the man. 'Or me . . . dream?'

'Answer my master's question! Hurry up!'

'Lamas . . . Wutai Mountains . . .' he finally succeeded in saying. 'Manjusri Monastery, Bodhisattva Peak.'

Doublet frowned.

'Stop talking jibberish!'

'These monks are lamas from Tibet,' explained Trinket. 'They don't speak very good Chinese.'

'So you're a bonze are you!' (This was the common term for a Buddhist monk of any denomination.)

Doublet gave him another kick.

'Why haven't you shaved your head then?'

'Me lama, not shave head . . .'

'Rubbish!'

She kicked him again in the small of the back, this time on the Vital Point known as the Celestial Gully, causing him the most excruciating pain. He let out a piercing scream. The worse the pain grew, the louder he screamed.

The other lamas had by now regained consciousness. They were greatly alarmed to hear their companion squealing like a pig in the slaughterhouse, and exchanged a few quick words in their own language.

'Yes miss!' cried the lama. 'Me bonze, yes miss, please to stop pain!'

'It all depends on my master. What do you say, master? What is he?'

Trinket laughed.

'A nun!'

The poor lama was truly in agony.

Trinket and Doublet both burst out laughing. Finally Doublet took pity on him. She tapped her foot lightly on the point known

as the Gate of Corporeal Energy, situated just below his neck, and
his pain ceased. But he kept on jabbering.

'Me nun! Nun! Me! Nun! Me!'

Trinket could not stop himself from laughing.

'If you really are monks,' he asked, 'why did you try to rob
us?'

'Never do again!'

'What are you doing down here in the first place? Why aren't
you up in your temple chanting your Sutras and saying your
prayers?'

'Guru . . . send us,' was their somewhat gloomy response.

'To steal pearls?'

'No . . . go to Peking.'

At this point one of the lamas (the fattest one) coughed loudly.
Trinket saw him give his companion a meaningful look. He had
assumed the three to be typical miscreant lamas on the rampage.
Lamaist Buddhism enjoyed the patronage of the Manchu Court,
and in Peking lamas seemed to think they possessed some kind of
diplomatic immunity, and could get away with all manner of mis-
behaviour as a result. Trinket had intended to enjoy himself a little
giving these three a hard time, and then let them go. But there was
something in that fat lama's look that alerted him to some deeper
plot afoot.

'These three are up to no good,' he muttered to Doublet.
'Give them each a good kick, and let's get out of here as quickly as
possible.'

Doublet duly landed a foot on the fat one's Celestial Gully
and he too started screaming his head off. Then she went up to her
previous victim.

'Please no kick!' he begged her pitifully. 'Me tell. Guru send
us Peking, carry letter.'

'A letter?' echoed Trinket.

'No can see. You see letter . . . Guru . . . kill us!'

'You give me the letter,' said Trinket, 'or I'll kick you!'

The lama assumed that whatever the maid could do, the
master was bound to do better. He was taking no chances.

'Me . . . not have . . . letter . . .'

'Give it to me!'

The lama stumbled over to his fat companion and the two of
them started jibbering in Tibetan. The fat one had some difficulty

talking, because he was still squealing with pain like a stuck pig. The resultant combination of noises was especially hideous.

Something about the fat lama's body language made Trinket feel sure that he was trying to prevent his companion from handing over the letter. Trinket walked up to him and booted him savagely in the head. He went out like a light. The other one now promptly extracted a little oilskin package from within his gown, and handed it over with trembling hands. Doublet produced a little knife and cut open the package. Sure enough, it contained a letter. On the envelope were two columns of Tibetan writing.

'Who is this letter for?' asked Trinket.

He ripped it open with a finger. The two lamas howled in protest. Inside was a sheet of yellow paper, covered in squiggly Tibetan writing. The bottom of the page was stamped with a talismanic charm in red ink—most peculiar and utterly indecipherable.

'What does it say?' asked Trinket.

'Come on,' added Doublet. 'You heard him. My master wants to know what it says. You'd better tell him, or I'll kick you and close your points and never open them again. Well, not for three days anyway.'

The lama took hold of the letter.

'Says . . . man . . . cannot . . . be . . .'

The other of the two conscious lamas suddenly started squawking loudly in Tibetan. Doublet landed him a quick kick to the Celestial Gully and his squawks were instantly transformed into pathetic moans.

The original lama (the one still holding the letter) paled. He began shaking uncontrollably.

'Says . . . man . . . cannot be found. Search everywhere. No find. Not on Wutai.'

Trinket studied the man. His eyes were glinting, his face was twitching, he was stammering so badly he could hardly get out two syllables in succession.

'I may not have been able to understand all that cock-a-doodle-doo jibberish of yours,' Trinket thought to himself, 'but I can tell that you're making it all up. And you're lousy at it too!'

'He's lying!' he said out loud to Doublet.

'Then we'll have to give him the works!'

She raised her foot in the general direction of the lama's Gully.

'Please not!' he yelped. 'Please to kill . . . not to kick! Guru say . . . we tell letter . . . we *dead*! So . . . please to kill!'

'Forget him.' said Trinket. 'Let's just go.'

He and Doublet climbed back onto the cart. The driver had watched in silent admiration as the two youngsters put paid to the three fully grown, and extremely aggressive, lamas.

'When we get to the next town,' Trinket whispered to Doublet, 'you'd better change into something different. And put the pearls away somewhere safe.'

'Yes, master. How would you like me to dress?'

Trinket smiled.

'Like a boy.'

Trinket the Benefactor

Ten miles further down the road, they came to a large town. There, Trinket dismissed the driver and took lodgings at an inn. He gave Doublet some money to go and spend on clothes. Presently she returned, looking for all the world like a handsome young page-boy.

They now made a much less conspicuous duo. Mr Trinket Wei and his page. They continued on their way, and in a day or two had arrived at the mountainous border between Hebei and Shanxi provinces. Travelling due west from the town of Fuping in Hebei, across the range of hills known as the Long Wall (because it follows an old southern spur of the Great Wall), they came to Dragon Pass, which forms the easternmost approach to the Wutai Mountains. Here they had to negotiate steep mountain paths, winding their way between precipitous peaks, until finally they reached the very first temple on the eastern slopes of Wutai, the Bubbling Spring Temple.

That evening Trinket and Doublet put up at a little village inn near the temple. They had a good meal of lamb stew with dumplings, followed by some preserved fruits. Trinket reflected ruefully on the unhelpful, almost disrespectful, attitude of the monks when the two of them had looked in briefly at the temple. They reminded him strongly of the snobbish bonzes he had encountered in his boyhood in the temples of Yangzhou. One had to be a very important person indeed to get their attention at all. It was going to be tough for a young nobody like himself to find the Old Emperor at the Pure Coolness Monastery. He was going to need all the help he could get. Perhaps it might improve his chances if he flashed his money around a bit.

With this in mind, he decided to go back to Fuping and break down one or two of his five-hundred tael notes. While they were there he and Doublet bought themselves some smarter clothes. But then Trinket reflected that if he was to pose as a wealthy Buddhist benefactor he would need some practice. A quick trip to the local Fuping temple, the Temple of the Goodly Auspices, and a bit of a dress rehearsal, would be just the ticket. In he went and kowtowed before the holy image of Buddha. As the Camerarius was producing the register of would-be benefactors, Trinket handed him a fifty-tael lump of silver. The monk was hugely impressed by this initial act of largesse, and promptly led Trinket off to sample the establishment's vegetarian fare.

At his meal Trinket was joined by the Abbot, who preached him a little sermon on the untold joys that devotion and generosity would bring him in later life, or indeed in later lives.

'Holy Father,' said Trinket (as ever a quick learner when it came to picking up the relevant lingo), 'I am on my way to Wutai, on a sort of pilgrimage. I wish to pay for a Mass to be said for certain departed souls. I would greatly appreciate your guidance in this matter.'

Predictably the Abbot's first instinct was to detain this well-heeled pilgrim on his own premises.

'My son, why travel the mountain trails to Wutai, when you can just as easily show your devotion here? The Lord Buddha is present here too, you know.'

Trinket shook his head vigorously, insisting that he absolutely must proceed to Wutai. Then, producing another fifty taels of silver, he enquired of the Abbot if he could possibly hire the services of a companion.

'Of course! The easiest thing in the world!' exclaimed the Abbot. He already had someone in mind, needless to say—his own cousin, who though not in holy orders, had been put in charge of the temple estates and produce. The cousin's nickname was Wurtle (on account of his similarity to a Turtle, so it was said). He was a plausible if somewhat scabrous sort of fellow, a bit of a scamp, and Trinket recognized him instantly as a kindred spirit of sorts. He sent him off to purchase whatever paraphernalia he considered necessary for the 'offering', and to buy himself some decent clothes. The three of them then set off back south on the main track across the hills towards Wutai, followed by eight bearers, each laden with gifts for the Lord Buddha. They crossed Dragon Pass once more, and entered the Wutai Mountains proper for the second time.

They passed by Bubbling Spring Temple again, then walked on past one monastic establishment after another, until finally they arrived at the Monastery of the Holy Precinct. Here they lodged for one night, and set off again the next morning in a northerly direction, reaching the Monastery of the Golden Pavilion, then veering off towards the west.

A mile or two further on they came to their destination, Pure Coolness Monastery, which stood on the crest of a mountain of the same name. Despite its reputation, it was no more impressive than the other monasteries; in fact if anything it seemed more dilapidated. Trinket was rather disappointed.

'Surely the Old Emperor could've chosen something a bit grander than this? Perhaps that stupid old Hai Dafu got his facts muddled up and he's not here at all?'

Wurtle went ahead and spoke with the Camerarius, who, impressed by the evident wealth of the party and their obviously generous intentions, went in at once to report their arrival to the Abbot, Father Aureole. The Abbot came out immediately to welcome the guests.

Trinket was even more disappointed by the Abbot's appearance than he had been by the monastery's. Father Aureole was a thin, scrawny monk, and had a generally down-at-heel and unprepossessing look about him.

'Holy Father,' Trinket began, 'I have come here to request a seven-day Mass for the salvation of my deceased father's soul, and for the souls of several of my deceased friends.'

The Abbot politely inquired why his guest had chosen his own humble establishment in preference to the many temples in Peking, or indeed on other parts of Wutai.

Trinket had rehearsed his answer to this question on the way there.

'My mother had a vision in a dream. My late father came to her and requested her to hold the Mass in this very place. No other place would do to save him from the endless torment of Hell!'

In actual fact, Trinket did not have the slightest idea who his own father was, or whether the individual responsible for conceiving him was living or dead. He found the whole idea highly entertaining.

'Why, dad, you old bugger,' he was silently joking to himself, 'whoever you are—you never cared two hoots for old Trink! You never came anywhere near him! You deserve to rot in Hell anyway! You don't know how lucky you are to have me, old Trink, paying for a Mass for your soul!'

'My son,' came the Abbot's somewhat fatuous response to Trinket's brief tale, 'dreams can be mere illusion!'

'But Father,' insisted Trinket, 'even so, even if it is an illusion, my heart will never find peace until I pay for this Mass. It was my mother's own wish. She said there was a karmic bond between herself and Your Reverence . . .'

'Nice one!' he chuckled silently to himself. 'Sort of implies that this bald-pated turtle-head of a bonze once sneaked off to Yangzhou and jumped on my mum!'

'But my son,' continued Father Aureole, 'what you may not have realized is that this monastery of ours is a Zen establishment. We devote ourselves mainly to silent meditation and the quest for wordless enlightenment. Of course, we can and do say Masses. But that is not really our main line. You'd be much better served if you went to one of the Pure Land temples on Wutai, like the Golden Pavilion.'

Trinket was perplexed to get such an unenthusiastic reception from Father Aureole, when the old Abbot at Goodly Auspices had been falling over himself to hang onto him and his money. He repeated his request once more, but the Abbot was adamant and finally rose to his feet, instructing his Camerarius to see them out and show them the way to the Monastery of the Golden Pavilion.

Trinket insisted on leaving large quantities of gifts behind, and the Abbot expressed his thanks—rather perfunctorily, given the scale of the donation. There were over three hundred items, Trinket explained, something for everyone, even the lowliest kitchen-boy or garden-hand.

'That is excessive,' insisted the Abbot. 'There are only fifty of us here. I must ask you to take the greater part of your presents with you.'

'May I in turn ask a final favour of you, Father?' said Trinket. 'My mother most particularly asked me to hand over the gifts in person. Would it be possible to assemble all of your monks together? It was my mother's wish.'

When he heard this a strange look came into the Abbot's eyes.

'Buddha is compassionate!' he intoned. 'Let it be according to your mother's wish, my son.'

With these words he walked back into the inner precinct of the monastery.

Trinket watched uneasily as the Abbot's spare frame disappeared. He picked up his teacup and awkwardly drank a sip. Wurtle, who was standing behind him, muttered a few uncomplimentary remarks, to the effect that 'with an old fogey like that in charge, it was no wonder the place was falling apart', and more along the same lines.

A bell rang from within, and the Camerarius asked them to proceed to the western hall. There Trinket found all the monks assembled. He gave each of them a present, and as he did so studied their faces one by one.

'I've never set eyes on the Old Emperor,' he thought to himself, 'but he's the Emperor's father, and there must be some kind of family resemblance. What I'm looking for is an older, bigger version of Misty.'

But not one of the monks answered this description.

Then Trinket reflected that if the Old Emperor were living in this monastery, he would hardly be subject to the same regulations as the other monks. He had doubtless been excluded from the summons. But however hard he pestered the Camerarius with questions (and terrifying threats of having his tongue cut out in Hell if he lied), he was unable to extract any information from him.

Lamas on the Hill

Just as Trinket was feeling most despondent, a monk came tearing into the room, crying to the Camerarius:

'Brother, there are a dozen lamas outside wanting to see the Abbot!'

He added, *sotto voce*:

'They're armed! And looking *very* unfriendly!'

The Camerarius frowned.

'We should always welcome fellow believers in the Dharma,' he said, 'even if they are followers of a different school. But what do these men want? You go in, and report to the Abbot. I'll go out and take a closer look.'

He turned to Trinket.

'Excuse me for a moment.'

'They're probably after us,' mused Trinket, reflecting that with a fighter like Doublet by his side, he would be more than a match for a dozen lamas.

The next instant he heard a great tumult outside and the sound of a large crowd of people bursting noisily into the Great Buddha Hall.

'Let's go and see what's happening!' he cried, and dragged Doublet and Wurtle off with him in the direction of the noise. They arrived to find the unfortunate Camerarius surrounded by a dozen lamas in saffron robes, jabbering wildly at him:

'Must search! Man . . . here . . . in Pure Coolness!'

'You . . . wicked! Why hide man?'

'Give man . . . or else . . .'

Trinket stood to one side, arms akimbo, thinking to himself: 'Here's your man! Here I am! Come and get me!'

But the lamas, although by now they could see Trinket quite plainly, were paying him no attention whatsoever.

The Abbot now made a dignified entry.

'What is all the excitement about?' he asked.

'Your Reverence,' gasped the Camerarius, 'these men—'

The moment they heard the word Reverence the lamas crowded round Father Aureole.

'You . . . Abbot? Give man, or . . . burn monastery!'

'Brothers,' replied the Abbot, 'would you be so good as to tell me where you have come from? And what brings you here?'

'Tibet!'

The lama who answered wore a red cassock over his saffron robe.

'Dalai Lama send us to China,' he continued. 'Our lama . . . young one . . . kidnapped . . . hiding here. Abbot give man . . . or burn monastery!'

'This is all very strange,' replied Father Aureole, 'and most irregular. This is a Zen cloister. We normally have very little to do with our Lamaist brethren. Should you not be looking instead in the other Lamaist monasteries on Wutai, of which there are quite a number?'

'Our man . . . *here*! You give . . . we go!'

The Abbot shook his head.

'I'm afraid we have no such person as you describe here.'

'Then please to look!'

'This is holy ground!'

The Abbot shook his head again.

Two lamas seized hold of him by the collar of his gown.

'Give . . . no give? Look . . . no look?'

'Monks . . . hide women! Sex! Bad secrets! Afraid of look-see!'

One of the other lamas was beginning to get carried away.

By now a dozen Pure Coolness monks had come into the hall, but were prevented by the lamas from approaching their Abbot.

'Master,' whispered Doublet, 'shall I deal with them?'

'Hold on,' Trinket whispered back.

It had finally begun to dawn on him what the lamas were up to. Like himself, they were searching for the Old Emperor.

There was flash of steel, and two lamas drew their swords. One held the tip of his weapon against the Abbot's chest, the other held his to the small of the Abbot's back.

'We kill!'

Father Aureole did not so much as twitch a muscle of his face.

'Amida Buddha!' he replied. 'We are all believers in the same faith. There is surely no need for any of this!'

The two lamas pressed their swords closer towards Father Aureole, but he stepped nimbly to one side and they all but collided with one another. A cry went up, and a motley assortment of thirty or forty more men came bursting in through the main door of the hall, some of them dressed in ordinary Buddhist monks' habits, some in lama garb. There were even one or two laymen in long gowns. Among them was one elderly, white-haired lama in saffron, who cried indignantly:

'Abbot killing lamas!'

Father Aureole protested and addressed himself to another monk in his fifties, also one of the newly arrived:

'Father Crystal, I am indeed honoured that you should have come all this way!'

The man he was addressing, Father Crystal, was the Abbot of Buddha Light Monastery, the oldest foundation on Wutai, dating back to the days of the Northern Wei dynasty in the fifth century. It antedated the very name Wutai Mountains. In fact, the mountains had at first been called the Mountains of Pure Coolness (it was beautifully cool up there during the summer months) and had only subsequently (during the Sui dynasty, or sixth century) been called the Wutai Mountains, from the five (*wu*) terraces (*tai*), or terrace-shaped peaks, that formed the range. The Buddha Light

foundation was ecclesiastically speaking far senior to the Pure Coolness Monastery, and its Abbot, Father Crystal, was tacitly acknowledged as the highest ranking cleric in the whole of Wutai. He was,
in actual fact, a fat, swarthy individual, with a twittering way of
speaking.

With the arrival of all these newcomers, the atmosphere had
calmed down sufficiently for conversation to take place.

'Allow me to introduce two friends,' began Father Crystal. He
pointed to the elderly lama as he went on: 'This is Brother Bayen,
from the great lamasery of Lhasa. He is a Great Lama and one of
the Dalai Lama's most trusted and influential advisers.'

'It is my most excellent karma to meet you, Brother Bayen,'
said Father Aureole.

Brother Bayen nodded. He definitely looked the proud sort.

'And this gentleman,' continued the Abbot of Buddha Light,
indicating one of the laymen in long gowns, 'is His Excellency Mr
Huangfu, a civil official from the Western Marches of Sichuan
Province.'

Huangfu made some reference to Father Aureole's great
Martial Arts fame, and Father Aureole greeted the layman courte-
ously. Trinket was almost disappointed to see things calming down
like this. He had been secretly hoping to watch the encounter esca-
late into a free-for-all fight, one which might even have offered him
a chance of determining the Old Emperor's whereabouts.

Brother Bayen, the elderly Tibetan lama, now demanded that
Father Aureole hand over their 'little disciple'. When the Abbot
politely but firmly insisted that he could not, since he did not have
him there in the first place, Bayen rolled his eyes and burst into a
torrent of barely intelligible broken Chinese, the general drift of
which seemed to be: 'Hand him over, or you'll regret it!'.

Father Crystal now offered to mediate. He proposed that the
only foolproof way to establish the truth of the matter was for
himself and Mr Huangfu to conduct a 'guided tour' (in other words,
a search) of the monastery. Father Aureole did not look pleased.

'To hear such an outrageous suggestion from our Tibetan
friends did not come as a surprise!' he protested. 'But from a distinguished fellow Chinese monk such as yourself? Would we not
be better advised to search *your* monastery first . . .'

Father Crystal gave one of his twittering laughs.

'Come, come! If we find no one here, I shall of course be more
than happy to agree to such a request from our lama brothers . . .'

'Man . . . here!' blurted out Bayen. 'Someone . . . see him! Or we not dare pesstrass on your troperty . . .'

He was trying hard.

'And who was it that saw him?' asked Father Aureole.

'Mr Huangfu see. Him very big famous person. Him not lie.'

'Of course not,' thought Trinket silently to himself. 'And him obviously happen to be part of your group . . .'

But what he said out loud was:

'Tell me, how old was this little lost lama of yours?'

Bayen, Father Crystal, and Mr Huangfu had until now paid no attention to the two well-dressed boys standing to one side. Their eyes now focused on Trinket in all his finery, and his smartly attired, and very handsome, page-boy.

'About the same age as yourself, as a matter of fact!' twittered Father Crystal.

'I thought so!' declared Trinket. 'That sounds like the one we saw just now—going into the Buddha Light Monastery . . .'

Brother Bayen and his friends pulled a face. Father Aureole secretly rejoiced.

'Stuffings and nonsense!' cried the irrepressible Brother Bayen, and made a lightning pass at Trinket. Father Aureole intercepted him with a flick of his right hand. Seeing that the two men were about to come to blows, Huangfu bellowed:

'We must talk this through! There's to be no rough play!'

His words were hardly out when they came echoing back in force from outside.

'No rough play!'

Judging from the strength of the chorus, there were several hundred men out there. The monastery was evidently surrounded. Father Aureole paused to reflect.

'Your Reverence . . .' Huangfu continued, smiling diplomatically. But what he went on to say contained nothing new. 'If you have nothing to hide, what's to be lost by permitting a civilized tour of inspection?'

Father Aureole could see that his men were outnumbered. He had once been a Martial Arts Master himself, but of late he had devoted more and more of his energies to Zen meditation, and few of his fellow monks were fighters of any kind. His recent observations warned him that Brother Bayen was a fighter to be feared. His attempted left-handed Chicken Claw gouging attack on Trinket indicated mastery of an especially ferocious style of fighting.

Huangfu was clearly not a man to be trifled with either, judging by the power of his voice! Not to mention the troops massed around the building.

'It really doesn't matter if we do find one or two nice-looking wenches on the premises,' Huangfu put in, seeing Father Aureole pause. 'What's a bit of flesh between friends!'

This was definitely adding insult to injury.

Father Crystal twittered.

'Brother Abbot, why not let them in?'

But Bayen was not even waiting for the invitation. He was already leading the way. Father Aureole was helpless to do anything but follow.

Bayen, Father Crystal, and Huangfu whispered among themselves, and dispatched their men to search every room of the monastery. The monks watched them with stony hostility. Trinket and Doublet walked immediately behind Father Aureole. They could tell how angry he was from the way the sleeves of his gown were trembling.

Suddenly they heard voices coming from the western row of cells.

'Is this him?'

Huangfu hurried over to see two men emerge from a cell, dragging with them an emaciated ascetic of middle years.

'What do you mean by laying hands on me?' he was protesting.

Huangfu shook his head and the two men apologized and let the man go.

Now Trinket knew beyond a shadow of a doubt that they had come to find the Old Emperor, and not some 'little lost lama'. Why else would they have seized such a man? The same thought had clearly occurred to Father Aureole.

'Does that brother look like a young lama?' he asked, with a quizzical smile.

Huangfu's men now produced another middle-aged monk. Their commander looked him up and down, and shook his head again.

'So he obviously knows what the Old Emperor looks like!' thought Trinket to himself. 'Sooner or later they're bound to find him. I must protect him! After all, he *is* the Emperor's father, and the Emperor *is* my friend!'

But he could think of no way of dealing with this enemy.

The search-party of twenty or thirty, led by Bayen and friends, and followed by Father Aureole, had now reached a small compound independently situated in the north-east corner of the monastery grounds. It was firmly locked.

'Open up!' they shouted.

'This is the personal retreat of a very distinguished monk,' said Father Aureole. 'He has been in seclusion in this hermitage for seven years. I must ask you not to intrude upon his meditations.'

'Come, come!' twittered Father Crystal. 'We will only interrupt his thoughts for a few minutes. It is not as if he himself were guilty of some lapse of concentration.'

'Break door!' shouted one of the taller lamas. 'Man here!'

He began kicking at the door.

In a flash Father Aureole was standing between him and the door, and the lama's foot made contact not with wood but with the Abbot's stomach, which was tense as steel. The lama gave a cry of pain as his leg shattered and he was thrown backwards through the air. At the same time, Bayen uttered a series of guttural croaking noises and leapt once more into his classic Chicken Claw position, threatening to pounce on Father Aureole. But the Abbot stood firm before the door, and dealt the elderly lama two hefty blows with left and right.

'Prajna Hand! Excellent kungfu!' cried Huangfu, promptly extending the index finger of his left hand and aiming a pinpoint attack at the Abbot's forehead. Father Aureole darted to the side, and Huangfu's finger drove forcefully into the heavy wooden panel of the door. Once again Father Aureole had demonstrated his mastery in the art of Prajna Hand karate.

Bayen and Huangfu now closed in on their adversary from both sides. Again and again they attacked, cheered on by their men; but each time the Abbot turned them back, using his precise, unostentatious, but deadly karate skill.

Bayen was growing angry and desperate. He threw himself once more into the attack. With a sudden grunt he raised his left hand and leapt through the air, his white hair fluttering in strands around him. All he succeeded in clutching hold of was the Abbot's moustaches, while he himself received a blow on his right shoulder. The pain seemed nothing at first, but gradually his right arm grew heavier and heavier until he could no longer even lift it up. He staggered off to one side, bellowing savagely. Four of his subordinate lamas drew their swords and rushed into the attack.

Father Aureole now landed a couple of well-placed aerial kicks that put two of his new attackers out of action. A third he despatched with a blow to the chest, which sent the man reeling. The fourth and last was swinging his sword through the air when Aureole flicked his sleeve and caught him by the wrist. Even as he did this he saw Bayen move back into the fray, his hands weaving up and down through the air. Father Aureole ducked to the right, but not quickly enough to escape the massive force of the Tibetan's assault.

He aimed a counter-blow, but felt a strange pain on his right cheek. It was Huangfu's finger.

Things were taking a nasty turn. Doublet took one look at the blood pouring down the Abbot's cheek and whispered to Trinket:

'Shouldn't I help him *now*?'

'Wait a little longer!'

Trinket's prime concern was still to locate the Old Emperor. Supposing Doublet succeeded in routing the enemy (which was admittedly unlikely—one girl against a heavily armed army!), then they would have lost their chance of tracing Shun Zhi.

Meanwhile, somewhat late in the day, the monks of the monastery had come to their Abbot's aid, wielding as weapons whatever sticks or broken bits of furniture they could lay their hands on. From the start, they were outclassed, and as the blood began to pour from their wounds their Abbot cried out to them to desist.

'Kill all!' bellowed Bayen.

The lamas attacked more viciously than ever, and hacked the heads off four of the monks. The remaining monks had now lost their taste for the fight. Bayen and Huangfu closed in again on Father Aureole, and after a final struggle they had the Abbot lying powerless on the ground, his Vital Points closed, his left leg pinned in a ten-pronged Chicken Claw attack by the lama.

Bayen now gave a mighty laugh, and kicked at the door with his right foot. There was a great crash as it flew open.

'In . . . go!' cried Bayen. 'See . . . inside!'

It was pitch-black inside the little hermitage, and silent as the grave.

'Tie up . . . and bring out!' shouted Bayen.

'Yes, master!' cried two of the lamas, and went charging in.

The Hermitage

With a sudden flash of light, a golden cudgel-like object came swinging out through the hermitage doorway—*bong-bong*—and dealt each of the two lamas a devastating blow on the head. They fell silently to the ground, and the contents of their brains spilled out from their broken heads.

Stunned by this turn of events, Brother Bayen began cursing and swearing. Three more lamas went into the attack, this time drawing their swords to protect their heads. The one in front had no sooner reached the doorway than out came that golden cudgel again, smashing past his sword and onto his head. The second lama went bravely on, sword raised, but he too had his brains spilled like soft noodles. The third dropped his sword to the ground in terror and fled. Bayen ranted and raved, but was certainly not planning to step into the breach himself.

'Onto the roof!' cried Huangfu. 'Take off the tiles and throw them inside!'

Four of his men obeyed these instructions, while others gathered stones and began hurling them through the open doorway.

Most of the stones were batted back out again by the wielder of the golden cudgel. But the tiles seemed to have more success, and several of them landed inside. Sooner or later the occupants of the hermitage would surely be forced out.

Suddenly, with a great bull-like bellowing, a massive monk came striding out of the doorway, his left arm clutching the form of another monk, while his right hand brandished the golden cudgel that had just wrought such havoc. This man must have been a good head taller than the average stature, and presented a terrifying spectacle. He was somewhat like a temple door-god come to life, with his great livid face, his bristling beard and moustaches, his huge hands and feet. Through his tattered monk's robe a glimpse could be caught of his muscular torso, his broad arms, and his knotted midriff.

Bayen and Huangfu found themselves instinctively retreating before this giant.

'He . . . only one man!' shrieked Bayen. 'He . . . only one big fat! Why frightened? Everyone . . . go fight!'

'Take care!' cried Huangfu in some alarm. 'Don't harm the other one—the one he's carrying!'

Trinket studied this second monk more closely. He was a

tallish, lightly-built man in his mid thirties, with fine features and a general air of distinction. Throughout the confrontation he held his eyes averted, cast firmly towards the ground. Trinket's heart missed a beat.

'That's him!' he thought to himself. 'That's the Emperor's dad! He's even better looking than Misty! Funny, somehow I expected him to be a lot older.'

Meanwhile, a dozen lamas had launched a concerted attack on the giant. He swung his golden cudgel, and—*bong-bong-bong*—one by one the lamas bit the dust. Huangfu now extracted a whip from his sash, while Bayen seized a pair of short-handled metal fighting-mallets from one of his followers. The two of them closed in on the big monk.

Huangfu flicked his whip and watched its barbed tip curl around the monk's throat. The monk gave a great yell and aimed his cudgel squarely at the Tibetan. Bayen parried firmly with both mallets but, as he felt the cudgel's impact, both his arms went numb and the two mallets fell from his hands.

Meanwhile, another lama was launching an attack on the middle-aged monk.

'Quick!' whispered Trinket to Doublet. 'Now!'

Doublet darted into action, immobilizing the lama with one well-aimed finger. Then she turned to deal with Huangfu, who ducked to one side to avoid her. She homed in instead on Bayen, landing a neat finger dead in the centre of his chest. The Tibetan howled with pain and fell flat on his back. Doublet continued, striking out left and right, and in a matter of minutes she had a dozen or so of their men on the ground.

'Oh . . . please . . . dear son . . .' twittered Father Crystal.

'Oh . . . please . . . dear father!' laughed Doublet, poking a quick finger in his ribs.

Huangfu now whirled his whip around him, and Doublet danced round the outside of the circle it formed. Faster and faster moved the whip, faster and faster danced Doublet. Then Huangfu cried out 'Clever little fellow!', and in the same moment straightened the whip out and flicked it at Doublet. She shot forward under it and reached one deadly finger into Huangfu's midriff. He parried with his left palm, while his right hand gave the whip a little nudge that brought the tip curling round into the small of Doublet's back. Doublet scrambled away, but things were beginning to look dangerous.

'No you don't!' yelled Trinket, searching the ground for particles of sand or grit or anything he could lay his hands on, to throw in Huangfu's eyes. Unfortunately the ground had been swept immaculately clean.

Meanwhile, the giant advanced on Huangfu.

Trinket reached into his inside pocket, frantically grabbing the first thing he could find and throwing it in Huangfu's face. Pieces of paper went fluttering through the air. And in that one split second when Huangfu was brushing them away, the giant brought down his golden cudgel. Huangfu tumbled out of range, but as he did so Doublet kicked out with her left foot and connected with his Great Solar point. He gave a cry of pain and rolled helplessly backwards. There was a great crash and flying sparks as the giant's golden cudgel struck the ground inches from his head.

'Excellent kungfu!' cried Trinket. Drawing his dagger, he rushed up and held the point of it to Huangfu's left eye.

'Order all of your men out of here! Now!'

Huangfu was incapable of moving and in no position to negotiate. He gave the order.

The big monk glared at him. Then he gazed at Doublet for a moment, before giving a grunt of approval.

'Hm, cute kid!'

Swinging his golden cudgel in his left hand, and still clutching the middle-aged monk under his right arm, he retreated back into the hermitage, and was gone before Trinket was able to speak with the monk he was carrying.

Doublet was meanwhile releasing Father Aureole's points. When she had finished, she gathered up the pieces of paper and handed them back to her master. Trinket laughed when he saw what they were: wads of banknotes!

Slice, No Slice

Huangfu was obliged to order his men (the several hundred of them still surrounding the monastery) to withdraw and wait for him at the foot of the hill. Father Aureole could finally breathe in peace. He made as if to release Father Crystal's points, but before he could do so, Trinket stopped him and led him away into one of the monastery's side chapels.

'Father,' he said, 'do you believe their story? Do you think those men *really* came here looking for one of their own lost disciples?'

Father Aureole did not reply. Trinket whispered in his ear:

'*I* know why they came. They were looking for His Majesty. His Majesty the Monk . . .'

Father Aureole gave a start. Then he slowly nodded his head.

'So you know about that, my son.'

'That's why I came here,' said Trinket. 'To protect him. The rest was all pretence.'

'I myself wondered, I must confess.'

'I think it would be very dangerous to set those two free,' Trinket continued.

'There must be no thought of killing them,' replied the Abbot. 'Today has seen enough blood spilled in this holy place! Amida Buddha!'

'I agree. Simply tie them up, and question them. We must find out why *they* were looking for His Majesty.'

'But we are simple monks,' protested Father Aureole. 'Somehow it doesn't seem right to treat them in this way.'

'And is what *they* did right? If we don't do something about them, they'll come back and burn your monastery down.'

Father Aureole pondered for a while, then nodded his agreement. He clapped his hands, and a monk came in answer to his summons.

'Bring Mr Huangfu here. I wish to speak to him.'

'No!' objected Trinket. 'He's too crafty. Question the lama first.'

'Yes, of course.'

Two monks dragged Bayen in and threw him roughly on the ground.

'Show some respect to our distinguished guest!' protested Father Aureole.

'Yes, master!' chorused the two monks as they withdrew.

Trinket meanwhile had picked up a chair and with his dagger began sharpening the chair legs. He peeled off layer after layer, and the blade sliced through the wood as effortlessly as if he had been peeling the skin off a pear. Father Aureole watched him mystified. Then Trinket went up to Bayen, patted his head with his left hand, and with the dagger in his right hand began making a movement— just like the peeling he had just completed.

'No!' shouted Bayen.

'On no account!' concurred Father Aureole.

'What do you mean?' protested Trinket angrily. 'I know these Tibetan lamas. They all practise Steel Head kungfu! Nothing can get into their brain-boxes! I tried it on one of them once in Peking. I peeled away for hours, and he never so much as budged an inch. Tell me, Brother Bayen, are you the real thing? Or are you a fake? There's only one way to be sure, and that's to test you out!'

'No slice!' stammered Bayen. 'No slice! Bayen . . . tell truth!'

Trinket fingered his scalp.

'But how will I *know*?'

'If Bayen lie, *then* slice!' suggested the lama hopefully.

Trinket pondered this option a moment.

'Very well. My first question is: who sent you here?'

'Great Lama Tsereng-bLo-do of Manjusri Monastery . . . sent here.'

'Holy name!' cried Father Aureole. 'That's right here on Wutai. Since when have the Lamaists of Wutai fought against us? Why did the Great Lama send you to make trouble here?'

'I no make trouble!' protested Bayen. 'Brother Tsereng . . . send me find monk. Monk . . . steal precious Sutra from Lhasa, belong Dalai Lama! He hide in Pure Coolness, so we come . . . take him away.'

'Holy name!' cried the Abbot again. 'I never heard of such carryings-on!'

'One lie, and I slice!' threatened Trinket, brushing Bayen's scalp with the blade of his dagger.

'No lie!' blurted out Bayen. 'No lie! Ask Brother Tsereng! We pretend look for young lama . . . really look for . . . older monk. Mr Huangfu, he know monk, he come with us. Brother Tsereng say . . . this monk steal precious Lama Sutra, Mahaparamarthasatya Sutra! I find monk . . . number one good thing . . . return Lhasa . . . Dalai Lama give big reward!'

From the look on Bayen's face during this lengthy recital, Trinket reckoned that this time he probably was telling the truth— the truth, that is, as far as Bayen himself was aware of it. The old lama had evidently been fed this story because the others did not want him to know about the Old Emperor. Trinket now produced the letter that they had taken from the three lamas on the road earlier, and thrust it in front of Bayen's eyes.

'Read this for me!'

As he said this, he pressed the edge of the dagger-blade against the lama's scalp.

'Yes! Yes!'

Bayen began uttering a long string of outlandish Tibetan syllables. Trinket nodded.

'That's right. Very good. Now do you mind saying all that in Chinese for the Father? He doesn't happen to understand Tibetan . . .'

'Letter say . . .' began Bayen. 'Letter say . . . great person . . . at Pure Coolness Monastery. Latest news . . . Mystic Dragons . . . come get him. . . . Must get there first . . .'

Trinket nodded.

'Anything else?'

'Letter say . . . Peking Great Lama Dahar . . . he send more men in case Mystic Dragons arrive. . . . If Great Lama Sangge already in Peking . . . he top fighter in whole world, can help. . . . Others no hand stance in Hell!'

Trinket burst out laughing.

'Tamardy! Hand what stance, you stupid lump of lama pudding!'

It was not often that Trinket had a chance to correct other people's idioms.

'Yes . . . no . . . yes . . .' jabbered Bayen. 'No . . . no . . . no . . . no handstand in Hell . . .'

'You mean he wouldn't stand a chance in Hell, you big baboon! What else?'

'No else!'

'And Mr Huangfu? Who's he when he's at home?'

The lama looked puzzled at the question. 'Brother Tsereng . . . He not at home . . . Send for him. He come yesterday.'

Trinket nodded. He turned to Father Aureole.

'I should like to question that Father Crystal, the fat monk from the Buddha Light Monastery. If you'd rather not be present, you can listen from outside.'

Father Aureole hastened to take his leave, and repaired to his cell.

Father Crystal was all smiles as he came in.

'What superb kungfu, my young friend!' he twittered.

'Up your mother's!' snapped Trinket. 'Who asked you to lick my arse?'

He gave him a boot up the pants. It hurt, but Father Crystal kept on smiling.

'Of course, no true hero likes to be praised! But I meant it, truly—'

'Shut up and answer this question. Who sent you here to put on this stupid little performance?'

'My son, I would never dream of lying to you. It was Brother Tsereng-bLo-do, the Great Lama of the Manjusri Monastery, who presented me with two hundred taels to accompany his fellow lama Bayen here. They were looking for someone, I believe. But I just did it to earn a little money . . .'

Trinket gave him another boot.

'Bullshit! Think you can pull that one on me? Now, give me the truth!'

'Yes, yes, my son. . . . Actually, it was three hundred taels.'

'You mean a thousand.'

'Five hundred, to tell the absolute truth.'

'And what about Huangfu?'

'A nasty piece of work. Brother Bayen brought him along. As soon as you let me go, I'll take him to Wutai County and have the magistrate there punish him properly. I think we çan pin all the deaths on him—'

'Why not on you?'

Next it was Huangfu's turn. He was a tough customer and refused to say a word. Trinket tried the dagger trick, but it had no effect. He sent for Doublet and told her to close his Celestial Gully point. Huangfu groaned with pain. But still he refused to answer Trinket's questions.

'Go on, kill me! But stop the torturing! That's no way for a real man to behave!'

Trinket had a grudging respect for that kind of talk. He told Doublet to open the point. Having dismissed Huangfu, he sent for Father Aureole again.

'We'll have to discuss all of this with a certain Very Important Person,' he declared. 'Then we'll know what to do.'

Father Aureole shook his head.

'He absolutely refuses to set eyes on any outsider.'

Trinket started getting angry.

'Don't give me that! He's just set eyes on a whole mob of people! And if we hadn't stepped in, he'd have been carried off altogether. Listen, a few days from now we'll have a whole new batch of lamas from Peking coming here, and this Great Fighting Lama whatever-his-name-is, and the Mystic Dragons, and the Spastic Turtles—and then our Very Important Person really *will* be up the creek!'

'I suppose you're right.'

'Of course I'm right. You go and have a word with him. Tell him it's a matter of life and death.'

Father Aureole shook his head.

'I have already given him my word that none of us—not even I myself—will speak to him.'

'All right then. I'll go. I'm not one of you.'

'No no! If you go in there, his friend, the big monk, Brother Headlong we call him—he'll kill you with one blow!'

'Not me he won't!'

Father Aureole glanced at Doublet.

'Even if your serving-boy manages to deal with Brother Headlong, Brother Wayward still won't speak to you.'

'Brother Wayward? Is that his new name? Is that what you monks call him?'

'Yes, it is. I thought you knew.'

Trinket sighed pointedly.

'I see. Very well then. There seems to be nothing I can do. Since you can't come up with anything either, not even a "handstand in hell"—we'll just have to stand back and watch your monastery being destroyed.'

Father Aureole frowned, and rubbed his hands together in great perplexity. An idea suddenly occurred to him.

'I'll go and speak to Venerable Yulin. Perhaps *he* can think of something.'

'And who's he?'

'He is Brother Wayward's Shifu.'

'Excellent. Let's go and see him together.'

Beyond the Dusty World

And so Father Aureole led Trinket and Doublet out through the back entrance of the monastery and onto the hillside behind. About half a mile further up they came to a little tumbledown temple, without a name-board above its entrance. Father Aureole walked in and through to the meditation chamber at the rear, and there found an elderly, white-haired monk sitting on his prayer-mat, his eyes closed in deep meditation. He seemed totally unaware of the three of them as they came in.

Father Aureole sat down respectfully on a prayer-mat at the side, lowering his gaze and bringing his hands together in a gesture of prayer. Trinket did likewise (privately chuckling to himself at his newly acquired monkish ways). Doublet stood behind him. It was deathly silent in the little temple, which was apparently uninhabited except for this one old monk.

An age seemed to go by, and still Venerable Yulin did not so much as move a muscle. Father Aureole sat motionless too. Trinket was beginning to get pins and needles, and kept restlessly jumping up and sitting down again, inwardly cursing the old bonze and his ancestors.

Another age went by, and the old man finally took a deep breath and slowly opened his eyes. He did not register any surprise at the fact that he was not alone, but merely nodded.

'My Revered Brother in the Dharma,' began Father Aureole, 'it seems that Brother Wayward's worldly karma is not yet extinguished. Trouble is at hand.'

He proceeded to tell the old bonze the whole story. Yulin listened in total silence, then closed his eyes, and seemed to drift back into a meditative trance.

Trinket's impatience finally got the better of him, and he jumped to his feet.

'Cut the karma!' he cried angrily. 'Time's running out!'

His imprecations were, however, cut short by Father Aureole, who gesticulated to him urgently, and indicated that he should be quiet and sit down.

Half an hour of further meditation passed (on the part of Yulin). With every minute Trinket's opinion of the bonze sank lower and lower.

Finally the old man opened his eyes again and spoke.

'Mr Wei, my son, have you come from Peking?'

'I have.'

'Have you been waiting upon His Majesty?'

Trinket started.

'How did you . . . know that?'

'I was just guessing.'

'What a weird old boy!' thought Trinket to himself, and silently resolved to show him a little more respect.

'So what has His Majesty asked you to come and talk to Brother Wayward about?'

'He seems to know everything!' Trinket thought to himself. 'No use trying to pull the wool over *his* eyes!'

'When His Majesty learned that his father was still alive, he was both happy and sad. He sent me here to kowtow and to bring a devoted son's heartfelt greetings. His Majesty would be overjoyed if . . . if His Old Majesty were willing to return to the Palace.'

He made no mention of Kang Xi's intention to pay a visit to Wutai himself, if the news that his father was there proved to be true. He was keeping that back for the time being.

Yulin asked to see something in writing from the Emperor, and Trinket produced Kang Xi's handwritten letter and presented it to him respectfully with both hands.

Yulin read it and handed it back to Trinket.

'So you are Lieutenant-Colonel Wei of the Palace Guards? My humblest respects!'

Trinket's sense of satisfaction was somewhat marred by the expression on the old bonze's face as he said this, which mingled disdain with detachment, and seemed devoid of any actual respect, let alone humility.

'So tell me, my son, what do you plan to do now?'

'I should like to kneel before the Old Emperor, and hear his instructions.'

'He used once to be ruler of all that he surveyed,' commented Yulin. 'But since he entered the Gate of the Dharma, he has left the red dust of the world behind him. You must never utter the words "His Old Majesty" or "Old Emperor" again. Someone might hear, and his tranquillity would be for ever disrupted.'

Trinket fell silent.

'I must ask you,' Yulin continued, 'to report back to His Majesty, that Brother Wayward wishes to see no one, neither you nor any other intruder from the dusty world.'

'But my Master the Emperor is his son!' exclaimed Trinket. 'He's not an intruder!'

'For one who has entered within the portals of the Lord Buddha,' pronounced Yulin, 'family is no longer family. From that time forth, wife and children are all of them intruders.'

Trinket found this very hard to accept. He went on to offer his services as a simple guard in attendance on the Old Emperor, but Yulin politely brushed the idea aside, brought the palms of his hands together, closed his eyes, and drifted off again.

Father Aureole rose to his feet, retreated to the door, and bowed to Yulin. Trinket pulled a face, stuck his tongue out and, putting the thumb of his right hand to his nose, twiddled his four fingers at the old bonze as if to say, 'Here's to you, you old fart!'

Yulin's eyes were closed, and he saw none of this.

When the three of them were outside again, Father Aureole spoke to Trinket:

'The Venerable Yulin is an extremely distinguished and enlightened member of our order. Now I must go and tell Father Crystal and the others they can leave. It has been a great privilege to meet you, my son. I must be on my way.'

He brought his palms together and bowed deeply. Clearly he had no intention of welcoming Trinket and his friends back to the monastery.

'Very well then,' replied Trinket, greatly mortified. 'Since you've obviously got a cunning plan up your sleeve, I'll just leave you to it!'

He sent Doublet to fetch Wurtle and their bearers, and they all set off back down the hill to the Holy Precinct Monastery.

A Strong Bond

Back in his room in the monastery, Trinket sat, chin on hand, lost in thought.

'So: I've seen His Old Majesty, and he's not a bit old—but he's in serious danger! What with the lamas and the Mystic Dragons all after him, and that old fart of a bald turtle Yulin, who's a pretentious idiot, and Father Aureole, who's no use to man or beast . . . I give the Old Emperor a few days at the most. What am I going to tell Misty? I mustn't let him down! What *am* I going to do?'

He looked up at Doublet, and saw that her face was locked in a frown.

'What's the trouble?' he asked her.

'Oh, nothing.'

'Come on, I can see there's something troubling you. Tell me what it is.'

'No, really, it's nothing.'

'I know what it is: you're cross with me for not telling you that I actually worked for the Emperor in the Palace?'

'How could you?' burst out Doublet, her face flushing. 'How could you do such a thing? The Tartars are wicked, wicked people! And to think that you're one of them!'

Tears were running down both her cheeks. Trinket stared at her a moment.

'Silly girl! There's no need to cry!'

'My Lady gave me to you,' sobbed Doublet, 'to serve and obey. But how can I? My father and mother, my two brothers, were all of them killed by the very people you work for . . .'

She started wailing out loud.

For an instant Trinket seemed at a loss what to say. Then suddenly he made up his mind.

'All right then. I'd better tell you the truth. All of that Palace stuff is just a front. Really I'm working for the Triads. I'm Lodge Master of the Green Wood Lodge, and I'm working on a top-secret mission in the Palace, collecting information . . . If the Tartars ever get to know, my life will be in danger.'

Doublet held her hand to his lips and whispered:

'Shush! I'm sorry. I should never have made you tell me.'

A smile of joy lit up her tear-streaked face.

'So you are a good person after all! I knew you had to be! How stupid I've been . . .'

'No, on the contrary, you're very clever.'

He took her hand, and sat her down next to him on the kang. He told her all about the two Emperors, whispering into her ear, and painted the Old Emperor's present situation in a desperate light. Then he talked about the two of them.

'You and I will never part,' he said. 'We'll always be together.'

Doublet blushed.

'I'll never leave you,' she whispered. 'Unless, of course, you send me packing . . .'

Trinket raised his hand to his throat and made a sideways chopping motion.

'If I ever send you packing, may my head be chopped from my body!'

Doublet copied his gesture, and they both burst out laughing.

Doublet had always conformed to the role of servant, and hardly ever allowed herself to smile, let alone laugh, in her master's presence. The open way in which he had just spoken to her made her feel strangely happy. The bond between them grew stronger and more intimate as a result.

Dangerous Thoughts breed Danger

Trinket and Doublet sat there for a long while discussing the Old Emperor's predicament and the possible ways of saving him from the threat of capture. Finally Trinket hit upon the idea of pre-empting their rivals by kidnapping him first themselves. With this plan in mind, they set off back to the Pure Coolness Monastery.

'We'd better wait for dark,' said Trinket.

They hid among some trees and waited for night to fall.

'Luckily for us,' whispered Trinket, 'the Abbot's the only trained fighter in the monastery, and he's wounded and certain to be resting in bed. You had better immobilize that big fat monk, Brother Headlong, and I'll look after His Old Majesty. Just watch out for that golden cudgel of his!'

Doublet nodded.

Under cover of darkness they crept stealthily through the monastery grounds to the little hermitage where Shun Zhi was staying. The wooden double-door was closed, but the damage done to it earlier had still not been repaired and Doublet was easily able to pull open the left leaf. As she did so there was a golden flash and a great bellow, and the golden cudgel came shooting out of the doorway. In that instant, as the cudgel was raised to begin its devastating descent, Doublet dived in underneath it and shot out two fingers, aiming with deadly accuracy at two Vital Points on the giant's chest. Even as she did so she whispered:

'Very sorry!'

At the same time she caught hold of the great cudgel with both hands. Brother Headlong sank slowly to the ground. The cudgel must have weighed at least a hundred catties, and it was a good thing Doublet got hold of it, or it would have come falling down and crushed her feet.

Trinket meanwhile opened the other half of the door and darted in. In the dark interior he could just make out the figure of a man sitting on a prayer-mat. He fell to his knees and kowtowed.

'Your humble servant Trinket, Majesty. I'm the one who came to save you earlier today. Don't be scared.'

Brother Wayward said not a word.

'Your Majesty,' continued Trinket, 'it is of course an excellent thing that you should spend your days in prayer and meditation. The trouble is, there are evil men outside who want to lay hands on you and take you away, so it would be much safer if we could move you somewhere a little more out of their reach.'

Still no response.

'So, if you don't mind, I'd like you to come along with me.'

Brother Wayward just sat there, cross-legged and silent. Trinket's eyes were used to the dark by now, and he could see that Brother Wayward was sitting in exactly the same position as his teacher, the Venerable Yulin, had been. He could not tell if he was in a deep meditative trance and therefore unaware of Trinket's presence, or just consciously trying to ignore him.

'Your presence here, Your Majesty, is no longer a secret. Those men have gone for the time being, but others will be back. We must get you to a safe place.'

Silence.

Then suddenly Brother Headlong spoke.

'It was very kind of you young people to come to my Master's rescue earlier today. My Master is meditating, and when he is meditating, he never speaks to anyone. Where are you wanting to take him?'

His voice, usually a great bellowing roar, had been reduced to a hoarse croak.

Trinket rose to his feet.

'Anywhere away from here. Anywhere your Master would like to go. Anywhere those wicked people can't get hold of him. Then you can both carry on meditating to your hearts' content.'

He told Doublet to release Brother Headlong's points, which she did by pressing him in the small of the back and below his ribs. Brother Headlong now addressed his Master, in a tone of great reverence:

'Sire, these children want us to take refuge from here.'

Finally Brother Wayward spoke. It was the first time Trinket had heard his voice. It was ringing and clear.

'My teacher said nothing about leaving this monastery.'

'But they are right,' insisted Brother Headlong. 'It is very dangerous here.'

'All things are born in the mind,' replied Brother Wayward. 'Dangerous thoughts breed danger. Peaceful thoughts breed peace.

All the killing earlier today has created a great deal of bad karma. We must have no more of such wild behaviour.'

Brother Headlong was silent for a moment, then replied:

'Your words are true, Master.'

He turned to Trinket.

'My Master refuses to leave. You have heard him.'

Trinket frowned.

'Then they'll take him and slice him up into little pieces! Do you want him to die?'

'Death comes to us all sooner or later,' replied Brother Head- long. 'What difference does a few years more or less make?'

'What difference?' disagreed Trinket boldly. 'Are you telling me there's no difference between being alive and being dead? Or between being a man and being a woman? Or between being a monk and being a putrid turtle?'

'Indeed,' replied Brother Headlong. 'All living things are equal.'

'Stone the crows!' thought Trinket to himself. 'No wonder they're called Headlong and Wayward! At this rate I'll never get them out of here! I can hardly immobilize the Old Emperor and carry him out on a stretcher . . .'

He ransacked his brains for a plan. Finally, in despair, he blurted out:

'Well, if all living things are equal, I suppose that means that Lady Donggo and the other Empress were equal too? In which case, why all the fuss in the first place? Why go to all the trouble of leaving the dusty world behind and becoming a hermit?'

That did it. Brother Wayward leapt to his feet.

'What . . . what did you say?'

His voice was trembling. Almost before he had spoken, Trinket had regretted his words. He fell to his knees.

'Your Majesty, I beg you—don't be angry at my foolishness!'

'The past is over and forgotten,' replied Brother Wayward. 'It is many a year since I was last addressed as Majesty. Rise, there is something I wish to ask you.'

Trinket rose, thinking to himself, 'At least I've managed to get him talking.'

'Tell me,' continued Brother Wayward, 'when did you learn about the two Empresses?'

'I heard the eunuch Hai Dafu talking to the Empress Dowager.'

'You know about Hai Dafu? Tell me, how is he?'

'The Empress Dowager killed him.'

Brother Wayward drew in a sharp breath.

'He's dead?'

'Yes. She used Soft Crush karate to kill him.'

'But . . . she never knew any Martial Arts.'

The Old Emperor's voice trembled.

'How do you know all this?'

'They fought in the garden outside the Empress Dowager's palace. I saw it with my own eyes.'

'Who exactly are you?'

'My name is Trinket Wei. I'm Deputy Intendant of the Palace Guards.' He added: 'I'm here at His Majesty's express command. I have a letter in His Majesty's own hand.'

He held out the letter for Brother Wayward, who stared at it a moment before taking it. After a long silence he sighed.

'Is the Young Emperor well? Is he . . . happy being Emperor?'

'As soon as the Young Emperor learned that Your Majesty was alive,' replied Trinket, 'he wanted to grow wings and fly here to be with you! But then . . . then he remembered his duties, and knew that he had to stay at Court. So he sent me instead. The moment I've reported back, he will come himself.'

'There is no need for him to come.' The Old Emperor's voice was shaking. 'He is a good ruler. He puts affairs of state above his own feelings. Not like me . . .'

He sounded as if he might choke at any minute. Trinket could hear that he was weeping. He decided to make use of this opportunity to communicate what he knew.

'Old Hai Dafu worked the whole thing out. It was the Empress Dowager who killed them all. First she killed Prince Rong, then the Empress Donggo, then her sister, Lady Zhen. After that she killed the Young Emperor's own mother, the Empress Kang. As soon as the Empress Dowager realized that the cat was out of the bag (because Old Hai knew all about it), she killed him as well. Then she sent a gang of men here to try and kill Your Majesty! She'll stop at nothing!'

Shun Zhi had already learned from Old Hai that *someone*, a kungfu specialist of an especially sinister sort, had been responsible for the deaths of his baby son, his beloved consort, and her sister. After reporting this to his Lord and Master, Old Hai had returned to the Palace to continue his investigations into the identity of the murderer. But the Old Emperor simply could not bring himself to believe that it was his wife, the present Empress Dowager, who had done it. He sighed.

'But she knows nothing of the Martial Arts. It *can't* have been her.'

'You wouldn't say that, Your Majesty, if you'd been there in the garden.'

Trinket then gave him a detailed, word-for-word account of what he had seen and heard pass between the Empress Dowager and Old Hai that night.

Shun Zhi had always been a devoted son and an upright man. His passion for the Empress Donggo (she whom the Old Whore had called the Fox Lady) had quite swept him off his feet. It was after her death that he had totally lost interest in being the Lord-of-all-beneath-the-Heavens, and had instead taken refuge in this hermitage. All these years he had devoted himself to the practice of Zen meditation. But Empress Donggo was still deeply etched in his memory, and Trinket's words had awoken all his old passion. For the moment, the spirit of transcendent detachment was driven from his mind. As Trinket went over the details of the plot uncovered by Hai Dafu, the Old Emperor's heart filled with grief and rage.

'She'll stop at nothing,' Trinket repeated. 'First she'll kill you, then she'll kill the Young Emperor. Then she'll dig up the Empress Donggo's grave, and have all the copies of her *Sayings* destroyed. She says they're full of rubbish and any family found with a copy of it should be put to death!'

This last part was entirely his own fabrication. But it stirred Brother Wayward to even further indignation.

'Vile woman!' he cried, angrily slapping his thigh. 'I should have had her deposed! Look at the havoc she is wreaking!'

When he was Emperor, he had in fact wished to depose her and put his beloved Empress Donggo in her place. But his own mother had prevented him from doing so.

'So you see, Your Majesty, to save your own son's life, and to save the grave of the Empress Donggo from being defiled, we *must* stop her! Even if *you* think that death and life are one and the same, it's still important to stop that woman from killing other people.'

Shun Zhi had always been an impulsive sort of person. Having come to the throne at the age of seven, he had been no more than twenty-four years old when he sought refuge in the hermitage on Wutai. He was still now only a year or two over thirty. He believed Trinket implicitly.

'Thank goodness you told me all of this! You are right! Brother Headlong, we must leave at once. Otherwise a disaster will occur.'

'Yes, Master!'

Brother Headlong grasped his golden cudgel in one hand, and with the other pushed open the door of the hermitage. There, standing in the doorway, he saw the figure of a man. In the darkness, he was unable to make out the man's face.

'Who are you?'

He raised his golden cudgel.

'Where are you going?' was the man's response.

Recognizing the voice, Brother Headlong gave a start, threw his cudgel to the ground, and brought his hands together in salutation.

'Shifu!' he cried.

Brother Wayward echoed his cry.

It was the Venerable Yulin.

'I heard everything that was said just now.'

He enunciated his words slowly.

'Oh dear!' thought Trinket silently to himself. 'This could mean trouble.'

Yulin continued, speaking in a sombre tone:

'The karma of this world allows no such thing as escape. It must be fulfilled. Every action has its ineluctable and immutable consequence. Try to escape it, and it will follow you.'

Brother Wayward was already kneeling at his feet.

'Yes, Shifu! You speak the truth. Your disciple understands.'

'I fear that your understanding is still deficient. If your wife of former times is indeed seeking you out, if she bears an ill will towards you, if she feels hatred for you, if she wishes to take your life; then you must look deep within yourself, you must let her hate, you must let her kill, you must let this karma be fulfilled. Try to escape from her, and the karma will remain; send someone to kill her, and you will create yet more karma.'

'Yes, Shifu,' said Brother Wayward, his voice trembling.

'Up yours, you fat bald-pated turtle-bonze!' Trinket muttered quietly to himself. 'Damn you! Sod you! Blast you to smithereens! Slice your bald pate open and cram your fat smelly head full of your own stinking karma!'

Yulin continued:

'The Tibetan Lama and his associates, however, are a different story. They and their plotting must be stopped. They want to lay hands on you and then, having done so, they will use you to control the Young Emperor. They will do wicked things and cruelly abuse the common people. They will create evil karma. We cannot simply stand by and let them wreak havoc. So, this place is no longer safe; for the present, you must come with me and move to the small temple up the hill.'

He turned and set off at once, and the two Brothers followed him, with Trinket and Doublet (whose presence the Venerable Shifu continued completely to ignore) trailing behind them. When they came to Yulin's little hillside retreat, the Shifu sat down again cross-legged on his prayer-mat and recommenced his meditations. Wayward sat on the mat next to his Shifu and followed his example. Headlong took a good look around first, and then did likewise. Yulin and Wayward brought their hands together immediately and closed their eyes, and sat there totally motionless. Headlong kept his eyes wide open at first, and sat staring into space, then finally he too closed his eyes, letting his hands rest in his lap. After a few minutes, one of his hands strayed towards his cudgel, just to make sure it was still there.

Trinket pulled a face at Doublet, and then he too went through a whole performance of sitting on a mat. Doublet sat next to him. Trinket was Restless Monkey Incarnate, and he would rather have died than sit motionless on a prayer-mat for more than a minute or two. But there was no question of running off and abandoning the Old Emperor. He kept wriggling around, and taking hold of Doublet's hand and tickling her palm. She managed not to laugh, but pointed warningly in the direction of the meditating monks.

After an hour or so of this, Trinket suddenly had one of his brainwaves.

'The Old Emperor may be a monk, but surely even monks occasionally have to relieve themselves. . . . I'll wait till he needs a piss, and then I'll try and trick him into escaping.'

This new plan set his mind considerably at ease.

After another period of meditative silence, they suddenly heard the unmistakable sound of tramping boots in the distance. It sounded as if a mighty horde of aggressors was on its way up towards the monastery. Headlong's face twitched. He instinctively reached for his cudgel, and opened his eyes wide. He saw that his Master and Shifu Yulin were still frozen, and after a moment's hesitation he let go of the cudgel and closed his eyes again.

Trinket could now quite clearly hear the sound of rampaging going on within the monastery.

'When they can't find him there,' he thought to himself, 'they're bound to come up here. And what are you going to do about that, Bald Pate?'

Sure enough, less than an hour later, they heard the mob burst out onto the rear hill and begin making its way through the darkness towards the little temple. There were cries of 'Search! Search!'

Headlong now leapt to his feet with his cudgel in one hand, and stood barring the doorway. Trinket stole across to the window and looked outside. By the light of the moon, all he could make out was a crowd of heads. Back inside, Wayward and his Shifu were still sitting motionless.

'What should we do?' whispered Doublet.

'In a minute,' Trinket whispered back, 'when they break in, we'll escape with the Old Emperor out the back!'

After a brief pause he continued:

'If we get separated, we'll meet up again at the Holy Precinct Monastery.'

Doublet nodded.

Brother Headlong guarded the doorway of the little temple single-handed against the yelling saffron-robed mob, his bulky frame all but blocking the entrance. In the ensuing confusion, by some miracle, nine pairs of grey-robed monks appeared as if from nowhere, succeeded in squeezing past him, and sat down cross-legged inside the temple. Trinket found all of this highly intriguing. Another monk in the place, and there wouldn't be room to move. If the eighteen new arrivals were fighters of the same calibre as Father Aureole, they would be able to hold the building against all comers.

Suddenly, above all the shouting, an old man's voice could be heard outside, crying:

'So the Shaolin monks want to take this on their heads, do they?'

Not a word came by way of reply from the eighteen monks within.

'Very well, then,' continued the old man's voice from outside.

'If the Eighteen Lohans of Shaolin are determined to make a show
of this, we'd best be off!'

Just as he had advised, the crowd then disbanded.

Trinket studied the new arrivals. Some of them were ancient,
wizened bonzes well into their seventies and eighties, some of
them were middle-aged monks. There were tall and short, good-
looking and ugly; and judging from the protuberances sticking out
through their gowns, they were all armed with weapons of some
kind.

'So these are the Eighteen Fighting Lohans of Shaolin! No
wonder that old Bald Pate Yulin wasn't scared! He'd got it fixed up
all along! He knew he had this lot to back him up! This is too weird!
I'm out of my depth! I'm wasting my time here!'

He went over to Wayward, and knelt on the ground before
him.

'Your Holy Majesty, I don't think I'm needed any more. I'd
best be on my way. Do you have any instructions for me to take
back?'

Wayward opened his eyes and gave a little smile.

'I am obliged to you for your trouble. Please tell His Majesty
not to bother coming to Wutai. He would only be disturbing my
peace. Even if he were to come, I would not be able to see him.
Tell him, if he wishes to keep the Empire at peace, he must remember one thing: *never raise taxes*. Tell him never to forget that. Then
he will have done well by me, and I shall be happy.'

'Yes, Sire!'

Wayward reached into the bosom of his gown and produced
a little package.

'I want you to give this little Sutra to your Master. Tell him,
in all things, to follow the course of Nature. Never try to force the
outcome of events. If we Manchus can bring blessings and pros-
perity to the Chinese people, well and good. If not, and they want
us to leave, then we should go back to the place from which we
came.'

He patted the Sutra.

'I know what *this* is,' thought Trinket to himself, remembering Auntie Tao's tale. 'It's another copy of the *Sutra in Forty-Two
Sections*!'

He held out his hands to receive it.

Wayward was silent a moment, then told Trinket to depart.
Trinket made his way to the door, but just before leaving he turned
to old Yulin and muttered:

'Hey, old bonze, with all that sitting you have to do, don't you ever need to piss?'

When Trinket arrived back at the Holy Precinct Monastery, he opened the little package. Sure enough, it was another copy of the Sutra, this time bound in yellow silk.

'So should I give it to the Emperor or not?' wondered Trinket. 'I've got five copies already, and this one makes six. Two more, and I'll have the whole set. Such a shame to give it away. Luckily, old Wayward said that even if the Emperor *does* go to Wutai, he definitely won't see him, so *he'll* never know even if I don't pass on the Sutra.'

But then he reflected that Kang Xi was his friend, and to pocket something belonging to a friend went against all the values of River and Lake. Perhaps he had better give it to him after all.

Fat Dhuta and the Eighteen Lohans of Shaolin

The next morning, Trinket led Doublet, Wurtle, and the rest of the party down the mountain, feeling extremely pleased at the way things had turned out. He had not only succeeded in completing his Wutai mission, by finding and speaking to the Old Emperor, as Kang Xi had wished; he had also acquired a delightful new companion. Doublet was at the same time beautiful, sweet-natured, and a brilliant kungfu fighter.

They had walked about three or four miles, when they came upon what looked like a pilgrim travelling in the opposite direction, going up the mountain. He was very tall, almost as tall as the crazy Brother Headlong. But Headlong was strongly built, whereas this man was quite extraordinarily skinny. His gruesomely cadaverous appearance made the scrawny old abbot, Father Aureole, seem positively fat by comparison. His head was an oblong box of bones, with a pair of cavernous eyes hollowed into it, and long hair dangling down to his shoulders, fastened around the forehead with a copper band. His loose cotton gown flapped around him as he walked, like a robe draped over a clothes-rack.

Somewhat daunted by this strange apparition, Trinket averted his gaze, and moved to the side of the road to let the ascetic pass. But the man stopped right in front of him, and asked:

'Are you on your way down from Pure Coolness Monastery?'

'No,' replied Trinket. 'As a matter of fact, we've come from the Monastery of the Holy Precinct.'

The Dhuta (for so such ascetics were called) reached out his left hand, and placed it on Trinket's shoulder. Then he twisted him forcibly around, and looked him in the face.

'Would you by any chance be Laurel Goong-goong from the Imperial Palace?' he asked.

As he asked the question, he pressed his hand down on Trinket's shoulder, causing the boy's entire body to go limp and immobilizing him in an instant.

'What a ridiculous suggestion!' he cried. 'Do I look like a eunuch? I'm Mr Wei from Yangzhou.'

'Hands off my master!' shouted Doublet. 'How dare you treat him like that!'

The Dhuta reached out his right hand, and grasped her by the shoulder too.

'*You* sound like a eunuch,' he said.

Doublet lowered her shoulder, and at the same time jabbed her index finger smartly at his Celestial Gully point, hitting the spot with her usual precision. But there was no give in the Dhuta's body. It felt as hard as an iron plate. Instead, Doublet herself felt an excruciating pain. The impact had all but shattered her finger. She gave a cry, and in that same instant a searing pain shot through her shoulder as the Dhuta's giant hand swooped down on it.

He chuckled darkly.

'Not a bad fighter, for a little eunuch! Not at all bad!'

Doublet now delivered a flying kick with her left foot, catching him squarely in the groin. It was like kicking a rock.

'Aiyo!' she cried, the tears running down her cheeks.

'Good move, little eunuch!' said the Dhuta. 'Excellent!'

'I'm *not* a eunuch!' she protested. '*You're* the one who's a eunuch!'

'Do I look like a eunuch?' said the Dhuta with a nasty-looking leer.

'Get your hand off me!' screamed Doublet, ' If you don't let go, I'll cry rape!'

'Think I'm frightened of you?' cried the Dhuta, and with Trinket in his left hand and Doublet in his right, he hoisted them both up into the air and set off up the mountain, striding at a great pace.

Trinket and Doublet began screaming and shouting, but the Dhuta ignored them both, and began to run uphill at a phenomenal speed, carrying them with as much ease as if they were weightless. Wurtle and the bearers watched, transfixed with amazement.

The Dhuta took a precipitous path up the mountainside, scrambling up it as if it was a flat surface. Trinket heard the wind whistling past his ears as they flew along.

'This Dhuta's like a cross between a troll and a mountain goat!' he muttered to himself.

After a while, the Dhuta deposited them on the ground, and pointed to a towering mountain ahead of them, its peak lost in a vista of foggy cloud.

'If you don't tell me the truth, I'll take you up there and drop you from the very top.'

'All right, I'll tell you the truth,' replied Trinket promptly.

'Smart lad!' said the Dhuta. 'So, who are you actually? And who is this little boy?'

'Well . . . as a matter of fact, Your Reverence, she isn't a little boy . . . she's my . . . my . . .'

'Well?'

'My . . . my wife!'

Both the Dhuta and Doublet started when they heard the word 'wife'. Doublet flushed a rosy pink.

'Your wife?' asked the Dhuta suspiciously.

'Yes! And now I really *am* telling you the truth,' declared Trinket. 'You see, I'm not really from Yangzhou: I'm actually from a very rich family in Peking, and I went and fell madly in love with the girl next door. We got secretly engaged in my garden, but her father wouldn't let us get married, so we had to elope. How could a pretty girl like her be a eunuch? If you don't believe me, take off her hat and see for yourself.'

This the Dhuta promptly did, uncovering a head of fine long hair. In those days, Chinese men had to shave the front half of their head and grow a pigtail, except for Buddhist monks and Dhutas (who shaved the whole head), and Taoist monks (who let their hair grow long). There was no doubt left in the Dhuta's mind. Doublet was a member of the female sex.

'Holy Father,' Trinket continued, 'please don't land us in trouble! We'll be put to death. I'll give you a thousand taels to let us go!'

'You're obviously not a eunuch,' mused the Dhuta out loud. 'No eunuch would have the guts to elope with a girl. Hm, you seem quite a brave little fellow . . .'

He let go of him.

'So what are you doing here on the Wutai Mountains?'

'We came to pray to Lord Buddha, and to ask for his bless-ing: I want to do well in my exams,' said Trinket, 'and then she—my wife—can be a proper lady.'

Needless to say, all this stuff about a 'secret engagement' and 'doing well in the exams' was something Trinket had picked up from the Yangzhou storytellers.

The Dhuta pondered this for a moment. Finally he said:

'I seem to have mistaken you for somebody else. Off you go now, both of you!'

Trinket was delighted.

'Thank you very much, Holy Father,' he said. 'We'll certainly remember you in our prayers.'

He took Doublet by the hand and they set off down the mountain again. They had only walked a few steps when the Dhuta cried out after them:

'Wait a minute! There's something not quite right here! Come back, both of you! You, little girl, you're not a bad fighter. You caught me with your finger right on the Celestial Gully, and landed me a very nasty kick in the groin. . . . Not bad.'

He was rubbing his Vital Point while he was saying this. He continued:

'Who taught you your kungfu? And which School is it?'

Doublet was not accustomed to lying. She flushed and shook her head.

'It's a family tradition. Her mother taught her,' Trinket told him.

'What's her mother's name?'

'Well . . . I'm afraid I really can't tell you that.'

'Why not? Go on, tell me her name!'

'My family name is Zhuang,' said Doublet.

'Zhuang?' repeated the Dhuta, shaking his head. 'That's not right, you're lying to me! I've never heard of a Shifu called Zhuang.'

'There are so many Shifus in this world . . .' put in Trinket.

'Who asked you? Don't interrupt!' said the Dhuta angrily, tapping Trinket on the shoulder.

He had only tapped lightly, for fear of hurting the boy. But the moment his hand made contact with Trinket's shoulder, he sensed an immediate counter-motion, an almost impalpable shift-ing of Inner Force. Trinket had used the move known as Grass

Bending in the Wind, twisting his shoulder, turning his body around, then raising his left hand to guard his face, while preparing his right for a sudden attack. The Dhuta was taken aback by this well-executed move. He snatched at Trinket's chest, and Trinket instantly jabbed with his right hand, a move known as Mystic Snake Quits Its Lair. He struck with precision at the Dhuta's neck, but it was like driving his hand into an unyielding piece of iron. He screamed with the pain.

Doublet now flew into the attack with both hands. The Dhuta succeeded in closing the Vital Points on Trinket's chest, then turned around to face his new opponent. Doublet crouched low and leapt high into the air, moving and striking with extraordinary speed and dexterity, but the Dhuta was more than a match for her. He ended up seizing hold of both her hands, and closed her points with a corkscrew motion of his left elbow.

He turned to Trinket.

'So—you said you were a rich young man from Peking. How come you know the Catch-Can of the Mystic Dragon School of Liaodong?'

'Is there a law against it? Are only poor people allowed to practise it?' answered Trinket, playing for time.

But he was thinking to himself: 'What does he mean by the Mystic Dragon School, I wonder? Ah . . . yes, the Old Devil once told me about the Old Whore only pretending to use Wudang moves, when actually she was using Snake Island karate. I bet Mystic Dragon Island is just a fancy name for Snake Island. It must be! They call themselves Dragons because Snakes would sound too common. Misty learned some of his stuff from the Old Whore, so he must have passed it on to me. That's where I got it from.'

'Well?' said the Dhuta. 'Who is your Shifu?'

Trinket's thoughts ran on: 'I can't tell him that the moves were taught me by the Old Whore. If I do that, I'm done for: that's as good as confessing that I'm a Palace Eunuch.'

So instead he replied: 'I was taught a bit by one of my uncle's girlfriends, a fat lady called Liu Yan.'

The Dhuta was visibly thrown by this.

'Liu Yan? A girlfriend of your uncle's? What uncle?'

'His name's Wei, Treasure Wei.' (Trinket to the power of ten!) 'He's a very smart Peking gentleman. A very good-looking man, who likes to throw his money around. The fat lady fell for him at first sight, and since then she's been coming to our house all the time, jumping in and out over the garden wall in the middle of the night. I kept pestering her to teach me kungfu, so she taught me a thing or two.'

The Dhuta was almost inclined to believe him.

'What about your uncle? Does *he* know any kungfu?'

'My uncle? You must be joking!' Trinket burst out laughing. 'Auntie Liu was always grabbing him by the collar, and dragging him all round the house.'

The Dhuta asked a whole series of questions concerning Sister Swallow's shape and appearance, which Trinket was able to answer with total accuracy, adding that she loved to wear red embroidered shoes. This last detail clinched it. The Dhuta was now convinced of the truth of Trinket's story. He reached out his hand and tapped him lightly on the midriff, intending to open his Vital Point and send him on his way. But as bad luck would have it, his hand never touched the point. It hit instead upon the very spot where Trinket had secreted the Sutra.

'What have we here?' asked the Dhuta.

'Just a wad of banknotes I stole from home.'

'Rubbish! It's much too thick!'

The Dhuta reached forward, extracted the packet from Trinket's inner pocket, and unwrapped it. He was stunned by what he saw.

'The Sutra! The Sutra!' he shouted, a big grin spreading all over his face.

He hurriedly wrapped the Sutra up again, and placed it in the bosom of his own gown. He grasped Trinket by the chest, and lifted him up into the air.

'Where did you get this?' he yelled at him.

This was no easy question.

'Well . . . it's a . . . a long story,' stammered Trinket nervously. 'I'll need some time to explain everything . . .'

He was playing for time again, trying to figure out a story that would not only convince the Dhuta of the Sutra's origins (that was easy enough), but also persuade him to relinquish possession of it.

'Who gave it to you?' the Dhuta asked loudly.

Trinket from his vantage point in mid-air caught sight of a party of seven or eight monks in grey climbing up the mountain-side. He was soon able to identify them as some of the Eighteen Shaolin Lohans whom he had seen in the temple behind the Pure Coolness Monastery. When the Dhuta swivelled him in a new direction, he saw a few more clambering up from the west. He counted. Yes, there were altogether eighteen of them. Trinket cheered silently to himself:

'Damn you, you putrid Dhuta! You'll never beat the Eighteen Lohans of Shaolin, not in a month of Zen Sundays!'

'Tell me, quickly!' the Dhuta barked. 'Where did you get it from?'

He noticed Trinket looking around and, following his line of vision, spotted the monks climbing slowly from the east, north, and west. But he did not seem particularly concerned.

'What are they doing up here?' he asked nonchalantly.

'The fame of your kungfu has probably reached them, and they want to be your disciples!' Trinket taunted him.

'I don't take disciples,' the Dhuta said, somewhat obtusely, shaking his head. 'Hey, you bonzes,' he bellowed. 'Scram! Go away!'

His mighty voice echoed across the valley.

But the monks continued climbing until finally they reached the spot where the Dhuta was standing. One of them, an old monk with especially long eyebrows, placed his palms together, and said:

'Reverend Father, are you the renowned Fat Dhuta from Liaodong?'

Trinket, still dangling in mid-air, couldn't help laughing. The old monk was surely mocking old Bag-of-Bones.

To his great surprise the Dhuta replied loudly in the affirmative.

'Yes, I am the Fat Dhuta. And I don't take disciples. Who are you?'

'I am Brother Cordial of the Shaolin Monastery,' replied the old monk. 'I have the honour of presiding over the Dharma Hall. These are my seventeen Brothers, who all hail from the same place.'

The Dhuta put Trinket down.

'Ah. . . . So you are the Eighteen Lohans of Shaolin. Well, if it's a fight you're after, I'm afraid I can't oblige. You can hardly expect me to take all of you on single-handed.'

'We have no cause to fight. We are all believers in the same faith,' protested Brother Cordial, still holding his palms together. 'It is our most excellent karma to meet you today. We have long heard tell of the unmatched kungfu prowess of the Two Dhutas of Liaodong—yourself and your brother-in-arms, the Thin Dhuta.

As for ourselves, we are unworthy of the name we bear. The Eighteen Lohans of old were holy men. We were merely given their name as a small mark of esteem by our friends in the Martial Arts fraternity.'

The other seventeen monks brought their palms together and bowed.

Fat Dhuta bowed back.

'What brings you here to Wutai?' he asked.

'There is a karmic bond between our Shaolin Monastery and this young gentleman,' said Brother Cordial, pointing to Trinket. 'We would like to ask you to show him mercy and release him.'

Fat Dhuta hesitated a moment, reflecting that he was greatly outnumbered. These were formidable fighters whom he could only hope to handle in single combat.

'Very well. I shall set him free out of respect for Your Holiness!'

He bent down and opened Trinket's point by rubbing lightly on his midriff. Trinket stood up at once and reached out his right palm.

'Give me back the Sutra,' he said to the Dhuta. 'It was given to me by a friend of these Eighteen Lohans. He asked me to take it . . . to the Shaolin Monastery and hand it over to the Abbot. So I'd like it back!'

'What?' Fat Dhuta screamed with fury. 'What's the Sutra got to do with the Shaolin Monastery?'

'Never you mind! You stole it from me!' Trinket had raised his voice. 'Hand it over or else!'

'Nonsense!' cried Fat Dhuta, turning around and setting off rapidly down the north face of the mountain.

Three of the Shaolin monks instantly leapt to their feet and tried to snatch him by the arms. Fat Dhuta dared not take them on, but eluded them effectively despite his great height by stepping nimbly to one side and dodging their threefold attack. This form of snatch is a branch of kungfu at which Shaolin monks excel. But the monks failed even to touch the hem of his gown. In an instant, four more monks had positioned themselves behind the Dhuta, barring his way with their interwoven open palms.

Fat Dhuta drew in a lungful of air and, letting out an ear-piercing scream, he thrust both palms forwards in the powerful move known as the Five Founding Fathers. Taking advantage of its phenomenal force, he spun round and dashed off towards the south. The four monks behind him opened their palms simultaneously, and attacked from left and right.

Meanwhile, Fat Dhuta caught a glimpse of three more snatching attacks coming at him from behind, as well as two karate blows on his left. He instantly leapt to his feet and threw himself kicking into mid-air. But the wide variety of claw-like snatches behind him—the Dragon, the Tiger, the Hawk—struck terror into his heart. He flailed his sleeves like a whirlwind, then landed on his left foot, seizing hold of Trinket with his right hand.

'Do you want him dead or alive?' he cried.

The Lohans—all eighteen of them—formed two circles, one inside the other. Fat Dhuta was trapped in the very centre.

'The Sutra is very important to this young gentleman,' said Brother Cordial. 'So please be so kind as to return it to him. If you do this virtuous deed, we will all appreciate your kindness.'

Fat Dhuta dangled Trinket high in the air with his right hand and, placing his left hand on the very crown of the boy's head, he broke through the double circle and strode off down the south face of the mountain.

The gravity of the situation was pretty clear. If the monks tried to stop the Dhuta, he would crush Trinket's head simply by applying a little extra pressure with his left hand. The monks standing in his path showed a momentary hesitation, but finally withdrew to one side.

Fat Dhuta went hurtling onwards to the south with Trinket, running faster and faster. The Eighteen Lohans glided closely behind him, hovering above the ground and moving at what seemed superhuman speed.

At this moment, Doublet, whose points had already been opened by the Shaolin monks, seeing that Trinket had been carried off, hurried in pursuit. She was a formidable fighter for her age, but not equal to the Shaolin monks in terms of her Inner Force. She found herself lagging a long way behind them. She was suddenly overcome by a sense of hopelessness, and burst into tears. Ahead of her she could see Fat Dhuta carrying Trinket with him, easily outrunning every single one of the Shaolin monks.

Fat Dhuta was now rushing with Trinket towards a high peak to the south. The Lohans spread out in a line chasing after them. By the time Doublet had reached the foot of the mountain, she was already out of breath. She looked up at the precipitous mountainside, wondering what terrible fate awaited her master. Suddenly a great rumbling interrupted her thoughts, and she saw a series of big rocks come rolling down the mountain. The Lohans evaded them by jumping to either side. Fat Dhuta was trying to deter his opponents from closing in, but his missiles failed to hit their targets.

Doublet took a deep breath before setting off up the peak.

The peak they were climbing was the southernmost peak of the Wutai Mountains. There are five main peaks on Wutai, and at the top of each of them is a monastery, each dedicated to a different manifestation of the Bodhisattva Manjusri, patron saint of the whole range. This one, criss-crossed with a maze of winding paths, was known as the Brocade Peak. Once Doublet reached the top, she saw the Shaolin monks positioned outside the monastery called the Monastery of Universal Salvation. Fat Dhuta and Trinket had already entered.

'Master! Master!' shouted Doublet, running directly into the monastery grounds, where she found Fat Dhuta standing under the eaves of the Great Buddha Hall, with Trinket still firmly grasped in his right hand.

Doublet dashed forwards.

'Master,' she cried, 'did he hurt you?'

'He wouldn't dare,' said Trinket.

'That's what you think?' bellowed Fat Dhuta furiously.

'If you dare to remove even one hair of my head,' said Trinket with a highly provocative smile, 'the Eighteen Shaolin Lohans will surely catch you, and change you back into the fat little dwarf you once were. Then you'll be in trouble!'

The colour drained from Fat Dhuta's face.

'What are you talking about?' he asked in a trembling voice. 'How . . . how . . . do you know?'

In fact, Trinket knew *nothing*. He had simply been improvising (in his usual fashion) his own explanation for the strange contradiction between Fat Dhuta's skinny appearance and his bulky name. He seemed to have stumbled upon the Dhuta's innermost secret by pure chance, and could sense the fear in the man's voice.

'I just know,' Trinket replied with an icy sneer.

'But the monks would never do me any harm,' said Fat Dhuta.

Without warning, he aimed a terrific kick with his right leg at a drum-shaped stone block, which flew with a great crash directly into the screen wall facing the gate of the monastery and instantly shattered into pieces, showering shards of stone everywhere.

The Dhuta turned to Doublet and bellowed:

'What are you doing here? Do you want to die?'

'If he lives I live, if he dies I die!' came the brave response. 'If you hurt him the least bit, I'll fight you till my last breath!'

'Tarmady!' blazed the Dhuta. 'What's so special about this little brat? Why do you care so much about what happens to *him*?'

Doublet flushed and hesitated before finally replying:

'My master is a good man, and you are wicked—that's why!'

'Amida Buddha! Amida Buddha!'

The voices of the Eighteen Lohans could be heard chanting outside.

'Honourable Fat Dhuta, please release the young gentleman, and give him back the Sutra! If you harm a child, you will be reviled on River and Lake!'

'Stop bothering me with your nonsense!' growled the Dhuta. 'Or I'll really give you something to worry about! I'll kill the child *and* destroy the Sutra.'

'Your Reverence, what are your terms for releasing the boy and returning the Sutra?' asked Brother Cordial.

'I can set him free, but I'm not going to return the Sutra, no matter what happens.'

The Eighteen Lohans outside all fell silent.

Fat Dhuta looked carefully all around the hall, figuring out how to make his escape. But suddenly a series of grey figures flashed before his eyes. The Eighteen Lohans had sneaked into the hall. Five of them were moving along the left-hand wall behind his back, another five along the right-hand wall. Once again he was surrounded.

'If you have the nerve, I'll fight you in single-handed combat!' he bellowed.

He raised his left foot and rested it on Trinket's head, giving a scornful sneer.

Turtle Stele

Breathing in the smell of the dirt on the Dhuta's sole, Trinket was both fearful and angry. Here he was, having his head trodden on by a smelly shoe, confused and unable to figure out what to do— his eyes darted around looking for some eye-catching object in the hall, anything around which he could concoct some drivel to attract Fat Dhuta's attention. Once he was distracted, then the Lohans could come to the rescue. Unfortunately Trinket's head was pinned to the ground and his field of vision was limited to what lay out in the courtyard. There he saw a big stone turtle with a large upright stone tablet on its back: an engraved stele with a long inscription.

'Fat Dhuta,' he called out, 'your dad's out there crawling around the courtyard, with a big boulder on his back! Don't you think it's a bit tough on him? Aren't you going to save him? You're not much of a son, are you!'

'What are you blathering on about? What's all this about my dad crawling in the courtyard?' replied Fat Dhuta angrily.

'And there are eight Sutras altogether, so what's the point of getting just one without the other seven?' continued Trinket.

'Where are the other seven?' asked Dhuta anxiously. 'Do you know?'

'Of course!'

'Where? Tell me! Or I'll squash your brain under my foot.'

'I didn't know until just a second ago . . .'

'A second ago? What are you trying to say?'

Trinket craned his neck to get a proper look at the stele. It was covered in rows and rows of squiggly seal-script characters, not one of which he could decipher (needless to say). This did not deter him in the slightest.

'There are in all,' he began to improvise, mimicking to perfection the tone of voice of someone reading from some ancient inscription, 'eight copies of the *Sutra in Forty-Two Sections*. Of these, the first copy is hidden in such-and-such Monastery on such-and-such Mountain in Henan Province—I'm afraid there are one or two bits I can't quite make out there . . .'

He made a great performance of squinting into the courtyard to get a better view of the inscription.

'The second copy is hidden in such-and-such Nunnery on such-and-such Mountain in Shanxi Province. . . . Fat Dhuta, I'm afraid I don't know the characters and they're rather worn. You're so clever at everything, I think you should try to have a look yourself.'

Fat Dhuta picked Trinket up by the scruff of the neck and edged his way closer to the doorway, from which vantage point he was able to get a clearer view of the stele. He peered at the inscription. It was certainly writing of some sort, but the Dhuta was quite unable to read it. He had never learned seal-script. Trinket meanwhile had begun again:

'The third copy is on such-and-such Mountain in Sichuan Province—I'm afraid I can't make that one out at all.'

Fat Dhuta had heard that there were eight copies of the Sutra, and that if (and only if) one could collect all eight of them one might be able to do something rather special (what it was exactly he had no idea). He also had absolutely no clue as to where they were, and no reason to doubt Trinket's charade. He relaxed his foot and dragged Trinket to his feet.

'And the fourth copy?'

Trinket squinted, and wagged his head from side to side.

'I just can't make it out . . .'

Fat Dhuta yanked him up, took three large steps forward, and deposited him right in front of the stele.

'I've got a terribly itchy scalp!' complained Trinket.

'What?'

'There are fleas in this place, and they're biting me to death! Fatty old friend, give my head a bit of a scratch. I'm itching too much to read the writing!'

Fat Dhuta removed Trinket's hat and began scratching his scalp with his massive fingers.

'Is that better?'

'No, over to the left! That's where they're biting me. You're too far over to the right!'

Fat Dhuta tried to oblige, but then Trinket protested that one of the fleas had jumped down his neck. The Dhuta gave up, released his wrist, and told him to scratch for himself.

'The little blighter,' exclaimed Trinket. 'It obviously hasn't had a meal for three or four years, it must be starved of blood. Once upon a time it was a fat, juicy, bouncing little thing, now it's all skin and bones . . .'

Fat Dhuta tried to ignore Trinket's taunts.

'Well, where's the fourth copy?'

Trinket strained his eyes once more.

'The fourth copy is on . . . such-and-such Mountain . . . in the . . . Dharma Hall of . . . the Shaolin Monastery . . .'

Fat Dhuta started.

'The Shaolin Monastery?'

Trinket knew he was scared of the Eighteen Lohans. He could see him glancing uneasily out of the corner of his eye.

'And the fifth?'

Trinket remembered Old Hai and the Old Whore talking

about the Wudang and Kongdong Mountains and their respective Schools of kungfu, so he decided to bury the fifth and sixth copies somewhere on their mystic peaks. Fat Dhuta's face was beginning to take on a scowling expression. The seventh copy, Trinket said, had fallen into the hands of the Mu Family, while the eighth was with some Satrap or other in Yunnan Province. . . . (If Fatty tried to beard Satrap Wu in his lair, thought Trinket, he'd be in for a bit of a scrap!)

This last invention of Trinket's suddenly brought a new expression to Fat Dhuta's face.

'Did you say the Satrap?' he growled.

Trinket hedged:

'I couldn't quite make it out, but I think so . . .'

Fat Dhuta was getting angry.

'Rubbish! That stone must be at least five hundred years old, and Satrap Wu's still alive!'

It was true. The stone, and the stone turtle it sat upon, were dark and worn and moss-covered, and must have been several hundred years old at least.

'Drat!' thought Trinket, aware that he had put his foot in it rather badly. He improvised again frantically:

'I told you I couldn't quite make it out. . . . It might be some other Satrap, not Satrap Wu at all! There must have been one in the olden days. Satrap Pooh, or Loo, or something! Wait a bit: there's some more writing underneath . . .'

Fat Dhuta's curiosity got the better of his anger (and his scepticism).

'Well, what does it say?'

Time to play the Snake Island card, Trinket calculated.

'It's really squiggly. . . . I can hardly make it out. Let me see now, something about Mystic Dragons. . . . Then there's something about "Long Life to Our Great Leader Hong" . . .'

Fat Dhuta went into a paroxysm of joy.

'I knew it! A miracle! It was prophesied in ancient times!'

'Yes, I think you're right,' said Trinket. 'Look down there, down in the left-hand corner. It says: "These words were spoken by the Great General Xu of the Mighty Tang dynasty, and this stone was erected by the Founder of the dynasty . . ." So it's a prophesy, made many years ago: one day, many days in the future, during the conquest of the Qing Tartars, a Great Leader will arise on Snake Island, and Long Life and Blessings will be his!'

Trinket had hit the jackpot. Fat Dhuta was hopping around with uncontrollable joy.

'I wonder what's written on the back of the stone,' said Trinket.

Fat Dhuta walked behind the stone tablet to have a look.

This was what Trinket was waiting for. He leapt up and ran for it. Fat Dhuta tried to grab him, but four of the Shaolin monks intercepted him, two on each side. He parried with his bare fists, and four more of the Lohans threw themselves into the fray. By now Trinket was safely out of reach.

There were now eight Lohans surrounding Fat Dhuta in a circle, striking out at him in a whirlwind of blows, each taking the other's place in rotation. It was clearly a formation they had mastered from lifelong practice. Fat Dhuta fought well, but he was hopelessly outnumbered. Eventually he conceded defeat and cried out:

'Enough! You can have the Sutra!'

At a command from Brother Cordial the eight Lohans moved their circle three feet further away from Fat Dhuta. He held out the Sutra. Brother Cordial, having first circulated his Inner Force and strengthened his Cinnabar Field, braced three fingers of his left hand in preparation for some deadly sudden attack, held out his right hand, and slowly took hold of the Sutra.

To the surprise of all watching, Fat Dhuta made no attempt at foul play, but handed the Sutra straight to Brother Cordial with a smile.

'Brother Cordial, it seems a little cowardly for famous fighters like yourselves to take me on—eighteen against one!'

'You must excuse us,' said Brother Cordial, bringing his palms together and bowing, having first placed the Sutra safely in the pocket of his gown. 'I'm afraid we would none of us have been a match for you in single combat.'

Again he made a gesture with his left hand, signalling the monks to take another step backwards. Some five or six of them were standing to the side guarding Trinket, for fear that Fat Dhuta might once again try to carry him off.

'Mr Wei,' said Fat Dhuta, 'I have a request.'

'What is it?'

'I would like to invite you to our island as an honoured guest of the Mystic Dragons.'

Trinket was startled at the idea.

'What? Me go to the Mystic Dragon Island? Not likely.'

'Your Sutra is now in Brother Cordial's keeping, and he will take it to the Abbot of the Shaolin Monastery,' continued Fat Dhuta. 'Come to the island, and our Sect members will treat you as one of our most distinguished guests. After you have met our Leader, I promise to bring you back safe and sound.'

Trinket looked very doubtful, and pulled a face. Fat Dhuta turned to Brother Cordial.

'Brother Cordial, please be my witness. Have I ever broken a promise?'

'We all know that you always keep your promise. The problem is Mr Wei. He has very important matters to attend to.'

'Yes,' cried Trinket. 'I'm terribly busy. Another day, when I have the time, I'll come and visit you and your Great Leader.'

'No, no, no. . . . Please!' said Fat Dhuta hurriedly. 'You've got it the wrong way round! You must say Leader Hong and his subordinate Fat Dhuta. In that order! No one in the whole world should ever be mentioned before our Great Leader! It would be highly disrespectful!'

'Even the Emperor?' asked Trinket.

'Even the Emperor,' replied Fat Dhuta. 'Another thing: in the Leader's presence no one else has the right to be called by titles like Dhuta or Lohan or Holy One. He is the one true Holy One in this world.'

Trinket stuck out his tongue.

'Sounds like I'm better off keeping out of this Leader's way!' he muttered inaudibly to himself.

'Our Leader is full of benevolence and love, his mercy reaches into the farthest corners of the earth. Our Leader is sure to admire a young hero such as yourself. He is certain to shower with you gifts, and, if he is pleased, he may even reward you by teaching you a secret kungfu move or two. Such knowledge would give you power; it would be something to treasure for the rest of your days.'

Fat Dhuta talked like a true fanatic. While he was speaking he was bent double and holding his mouth right next to Trinket's ear. Trinket did not like the sound of what he heard at all. Then Auntie Tao's remarks about the Mystic Dragon Sect flashed through his mind, and with them a host of images—the Mystic Dragon riders at the 'haunted' Zhuang mansion; the Empress Dowager and her sinister associates (Sister Swallow, and the man-maid), all of whom had some secret connection with the Mystic Dragons. He found himself feeling a sudden sense of revulsion towards the whole lot of them. By comparison, Fat Dhuta seemed positively decent. But Trinket still didn't trust him. There was something suspicious about his sudden change of attitude, from outright hostility to fawning flattery. This invitation of his might well turn out to be another sinister plot. Once the Lohans were out of the way, he might easily revert to his former behaviour.

Trinket shook his head.

'No, I'm not going!'

Fat Dhuta's emaciated face darkened.

'Since you refuse to visit our island,' he said gloomily, 'I shall have to bid you farewell.'

Trinket politely said goodbye, trying to urge Fat Dhuta to leave first, so that he could set off in the opposite direction.

Fat Dhuta shook his head uncooperatively.

'No, you go ahead. I still have work to do. I'm going to make a rubbing of the inscription.'

Poor Dhuta! He actually believed in the stele—or rather in Trinket's off-the-cuff, garbled version of it! Trinket couldn't help chuckling softly to himself as he went on his way.

CHAPTER 14

In which Trinket travels
to Snake Island, and is
initiated into the Sect of
the Mystic Dragon

An Ambush, and a Journey to the Sea

The Eighteen Lohans accompanied Trinket and Doublet down the mountain.

'Will you be going back to Peking immediately, Mr Wei?' asked Brother Cordial, handing the Sutra to Trinket. He added: 'We've been asked by Venerable Yulin to act as your bodyguards on the way there.'

Trinket was delighted.

'Excellent! I was just worrying what old Bones was going to try on me next. But if all of you come with me, who'll be left to protect Brother Wayward?'

'Don't worry about that, Mr Wei. Venerable Yulin has seen to that.'

Trinket was beginning to be rather impressed by Venerable Yulin. On the surface the old recluse seemed totally obsessed with Zen, to the exclusion of everything else. Even if the sky fell down all around him, it looked as though he would just carry on sitting there meditating with his eyes firmly closed. But all the while he was quietly taking care of things.

With their Lohan escort, Trinket and party encountered no further danger on their journey, and saw no more of Bag-of-Bones, nor of any other roving outlaw for that matter. Within a few days, they arrived at the outskirts of Peking, and there the Lohans took their leave.

'Now that you're in Peking, we must return to Shaolin,' said Brother Cordial.

'Brothers,' began Trinket, sinking to his knees and kowtowing to the monks. 'It . . . it was very kind of you to come with me all this way.'

Brother Cordial hurriedly reached out his hands to help him up.

'Say nothing of it, Mr Wei! Actually, thanks to you, this has been a most pleasant journey for us all.'

On the way down from Wutai, Trinket had hired nineteen mule-carts, one for Doublet and himself, and one for each of the Eighteen Lohans. He had instructed Wurtle to ride on ahead at full speed, so as to arrive at each of their stopping places a day in advance of the main party and arrange accommodation, tea, dimsums, and vegetable dishes for them all. No expense was to be spared. In every place they passed through, thanks to Trinket's foresight (and lavish tipping), the innkeepers and waiters treated the Eighteen Lohans like living Buddhas. Shaolin monks normally led very simple, austere lives, having transcended all desire for the good things of life; but on this occasion the Lohans could not help feeling gratified at the lengths to which Trinket had gone to ensure that they were treated with respect.

As for Trinket, he was an incorrigible talker, and once he got going there was no stopping him. But he also genuinely enjoyed making new friends, and giving them a good time. During the journey, he had many a pleasant conversation with the monks, and hit it off with them wonderfully well, with the result that when the time came for them to part, he was genuinely sad, and tears ran down his cheeks.

'There is no need to be so upset, my boy,' said Brother Cordial. 'One day, when you have a chance, you must come and visit us at the Shaolin Monastery.'

'Yes, I must!' sobbed Trinket.

Brother Cordial and the other monks cupped their hands together, and made their farewells.

By the time Trinket and his two remaining companions entered the city, it was too late to return to the Palace. Instead Trinket went to rather a grand hostelry called The Happy Return, just inside the West Straight Gate, and there he rented an upper room, planning to stay overnight before reporting to Kang Xi the next day.

'Fat Dhuta is obviously desperate to get hold of my Sutra,' he thought to himself, 'and he may have trailed me here. Without the Eighteen Lohans to protect us, Doublet and I wouldn't stand a chance. I'd better hide the Sutra for the time being. Tomorrow I can come back for it with an escort of guards, and take it to His Majesty. That sounds like a pretty foolproof plan!'

He despatched Wurtle to buy some necessities and sent Doublet out of the room as well, shutting the door behind her. He looked around carefully outside to make sure that Fat Dhuta was not lurking anywhere, and closed the windows. Then he wrapped the Sutra in oilskin, moved the table away from the wall, and took out his dagger. Prising a brick from the wall where the table had stood, he slid the package into the hollow, replaced the brick, and resealed it as best he could. When he'd finished, his handiwork was barely noticeable.

Early the next morning, Trinket sent Wurtle off to prepare their mule-cart. Trinket was feeling extremely pleased with himself at the successful completion of his Wutai duties, and in a mood for celebration. He thought he would take Doublet out for a slap-up breakfast, and then swagger into the Palace in style, wearing his guard's uniform, with his Yellow Jacket on top. He could already picture the look on the other guards' faces! Climbing onto the cart with Doublet and Wurtle, he addressed the driver in the convincing Peking brogue he had by now mastered.

'First of all, take us to the Polestar Inn in Xidan. They do a first-rate fried lamb's tail there,' he added for Doublet's benefit, 'and their mutton dumplings are delicious.'

'Yes, sir,' replied the driver respectfully.

The next thing he knew, the mule-cart was heading out through the West Straight Gate.

'Hey, I said go to Xidan!' cried Trinket. 'What are we doing heading out of the city?'

'I'm really sorry, sir!' apologized the driver. 'My mule's got this strange habit: the moment he sees the Gate, he wants to go for a little trot outside the walls. There's no stopping him!'

Trinket and Doublet burst out laughing.

The cart headed north after leaving the Gate, and continued for nearly half a mile without showing the slightest sign of stopping or turning back. Trinket grew more and more suspicious.

'What the hell are you playing at?' he shouted at the driver. 'Turn around and go back!'

'Yes sir, yes sir, I'm trying my best!' answered the man, making a great show of wheeling his mule around, and waving his whip wildly in the air. But the mule just kept on hurtling northwards, getting faster all the time.

'Turn round, you smelly creature!' shouted the driver. 'Whoa there! Stop, you stinking pile of tamardy dung!'

At this very moment, they heard the sound of hooves approaching fast, and two massively built horsemen came galloping up behind them, closing in on the cart from both sides.

'Now!' Trinket whispered to Doublet, who instantly leaned forward, and dug a finger into the small of the driver's back. The man immediately toppled over, and fell from the cart. He let out a cry of pain as the horse galloping up on that side of the cart trampled him into the dust. One of the riders now jumped from his horse and took the driver's seat. Doublet repeated her previous manoeuvre, poking him in the small of his back, but this man responded by grabbing her wrist. Doublet twisted her palm and struck him in the face, but the man fended off her attack with his left hand, seizing her shoulder with his right. They exchanged some eight or nine such moves as the mule-cart continued to career forwards.

'What's up?' the other rider yelled from the left.

Doublet lashed out with her right palm, struck her man on the chest, and threw him flying out of the cart. The man on horseback cracked his whip at Doublet, who grabbed the end of the whip and lashed it to the cart, which was still rolling along at full speed.

The man was instantly dragged screaming from his horse, and forced to let go of his whip.

Doublet had no idea how to drive a mule-cart. She passed the reins to Wurtle, and asked him to bring the cart under control. But this was a mule with a mind of its own, and he was no better at controlling it than she was. Trinket now jumped into the driver's seat, seized the reins and yelled to the mule, mimicking the driver's tone of voice. He applied what little basic technique he had learned from horse riding, loosening the left rein and tightening the right. The mule wheeled round obediently.

At this moment Trinket heard the thunder of hooves up ahead, and saw a party of some dozen horsemen come riding towards them. He tugged frantically on the reins, steering the mule off the road and down the slope to the right. The horsemen chased after him. A horse can easily outstrip a mule, and in a minute or two the cart was completely surrounded.

'What's going on?' shouted Trinket, observing that the riders were all armed. 'Is this a hold-up?'

'No, we're not robbers! We are here to deliver an invitation,' said one of riders, with a smarmy smile. 'Mr Wei, we have orders to invite you for a drink.'

Trinket's first reaction was a stunned silence. Then he asked: 'Who from?'

'You'll find out soon enough. A friend of yours, of course!'

Trinket found these strangers and their 'invitation' highly suspicious.

'Out of our way!' he shouted.

'As you wish!' cried another of the riders. Even as he spoke, he raised his sword, and swung it downwards with all his might, chopping clean through the mule's neck. The headless beast collapsed to one side, dragging the cart down with it. Trinket and Doublet leapt to the ground, and Doublet flew into the attack, flailing around her like the wind. She was too small to reach the bodies of her enemies, but she poked very effectively at their horses' eyes and began jabbing the Vital Points on the riders' legs.

The riders were soon thrown into utter confusion and the place echoed with the sounds of men shouting and horses neighing. Several of the men dismounted, and ran forward with swords drawn. Doublet responded with phenomenal speed, and in no time seven or eight of them were lying dead on the ground. The rest of the riders, about four or five, observed this girl's devastating kungfu with utter astonishment and were wondering what on earth to do next, when suddenly they saw another cart approaching at a fast trot down the road, and heard a woman's voice cry out from within it:

'Stop! Lay down your arms! We should all be friends here!'

Trinket recognized the voice at once.

'Ha!' he cried, beside himself with joy. 'There comes my wife!'

Doublet and the surviving men instantly stopped fighting. Doublet was greatly perplexed to hear her master referring to his wife. He had certainly never said anything about being married, although it was quite common at that time for young men to get married at the age of fourteen or fifteen.

The cart stopped in front of them, and out jumped—Fang Yi. Trinket beamed at her happily, stepped forward, and took her by the hand.

'Dearest sister, I've missed you so much. Where have you been?'

'Let's talk later,' said Fang Yi, shocked to see the tangled pile of dead bodies on the ground, and the blood streaming from the beheaded mule. 'How did this happen?'

'Miss Fang,' said one of the riders, bowing to her, 'we delivered the invitation as instructed, but I'm afraid we must have somehow offended Mr Wei.'

Fang Yi turned to Trinket.

'Did you really get the better of all these men? Your kungfu must have improved enormously since I last saw you.'

'Hardly,' replied Trinket. 'It was Doublet. She saved me. She killed them all.'

Fang Yi took a good look at this Doublet. She found it hard to believe that such a delicate, bashful-looking girl of fourteen or so could be a brilliant fighter.

'Tell me, little sister, what's your name?'

'Mistress,' answered Doublet, sinking to her knees, 'I'm your maid Doublet.'

Trinket burst out laughing. Fang Yi flushed.

'What . . . *what* did you call me?'

Doublet stood up.

'My master said you were his wife. Since I'm his maid, naturally you're my mistress.'

'Don't go believing what *he* says,' said Fang Yi, shooting Trinket a fierce glance. 'He just blurts out the first thing that comes into his head. How long have you been serving him? Surely you know his ways by now! Anyway, you can just call me Miss Fang.'

Doublet smiled. She glanced at Trinket. He was looking so proud and happy. She recalled the scene on Wutai, when he had told Fat Dhuta that *she* was his wife. Apparently he made a habit of calling young girls his wives. . . . A flush stole over her cheeks.

'All this time we've been apart, and you're as silly as ever!' said Fang Yi, shooting another look at Trinket, and ordering her men to prepare themselves to set off again. Doublet opened their Vital Points for them one by one.

'If I'd known the invitation was from you,' said Trinket with a smile, 'I'd have flown to your side.'

Fang Yi gave him a supercilious glance.

'I hardly think so,' she said. 'You'd obviously forgotten all about me.'

'How could I?' Trinket began to wax sentimental: 'How could I forget you for a single moment? If I'd known it was you, I'd have gone in a flash! You could have poured horse-piss or poison in my cup!'

'Flattery will get you nowhere!' said Fang Yi, fixing her fine eyes on him. 'Try and be serious for a moment. Suppose I were to invite you to come with me to the ends of the earth—and *then* drink poison? Would you really accept?'

A faint smile played on her lips. Trinket gazed at her. Standing there bathed in the rays of the morning sun, she seemed to him an indescribable, adorable vision of beauty. His whole body tingled with a feeling of warmth. He was glowing.

'Of course!' he said. 'If you asked me to climb the Mountain of Knives, or throw myself into a wok of boiling oil, I'd do it—for you!'

'Your word is still your wand?'

'Wizard Trinket at your service!' cried Trinket loudly, slapping himself on the chest.

The two of them burst out laughing.

Telling Doublet to drive her cart, Fang Yi got horses for Trinket and herself and they set off together, riding side by side. And so they headed slowly eastwards, with her surviving men following behind.

As they rode, Trinket asked after the Little Countess, Brother Xu, and the rest of their party.

'When we were separated, in the haunted house, how did you

manage to get away from those Mystic Dragons? Were you saved by Widow Zhuang?'

'Who's she?'

'The lady of the haunted house.'

'The lady of the house? We never even saw her,' replied Fang Yi, shaking her head. 'The Mystic Dragons were after you, but they didn't really mean to hurt you. As soon as they lost track of you, they set us free. The Little Countess and the others are a short distance ahead of us. You'll be seeing them soon.'

As she said this she turned to look at Trinket, with a cross little frown.

'That's the seventh time you've asked about her. All you seem to care about is the Little Countess.'

'That's not true,' Trinket defended himself smilingly. 'If *she'd* been here in your place, I'd have asked *her* about *you* at least seventy times.'

'You'd have needed ten mouths to do that,' replied Fang Yi flippantly. 'But then perhaps not: *you* probably do more talking than ten people put together.'

They travelled three or four miles in this fashion, skirting the northern walls of the city, and then heading due east away from Peking.

'Are we nearly there yet?' asked Trinket.

'No, we've still got a long way to go! Stop being so impatient!' said Fang Yi with more than a hint of anger in her voice. 'If I'd known you were pining for *her* so much, I'd have asked her to come and collect you instead of me.'

'I'll never mention her ever again!' declared Trinket, sticking out his tongue.

'You may not mention her, but you'll be thinking about her all the same!' cried Fang Yi. 'And that'll make me even crosser!'

She was beginning to sound extremely jealous. Trinket found it highly amusing.

At midday they stopped for some refreshment in a little county town, then set forth again, still heading east. This time Trinket dared not even ask where they were going. He only knew that they were by now a long way from Peking, and that it would be out of the question for him to see Kang Xi that day.

'Anyway,' he thought to himself, 'Misty didn't set a deadline for my return. For all he knows, I might have stayed on at Wutai for a few more days, or been carried off by Fat Dhuta.'

As they travelled, he and Fang Yi chatted on every subject under the sun. In the Palace, they'd been closeted together in the same room, but the Little Countess had always been with them, which had cramped their style, and made Fang Yi rather reserved. Now, as they rode slowly along side by side (with the rest of the party tactfully lagging a long way behind them), she behaved quite differently, talking happily and smiling gaily. In the Palace, Trinket had made a big thing of calling Fang Yi his wife, but that had been mainly to tease her. Perhaps he had been a tiny bit flirtatious. But he was only very slightly in love, if at all. Today it was different. Meeting her again, seeing once more the tantalizing expression on her face when she got angry, the delightful way she had of talking and smiling, he couldn't help falling head over heels in love with her. After half a day's ride, she was flushed with exertion, and tiny beads of sweat stood out on her face. Trinket found her beauty utterly bewitching. He kept staring at her, transfixed.

'What's the matter with you?' asked Fang Yi lightly.

'Dearest sister! You . . . you just look so beautiful. I think . . . I think . . .'

'Think what?'

'Don't get angry when I say it,' said Trinket.

'If you're serious, I won't get angry; but if you're being silly again—'

'I think . . . if you *really were* to become my wife, I'd be the happiest person alive!'

Fang Yi glowered coldly at him, and turned away.

'Dear sister, what's wrong?' he asked anxiously. 'Are you cross with me?'

'Of course I am! Very cross indeed!'

'But I'm being very, *very* serious,' said Trinket. 'I *really* mean it.'

'And what about me? Listen to you! *Really* this . . . *really* that. . . . Anyone would think you were the only person in the world who mattered! What about me? Don't I *really* exist? Didn't I *really* mean what I said? In the Palace, I promised to serve you for the rest of life! Don't you think *that* was real?'

At that moment Trinket was blissfully happy. If he'd been riding on the same horse as Fang Yi, he would have squeezed her tight, and kissed her on her lovely cheek. As it was, he just took her left hand in his right.

'I'll be faithful to you for a thousand years, no, ten thousand years!'

'How could you possibly? Silly boy!'

Fang Yi gave a peal of laughter, and turned away. But she left her hand in his, and Trinket felt as if he would burst with joy.

Time flew as they rode along and chattered together on their journey. That evening, they stopped at a largish country town and took lodgings for the night in an inn. The next morning, Trinket asked Wurtle (who had been keeping discreetly in the background) to hire a large cart, and now he and Fang Yi were able to sit side by side during their journey. When he talked of love, and put his arm round her waist and kissed her on the cheek, she did not resist. But she refused to allow him any further intimacy. Trinket had no first-hand experience of such things, and was more than satisfied with what she granted him. His only desire in life was that their journey would never come to an end, and that the cart would rumble on and on to the end of the world with him sitting inside it, his arm round his fair love.

The joys of sweet love had chased all thought of duty from Trinket's mind: his Imperial commission, the *Sutra in Forty-Two Sections*, even the Old Emperor on the Wutai Mountains—all these things were quite forgotten. In his dazed state of infatuation, Trinket was oblivious of the passage of time, and of how far they had been travelling.

One evening, their cart finally arrived at the sea. Fang Yi took him by the hand and walked with him to the shore, talking to him softly.

'Why don't you and I sail across the sea? Would you like to do that? Shall we explore the world together? We could live a magical life, like a pair of immortals? What do you say?'

As she spoke, Fang Yi held his hand and rested her head softly on his shoulder, leaning on him gently.

Trinket put his arm round her waist, for fear that she might fall. Her silken hair brushed against his face, he felt her slender body tremble slightly. He was somewhat taken aback by this sudden proposal. The whole idea of setting sail and crossing the ocean struck him as decidedly dangerous. But in the circumstances, in the glowing halo of romance that enveloped them, how could he possibly say no?

Snake Island

A large ship was anchored just off shore. When the sailors on board saw one of Fang Yi's men wave a blue handkerchief, they sent a small boat to pick up first Trinket and Fang Yi, and then the rest of them. Wurtle had never seen the sea before and was convinced he'd be seasick. He begged to be left behind, and Trinket gave him a hundred taels, and sent him back happily on his way to Shanxi.

Once on board the ship, Trinket was taken to a luxuriously furnished cabin, fit for a prince, with a thick carpet laid on the floor and sumptuous food and drink set out on the table.

A momentary doubt flickered through his mind: 'She couldn't be up to something, could she?' But the thought went as quickly as it had come.

At this moment, two attendants entered the cabin and handed him and Fang Yi hot towels, before serving bowls of noodles topped with slices of chicken. The chicken had an exquisite, almost other-worldly flavour. There was a sudden movement, and they knew that the ship had set sail.

Trinket found life on board utterly blissful. Fang Yi was by his side all day, drinking and playing 'guess-finger' games, chattering away with him freely until midnight, when she would see him to bed, and settle herself in the next cabin. In the morning, she would come over to help him dress and comb his hair.

'She still thinks I'm a eunuch,' Trinket mused to himself one day. 'She still thinks this being together is all a sham, and that we could never be like a real married couple. I wonder when I should tell her the truth?'

A few days later, what seemed like a perfect opportunity presented itself. They were standing together at the cabin window, watching the spectacle of the sun rising above the eastern sea, its golden beams swimming like so many sea snakes on the surface of the water.

Fang Yi heaved a sigh.

'When I went to Peking to kill the Tartar Emperor, I honestly believed it was my destiny to die there in the Palace. Then by the grace of Heaven, I met you! And now here we are, having this wonderful time together. I wish you'd tell me something about yourself, who you are, and where your family comes from.

How did you end up in the Palace? Where did you learn your kungfu?'

'There are a couple of things I was planning to tell you,' replied Trinket with a slightly nervous smile. 'But I was afraid they might come as a bit of a shock. Or else you'd be so happy you'd faint with joy!'

'If I'm happy, so much the better,' whispered Fang Yi, moving closer to him. 'But whatever it is, just tell me the truth. I . . . I . . . I won't mind. I promise.'

'In that case,' said Trinket, 'I'll tell you the whole truth. Here goes. First of all, I was born in Yangzhou. My mother worked in a whore-house.'

'A whore-house?'

Fang Yi started. She looked him in the eye.

'What did she do there?' Her voice was trembling. 'The washing? The cooking? The cleaning? Or perhaps she served tea? How did she end up in such a dreadful place?'

Trinket saw the horror on her face. His heart sank. If she was so appalled by the mere mention of the word 'whore-house', how could he possibly tell her that his mother was a whore? She would never show him any respect or love ever again.

He managed a short laugh.

'Oh, don't get the wrong idea! My mother was only a little girl at the time. She was hardly even seven years old when she first went there.'

'Seven?' asked Fang Yi, recovering her composure slightly.

'Well, you see,' Trinket continued, playing for time while he tried to work up a decent pedigree for his mother, 'the Tartars killed so many Yangzhou people after the conquest—I'm sure you know all about the Ten Day Massacre of Yangzhou. My grandfather was an important official in Yangzhou during the Ming dynasty, and he was brave too. He died defending the city against the Tartars. My mother was just a little girl then. When he was dead she had no one to turn to, so she started roaming the streets of Yangzhou, and was taken in by this man, a kind man, a rich man, who happened to be . . . a customer at this whore-house. First he took her on as his little maid, then later when he found out whose child she was he adopted her as his own daughter. A few years later my mother married my father. He was from another rich Yangzhou family.'

'Ah, I see!' said Fang Yi, only partially believing this rigmarole. 'You gave me a bit of a turn at first. I thought your mother actually worked in the whore-house as some sort of servant, you know, waiting on those . . . horrible, bad women.'

Trinket had grown up in the whore-house, and had never thought of his own mother (or any of the other whores) as 'horrible' or 'bad'. He could barely contain his anger.

'Who the hell do you think you are?' he muttered silently to himself. 'Tamardy! If you ask me, you snotty-nosed Mu Family girls are much worse sluts than the whores in Vernal Delights ever were!'

He had wanted to tell her the plain truth about himself, but now he was stuck with his story and had to go on to describe his father's fabulous wealth, and the opulent decor of his family home, the details of which were in fact borrowed straight from Vernal Delights.

Fang Yi still seemed unimpressed.

'I thought you were going to tell me something to make me very happy? Surely it can't have been that!'

Trinket's resolution to tell her that he was a fully equipped man, not a eunuch, had quite evaporated.

'Yes, that was it,' he replied as casually as he could. 'I can see you're not happy at all.'

'Yes I am,' replied Fang Yi casually, obviously not meaning it.

After a few moments of silence, they saw land on the horizon in the north-east, the direction their ship was heading. An hour later, they were very close to the shore of an island, and they could distinguish lush green trees and an endless vista of beautiful beaches covered with fine snow-white sand.

'We've been at sea so long,' said Fang Yi. 'And so cooped up. Shall we take a look around the island?'

Trinket agreed to this with alacrity. Fang Yi called the ship's captain to the cabin and asked him about the island.

'This is the famous Fairy Island of the Eastern Sea,' he replied. 'People say magical fruits grow here. Anyone who eats them becomes immortal. But only the lucky few ever find them. Why don't you and Mr Wei try your luck?'

Fang Yi nodded. When the man had left the cabin she murmured softly to Trinket:

'I don't want to be immortal, or a fairy. I'm happy just being with you.'

Trinket was ecstatic.

'Let's spend the rest of our lives together on this island.'

'Yes, let's,' whispered Fang Yi, leaning gently against him.

They went ashore and walked along the fine sand. A faint scent of flowers drifted to them from the trees, as if they really had entered some fairyland.

'I wonder if anyone lives here?' asked Fang Yi.

'I don't believe so,' replied Trinket with a smile. 'Not until today. But now the island is inhabited by a beautiful fairy, and her obedient little servant—me!'

'Why couldn't I be *your* maid instead?' said Fang Yi with an enchanting smile.

The word 'maid' instantly reminded Trinket of Doublet, who was nowhere to be seen. He felt guilty for having neglected her during the past few days; but then again, he reflected, how much harder it would have been for him to be intimate with Fang Yi, if Doublet had been there.

Trinket and Fang Yi walked hand in hand through the trees, and the scent of flowers grew stronger all around them.

'The flowers here smell so sweet,' said Trinket. 'Do you think they're magical?'

He walked on among the trees, when suddenly he heard a rustling in the grass and saw something yellow moving in front of his eyes. To his horror, seven or eight yellow-and-black-striped venomous-looking snakes came slithering out of the undergrowth.

'Aiyo!' he cried, and, dragging Fang Yi after him, turned around and ran, only to find the path behind them blocked by another seven or eight snakes, this time blood-red in colour, hissing and sticking out their tongues. Their heads were triangular, and they looked extremely poisonous.

Fang Yi shielded Trinket, drawing her sword and brandishing it at them.

'Run!' she shouted to Trinket. 'I'll take care of the snakes!'

Trinket naturally refused to escape on his own. He drew his dagger, crying:

'Come this way!'

He dragged her with him off to one side. After stumbling no more than a couple of steps, he felt something cold, and to his horror saw that it was a snake dangling in one of the trees, and beginning to coil itself around his neck. He was petrified, and started shouting loudly for help. Fang Yi reached out her hand and tried to grasp the snake by its body, but it whipped round, and sunk its teeth into her arm.

Trinket swung his dagger through the air, and sliced the snake in two.

By now there was a huge, writhing mass of poisonous snakes entwined around their legs. Trinket continued to slice at them with his dagger, but soon he too was bitten (on his left leg), and virtually immobilized.

Fang Yi threw her sword to the ground, and held him tightly. 'We shall die here together!' she sobbed.

With his sharp dagger, Trinket was able to slice through the snakes one at a time, but the more he sliced, the faster they multiplied. The two of them struggled their way out into the open, their bodies covered with snake-bites. By now Trinket was beginning to feel dizzy, and gradually he sank into an almost comatose state. Fang Yi gazed desperately out to sea, where she could see the little boat that had carried them to shore making its way back towards the large ship. She shouted to the sailors a couple of times, but they could not hear her.

She rolled up Trinket's trousers, and bent down to suck the poison from his leg.

'No!' gasped Trinket. 'Don't! You . . . mustn't!'

Suddenly they heard footsteps approaching behind them.

'What are you doing here?' asked a voice. 'Are you trying to get yourselves killed?'

Trinket struggled to turn his head and saw three middle-aged men.

'Snakes!' he moaned. 'We've been bitten! Please, I beg you, help us!'

One of the men produced a herbal substance from an inside pocket, chewed on it, and then applied it to Trinket's wounds.

'Put . . . put some on her wounds first,' stammered the barely conscious Trinket. His legs were by now black and had lost all feeling.

Fang Yi took the medicine herself, and applied it to her own wounds.

'Dearest . . .' murmured Trinket, but before he could even finish the sentence, he lost consciousness altogether, and slumped backwards onto the ground.

Doctor Lu

As Trinket gradually came to, the first thing he became aware of was that his lips and tongue were parched, and that he had a bad pain in his chest. He groaned.

'Excellent!' exclaimed a voice. 'He's waking up!'

Trinket slowly opened his eyes, and saw a man preparing to feed him from a bowl full of some medicinal broth. The medicine, whatever it was, gave off a nasty stench and tasted extremely bitter, but he drank it down without hesitation, then turned to the man.

'Thanks for saving my life!' he said. 'What about . . . her? Is she all right?'

'She is out of danger,' replied the man. 'The two of you are very lucky. If we had come any later, both of you would have died. What you did was extremely reckless. Why did you come to the island?'

Trinket was hugely comforted to learn that Fang Yi was alive and well, and thanked the man profusely. Then he became aware that he himself was lying on a bed, naked under a bedspread, and that he was quite unable to move either of his legs. The man beside the bed, administering the medicine, was a hideous sight, his face pitted with scars, but in Trinket's eyes he was a blessed saviour. Trinket breathed a sigh of relief.

'One of the sailors told us that there were magical fruits here on the island,' he said, 'and that if we ate them, we would live for ever.'

The man laughed drily.

'I see. In that case, why didn't they come and pick the fruits themselves?'

'It must have been a plot!' cried Trinket. 'Oh dear! One of my friends is still on board their ship. She . . . she may be in trouble too. Please think of some way of helping her.'

'The ship left three days ago, I'm afraid. It's too late.'

'Three days ago?' Trinket sounded puzzled.

'Yes. You've been unconscious for three whole days and nights.'

Trinket couldn't help feeling most concerned at the thought of Doublet, all alone in the middle of the sea, at the mercy of those wicked sailors. However good a fighter she was, she would have great difficulty escaping.

'It's no use worrying about that now,' urged the man. 'You must rest. The snakes on this island are extremely poisonous. You will need at least seven days of medication to neutralize the poison inside you.'

He asked Trinket for his name, and introduced himself as Mr Pan.

After another three days, Trinket was able to get up and walk slowly, propping himself against the wall. Mr Pan took him to visit Fang Yi, who was being taken care of by some women, but who still looked pale and weak. When they met, a combination of happiness and sorrow overtook them. They clung onto one another, weeping with emotion.

On the morning of the seventh day, Mr Pan came to visit Trinket again.

'Our doctor, Doctor Lu, has just returned to the island, and I've asked him to come and see you.'

Shortly afterwards, an agreeable man in his mid forties, identifiable by his dress as a member of the scholar class, entered the room, and began asking Trinket in detail about the snake-bites.

'All the inhabitants of this island are issued with a quantity of Realgar Elixir,' explained Doctor Lu. 'Provided you've taken the Elixir, it acts as an antidote. Even if a snake attacks you, it will not dare bite you but will escape instantly.'

'I see!' said Trinket. 'So that's why Mr Pan and the others weren't afraid of the snakes.'

Doctor Lu checked his wounds and then produced six pills, three for Trinket and three for Fang Yi, one to be taken every day for three days. Trinket took out a two-hundred tael banknote, and handed it to the doctor as a token of his appreciation.

At first Doctor Lu was taken aback, but Trinket insisted on his keeping the money, and in the end he did so with gratitude. Doctor Lu invited the two of them to stay at his house that night, and his invitation was joyfully accepted. That evening, Trinket and Fang Yi were fetched in two bamboo chairs, with bamboo carrying-poles along both sides—the islanders led a simple life, and did not have anything as sophisticated as a real sedan-chair.

They were borne along the side of a stream, and the sound of gurgling water, and the sight of the lush green trees all around them, greatly revived them. Their good spirits were only marred by the thought of the countless poisonous snakes that must be writhing among the great trees and tall grasses. Finally, after some two or three miles, the chairs stopped in front of three bamboo houses, their roofs and walls all solidly constructed of bamboo poles as thick as a large bowl in diameter. Nowhere, either in the regions to the south of the Yangtze River, or north of the Yellow River, had Trinket and Fang Yi ever seen houses like these.

Doctor Lu came out to welcome them into his house. In the living-room, a middle-aged woman came out to greet the guests. This was Doctor Lu's wife. She held Fang Yi's hands in hers, and spoke to her warmly. Doctor Lu invited Trinket to take a seat in his study, where the bamboo shelves were piled high with an endless array of old thread-bound books, and the walls were covered with calligraphic scrolls and paintings. It was clearly the room of a scholar and connoisseur of art.

'Residing as I do on this remote wilderness of an island, I am, alas, both ignorant and uncouth,' declared the doctor. 'You, Mr Wei, hailing as you do from the fertile plains of central China, proud scion of the Chinese race, are doubtless a young man of broad culture, and have a keen appreciation of calligraphy and the pictorial arts. Would you deign to glance at these humble scrolls of mine, and tell me if you think they pass muster?'

Trinket found his bookish language almost incomprehensible, but his eyes followed the doctor's fingers as they pointed in the general direction of the scrolls. The first thing he saw was a landscape painting, then a painting of a white stork and a tortoise. He smiled.

'Not a bad old turtle!'

Doctor Lu gave him a decidedly old-fashioned look. Then he indicated a vertical scroll covered in an antique style of calligraphy.

'Mr Wei, what do you think of this example of the Stone-Drum style?'

Trinket looked at the inscription, with characters that twisted and twirled all over the paper like Taoist talismans, and nodded his approval.

'Good, very good!'

'And what of this rubbing? It is one of the famous stone inscriptions from the Qin dynasty, carved on Langya Terrace,' continued Doctor Lu, pointing to another scroll.

Thinking that variety was probably a desirable feature of his performance as a connoisseur, Trinket shook his head.

'Not quite up to scratch . . .'

'Mr Wei, would you be so kind as to indicate for my enlight-enment the outstanding faults in this inscription?' asked Doctor Lu solemnly.

'Not exactly outstanding faults,' replied Trinket, thinking he'd latched onto some specialist jargon. 'I'd say they were more *in*standing . . .'

Doctor Lu was appalled. He managed to murmur:

'Brilliant, brilliant! Most . . . interesting!'

He turned to another scroll written in the free Grass style.

'How do you find this one, Mr Wei?'

Trinket cocked his head to one side and subjected the scroll to his expert appraisal. He shook his head.

'Dreadfully dry. I can't understand why the painter didn't put more ink on his brush. And all those straggly lines all over the place look a real mess!'

Doctor Lu was horrified. The colour drained from his face. A fine piece of Grass-style calligraphy should alternate 'hollow' and 'solid' strokes, the former being 'dry' (written with a brush lightly laden with ink), the latter 'moist' (black and thick). In this way the two kinds of stroke complement each other, and enhance each other's beauty. The 'straggly lines' are what calligraphers call 'silken threads'. The well balanced interweaving of these 'threads' between individual strokes or characters lends to the aesthetic harmony of the piece as a whole. In just a few words, Trinket had betrayed his utter ignorance of the art of calligraphy.

Doctor Lu pointed to another scroll.

'This is a rubbing of an inscription in the ancient Oracle-Bone script. Unlettered as I am, I can recognize none of these words. I crave your instruction, Mr Wei.'

Trinket found himself looking at some tadpole squiggles which somehow reminded him very much of the inscription he had seen on the stone tablet in the Monastery of Universal Salvation, in the Wutai Mountains—the one he had interpreted so fluently for the benefit of Fat Dhuta. He had a sudden brainwave.

'I can read this!' he exclaimed. 'It says: Long Life to Our Great Leader Hong of the Mystic Dragon Sect! Blessings be on Him!'

'Heaven be praised!' cried the doctor. 'You really do know the words.'

Trinket grew suspicious at the doctor's joyful expression, and his trembling voice.

'Why's he so happy all of a sudden,' he thought to himself, 'just because I can decipher a few words? Unless of course he's a Mystic Dragon himself? Oh no! Wait a minute. Snakes . . . snakes . . . magical snakes . . . mystic dragons! Is this Snake Island?'

'Where's Fat Dhuta got to?' he blurted out.

Doctor Lu started, and retreated a couple of steps.

'You . . . you know?' he cried in a panic-stricken voice.

Trinket nodded, although in fact he knew virtually nothing.

'So long as you know, then everything's fine,' said Doctor Lu in a serious tone of voice.

He walked to his desk, ground some ink, and spread out a sheet of paper. Then he dipped his writing-brush in the ink, and gestured to Trinket to come over to him.

'Would you be so kind as to explain some of the words in the rubbing for me? Write them down. Tell me which is the word "Hong" and which is the word "Sect"?'

Trinket uttered a silent cry of despair. He would rather die than try to write. But the doctor's face looked grim, he dared not refuse. He walked up to the desk, sat down, and reached out his hand to take hold of the writing-brush. Then he clutched it tightly— like someone holding a chopstick, or a butcher with a knife about to slaughter a pig, or someone with a hammer about to drive a nail into the wall. The last thing he resembled was a calligrapher holding a brush.

Doctor Lu tried to control his rage.

'Very well then,' he said slowly, 'write your name first.'

All of a sudden Trinket leapt to his feet, and flung the brush to the ground. Ink splashed everywhere.

'I don't know how!' he shouted hysterically. 'Not a dog's fart! I can't even write the word fart! All that stuff about "Long Life to Leader Hong" was a load of rubbish. I just made it up to fool old Bones! So if you want *me* to write, you'll have to wait for my next life. You may as well just kill me now!'

'You don't know how to write a single word?' said Doctor Lu coldly.

'Not a word! Not even "smelly turtle" or "stupid jerk"!'

Trinket's game was up. He felt a mixture of shame and anger. Here he was stuck on Snake Island, doomed to death, with no hope of escape. He might as well try and score a few verbal points at Doctor Lu's expense.

Doctor Lu lapsed into silence. He took up the writing-brush and began writing some tadpole-like characters on the paper.

'What word is this?' he asked.

'Pop your mother's!' howled Trinket. 'I already told you—I said I can't read and I meant it!'

'Good!' muttered Doctor Lu, nodding his head. 'Now at least we know where we stand. So Fat Dhuta fell for your little trick. But what do we do now? We have already reported the inscription to our Leader, damn you!'

Suddenly he leapt forwards, caught Trinket by the neck with both hands, and began squeezing him, tighter and tighter.

'It is all *your* doing!' he spat out bitterly. 'Now we are guilty of deceiving our Leader! Our own lives are in danger! Sooner or later every one of us will come to a horrible end. So we might as well all die now, and save ourselves the endless torment!'

Trinket was suffocating. His face was swollen and purple, his tongue was protruding from his mouth. A little more pressure from the doctor's hands, and the boy would be dead. But Doctor Lu seemed to lose his nerve. He loosened his fingers, threw Trinket to the ground, and stomped out of the room in a rage.

A long time passed before Trinket was able to overcome his terror and rise to his feet again. Mentally he reviled Doctor Lu a hundred times as a 'dead turtle', and a 'mother-fucking scumbag'. But his thoughts soon turned to escape. It was no use trying to hide in the woods; that would only be to endanger his life yet again. He went to the bamboo door and tried to push it open, but it was locked from the outside. Then he moved over to one of the windows and gazed down. Beneath the house lay a deep gorge, with no visible way out of it. He turned around and looked at the scrolls hanging on the walls.

'This stuff makes me want to puke!'

He took the writing-brush, dipped it in the ink, and began doodling an endless series of turtles of various shapes and sizes all over the doctor's precious scrolls. Eventually he grew tired of doing this, threw the brush on the ground, curled up in a chair, and was soon fast asleep. It was already the middle of the night when he got up, and still no one had come bothering him. He was starving.

'Now I suppose turtle Lu is trying to starve me to death,' he thought.

A long while later, he heard the sound of approaching

footsteps, and a light shone through a crack in the bamboo door. The door opened, and Doctor Lu entered the room with a candlestick in his hand, his head tilted to one side, his eyes fixed on Trinket, who could read no recognizable emotion on his face, but was terrified none the less. As he put the candlestick down on the table, the doctor caught sight of the turtle-graffiti on his scrolls. They were ruined beyond repair. He burst into an uncontrollable rage.

'You . . . you . . .' he howled, his hand raised to strike. But then he checked himself in mid-flight.

'You . . . you . . .'

His voice was so choked with emotion, he could not utter another word.

'What do you reckon?' quipped Trinket with a nervous smile. 'Did I do a good job?'

Doctor Lu heaved a deep sigh and sank to the ground.

'Wonderful!' he muttered. 'Just wonderful!'

Improvisations on a Tadpole Theme

To Trinket's intense surprise, Doctor Lu, so far from hitting him, appeared to be complimenting him on his 'work of art'—his Turtle Improvisations on a Tadpole Theme. But the doctor's lugubrious expression soon betrayed his underlying pain. Trinket felt a certain sense of remorse.

'Doctor Lu, I'm so . . . so sorry I've ruined your paintings.'

'It doesn't matter,' replied the doctor, burying his head in his hands. After a long while, he turned to Trinket.

'You must be hungry. Let's go and have some refreshment.'

In the main room, a sumptuous meal—four dishes (including one chicken dish and one fish dish), and a pot of soup—had been set on the table. Doctor Lu's wife accompanied Fang Yi into the room, and the four of them sat down together to eat.

'Maybe he really is pleased with me. Maybe this nosh is his way of thanking me for my turtle-art,' Trinket mused to himself. But he soon dismissed the idea, and did not venture to bring up the subject during their meal for fear of upsetting the doctor, who still looked distinctly moody.

The meal was finished in silence, and Doctor Lu led Trinket back to his study. He picked up the writing-brush from the floor, and wrote the words 'Trinket Wei ' on a piece of paper.

'This is your name. Can you write it?'

'The words know me, but I don't seem to know them,' answered Trinket. 'No. I can't.'

Doctor Lu cleared his throat and gazed out of the window, lost in deep thought. A moment later he took the candlestick in his left hand, and walked over to the rubbing in the Tadpole script hanging on the wall. He examined it again in minute detail, following the characters one by one with his finger and mumbling them quietly to himself. Then he returned to the table and began writing something energetically on a sheet of paper. As he wrote he kept going back and counting the number of characters on the rubbing, then checking it against the number on his own scroll; time after time he altered his own text, then went to examine the rubbing again.

'These three characters look exactly the same,' he mumbled to himself. 'But these two are only a passable approximation. They have to be a perfect match.'

Again he was lost in deep thought for quite some time. Then he made a few more alterations on his own scroll, and gave a cry of joy.

'That's it!'

Trinket had no idea what was going on. He had eaten, and was no longer hungry: that was the main thing. He paid Doctor Lu little attention. The doctor spread out another sheet of paper and began writing.

This time he wrote slowly and with great care—it was evidently a fair copy. When he had finished, he read it through softly, his head swaying gently to the rhythm of the text. Trinket was able to catch the odd phrase such as 'Mystic Dragon Island', and 'Long Life to Our Great Leader Hong'. Then towards the end, he heard him mumble something about the locations of the first copy and second copy. Suddenly it dawned on him. The squiggly text on which the doctor was lavishing such calligraphic effort was simply Trinket's own impromptu version of the stele he had spotted in the courtyard of the Monastery of Universal Salvation, the version he had invented for the benefit of Fat Dhuta. Old Bones must have swallowed his nonsense literally, made a rubbing of the (to Trinket) unintelligible squiggles on the stone, and committed the Authorized Trinket Version of their meaning to memory; then he had communicated the whole thing to the doctor—the rubbing of the text and the word-for-word oral interpretation—on his return to the island. Trinket had turned down Fat Dhuta's earlier invitation to the island. But an ironic twist of fate (in the form of that romantic cruise on the boat) had now brought him to the island anyway, where his little stele-prank had been shown up for what it was! And the worst thing about it was that the Great Leader (whoever he was) had been officially told about the stele and its wonderful prophesies! The Leader was sure to fly into a hideous rage when he found out that he had been duped, and would have both Trinket and Fang Yi thrown into some terrible pit, to be consumed alive by thousands of poisonous snakes! Trinket shuddered with terror at the very thought.

Doctor Lu turned round with a smile of satisfaction.

'Mr Wei, we must compliment you on having been able to decipher the Tadpole inscription on the stone tablet. It must have been a Blessing vouchsafed to Our Great Leader, that such a Divine Prodigy as yourself appeared at such an opportune moment!'

Trinket cleared his throat.

'There's no need to tease me. Me, know Tadpole script? You'll be telling me I know Frog's-Leg script next, or Toad script. . . . I just made the whole thing up to fool old Bones.'

The doctor smiled.

'Mr Wei, you are being too modest! What we have here is indeed the inscription on the stone tablet exactly as you recited it. See, I have copied it down. Please listen carefully and tell me if there are any mistakes.'

The doctor began:

In the Second Year of the Zhen-Guan Period of the Tang Dynasty, the year Six Hundred and Twenty-Nine according to the Great Western Calendar, the Tenth Lunar Month, the Day Jia-Zi, His Majesty's four loyal subjects Lord Li Jing, General Cheng, the Minister of War Li, and the Governor of Xuzhou Qin Shubao, being assembled on the Embroidered Peak of the Wutai Mountains, did behold in the rosy firmament of the eastern heaven, inscribed in great characters of gold that shone mightily against the clouds, the following marvellous proclamation:

'One thousand years from now, there will come to pass the great conquest of the Qing Tartars. In the eastern sea there lies an island, its name is the Isle of the Mystic Dragon. On that isle will preside a Great Leader, and his name will be Hong. He will hold sway over his subjects with mighty awe, wielding magical power over them. They will practise strange rites, and great will be their power that will be restored thereby. Long Life and Blessings to the Great Leader! May He Live For Ever!'

A little while later, and the heavens were emblazoned with further characters in black:

'To the Great Leader Hong will be vouchsafed transcriptions of the Sutra in Forty-Two Sections. There will be in all Eight transcriptions of the Sutra. These will be concealed in the following locations: the First will be concealed in the Great Spirit Monastery, on Ox Mountain in the province of Henan; the Second will be concealed in the Heavenly Heart Nunnery, on Brush Stand Mountain in the province of Shanxi; the Third will be concealed in the Taoist Priory of the Pierced Cloud, on Green City Mountain in the province of Sichuan; the Fourth will be concealed in the Shaolin Monastery, on Mount Song in the province of Henan; the Fifth will be concealed in the Taoist Abbey of Truth and Might, on Wudang Mountain in the province of Hubei; the Sixth will be concealed in the Kasyapa Monastery, on Mount Kongdong in the Western Marches; the Seventh will be concealed in the estates of the Mu Family in Kunming, in the province of Yunnan; and the Eighth will be concealed in the Palace of the Satrap Wu, Prince of the West, also in Kunming, in the province of Yunnan.'

These words of prophesy we have most reverentially inscribed upon this tablet of stone, that they may bear witness to men of future ages.

Doctor Lu recited the words singsong fashion, and when he had finished, turned to Trinket.

'Is that correct?'

'Yes, but tell me,' said Trinket, remembering the objection raised by Bag-of-Bones. 'If this stone tablet was carved in the Tang dynasty, how did they know about Satrap Wu?'

'The Almighty in his wisdom knows *all*. If he knew about Our Great Leader Hong, of course he knew about Satrap Wu.'

'Fair enough,' Trinket nodded.

But he was meanwhile laughing to himself and thinking:

'I hope the Almighty-in-his-washroom (or whatever) knows what you're on about, because *I* certainly don't!'

'The inscription needs to be recited with complete accuracy,' Doctor Lu went on. 'Heaven blessed you with an extraordinary ability to read Tadpole script. You are a prodigy. But in order to avoid any possibility of misinterpretation in later times, I want you now to memorize the whole inscription, so that you can recite it perfectly by heart when you are summoned into the presence of Our Great Leader Hong. Our Leader is sure to be pleased, and will reward you generously.'

Trinket finally realized what Doctor Lu had in mind. He nodded several times in succession.

'I see, I see!'

He was able to piece together what had happened. Fat Dhuta and Doctor Lu had reported to Leader Hong that they had found a child prodigy who had been able to interpret the Tadpole inscription, and the Great Leader had demanded to set eyes on the prodigy for himself. Now that Doctor Lu knew that the Authorized Trinket Version of the inscription was a fake, he had decided to create another inscription of his own (along the lines of the Authorized Version), in order to cover up their deception of the Great Leader. He had taken enormous care to make his new version tally with the number of characters in Fat Dhuta's rubbing.

'Now, I'm going to read it to you again sentence by sentence,' said Doctor Lu, 'and you are to repeat it after me, until you have memorized every word perfectly.'

Trinket really had no choice. And anyway, he found the whole idea of being in cahoots with Doctor Lu and fooling the Great Leader rather appealing. It might be a lot of fun. So he did as he was told, and repeated the sentences after Doctor Lu. He had always had an excellent memory, and was able to memorize large chunks of normal speech with ease. Doctor Lu's inscription was short, but it was full of difficult bookish expressions ('rosy firmament' and 'vouchsafed', for example, were quite beyond Trinket's normal vocabulary). Luckily Doctor Lu was an extremely patient teacher. By the thirtieth repetition, Trinket had managed to get it off pat.

He spent what was left of that night at Doctor Lu's house, and recited the text perfectly by heart once more the following morning, much to the satisfaction of the doctor, who now took his brush, spread out another sheet of paper, and began writing down all the Tadpole-script characters, teaching him how to decipher (and how to write) the squiggly words, even the ones for 'rosy firmament' and 'vouchsafed'. It was torment for Trinket, who was a reluctant and restless student at the best of times. But somehow Doctor Lu succeeded.

Doctor Lu knew that the original inscription, the one on the stone in the monastery courtyard, had meant something quite different. His only concern was to make up a text with exactly the same number of characters as the rubbing, and with a content designed to please the Leader—at least for the time being. There

were discrepancies between the two texts which a careful examination (especially by a man as intelligent as the Leader) would soon
uncover. But in the limited time available, this was the best he could
do. Let the future take care of itself!

Trinket's progress at writing was extremely slow. By noon
that day he had learned a total of four Tadpole characters. Luckily
the original graphs themselves were weird enough, so even in
Trinket's ungainly hand they looked almost plausible. He learned
three more graphs in the afternoon, and two more that night, which
made a grand total of nine in one day. But he kept screaming and
yelling during his practice, and threw his brush on the ground more
than once. Doctor Lu threatened and cajoled him, and it was only
when he thought of asking Fang Yi to sit next to the boy that Trinket
finally settled down a bit and tried to work at it. All this time Doctor
Lu was fretting that the Leader would summon Trinket before he
had learned the whole inscription, in which case not only would
Trinket lose his head, but Doctor Lu and the whole of his family
would be put to death as well.

But there was no hurrying Trinket. The more Doctor Lu
pressed him, the slower was his progress. The tadpoles just seemed
to swim around in Trinket's head in ever widening and more con-
fusing circles. A few days later, although Trinket had totally recovered from his snake-bites, he could still barely decipher thirty
Tadpole graphs.

A Summons

The doctor heard Fat Dhuta's voice at the door.

'Doctor Lu, our Leader has summoned Mr Wei.'

The doctor's face turned pale, his hands trembled, and he lost
hold of his writing-brush which fell onto his robe and splashed him
with ink.

In came Bag-of-Bones. Trinket greeted him with a smile.

'Bones, it's been so long!'

From the drawn expression of Doctor Lu, Fat Dhuta could see
that all was not well.

'I should have known right at the start that this boy was only
mucking around!' he muttered. 'It's just that I so badly wanted to
achieve something for the cause! And all I've done is to dig my own
grave!'

'You've only got yourself to worry about!' grumbled Doctor

Lu. 'What about me? There are eight people in my family to think about!'

Fat Dhuta heaved a long sigh.

'It's our fate. It must have been predestined. Even if this hadn't happened, our Leader might not have allowed us to live very long.'

'One moment, Fat Dhuta,' said Doctor Lu gloomily. 'I have something to say to my wife.'

A little while later, Doctor Lu returned to his study, with traces of tears visible on his cheeks.

'Brother Lu, please give me one of your Ascension Tablets,' said Fat Dhuta.

Doctor Lu nodded, produced a little porcelain phial from inside his gown, removed the stopper, and tipped out a tiny red pill.

'Remember, the moment you put this into your mouth, you're a dead man,' he said grimly.

'I won't forget!' replied Fat Dhuta with a wry smile, reaching out his hand to take the pill.

Trinket, who had witnessed a very different Fat Dhuta on Wutai, in full fighting form against the Eighteen Lohans, shivered to see him contemplating the possibility of suicide, rather than face the wrath of an unforgiving Leader.

As the three of them left the study, Trinket heard the sound of weeping issuing from the women's quarters.

'Where's Miss Fang?' he asked. 'Isn't she coming with us?'

'Quite the little ladies' man!' quipped the Dhuta. 'On Wutai you had that girl Doublet, now you've got this Miss Fang! Come on—let's go!'

He lifted Trinket up in the air with his left hand, and strode off in an easterly direction, quickening his pace until he was soon going as fast as a trotting horse. Doctor Lu kept up with them, moving with an athletic stride that contrasted strangely with his gloomy preoccupied air.

The three of them soon turned and began heading towards a peak on the northern end of the island. There were poisonous snakes all around them—some hanging from the trees, some crawling in the grass and on the road itself—but strangely the three of them passed through them all unscathed. They had rounded two hills, when they saw a cluster of large bamboo buildings on the very top of the peak a long way ahead of them.

The road narrowed as they climbed towards the peak, and

there was no longer room for Doctor Lu to walk alongside Fat Dhuta. He therefore fell several yards behind.

Fat Dhuta then whispered in Trinket's ear:

'So what's happened to the copy of the Sutra you found?'

'I don't know. *I* haven't got it,' replied Trinket.

'Don't worry, I know that. I've already had a good look. Where have you put it?'

'I suppose the Shaolin monks must have given it to their Abbot,' said Trinket, thinking that Fat Dhuta would never dare try to seize the Sutra from the Abbot of the Shaolin Monastery. Since Fat Dhuta had in fact himself surrendered the Sutra to Brother Cordial, he was ready to believe Trinket's story.

'When you see our Leader, whatever you do, don't mention the Sutra,' muttered Fat Dhuta. 'If he asks you for it, and you can't oblige, he'll throw you into a cave crawling with poisonous snakes.'

Fat Dhuta was obviously terrified of the Leader, and nervous lest Doctor Lu should overhear their conversation. Trinket turned to him and whispered:

'*You're* the one who gave the Shaolin monks the Sutra—he'll throw *you* into the snake-cave for sure. Or send you to Shaolin to get it back . . .'

Fat Dhuta trembled with fear, and fell silent.

After proceeding for about the time it would take to consume an average meal, they reached the top of the peak, where they saw four youths dressed in blue approaching hand in hand, each with a long-sword strapped to his back.

'Comrade Dhuta, what's this boy doing here?' asked the youth furthest to the left.

'Our Leader has summoned him,' replied Fat Dhuta, depositing Trinket on the ground.

From the other side came three girls all in red, laughing and simpering, each of them also equipped with a long-sword. They saw Trinket and his companions.

'Is this your love child?' said one of them, turning to Fat Dhuta with a grin and pinching Trinket on the cheek.

'Very funny,' replied Fat Dhuta. 'This boy has been especially summoned by our Great Leader, who wants to question him on some important matters.'

Any further banter was forestalled by the sudden ringing of a bell. The boys and girls turned around and dashed towards one of the bamboo buildings.

'The Leader is calling an assembly,' Fat Dhuta explained to Trinket. 'Mind your tongue when you meet him.'

Poor Dhuta, thought Trinket. It was pathetic that such a formidable fighter should seem almost nervous in the presence of these children.

The Great Leader

People were flooding towards the bamboo building from every direction. Fat Dhuta and Doctor Lu led Trinket in, and after walking down a long covered walkway, they found themselves at the entrance to an enormous hall, big enough to accommodate more than a thousand people. Trinket had spent quite a long time in the Imperial Palace, and he was accustomed to large halls: but even he was impressed by this one.

Inside the hall he found groups of young acolytes dressed in different colours. They stood in five different parts of the hall according to their colours—the boys in blue, white, black, or yellow, the girls in red. Each one of them had a longsword strapped on their back. Each colour group was approximately a hundred strong. At the far end, in the centre of the hall, stood two bamboo chairs set with brocade-covered cushions; on both sides of the chairs stood several dozen adults, both men and women, ranging in age from thirty to seventy, all unarmed. Altogether between five and six hundred people were gathered in the hall, but there was dead silence. Not a single cough could be heard.

'Tamardy!' Trinket exclaimed silently to himself. 'Who does this big guy think he is! The Emperor or something?'

After an interval, he heard the bell ring nine times, and footsteps could be heard coming from the inner hall.

Ten men walked in, all in their thirties, each dressed in one of the five colours, and took up their positions on either side of the bamboo chairs. After another interval a great bell sounded, followed by the tinkling of hundreds of little silver bells. Everyone in the hall knelt, and the chanting began:

'Long Life to Our Leader! Blessings be on Him!'

Fat Dhuta tugged Trinket lightly by the collar, signalling him to kneel down. Trinket reluctantly complied. He glanced up, and saw a man and a woman walk out from the inner hall and seat themselves down on the chairs. The silver bells tinkled again, and everybody rose to their feet.

The man looked positively ancient. He had a long white beard hanging down to his chest, and his face was covered with scars and wrinkles. He was altogether rather an ugly sight. So this, mused Trinket, was the Great Leader of the Mystic Dragons. The woman, on the other hand, he was happy to note, was ravishingly beautiful. She looked about twenty-three or twenty-four years old, and had an enchanting smile.

'Wow!' Trinket whistled silently to himself. 'She's even prettier than Fang!'

A man in blue standing to her left now took two steps forward, and, holding a blue sheet of paper in his hand, began to declaim:

'Let us read the Treasured Teachings of Our Most Merciful and Mighty Leader. It is written: "United we stand, United we will triumph! Our Power will reign Supreme!"'

Everyone in the hall repeated this in unison.

'United we stand, United we will triumph! Our Power will reign Supreme!'

Trinket was staring goggle-eyed at the handsome lady. The chanting shocked him out of his reverie.

'Long Life to Our Leader! Courage to all Comrades! With Him we will Surmount Every Challenge! With Him we will Conquer the World! We will Live for Him, and Die for Him! Obey His Every Command! May His Grace Shine upon us like the Light of the Sun and Moon!'

The man in blue continued declaiming, and the assembly chanted the words after him in chorus.

'The Leader's Treasured Teachings my arse!' thought Trinket to himself. 'Our Triad passwords sounded better than this load of crap!'

The chanting finished with the words: 'Obey His Teachings! Follow Him to Victory!'

The acolytes were especially enthusiastic in their chanting. Leader Hong's ugly face registered no emotion whatsoever, while the exquisite lady by his side smiled sweetly as she murmured the chants along with the others.

The assembly fell silent again.

Madame Hong and the Dragon Marshals

Still smiling, the fair lady glanced across the hall.

'Black Dragon Marshal, you are due to present the Sutra today.'

She spoke slowly, enunciating the words clearly and with an attractive intonation.

She held out her left hand and opened her palm. Trinket could see even from a distance that her hand was superbly smooth and white; it looked as if it had been carved from a piece of flawless white jade.

'She'd make a lovely wife!' he found himself thinking at once. 'None of the whores at Vernal Delights were a patch on her! She'd have had all the old men breaking the door down!'

An elderly man in black standing to the left of the two 'thrones' now moved a couple of steps forward.

'I wish to report to Madame that we have received news from Peking about the whereabouts of four of the Sutras.'

His voice was trembling with fear.

'Our people are working according to the Leader's instructions and sparing no effort—not even their lives—to lay hands on the Sutras and present them to the Leader and Madame.'

'What a pity she's married to the Leader,' thought Trinket. 'What a waste to have such a beautiful flower growing in such a pile of shit!'

'Your Leader has extended the deadline three times,' said the lady with a sinister little smile. 'But you always delay. You aren't working hard enough. Don't you think you're being a bit disloyal to the Leader?'

'I owe everything to the Leader and to Madame,' grovelled the man referred to as the Black Dragon Marshal, prostrating himself lower and lower to the ground. 'There have been certain obstacles. Two of the six people I sent to the Palace have given their lives: Deng Bingchun, and Liu Yan. I beg for more time.'

So, mused Trinket, the Fat Sow (Liu Yan) and the cross-dressing maid (Deng Bingchun) were acting on orders from this Black Dragon Marshal. It seemed that the Marshal was even higher up in the Mystic Hierarchy than the fake Empress Dowager.

The lady waved her left hand to Trinket.

'Come here, little man,' she said, with that irresistible smile of hers.

At first Trinket was too shocked to respond.

'Me?' he finally mumbled.

'Yes, you.'

Trinket glanced quickly at Doctor Lu and Fat Dhuta who were still standing next to him.

'Madame is summoning you,' said the doctor. 'Go on, salute her respectfully.'

'And what if I decide to fart in her face?' Trinket thought to himself. But he did as he was told.

'Long Life to Our Leader and to His Wife!' he said, bowing deeply. 'Blessings be on You Both!'

'You're a clever little man, I must say!' said Madame Hong, visibly amused. 'And who told you to add "and to His Wife"?'

Actually Trinket had emended the immutable Mystic Mantra without thinking too much about it. After all, it didn't cost him anything to be a little obsequious. And this beautiful lady clearly had a lot of authority.

'The Leader's Long Life wouldn't be much fun without His Wife to keep him company,' he replied. 'How lonely he would be if His Wife rose to heaven a hundred or two years before he did!'

Madame Hong shook with laughter on hearing this, and even the Leader could not help laughing, rocking his head from side to side and twiddling his long beard.

Members of the Mystic Dragon Sect, whatever their rank, stood in absolute terror of the Leader, and never under any circumstances ventured to talk frivolously in his presence. They were astonished, and hugely relieved, to see Trinket emerge unscathed.

'So it was your own idea to add the few extra words?' asked the smiling lady.

'Yes. I had to, because your name was on the Tadpole inscription too.'

Doctor Lu's heart sank.

'After all the trouble I went to, to teach him the inscription!' he thought. 'Now that he has added *her* name, our inscription will not have the same number of words as the original. They will soon discover our secret!'

Madame Hong was equally surprised at Trinket's words.

'You mean, my name was on the stone tablet?'

'Yes.'

No sooner had Trinket said this than he realized what a spot he'd be in if she asked him to recite the inscription. But luckily for him, she did not.

'Your surname is Wei, isn't it? And you come from Peking?'

'Yes,' Trinket replied.

'Comrade Dhuta told me that you once met a fat lady called Liu Yan in Peking, and that she taught you some kungfu skills. Is that right?'

Figuring that Fat Dhuta must have reported everything he had said to the Leader and Madame Hong, except for the whereabouts of one of the Sutras (the one supposed to be in the Shaolin Monastery), Trinket resolved to keep on lying. After all, the Fat Sow was dead, and could not contradict him.

'Yes,' he answered. 'Auntie Liu was a good friend of my uncle's; she often used to drop by.'

'What for?' Madame asked with a sly little smile.

'She used to like chatting and joking with my uncle. Sometimes they even used to cuddle and kiss a bit. They didn't know I was watching,' said Trinket, thinking that details like this might make his story more plausible.

'You naughty boy! Spying on other people like that!' Madame Hong was still smiling. Then she turned to the Black Dragon Marshal, and her tone of voice altered. 'Did you hear what he said? I don't think the boy is lying.'

Trinket saw the Black Dragon Marshal's countenance change. Shaking with abject terror, he threw himself on his knees and knocked his head again and again on the ground.

'I . . . I have been negligent,' he said, 'and for that I deserve the harshest punishment. But I beg you to have . . . mercy on me so that I can atone for my fault with good service.'

Trinket was puzzled. What had his story about the Fat Sow messing about with his 'uncle' got to do with this old man? Why was he so terrified?

'Atone with good service? What good service have you ever performed?' The smile was still there, but fainter. 'I thought that the people you sent to Peking on this mission were doing their duty properly, working loyally for their Leader. But it seems they were just indulging in debauchery.'

The Black Dragon Marshal kept knocking his head on the ground, and blood was pouring from his forehead. Trinket felt sorry for him and wanted to put in a good word for him, but could think of nothing to say.

The Black Dragon Marshal hobbled forward on his knees.

'Leader, I braved so many dangers with you!' he cried.

'What's the use of talking about the past?' sneered Madame Hong. 'You're getting old. It's high time you stepped aside.'

The Black Dragon Marshal raised his head and turned to Leader Hong.

'Leader, have you no feeling left for an old Comrade?'

'There are too many useless old men in our Sect,' replied the Leader. His voice was expressionless, and there was not the least trace of emotion on his face. 'It's time for some reorganization.'

This was the first time that Trinket had heard his voice. It was deep and muffled. Suddenly a loud chorus rang out from the massed acolytes:

'Obey His Teachings! Follow Him to Victory!'

The Black Dragon Marshal heaved a desperate sigh, and staggered to his feet.

'Out with the Old! In with the New!' he said. 'It seems it is time for us old people to step aside. Time for us to die.'

He turned around.

'Bring it to me.'

Four acolytes in black standing in the doorway hurried into the hall, each bearing a wooden plate with a brass cover. They placed the plates on the ground in front of the Black Dragon Marshal and retreated quickly. Everyone else in the hall took a few paces back.

'Obey His Teachings! F'ollow Him to Victory!' mumbled the Black Dragon Marshal. Then suddenly: 'Ha ha. . . . Not this time I won't!'

He stretched out his hand and, taking one of the brass covers by its knob, lifted it up. Something wriggled out from under the cover. It was a bright banded little snake. There was a sudden flash of light, and the blade of a knife struck from the side, slicing the snake clean in half. It fell twitching back onto the plate.

Trinket cried out in surprise, as did the whole assembly.

'Who did that?'

'Who's the rebel?'

'Get him!'

'Treason! Who dares defy the Leader?'

Madame Hong suddenly stood up with her arms folded, and swayed her body three times from side to side. This was clearly a prearranged sign. It was immediately followed by the clanking sound of swords being drawn from their scabbards. A massed phalanx of acolytes came rushing up to the front of the hall, and, dividing themselves neatly into small groups, according to the colour they were wearing, proceeded to surround each of the fifty or sixty Marshals, including Fat Dhuta and Doctor Lu.

'You must have spent months rehearsing this, Madame,' said a black-bearded Taoist in his fifties, laughing. 'It seems a rather heavy-handed way of dealing with old folks like us.'

'Don't be insolent to the Leader and Madame,' shouted two of the eight young girls in red who had surrounded him, their swords pointed at his chest.

'Madame,' continued the Taoist. 'It was I who did it. I, Rootless the Taoist, killed the snake. Punish me. There is no need to put the blame on anyone else.'

'So you confess. Very good.'

Madame Hong smiled as she returned to her chair.

'But why? The Leader has been so good to you; he appointed you Red Dragon Marshal, above all other Comrades except for himself. Why would you want to turn against him?'

'I have no desire to turn against him. I just wish to beg mercy for the Black Dragon Marshal. He has done so much for our Sect over the years. It seems wrong to kill him just because some of his subordinates have failed to perform their duties.'

'What if I decline your request?'

Still the smile.

'It is true that the Leader founded the Mystic Dragon Sect,' replied Rootless the Taoist. 'But thousands of other Comrades also braved dangers and played their part. Altogether one thousand and twenty-three of us elders took part in the armed struggle then, and now less than a hundred remain. Some died at the hands of our enemies. Others were eliminated by the Leader. I beg the Leader to be merciful to us and not to demand our lives. If he has had enough of us, and wants to replace us, he can just dismiss us.'

'Since it was founded, no one has been allowed to leave the Sect alive,' said Madame Hong grimly. 'You must be out of your mind.'

'So you reject my request?'

'I regret that our rules do not allow this to happen.'

'I see.' Rootless the Taoist laughed. 'So you are going to put us all to death.'

She smiled.

'Not necessarily. The Leader will always be good to any loyal Comrade. Total loyalty to the Leader is the only thing that matters.'

She turned to the others with a smile and continued:

'Raise your hands if you are loyal to the Leader.'

The acolytes in the hall all raised their left hands at the same time, and so did all the elders, including Rootless the Taoist. Trinket raised his hand too.

'We vow unshakeable loyalty to the Leader,' they cried in one voice.

'Very good,' said Madame Hong, nodding her head. 'So everyone in this room is loyal to the Leader, including apparently this boy who doesn't even belong to our Sect.'

('Yes, I took the oath—to be loyal to an ugly old turtle!' Trinket muttered silently to himself.)

'So that means there isn't a single traitor here. It's curious, isn't it? There must be something wrong somewhere. I think I'd better look into this carefully. I'll need to ask a few questions. Sorry to have to put the older Comrades to such inconvenience.'

She turned to the acolytes:

'Tie them up!'

'Wait a moment!' cried a big burly man.

'What do you propose, White Dragon Marshal?' Madame asked.

'Nothing. I just feel it's unjust.'

'Are you accusing me of being unjust?' she asked, clicking her tongue.

'No, I would never dare do that. I have followed the Leader for twenty years and have fought bravely by his side. These boys and girls weren't even born when I risked my life for the Sect. Why do you consider them loyal to the Leader but not us?'

'So you are indispensable to the Sect, are you, White Dragon Marshal?'

'The Mystic Dragon Sect was founded by the Leader. We're only his followers, but—'

'But what?'

'If we deserve no credit, then these young people deserve even less.'

'And that includes me?'

'In a way,' he answered hesitantly.

'If none of us can claim any credit, then you can't blame me for killing you, can you?' she said slowly. There was a murderous look in her eyes, though her smile was as sweet and charming as ever.

'My life is unimportant, of course,' cried the White Dragon Marshal angrily. 'But if you execute others who are loyal or who have rendered meritorious service, you will be destroying the very foundation and future of the Sect.'

'I see. Oh dear, I'm feeling so tired . . .'

Her languid yawn was, in fact, a secret sign to commence the execution. On hearing it, the seven boys dressed in white surrounding the White Dragon Marshal thrust their swords into his body in one concerted movement. As they withdrew the swords, blood spurted from the seven wounds, and splashed all over their white clothes.

'My Leader,' cried the White Dragon Marshal in pain, 'you . . . you . . . you have a heart of stone.'

So saying, he fell dead to the ground.

The seven boys marched smartly out of the hall.

The other elders all trembled with fear. The White Dragon Marshal was a veteran kungfu expert, and yet even he was powerless against the swords of these boys. Clearly they had received secret training from the Leader and had practised the manoeuvre many times.

Madame Hong put her left hand lightly to her pretty little lips and yawned again. Even when yawning she managed to look seductive. The Leader showed not the slightest sign of emotion; it was as if nothing had happened.

'Blue Dragon Marshal, Yellow Dragon Marshal,' said Madame Hong softly. 'Do you think White Dragon Marshal deserved his punishment?'

'He had been planning this rebellion for a long time,' said an old man with small eyes and a pointed chin. 'I reported it to you several times, Madame. But you insisted on giving him another chance, because he was an old Comrade. You were too forgiving! White Dragon was evil! It was kind of you to let him die such a quick death.'

'What an arse-licker!' thought Trinket.

Mutiny on Snake Island

'What about you, Blue Dragon?' said Madame Hong with a smile. 'What do you think?'

'Stand back!' cried a tall, thin man in his fifties, glaring at the

acolytes in blue who were standing around him. 'If the Leader
wants me killed, I can do it myself.'

The eight boys reached out their swords until the tips of the
blades were touching the edge of his gown.

'Ha ha ha!' the man laughed contemptuously, and raising his
hands slowly, he took hold of the front of his gown. 'Leader Hong,
Madame Hong, when I swore with the other Dragon Marshals to
devote myself to the Sect, I never dreamed that things would come
to this. Yellow Dragon is a vile coward . . .'

With a rapid movement of his hands and the sound of tearing
cloth, Blue Dragon ripped his long gown in two, and flailing his
arms outwards he wound the long strips of cloth around the boys'
swords and sent them clanging across the room. Next came a flash
of light, and he produced two twenty-inch short-swords of his
own, one in each hand. He moved into the attack like a deadly
whirlwind. There was a nasty sound of tearing flesh as he drove his
twin swords into the boys' chests one after the other. They fell to
the ground in a neat circle around him, blood spurting from their
wounds.

Gasping with horror, Madame Hong clapped her hands
several times, and in answer to this summons, more than twenty
more boys came forward and surrounded the Blue Dragon Marshal
again, each pointing a sword at him.

'Ha ha ha!' laughed Blue Dragon again. 'Madame, these
little brats of yours are no damned good! Our Leader will
need something a bit better than *them* if he wants to achieve
Victory . . .'

The Leader seemed as unconcerned about the killing of the
eight boys as he had been about the killing of White Dragon. He
sat in his chair motionless and unmoved. Madame Hong glanced
at her husband, almost with a feeling of remorse. Then she gave a
pretty smile and sat down.

'Blue Dragon Marshal,' she said, 'you're certainly a master
with the sword . . .'

Suddenly there was a resounding series of clangs as swords
fell from the hands of the acolytes in the hall and crashed to the
ground. One by one the young fanatics fell dizzy and exhausted to
the floor. In a matter of seconds, the hall was strewn with prostrate
bodies.

'What . . . what's going on?' cried Madame Hong fearfully.
She herself felt weak, and slipped from her bamboo chair.

'Leader,' said the Blue Dragon Marshal, standing erect and proud, with a hideous grin on his face. 'When you had so many of us put to death, did you never think you would see this day?'

He clanked one of his swords against the other, and, stepping over the bodies, walked towards the Leader.

'Not exactly,' the Leader said contemptuously. He clutched one of the arms of his chair and snapped off a piece of it. The Blue Dragon Marshal took two steps backwards, changing countenance in an instant.

'Leader,' he said, 'our great Sect is being broken up and divided against itself. I suppose you now realize who is the source of all the trouble, don't you?'

The Leader cleared his throat. Suddenly he slipped from his chair to the floor. Just as the Blue Dragon Marshal hastened forwards in delight, something came whistling towards him at high speed. It was the broken arm of the Leader's bamboo chair, thrown with such phenomenal strength that, although the Blue Dragon Marshal managed to catch it on the blade of his sword and slice it in two, one half of it impaled itself in his chest, breaking five or six of his ribs and piercing through to his lung. He cried out in pain, and panted hoarsely for breath. He staggered, and his swords dropped from his hands, straight into the prostrate bodies of the two boys lying beneath him.

A chorus of cheers rose from the hall to see the Leader getting the better of Blue Dragon.

The Leader now tried struggling to his feet, propping himself up with one hand; but no sooner was one leg straight than he felt weak in the knees and tumbled clumsily over onto the ground again. Then the others began to realize that they had all, including the Leader, been given a poison which had incapacitated them.

The only person left standing in the hall was Trinket. He was only short, but he towered above the body-strewn hall like a giant. He had no idea what everyone was doing lying on the ground. When he had recovered from his surprise, he tugged at Fat Dhuta's gown.

'Didn't the poison have any effect on you?' asked Fat Dhuta incredulously.

'Poison? I . . . I don't know,' said Trinket, puzzled. He tried hard to help Fat Dhuta up onto his feet, but Fat Dhuta was too weak and had to sit down again.

'Comrade Xu,' said Doctor Lu abruptly, addressing Blue
Dragon, 'what . . . what kind of poison did you use?'

The Blue Dragon Marshal seemed drunk. He was swaying
from side to side, holding onto a pillar for support, and coughing
persistently.

'Too bad,' he said between coughs. 'Too . . . too bad! I was
so nearly there! And I failed. I'm . . . I'm really useless.'

'Was it Seven Worm Disabling Potion?' Doctor Lu asked
again. 'Or Thousand Mile Devitalizing Scent? Or . . . was it
Blood . . . Blood and Bone . . . Combustion Powder?'

He had mentioned three potent types of poison, and when
he came to the last one, his voice trembled in grave fear. The Blue
Dragon Marshal was coughing badly and unable to reply.

'Why is that Mr Wei hasn't been affected?' Doctor Lu seemed
quite bewildered. 'Ah!' He suddenly cried, as if he had at last understood the truth. 'You put some Floral Serpent Bane on the tips of
your swords. What a superb stratagem! Mr Wei, would you be so
good as to go and smell the Blue Dragon Marshal's two swords,
and see if you can detect the scent of flowers?'

Trinket was damned if he was going to start sniffing poisoned
swords.

'I can smell it from here,' he told Doctor Lu. Trinket had
already detected a faint but intoxicating fragrance in the air.

'Ah, there we have it then!' said Doctor Lu, beaming happily.
'Floral Serpent Bane is a secretly distilled perfume, which produces
a pungent smell when it comes into contact with blood. This
normally has a pleasant, relaxing effect. But . . . on the island
we regularly take Realgar Elixir to protect us against snakes, and
when the Bane reacts with the Elixir, it will make us feel weak for
twelve hours or so. Superb, Comrade Xu! You had it all planned.
And you yourself must have stopped taking the Elixir several
months ago.'

Blue Dragon was sitting on the dead bodies of the two
boys.

'But in the end Hong Antong's evil hands got the better of
me!' he said, shaking his head. 'Man proposes, but fate disposes!'

'How dare you call the Leader by his holy name!' cried one
of the boys. 'Madman! Heretic!'

Blue Dragon rose slowly to his feet, picked up a sword from
the floor, and staggered towards the Leader.

'So they won't let me call you by your name?' He was

overtaken by another coughing fit. 'Let's see, shall we. . . . When you're dead, perhaps then they will!'

The boys cried out in alarm. Then came the deep, hoarse voice of the Yellow Dragon Marshal.

'Kill Hong Antong, Comrade Xu, and all of us will revere you as the new Leader of the Mystic Dragon Sect. Say after me, everyone: We swear to obey Leader Xu's Command, to follow Him with Unswerving Loyalty.'

There was a brief silence, then twenty or thirty voices could be heard repeating the oath, some firmly, others more hesitantly.

Blue Dragon took a few steps forward, and started coughing and swaying again. He was badly injured, but he knew that come what may he must kill the Leader first.

Madame Hong suddenly laughed.

'You're finished, Blue Dragon,' she said in her ever sweet and softly mesmerizing voice. 'Your legs are weak and the blood is draining from the wound in your chest. You're going to die. Sit down, you must be very tired. Sit down, that's right, sit down and have a rest. Put down your sword and come over here. Sit down beside me, so that I can treat your wound. That's right, sit down, and put down the sword.'

Blue Dragon took a few more steps and finally sat slowly down on the floor, letting his sword slip from his grasp.

Realizing that Blue Dragon was all done in, Yellow Dragon decided to try another volte-face.

'You, our Leader? You little rat!' he jeered. 'Just take a piss and have a good look at yourself! You're no Leader!'

'What a mean, shameless fellow you are, Yellow Dragon!' shouted Rootless the Taoist, the Red Dragon Marshal. 'Tacking with the wind. Once I can move again, the first thing I'll do is to have your head!'

'Why are you so angry? I . . . I . . .' protested Yellow Dragon, but seeing Blue Dragon struggling shakily to rise to his feet, he decided it imprudent to say any more. All eyes in the hall were focused on him.

'Comrade Xu,' said Madame Hong softly, 'you're very tired, you'd better sit down. Look at me, I'll sing you a little song. Have a good rest. I'll sing you a little song every day from now on. Do you think I'm beautiful?'

'Yes, you . . . you're very beautiful . . .' mumbled Blue Dragon. 'But I . . . I don't dare look at you . . .'

He was too weak to stand and sat on the floor again. But he knew that if he stayed sitting and did not kill the Leader, all the elders would be in grave danger. The Leader had the most powerful Inner Force. He would be the first to recover, and then he would kill all the elders.

'Doctor . . . Lu . . . I can't move,' he said. 'You must think . . . of a way out . . .'

He was coughing again. Doctor Lu turned to Trinket.

'Mr Wei,' he said, 'the Leader is merciless. As soon as the poison wears off, he will dispose of us all. You'd better kill him and Madame Hong now!'

Trinket to the Rescue

Trinket had already seen the danger Doctor Lu was telling him about, of course. He picked up a sword from the floor and slowly walked towards the Leader.

'Madame Hong is a fox,' warned Doctor Lu. 'She's a witch. Don't look at her. Never look into her eyes.'

'All right,' said Trinket, holding the sword and walking a few steps further forward.

'Don't you think I'm beautiful, little man?' murmured Madame Hong in her soft, bewitching voice. Trinket immediately turned to look at her.

'Don't!' cried Fat Dhuta. 'She's an evil woman!'

Trinket shuddered and closed his eyes tightly. Madame Hong gave a soft laugh.

'Look at me, little man! Go on, you can see your reflection in my eyes!'

Trinket looked into her smiling, glistening eyes. His heart melted. He raised his sword and advanced towards the Leader, thinking to himself, 'How could I ever harm a beautiful woman like you? But I still have to kill your husband.'

Suddenly a voice rang out from his left side.

'Don't, Brother Wei!'

It was a very familiar voice. Startled, Trinket turned around and saw a pretty girl lying on the floor, dressed in red. It was the Little Countess, Mu Jianping. Trinket was utterly astounded. She was the last person he would have expected to find there.

'What are you doing here?' he asked her, hastening to lift her up.

She ignored his question, but repeated that he must on no account kill the Leader.

'Have you joined the Mystic Dragons?' said Trinket, in amazement. 'What's going on?'

Her body was as soft as if every bone in it had melted. Resting her head on Trinket's shoulder, she whispered into his ear.

'If you kill the Leader and Madame Hong, that will be the end of me. These old men are sure to kill all of us.'

'But surely if I ask them not to hurt you, they'll listen to me,' said Trinket.

'Oh no they won't!' cried the Little Countess. 'Anyway, the Leader has given us all the drug, and no one but he has the remedy for it.'

Trinket was so happy to see her again after such a long separation, and now, with her sweet body in his arms and her soft voice in his ear, he found it hard to go against her wishes.

'But if I don't kill the Leader,' he said, holding her tightly and whispering back, 'he'll kill me instead, as soon as the poison wears off.'

'Why would the Leader and Madame Hong want to do that, if you were the person who saved their lives?' said the Little Countess.

Trinket agreed with her. The best solution would be to spare the Leader and his wife, and at the same time somehow to save the lives of Fat Dhuta, Doctor Lu, and Rootless the Taoist.

'All right, doll,' he said to the Little Countess, giving her a kiss on her left cheek. 'Even if the Leader kills me, I'll do my best to save you.'

Her face flushed and a joyful look came into her eyes. He laid her gently back on the floor and turned to Doctor Lu.

'Neither the Leader nor Madame Hong should be killed,' he said. 'The inscription prophesies Long Life and Blessings for both of them. It must be obeyed.'

'That inscription is a fake!' protested Doctor Lu heatedly. 'Stop fooling around. Dispatch them both at once or we will all die a horrible death.'

Trinket shook his head.

'You mustn't talk like that, Doctor Lu. Have you got the antidote? No, we must help the Leader and Madame to recover from the poison as soon as possible.'

'You're right, little man,' said Madame Hong softly. 'You

really are very clever. A young hero like you must have been sent
by Heaven to assist the Leader. We are very lucky to have you in
the Sect.'

Her words gave Trinket a thrill of pleasure.

'But Madame, I'm not a member of the Sect.'

'That's simple enough,' she replied. 'You can join the Sect
right away; I'll be your sponsor.'

She then turned to the Leader.

'What position should we appoint this young hero to, con-
sidering the remarkable service he's rendered to the Sect?'

'Since White Dragon has been executed for treason,'
answered the Leader, 'we should make this young person the next
White Dragon Marshal.'

'An excellent idea!'

Madame went on to explain the workings of the Sect to
Trinket.

'Under the Leader, there are the Five Dragon Marshals—the
Blue, the Yellow, the Red, the White, and the Black. It is an unprecedented honour for you to be made a Marshal as soon as you join
the Sect. It shows that the Leader thinks very highly of you. We
know that your family name is Wei. What other names do you
have?'

'Trinket,' he replied. 'And on River and Lake they sometimes
call me Little White Dragon.'

The *nom de guerre* given him by Whiskers strangely foreshad-
owed his impending elevation.

'What a miraculous coincidence!' purred Madame Hong. 'Fate
certainly moves in mysterious ways!'

'Beware, Mr Wei,' cried Doctor Lu agitatedly. 'Don't you see?
Even if they do make you White Dragon Marshal, they will dispose
of you whenever they feel like it. Look what they did to the last
White Dragon! Kill them! Act now, and we will make *you* our new
Leader!'

Fat Dhuta, Xu the Blue Dragon, and Rootless the Taoist all
gasped at the sheer audacity of the doctor's proposal. But this might
be the only way out. Somehow they had to lure him into taking
the plunge. He must kill. The important thing was to get rid of the
present Leader and his wife. Afterwards, even if this boy did
become the new leader, they could easily control him.

'Yes, yes!' they cried in unison. 'We swear to obey Leader
Wei's Command, to follow Him with Unswerving Loyalty!'

This was beginning to sound rather interesting, thought Trinket. He glanced at Madame Hong out of the corner of his eye. She was half sitting, half reclining on the bamboo chair, her body softly wrapped around it as if there was not a hard bone in it. He took in the gentle curve of her breast, the rosy glow of her cheeks, the moist gleam that shone from her eyes. His mind wandered.

'Being Leader wouldn't be much fun. But she's gorgeous . . .'

But after a moment's reflection he dismissed the idea. The whole thing was altogether too dangerous. These Dragon-folk were capable of anything. They'd use him, and then dump him. If there was one thing he wanted above all else, it was to stay alive.

'I have another idea,' he said, turning to the Leader and Madame Hong and addressing them both. 'Will you agree to forget what's happened today? Will you forgive Doctor Lu and Blue Dragon for everything?'

Then turning to Doctor Lu, he continued:

'And I want you to give them the antidote for the poison. Then everyone can make up.'

'Very well,' the Leader hurried to answer before Doctor Lu could speak. 'Let's do as White Dragon suggests. He wants us to live in harmony, and let bygones be bygones. I'm ready to forgive and forget.'

'Wonderful!' cried Trinket with delight.

Doctor Lu could see that Trinket was not going to do it. He heaved a long sigh.

'In that case, I should like our Leader and Madame Hong to swear an oath.'

'I, Su Quan, will forgive and forget everything that has happened today,' declared Madame Hong. 'If I ever go back on my word, may I fall into the Dragon Pool and be bitten by ten thousand snakes.'

'May I, Hong Antong, the Leader of the Mystic Dragon Sect,' declared the Leader in his deep voice, 'fall into the Dragon Pool, and my flesh and bones be consumed by ten thousand snakes if I ever blame any old Comrade for what has happened here today.'

'What do you think, Blue Dragon?' asked Doctor Lu.

'I . . . I'm dying anyway . . .' gasped the Blue Dragon Marshal.

'What about you, Rootless?' Doctor Lu inquired.

'Very well,' said Rootless the Taoist loudly. 'Our Leader was once a great man, and we supported him loyally. Ever since he took Madame as his wife, he has changed. That was when he started promoting these children, and eliminating old Comrades like us. Actually, Blue Dragon was only trying to protect himself.'

'Long Life to Our Leader! Blessings be on Him!' cried all the boys and girls in the hall.

'Mr Wei,' said Doctor Lu, 'it is very easy to dispel the effects of the poison. Go outside, fetch some cold water, and give each of them some to drink.'

Trinket went outside, but could not see any water. Rounding the building, he saw a row of over twenty stone vats filled with water for putting out fires. He immediately filled up a bucket and brought it into the hall. He gave the first ladle of water to the Leader, the second to Madame Hong, and the third to Rootless the Taoist.

'You're a great hero,' he said to Rootless.

He then helped Fat Dhuta, Doctor Lu, and the Little Countess drink the cold water. They all threw up on taking it, and gradually recovered movement in their limbs. When Doctor Lu was able to get to his feet, he went to help Blue Dragon and treated his wounds. Fat Dhuta and the others started ladling out cold water for their friends. Before long, Mu Jianping got up and gave water to a few of the girls from her Branch. Soon the hall stank of vomit.

'Go and rest, all of you,' said Madame. 'We'll meet again tomorrow.'

'I forgive you all,' said the Leader. 'There must be no more quarrelling, and no taking of revenge. Anyone who offends against this order will be severely punished.'

The assembly vowed obedience, but their hearts were filled with suspicion and anxiety.

'Come with me, White Dragon Marshal,' Madame Hong said softly, beckoning to Trinket, who at first had no idea that she was calling him.

The Leader and Madame walked out of the hall together, followed by Trinket the White Dragon Marshal. Those Sect members who were now able to move bowed to them as they passed, shouting:

'Long Life to Our Leader! Blessings be on Him!'

Trinket the White Dragon Marshal

They walked along a black flagstone road, round to the left of the assembly hall. After passing through a large grove of bamboos, they came to a level terrace. On the terrace, several more large bamboo buildings had been constructed, and a dozen armed youths stood guard at the front and rear entrances. They all bowed to the Leader as he approached.

Madame led Trinket inside one of the bamboo buildings.

'This is Mr Wei,' she told a boy in white. 'He's the new Marshal of your White Dragon Branch. Show him the way to the east wing where he can rest, and attend to him well.'

Casting Trinket a smile, she went on into the inner house. A number of boys in white greeted Trinket with a bow. Trinket, having been both a senior Palace Eunuch and a Triad Lodge Master, was by now quite used to this kind of subservience and merely nodded in reply.

The boys led him into the east wing and served him tea. The 'wing' was in fact a palatial apartment furnished in the grandest style, with gold and jade antiques on the tables and shelves, calligraphic scrolls and paintings hanging on the walls, and the most elegant brocade coverlets spread on the bed. It was known as the Abode of Immortal Bliss, and was reserved for the Leader's most honoured guests.

That afternoon, Trinket asked the boys in white to tell him something about the way the Sect was organized. He learned that each of the five Branches (or Dragon Gates as they were called) of the Mystic Dragon Sect consisted of a Marshal, twenty or so elders, a hundred acolytes (boys and girls), and several hundred rank and file members. The elders were distinguished veteran generals who had rendered outstanding service to the Sect; but recently, the Leader had gone to great lengths to promote new recruits, and so acolytes in their twenties were often appointed to positions immediately under the Marshals. For this reason, they were not in the least surprised that young Trinket had become the new White Dragon Marshal.

The next morning the Leader and Madame Hong called another assembly in the hall. There was a general air of apprehension. Despite his promises of the previous day, the Leader was both inscrutable and unpredictable. Anything could happen. He and Madame Hong seated themselves. Trinket was asked to stand fourth among the five Marshals.

'How is the Blue Dragon Marshal?' asked the Leader.

Doctor Lu bowed.

'His injuries are serious, Leader. He is not yet out of danger.'

'Here are three Breath of Life Pills,' said the Leader, producing a little red porcelain bottle from his bosom. 'Give them to him.'

Without even the slightest movement, the Leader released the bottle, and it flew slowly through the air in the direction of Doctor Lu, who caught it in his outheld hand.

The doctor prostrated himself.

'You are most gracious, Leader.'

He knew how precious these Breath of Life Pills were. Some time ago, the Leader had sent far and wide to search for the rarest herbs—including three-hundred-year-old ginseng, the gall bladder of the white bear, and pods of the snow lotus. Boiling up the ingredients and making them into pills was a long and difficult process. Only a dozen had ever been made. With these, Xu should make a full recovery.

The other elders also bowed and thanked the Leader, thinking that if he had forgiven the Blue Dragon Marshal, they themselves must be out of danger. The atmosphere in the hall lightened noticeably.

'I understand that on the Wutai Mountains you came across a stone tablet with a Tadpole inscription. Is that right, White Dragon Marshal?' asked Madame Hong.

'Yes,' Trinket answered, bending at his waist.

'I made a rubbing of the inscription,' said Fat Dhuta, producing an oilskin packet from inside his gown. He opened the packet, took out a large rubbing, and hung it on the eastern wall of the hall. The strange, squiggly white characters on a black background were quite unintelligible to the assembled company.

'Read us out the characters if you know them, White Dragon Marshal,' said Madame.

'Certainly,' said Trinket and, looking at the rubbing, he began to recite loudly the text concocted by Doctor Lu:

'In the Second Year of the Zhen-Guan Period of the Tang Dynasty . . .'

He recited the text slowly, and whenever he was having trouble remembering a word, pretended not to be able to decipher one of the characters on the rubbing. When he came to the bit about 'Long Life and Blessings to the Great Leader! May He Live For Ever!', he changed the words to 'Blessings to the Great Leader and His Wife.'

The 'and His Wife' sounded a bit crude. The learned doctor

would doubtless have come up with a much more elegant turn of phrase.

'You see! I'm actually in the inscription, Leader,' said Madame Hong, beaming with joy. 'The White Dragon Marshal couldn't possibly have made it up.'

The Leader also seemed very happy. He even smiled and nodded his head.

'Excellent! So our Sect was prophesied as long ago as the Tang dynasty.'

'Long Life to Our Leader! Blessings be on Him!' resounded through the hall. Even Rootless the Taoist and the other elders seemed impressed.

Trinket finally came to the last part of the inscription where the location of the eight copies of the Sutra was divulged.

'How strange that they even predicted Satrap Wu,' said Madame Hong. 'It seems that the eight Sutras are ours by right, Leader. It's just a matter of time.'

'Yes.'

The Leader smiled and played with his beard.

'Long Life to Our Leader! Long Life to Our Leader!' rang out again.

When the chanting had subsided, the Leader gave the order that the altar be set up—he now wanted to install Trinket ceremonially as Marshal of the White Dragon Branch. Trinket noticed how different their ritual was from that of the Triads. On top of the altar stood five golden plates, each containing a small snake of a different colour: blue, yellow, red, white, and black. Their bodies were coiled, but their heads were raised and their tongues flicked in and out.

Trinket bowed before the Five Miniature Mystic Dragons, then he kowtowed to the Leader and Madame Hong. He was congratulated by Rootless the Taoist and the other elders. Madame Hong then poured him three cups of the famous Realgar Elixir.

'Drink this elixir, and the Mystic Dragons on this island will recognize that you are one of us; they won't bite you any more.'

The Leader presented Trinket with a string of realgar beads and ordered him to wear it underneath his clothing, saying that this too would protect him from any kind of poison. Then the elders and acolytes of the White Dragon Branch came over together to pay their respects to their new Marshal.

'Since the Blue Dragon Marshal is sick and in need of rest,' announced the Leader, 'and since Comrade Dhuta has made a contribution by making the rubbing of the inscription, Comrade Dhuta will be in charge of the Blue Dragon Branch until the Blue Dragon Marshal has recovered.'

Fat Dhuta bowed.

'The five Marshals and Doctor Lu should proceed to the inner hall,' commanded the Leader. 'I wish to hold a council.'

He and Madame Hong immediately descended from their seats and made their way to the inner hall, with the six others following at their heels.

The Five Dragon Disc

The inner hall was situated behind the main hall, and smaller in size. The Leader and Madame Hong sat down on two large bamboo chairs in the centre. Fat Dhuta, as acting Blue Dragon, and three other Marshals sat on four of the five stools placed in front of the bamboo chairs.

'Please be seated, White Dragon Marshal,' said Fat Dhuta.

Trinket hesitated, seeing that Doctor Lu was still standing.

'Go ahead, White Dragon Marshal,' said the doctor with a smile. 'An ordinary Comrade such as myself has no right to be seated in the Hall of the Hidden Dragon.'

Trinket sat down, and Doctor Lu remained standing next to the Black Dragon Marshal.

Suddenly, the four other Marshals rose to their feet. Without even thinking, Trinket stood up too.

'Obey His Teachings!' they chanted in unison.

Trinket promptly joined in: 'Follow Him to Victory!'

His high-pitched voice stood out from the others. The Leader nodded his head, and they all resumed their seats.

'The inscription tells us that the eight copies of the Sutra were scattered in different places,' began the Leader. 'But according to the Black Dragon Marshal's report, four of those copies are now in the Palace. How has this come about?'

'One was originally in the Shaolin Monastery, one was in the Mu Family estate and two were elsewhere,' answered the Black Dragon Marshal. 'Later all four were seized and taken to the Palace by the Tartars.'

The Leader brooded for a moment. Black Dragon looked extremely nervous.

'Have you any news from your brother-in-arms?' said the Leader, turning to Fat Dhuta.

'Leader,' replied Fat Dhuta respectfully, 'Thin Dhuta once told me he'd come across something in the possession of the Head of the Bordered Blue Banner. But it never came to anything.'

'The Bordered Blue Banner?' ran Trinket's thoughts. 'Where have I heard that before? Isn't that where Auntie Tao's Master used to work? And Fat Dhuta . . . so, he's got a brother-in-arms called Thin Dhuta . . .'

The Leader spoke again.

'Tell him to speed up his investigation. There must be no more slacking.'

'Yes, Leader! Yes, Leader!'

'Since there's been no progress, perhaps we should send someone new,' said Madame Hong.

'Wonderful idea,' commented the Yellow Dragon Marshal hastily. 'Why not send the new White Dragon Marshal? Look at the red glow between his eyebrows—after the Leader and yourself, he must be the one among us most favoured by fortune.'

'But he's only a child,' said the Leader, smiling and playing with his beard. 'Can he be entrusted with such an important mission?'

Being a Dragon Marshal was not a career that appealed enormously to Trinket on any long-term basis, especially since it apparently involved being marooned on this snake-infested island. It was of course great fun goggling at the gorgeous Madame Hong, but if he did too much of that, the Leader would undoubtedly notice and find some way of eliminating him. In the circumstances, going to Peking on official business seemed by far the best option.

'Leader, Madame Hong,' he said, 'I'm not good at much, I know, but I reckon I could sneak into the Palace and steal those four Sutras for you.'

The Leader nodded.

'According to Black Dragon,' said the Leader very slowly, 'the people he had working for us in the Palace came to hear of a boy eunuch close to the Young Emperor, someone with a name like Laurie . . .'

Trinket's heart missed a beat. For a moment he wondered if the Leader had seen through his entire story.

'It seems the Young Emperor sent this Laurie to the Wutai Mountains to meddle in our Sect's activities there,' the Leader continued. 'We sent several groups after him, but none of them managed to find him—not even Comrade Fat Dhuta. And now we've found you instead . . .'

The Leader paused.

'Didn't I say that fortune had smiled on him!' mumbled Yellow Dragon.

The Leader nodded.

'White Dragon Marshal,' he continued, 'when you get into the Palace, I want you to find out what the Emperor had in mind in sending this eunuch of his to Wutai.'

'Yes, Leader!' responded Trinket smartly. By now he was in a cold sweat.

'The eight copies of the Sutra contain secret doctrines,' said Madame Hong. 'Important doctrines concerning the preservation of Long Life. Our Leader is certainly destined to receive them. Do this for the Leader, White Dragon Marshal, and he will certainly grant you another reward.'

Trinket stood up and bowed low.

'I will always be grateful to the Leader and to Madame,' he declared. 'I will devote my life to my country and die on the battlefield.'

Trinket, as usual, had dredged something up for the occasion from his repertoire of storytellers' tags. An appropriate declaration for a general setting off on a campaign, perhaps. But not quite the thing for the present context.

'Loyally said!' Madame Hong smiled. 'You can choose a few people to go with you.'

Trinket was not too keen on the idea of other Comrades breathing down his neck.

'We don't need too many people. Don't want to give ourselves away. Perhaps one or two girls from the Red Dragon Branch—they could always disguise themselves as Palace maids.'

He had in mind the Little Countess, of course.

'I'm afraid my girls are not much use,' remarked Rootless, the Red Dragon Marshal. 'But you're welcome to them. Choose whichever ones you want, provided the Leader and Madame approve.'

'Leader, Madame,' began Doctor Lu, 'I committed a grave

error yesterday. Thanks to the Leader's magnanimity, my life has been spared and—'

'Please don't keep harping on about what happened yesterday,' said the Leader, waving him aside with a frown. 'None of you are ever to mention it again.'

'Thank you, Leader,' said Doctor Lu. 'What I was wanting to say was, I should like to go with the White Dragon Marshal myself. It would be a way of showing my gratitude.'

'You are certainly a resourceful and cool-headed person,' replied the Leader. 'And adept with both sword and pen. You know how to cobble together a plausible enough text too. Very well, Comrade Lu, you can go with the White Dragon Marshal.'

Doctor Lu pondered that phrase of the Leader's about cobbling together a text. It appeared the Leader knew only too well that the inscription was a forgery.

'Leader, Madame,' said Fat Dhuta, 'I too am willing to go with the White Dragon Marshal to Peking and render you service.'

The Leader nodded his approval. Then he noticed that the Yellow Dragon Marshal was about to offer as well.

'We can't have too many people going, or we will give the whole thing away. Only Doctor Lu and Fat Dhuta. The two of you are to act on the White Dragon Marshal's orders.'

'Yes, Leader!' Doctor Lu and Fat Dhuta bowed.

Madame then produced a miniature dragon from her bosom. It was very colourful, cast from bronze, gold, copper, silver, and iron: the five metals representing the five Branches of the Sect.

'This is the Leader's Five Dragon Disc, White Dragon Marshal,' she said. 'It's yours for the time being. When they see it, members of the Sect will obey you just as they do the Leader. It gives you absolute power over their lives. You are to return it when you have completed your mission.'

'Yes,' replied Trinket, accepting the disc respectfully in both hands.

Trinket had fresh worries on his mind. Originally he had thought he could forget about the Mystic Dragon Sect once he had returned to Peking. But now that he had this Five Dragon Disc, he would probably be in for a whole lot more trouble.

'White Dragon Marshal, Doctor Lu, and Fat Dhuta, I want you to stay here for a while,' Madame Hong ordered. 'The rest of you may leave.'

Rootless, Black Dragon, and Yellow Dragon saluted and left.

The Leader now produced a black porcelain bottle, and tipped out three bright red pills.

'To reward your courage in undertaking this Peking mission,' he said, 'I now bestow on each of you a Leopard Embryo Pill.'

A combined expression of delight and awe suddenly entered the faces of Fat Dhuta and Doctor Lu. They bent their right knees to thank the Leader, then each of them took his pill and swallowed it. Trinket copied their actions exactly. Seconds after swallowing his pill, he felt a wave of warmth rising from the pit of his stomach, circulating slowly through his bloodstream and diffusing an indescribably pleasant sensation of well-being throughout his entire body.

'White Dragon Marshal, stay for a while,' Madame Hong commanded. 'You two may leave.'

Fat Dhuta and Doctor Lu retreated from the inner hall.

Three Beauties and Three Heroes

Madame Hong gave one of her disarming smiles.

'What weapons do you normally use, White Dragon?' she said.

'I've only ever learned how to use my dagger,' he replied.

'Show it to me.'

Trinket extracted the dagger from his boot, and held it out, handle first, to Madame Hong.

'A fine weapon!'

She pulled out one of her hairs and passed it lightly over the blade, which sliced it clean in two. The Great Leader made an approving noise. Trinket, ever quick to see an opportunity for ingratiating himself, immediately offered his dagger to Madame Hong as a present.

'A fine dagger such as this needs a beautiful owner,' he said, vaguely remembering some storyteller's proverb. 'And where could it find a more beautiful owner than you?'

Madame Hong simpered.

'What a dear boy! Come here, I'll teach you something *very* special in return. Three kungfu moves. They are known as the Three Beauties.'

She took out a silken handkerchief and used it to bind the dagger to her right calf. Then she turned to the Great Leader.

'Would you be so kind as to demonstrate the moves, Leader?'

The Leader graciously stepped forward. Suddenly, he shot out his left hand, gripped Madame Hong by the back of her neck, and hoisted her up into mid-air. Trinket's breath was taken away by the sheer speed of the move.

Madame Hong now twisted herself around, and kicked out with her right foot against the Leader's stomach. He in turn pulled back, and she then curved into the hollow made by his withdrawal, throwing her left arm around his neck and taking hold of her dagger with her right hand, pressing the point of it against the small of his back.

'That move is known as the Twirling Princess!'

Trinket clapped his hands in delight.

The Leader gently lowered Madame Hong to the ground. She replaced the dagger, did a quick little somersault, and landed prostrate on the ground. The Leader now thrust his right foot forward, placed it above her back, and made as if to point his sword against the back of her neck.

'Surrender?'

Just as Trinket thought she must have no other option, Madame Hong moved her head to the side and the Leader found himself thrusting into empty space. Another somersault and she had flipped between the Leader's legs and was holding the dagger at his back again.

'Excellent kungfu!' cried Trinket.

They carried on with this breathtaking display, demonstrating the second Beauty, named after another Princess, and then the third, known as the Princess Flying Swallow, a series of hair-raising (and deadly) moves in which Madame Hong came so close to slicing through the Leader's throat that she had Trinket gripping the back of his chair in suspense.

Madame Hong went through the intricate details of the Three Beauties for Trinket's benefit, and the Leader helped him to practise them. Flying Swallow was a particularly dangerous move to execute. The slightest mistake could result in self-destruction.

The Leader seemed in high spirits.

'Now it's my turn! I too should like to teach you three moves. Mine are called the Three Heroes. The Three Beauties are designed to kill. Mine are designed to make your enemy surrender.'

'You never mentioned your Three Heroes to me before!' complained Madame Hong.

'I made them up just now as I was watching you do the Three Beauties. I'd like to test them out. You can be my judge.'

Madame Hong cast him a quizzical glance.

'Our Leader does seem in a jolly mood today!'

'Even the greatest Hero was never a match for Beauty—such as yours . . .'

Madame Hong gave a little laugh, and purred:

'Please! Not in front of the boy!'

The Leader cleared his throat.

'Now, I want you to pretend that I am the White Dragon Marshal.'

Madame Hong reached out her left hand and lifted the Leader off the ground—all two hundred pounds of him. It seemed to cost her no effort at all.

'On guard!' cried the Leader.

He turned his left hand slowly and gave Madame Hong a tickle under the left armpit. She began laughing and the strength went out of her at once. She lowered him to the ground. He then gripped her round the neck with both hands, lifted her up into the air, and threw her over his shoulder. It was all done slowly and effortlessly. Trinket watched it all, and found it unbelievably grace-ful. The Leader's kungfu was majestic, it was nothing short of tran-scendental. It made Madame Hong's seem elementary.

Madame Hong stood up and gave a little laugh.

'That was for the benefit of White Dragon,' said the Leader. 'If he ever finds himself in a fix, he can get himself out of it by light pressure—it doesn't have to be tickling—on the Ultimate Source point beneath the armpit. That Vital Point connects directly through the Lesser Yang meridian with the heart. First his opponent will lose his grip. Then if White Dragon is feeling strong he can try the throw—using slight pressure to close the Little Ocean and Ultimate Source points as he does so. That way he'll have his enemy on the ground and immobilized.'

Trinket clapped his hands in delight.

Now the Leader lay face down on the ground and asked Madame Hong to tread on him, placing one foot on the small of his back. Meanwhile, with her right hand she took a wooden door-bar that was leaning against the wall, and held it to the back of his neck.

'Surrender?'

The Leader laughed.

'I already have! Now I will kowtow to you.'

He made as if to kneel before her, but at the same time stealthily reached out with his right forearm and lowered it very slowly onto the door-bar. There was a crunching sound and the bar snapped in two.

Trinket was astonished at the sheer force in that slow, almost imperceptible movement.

'You won't have my strength,' commented the Leader, 'but you can use that special dagger of yours.'

Next he did a sudden somersault between Madame Hong's legs. It was only a feint, though. The next instant he had her by the ankles, twirled her round, and raised her into the air so that she was to all intents and purposes standing on her head.

'Put me down!' she cried. 'What *are* you doing?'

He gave a loud laugh.

'White Dragon, you're too small to do this one. But you could try dragging your opponent along the floor instead, and then use that dagger of yours. Then kick him on three Vital Points in the chest—the Reservoir of the Soul, the Seal of the Soul, and the Walkway—to prevent him from any sort of retaliatory move.'

Trinket liked the sound of that.

Next, for the third Hero, the Leader proceeded to place both his hands behind his back, and invited Madame Hong to attack him again. She moved behind him, seized hold of his wrists with one hand, and, taking one of the broken halves of the door-bar in her free hand, rammed it against his neck.

'Now she's got me in a very dangerous clinch!' said the Leader with a cunning smile. 'With the slightest pressure on my wrists, she can drain me of my strength. So . . .'

Trinket heard Madame Hong let out a little cry, then laugh and let go of the Leader's wrists. She jumped clear, her face flushed.

'That's a dirty move! Not in front of the boy, please!'

The Leader laughed.

'What's dirty about the Groin Flip?'

He continued in a serious tone of voice.

'The sexual organs are, of course, among the most sensitive and vulnerable parts of the human body. Every school of kungfu has a move like this, even the Shaolin and the Wudang schools. But what I did just now was the Inverted Groin Flip. I had to, because of the grip she had me in.'

He paused for a moment.

'Of course, your opponent may anticipate the move, and try stabbing you in the back of the head. In that case you have to try something a little different . . .'

Once again he put his hands behind his back and let Madame Hong hold him by the wrists. Suddenly he tensed his fingers and poked them into her breasts.

She recoiled, crying:

'Very heroic!'

The Leader smiled.

'There are two deadly Vital Points on the chest: the Nipple Centre, and the Nipple Root. Both men and women have them.'

Again he invited Madame Hong to come at him and seize him by the wrists. This time, having feinted another lunge at her breasts, he did a somersault, leapt into the air and ended up on her shoulders with his thumbs pressing her Greater Yang point, his index fingers on her brow, and his middle fingers on her eyes. Another backwards somersault, and he landed about ten feet clear of her.

Trinket was hugely impressed. This was like being at the circus. But it all looked much too hard for him, and he said so.

'The three moves I've just shown you,' said the Leader, 'involve three main branches of kungfu: Catch-Can, Striking the Points, and what we call Flying. Each branch takes between eight and ten years to learn, if you want to master them properly. But if all you want to do is learn enough to do these three moves, that's a lot easier.'

He proceeded to break the moves down into their individual components, and took Trinket through them, patiently correcting any mistakes he made. The one part he did not dare try was jumping up onto the Leader's shoulders.

'Leader,' said Madame Hong, 'my Three Beauties took me years of instruction from my Shifu, and years of practice; you made up your Three Heroes in a few minutes. And yet they are more deadly than mine! You are truly a Great Master!'

The Leader acknowledged her compliment with a modest clasping of his hands.

The previous day in the great assembly, Trinket had been very unimpressed by the Leader. This acrobatic display had completely changed his opinion.

'Leader,' said Madame Hong, 'my Beauties have names. What about your Heroes?'

'Yes, I'd better think of some,' replied the Leader.

He quickly coined three appropriately heroic names for them, slipping in a little sexual innuendo which seemed to cause Madame Hong both embarassment and pleasure.

Trinket spent some time practising both sets of moves, and the Leader and Madame Hong gave him some more coaching. This lasted until midday.

Madame Hong insisted on giving Trinket back his dagger, saying that he might need it on his mission to the Palace.

'You are the only person that the Leader has taught kungfu, apart from myself! It is a great honour. You must serve him loyally.'

Trinket acknowledged his great blessing.

'Tomorrow you can set off by ship with Doctor Lu and Fat Dhuta. You can say your goodbyes now.'

Trinket did so, and walked out to find the others.

Leopard Embryo Pills

All this time Fat Dhuta and Doctor Lu were sitting in the rockery outside the hall waiting and wondering if something untoward might have happened to Trinket. Not until they saw him walk out with a grin on his face did they set their minds at rest.

'The Leader and Madame Hong have taught me some excellent kungfu!'

'Congratulations, White Dragon Marshal!' said Fat Dhuta and Doctor Lu together. 'Such an honour!'

'I know,' replied Trinket in a tone of joyful pride.

'Did they mention when they would grant us the antidote for the Leopard Embryo Pills?'

'Antidote?' asked Trinket curiously. 'Are you . . . are you . . . saying that the pills are a kind of poison?'

'Not exactly,' said Doctor Lu, looking fearfully back at the bamboo structure. 'Let's talk about it when we get home.'

As the three of them walked to the doctor's home, Trinket could not help noticing how miserable the two of them looked.

'What's up with these Leopard Pills?' he asked, when they had arrived. 'Are they a poison, or a magic elixir, or what?'

Fat Dhuta heaved a sigh.

'We'll have to wait and see! But our lives are entirely in your hands.'

'Why?' asked Trinket, greatly perplexed.

Fat Dhuta gave Doctor Lu a questioning glance. The doctor nodded.

'Hasn't it ever struck you as strange, White Dragon,' continued Fat Dhuta, 'that everyone calls me Fat Dhuta, when I'm so skinny?'

'Oh yes, I thought it was strange ages ago,' replied Trinket. 'I guessed it was some kind of joke. But I don't think the Leader is the joking type.'

Fat Dhuta heaved a long sigh.

'This is my second dose of the pills. Last time was such a terrible experience, I still have nightmares about it. You see, I used to be short and fat.'

'Oh I get it!' said Trinket. 'You mean the first pill made you tall and thin? But that's great! I'm sure you're much better looking now than you used to be!'

'In theory, perhaps,' said Fat Dhuta with a bitter smile. 'But can you imagine how terrible it is to be stretched three feet in three months, till every inch of your skin is oozing blood? I would have been a couple of feet taller still if I hadn't, by a stroke of luck, returned to the island and been granted a dose of the antidote by our merciful Leader.'

Trinket suddenly started.

'But now we've all taken the pills! *I* don't mind being a couple of feet taller, but *you* two . . . you'll both be way too tall if you grow even a few more centimetres.'

'This Leopard Pill is a miraculous medicine,' said the Dhuta. 'It can make you very healthy and strong, but if after a year you don't take some antidote, the poisonous ingredients in the pill gradually come into effect. It doesn't necessarily make you taller. My brother-in-arms, Thin Dhuta, used to be extremely tall and thin; now he's all swollen and fat.'

'All you need to do is swap names,' said Trinket with a smile, 'and everything will be fine!'

Fat Dhuta shook his head.

'That wouldn't be any good.'

He sounded almost angry.

Trinket hastened to apologize.

'Fat Dhuta, I'm really sorry! I said a stupid thing. Don't be mad at me!'

'How could I be angry?' said Fat Dhuta. 'You have the Five Dragon Disc. I must always obey you. And anyway, I know you meant no harm. It's just that my brother-in-arms and I are two different people—we look different, we sound different, we have entirely different personalities. Changing my name would never turn me into Thin Dhuta, or him into Fat Dhuta.'

'I understand.' Trinket nodded.

Fat Dhuta continued:

'Five years ago, our Leader sent me and Thin Dhuta on a very difficult mission. By the time we'd completed it, it was already three days beyond the due date. We travelled back to the island by ship as quickly as we could, but the poison had already started to work. The pain was unbearable. My brother-in-arms has a very hot temper. In a fit of rage he kicked the mast of the ship and broke it. After that our ship drifted aimlessly on the ocean. Days passed, and with every day I became taller and thinner, while he became shorter and fatter. We drifted for two months, and gradually ran out of food. So first we killed the captain, then the sailors one by one, and ate them. Luckily, we met another ship and were saved. We made them take us straight to Mystic Dragon Island. Once the Leader knew that we had completed our mission, and had not meant to return late, he gave us the antidote and spared our lives. But it was too late.'

Trinket was horrified by Fat Dhuta's story. He turned to Doctor Lu, whose serious expression confirmed the truth of it.

'In that case we have exactly a year to find all eight copies of the Sutra and get back to the island?'

'Of course, that would be wonderful,' answered Doctor Lu. 'But it won't be so easy. If we can lay our hands on just one or two copies and be back in time, I am sure the Leader will give us the antidote.'

Trinket was thinking to himself:

'I've got six copies of the Sutra already. At a pinch I can give the Leader one or two of mine.'

His sense of panic was instantly dispelled. He laughed.

'If our Leader doesn't give us the antidote, maybe I'll turn into an old grandpa, and you'll turn into little children. That would be fun!'

Doctor Lu shuddered.

'I have racked my brains about these pills,' he commented. 'They seem to be compounded from a number of rare and extremely powerful ingredients—like leopard and deer embryos, human placenta, and seal kidneys. They have the effect of reversing the body's existing tendencies. I think our Leader was originally trying to use the drug to reverse the ageing process. But with other people it has turned out to have the most unpredictable results—'

'You mean he hasn't taken the pills himself,' said Trinket. 'He's been testing them out on other people first?'

'I'm simply guessing,' Doctor Lu hastened to reply. 'It may not be true, so please do not breathe a word about this, White Dragon Marshal.'

'Don't worry,' said Trinket. 'I guarantee I'll be able to get hold of the antidote for you. Trust me! Please wait here a moment. I want to go and talk to Miss Fang.'

He very much wanted to tell Fang Yi that he had seen the Little Countess the day before. But Doctor Lu told him that Madame Hong had already summoned her:

'She says you are not to worry about Miss Fang's safety here on the island. Madame Hong sent someone to fetch her, and left my wife a message to this effect. Miss Mu Jianping from the Red Dragon Branch will be staying here as well.'

Trinket groaned to himself. Madame Hong obviously did not trust him.

'It is one of our rules,' said Doctor Lu. 'You cannot take your family with you when you are on a mission.'

'But they're not my family,' said Trinket with a bitter smile.

'Almost,' replied Doctor Lu.

Trinket's hopes of leaving the island with the two girls were completely dashed. The Leader and Madame Hong were not only using drugs to control him; they were taking his two wives hostage as well!

The next morning he woke up to the sound of the blowing of horns, and a large number of men shouting outside the door. This was followed by the tinkling of musical instruments. He rushed outside to find three or four hundred acolytes and elders dressed in white, lined up outside his door.

'Every Success to Our Marshal!' they shouted together.

Next arrived a group in blue to bid farewell to Fat Dhuta, their acting Marshal.

The three of them boarded the ship. Just as Trinket was exchanging farewells with Rootless the Taoist and the Black Dragon Marshal, he heard pounding hooves and saw two horses galloping towards the jetty. To his astonishment and delight, he saw that the two riders, both dressed in white, were Fang Yi and the Little Countess. His heart started thumping wildly.

'Maybe Madame has changed her mind, and is letting them go with me after all,' he thought to himself.

The two girls dismounted from their horses, and took a few steps forwards.

'In the name of our Leader and Madame, we come to bid farewell to our White Dragon Marshal,' said Fang Yi loudly.

Trinket's heart sank.

Fang Yi bowed and continued:

'By Madame's gracious permission, we have both been trans-ferred from the Red Dragon Branch to the White Dragon Branch, and are now under your command.'

At that moment it dawned on Trinket that the girls had been members of the Red Dragon Branch all along. They had been acting on the Leader's instructions, and their mission had quite simply been to get him, by one means or another, to the island. Where Fat Dhuta had failed to get him there by force, they were to use gentler means. . . . The ship they had travelled on must have belonged to the Sect as well. It had all been a plot. He was totally disillusioned. The happy words of endearment that had already formed themselves on his lips evaporated into a stunned silence.

And what about Doublet? What might they have done to her?

He turned to the doctor.

'Doctor Lu, what about my maid Doublet? She was with me on the ship when I came to the island. Where is she now?'

Doctor Lu hesitated. 'Don't worry. The Leader has taken good care of her.'

'What does that mean? Where is she? Send someone to get her. I'm taking her with me.'

'But—'

'But what? Just do it!' yelled Trinket angrily.

Doctor Lu dared not disobey. Quietly he instructed a subor-dinate of his, who jumped ashore and went running off.

Shortly afterwards, two horses came riding up at lightning speed. The rider in front had a slender build, and was soon recog-nizable as Doublet. With a cry of 'Master!' she vaulted nimbly from the saddle before the horse had even come to a halt, and landed weightlessly on the deck. In the eyes of a veteran like Rootless the Taoist, her 'flying' skills were nothing outstanding, but in view of her youth, and the elegance with which she executed the leap, everyone applauded heartily.

Trinket was very happy to see Doublet again. He held her by her hands. Her face was pale and drawn, and her eyes were red from much weeping.

'Have they treated you badly?' he asked.

'No . . . no . . .' wept Doublet. 'They . . . they just locked me up. But I missed you so.'

Trinket comforted her.

'Everything is fine now. We're leaving this place.'

'There are so many . . . horrible snakes here!' Doublet burst into tears again.

Trinket glanced at Fang Yi, and recalled how she had lured him into the woods to be bitten by poisonous snakes, and how she had pretended to be affectionate towards him on the ship. He could feel himself about to explode with rage.

'Set sail!' he ordered.

As the sailors were raising the anchor, the people on shore let off firecrackers, and continued to shout 'Every Success to Our White Dragon Marshal!' and 'Obey the Leader's Teachings! Follow Him to Victory!' as the ship moved slowly away from the jetty.

'If I didn't know that Fang Yi was a member of the Sect, I'd be missing her dreadfully,' he thought to himself. 'But as it is, I couldn't care less!'

Even so, when he thought of her tenderness on their journey to the island, he couldn't help feeling disconsolate.

His thoughts ran on:

'How could the two of them have become involved with the Sect? It's very strange. They must have been captured in the haunted house, and then forced to join. Although Widow Zhuang promised to try and save them, she must have failed. If the Little Countess has taken the drug, then Fang Yi must have taken it as well. She probably had to cheat me into going with her to the island, or else die. . . . I suppose I can't blame her for what she did. But she certainly had me fooled, the little tart! Oh tamardy! I don't know! I may be the White Dragon Marshal, but I haven't got a clue what this Mystic Dragon Sect is all about!'

It suddenly occurred to him that the old man in command of the riders in the haunted house might have spilled the beans and informed on him to the Leader, in which case the Leader would know that he, Trinket, was in fact Laurel (or vice versa!). But it seemed that this had not happened, probably because the old man had been too frightened to admit his failure in bringing back Laurel alive.

And another thing—Fat Dhuta had kept quiet about the inscription being a fake.

Trinket had so many questions. . . . Why had Madame Hong taken such a liking to him? Or the Leader, for that matter?

It was all very puzzling.

CHAPTER 15

In which Trinket returns to Peking and meets the Princess Ning; is made a Manchu Bannerman Colonel and sent to the Shaolin Monastery; encounters the Wang Wu Clan en route; and, as Father Treasure, meets Two Interesting Young Ladies

Back in the Palace

Some days later their ship berthed at Qinhuangdao and they disembarked and continued their journey by land.

'I've got to think of some way of getting inside the Palace,' Trinket told his companions when they finally reached Peking, 'but I don't know how long this job is going to take. I think we'd better first look for somewhere safe to stay.'

Doctor Lu made this his responsibility and rented a house for them in Hair Lane in a quiet part of the North City near the Gate of Military Proclamation. As soon as they had moved in there and were comfortably settled, Trinket went off on his own to make contact with his Triad friends at their headquarters in Sweet Water Lane; but the place had now become a tea emporium and and his muttered password evoked only a blank stare. It was clear that the new occupant was not a Triad and that the Triads had moved their headquarters to somewhere else in the city.

He made his way to the Bridge of Heaven, reasoning that even if Xu Tianchuan, the Eight-Armed Ape, wasn't at his usual stand, having perhaps, like himself, been forced to join the Mystic Dragon Sect, he was bound to run into one or other of the Brothers some-where in that area. But though he tramped round the whole of it three times, he didn't catch sight of a single one of them.

Abandoning the search, he made his way to the inn near the West Straight Gate where he had stayed last time he was in the city and where he had hidden the copy of the *Sutra in Forty-Two Sections* entrusted to him by the Old Emperor. By generous tipping he was able to obtain the same upper room, which by a stroke of luck was unoccupied, and after a brief rest on the bed, having first made sure that there was nobody around outside, he used his dagger to prise the brick out of the wall behind which the Sutra was concealed. To his relief it was still there in the hole. He took it out and undid the oilskin wrapping. After a brief inspection to make sure it was unharmed, he thrust it into the inside pocket of his gown, replaced the brick, slipped out of the inn, and hurried off to the Palace.

A little trouble with the guard on the Palace gate was quickly resolved when he identified himself and explained that he was dis-guised as a commoner because he had been on a secret mission and was hurrying back to report. Back once more in his own room in the Palace, he changed into his eunuch's uniform, wrapped the Sutra in an old cloth, and went straight to the Upper Library to see the Emperor.

Apprised of his coming, a beaming Kang Xi stood in the doorway of the inner library to welcome him.

'Tamardy, Laurie!' he cried joyfully. 'What a long time you've been away! Bugger in!' (Kang Xi's ventures into the vernacular were sometimes a little wild. Fortunately it was only Trinket who ever heard them.)

Trinket knelt and kowtowed.

'Congratulations, Your Majesty! It's very good news.'

Kang Xi knew that this meant his father was alive and well. A surge of emotion caused him to reel momentarily, so that he had to clutch the side of the doorway to steady himself.

'Come inside,' he said. 'I want to hear everything.' His voice was trembling.

After following him inside, Trinket closed and barred the door and looked carefully behind the bookcases before embarking on his story.

'Well, I saw His Old Majesty in the Wutai Mountains,' he began in a low voice.

Kang Xi grasped his hand.

'So . . . so he *did* go there and become a monk. What did he say?'

Trinket told him about his meeting with the Old Emperor. He also told him about the attempt made by the Tibetan lamas to kidnap him and how he, Trinket, helped by the Eighteen Lohans from the Shaolin Monastery, had frustrated them. He may perhaps have embroidered the facts a little, particularly when speaking of the part he had played himself in that affair. The young Emperor was horrified.

'How terrible! I must send a thousand of the guards there immediately.'

Trinket shook his head.

'I don't think His Old Majesty would want that.'

He went on to tell him how the Old Emperor had praised his son, saying that Kang Xi was a better Emperor than *he* had been and must always continue to work for the welfare of his people. Kang Xi broke down and wept. When Trinket handed him the Sutra the Old Emperor had given him, tears fell on the cloth wrapping. They fell even faster when Kang Xi saw the inscription, *Never Raise Taxes*, on the flyleaf and recognized his father's own writing.

'Tamardy!' thought Trinket. 'If he's going to carry on like this, I might as well cry too for company. A few tears don't cost anything: they might even add a bit to my reward.'

He had always cried easily. In Yangzhou, across his mother's knee, the tears had started falling even before her cane had made contact with his bottom. Soon he was putting on a very convincing performance.

Somewhat surprised at seeing Trinket's real tears, Kang Xi checked his own weeping and asked the reason for them.

'Boo-hoo,' sobbed Trinket, 'I was just thinking how kind His Old Majesty was to me when I saw him on Wutai. If I hadn't known how anxious you'd be if I didn't return, I'd have stayed on to look after him. I'm worried that someone else might try to harm him.'

'I'm worried about that too,' said Kang Xi. 'I tell you what, Laurie. It's a good thing my father has taken a liking to you, because although I really need you here, a good son ought to put his father's needs first and—'

Trinket's jaw dropped.

'Holy ting-a-ling bells!' he thought. 'Idiot! Why did I say that? He's going to send me back to Wutai to be a monk and look after his dad.'

And this was just what Kang Xi now proposed.

Trinket began sobbing again, this time with genuine feeling.

'I can't bear the thought of leaving you,' he said between sobs—not because he thought there was the slightest chance of Kang Xi changing his mind, but by way of explaining his tears.

Kang Xi patted him kindly on the shoulder.

'There, there, Laurie! I'll be visiting the monastery from time to time. It's not as if you'll never see me again. I'll probably be paying a visit there in a month or two. Anyway, there's nothing to stop you becoming a layman again in the course of time. You can learn to read and write while you're in the monastery, so that when the time comes I'll be able to give you a really important post.'

Trinket knew that 'when the time comes' meant when Shun Zhi, who might yet live forty years, had died, so he was scarcely comforted. He didn't, in any case, want to end his days as a high-ranking Manchu official. However, his busy mind was soon thinking of ways in which he could deceive the Old Emperor into releasing him. For example, he might impress on that tender soul how much the Young Emperor was pining for his favourite eunuch, unable to eat properly and losing weight. The prospect cheered him and he promised Kang Xi continuing devotion in his new role.

To show his pleasure, Kang Xi gave Trinket *carte blanche* to reimburse himself from the Privy Purse for the expenses he had incurred on this last mission. But Trinket confessed that he had already helped himself rather generously while supervising, with Songgotu, the confiscation of Oboi's estate, and that, moved to repentance by the teaching and example of the Old Emperor, he had used the money pocketed on that earlier occasion, which strictly speaking was the Emperor's own, for pious donations during his Wutai visit.

'I shall be nicely covered now if there's ever an inquiry,' he thought. But Kang Xi, suspecting nothing, was impressed.

Kang Xi was curious to hear more about Wutai and its temples, but their conversation was interrupted by the sound of footsteps outside and a ringing female voice.

'Emperor–brother, when are you going to give me that fight?'

This was followed by some hefty knocks on the door and the rattle of someone trying impatiently to get in.

'Better open it,' said Kang Xi with a somewhat rueful smile.

The Tomboy Princess

A fifteen- or sixteen-year-old girl dressed entirely in crimson brocade rushed like a whirlwind into the room as soon as Trinket had unbarred the door. She had a fine, oval face with strikingly thin lips and a lively, somewhat imperious expression. Because of his fear of the Empress Dowager, Trinket avoided the Hall of Maternal Tranquillity as much as possible and had never met most of its occupants; but he knew that one of them was the Empress Dowager's own daughter, Princess Ning, and guessed that this was her.

'Emperor–brother,' said the Princess, 'you promised to give me a fight. Why do you keep putting it off? Are you afraid?'

'*Afraid*?' said Kang Xi, laughing. 'I doubt you're even a match for my pupil here. I'm sure you're not good enough for *me*!'

He winked at Trinket, who gathered that he had been given a new role to play. He began formally presenting himself.

'I'm Laurie, Your Highness. His Majesty has been good enough to teach me some kungfu. May I humbly—'

As he bowed down low she gave a little laugh and, without any warning, just as his head had reached its lowest level, shot out a foot and caught him squarely on the jaw, driving it upwards so that his teeth bit almost through his tongue. When he opened his mouth and cried out in pain, the blood flowed freely down the front part of his gown.

Kang Xi was aghast, but the Princess only laughed.

'This pupil of yours is useless, Emperor–brother,' she said. 'He couldn't even dodge the little kick I gave him. I don't suppose *you're* much better.'

'Are you all right, Laurie?' Kang Xi asked with concern. 'Your tongue must be very painful.'

'Not too bad,' said Trinket, trying hard to smile, though his tongue hurt so badly he could hardly speak.

'Dod doo bad,' the Princess mimicked. 'I'be odely half dead and I'be feeling very sad.'

She grabbed her Imperial brother by the hand.

'Come on!' she said. 'Let's have this fight!'

The Princess had once or twice in the past watched the Empress Dowager giving Kang Xi lessons in kungfu and begged that she might have some herself; but the Empress Dowager, though not refusing outright, had been unwilling to give her much of her time, so she had gone off and badgered members of the Palace Guards to teach her. As they did their best to humour her and fell down each time she touched them, she considered herself a champion. But though she had picked up a good deal of the lingo, there was precious little else that she had learned from them. As a fighter she was negligible and had been beaten easily when she challenged her brother to a fight. Having recently got her Guards instructor to teach her a little Catch-Can, she was now anxious to make another trial of her skill. But Kang Xi was in no mood to indulge her.

'Not now,' he said. 'I'm really too busy. Train a bit longer and we'll have a match another time.'

The Princess frowned.

'You promised. Refusing a challenge counts as defeat.'

'All right,' said Kang Xi. 'I concede defeat. Princess Ning is the champion. Her punch can knock out the Tiger of the South and her kick eliminate the Dragon of the North.'

'You mean the *Little Worm* of the North,' said the Princess, aiming another kick at Trinket, which this time, however, he side-stepped with the agility of a trained fighter.

The Princess could see that her brother wasn't going to fight with her; and since Trinket was about her size and ap-peared to have had some training, she decided that he would do instead.

'Very well,' she told Trinket. '*You'll* have to fight me, since your teacher's too scared.'

'Yes, Laurie, *you* go and play with her,' said Kang Xi, who had always had a soft spot for his tomboyish sister and didn't like to disappoint her. 'We can continue our discussion tomorrow.'

As they were on their way out, she suddenly stopped, squared up to Kang Xi, and raised her fists.

'Watch this, Emperor–brother!'

She tried to execute a Double Drumbeat on him, driving her fists against his temples; but Kang Xi was too quick for her, parrying with an Opening the Window defence which sent her reeling. Trinket could not help laughing at her discomfiture, which so enraged her that she seized his ear and twisted it painfully, then marched, still holding him by it, out of the Library and down the long corridor outside, past the eunuchs and guards, who, though they dared not show it, were no doubt entertained by the spectacle of the Emperor's favourite bowed down and trotting along behind her.

'All right, all right,' said Trinket. 'Let go of my ear and I'll follow you anywhere!'

'You're a dangerous criminal,' said the Princess. 'Now that I've arrested you, I can't possibly let you go. I shall have to immobilize you.'

She pointed a finger and jabbed it into his chest.

'Oh, I'm paralysed!' said Trinket, entering into the spirit of the thing by sitting down hard on the ground and freezing into immobility.

'Get up!' she said, and gave him a few gentle kicks. Then, as he still hadn't moved, she kicked him again, this time very hard, in the kidneys. Trinket decided that enough was enough and jumped up with a great 'Ow!'

'That one released me,' he said. 'I don't think even your Emperor–brother could have done that.'

'Smarmy villain!' said the Princess. 'Who said I know anything about Vital Points?' (She didn't.)

But secretly she was rather pleased that he was playing along with her.

'Follow me!' she said.

She led him to the room in which he and Kang Xi used to do their sparring. When they were inside, she told him to bar the door.

'I don't want anyone stealing my methods,' she said.

'Silly bitch!' thought Trinket. 'What do you know about kungfu that anyone would *want* to steal?'

He closed the door; but when he turned to get the door-bar,

he found the Princess holding it. He thought she had picked it up to hand it to him, but the next moment there was an explosion in his ears and a sharp pain in the crown of his head and he fell down unconscious. When he came to, she was standing over him grinning, one hand on her hip, the other still holding the door-bar.

'You really are useless,' she said. 'A kungfu fighter needs eyes in the back of his head. You don't seem to have learnt *anything*.'

His head felt as if it was split in two, and from the sickly smell that filled his nostrils he knew that the stickiness which prevented him from opening his left eye properly must be caused by blood from his broken crown.

'Get up and fight, if you're a man!' shouted the Princess, aiming a blow at his shoulder.

He got to his feet and tried to wrest the door-bar from her, but while they were struggling it caught him a crack on the right cheek-bone which made him see stars.

'Bandit!' she cried. 'Highwayman! Scum like you must be exterminated!'

She swung the door-bar in a great sweep and Trinket went down again, this time on his face. Pleased with her handiwork, she raised the bar in both hands and aimed at the back of his head. It would undoubtedly have brained him if he had not rolled away in time. As it was, it hit the floor with a mighty thump and hurt her hand.

'Horrible little eunuch!' she screamed in rage. 'How dare you dodge away when I'm trying to hit you!'

More blows followed when he had struggled once more to his feet, including one that nearly broke his arm.

'This isn't playing,' thought Trinket. 'She's out to kill me. The Empress Dowager must have put her up to this!'

Princess or no princess, he wanted to stay alive. In desperation he went for her eyes, and when she recoiled in fear, tripped her up with his foot, picked up the door-bar, and raised it up to strike. But almost at once he knew that he couldn't do it. If he did, he would be guilty of high treason, the penalty for which was considerably worse than death by door-bar.

'Horrible little eunuch!' said the Princess while he hesitated. 'Help me up. You're no match for me. I just tripped over, that's all.'

Almost without thinking what he was doing, he helped her

to her feet. The blood from his head-wound was trickling down over his face and blinding him. He tried wiping it with his sleeve.

'Useless creature, let me wipe it for you,' said the Princess. 'On River and Lake, people are supposed to help each other when they are in trouble.'

She took out a snow-white handkerchief and set about wiping the blood from his face. They were standing very close and he could smell the scent she was wearing. Suddenly he realized that she was rather pretty.

'I was wrong,' he thought. 'She's not trying to kill me, she really is playing. It's just that she's overdoing it a bit.'

But his martyrdom was not over yet.

'Turn round,' she said, and he did so obediently: but instead of a gentle touch on his head he felt a sharp pain in the small of his back and an encircling leg round both of his which brought him once more face downwards on the floor. Next moment she was stabbing the back of his legs with a knife she had extracted from one of her little boots.

'Is *that* painful?' she asked. 'If you say "Not too bad" again, I shall do it harder.'

'It's very painful indeed,' said Trinket. 'If this really was River and Lake, you'd release me, now that I'm in your power.'

'Ah, some crimes can't be forgiven,' said the Princess. 'A great pirate like you must first be made to confess.'

She bound his feet with his own belt, then tied his hands behind him with a strip of cloth cut from his gown. With mounting horror he watched her go to a table at the side of the room on which were some candlesticks and a tinder-box and light one of the candles. She was going to burn him! She did in fact hold the candle-flame to a corner of his gown, but soon grew impatient when it didn't at once catch fire. Then her eye lit on his long, glossy pigtail and she gleefully set fire to that. A flame leapt up and engulfed his head, and the whole room was filled with the acrid smell of burning hair. Such was his panic that he managed, trussed up as he was, to struggle to his feet and ram his burning head into her stomach. The flames were extinguished and the Princess was temporarily winded; but having recovered herself, she kicked him in the head and, for the third time, he fainted.

This time when he came to, she was standing over him with a packet of white stuff in her hands.

'This is salt,' she said. 'I got this tip from the guards. They say it's very good for getting a confession.'

Using her knife again, she cut away the front of his gown and made a few incisions in his chest into which she proceeded to rub some of the salt. Then she rolled him over and sprinkled some of it into the cuts she had made in his legs. His whole body was now in such anguish that he was nearly mad with pain. He knew now that she was only playing but that, to this spoiled, unfeeling girl, eunuchs and maids-of-honour were scarcely human, and killing one of them was of no more consequence than squashing an ant. The thought that he was only an ant to her made him furious. Rage gave him superhuman strength. Wriggling about as she bent over him, he kicked out with both his feet and caught her in the solar plexus, knocking all the wind from her body and laying her out temporarily unconscious. In the brief respite this gave him he managed, by several contortions, to extract the dagger from his boot with one of his bound hands and cut through the belt which bound his feet. Then he plunged the dagger into a leg of the table, sat on the floor with his back to it, and freed his hands by rubbing the cloth which bound them against the blade. Though the whole of his body was in agony, a great happiness swept over him. He went over to the Princess and kicked her once more in the stomach. '

Curiously, this second kick had the effect of bringing her back to consciousness. She gave a little sigh, opened her eyes, and got up slowly on her feet.

Almost at once she began cursing him:

'Horrible little eunuch . . . !'

But Trinket's wrath was now thoroughly roused and he slapped her hard on both cheeks. Then he punched her in the chest and sent her sprawling by sweeping her feet from under her with his leg. When she tried to get up, he sat down on her facing her feet and began fiercely pummelling every part of her that he could reach, legs, back, and bottom.

'Stinking little tart!' he cried, as his fists flailed down on her. 'Whore's abortion! I'll *kill* you!'

'Don't you dare!' she screamed. 'I'll tell my mother. I'll tell the Emperor. I'll have you executed by a thousand cuts.'

This gave him pause. Execution by a thousand cuts, sometimes known as the Slow Process, was a particularly nasty form of death, a lingering farewell to this world, during which bits of the body were sliced away one by one. But then he thought that now he'd started, he might just as well go on, so that, whatever the consequences, at least he would have had the satisfaction of giving her a good thrashing.

'I don't give a damn,' he said. 'Damn you! And *all* your ancestors!'

He laid into her again, but after a few more thumps she gave a little giggle.

Trinket stopped in surprise. He pulled his dagger from the table-leg and, using his free hand to turn her over, pointed it threateningly at her throat.

'What's so funny?'

The Princess's face was full of smiles.

'You can go on hitting me if you like,' she said coyly, 'only not quite so hard.'

Trinket was mystified. Was this some sort of trap? He put his dagger away and placed a foot on her chest.

'Don't try anything,' he said. 'I'm not falling for any more of your tricks.'

She tried to raise her head, but he pushed her back by her forehead. Then she let fly a kick. It caught him on one of the salt-filled cuts, which were already throbbing painfully. In a fury he began slapping her—left, right, left, right—on both sides of her face.

'Don't hit my face,' she said. 'If you hurt my face, the Empress Dowager will notice it and start asking questions.'

He gritted his teeth and gave her a couple of savage pinches on her left arm.

'Aiyo, aiyo!' she cried and frowned a little: but there was a look almost of happiness in her eyes.

'Tamardy!' said Trinket. 'You liked that, didn't you!'

She kicked again. This was too much. He tied her hands and feet up with both their belts, knelt on her shoulders, and began pinching her all over as hard as he could.

She laughed.

'Horrible little eunuch! I mean dear eunuch, darling eunuch! Have mercy!'

Trinket got up, panting. His body hurt all over and he felt he was going to faint. His anger had subsided somewhat, giving way to a sensation rather like the one he had experienced when he was with Fang Yi on the voyage; but he still couldn't make her out.

'This is fun,' she said. 'Can't we go on playing?'

'*Fun?*' said Trinket. 'Your "playing" has just about killed me.'

'I can't hurt you while I'm tied up,' said the Princess. '*You* can go on hitting *me* though if you like.'

He spat.

'You're no Princess,' he said. 'You're a little tart.'

'Are you really not going to play any more?' she asked. 'Let's meet again tomorrow, then.'

He shook his head.

'I can't come tomorrow. It will take me more than a day to get over these injuries. More like a month, I should think.'

He began untying the belts round her hands and feet.

'You *must* come tomorrow,' she said. 'I shall be waiting here for you at the same time. If you don't come, I shall show the Empress Dowager what you've done to me.'

She rolled up one of her sleeves and showed him her arm. It was entirely covered with black and blue bruises where he had pinched her.

'All right,' he said. 'I'll come on condition that you don't hit me any more.' After some argument she agreed.

'Whenever I try playing with one of the guards or one of the other eunuchs,' she said, 'they won't fight back properly. The only person who's ever given me a proper fight is the Emperor, and even he has never really hurt me like you did. So don't worry, Laurie, I shan't kill you. I can't afford to lose you.'

Quite suddenly she leant forwards and gave him a kiss, then turned and fled, blushing, from the room.

Trinket sat down heavily, his head spinning. She must be a bit mad, this Princess. The more you hit her and swore at her, the more she seemed to like it.

'Tamardy!' he thought. 'Can she really have taken a fancy to me? I'm supposed to be a eunuch!'

But for the time being he was feeling too muzzy to think properly. Slowly getting to his feet, he dragged himself off to his room, where, utterly exhausted, he threw himself down on the bed and went straight to sleep.

He must have slept for about five hours, because it was already getting dark when he awoke. His whole body hurt so much that he could hardly help crying out, and when he got up and went to wash the salt out of his wounds, he found that the blood from them had congealed and stuck to his clothes, making it agony to undress. He did eventually succeed in undressing, all the time cursing the hateful girl who was responsible for his suffering, and when he had washed and dried the numerous cuts and stab-wounds she had inflicted, he sprinkled them liberally with wound-powder.

Emperor and Shifu

Trinket went on duty next day sporting two black eyes. His nose, cheeks, and lips were swollen and his eyebrows and most of his hair, including his long, glossy pigtail, had been burnt away. Kang Xi knew that this was the handiwork of his precious sister, but was shocked by the extent of the damage.

'Did the Princess do this?' he asked. 'I hope you're not seriously injured.'

'It's not too bad,' said Trinket, managing a rueful smile. 'I'm afraid I let you down badly, Majesty. I'll have to train at least another three years before I can be a credit to you.'

Kang Xi was relieved that he was taking his beating in good part. He had been worried that Trinket might ask him to side with him against the Princess, which he could not possibly have done, since she was a member of the ruling class whose prerogative it was to beat servants as and when they pleased. In that case Trinket might have carried his resentment with him to the Wutai Mountains and been considerably less enthusiastic about serving the Old Emperor.

'You're a good fellow,' he said. 'I really must do something to reward you. What would you like?'

'Perhaps you could give me a few tips that I could use in future combat,' said Trinket.

Kang Xi was rather tickled.

'All right,' he said, and proceeded to demonstrate a few of the methods he had learned from the Empress Dowager. When Trinket thought he had mastered them, he dropped to his knees and kowtowed, knocking his head altogether eight times on the floor.

'Majesty, will you be my Shifu, and have Trinket Wei as your first pupil?'

Since his return from the island he had noticed that, though Kang Xi had not grown physically during his absence, he had gained considerably in authority and self-importance and was no longer the carefree Misty with whom he had romped and wrestled in the past. Kang Xi, for his part, saw that they could no longer pretend to be equals, even when they were alone, and rather welcomed the new teacher–pupil relationship that Trinket was offering him.

'All right,' he said. 'I was the one who started this and an Emperor shouldn't go back on his word. I accept you as my pupil. Only you must never let anyone else know about this.'

He called for service, and two guards and two eunuchs came running in. Kang Xi made them stand in a row, shoulder to shoulder, then, taking a pair of scissors from his desk, he walked along behind them, selected the largest, glossiest pigtail of the four, and cut it off. It belonged to one of the eunuchs. The wretched fellow, scared out of his wits, dropped down on his knees and began kowtowing.

'Your Majesty, Your Majesty,' he whimpered, 'forgive me, forgive me.'

'Don't be afraid,' said Kang Xi. 'I award you ten taels compensation. Now be off with you all!'

The pigtail-less eunuch got up, and the four of them, totally nonplussed, walked backwards, bowing, from the room. The ways of Heaven and the whims of Princes were alike unfathomable. Who were they to question them?

'You'd better take this,' Kang Xi said, handing Trinket the pigtail when the two of them were once more alone together. 'You won't need any hair when you're a monk, but in the meantime this will make you look a bit more presentable.'

Trinket kowtowed his thanks and stood watching him expectantly. The young Emperor had sat down at his desk and appeared to be lost in thought. Here he was, pretending to be Trinket's teacher, Kang Xi was thinking, yet in actual fact *neither* of them was much good at kungfu, or would be of much use to his father in a crisis. Who were the great masters of self-defence? Probably the most dependable to have around you in times of need were the monks of the Shaolin Monastery, where the arts of self-defence had been preserved and cultivated for centuries. A plan began forming itself in his mind.

'You can go now,' he told Trinket. 'Come and see me again tomorrow.'

Mistress and Slave

When Trinket got back to his room, he sent for one of the Imperial Physicians, who assured him, after examining his wounds and applying medication to them, that although they were so painful,

they were only superficial and ought to heal up in a couple of weeks
or so; then, after finishing his lunch, he went off to keep his appointment with the Princess. Rather surprisingly, though apprehensive
that she might try to hurt him again, he found himself quite looking
forward to seeing her.

As soon as he entered the room, she was on him with a shout;
but this time he was ready for her. He warded off the blow and
soon had her bending forwards with an arm twisted behind her
back.

'Horrible little eunuch!' she cried. 'A bit livelier today than
yesterday, aren't you!'

'My name's Laurie, if you don't mind,' said Trinket. 'Just say
"Laurie", will you, or "*dear* Laurie", unless you want me to break
your arm.'

But the Princess was unwilling to admit herself beaten, and
put up a struggle. He gave her a few thumps, and she smilingly
informed him that she only felt really happy when she saw his
blood flowing. This made Trinket completely lose his temper, and
he gave her such a trouncing that she ended up helpless on the floor.
After much pleading, and only after she had promised not to try
hitting him again, he consented to help her up and support her on
her way back to her apartment, which was on the west side of the
Hall of Maternal Tranquillity where the Empress Dowager lived. As
soon as they arrived at the entrance, he turned to go.

'No, come inside,' she said. 'There's something I want to
show you.'

There were four eunuchs and four Palace ladies on duty
outside, so he couldn't argue. He had to submit while she took him
by the hand and led him through to her bedroom. Soon two Palace
ladies came in with hot towels. The Princess took one and wiped
her perspiring face with it, then handed one to Trinket. The women
goggled somewhat to see the Princess treating a mere eunuch
almost more politely than she did her own mother.

'What are you staring at?' she shouted, going for the eyes of
the nearer one with her nails. Fortunately she missed the woman's
eyes, but left deep red scratch-marks beside her left eye, from which
the blood trickled down to her chin. The two women dashed from
the room in terror.

'You see what whining slaves they are!' said the Princess.
'Nobody will stand up to me but you.'

Trinket wondered what she was planning to do next.

'I'm tired of always being a mistress,' she said. 'Today we'll change places. You can be the master and I'll be your slave.'

Trinket objected, but when she threatened to scream blue murder and then claim that he had assaulted her, he submitted in order to keep her quiet.

She sat him down in a chair and made him a deep curtsey.

'Now, Prince Laurie,' she said, 'I'm sure Your Highness would like to rest. Let me help you undress.'

'No, thank you,' said Trinket. 'I don't feel like sleeping yet. You can give me a very gentle massage if you like.'

'Very good,' said the Princess eagerly, and kneeling with one knee on the floor, she laid one of his legs across her other knee and began to massage it, taking great care to avoid the parts that were still sore. After a while she took his boot off and began massaging his foot.

'Thank you, slave,' said Trinket, pinching her gently on the cheek. 'I think you made a very good job of that.'

The Princess was delighted.

When she had finished giving the same treatment to the other leg, she asked him to lie down.

'Now, Prince Laurie, if you will lie down on the bed, I'll massage your back for you.'

Trinket could see that he would never get away until he had let her go through with this, so he got up on to what was the most luxuriously appointed, ravishingly perfumed bed he had ever come across and lay down on his side. The Princess drew a quilt over him and began gently pummelling his back.

Trinket was growing drowsy and just beginning, in his drowsiness, to enter fully into the spirit of his new role, when there was a chorus of voices outside the apartment:

'Her Imperial Majesty the Empress Dowager!'

He sat up with a start.

'There's no time to get away,' said the Princess in a great panic. 'Get under the bedclothes and don't move!'

Trinket quickly lay down again and disappeared beneath the quilt. Through it, almost fainting with terror, he could hear the muffled sound of someone thumping on the door. The Princess drew the bed-curtains together and ran to unbar the door. As soon as it was open, the Empress Dowager came striding in.

'Barring the door in broad daylight! What does this mean?'

'I'm feeling very tired,' said the Princess, forcing a smile. 'I was just about to lie down and have a sleep.'

The Empress Dowager seated herself in a chair.

'What mischief are you up to this time?' she said. 'Your face is as white as a sheet.'

'I told you,' said the Princess. 'I'm very tired.'

As the Empress Dowager looked around her, her glance lit on a pair of men's boots by the side of the bed. She also thought she could detect a slight movement of the bed-curtains.

'Go and wait outside, all of you,' she said to the eunuchs and women who attended her. When they had all trooped out, she ordered the Princess to shut and bar the door. The Princess did this with an ill grace, then, following her mother's steely glance, she noticed the boots beside the bed and coloured.

'Oh, *those*,' she said lightly. 'I've been dressing up. I was going to ask you what you thought. I think I make rather a handsome boy.'

'I'd like to see what that boy in the bed looks like,' said the Empress Dowager grimly, striding over, drawing the curtains apart, and lifting up the quilt. She seized the hapless Trinket by the collar and raised him up from the bed. He was shaking in every limb but was careful to keep his head turned away from her.

'Don't hurt him!' cried the Princess. 'He's one of the Emperor's favourite eunuchs.'

The Empress Dowager was not seriously worried by her discovery. She assumed that the Princess, having reached an age at which the first stirrings of sexual awakening are felt, was playing at 'mothers and fathers'—harmlessly, in this case, since the playfellow she was experimenting with was a eunuch. She forced him to turn his face towards her and dealt it a couple of slaps.

'Now be off!' she said. 'And don't let me see you anywhere *near* Her Highness again!'

But then she looked more closely and realized who it was.

'Oh!' she said in surprise. 'So it's *you*?'

'No,' said Trinket somewhat illogically, 'it's not.'

The Empress Dowager took a firmer grip on his collar.

'Since you seem to deliberately run towards trouble,' she said, 'you can hardly blame me for the consequences.'

'I *asked* him to lie down in my bed,' said the Princess. 'It really isn't his fault.'

The Empress Dowager ignored her and, raising her free hand

high up in the air, prepared to deliver a blow that would send Trinket speeding from this world to the next. In frantic desperation he resorted to one of the disreputable kungfu tricks that the Leader of the Mystic Dragon Sect had taught him—the third of the Three Heroes. He caused her to disengage by putting his hands behind him and squeezing her breasts. Then, stamping with his feet on the edge of the bed, he executed a clumsy back-somersault which landed him on her shoulders. As he straddled her neck from behind, he pressed his thumbs against the Greater Yang point on her temples and held a finger over each eye.

'If you move,' he said, 'I'll gouge your eyes out.'

The Princess burst out laughing.

'Naughty, naughty!' she said. 'Let the Empress go, Laurie!'

Trinket raised his right foot and drew the dagger from his boot. Then he slid down from the Empress Dowager's shoulders, all the time keeping the dagger aimed at a Vital Point on her back.

While he was executing these manoeuvres, the Five Dragon Disc had slipped out of his inside pocket. It now fell to the floor with a metallic clink. The Empress Dowager looked down at it and gasped.

'That—that thing!' she cried. 'How did it get here?'

Trinket already knew that she must have some connection with the Mystic Dragon Sect from the fact that she had harboured two of its members, Liu Yan, otherwise known as Sister Swallow, and the cross-dressing Deng Bingchun, both of them disguised as her ladies-in-waiting. He wondered if she would know about the disc and submit to its authority. It was worth a try.

'What do you mean, *that thing?*' he said. 'How dare you! Don't you recognize the Five Dragon sign when you see it? Don't you know what it means?'

'I do, I do,' said the Empress Dowager, trembling all over.

'Very good, then repeat after me,' said Trinket: 'Long Life to Our Leader! Blessings be on Him!'

'Long Life to Our Leader! Blessings be on Him!' .

'Obey His Teachings!' Trinket intoned. 'Follow Him to Victory!'

'Obey His Teachings! Follow Him to Victory!' she echoed reverently.

Inwardly sighing with relief, Trinket put away his dagger and seated himself imperiously on the bed.

The Empress Dowager turned to the Princess.

'Go outside!' she said. 'And don't breathe a word of this to anyone, or I shall kill you.'

She looked as if she meant it, too.

The Princess glanced wonderingly at Trinket.

'Is this some secret business of Emperor–brother's?' she asked.

'Yes,' said the Empress Dowager. 'And when you see him, you mustn't let on that you know about it, or he will be very angry.'

'I'm not that stupid,' said the Princess, and obediently left the room.

After a few moments, during which Trinket and the Empress Dowager looked at each other in silence, the Empress Dowager suggested, very deferentially, that if they wanted to talk, it would be safer if they did so in the Hall of Maternal Tranquillity.

Trinket nodded. But first, he thought, he had better explain the disc.

'I'm the new White Dragon Marshal,' he said, in a very low voice. 'I'm here on the Leader's instructions. He gave me the disc when he sent me out on my mission.'

The Empress Dowager bowed to him submissively.

'Your servant,' she murmured.

'So she's only an ordinary Comrade,' he thought. 'I'm actually higher up than her.' He found it hard to imagine how a person of such exalted rank came to be a rank and file member of the Sect.

While he was musing on this, she mistook his silence to mean that he was feeling resentment. The red marks where she had slapped him were still plainly visible on his face.

'I had no idea until now who you were,' she said. 'I hope you will forgive me for anything I did or said while I didn't know.'

She wondered for a moment if this boy really could be who he said he was; but then she remembered hearing that the Leader and his wife had lately begun a campaign to import new blood into the Sect and that several of the old guard had been killed or fallen into disgrace.

'Probably he really is the new White Dragon Marshal,' she thought, 'but in that case I'm in for a hard time. I know how much he hates me. Better kill him now, before he can do me any harm. No one need know I did it.'

At the mere idea of it, an evil gleam came into her eye. Trinket noticed it with alarm.

'She's going to kill me,' he thought. 'I must say something to scare her.'

'I suppose you know who taught me that trick I played on you just now,' he said.

'It wasn't . . . it wasn't the Leader, was it?' she asked nervously.

'They both taught me a lot,' boasted Trinket. 'The moves the Leader taught me were all lethal. I decided to combine one of his Three Heroes with one of her Three Beauties—it's called Princess Flying Swallow—because I didn't want to kill you. Even so, I didn't do it properly. To do it properly I should have gouged your eyes out. I left that bit out so you didn't get hurt.'

The Empress Dowager shivered.

'You are very kind,' she said. 'I shall try to find some way of showing you my gratitude.'

'I've brought Fat Dhuta and Doctor Lu with me on this mission,' said Trinket nonchalantly, at the same time picking up the Five Dragon Disc and putting it back in his inner pocket.

'Oh,' said the Empress Dowager, instantly abandoning all thought of killing him. She knew these two senior members of the Sect and was aware how formidable they were. If they were his subordinates in this mission (whatever it was), she would, by killing him, be signing her own death-warrant.

'Marshal Zhong was a traitor and had to be killed,' said Trinket. 'I'm his replacement. And the Leader was so dissatisfied with Black Dragon's failure to get the Sutras, that he's given *me* the job.'

The Empress Dowager could see that she would soon be having to answer questions about these Sutras—something she had been dreading ever since the three copies she had been at such pains to acquire had gone missing.

'The Sutras, yes, that's a long story,' she said. 'If you don't mind coming with me to the Hall of Maternal Tranquillity, I'll try to explain what has happened.'

Trinket nodded and rose to his feet to go. Having removed the door-bar and opened the door, the Empress Dowager stood politely aside for him to go through; but Trinket knew better than to go first.

'Her Imperial Majesty is about to leave,' he sang out in his best official voice, whereupon the Empress Dowager, murmuring, 'Excuse me!' as she did so, stepped out into the throng of eunuchs and ladies-in-waiting, who followed in a little column behind her as she made her way, with Trinket at her heels, to the Hall of Maternal Tranquillity. There she led Trinket into her bedroom, and, having dismissed her attendants, shut and barred the door.

When he was seated, she gave him ginseng tea to drink, waiting on him like a servant. He began to detect something that she and her daughter had in common: they both seemed to feel some need to be humiliated and to wait on people.

While Trinket was sipping his tea, the Empress Dowager got out a small jade bottle containing thirty precious Body-Strengthening Pills, a present to her from the King of Korea, she said. Eight of them were for Trinket, the others he was to give to the Leader and Madame Hong when he next saw them. This brought up the subject of the Leopard Embryo Pills, and she asked him anxiously whether by any chance he had brought her the annual antidote; from which he deduced that she, too, had been made to take the pills and that her dependence on the antidote was the Leader's way of exercising remote control over her.

No, said Trinket, he hadn't brought the antidote, but he was sure that if she continued to be loyal and obedient, it wouldn't be long coming.

'Those Sutras you mentioned,' said the Empress Dowager, thinking that she had best get a word in about them first, before she was asked anything. 'I sent Deng Bingchun and Swallow with three of them to give the Leader. I hope he got them all right.'

'Not that I know of,' said Trinket. 'In fact, the Leader was complaining that Black Dragon had failed to bring him a single one of them. Black Dragon was very nearly made to kill himself.'

The Empress Dowager's face assumed an expression of astonishment.

'How strange! I gave Deng and Swallow explicit orders to take them to Snake Island. That was before you were obliged to kill Swallow, of course.'

'Deng Bingchun—is that the bald fellow you had here?' Trinket asked innocently.

'Yes,' said the Empress Dowager. 'When you get back to Snake Island, ask to see him. He'll be able to tell you what happened.'

'Clever!' thought Trinket. 'Deng Bingchun gets the blame. She knows dead men tell no tales.' But what he actually said was:

'Well, you've already done very well to get those three. Now we've got to find the other five. I'll tell the Leader how well you've done next time I see him and put in a good word for you.'

The Empress Dowager made him a deep curtsey.

'That's very good of you. I really am most grateful. In fact, if you will allow me, I'd like to apply for a transfer from the Black Dragon Branch to the White Dragon Branch so that I can be under your command.'

'No problem,' said Trinket. 'But first I'll need a full account of everything you've done since you first joined the Sect. I want to know everything.'

'Certainly,' said the Empress Dowager. 'I promise not to conceal anything from you, Marshal.'

The Bannerman Colonel

Before the Empress Dowager could begin, there was a sound of footsteps and the discreet cough of a lady-in-waiting outside the door.

'Your Majesty, His Majesty the Emperor wants to see Laurie Goong-goong on important business. He says could you send him over right away, please.'

Trinket nodded to her to comply.

'It's all right,' he whispered. 'We can finish our talk later.'

'Thank you,' she whispered back; then, loudly, 'The Emperor wants to see you. You'd better go now.'

'Yes, Your Majesty. Thank you, Your Majesty,' said Trinket in his official Goong-goong voice.

When he got outside he found eight Palace Guards waiting for him. Wondering what on earth could have happened, he almost ran on his way to the Upper Library.

'Thank goodness you're all right!' said Kang Xi joyfully when he saw him enter. 'I was really worried when I heard that that vile woman had gone off with you. I was afraid she might try to murder you.'

'Thank you for worrying about me, Shifu,' said Trinket. 'Actually the Old Wh—I mean, Her Majesty—only wanted to find out where I'd been all this time. I didn't dare tell her I'd been to the Wutai Mountains in case she suspected something, so I said I'd been to the South to buy some knick-knacks for you.'

Kang Xi laughed.

'Good. That should put her off the scent. She'll think my

interests are childish still.'

He picked up a large yellow envelope from his desk.

'Before you go to Wutai, I want you to go south to Mount Song, and make your way to the Shaolin Monastery. This is a Secret Edict for the monks there which I want you to deliver for me. You are to pick forty of the Palace Guards and a thousand men of the Valiant Regiment to go with you. The Edict is to be opened and read when you get there. It will tell you what you are to do next. I'm awarding you Manchu nationality and appointing you Second-in-Command of the Valiant Regiment of the Plain Yellow Banner and Deputy-Intendant of the Palace Guards, the two appointments to run concurrently. Your rank will continue to be that of Lieutenant-Colonel.'

Trinket kowtowed.

'So I'm a Manchu now, am I?' he thought. 'Thanks a lot! I suppose this is my consolation prize for offering to be a monk. I get the sweetie first and the nasty medicine after. It should be the other way round!'

Kang Xi had the Plain Yellow Banner commander, Colonel Chalju, summoned and explained to him that Trinket was now to become his deputy in the Valiants. Chalju understood perfectly well that, as the Emperor's favourite, Trinket would now in effect be the commander, but was perfectly happy to play second fiddle to him: he had suffered greatly under Oboi's regency and was glad to welcome the young hero who had removed his tormentor. Kang Xi handed Trinket the gold token of his command and told him that his marching orders were for that very evening and that there was no need to see him again before he left the city.

Kowtowing once again, Trinket took his leave, mentally noting that the Empress Dowager's story would now have to wait until he got back to the Palace, whenever that might be, and that there would now be no time to find out how Auntie Tao was doing. After seeing his friend Dolong, the Chief Intendant of the Palace Guards, and arranging for two of the latter's trusted lieutenants, his own friends Zhang Kangnian and Zhao Qixian, to select another thirty-eight for the expedition, he slipped off to Hair Lane in the West City, leaving Chalju to decide which of the Valiants should go with him. He told Fat Dhuta and Doctor Lu that he had managed to gain an entry into the Palace and that the business of stealing the Sutras was well in hand.

'Better lie low here until you hear from me again,' he told

them. 'We don't want anyone to find out what we are up to.'

They were pleased to learn that he had made such a good start and gladly agreed to do as he had said.

He made Doublet dress up as a boy. She was to go with him on the expedition as a sort of junior batman.

Gambling on the March

When he got back to the Palace, accompanied by Doublet, he found that Chalju had thought of everything. As there was no uniform available that would fit him, Chalju had rustled up four highly skilled tailors to whom he had given a spare uniform of his own and whom he had told to sit in one of the wagons while they were on the march and alter it to fit someone of Trinket's size. If they showed any sign of idling, he told them, they would discover what an army-style flogging was like.

Although it was evening by the time the troops were ready, the Emperor had insisted that they should start immediately, so Trinket had to get them outside the city before nightfall. After leaving by the South Gate, they had in fact only marched seven miles or so before it was necessary to pitch camp.

The Valiants, recruited exclusively from the Manchu aristocracy and fed and housed ten times better than ordinary troops, were the Emperor's own household regiment. Cooped up for long periods in the Capital, they looked on this tour of duty outside, particularly when they learned that no fighting was involved, as a government-paid holiday, and all were in festive mood and looking forward to the trip.

After supper and a drink or two, Trinket, feeling little inclined to sleep, had the forty Palace Guards and the officers of the Valiant Regiment summoned to his capacious headquarters tent. Being still ignorant of the purpose of the expedition, they assumed that he had summoned them for a briefing; but it was something quite different that he had in mind.

'Well, boys,' he said, grinning round at them, 'we've got nothing else to do tonight: why don't we roll the dice? I'll be the banker for you.'

They stared at him open-mouthed, supposing that he must be joking. But when he took four dice out of an inner pocket and rolled them on the table, they responded enthusiastically. The officers among them knew that it was against army regulations to gamble while on active service, but as they were not engaged in any sort of action, they saw no reason why they should mention this to their diminutive commander and deprive him of his fun.

Trinket took out a wad of notes and threw them down in front of him. Altogether there must have been five or six thousand taels' worth.

'All right,' he said, 'who's going to have a go at winning this lot?'

Back in Yangzhou he had watched fascinated while the professionals in the gaming-houses plied their trade, and had dreamed of one day doing the job himself. He could remember quite a few bits of their patter:

> *Silken gown or cotton rags, come and play!*
> *This could be your lucky day.'*

Or:

> *The good sport loses with a smile;*
> *The bad'un runs off with his pile.*

He sang these out now as he took up the dice from the table, blew on them for luck, and shook them in his hand.

Soon money was being slapped down on the table, some on the Gate of Heaven (the side of the table opposite the banker) and some on the Upper and Lower Gates, and the atmosphere grew more and more lively as the men shouted their calls and money began rapidly changing hands. Some of the gamblers lost all they had and went off to their tents to borrow from those who weren't gambling, so that they could go on betting. At one point Trinket's throw showed all four dice with red spots uppermost, which means that the banker takes all, and a universal groan went up from those present; but just as Zhao Qixian, who was acting as croupier, reached out to take the money, Trinket stopped him.

'This is the first time I've ever been on the march, and it's the first time I've ever been banker,' he said. 'This is my present to you all.'

There were cries of admiration:

'Good for the little Colonel!'

'Now there's a real sport!'

'Any of you want to raise your bets?' Trinket asked them.

His generosity had made them all feel lucky and the piles on the table quickly grew, as many of them added to what they had already wagered. Suddenly a voice rang out from the rear:

'The Gate of Heaven!'

Simultaneously a melon-shaped object landed on the table with a thump. The men gazed at it in horror. It was a bloody human head. From the cap which still adhered to it they could see that it was one of the Palace Guards.

'It's Getong!' said Zhao Qixian. 'He was on sentry-duty tonight.'

When the soldiers looked round, they saw a dozen or more men dressed in blue, each of them holding a long-sword, standing in the entrance of the tent. They had all been so intent on their gambling that none of them had seen these intruders arrive. And as none of them were carrying arms, they were at a loss to know what to do.

One of the blue-dressed intruders, a young man of twenty-five or so, stepped up to the table. He was empty-handed and appeared to be unarmed.

'Well, Colonel,' he said, 'do you accept the bet?'

'Seize him!' shouted Zhao Qixian, and instantly four guards moved to lay hands on the young man; but before they could touch him, he had seized two of them by their necks and banged their heads together, so hard that both of them fell down unconscious on the ground. At the same moment, there was a flash of steel and the other two guards uttered cries of pain as two of the blue-clad swordsmen transfixed them from behind. The guards slumped to the ground and the two men in blue, one a man of middle years, the other wearing the long hair and robe of a Taoist, withdrew their swords, which they then hurled like javelins at the table. The swords sank quivering into the wooden surface, one on the left, one on the right-hand side.

'I'm betting on the Upper Gate,' said the middle-aged man.

'And I'm betting on the Lower Gate,' said the Taoist.

At a gesture from the young man, who appeared to be their leader, four more of the blue-dressed swordsmen came forwards and stood on either side of Trinket, pointing their swords at his body.

'You're crazy, breaking into the middle of an armed camp,' Zhao said to the intruders. 'You don't stand a chance of getting out alive. Aren't you afraid of being killed?'

Somewhat surprisingly, one of the four men in blue who were

covering Trinket with their swords let out a giggle.

'*We* aren't afraid. Shouldn't *you* be?'

It was a high female voice. Trinket looked up into the smiling face of a fifteen-year-old girl. She had large, lustrous eyes and a rather gentle expression. A moment before he had been terrified, but now he felt suddenly heartened.

'If I'm afraid, it's because of *you*,' he said, smiling back at her. 'I'm only afraid of girls.'

'Why are you smiling, then, if you're afraid?' she said.

'I won't smile if you don't want me to,' he said, and his face instantly assumed a very serious expression, so droll that it provoked another giggle.

The young leader of the group laughed scornfully.

'You can see the Manchus are finished if they appoint little babes like this to command their forces,' he said. 'Come on, little Colonel! Are you going to throw those dice or not?'

'What do I have to pay you if I lose?' said Trinket.

'Need you ask?' said the young leader. 'If you lose to Upper or Lower Gate, you must give them a sword; if you lose to the Gate of Heaven, you pay with your head.'

At this point he expected Trinket to begin begging for mercy; but whatever he might be like in other situations, Trinket at the gaming-table, particularly when there was a pretty girl present to show off in front of, was no coward. In any case, with four swordpoints an inch or two away from his body, he calculated that they were probably going to kill him anyway, so he might as well go out in style.

'All right,' he said, 'a head for a head, then. A sword for a sword, a head for a head, and trousers for trousers. You throw first.'

The young leader was a bit taken aback by this response, and the middle-aged man muttered something about the need to hurry and not fool about if they wanted to get away before the whole camp was alerted; but the young leader realized that he would lose face if he didn't go through with what he had started, so he picked up the four dice and threw. Six. The Taoist and the middle-aged man threw after him. Each of them got eight.

Trinket picked up the dice and held them out to the girl.

'Will you blow on them for me?'

'What for?' she asked, but blew just the same.

'Thank you,' he said. 'If a girl blows on them, I'm sure to win.'

His throw scored six.

'Six beats six, and I lose to Upper and Lower Gate,' he said, reaching for Getong's head and placing it in front of him.

'Zhao,' he said, 'go out and get me a couple of swords, please.'

Zhao Qixian made off to do his bidding, but was called to a halt at the entrance of the tent by one of the men in blue, who shouted at him and pointed a sword at his chest.

'All right,' said Trinket. 'If I'm not allowed to get swords, you'll have to take money instead. Let's say each of these is worth a thousand taels.'

He took two thousand taels' worth in banknotes and silver from the pile in front of him and placed half beside each of the swords. Once more the young leader of the intruders gave a scornful laugh.

'Do you really think you can get away with *that*?' he said. 'Those swords are worth all the money on this table.'

He made a sign to his followers and six or seven of them leapt forward and swept up all the money. Then he took a sword from one of them and pointed it at Trinket's throat.

'Tell me, scum,' he said, 'are you a Manchu or a Chinese? What's your name?'

Trinket knew that this was a challenge, and that he must now either fight or surrender. He didn't want to fight, but it seemed silly to surrender after having braved it out so far.

'I'm a Lieutenant-Colonel in the Plain Yellow Banner,' he said cheerfully. 'My name is Trinket Wishy-Washy. If you want to kill me, kill me. If you want to play with me, play with me. But I must say, I don't think it's very sporting of you to take on someone so much smaller than yourself.'

The young man quite admired his courage.

'You're right. Sister,' he said, turning to the girl, 'you're about this fellow's size. You can take him on for me.'

'Certainly,' said the girl. 'Come on, Colonel Wishy-Washy, let's see what you can do.'

'Outside!' shouted the other three who had been covering Trinket, and gave him a prod. Then, at a sign from their young leader, they drove their three swords into the table for him to choose from.

Trinket had never in his life fought with a sword and knew that he wouldn't stand a chance.

'I think she's smaller than me,' he said. 'It's still not fair.'

The young leader seized him by the collar and shook him.

'If you're too scared to fight with my sister, kowtow to her and ask her for mercy!'

'No problem!' said Trinket lightly. 'You know what they said to the man who kept his gold below his knees: As long as there are ladies around, *keep kneeling!*'

There was a roar of laughter from the blue-clad men as he dropped to his knees at her feet. In a flash he had twisted around, jumped up, and was standing behind the young leader holding a dagger at his back.

'Surrender?' he said.

He knew that clowning was a good way of putting your opponents off their guard and had used this ploy to get his dagger out of his boot while he was grovelling servilely on the ground.

Seven or eight of the swordsmen pointed their weapons at his breast and shouted to him to release their leader, but they could do no more.

'Release him?' said Trinket. 'I suppose I could. But that wouldn't help very much.'

He made a sudden sweep round with his dagger and there was a series of clangs as it severed their sword-blades in turn and the cut-off parts dropped to the ground. He returned his dagger to the young leader's back as the men stepped back, gazing in amazement at their useless swords.

'Now,' said Trinket, 'just put that money back, will you!'

The men who had taken the money put it back on the table without hesitation.

Just then there was a confused medley of sounds outside the tent, shouts of 'Surrender!' and 'Don't let them get away!', and a surge of fully armed soldiers burst into the tent, some of them carrying extra weapons for the unarmed officers and guards inside.

What had happened was that two officers had slipped out unobserved while the attention of everyone in the tent, including the blue-clad intruders, was focused on Trinket and the young leader, and had managed to call out a sufficient number of infantry-men to surround the headquarters tent with a human ring three or four men deep. All this had been done so silently and expeditiously that the tent was completely encircled before a sound was heard by any of those inside.

'Never mind me!' shouted the young leader. 'Fight your way

out and get away if you can!'

But already each of the blue-clad intruders was surrounded by five or six armed men. However skilled or valiant they were, there was nothing they could do but surrender. They had to drop their weapons (damaged or not) and submit to being bound.

Trinket suspected that skilled fighters such as these who considered themselves enemies of the Manchu Court were likely to be connected with the Triads in some way, and wondered if he could find some means of freeing them.

'Look, friend,' he said to the young leader, 'you could have killed me when you came in here, but you didn't. If I kill *you* now without giving you a second chance, I'll be like the unsporting bastard who runs off with his pile the first time he makes a lucky throw. Why don't we have another go at betting for heads, like the game you started just now?'

The young leader now had seven or eight soldiers in front of him pointing their weapons at his chest, so Trinket put his dagger away and sat down at the table again, chuckling at the prospect of some more gambling.

'If you want to kill me, get on with it,' said the young leader. 'Don't play about with me.'

Trinket ignored him and picked up the dice, still chuckling.

'I'll be banker again and we'll play for heads. Each of you throws in turn. If you win, you go free, with a hundred taels to see you on your way. Anyone who loses—Zhao, get a sharp sword, will you, and stand over here!—anyone who loses gets his heads cut off straight away. That will pay them back for killing poor old Getong and the other two.'

He proceeded to count the intruders. There were nineteen of them, so he made nineteen little piles of silver ingots, each to the value of one hundred taels. To the prisoners, who had considered themselves dead men as soon as they surrendered, this was unexpected clemency. The Taoist told Trinket that, for a Manchu, this was very handsome.

'Wishy-Washy always believes in fair play,' said Trinket. 'That young lady saved my life by blowing on the dice for me. Your little head is safe, sweetheart. You don't have to throw. You can take the money and go.'

He told one of the officers to see that she had safe conduct through the camp.

The girl's face, which had been deathly pale, turned a deep

red, and she slowly shook her head.

'I don't want to,' she said, speaking in a very low voice. 'I can't. The nineteen of us have sworn to live and die together.'

'That's very noble of you,' said Trinket. 'Well, actually, it makes things much simpler. If you've sworn to live and die together, *you* can throw for the lot of them. If you win, all nineteen of you take the money and go. If you lose, all nineteen of you get the chop. Pretty straightforward, isn't it?'

The young leader wasn't too sure what the others would think about it and looked round at them inquiringly, but as several of them expressed their approval, he nodded at the girl.

'Have courage, sister!' he said. 'Whatever you throw, it's fated to happen, anyway.'

The girl reached for the dice. Her eyelids with their long lashes were lowered, but as she picked the dice up, she raised her eyes for a moment and darted a pitiful look at Trinket. Her hand was trembling violently. She closed her eyes tightly again as the dice fell from her hand and rattled smartly on their tray. She dared not look; but though she knew nothing of dice or gambling, she could guess that the Manchu soldiers' loud laughter and their shouts of 'Three! Three! Three!' must bode ill for herself and her friends. And when she did at last open her eyes, she saw that the faces of her companions were ashen. In this kind of gambling three is nearly the lowest score it is possible to get. The nineteen of them almost certainly faced death.

Suddenly one of the men began to shout.

'It's *my* head, why should someone else throw for me? I want to throw for myself.'

'Don't be such a coward!' said the Taoist angrily. 'You are disgracing our Wang Wu Clan.'

'It's my parents who gave me life, not the Clan,' said the man. 'None of you has the right to decide for me.'

'Why didn't you say so before then, instead of waiting until our sister-in-arms had thrown?' said the Taoist, even more angrily.

'That commander said we were each of us to have a throw,' said the man. 'The rest of you may have agreed to let her throw for us, but you didn't hear *me* say anything.'

'Throw for yourself then, Yuan,' said the young leader icily. 'From now on you are no longer a member of the Clan.'

'So be it,' said the man.

'Does anyone else want to throw for himself?' Trinket asked, looking round at the other members of the group.

Two of them moved their lips slightly as if they wanted to say something, but after a little hesitation decided not to.

'Right, then,' said Trinket. 'The Wang Wu Clan are obviously a very brave bunch. I'm not so sure about this Yuan—but of course he's not a member any more. Pour out some wine, somebody! I'd like to have a drink with these friends first, just to show there are no hard feelings.'

An orderly fetched and filled nineteen cups and, after setting one of them down in front of Trinket, handed one to each of the remaining eighteen members of the Clan.

'No Manchu can be a friend of *mine*,' said the young leader, 'but since you have behaved to us like a gentleman and spoken well of our Clan, I am willing to drink with you.'

Trinket raised his cup. The man called Yuan turned his head away and looked rather green while they were drinking.

'Now,' said Trinket, 'eighteen officers with sharp swords, please! If I throw three or anything higher than three, these eighteen friends of ours here must end up a head shorter!'

With an enthusiastic shout a number of officers leapt forward, and soon there was one of them standing, with sword upraised, behind each of the seventeen men and one girl whose lives depended on the throw.

Trinket was secretly worried that he was too out of practice to control the dice, but after blowing and shaking and prolonging the whole operation as long as he dared, he was delighted to see that what he had thrown was two Twos, a One, and a Five: the 'bent five'. A 'bent five' is equivalent to zero: anything can beat it. The prisoners' joy can be imagined, but the soldiers, though they dared not say anything, looked grumpy and suspicious. Trinket saw, and feigned disappointment.

'Tamardy!' he swore. 'It's my hand that ought to be cut off!' And he put his right hand on the table and dealt it several hard slaps with his left.

While the blue-clad clansmen were wondering if a Manchu's word could be trusted, Trinket began pushing the piles of silver towards the edge of the table.

'Go on,' he said. 'You've won the money. Aren't you going to take it?'

The young leader at first refused, but when he was given to understand that Colonel Wishy-Washy would regard his refusal as an insult, he deemed it best not to waste time by arguing and picked up the first little pile with muttered thanks. The others followed his example and began walking from the tent. When it came to the girl's turn, she gave Trinket a little smile as she thanked him and picked up the money. For a brief moment they exchanged glances, then she blushed and turned to go; but when she had gone a few steps she stopped and turned to him again with a smile.

'Do you think I could ask you for those dice?' she said timidly.

'Of course,' said Trinket, handing them to her and giving her fingers a little squeeze. 'Is this so that you can play dice with your friends?'

'No,' she said. 'To remind me how frightened I was! Thank you.'

And she hurried from the tent.

The man called Yuan showed signs of leaving with the rest.

'Hey!' Trinket shouted. 'What about your throw?'

The man turned pale.

'I thought you wouldn't want me to, now that you've given the dice away,' he stammered.

'You don't need dice to gamble with,' said Trinket. 'You can bet on anything. For example, we could bet on how much money there is on this table. What's your guess?'

'I couldn't possibly say,' said the man.

Trinket banged the table angrily.

'This rebel scum thinks he can make a fool of me! Take him outside and cut his head off!'

Yuan, now grey-faced, slumped to his knees.

'No, General, no!' he pleaded. 'Have mercy!'

'General, eh?' thought Trinket. 'Thanks for the promotion!'

'All right then,' he said. 'We're going to ask you some questions. If you answer them truthfully, I might let you go. But the tiniest little lie, and you get the chop. Understood?'

He had the man manacled and put in leg-irons, then, having first reimbursed the officers and the guards with the money they had lost in gambling, he cleared the tent and ordered Zhang and Zhao to proceed with the interrogation.

From Zhang and Zhao's preliminary grilling it emerged that the Wang Wu Clan were followers of Situ Bolei, a high-ranking officer who, during the last days of the Ming, had commanded one of the detachments guarding the Great Wall under the overall command of Wu Sangui. When Wu Sangui defected to the

Manchus, Situ Bolei had resigned in disgust and withdrawn to the Wang Wu Mountains on the borders of Henan and southern Shanxi provinces, with those of his officers and men who shared his opinions. This group of patriots, continuing to drill and train under their old commander, had evolved a distinctive method of fighting which even Zhang and Zhao had heard of. The young leader of the blue-clad intruders was Situ Bolei's son, Situ He. The girl's name was Zeng Rou. Her father had been one of the old man's staff officers who had died some years previously and entrusted his daughter's care to his old commander. The Clan had recently learned that Wu Sangui's son was visiting Peking and had sent this group of fighters to make their way there and kidnap the son as a means of coercing the father to revolt. Coming upon this large Manchu encampment on their journey north and finding it ill-guarded and with loud sounds of gambling coming from the head-quarters tent, their young leader had been unable to resist the temptation to profit from the Manchus' negligence by slipping inside the camp and taking a few Manchu lives before continuing on his mission.

Conscious that his men must be feeling somewhat aggrieved that he had allowed the murderers of three of their comrades to go free, Trinket had been trying to think of some way of giving them satisfaction. The mention of Wu Sangui now gave him an idea how this might be done.

'How dare you pretend you were going to kidnap Wu's son!' he shouted, angrily thumping the table. 'It's obvious you were in his pay all along and just going to Peking for instructions. Tamardy! This turtle's egg is still holding out on us. Let's have some soldiers in here; I want this man beaten!'

Seven or eight men came running in, threw Yuan face down-wards on the ground, and proceeded to administer a military-style flogging, which soon reduced his back and buttocks to a bloody mess.

'Now,' said Trinket, 'perhaps you're ready to talk. How many of you are there living on Wang Wu Mountain?'

'About four hundred,' Yuan answered faintly.

'Including families?' Trinket asked.

'Two thousand, maybe.'

'Granny's twat!' Trinket shouted, banging on the table. 'There must be more than that. Beat him again!'

'Don't beat me! Don't beat me!' pleaded the wretched Yuan.

'I think there must be four thousand—no, *five* thousand.'

'Four thousand, five thousand,' said Trinket. 'If you mean nine thousand, why don't you say so?'

The interrogation, reinforced by further shouts and threats of beating, continued in this fashion, until the final deposition, duly taken down in writing by a regimental clerk, contained the following information:

1. The Wang Wu Clan numbered thirty thousand trained and fully-armed men.

2. Their leader, Situ Bolei, had been to Yunnan from the Wang Wu Mountains to plan a rebellion against the Manchus with his former commander Wu Sangui.

3. The rebellion was to begin with the simultaneous mobilization of Wu Sangui's troops in Yunnan and the invasion of Peking and massacre of the Manchus there by the forces from the Wang Wu base. (Trinket, whose ideas of geography were exremely hazy, was under the impression that the Wang Wu Mountains, which are actually five hundred miles from Peking, were only a few miles from where he was sitting.)

Zhang and Zhao had exchanged uneasy glances during the course of this interrogation, but when they expressed their doubts, Trinket assured them that this whole operation, including the freeing of the prisoners, was part of a deep plan concocted by the Young Emperor. They remembered how, on a previous occasion, Kang Xi had countenanced the deliberate freeing of three members of the Mu Family and were easily persuaded not only that Trinket was acting in a fully approved manner, but also that there would probably be big rewards for those who carried out his orders.

That very night two of Trinket's staff officers were dispatched to Peking with the deposition and a hastily drafted memorial, together with the prisoner, guarded by a detachment of ten Palace Guards and three hundred of the Valiants.

Kang Xi's response was both swift and unexpected. At noon next day, when the troops had struck camp and were proceeding slowly on their southward march, they were overtaken by two mounted members of the Palace Guards, galloping at a tremendous pace. They were carrying a Secret Edict from the Emperor, which Trinket gathered his staff round him to receive. Though beginning with a full list of Trinket's titles, it was not written in the usual Court language but in wording that he could actually understand when it was read out to him:

'. . . You are supposed to be going to the Shaolin Monastery to carry out my orders. Who told you to meddle with things that don't concern you while you were on your way? You have been listening to the lying gossip of someone who wants to undermine the reputation of a loyal officer. What sort of effect is this going to have on the Satrap when he gets to know about it? If I hear another word of this nonsense, the whole lot of you will be coming back to Peking without your heads. Hear and Obey.'

Trinket kowtowed fearfully, the cold sweat running down his back. Zhang Kangnian and the other officers looked rather pale.

'Silly little bugger!' they thought. 'He's lucky to have got away with a telling-off.' And they slunk away, unwilling to share his embarrassment.

The march proceeded. Towards evening the detachment which had escorted Yuan to Peking caught up with them. There was no further gambling this night, or on any of the nights which followed, after they had pitched camp.

Father Treasure

After some days, Mount Song and the Shaolin Monastery came in sight. Father Wisdom, the Abbot, who had been warned that he was to be the recipient of an Imperial Edict, was waiting at the foot of the mountain with all his monks and escorted them up to the monastery. There Trinket took out the Edict, broke open the seals, and handed it to Zhang Kangnian to read out. This Edict, unlike the last one, was composed in extremely flowery language which Trinket found quite incomprehensible. It was only towards the very end that he began to understand the words that were being read. After announcing the gifts that the Emperor was making to the inmates of the monastery, the Edict went on to say that Trinket (it gave him all his new titles) was to have his head shaved there and then and to be received as a monk in the Shaolin Monastery as the Emperor's proxy.

This came as a thunderbolt. Trinket had agreed to become a monk and go to Wutai in order to look after the Old Emperor; but he had not expected to be leaving the secular world so abruptly, or leaving it in this particular place. He looked on glumly while the officers distributed the Emperor's gifts and while Zhang handed the Certificate of Induction to Father Wisdom, and there were tears in his eyes when he knelt on the ground to be shaved.

'This is a great honour for our monastery,' said Father Wisdom as he took up the razor. 'As you are the Emperor's proxy, no one here, including myself, is worthy to be your instructor. I shall put you down as a disciple of my own late Master of blessed memory, so that you will be equal with me in seniority. The name in religion I give you is Treasure, because you will be accumulating spiritual treasure here for His Imperial Majesty. To the Brothers you will be known as Father Treasure.'

He motioned with the razor three times over Trinket's head, then handed it to a barber monk, who removed from Trinket's pate the frizzled remnants that Princess Ning had left him. While the barber was engaged in this, Father Wisdom filled in the blanks in the Certificate of Induction. Trinket, in addition to being a Palace Eunuch, a Triad Lodge Master, a Mystic Dragon Marshal, a Manchu Colonel (and of course a genuine, authenticated Yangzhou street urchin), was now a monk. He had entered the Holy Gate of the *sangha*, the monastic community of Buddhist believers. Suddenly a great wave of misery welled up inside him and he burst into tears. But just at that moment the assembled monks began chanting the names of the Buddha, so the sound of his sobs went unheard.

When the chanting finished, Father Wisdom introduced the Brothers to him, one by one. All of them called him 'Father'. When he found himself being called 'Father' by old men with long white beards, he could not contain his amusement and the Brothers smiled kindly to see this little monk laughing loudly while the tears were still wet on his face. Some of them, of course, knew him already, having met him on Wutai.

Their mission having been accomplished, it was time now for the soldiers to leave. After taking his farewell of the officers, Trinket led Zhang Kangnian to one side and handed him three hundred taels with which to arrange board and lodging for Doublet somewhere in the vicinity of the mountain. Women were not allowed in the monastery: and though Doublet was disguised as a boy, the Shaolin monks who belonged to the Eighteen Lohan group had seen her on Wutai and knew that she was a girl, so she had remained behind when Trinket and the senior officers were escorted up the mountain. She had been expecting him to return within a matter of hours; but now he didn't know *when* he would be returning and the best he could hope for was that, if he kept her nearby, he would be able to steal visits to her from the monastery from time to time.

The days which followed were for the most part days of idleness. Father Wisdom decided that, provided Trinket observed the Five Major Precepts, it should be left to his own discretion whether or not he joined in chanting the offices and in the various other activities of the Brothers. The Five Major Precepts, he explained, were the prohibitions against taking life, stealing, fornicating, lying, and drinking alcoholic beverages. Trinket asked if gambling was forbidden, a question for which the unworldly Abbot was unprepared. However, after thinking for a bit he smiled amiably and replied that it wasn't among the prohibitions, so he supposed it was all right; though of course the Brothers wouldn't be able to gamble with him. Trinket didn't think he would derive much pleasure from gambling with himself; and since he had no intention of taking part in the offices, foresaw that the time he spent in this monastery was going to be very, very boring.

Yet in the event he found there was some relief. The Shaolin Monastery had for centuries been the Empire's most famous centre for training and research in the arts of self-defence, and most of the monks spent a good deal of their time in practising and training themselves in these arts. At first, when Trinket was wandering idly round the monastery and came upon a group of them practising, they would stop what they were doing and stand respectfully to attention. It was not entirely out of respect that they did this: many of the Shaolin methods were closely-guarded secrets and the trainee monks had had it drummed into them that they were never to allow strangers to see them practising. However, they had been told that Trinket was equal to their Abbot in seniority, so when he begged them to continue and behave as if he wasn't there, they soon got used to his presence and he was able to spend a great deal of his time watching them practise. It occurred to him that the reason why Kang Xi had arranged for him to begin his life as a monk in the Shaolin Monastery was so that, before he went to Wutai, he might improve his credentials as a protector of the Old Emperor by acquiring some of these skills. While he was stuck there it seemed a waste of opportunity not to do so, and for a day or two he was enthusiastic about the idea; but, needless to say, he was too lazy to persist with any sort of training for long.

Green Girl and Blue Girl

Spring had come, and one day the weather was so inviting that Trinket was suddenly filled with a longing to escape for a while from the tedious company of the monks. He decided to go down the mountain and visit Doublet. She must be lonely, he thought; and besides, if he were to buy the ingredients, she would be able to cook him the meat and fish dishes for which, after weeks of enforced vegetarianism, he had developed a craving.

On his way down, as he approached the halfway pavilion, where visitors were first received before proceeding up to the monastery, he could hear the sounds of a quarrel—men's voices mixed with the higher-pitched voices of women. Anxious not to miss any excitement, he hurried forward and found that it was the four monks who were permanently employed there as receptionists engaged in altercation with a pair of females, one of them a young woman of about twenty entirely dressed in blue, the other a girl of sixteen or so in pale green. Trinket, knowing that these four Brothers were the gentlest of men whose courtesy and tact had recommended them for the job, wondered how they came to be quarrelling. The senior of them, Brother Clarity, ran to meet him and begged him to intervene.

Suddenly, as Trinket approached the girls, he was smitten with a sensation the like of which he had never in his life experienced before. It was the girl in green. She was quite simply the most beautiful girl he had ever seen. He stood gazing at her, wide-eyed and open-mouthed.

'I'd like to marry that girl,' he thought. 'I *will* marry her. Even if it means going through fire or flood or boiling oil, I'll have that girl for my wife!'

Embarrassed by his stare, the Green Girl blushed and turned away her head. The blue one at first looked indignant; but when she saw the fierce working of his face, one moment grinning, the next moment rolling his eyes and grinding his teeth, she concluded that he was a harmless idiot. With some astonishment she heard the monks calling to him to rouse him from his trance:

'Father Treasure! Father Treasure!'

'*Father*?' she said. 'Is this little monk your superior?'

'He is indeed, young lady,' said Brother Clarity. 'Next to our Lord Abbot, he ranks highest in this monastery.'

'Don't believe him, sister,' said the younger girl. 'He's pulling your leg.'

'*Are* you a high-ranking monk?' the Blue Girl asked Trinket.

'I'm certainly am, darling, worse luck,' said Trinket, who had by this time come out of his trance.

'I thought we came here to learn something from the greatest Martial Arts centre in the Empire,' said the Blue Girl. 'But the first four monks we meet can't even fight properly, and this so-called Father of theirs is a little guttersnipe. We're wasting our time. Come on, let's go!'

Trinket noticed that Brother Clarity and one of the other Brothers had red marks on their faces where they had been hit and realized that the girls must have laid into them as soon as they arrived. Brother Clarity for his part was worried that if the girls left now with so bad an impression, they might spread the word outside and the reputation of the monastery would be damaged.

'Please don't go, young ladies!' he begged them. 'We four are only receptionists; we don't pretend to be any good at Martial Arts. I think before you go you ought at least to tell us where you come from and who your teacher is. If you will wait a moment, I will fetch some Brothers from the monastery who are better qualified to help you.'

He turned to run, but before he had gone a few steps, a blue streak appeared behind him and he was sent flying head over heels. There was a cruel laugh and next moment the Blue Girl was over him and—*click! clack!*—had dislocated his right shoulder and his arm. She then proceeded to deal with the three other monks in the same fashion.

Scared out of his wits, Trinket was still wondering what to do when he felt a tightening of his collar and his whole body went numb. Whoever had grabbed hold of him must simultaneously have done something to a Vital Point on his neck. He could see the Blue Girl standing in front of him, so he knew that it must be the Green Girl who was holding him. The thought of being touched by her, however roughly, gave him pleasure. He could smell the perfume she was wearing.

'Mm!' he murmured. 'I like your scent!'

This seemed to infuriate the Blue Girl.

'What a vile little creature this monk is!' she said. 'I think you'd better cut his nose off.'

'No, I think I'll poke out his horrible little leering eyes,' said the Green Girl.

'I hope it takes a nice long time,' thought Trinket dreamily; but then he felt excruciating pressure on his left eye and realized that she was serious.

'Ow!' he cried. 'Mother's!'

Wildly fumbling behind him in an effort to push her off, he unthinkingly employed the Hero trick which the Leader had taught him and which he had afterwards practised on the Empress Dowager, squeezing the Green Girl's young breasts so that she was forced to back away. As she stepped back, with a cry of shame and rage, she seized both his arms and gave them a violent twist. There was a sickening crack and both his elbows were disjointed. Then she drew a sheath knife from her waist and went for him. He threw himself to the ground and rolled under a stone picnic-table for cover, but she kicked him out and made a stab at his back.

'Sister, sister,' cried the Blue Girl, 'you mustn't kill him!'

But the Green Girl went on stabbing. Though Trinket was wearing his weapon-proof waistcoat, the blows hurt him badly and he cried out in pain. Believing that she had killed him, the Green Girl completely lost her head. Her virgin purity had been violated and she had killed a Shaolin monk. Unable to face the consequences, she turned the blade of the knife towards herself and drew it across her throat. Immediately the blood gushed up from the wound. The Blue Girl caught her as she fell and held her in her arms.

'Oh sister, what have you done?' she said. 'You mustn't die!'

'Holy name! We must save her. There's no time for delay.'

The speaker was a venerable monk with a long white beard who must all this time have been hurrying to the scene.

'I fear she's past saving,' said the Blue Girl; but the old monk, ignoring her, reached down over her shoulder and pressed with his fingers on several points round the bleeding wound.

'Forgive me, young lady, but we have to act quickly.'

There was a rending sound as he tore a strip from his habit which he then bound round the Green Girl's throat. Then he took her in his arms and hurried off with her along the path that led up to the monastery, with the Blue Girl following at his heels.

Trinket struggled to his feet and tried to follow too, but his arms were hurting abominably and the effort made great drops of sweat stand out and roll down from his forehead. Fortunately he had not gone very far when a number of the monks came running towards him and helped him and the other four injured monks back to the monastery. In the Shaolin Monastery the treatment of injuries was considered a branch of the Martial Arts and there were monks specializing in dealing with fractures and dislocations, who were able, with a minimum of manipulation, to get Trinket's injured limbs back into joint.

As soon as they had finished with him, Trinket wanted to go and see the Green Girl, but he was told that his presence was required by the Abbot. This message was conveyed to him by eight Brothers from the Vinaya Hall, the disciplinary centre of the monastery. At first he refused, and they were obliged to traipse after him to the infirmary. The Blue Girl was standing guard outside, but the aged monk who had rescued her happened to come out at that moment and was able to assure him that the Green Girl had not died—her wound was by no means dangerous and would certainly respond favourably to treatment—so he abandoned his idea of going in to see her, and resolved to come back later.

'It was all that young monk's fault,' the Blue Girl shouted, pointing her finger at Trinket. He stuck out his tongue at her and accompanied his escort to the hall.

An intimidating scene awaited him. Fifty or sixty monks wearing their cassocks were drawn up in two ranks facing each other on either side of the hall. At the head of the hall, below the Buddha image, were two thrones, the left-hand one occupied by the Abbot, Father Wisdom, in full canonicals, the right-hand one by a tall, forbidding figure whom Trinket had not previously encountered. This was Father Perception, the Master of Discipline. The four unfortunate receptionists stood in a row facing them. As Trinket walked with his escort between the ranks of silent monks, he felt he was entering a court of law.

'You must first pay your respects to the Lord Buddha,' said Father Wisdom when Trinket stood before him. Trinket kowtowed to the image.

'Now,' said Father Wisdom, 'will you kindly tell the Master of Discipline exactly what took place this morning at the halfway pavilion?'

'I was on my way down the mountain when I heard the sound of quarrelling, so I went to have a look,' said Trinket, 'but

I've no idea what they were quarrelling *about*. Brother Clarity could tell you that.'

Brother Clarity embarked on a rather long-winded account of the monks' altercation with the two girls, ending with the girls' refusing to say who they were and then striking him and another Brother in the face. The Abbot seemed to think it very important that they should establish what school of Martial Arts the girls had been trained in and summoned the head monk of the Prajna Hall to advise them.

When this venerable individual arrived, he turned out to be none other than the old monk who had applied first aid to the Green Girl and carried her off to the infirmary. His name was Brother Simple. He had lived in the monastery since he was seven years old and had an encyclopaedic knowledge of every aspect of the Martial Arts but an almost total ignorance of the world outside, so that in practical matters he often seemed half-witted. Questioned about the blows sustained by two of the receptionists, he mentioned several systems of self-defence which might employ this form of attack and gave a number of impressive-sounding technical terms to describe what Trinket thought of as a simple smack in the face. When Trinket mentioned the way in which the Blue Girl had dislocated the monks' shoulders, Brother Simple produced even more possibilities and a great deal more technical terminology from his vast store of knowledge. After some discussion it was concluded that the girls' training was eclectic and that they did not belong to *any* particular school.

The Master of Discipline was more interested in the Blue Girl's charge that Trinket had indecently assaulted her companion. Trinket's flippant answers when pressed about this did little to endear him to this austere individual, but at least they made it clear that when the 'assault' occurred which had driven the Green Girl to try and take her own life, he had been struggling for his survival. This was confirmed when they saw the holes that her knife had made in his habit. The Master of Discipline having first expressed the view that Father Treasure, though he had conducted himself throughout with unseemly levity, was not actually in breach of the rule of chastity, Father Wisdom delivered his own judgement: the four receptionists should be temporarily relieved of their duties in the halfway pavilion so that they could devote more time to training, and the two young women should exceptionally be allowed to reside in the monastery until the younger one's injury was healed. As Trinket had been found innocent of unchasteness, he might take a seat beside him.

'How many years' training have you done already?' Trinket asked the receptionists when he had seated himself next to the Abbot. It turned out that all four of them had done more than twelve years.

'There's something wrong here,' he said. 'This monastery is supposed to be the great Martial Arts centre of the world; but here are four Brothers who've trained all these years, and yet a couple of girls who haven't had any proper training at all can make monkeys of them.'

'We all have our strengths and weaknesses,' said Father Wisdom. 'These four Brothers just happen not to be good at Martial Arts; but they are very good at dealing with outsiders, which itself is a work of merit.'

But Brother Simple seemed unconvinced.

'Father Treasure is right,' he said, looking desperately worried.

When the session had ended and the Brothers were dispersing to their duties, the old monk was still muttering to himself and worriedly shaking his head.

As soon as he could get away, Trinket slipped round to the infirmary. The Green Girl was lying motionless in one of the beds, whether sleeping or unconscious he couldn't tell. Her face was almost as white as the bandages with which her neck was swathed. An arm lay outside the coverlet, whose dimpled hand he reached out to touch; but just at that moment there was an angry shout which caused him to draw back:

'Don't you dare touch her!'

It was the Blue Girl who had just appeared at the other end of the room. He turned and fled. His joints ached at the mere thought of experiencing those 'eclectic' methods of Martial Arts a second time.

He was round again first thing next morning. The old monk who looked after the infirmary came out to greet him.

'Is the young lady any better?' Trinket asked him.

'She's gone, Father. She came to in the middle of the night, and when she saw where she was she said she wasn't going to stay a moment longer in the same monastery as that little . . . that little . . .'

Trinket could guess whom she meant.

'Yes, yes.'

'So, well, she managed to get up on her feet and the other young lady helped her to leave. I've no idea where they were planning to go.'

Trinket nodded miserably. He didn't know where the Green Girl had gone. He didn't even know her name. But then he reflected that a girl who was so beautiful and who had such remarkable accomplishments would surely not be too hard to trace. Sooner or later he would track her down. Meanwhile he went off to tease Brother Simple. Even life in the monastery still had its amusements.

For a whole month after the Green Girl's disappearance, no day went by without his thinking about her two or three times.

Green Girl and Blue Girl again, in Strange Circumstances

The weather was now getting warmer and he miserably reminded himself that it was already three months since he became a monk. It was high time, he decided, for a break.

Taking a supply of money with him, he left the monastery and struck out on a path that led down the slopes of Shaoshi Mountain to the market town of Tantoupu. At an outfitter's in the town he bought himself a complete new set of clothing, including hat and shoes, which he carried off to a cave he had passed on his way across the mountain. There he changed into his new purchases, made his monk's clothes into a bundle, and went off to admire his reflection in the still, deep part of a mountain stream. Satisfied with what he saw there, he made his way back to Tantoupu, carrying his bundle with him.

The first thing he did when he was back in the town was to find a good restaurant, where he treated himself to a substantial meal of chicken, duck, fish, and pork. Then, having satisfied his most pressing craving, he set out to look for somewhere where he could hear once more the shouts of gamblers and the merry rattle of dice. After walking the length of seven or eight little back streets, he heard a cry of 'Aces up!' from the depths of a house he was passing. The sound was sweet music to his ears. He knocked at the door. A man of forty or so with a rakish tilt to his hat came out to answer.

'What do you want?'

Trinket took out a silver ingot and juggled it in his palm.

'I've got itchy fingers,' he said. 'I want to lose some of these.'

'This isn't a gaming-house, sonny,' said the man, 'it's a whore-house. And if it's girls you're after, you'd better come back in two or three years' time.'

Trinket was not to be discouraged.

'That's all right,' he said. 'Find me a few of the free girls, enough to make up three tables, and we'll have a party.'

He pressed the ingot, weighing all of two taels, into the man's palm and gave him a wink.

'To buy yourself a drink, friend.'

At the feel of the money the man's manner underwent an instant transformation.

'Why, thank you, sir. Come inside, sir,' he said affably; and as Trinket entered, he turned and bawled in a great voice to those within:

'Visitor!'

The bawd came hurrying out, all smiles when she saw this fifteen-year-old in his expensive, flashy clothes.

'Here's a young lad who's stolen from his parents and gone on the town to spend the money,' she thought. 'We'll pluck you well, my pigeon, don't you worry!'

She took him by the hand.

'I expect you want to see the girls, my dear. We ask for a little present first, that's the rule. Like a deposit.'

The smile fled from Trinket's face.

'Who are you trying to fool? I'm no innocent babe, lady. I was *born* in the trade.' He slapped a wad of notes, three or four hundred taels' worth, on the table. 'One tea-round, five pennyweights a girl; flower-top, three taels; server of the big pot, five pennyweights; and five pennyweights for the auntie. And I'm feeling generous, so make it all double.'

The bawd's jaw dropped. Only someone brought up in a brothel could have so fluent a command of the language.

'How silly of me! I should have seen at once you were a pro-fessional. Now just say what you want, my dear, and we'll do our best for you.'

'I suppose in a small place like this you wouldn't have any Suzhou girls or any from Datong?' said Trinket.

The bawd looked embarrassed.

'Well, yes and no. We've got one who passes for a Suzhou girl, but she isn't really. She can fool our ordinary customers, but I wouldn't recommend her for *you*, dear.'

'Never mind,' said Trinket cheerfully. 'Call them *all* in. Tell them three taels each, with my compliments.'

Soon the room was full of twittering, excited young women. No beauties these: most of them were big-footed country girls, crudely made up, and far too gaudily dressed. But Trinket was happy. All his young life he had dreamed of playing the big shot, the seriously rich customer who treats all the girls, and for whom the brothel puts on its smiling best. He sat in their midst, a girl in either arm, on one of whom he planted a big kiss, savouring as he did so a very strong reek of garlic.

There was a movement in the doorway as two more young women came elbowing their way in.

'Two more!' he said. 'Welcome, welcome! Come over and let me give you both a smacker!'

Next moment he jumped up with a cry of dismay, upsetting the two girls at his sides. The two who had just come in were the Blue Girl and the Green Girl! The Blue Girl laughed mirthlessly at his confusion.

'We've been following you ever since you got to town,' she said, 'wondering what mischief you would get up to next.'

Trinket's back was clammy with cold sweat.

'You—no, not you, the other one—are you . . . I mean, is it . . . is your throat better now?' he asked faintly.

The Green Girl ignored him. The Blue Girl continued as if he had said nothing:

'We've been waiting outside the monastery day after day for you to come out. Now our patience has at last been rewarded and we are going to have our revenge. We are going to cut you up into little tiny pieces.'

'When I grabbed you that time,' Trinket said to the Green Girl pleadingly, 'it wasn't . . . I mean, I didn't . . . I think . . .'

The Green Girl reddened and her eyes flashed.

'And what about what you said just now when we came in?' said the Blue Girl angrily.

'Don't talk to him, sister, he isn't worth it,' said the Green Girl. 'Let's kill him now and get it over with!'

She drew her sword from its scabbard. There were screams from the girls as the blade flashed out, catching the tip of Trinket's hat as he ducked to avoid it. The hat fell off, revealing his bald head.

'I advise you two to get out of here,' Trinket shouted, crouch-

ing behind one of the girls. 'This is a whore-house. Only prosti-
tutes come in here. What about your reputations?'

The Blue Girl and the Green Girl were now both slashing with
their swords. In the crowded room they narrowly missed decapi-
tating one of the young whores.

'I told you, this is a whore-house,' Trinket shouted. 'Don't
you understand why I came here? I'm going to undress now. I'll be
taking my trousers off in a minute.'

He had already begun unbuttoning and tossed a garment out
to show that he meant business. The Green Girl turned and fled.
The Blue Girl stared angrily for a second, then turned and followed
her. The bawd and one of the tapsters were knocked over as she
and the Green Girl rushed out of the house.

Trinket knew that he had only gained a momentary respite.
The girls would wait outside and cut him down as soon as he
emerged. Inside the brothel, meanwhile, it was pandemonium.

'Calm down, everybody!' he shouted 'There's ten taels for
every one of you. That's a promise. Only just calm down!'

At once there was silence. He took out twenty taels and gave
it to one of the tapsters.

'Get me a horse from somewhere, and have it waiting for me
at the end of the lane.'

The man ran off to do his bidding. Trinket took out another
twenty taels and held it out to one of the young whores.

'Here's twenty taels if you'll change clothes with me.'

The young woman was only too willing to oblige.

'Those two who came in just now are my wives,' said Trinket.
'They shaved my hair off to stop me going out, so that I wouldn't
be able to go to places like this. Now they've found out that I
escaped, they're trying to kill me.'

The bawd and the young whores were fascinated. They were
used to wives following their husbands to the brothel and quarrelling with them outside; but shaving a husband's hair off to keep
him at home, and going out sword in hand to kill him—such things
were quite outside their experience.

Meanwhile Trinket was changing into the young woman's
clothes. The others entered into the spirit of the thing, some of them
fetching rouge and eye-black to make up his face for him while
others offered advice. Male customers drifted in from other parts
of the house to watch the fun. To hide his baldness, Trinket tied a
floral kerchief over his head.

Presently the tapster returned to say that he had got a horse.

'You want to be careful, sir. Your older missus is outside the front door and your Number Two is round the back. They've both got their swords drawn waiting for you.'

'Spiteful bitches!' said the bawd. 'The likes of them take the food out of our mouths. We should all be starving if they had their way. I'd divorce them, my dear, if I was you. Then you can come here and enjoy yourself whenever you like.'

'Good idea,' said Trinket. 'But right now, could you do me a favour? Could you go to the front door and give that bitch in the blue dress there a piece of your mind? Keep her occupied. Don't go outside though, or you might get yourself hurt.'

This was a task that the bawd was both willing and well qualified to perform. Soon such a violent stream of abuse was issuing from the front of the house that even Trinket might have learned from it if he had been listening. But he was too busy handing out the promised money to the whores.

'When I give the word, I want you all to rush out of the back door with me,' he said. 'If we go out together, those filthy wives of mine won't be able to catch me.'

Emboldened by the sight of so much silver, the young whores, fairly hopping with excitement, enthusiastically agreed. Just at that moment there was a sudden break in the stream of invective from the front, followed by a cry of pain.

'Ow! Aiyo!'

Trinket concluded that the Blue Girl had finally lost patience with the bawd and stepped inside to strike her.

'Now!' he said, and the twenty-odd whores, with him in their midst, streamed through the back door in a promiscuous mass, while the Green Girl, sword in hand, stood helplessly by, not knowing what to make of this sudden exodus.

The Blue Girl, however, sensing that something was up, abandoned the bawd and rushed round to the back of the house. But Trinket was already astride the horse and galloping away. The whores laughed jeeringly and taunted the 'jealous wives'.

'Run after him! Hurry!' the Blue Girl shouted; but it was obviously too late.

Once out of the town, Trinket began taking off the whore's clothing garment by garment and tossing it away as he rode along. He had left his bundle of monk's clothes behind in the brothel, so when he dismounted on the lower rear slopes of the mountain, leaving the horse to make its way back alone, he had to climb up to the monastery in his underwear. He managed somehow to sneak inside unobserved and, hiding his face in his hands, to make his way back to his cell. Once inside his cell, he washed the make-up from his face and put on a fresh habit.

'Now,' he thought, 'if those two wives of mine come back here to make trouble, I'll just deny the whole thing.'

CHAPTER 16

In which Father Treasure is further involved with the Green Girl; a Mongol Prince and a Tibetan Lama visit the Shaolin Monastery; Father Treasure is made Abbot of Pure Coolness Monastery; Kang Xi visits the Wutai Mountains; and a White Apparition tries to assassinate the Emperor

Trinket, Brother Simple, and the Green Girl

About noon next day, as Trinket lay sprawled on his bed thinking dreamily of the Green Girl, a nervous-looking Brother Clarity slipped into his cell.

'Father Treasure,' he said, 'I think you'd better not go outside the monastery for a day or two.'

'Oh?' said Trinket. 'Why?'

'One of the brothers from the kitchen was outside gathering sticks this morning when he ran into two young women with swords in their hands. They asked him if he knew you, and when he said he did, they started asking questions about you.'

'What did they want to know?' said Trinket.

'They asked what times you generally go outside and where you generally go to. It was pretty clear they meant you no good and were lying in wait for you. As long as you stay in the monastery though, I shouldn't think they'd dare come inside.'

'But this is the famous Shaolin Monastery,' said Trinket. 'What are people going to think when they hear that a big shot Shaolin monk is too scared to go outside his own monastery because of a couple of girls?'

'I know,' said Brother Clarity. 'To tell the truth, though, I've already spoken to the Abbot about this. It's on his instructions that I've come. He said to tell you that as long as you don't go out, he thinks they're bound to give up after a day or two; and he's sure no one will think any the worse of us for ignoring them.'

'Well, I still think it looks bad,' said Trinket. 'Brother Simple said they don't belong to any particular school of Martial Arts. Girls with no special training getting the better of Shaolin monks! It makes us look ridiculous.'

'I agree,' said Brother Clarity, thinking ruefully of the things they had done to his joints. 'I'm only passing on the Abbot's orders. He's determined that this matter should be dealt with peaceably.'

When Brother Clarity had gone, Trinket continued his musings about the Green Girl. He didn't *want* to avoid her, he wanted to be near her. In fact, he wanted to marry her. The trouble was that the Green Girl had made it abundantly clear that she wanted him dead, and if he got near enough for her to do so, she would undoubtedly kill him. Somehow or other he must acquire the ability to disarm her—and, of course, her companion—so that he could have her in his power. What he would do then to convert her from an unwilling captive to an affectionate wife he didn't yet know; but he could only take one step at a time. He decided he would go to Brother Simple and see if that great authority on the Martial Arts could come up with some brilliant method for disarming enraged young swordswomen and getting them into one's power.

He found Brother Simple striding up and down the Prajna Hall clutching his head in both hands, his eyes upturned to the ceiling. The poor man had taken to heart what Trinket had said after his interrogation in the Vinaya Hall a month earlier about Shaolin monks with years of training being no match for untrained girls. He had been puzzling about it ever since, wondering if there could in fact have been some secret system in what he had taken to be the girls' eclectic methods and convinced that among all the dozens of systems of self-defence and thousands of figures, positions, throws, feints, holds, attacks, and counter-attacks he had committed to memory there must be something which could have neutralized them. The hours he spent each day in contemplating this problem had only made his mind the more confused, so that when Trinket came to call on him, he was close to mental breakdown.

Trinket coughed a few times, but the old man appeared not to have heard him and continued to pace up and down.

'Brother Simple,' said Trinket; but Brother Simple had still not heard.

Trinket walked up behind him and tapped him on the shoulder. Almost as he did so a shock ran through his body and he found himself being hurled across the room against the wall. He opened his mouth to cry out, but no sound came. At once Brother Simple was on his knees beside him apologizing.

'Oh dear! Oh, Father Treasure! Oh, I am so sorry, I have hurt you! I must beg you to punish me, very, very severely!'

It took Trinket a while to get his breath back.

'That's all right,' he gasped. 'Please get up. It was my fault.'

But Brother Simple remained kneeling and continued to apologize. Trinket managed to struggle to his feet by holding on to the wall and then helped the old monk to get up off his knees.

'What was that bit of kungfu you used on me just now?' he asked curiously.

'It's one of the forms of defence taught in Prajna Hand karate,' said Brother Simple.

'Is it something you could teach me fairly quickly?' Trinket asked him.

Brother Simple shook his head doubtfully.

'Prajna Hand karate would certainly be effective against the young ladies, but, er . . .'

'But it would take twenty or thirty years to learn properly, is that what you were going to say?'

'Twenty or thirty years? Let me see. Perhaps . . .'

'Perhaps twenty or thirty years wouldn't be long enough.'

'Perhaps not.'

'Look,' said Trinket, 'couldn't you just teach me those parts of Prajna Hand that I would need to use if I was going to take on those girls?'

Brother Simple looked startled. Evidently such a possibility had never occurred to him and he was somewhat overwhelmed by the boldness of the concept. His face brightened, but after a moment or two of reflection he began to look worried and glum again.

'Oh dear, oh dear!'

'Why the "oh dears"?' said Trinket.

'I shall need to know *all* the forms of attack these young ladies are capable of and match each of them with a Prajna Hand defence before I can begin instructing you. You and the four brothers who were with you that day will have to have another encounter with them. That could be dangerous.'

Trinket laughed.

'I don't think *that* will be necessary. If you want to know more about their method of fighting, why don't you go and find out for yourself?'

'You mean *fight* them?' said Brother Simple. 'Oh dear me, no! Our vows forbid us to *seek* conflict with anyone.'

'All right, then,' said Trinket. 'Just come outside with me and the two of us will walk around together. Perhaps we shall find that the girls have already gone, in which case we shan't need to bother.'

He seized the old monk by the hand and hauled him off after him.

Brother Simple had seldom been outside the monastery walls since he was a lad and found much to marvel at as they walked around. He was just making an inane remark about some pine trees when there was a shrill cry and a blade flashed out from behind one of them.

'Here he is!' screamed the voice.

The blade was aimed at Trinket, but Brother Simple effort-lessly stretched out his arm and grasped the wrist of the person wielding it before it could do any damage. As he did so, he called out the names of the movements:

'That was a Wild Tiger attack. This defence is a Flower-Picker's Catch-Can.' But he quickly released the wrist. 'Oh dear! I shouldn't have used that defence. You'd find that one too difficult.'

The wielder of the sword was the Blue Girl. As soon as her wrist was released, she drew the sword back and aimed it in a wide sweep at the old monk's waist. Meanwhile, however, the Green Girl had also run out of the trees with sword upraised to cut down Trinket; but as Trinket had at once dodged behind Brother Simple's back, her blade was descending on the old monk's shoulder at the same time as the Blue Girl's sword was sweeping towards his waist. He had little difficulty in fending off this double assault, but it cost him considerable effort to name the two forms of attack and the way in which he had countered them. He appeared to be under the impression not that he was fighting for his life but that he was giving a lesson in unarmed combat; but the girls mistook his muttering for taunts and in their anger began hacking at him wildly.

'Father Treasure,' he called out between gasps as he warded off their blows, 'tell the young ladies to go a little slower. My old brain isn't fast enough to identify all these attacks!'

But Trinket, nearly helpless with laughter, had slipped off to lean against a pine tree, from which vantage point he could devour the Green Girl with his eyes. The Green Girl, not seeing Trinket, thought he must have run away and stopped for a moment to look round. When she caught sight of him leaning against the tree and gazing at her she reddened and, abandoning the combat with Brother Simple, turned to run at him with her sword. But even as she did so, the old monk aimed the middle finger of his right hand against a Vital Point under her ribs. The effect of this was almost instantaneous. Halfway to the tree she twisted about, dropped her sword, and fell down, paralysed from the neck downwards, upon the ground. Trinket ran up and knelt beside her.

'How beautiful you are!' he said. 'Just to look at you almost makes me want to die!' And he touched her cheek.

Speechless with shock and anger, she fainted away.

Trinket got up.

'Brother Simple,' he called, 'why don't you do that to the other girl as well? Fighting isn't a very good way of finding out their methods. If they're both immobilized you can find out what you want by just asking them.'

'You're right, Father,' said Brother Simple. 'We should always avoid violence if we can.'

The Blue Girl paused and stepped back. She knew she was no match for the old monk and that, if there was to be any hope of rescuing her companion, it was essential for her to remain free. She darted towards the trees, just pausing a moment to look back.

'If either of you harms a hair of her head,' she shouted, 'I'll burn your monastery to the ground.'

And with that she plunged into the trees and disappeared.

'Why should we want to harm her hair?' Brother Simple asked, naively. 'Do you think she will burn the monastery if one of the young lady's hairs should just chance to drop out?'

Trinket ignored his dumb question. He was gazing down at the green-clad figure on the grass, wondering how he could take advantage of this heaven-sent opportunity to have her in his power. Somehow or other the old monk must be persuaded to let him keep her. He placed his palms together and raised his eyes heavenwards in what he hoped was a convincingly pious attitude.

'The Lord Buddha's holy name be praised, Brother Simple!' he said. 'He has delivered this girl into our hands for the greater glory of the monastery.'

'Oh?' said Brother Simple. 'How do you make that out?'

'Don't you see? We can take her back with us. Then you will have plenty of time to find out all you need to know about her combat methods and work out the appropriate ways of countering them. Once we know that, no one will be able to say that the Shaolin monks are no match for a couple of half-trained girls.'

He took off his monk's habit and wrapped it round the recumbent figure, then, gathering her up in his arms, began marching off with her.

'Come on!'

Brother Simple felt that there was something not quite right about this, though he couldn't have said exactly what it was; nevertheless, Trinket was his superior and he was enjoined by his vows always to obey his superiors in religion, so he simply picked up the Green Girl's sword from the grass and trailed along, somewhat unhappily, behind.

Just outside the side gate of the monastery Trinket drew a flap of the monk's habit over the Green Girl's face, so that none of her was visible. Even so, his heart beat faster as they entered, for he knew that if any of the monks saw him like this, their suspicions would be aroused and there would be serious trouble. Fortunately he got to the Prajna Hall without an encounter, and once he was inside, the monks on duty there, seeing him followed by their own superior, made way for him with meekly downcast eyes and did not venture to question what he was doing. Trinket made straight for Brother Simple's cell and laid the still-unconscious Green Girl on the bed.

'I think I'd better be with her on my own when she comes to,' he told Brother Simple. 'You've seen how stubborn and violent she is. I shall try to talk her into a better frame of mind so that she is more willing to help you with your investigation.'

Obediently Brother Simple went outside his own cell and allowed Trinket to close the door on him.

When, some minutes later, the Green Girl came to her senses, she saw Trinket standing over her holding his dagger an inch or two from her nose. She was on the point of calling out when he stopped her.

'Don't make a noise! If you call out, I shall cut your nose off. Just listen to me and answer my questions and I promise not to harm you.'

The Green Girl turned pale with anger.

'Will you do as I say?'

She looked even angrier.

'Kill me!' she said in a scarcely audible voice.

'Oh no,' said Trinket. 'You're so beautiful, I can't stop thinking about you. I can't kill you and I can't let you go. Either way I should die of longing.'

The Green Girl's face turned very red, then, almost immediately, very pale again.

'I think I'll just have to cut your nose off,' said Trinket. 'Then you won't look so beautiful.'

She closed her eyes tight, but a big tear escaped from the corner of each of them and ran down towards her ears.

'Don't cry, don't cry!' said Trinket in a panic, laying down the dagger. 'Of course I won't cut your nose off. I'd sooner cut off my own. Just tell me what your name is.'

The Green Girl shook her head.

'Look,' said Trinket, 'I have things to say to you. How can you talk to someone when you don't even know what their name is. Can't you just tell me your name?'

Again she shook her head. Her eyes remained tightly closed.

'Well, I shall have to call you something,' said Trinket. 'I think I'll call you "No Way". "No" because you keep shaking your head, and "Way" because that's my surname (get it?), and I'm quite determined to marry you, so you might as well get used to the idea of being Mrs Wei.'

'I shouldn't think there could be another monk in the world who speaks such rubbish as you do,' said the Green Girl. 'You know that monks can't marry. Probably you'll burn in hell for just thinking of such a thing.'

Trinket fell down on his knees, so heavily that the Green Girl opened her eyes to see what he was doing. She saw that he was kneeling, his face towards the window and his palms together, in an attitude of prayer.

'I call on the Rulai Buddha, the Amida Buddha, Guanyin the Bodhisattva of Mercy, Manjusri the Bodhisattva of Wisdom, the Puxian Bodhisattva, the Jade Emperor, and all the host of Heaven to bear witness. I, Trinket Wei, whatever the price, even if it means suffering all the tortures of hell for a thousand, thousand years, vow that I will in this life or a life to come have this girl here for my wife.'

She thought that he was fooling, but when he got up again and she saw the strange look in his eyes, she knew he was deadly serious.

'But I hate you,' she said. 'I detest you. You can kill me if you like or you can beat me every day until I die, but I shall never, never consent to be—what you said. After the way you've shamed and humiliated me, my only wish is that I might one day have you in my power so that I could kill you and afterwards kill myself.'

'*I* don't want to kill *you*,' said Trinket. 'I'd rather kill myself. Look, just do one thing for me. Just tell me what your name is and I'll let you go. I swear I will.'

'I don't want you to let me go,' she said. 'You've dishonoured me so much that I don't want to go out of here alive. Why don't you just cut my throat and have done with it?'

As she was saying this, he caught sight of the red line round her neck where the self-inflicted wound had only recently healed. A pang of remorse went through him and a strangled cry, halfway between a sob and a groan, rose up in his throat, so strange that the Green Girl felt quite frightened.

'I know I've done you wrong,' he said, falling once more on his knees beside the bed. 'I'm sorry! I'm sorry! I really didn't mean to.'

He held his arms out on either side of his face and began bringing them together, dealing himself heavy slaps on both his cheeks at once.

'You mustn't mind me,' he cried between slaps. 'I'm a stupid, silly idiot. I deserve to be beaten.'

After dealing himself a dozen or more of these double slaps, he got to his feet again and walked over to the door. He opened it to find Brother Simple patiently standing in exactly the same spot as before. The old monk had heard every word spoken inside the cell, but was far too unworldly or too simple to understand their meaning. He assumed from the earnestness of the tone that what Trinket was urging on the girl was a message of salvation. His admiration for Trinket's saintliness had grown even stronger when he became aware from the sounds inside that Trinket was striking his own face. The Buddhism of the Shaolin Monastery was of the Zen variety, and Brother Simple had heard many stories of Zen Masters shouting at novices or striking them to bring about a spiritual awakening; but striking one's own face for this purpose was rare indeed and worthy of the Holy One himself.

'Brother,' said Trinket, interrupting the old man's rapt meditation on his saintliness, 'I want to release her Vital Points. How do I go about it?'

'The point I closed is the Big Bag on the tract that connects the Greater Yin of the foot with the spleen. To release it, you have to reverse the flow of blood temporarily by applying pressure to the Basket Door and Sea of Blood points on the young lady's legs.'

'Whereabouts on her legs?' said Trinket.

The old monk bared his own legs one after the other and showed Trinket where the points were, behind the bend of the knee. When he had shown him several times exactly how the pressure was to be applied, Trinket went inside the cell again and closed the door. But the Green Girl had been listening to their exchange and wasn't having any.

'I don't want my points opened,' she said. 'I don't want you to touch me.'

Trinket went outside again to ask if a point could be opened without bodily contact being made. Brother Simple knew of at least one way it could be done, with a flick of the sleeve, but the art required many years of inner cultivation. It seemed not to occur to either of them that the easiest way of resolving the problem was for Brother Simple to go inside and do the job himself.

Trinket went back inside and looked around. On a table beside the bed there were some books and one of those instruments called 'wooden fish' which monks beat as an aid to their chanting. He picked up the little hammer which lay beside it, gently uncovered one of the Green Girl's legs, and began delicately poking in the prescribed manner at the point on it which Brother Simple had indicated.

'You see,' he said. 'I'm not touching you.'

He had in fact found the correct position, but he was being too gentle to do any good.

'Can you feel anything?' he asked her.

'Useless creature!' said the Green Girl scornfully. 'Making disgusting, guttersnipe remarks is all you're any good at.'

This was too much. He struck her angrily, this time quite hard, provoking an 'Ow!' which made him instantly concerned.

'Did that hurt?'

But she was too cross to reply.

He struck her again, in the crook of the other leg, but not quite so hard. This time a slight tremor ran through her whole body.

'It worked!' he cried joyfully. 'It worked!'

But just as he was congratulating himself on his new skill, he felt a sudden sharp pain. The Green Girl had sat up, seized his dagger, and stuck it, with all the force she could muster, into his chest.

'Aiyo!' he cried. 'You've murdered your own husband!'

As he slid down to a sitting position on the floor, she picked up her sword and ran to the door, planning to make a getaway. But instead of escaping, she ran straight into the arms of Brother Simple.

'Young lady, what have you done?' cried the old monk in distress.

She slashed at him with her sword, but her legs were still weak and he had little difficulty in immobilizing her once again with a single skilled flick of his long sleeve. He left her lying helpless on the floor and rushed into the cell where Trinket was sitting, his back against the bed and his legs stretched out in front of him, with a dagger sticking out of his chest. With the middle finger of his right hand Brother Simple flicked the Vital Points round the place where the dagger had entered, then he took hold of the dagger and, muttering 'Amitabha, Merciful Buddha!', gently drew it out. A rush of blood followed, but not nearly as much as might have been expected. The wound, though very painful, was quite a shallow one, for Trinket had been wearing his protective waistcoat and it was only because he had been struck with his own almost irresistible dagger that it had pierced through the fabric at all. An ordinary dagger might have bruised him severely but would not have broken the skin. The Green Girl, lying outside, immobilized but still fully conscious, assumed that she had killed him and tearfully begged the old monk to dispatch her quickly, convinced that, sooner or later, she must pay with her own life.

Ignoring the Green Girl's cries, Brother Simple rushed off to get wound-powder to apply to the cut in Trinket's chest. Later, as he was applying it, he told Trinket that his wound was by no means serious. He had been providentially saved: a reward, no doubt, for the saintly way in which he had attempted the Green Girl's conversion.

Now that he knew he was out of danger, Trinket's chief concern was that Brother Simple should not let the Green Girl get away.

'Oh, I'm dying, I'm dying,' he groaned, sufficiently loudly for the Green Girl to hear him. Then, beckoning to Brother Simple to come closer, he whispered in the old man's ear, 'You can open her Vital Points now. Only, when you've done it, don't let her go. Don't forget you've still got to find out about her methods. Go on, go on!'

Somewhat puzzled by these instructions, the old monk went outside to do his bidding.

Through the open door the Green Girl had witnessed the conspiratorial whispering from where she lay, but had been unable to hear what was said. She concluded that the evil little monk, knowing that he was dying, must be plotting for some horrible vengeance to be executed on her after his death, or, worse still— since he had more than once vowed that he would one day make her his wife—that he was planning for her to be forced into marrying him before he died. As soon, therefore, as she was released from her immobility, she reached for her sword and once more attempted to take her own life. But before she could do herself any harm, the old monk's sleeve shot out and the sword dropped out of her hand. She leapt up and tried to claw at his eyes, but Brother Simple effortlessly knocked her wrist back with his arm.

'The Eye Hazer,' he said in his classroom voice, 'favoured by the Jiang Family of Jiangnan.'

She kicked out at his lower belly, but he merely swayed a little to one side so that she was kicking at thin air.

'Footfall in the Empty Valley,' he chanted, 'used by the Shato tribesmen of Turkestan, though I suppose they must have their own Turkish name for it. Such is my ignorance, I am afraid I have never been able to discover what it is. Do you know, by any chance, young lady?'

Ignoring his question, she followed up with several punches and kicks, all of which he blocked or evaded with the greatest of ease. At first he tried naming them, but when, with her increasing exasperation, her attacks grew wilder and more agitated, he was unable to keep up his commentary and had to content himself with identifying them mentally and trying to remember what she had done.

The Green Girl was growing tired and dizzy, and since every single attack she made was frustrated and there was not the slightest chance of her overcoming the old man, whose skill in combat was clearly a hundred times greater than her own, she presently broke away from him, retreated a few steps, and plumped herself down on one of the benches which had been placed at intervals along the wall of the cloister.

'Oh, aren't you going to fight any more?' asked the old monk, surprised.

'What's the point?' she said. 'You will always beat me.'

'But I am all the time studying *how* to beat you,' he said. 'How can I finish my research when I haven't seen all your methods of attack? My dear young lady, if you won't fight me, could you perhaps give me a demonstration and I will sit and watch. Do, please, go on.'

'So that's your game!' thought the Green Girl. 'You have provoked me to fight you so that you can study my methods and think of ways to beat them. I'll take very good care that you don't learn any more from me!'

She rose from the bench and began punching the air with her fists and kicking and stamping with her feet like a little child in a rage. Brother Simple, who had taken her place on the bench to watch this 'demonstration', gazed at her in astonishment.

'Good heavens! Extraordinary! Remarkable! Oh dear, I don't understand!'

The forms of attack were so unfamiliar and followed each other in such rapid succession that he suspected some mysterious, half-magical form of combat which had escaped him throughout all his years of study. His brain was whirling, a dreadful spiritual blackness possessed his soul as he reflected that the vast corpus of learning it had taken him a lifetime to acquire was perhaps invalid, and by the time the Green Girl ended her wild dance and sat down, exhausted, on the floor, the poor man was so dizzy and his mental faculties in such confusion that he fainted.

The Green Girl, scarcely believing her eyes, watched him keel over, then, when it became clear that he really was unconscious, she seized the opportunity to pick her sword up and run away. As she sped through the Prajna Hall, the monks there looked at this fleeting female vision in astonishment, but, lacking the authorization of their superior, dared not do anything to stop her, so that she actually succeeded in getting out of the monastery unchallenged.

It took some time for Brother Simple to regain consciousness. When he finally came to and saw that the Green Girl had gone, he felt that he had been defeated by superior knowledge and went in to see Trinket, full of shame and confusion, to confess his failure.

'Father Treasure,' he said, 'I am very ashamed. In the demonstration just given by that remarkable young woman, I was unable to identify a single movement. I am unworthy to teach Martial Arts in this monastery any longer.'

Trinket had witnessed some of the Green Girl's performance through the open doorway and, when he saw the old monk's tragic expression, could not refrain from laughing. Unfortunately, laughter proved so painful that the sweat stood out on his forehead and he had to press his hands against the place on his chest where he had been stabbed before he was able to answer.

'That wasn't kungfu you were watching, Brother,' he said. 'She was just throwing her arms and legs about to fool you, like a little brat having a tantrum.'

The old monk looked surprised.

'Do you really think so, Father? Well, well. Bless my soul!'

Trinket was obliged to hold his chest again for fear of laughing.

Matters of the Heart

The by no means dangerous stab-wound on Trinket's chest responded rapidly to the Shaolin Monastery's excellent wound-dressings and by the end of a fortnight it had very nearly healed. As to the circumstances in which he had been wounded: the three or four monks of the Prajna Hall who had seen the girl kept their own counsel, and the rest, because Trinket was the Emperor's proxy and a very senior monk, were not inclined to ask questions, so the episode passed without comment.

While Trinket was recovering, Brother Simple wrote down as many of the forms of attack used by the two young women as he could remember and worked out appropriate ways of countering them, with a view to demonstrating them to Trinket when he was better.

As soon as he was sufficiently recovered, Trinket agreed willingly enough to undergo some training, but after only a few days his enthusiasm was waning, and Brother Simple, for his part, although he had tried to accommodate his pupil by taking short cuts, was coming to the conclusion that it was only by going back to the very beginning of the course normally prescribed for Shaolin novices and training systematically that Trinket would ever get anywhere.

'What we are doing at present,' he said, 'would only serve against the two young women. It would be useless against anyone who had received a proper training.'

'But I only want the moves for using against the two girls,' said Trinket.

'You may never see them again,' said Brother Simple. 'In that case, isn't this rather a waste?'

'But I *must* see them again,' said Trinket. 'I mean I *must* see the Green Girl again.'

Brother Simple was puzzled. But then a thought struck him.

'Did she poison you, by any chance? Do you mean she has poisoned you and you need to see her to get the antidote?'

Trinket saw that it would be useless to try explaining matters of the heart to someone as unworldly as Brother Simple and decided to go along with his suggestion.

'That's exactly the trouble,' he said. 'I've got her poison in my bones, in every part of me. I've *got* to see her again if I want to get better.'

'Brother Radiant knows a lot about poisons,' said Brother Simple. 'Shall I ask him to come over and examine you?'

'No, no,' said Trinket. 'He couldn't do anything about it. It's got to be that girl.'

A Mongol Prince and a Grand Lama from Tibet

A few days after this exchange, Trinket and Brother Simple were in the latter's cell discussing some fine points concerning the swordsmanship practised by the two girls when one of the Prajna Hall monks came in to say that they were wanted by the Abbot in the monastery's main hall.

When they arrived, they found thirty or forty visitors there, three of them sitting with the Abbot, the rest standing. Of the three sitting with the Abbot, the first was a young man in his early twenties who, to judge from his dress, appeared to be a Mongol nobleman; the second was a tall, thin, red-robed lama of middle years; and the third was a fortyish military man wearing the uniform of a high-ranking officer. Of the thirty or forty men standing behind them, some were army officers, some were lamas, while a dozen or so of them were dressed in civilian clothes but looked as if they might have had some sort of military training and knew how to fight.

'Ah, Father,' said Father Wisdom as Trinket entered, 'our monastery has some distinguished guests today. This gentleman is His Highness the Mongol Prince Galdan; this is the Grand Lama sDe-srid Sangs-rgyas-rgya-mtsho from Tibet—in China he is known as Father Sangge; and this is Brigadier Ma Bao, who is on the staff of His Highness the Satrap of Yunnan.'

'And this,' he said, turning to the three men he had just introduced and pointing to Trinket, 'is my Brother in the Truth, Father Treasure.'

All those present were more than a little surprised at hearing this disreputable-looking juvenile introduced as an equal-ranking colleague of the Abbot. The Mongol Galdan laughed out loud.

'Such a little Father! Very amusing.'

Trinket pressed his palms together and bowed.

'Such a big Prince! Very funny.'

'What is funny about me, please? I should like to know,' Prince Galdan said angrily.

'What's amusing about *me*, then?' said Trinket. And he sat down unconcernedly in the chair next to the Abbot.

It was clear from the looks of the others present that they didn't know what to make of him.

'Well, gentlemen,' said Father Wisdom, 'to what do we owe the honour of this visit?'

'The three of us all happened to be passing through this area,' said the Grand Lama Sangge. 'We have heard of the famous Shaolin Monastery and we all come from obscure and backward places, so we decided to call on you in the hope that we might have the benefit of your instruction.'

Unlike the lesser lama Brother Bayen, whom Trinket had run into on an earlier occasion on Wutai, this one spoke like an educated Chinese and with a passable Peking accent.

'You are too polite,' said Father Wisdom. 'Mongolia, Tibet, and Yunnan all have distinguished traditions of Buddhist teaching. I cannot believe that we in this monastery can have anything to teach you.'

Sangge had, of course, been referring to the Martial Arts for which the Shaolin Monastery was famous. Whether the Abbot had misunderstood him or was only pretending to do so it would be hard to say.

'All the world has heard of the seventy-two incomparable fighting skills of the Shaolin Monastery,' said Prince Galdan. 'Could you not get your monks together to give us a little demonstration?'

'You mustn't believe all the things that people say about us,' said Father Wisdom. 'All our monks here, without exception, devote their lives to the pursuit of Zen as a means of obtaining enlightenment. Although it is true that a number of them devote some of their time to training in kungfu, they do so only as a means of keeping their bodies fit and their minds alert. We attach no special importance to such exercises.'

'Are you not being a little devious, Abbot?' said Prince Galdan. 'We would like only to see a demonstration of the seventy-two skills. We do not intend to steal them from you. Why be so grudging?'

'If you gentlemen wish to discuss the Buddhist *dharma* with us, I will gladly summon the Brothers,' said Father Wisdom, 'but not for a demonstration of martial skills. That is something expressly forbidden by the rules of our Order.'

Prince Galdan's eyebrows went up.

'It seems that the reputation of this monastery is a hollow sham. It is—how do you Chinese say?—not worth fart.'

'We are indeed taught that this world we live in is a hollow sham,' said Father Wisdom smiling gently. 'Not worth a fart, as you put it. What you say about the reputation of this monastery is of course correct.'

Prince Galdan had not expected so mild a response. He pointed, laughing, at Trinket.

'So. And this little monk, too, he is not worth fart?'

Trinket smiled cheerfully back at him.

'I'm certainly not worth as much as *you*, Your Highness,' he said. 'So, if I'm not worth a fart, it's safe to say that Your Highness *is* worth a fart. A big fart.'

Prince Galdan leapt up in a rage and was on the point of striking him. But then he reflected that the only reason this little monk had such high standing in the monastery must be that he was exceptionally skilled in Martial Arts. With some difficulty he restrained himself and sat down again.

'There are much worse things than not being worth a fart,' said Trinket. 'Owing hundreds and thousands of taels and not being able to pay them back, for instance—that's much worse.'

'How true!' said Father Wisdom. 'My brother has stated a profound truth. It is the law of karma that evil actions incur a debt of evil and good ones a good reward. Not to be worth a fart, that is to have incurred neither good nor evil karma. How much better to be owing neither good nor evil than to have incurred an infinite debt of evil karma! The parable is an excellent one.'

Brother Simple was glad to hear the Abbot praising his saintly young companion.

'I have learned much from Father Treasure since I have been working with him,' he said. 'Although he is so young, he has advanced far along the path towards enlightenment.'

The two older men's praise of this impertinent little monk struck Galdan as a deliberate provocation. He leapt up once more, determined this time to do him an injury. Before he could hurt him, however, Father Wisdom's long sleeve shot out and he stepped back and sat down heavily in his seat. How this had happened he did not understand. It felt as if he had been blown back by a small but powerful wind.

All this time Trinket had not even moved. This was partly from fright and partly because he was not expecting the attack and had not had time to respond. To Father Wisdom and Brother Simple, however, he appeared to have shown remarkable restraint. Father Wisdom now launched into a short homily, interlarded with quotations from the Buddhist scriptures, on the virtues of impassivity, ending with further commendation, in which Brother Simple joined, of Trinket's spiritual advancement. This so enraged Galdan that he suddenly interrupted with a barked-out order that none of the Chinese present could understand.

'*Hanisbal nimahong kanubidigar!*'

A number of the Mongol henchmen behind him raised their arms and there was a rapid succession of little flashes as nine metal darts sped one after the other through the air, three towards the Abbot, three towards Brother Simple, and three towards Trinket. Despite the lack of warning, neither Father Wisdom nor Brother Simple was hurt. Father Wisdom disposed of the three aimed at him by flicking his long sleeve; Brother Simple caught the three aimed at him by slapping his hands on them as if he was catching flies; but Trinket, once again taken unawares, sat motionless as the darts hit his chest and fell—*tink tink tink*—on the floor. Once more the wonderful waistcoat had saved him, though one of the darts had landed near the newly healed stab-wound on his chest and hurt so intensely that it cost him a great effort not to cry out.

There were gasps of amazement from the visitors. Most of them had heard of the 'adamantine body', the temporary immunity to weapons said to be attained by a very few Martial Arts practitioners after years of 'internal' training involving breath control, meditation, and various secret exercises, but none had ever seen it, and seeing it now (apparently) demonstrated by one so young struck them as doubly miraculous. The Grand Lama Sangge was the only one who affected to be unimpressed.

'Our young friend has made remarkable progress in the cultivation of the "adamantine body",' he said with a sort of sneering smile, 'but I believe the ultimate aim of people who undertake this training is the creation of a protective aura round the body which prevents weapons or missiles from even touching it. I think our young friend still has quite a long way to go before he attains *that* level of immunity.'

Trinket, still struggling not to cry out in pain, was incapable of answering and could only manage a rather twisted smile; but his silence merely added to the admiration of those present, for it seemed to them that only a person who had reached so high a level of inner training could afford to treat pettiness like the Grand Lama's with contempt. 'How would *you* manage if we threw a few darts at *you*?' they felt like saying, but were too polite to do so.

'After what we have just witnessed,' Sangge continued, 'I would agree that the Shaolin Monastery's reputation as an incomparable centre for training in the Martial Arts is fully justified. Certainly it could not be said that it is, as the Abbot here earlier suggested, "not worth a fart". The same cannot, I fear, be said about the *moral* reputation of a monastery which conceals females on its premises.'

Father Wisdom looked grave.

'Your Reverence is mistaken. We do not even allow female *visitors* to our monastery. The idea that we are hiding women here is absurd.'

'Yet such is the current rumour we have encountered on our travels,' said Sangge.

Father Wisdom smiled.

'As a man of religion, Your Reverence must know better than to be moved by current rumours. Father Treasure here teaches us all a lesson in how to remain unmoved.'

'But it is precisely this young Father who is said to be concealing a beautiful young woman in his cell,' said Sangge. 'According to what we have heard, he tied her up and brought her in here a prisoner—kidnapped her, in fact.'

Trinket was startled. First he wondered how the Grand Lama knew all this. Then he wondered how it was that he knew so much yet didn't know that the Green Girl had got away. After thinking for a moment it dawned on him. He must have got it from the Blue Girl. And the Green Girl had not yet made contact with her. That at least was good news.

'There aren't any young women in my cell,' he said, 'but if you want to, you are very welcome to look.'

'We will,' said Galdan. He turned to the men behind him. 'Search the monastery!'

The men began to move.

'Just a moment!' said Father Wisdom. 'Do you have a warrant to search?'

'*I* give the order,' said Galdan. '*I* give warrant. I do not need warrant.'

'There I am afraid Your Highness is mistaken,' said Father Wisdom. 'In Mongolia you can give all the orders you like, but you have no right to do so here.'

Galdan pointed to Brigadier Ma.

'He is Chinese officer, commission of Chinese Court. He gives the order to search. You disobey us? That is rebellion.'

'The Shaolin Monastery will not defy the Chinese Court,' said Father Wisdom. 'But the Brigadier is on the Satrap of Yunnan's staff. The Satrap's jurisdiction does not, as far as I am aware, extend to the province of Henan.'

'The little Father has already agreed that we should look in his cell,' said Sangge with a crafty smile. 'Why are you so unwilling that we should search the monastery? She couldn't by any chance be hidden in *your* cell, I suppose?'

Father Wisdom was deeply shocked.

'Amida Buddha! I trust Your Reverence is only joking?'

Suddenly a bearded figure spoke out from among the crowd of men standing at the back.

'With my own eyes I saw my sister being carried off by this little monk, Your Highness. Please do carry out this search. If she's not found here, we should burn down the monastery.'

It was a high female voice. Behind the layer of yellow grease and the copious whiskers Trinket had no difficulty in recognizing his old enemy the Blue Girl. Father Wisdom also recognized her.

'Are you not the young woman who came to this monastery and injured several of our Brothers? There was another young woman with you whom we allowed to stay here until she had recovered from a self-inflicted wound. Is she not with you now?'

To Trinket it now seemed evident that the game was up.

'Confess!' said the Blue Girl, addressing herself to Brother Simple in a strident voice. 'What I am saying is true, isn't it?'

'Young lady, I beg you,' the old monk said earnestly, 'do please tell us where she is. She has poisoned Father Treasure and only she can cure him. Be merciful. Entreat her to come here and save him. Father Treasure knows that life on this earth is an illusion, but we should like to keep him with us a little longer. Please, please—'

No one had the faintest idea what he was talking about, but at least it was clear from what he said that the girl they were supposed to be looking for could not be in the monastery.

'I *know* you kidnapped her,' said the Blue Girl. 'Probably you've killed her and disposed of the body. We shall never find her.' And she began to weep.

'You are right,' said Prince Galdan. 'It is certain. The little Father is very, very bad.'

'You're *evil*,' cried the Blue Girl, pointing her finger at Trinket. 'You saw my sister when you were in the brothel with those bad women. You must have taken a fancy to her then and afterwards killed her because she wouldn't submit to you. A monk who goes to brothels—there's no wickedness you wouldn't be capable of!'

Father Wisdom smiled incredulously and shook his head. But Trinket was growing really worried. It would not be long now before all his guilty secrets came to light. Providentially it was just at that moment that one of the group of officers standing behind Brigadier Ma's chair put in a good word for him.

'Excuse me, Miss, but I'm sure this young Father wouldn't do anything wrong like going to brothels and that. It looks as if someone has been misleading you.'

Trinket looked at the speaker and wondered why he had not noticed him before. It was Yang Yizhi, who had come to Peking with the Little Traitor and whom he had befriended at the party given by Prince Kang.

'How do you know?' the Blue Girl said scornfully. 'You're not going to tell me that you've met him before?'

'With respect, Miss, I have,' said Yang Yizhi. 'He did me a very great kindness once at Prince Kang's place in Peking. Before he entered holy orders, he used to be a eunuch in the Palace. That's why I can't believe he has been visiting brothels or doing any of those other things you accuse him of.'

There was a clearly audible 'Ah!' from the assembled company.

The Blue Girl could see that none of those present any longer believed her. Anger made her voice shrill.

'How do you know he is a eunuch? He said he wanted to make my sister his wife. He is a liar and a seducer. And this old monk is no better.'

The eyes of those present turned to Brother Simple, more than eighty years old, with a vague, slightly half-witted expression on his face, and they remembered the all but incoherent statement he had made a little earlier. Clearly the young woman was deranged. They began to regret that they had ever listened to her wild story or agreed to come to this monastery, only to make fools of themselves.

'Before he became a monk, this young Father was quite famous,' said Yang Yizhi. 'He is the Laurie Goong-goong who executed the traitor Oboi. When my master was slandered by bad men in Peking, it was thanks to this young Father here speaking up for him to the Emperor that his good name was cleared. My master still feels very much indebted to him.'

Everyone present had heard of the famous Laurie. There was another 'Ah!', and expressions of admiration were appearing on every face.

'How are you, Yang my friend?' Trinket asked Yang Yizhi.

'And how is His Grace? You really shouldn't have said all that stuff about me. It was nothing.'

It was obvious to all present that they really knew each other. Apart from the other officers who had accompanied Brigadier Ma from Yunnan, none of them had known Yang Yizhi by name.

The Blue Girl was by now looking somewhat chastened.

'Brother Yang,' she said (confirming Trinket's growing suspicion that she and the Green Girl were in some way connected with the Satrap), 'is this . . . this person *really* a eunuch? Did he *really* speak up for the Satrap?'

'He did indeed, Miss,' said Yang Yizhi. 'And there are many people in Peking who would tell you the same thing.'

The Grand Lama rose to his feet. The Blue Girl's charge was now quite discredited. It seemed there was nothing more to be said.

'Father Wisdom,' he said, pressing his palms together and inclining his head to the Abbot, 'I trust you will forgive us for what has turned out to be a somewhat unmannerly intrusion. We had better take our leave.'

'Won't you just stay for a simple meal with us?' said Father Wisdom. 'The, er, young lady—'

He wasn't going to invite a young female who had smuggled herself into the monastery in disguise to sit with them at table. Sangge laughed.

'Thank you all the same, but I think we will forego that pleasure. We don't want to embarrass you.'

The rest of the visitors followed him in making their farewells, and Father Wisdom, Brother Simple, and Trinket escorted them to the main gate of the monastery.

Just as they arrived at the gate, there was a sound of galloping hooves, and presently a party of sixteen Palace Guards dismounted twenty yards from where they stood and, arranging themselves in formation, advanced towards them on foot. The two officers leading them were Trinket's friends Zhang and Zhao.

As the senior officer among them, Zhang greeted Trinket by name, a trifle confusedly because he was not quite sure whether to call him 'Colonel' or 'Father'. All sixteen guards saluted him Manchu style, dropping on one knee and touching the ground with the knuckles of their right hands.

'Please get up, everybody!' said Trinket, delightedly. 'You can't imagine how glad I am to see you.'

Galdan knew that the Palace Guards ranked higher than most

civilian officials, so Trinket must evidently be a very important person. All the same, the fuss they were making of this young monk, while according only the curtest of nods to the Brigadier, so disgusted him that he was in a hurry to get away. Turning only to clasp hands in a brief gesture of farewell to the Abbot, he and his company set off at once on a rapid descent of the mountain.

Inviting the guards to accompany him into the monastery, Trinket walked in at the head of them with Zhang Kangnian at his side.

A Secret Edict

'I've got a Secret Edict for you,' said Zhang, speaking in a low voice so that the others couldn't hear. Trinket nodded.

There was, of course, a more formal Edict which Zhang read out when they were all assembled in the monastery's main hall. The Emperor was donating five thousand silver taels to be spent on refurbishing the monks' dormitories and re-gilding the image of the Buddha. There was also a fancy religious title which he was bestowing on Trinket in recognition of his spiritual services to the Empire. Trinket and Father Wisdom both kowtowed. Then followed what, for Trinket, was the most important part of the Edict. He was to leave the monastery not later than noon next day and proceed to the Wutai Mountains. He bowed down low. This was what he had been waiting for.

'I hear and obey.'

After they had taken tea, Trinket invited Zhang and Zhao to his cell, where they could be more private. As soon as they were inside, Zhang took out the Secret Edict and Trinket kowtowed and received it in both hands. It was fastened together with seals of sealing-wax.

'Fat lot of good this is, when I can't read,' he thought.

He couldn't get Zhang to read a Secret Edict; but then it occurred to him that Father Wisdom could be trusted to keep a secret, so he excused himself and went off to see the Abbot. Father Wisdom expressed his willingness to explain the contents, but when the seals were broken, it appeared that his help wouldn't be needed after all. The Secret Edict turned out to be a large folded-up sheet of drawing paper divided into four sections, in each of which was a picture.

The first one showed a mountain range with five peaks, which

Trinket could see was meant to be Wutai. On the north side of the southernmost peak there was a little building, above which were written the characters for 'Pure Coolness Monastery'. Because he had stayed in the monastery and seen the characters many times before, they had a familiar look. Seeing them in this context, he could easily guess what they were.

The second showed a little monk entering the gate of a monastery over which were written the same characters: 'Pure Coolness Monastery'. A small procession of bigger monks were following him. Over them were written the words 'Monks from Shaolin Monastery'. Trinket could read the characters for 'Shaolin'. The other ones he could guess.

The third picture was of a big hall in which a grinning little monk sat in the middle wearing the cope and crown of an abbot, with larger monks standing on either side of him. Trinket burst out laughing when he identified the little abbot as himself. It was some time before he could take his eyes off this picture and go on to the next.

In the fourth picture the little Abbot was kneeling down in front of a monk of middle years. From the thinness of his face Trinket guessed that this was Brother Wayward, as the Old Emperor Shun Zhi was called when he entered holy orders.

Apart from these pictures there was nothing else in the Edict. Kang Xi knew that Trinket could not read and had used his considerable skill as a draftsman to convey his message.

'Congratulations!' said Father Wisdom. 'The Pure Coolness Monastery is an even older foundation than the Shaolin and very greatly respected. You will be able to do great things there for the Truth.'

'How can I possibly be an *Abbot?*' said Trinket ruefully. 'I'll be sure to make a mess of things.'

'Don't forget that according to these drawings you are to take some of the monks from here with you,' said Father Wisdom. 'If you pick Brothers you know and can trust, they will surely do their best to help you and see that you don't make mistakes.'

After a moment or two of reflection Trinket began to appreciate what a lot of thought Kang Xi had given to his plan. He couldn't have sent soldiers to guard his father because, apart from the fact that his father would in any case refuse to have them, their presence would attract too much attention. There might even be some of them who recognized him as the ex-Emperor. And he couldn't have sent Trinket there from the Palace because that, too, would have been likely to excite suspicion. But the present Abbot of Pure Coolness Monastery, Father Aureole, was a former Shaolin monk, and what could be more natural than that he should be replaced by a monk from the same monastery? Moreover, this stay at the Shaolin Monastery had given Trinket time to get to know which monks would be most congenial to take with him and best able to help him guard the Old Emperor. The Young Emperor had thought of everything.

Trinket hurried back to his cell, where Zhang and Zhao were still waiting. He took out six thousand taels' worth of banknotes from his monk's chest to divide between them. This was a surprise. They had not expected the fabulous generosity of his Palace days to survive his transplantation to a religious environment. Was something expected of them? They still did not know why Kang Xi had sent him to the Shaolin Monastery to be a monk and, in view of Kang Xi's known interest in the Martial Arts, wondered if it had something to do with the monastery's incomparable collection of texts relating to this subject. Perhaps Kang Xi coveted them and had planted Trinket there to 'acquire' them for him.

'If you've got something big in mind,' said Zhang, 'you can count on us to help you. For example, if you want to get hold of their books, we could start a fire and get them away for you while we were "rescuing" them. You've only got to say the word.'

'No, that's all right,' said Trinket, somewhat alarmed by this offer. 'But there *is* something else I'd like you to do for me.'

'Anything. It'll be a pleasure.'

'Those men who left as you arrived—they're up to no good. Treason, probably. Keep an eye on them, will you, and find out what they're up to?'

'Easy. They can't have got very far.'

'Oh, and one other thing,' said Trinket, trying his hardest to sound nonchalant. 'There's a young woman dressed up as a man with them and she says she's looking for a friend, a girl of sixteen or so. Find out both of their names, will you, and anything else you can about them?'

'We will. You can count on it.'

They took their leave in haste, wanting to go about their business straight away. Sniffing out rebellion meant rapid promotion and generous rewards. The sixteen guards were soon galloping on their way.

Trinket selects His Companions

As soon as they had gone, Trinket went to see the Abbot to discuss the arrangements for his departure on the following day. It was agreed that he should take the Eighteen Lohans with him, an obvious choice because of their special fighting skills and because they had been to the Pure Coolness Monastery before; and he particularly wanted Brother Simple to accompany him. In addition to these, he chose seventeen other monks whom he had grown familiar with during his stay, making a total of thirty-six in all. Father Wisdom raised no objection to his choice. He had the thirty-six summoned into his presence straight away and gave them a little address in which he explained that they were being transferred to this other monastery and that they must henceforth obey Father Treasure as their new Abbot.

After taking leave of Father Wisdom, they set off early next day. Their first stop was in a little village near the foot of the mountain where Doublet had all this time been lodging and where Trinket left his companions for a while to go and see her. He found her much thinner and felt guilty that in all the six months she had been there he had never once visited her. This was the first time she had seen him shaven-headed and wearing his monk's clothes. The sight made her burst into tears.

'Why are you crying?' he asked her. 'Are you upset because I haven't been to see you all this time?'

'It isn't that,' said Doublet, 'it's just that you're . . . you're a *monk* now.'

She feared that he would have to stop seeing her and that their life together was now permanently ended.

'Oh, *that*!' he said. 'It's only pretend.'

Doublet brightened.

'Come on!' said Trinket. 'Get into your boy's clothes again. You're coming with me.'

When he rejoined his thirty-six companions, he had a little serving-lad with him.

Father Treasure, Abbot of Pure Coolness Monastery

On their arrival, after several days of travelling, at the foot of the Wutai Mountains, they were met by four monks from the Pure Coolness Monastery, who had been waiting there for some time to welcome them and conduct them up the mountain. The Abbot,

Father Aureole, had received his own Secret Edict at about the same time as Trinket got his, informing him that he was being elevated to the abbacy of the Cloud of Compassion Monastery in Chang'an, a larger and more ancient foundation than Pure Coolness, and that his replacement was to be Father Treasure from the Shaolin Monastery, previously known to him as Deputy Intendant Trinket Wei of the Palace Guards. He had therefore had ample time to prepare for the take-over and to arrange for the little welcoming party to be lodged at the foot of the mountain in readiness to meet his successor.

As soon as the hand-over ceremony was completed and Father Treasure installed, Father Aureole called the Pure Coolness monks up one by one and introduced them to their new Abbot. Trinket noticed that Brother Wayward and his two companions were missing from their number. The only indication of their continued presence was a written note from the Venerable Yulin offering his respects. The day after the installation Father Aureole left for Chang'an.

Trinket was now in sole charge of the monastery. Though he lacked both dignity and experience, his Shaolin friends were able to guide him through the various rites and ceremonies over which he had to preside, while the Pure Coolness monks, though at first finding it a little strange that they had been given so juvenile an Abbot, remembered how less than a year before he had saved their lives and were well-disposed towards their little benefactor. With so much help and goodwill, he was able to discharge the duties of his office without any serious hitch.

The chief of these duties was, of course, to watch over the safety of the Old Emperor. In answer to an enquiry, the Camerarius told him that Brother Wayward and his companions, Brother Headlong and the Venerable Yulin, were still living in the little temple where he had left them the previous year. He knew that there was little point in going there to discuss security with the Old Emperor, so, after talking the matter over with Brother Cordial, he gave orders for four thatched huts to be built, one to the north, one to the south, one to the east, and one to the west of the little temple at a distance of about three hundred yards from it, and for eight of the Shaolin Brothers to take turns in doing sentry duty in them all the time.

Now that these essentials had been taken care of, there was nothing much left for him to do but wait for the arrival of Zhang and Zhao with information about the Green Girl; but as the months went by and not so much as a word from that quarter was forthcoming, the time weighed heavy on his hands. His only diversions were practice bouts with Brother Simple, in which he would pretend that the adversary against whom he was contending was the 'young lady', as the old monk continued to call her, and visits to Doublet, whom he had settled in a little hermitage outside the monastery walls.

One day when he was feeling particularly bored and frustrated, he had gone off walking on his own. His walk had led him to a pretty spot in the mountains where there was a young willow tree swaying gracefully beside a brook. Suddenly the greenness of the tree made him think of his beloved.

'Ha!' he said. 'If you were really the Green Girl, I'd want to give you a hug. But you wouldn't like that, would you? I expect you'd try to knock me out with one of those Kunlun-style Thousand Cliff actions that Brother Simple told me about. Then I'd have to parry with a Holding the Bowl. Then you'd—oh, I don't care! Just kill me, if you like. I can't resist it!'

And he wrapped his arms round the tree in a passionate embrace.

He was interrupted by a rude laugh.

Whipping round, he saw two red-robed lamas, barely twenty yards from him, laughing and pointing.

The Abbot of Pure Coolness Monastery making love to a tree! It was too shaming! Blushing to the tips of his ears he hurried away.

A turn in the mountain track brought him in sight of three or four more red-robed lamas. He hurried past them, head averted, pretending to be admiring the view.

He was not particularly surprised at seeing the lamas. There were several lamaseries on the Wutai Mountains and hundreds of lamas. It wasn't until after he had got back and been met at the gate of the monastery by a worried-looking Brother Cordial that the significance of these encounters became apparent.

'Things don't look too good, Father,' said Brother Cordial.

'Oh?' said Trinket. 'What's the matter?'

Beckoning to him to follow, Brother Cordial began climbing the stone steps that led up to a vantage point on the peak beside the monastery. When they were both there, he pointed from one side to the little valley below. Scattered everywhere among the rocks and trees there were yellow blobs which, on looking harder, Trinket identified as little groups of four or five yellow-robed lamas.

'What—?' he gasped.

'Look!' said Brother Cordial, going over to the other side, 'there are more of them over here.' Trinket looked down towards the west. There were at least as many lamas there as well. From time to time, as the sunlight caught them, there were little winking flashes. They were carrying weapons.

'What do they want?' said Trinket. 'You don't think—?'

Brother Cordial nodded. 'Brother Wayward. The same as last time.'

They walked all round the peak, looking down on every side. The monastery was completely surrounded. Brother Cordial said he had calculated that altogether there must be something like three thousand of them.

'They're waiting for darkness,' he said. 'We've only got a few hours. No time to get help from outside.'

They descended and went inside the monastery.

'So,' said Brother Cordial. 'What are we going to do?'

Trinket hadn't the faintest idea.

'Tamardy!' he said. 'I know what *I'll* do. I'll go and have a nap.'

Brother Cordial's jaw fell and he stared at his little Abbot uncomprehendingly. But Trinket ignored him and strode off to his cell to lie down and think. Within less than half an hour a little deputation consisting of Brother Cordial, Brother Simple, and two other of the Eighteen Lohans were knocking at his door and asking to speak with him. Trinket sat up, gave a big yawn, and asked them what they wanted.

Lamas at the Gate

'Father Abbot,' said Brother Cordial, speaking for the others, 'those lamas who have gathered down below obviously intend no good to our monastery. The Brothers want to know what you are planning to do about it.'

'I thought about it a lot, but I couldn't come up with any plan,' said Trinket, 'so I decided to have a bit of a nap. "The calamity from which there is no escape has come upon us. We must except reversity with meekness and remit our throats to the knife."' (He was trying, not altogether successfully, to remember some words from a Sutra.)

Even Brother Simple was not convinced that this was the best answer to their predicament.

Trinket eyed Brother Cordial and asked him if he had a better idea.

'We could try to break out with Brother Wayward and the other two when it's dark and smuggle them through their lines somehow under cover of darkness,' said Brother Cordial. 'I don't think they intend any harm to the other monks.'

'All right,' said Trinket. 'Let's see if we can sell this to the Venerable.'

The five of them made their way to the little temple.

A young novice who attended to the needs of the three senior monks ran inside to announce them.

The Venerable Yulin had been told only that the new Abbot was a young monk from the Shaolin Monastery but had no idea of his identity. Seeing now, for the first time, that it was Trinket, he and the other two at once guessed that his presence in the monastery must be part of some plan of the Young Emperor's to protect his father. After exchanging greetings, Yulin made Trinket sit on the central prayer-mat while he and Brother Wayward stood respectfully on either side of him. Reflecting that he was being waited on by an ex-Emperor and that even Kang Xi could not be seated in the presence of his own father, Trinket had some difficulty in suppressing a smirk of satisfaction as he invited them both to sit down.

'Father Abbot,' said Yulin when they had done so, 'I should have called on you after your installation. It seems wrong that *you* should now feel obliged to call on *me*.'

'That's all right,' said Trinket cheerfully. 'I know you don't like being disturbed. I wouldn't have come *now* if there hadn't been an emergency.'

Yulin didn't ask him what the emergency was.

'Brother Cordial,' said Trinket, 'will you explain the situation to these reverend Brothers?'

Brother Cordial proceeded to explain, in grave and respectful terms, that they were being besieged by a couple of thousand lamas, whose object, he believed, and the Father Abbot had seemed at first to agree with him, was the kidnapping of Brother Wayward.

Yulin closed his eyes and appeared to be meditating. After a minute or two he opened them again and spoke.

'And what are you proposing to do about this, Father Abbot?'

'Our Lord Buddha said: "If *I* don't go to hell, who *will?*"' Trinket replied, ransacking his memory for a few more scraps of sutra. 'We should prepare to offer our necks to the sword. In other words, if *we* don't have our heads cut off, who *will?* If there was no life there'd be no death, and if there was no dust there'd be no spick and span. And vicey versy. The sword is a void. And the void is a sword. Let us offer *our* necks to *their* swords in that spirit. Therein lies wisdom. In the beginning was the Void. I mean, the Word. I mean, the Sword. Here endeth the first lesson.'

The Venerable Yulin said nothing. Brother Simple was impressed. The other three Shaolin monks, though decidedly *un*impressed, were beginning to suspect that Trinket was up to something. Brother Headlong, old warrior and former Captain of the Guard, was very nearly exploding. After some moments of silence he could restrain himself no longer.

'Father Abbot,' he blurted out, 'you've said yourself that you think these lamas have come here to kidnap Brother Wayward. And you know as well as I do that if the Tibetans and their friends can get hold of Brother Wayward they will use him to oppress our people. Maybe *our* lives are unimportant, but what about the millions of Chinese who will be oppressed? What about *their* lives?'

'You're right,' said Trinket. 'But there are thousands of these lamas. There's nothing much we can do to stop them.'

'We could try a break-out,' said Brother Headlong. 'If we put Brother Wayward and the Venerable in the middle of us so they didn't get hurt, we might be able to get through their lines to a place of safety.'

'Wouldn't that mean killing a lot of lamas?' said Trinket. 'Amida Buddha! We're supposed to save life, not take it. The Lord Buddha says, "It is better to save one life than to build a seven-storey pagoda." I don't know how many pagodas we'd be pulling down by fighting our way out!'

Just then there was a sound of running and one of the Shaolin monks burst in on them.

'Father Abbot, during this past half-hour the lamas have been moving up on us. They've stopped about three hundred yards below. We're completely surrounded.'

'Did you say they've stopped?' said Trinket. 'A miracle! They must have repented of their wickedness. Praised be His Holy Name!'

'No, you little—*no*, Father!' Brother Headlong bellowed. 'They're waiting for the darkness. As soon as it's dark, they'll move in for the kill.'

'All right,' said Trinket. 'You all seem to think that breaking out is our only hope. Let's try to break out, then.'

'No!' It was the first time Brother Wayward had spoken. 'I can't allow any more lives to be lost on my account. Many were lost last time, when they made their first attempt. Even if we could get out now, there would be more attempts later. These people will not give up. I have decided what to do. When the lamas come, I shall set fire to myself. Whatever plans they may have for using my person in order to oppress others will have to be abandoned when they see me burned to ashes before their eyes. Besides, in fighting and massacres and the sacking of cities, my people have done untold evil in this land. Perhaps today, by burning myself, I can atone for some of it.'

'Oh blessed words! *Shanzai*! *Shanzai*!' said the Venerable Yulin. 'Our brother has seen the light. *That* is what our Lord Buddha meant when he said, "If *I* go not into hell for them, *who* will go?"' (This time the Sutra was quoted correctly.) 'In a little while, when the lamas arrive, Brother Wayward and I will burn ourselves together. You and the Brothers, Father Abbot, must not do anything to stop us.'

'Silly old bugger!' thought Trinket, but managed to remain silent.

Brother Wayward rose to his feet and addressed Trinket and the five Shaolin monks entreatingly.

'I am quite resolved. This is a work of merit, you understand. You must all of you help me to carry it out successfully.'

He joined his palms and bowed.

It was obvious that nothing they could say would make him change his mind, so they took their leave and went back to the monastery.

Entering the Manjusri Hall with the five brothers, Trinket found Doublet waiting for him, half-hidden in a corner. From her little hermitage she had witnessed the warlike movements on the mountainside and sensed that her master might soon have need of her. He summoned the rest of the Shaolin monks to the hall and explained the situation to them. All of them agreed that it was quite out of the question that Brother Wayward should be allowed to carry out his resolve, but none could think of a way of stopping him.

'I've thought of a way,' said Trinket, 'but it will only work if you all do exactly as I say. First of all I want all thirty-six of you to pretend you're attempting a break-out. I want you to take the east track as if you're going down the mountain, fight for a bit when the lamas try to stop you, then pretend you've decided that it's hopeless and retreat back to the monastery. Make sure they know that you're doing this. Lots of shouting. *But*—and this is the important bit—while you're doing it, I want you to take some prisoners. If possible I'd like about forty prisoners. Any lamas will do: they don't have to be leaders or anything.'

The thirty-six had no idea what the point of this could be, but, with that unquestioning obedience that a monk owes his superiors, they set about carrying out his orders straight away. Trinket went up to the drum-tower to watch them skirmishing. After a few minutes he heard Brother Cordial shouting above the din:

'It's hopeless, we'll never get through this lot. Fall back to the monastery, everybody!'

His cry was taken up and passed on by the others. The convincing ring of despair in these shouted orders seemed to have fooled the lamas, for they did not bother to pursue the retreating monks as far as the monastery gate, confident, no doubt, that if they waited a bit, the whole community would soon be in their hands. Trinket hurried down to the gate to let the monks in. Incredibly, they had taken a total of forty-seven prisoners.

Trinket had the captive lamas brought into the Manjusri Hall, deprived of their clothes, and immobilized by expert handling of their points. Then the forty-seven naked men, unable to move head or hand, were herded into the fuel store and padlocked in.

'Now, this is where Zen monks transform themselves into lamas,' said Trinket.

He made the thirty-six Shaolin monks strip off and change into the robes that had been discarded by their captives. He picked the smallest robe for himself and got Doublet to help him into it, but it was still much too big for him and he had to cut several inches off the sleeves and the bottom of the skirt with his dagger.

'You've got to be a lama too,' he told Doublet.

The robe she put on needed more of the same rough tailoring.

'Now this is the plan,' he said, when all of them had finished dressing up and found hats that would fit their heads. 'We're going to raid the little temple and capture Yulin and Wayward and Headlong ourselves. We'll close their points, dress them up as lamas with these spare outfits, then, as soon as the real lamas start running about, get them down the mountain and out of danger.'

'Brilliant!' said Brother Cordial. 'This way there needn't be any killing.'

'Wrap your monk's clothes up in a bundle and carry them with you,' said Trinket. 'You'll be needing them again later.'

While they were doing this, he got Doublet to go to his cell and make up a little parcel of his money and a few valuables that he could keep about him. The next thing he asked the Shaolin monks to do was to provide themselves, each one of them, with a bucket of water and to smear ash over their faces. Then they had to sit down and wait for it to get dark.

As soon as Trinket judged that it was dark enough, he and his party of pseudo-lamas left the monastery and, keeping to the foot of the walls as much as possible, stealthily made their way to the little temple.

In the temple's tiny courtyard the Venerable Yulin, Brother Wayward, and Brother Headlong were sitting side by side on a hastily constructed pyre of straw and faggots, impassively waiting for the kidnappers to arrive. They had previously drenched their clothes and the faggots with cooking-oil and placed the means of igniting themselves within easy reach. As soon as the lamas came, the Venerable Yulin planned to make a brief address explaining the purpose of what they were doing, then the flames would leap up and a load of evil karma would vanish in smoke.

Unfortunately for this plan, the pseudo-lamas' assault was too sudden for even a short address to be possible. They had not dared to risk making a noise as they approached the temple for fear of alerting the real lamas below. It was only when these robed and hatted figures were actually entering the courtyard that they began, in a language which, by a stretch of the imagination, might conceivably have been Tibetan, to shout and jabber. Whether or not the pyre was ignited in those few seconds could have made little difference, since just at that moment thirty-eight buckets of water were simultaneously discharged on the seated figures. Dependable

Doublet at once darted up to the biggest of them, Brother Head-long, and immobilized him with a few expert jabs. The other two offered no resistance: Brother Wayward because he was incapable of doing so, the Venerable Yulin because he elected not to. Many hands drew off the monks' dripping habits and replaced them with lama habiliments. Then, stopping only to collect Brother Head-long's cudgels and set a light to the pyre, they hustled the three new-made lamas out of the temple and into the darkness outside. Despite the water that had been thrown on it, the oil-drenched fuel caught rapidly, and by the time they had gone no more than a hundred paces, the flames and smoke could be seen rising, high above the walls of the temple.

The lamas too had seen the fire, to judge from the hubbub below, and presently a large body of them came rushing uphill, torches in hand, presumably to put it out. Trinket and his party were clearly visible to them in the light of the flaming torches, but because of their lama costume, went unremarked.

'They'll never put that out,' said Brother Cordial, 'and when they don't find Brother Wayward, they'll think he's burned himself. They shouldn't give us any more trouble after this.'

Thanks to the disarray which the fire appeared to have created, they had little difficulty in getting down the mountain. Once they had left the lamas well behind, Trinket asked Brother Simple to open the points of their three captors and apologized to them for the rough and unmannerly treatment to which they had been subjected.

Brother Headlong would have burned himself out of loyalty, but had not really wanted to die; moreover, as an old soldier, he was impressed by the ingenuity of Trinket's plan of rescue. His response was therefore a warm one. The Old Emperor had been determined to die, but generously praised Trinket for rescuing him in a way which had involved no loss of life. The Venerable Yulin said nothing. Probably he regarded being burned and being rescued with equal equanimity.

Just at that moment there was another hubbub ahead of them and they became aware of a large body of people hurrying in their direction.

'Another lot of lamas, I'm afraid,' said Brother Cordial.

'We mustn't run away, we must run towards them,' said Trinket. 'Look as if we're glad to see them. Smile. Jibber-jabber a bit and point back up the mountain.'

It was good advice, but fortunately not needed. The party ahead turned out to be a party of pilgrims, all wearing yellow cloth bags round their necks with the words ON PILGRIMAGE printed or embroidered on them in large characters.

The leader of the pilgrims, a big fellow, stepped forward.

'What are you lot up to?' he shouted, in a far from friendly manner.

Under the pilgrim disguise Trinket had no difficulty in recognizing Dolong, Colonel of the Palace Guards. The unfriendliness, he realized, was due to the fact that he was himself disguised.

'Dolong, my friend,' he cried, 'don't you recognize me?'

Dolong grabbed a torch from a nearby pilgrim and held it in Trinket's face. He burst out laughing.

'Well I'm damned! It's young Wei. What are you doing here? And why are you dressed up like a lama?'

Trinket couldn't tell him much, but Dolong didn't press him. The 'pilgrims' gathered round, laughing and chattering. Soon Trinket was surrounded by what appeared to be, as far as he could make out, an entire company of Palace Guards in disguise. There were many of them that he recognized: Zhao Qixian, for example, who was supposed to be getting news of the Green Girl for him.

'So has the Emperor sent you?' he asked Dolong.

'The Emperor's *here*,' said Dolong. 'Both Their Majesties, the Emperor and the Empress Dowager. They've come to Wutai to make offerings at all the main shrines. Right now they're at the Holy Precinct Monastery. It's not only us, by the way. The Valiants are here as well, and the Vanguards. Altogether there must be well over thirty thousand men.'

'So the Emperor's here,' said Trinket. 'That's great!'

'But what's the Old Whore doing here?' he wondered.

Just at that moment Colonel Chalju of the Valiants arrived, also disguised, and was pleasantly surprised to find that the young lama talking to Dolong was Lieutenant-Colonel Wei, who for a while had been his Second-in-Command. Trinket took the opportunity of explaining the situation to the two officers, though taking care to say nothing about the Old Emperor, of whose very existence they were, of course, like everyone else, unaware.

'There are about three thousand Tibetan lamas up there,' he said, pointing to the mountain. 'They must have heard about the Emperor's arrival and be planning some mischief against him. They seem to be under the impression that it's the Pure Coolness

Monastery he's visiting, because they've got it completely surrounded. With all these forces you've got with you, do you think
it would be possible to take care of them without too many casu-
alties? Best of all would be if you could take them all prisoner. The
Emperor doesn't like to hear about people being killed.' This last
was spoken loudly for the benefit of Brother Wayward, who was
standing near enough to hear what they were saying.

'Shouldn't be difficult,' said Dolong. 'We'd have to clear it
with the C.I.C. first, of course.'

'Who's that?'

'Prince Kang.'

'Good,' said Trinket. 'He's a friend of mine.'

He called Zhao over and instructed him to tell Prince
Kang that an emergency had arisen which threatened the
Emperor's safety. They needed to use troops immediately, there
was no time to consult him. They would report to him as soon as
possible.

Zhao hurried away to look for the Commander-in-Chief,
while Dolong and Chalju went off to organize their forces, glad of
a chance to gain military distinction. When the safety of the
Emperor's person was involved, a successful operation was sure to
bring special honours. Trinket moved over to where Brother
Wayward and his two companions were standing.

'Reverend Brothers,' he said, 'the Golden Pavilion Monastery
is not very far from here. Shall we go there and change into something more suitable? We ought to be able to find a quiet place there
where you can rest and meditate without being disturbed.'

Brother Wayward nodded.

It was in fact a good two miles' walk to the Golden Pavilion.
Trinket went in ahead of the others to arrange things with the
Abbot. His way of doing this was to hand him a thousand-tael
banknote.

'My Brothers and I would like to rest for a while in your
monastery, Father Abbot. All of this money is for you if you don't
ask any questions. For every question you ask, I'll charge you ten
taels. If you ask a hundred, I'll want the whole lot back.'

'Certainly,' said the Abbot, 'certainly. You are very welcome.
Would you—?'

He was about to say 'like some tea?', but suppressed the question in case it cost him ten taels.

As soon as a quiet room and three sets of monk's clothing

had been found for Brother Wayward and his companions, Trinket and the Shaolin monks changed back into the monk's habits they had brought with them and settled down to take a much-needed rest.

Kang Xi meets Brother Wayward

They had not been sitting long when distant sounds of fighting could be heard and they knew that the Imperial forces had begun the task of rounding up the lamas. The sounds continued for an hour and then grew fainter. After another half-hour had gone by, there was, quite suddenly, total silence. This was broken, some minutes later, by the sound of marching feet approaching from a distance. The sound grew louder and stopped outside the monastery; then they heard talking and the sound of a smaller group entering the forecourt.

'The Emperor!' said Trinket, and, rushing to the door of the room in which Brother Wayward and the two others were resting, he took out his dagger and struck an impressively warlike pose: Trinket Guarding His Master against All Comers.

A dozen guards approached, armed with swords, though still in civilian clothes, and challenged him to lay down his weapon. Trinket maintained his pose, but dropped it hurriedly and put away his dagger when, seconds later, the guards were followed by a slight, youthful figure wearing the blue cloth gown of a commoner. At once he fell to his knees and kowtowed.

'Good news, Your Majesty! His . . . His *Reverence* is in here.'

Kang Xi waved away the guards.

'Go, all of you!'

As soon as the guards had gone, Trinket rapped a couple of times on the door.

'It's Father Treasure,' he said. 'Could I please see you for a moment?'

There was no reply. After waiting for what seemed like an eternity, Kang Xi became so impatient that he stepped forward and gave the door a couple of raps himself. He would have called out, too, had not Trinket frantically signalled to him not to say anything. After another silence they heard Brother Headlong's voice speaking from the other side of the door.

'Our Brother is feeling very tired, Father Abbot. He begs you to excuse him. And he says that he severed all earthly ties when he became a monk, so will you please tell your visitor to leave him in peace?'

'Yes,' said Trinket, 'but would you mind opening the door, please? I only want to see him for a moment.'

After some murmuring inside, Brother Headlong spoke again.

'He says, he hopes you won't be offended, but as this is the Golden Pavilion Monastery and you are only a guest here the same as us, he no longer owes you obedience.'

When Trinket looked back and saw the sheer misery on Kang Xi's face, he felt quite angry.

'We'll see about that,' he thought. 'Just wait till I fetch the Abbot. He'll soon have that door open!'

But just at that moment Kang Xi burst into tears. Trinket, who had perfected the art of producing tears to order at—or rather *across*—his mother's knee, was soon weeping noisily to keep him company.

'I wish *I* had a father,' he blubbered. 'I've got no one to look after me. Nobody loves me. I wish I hadn't been born.'

The door suddenly creaked open and there stood Brother Headlong, nearly filling the doorway. He looked only at Kang Xi.

'Come in, please!'

At once Kang Xi dashed in, threw himself, sobbing, at his father's feet and embraced his legs. Trinket heard the Old Emperor murmuring 'Silly boy!' and got a brief glimpse of him bending over and stroking his son's head; but before he could see more, the Venerable Yulin and Brother Headlong walked out of the room, shutting the door after them. They swept past him, eyes downcast and hands crossed on their breasts, without a look or a word. Brother Headlong must have thought this a poor way to treat someone who had not long since saved his life, for after a few steps he looked back, with what might have been a wink.

Trinket tried hard to hear what was being said inside. Once he thought he heard the Empress Donggo mentioned, but mostly it was murmuring too indistinct for him to make out. After a long time there was a sound of footsteps, the door opened, and for a while father and son stood hand in hand outside.

'You are a good boy,' said Brother Wayward, 'a better person than I ever was. I don't need to worry about you. And *you* mustn't worry about *me*.'

Then, gently withdrawing his hand, he went inside and closed the door. After a few moments they could hear him fastening the door-bar. Kang Xi threw himself against the door and for a while sobbed uncontrollably. And this time the tears that Trinket shed to keep him company were not entirely forced.

'Laurie,' said Kang Xi when he had somewhat recovered, 'my father thinks very highly of you, but he doesn't want you here looking after him any more. He says that if we try to do too much for him, he can no longer feel that he has left the world behind.'

This was good news to Trinket, but he tried to look disappointed.

The conversation with his father, now that the worst of the shock of parting from him was over, had left Kang Xi in a talkative mood. And since Trinket was the only human soul to whom he could ever unburden his true feelings, he entered now on a wide-ranging discussion of matters of state and policy, though much of what he said went well over Trinket's head.

One thing he did understand was that the Old Emperor was deeply concerned about the sufferings inflicted by his own people on the Chinese during the time of the conquest and was anxious that his son should make amends. The Ten Day Massacre of Yangzhou by the Manchus was mentioned, and Kang Xi said that one thing he was planning to do was to grant freedom from taxes to that city for several years. Trinket was appreciative, thinking how good this would be for his mother's business.

He grew apprehensive, however, when Kang Xi got on to the subject of Wu Sangui. Remembering the wigging he had earned on the journey to Shaolin for attempting to inculpate the Satrap in a non-existent rebellion involving the Wang Wu Clan, he feared that Kang Xi might still be feeling angry about it. He was relieved to find that the Emperor, far from being angry, was himself deeply suspicious of Wu Sangui's intentions; and though he had realized that the 'evidence' that Trinket had sent him on that occasion was probably spurious, his only reason for responding to it with a public reprimand was in order to put the Satrap off his guard; for the Satrap, he knew full well, had many agents and might well have a spy or two in the Imperial armies.

They were sitting side by side on the plinth that ran along the side of the courtyard. In order to explain his strategy for dealing with Wu Sangui, Kang Xi got up and found four stones to represent the Four Satraps—the collaborationist Chinese generals whom the Manchus had rewarded with semi-autonomous fiefdoms, each stationed with his own army in one of the outer provinces of the

Empire. Wu Sangui, Satrap of the West, was by far the most powerful, most ambitious, and potentially the most dangerous of them. Kang Xi had learned quite a few new profanities since Trinket saw him last—presumably the Princess had picked them up from the Palace Guards and passed them on to him—and he was using quite a few of them in discussing the threat that Wu Sangui posed to the stability of the Empire. Trinket mischievously suggested that they should commence operations against the Satrap by pissing on his stone. And Kang Xi, who, for all the Imperial gravity of his everyday demeanour, was still at heart a boy, gleefully took up the suggestion, hitched up his gown, and began untrussing his trousers.

'You too,' he said.

And so the two friends, Laurie and Misty, stood there, one on each side, solemnly watering Wu Sangui with their piss. Their eyes met as they were trussing themselves up again and they burst out laughing.

Kang Xi sat down again on the plinth, but Trinket remained standing and inclined his ear to listen. There seemed to be a lot of activity all of a sudden: no shouted orders, but the sound of large numbers of men assembling outside the monastery.

'It sounds as if the troops have arrived with their prisoners,' he said. 'They must have finished rounding up the lamas. Congratulations! What a bit of luck that you turned up when you did with all those forces!'

'Not entirely,' said Kang Xi. 'Thanks to you, I had warning that the lamas were going to make this attempt.'

'Thanks to *me?*' said Trinket, puzzled.

'Don't you remember? That time I sent Zhang Kangnian to the Shaolin Monastery with that Picture Edict I took so much trouble to draw, there was a large party of people leaving just as he arrived. You told Zhang, when you were seeing him off, to find out who they were and keep an eye on them because you thought they were up to something. Well, he managed to find out who they were. There were three groups in that party. One of them was led by a Mongol prince called Galdan. One was commanded by a staff-officer of Wu Sangui's called Ma Bao, and the rest were a party of lamas. It looks very much as if Wu Sangui was involved in the plot to kidnap my father.'

'So he *is* plotting rebellion,' said Trinket.

'Perhaps,' said Kang Xi. 'But I'm not ready for him yet. I need a few more years before I can take him on. Anyway, to get back to the story. When the three groups split up, Zhang followed the lamas and was able to find out that they were planning this attempt. Unfortunately I didn't receive the information in time to stop them getting here.'

Trinket thought he had better tell him about his father's decision to burn himself rather than allow himself to be made use of as a hostage. Kang Xi was horrified—and all the more grateful to his young friend for acting so resolutely.

But it was time to end this private interlude and return to public business. Kang Xi went up to the door and put a hand on it. He seemed to be struggling with his tears. Then he knelt down and kowtowed.

'Look after yourself, father!' he said in a low voice. 'I'm going now.'

Trinket kowtowed beside him.

Tantric Confabulations

When Kang Xi, with Trinket following him, entered the great Buddha Hall of the monastery, Prince Kang, Chalju, Dolong, Songgotu, and a number of other officers and courtiers were already gathered there waiting for his arrival. Several of them noticed—with surprise, for he was normally so grave and mature in public and never showed any sign of emotion—that his eyes were red and swollen with weeping. When they saw Trinket's tear-stained face as well, they assumed that he was responsible and wondered exactly what the nature of the boy-Emperor's relationship with his young favourite might be.

As soon as Kang Xi was seated, Prince Kang came forward and announced that the Imperial forces had captured and disarmed several thousand lamas found making a disturbance in the precincts of the Pure Coolness Monastery and were now awaiting the Emperor's instructions.

Kang Xi nodded.

'Bring in the ringleaders.'

Three elderly lamas were brought in and led before him. In spite of the manacles and leg-irons, their attitude was defiant. They had no idea that the stripling confronting them was the Emperor and continued to jabber to each other in their own language, completely ignoring his presence. Great was their surprise, therefore, when Kang Xi began jabbering at them himself in their own language. The surprise of the courtiers was almost as great, since none of them was aware that he had any knowledge of Tibetan. As a matter of fact he hadn't: the lamas were not Tibetans but Mongols and the language they were speaking was Mongolian, in which Kang Xi was reasonably proficient. After he had spoken to them for a bit, they hung their heads and were silent. Whatever it was, he seemed to have made his point.

'Take them into a private room,' said Kang Xi. 'I want to interrogate them in camera.'

The three lamas were led off to the monastery's scriptorium. Shortly after they had gone, Kang Xi left the hall himself, signalling to Trinket to follow.

When they were alone with the lamas in the scriptorium, Kang Xi made Trinket shut and bar the door. As soon as he had done so, Trinket took out his dagger and waved it meaningfully in the region of the lamas' eyes, noses, ears, and throats, rolling his eyes and intimating, by a series of blood-curdling gestures, that if they did not comply with what was required of them, these parts would be at risk. Thereafter, throughout the interrogation, he frowned and waved his dagger at them when Kang Xi sounded angry, and nodded and smiled at them when he spoke more gently.

After about half an hour the interrogation ended, the door was unbarred, and Kang Xi ordered the waiting guards to take the lamas away. Then the door was closed and barred again.

'Strange!' said Kang Xi.

Trinket didn't ask him what was strange, but waited for him to say in his own good time.

'Laurie,' said Kang Xi after a bit, 'how many people know that my father is here as a monk?'

'Apart from you and me, only Yulin and Brother Headlong,' said Trinket. 'The old eunuch Hai Dafu knew, but he died some time ago. That only leaves the Old—Her Majesty.'

Kang Xi nodded.

'That's right. Only five people know. Yet these Mongol lamas told me just now that they had orders from the Dalai Lama in Tibet, the Living Buddha, to kidnap my father. I kept asking them who this monk was that they'd been ordered to kidnap, but they didn't seem to know. In the end all they could say was that they thought he knew a lot of *dharanis*—that's what they call the magic spells they go in for in their kind of Buddhism—and the Dalai Lama wanted to learn them from him. That's all nonsense, of course, but they really seemed to believe it.'

'Maybe the Living Buddha doesn't know who your father is either,' said Trinket. 'Maybe he *does* think he's just a Pure Coolness monk who knows a lot of thingumajigs. But the person who put him up to it must have known all right. And that could only be the—'

Kang Xi nodded.

'The Empress Dowager. She killed the Empress Donggo and my mother, the Empress Kang. She hates my father. We know that she'll stop at nothing. She won't rest until she's killed him. And probably you and me as well.'

Trinket suddenly recalled his other identity as White Dragon Marshal of the Mystic Dragon Sect, and remembered that the Empress Dowager was a member of the Sect too. When she learned from the old eunuch Hai Dafu that Shun Zhi was alive and living as a monk on Wutai, she would almost certainly have passed on that information to the Sect's evil Leader. But Trinket couldn't possibly tell all this to Kang Xi. He must have been looking worried, because Kang Xi asked him what was the matter.

'Nothing,' he said. 'I was just thinking that it really *must* be her and remembering how dangerous she is.'

'I *hate* her,' said Kang Xi. 'I *hate* her. I'd like to have her cut into little pieces; but I've promised my father not to harm her.'

'But *I* haven't,' thought Trinket.

'I shouldn't worry, Your Majesty,' he said. 'A person as wicked as her is bound to come to a bad end sooner or later. You only have to wait.'

Kang Xi was sharp enough to see what he was getting at and shot him a meaningful look.

'Yes,' he said, 'you're right. Someone who has done so many bad things is sure to come to a bad end.'

He paced to and fro a while, pondering.

'I *must* think of some way of making sure that my father is safe from any more of these attempts.' He was speaking more to himself than to Trinket. 'All lamas everywhere owe obedience to the Living Buddha in Lhasa. What we really need is a Living Buddha in Lhasa who would take his orders from *us*.'

Trinket was growing nervous. He was prepared to become a pseudo-lama for several hours but didn't want to become a real one permanently.

'Please don't send me away to be a lama, Your Majesty!' he begged. 'I'd much rather just be one of the Palace Guards, so that I can stay near you.'

'Come to think of it, it wouldn't work anyway,' said Kang Xi. 'The Living Buddha has to be born there. No, I've thought of another way.'

He made Trinket unbar the door and follow him back into the hall. He called to Chalju and Dolong to come over to him.

'You have both done excellently today,' he said. 'I intend to reward you.'

They knelt down and kowtowed.

'I'm becoming very much attached to the teachings of the Lord Buddha,' Kang Xi went on. 'So far my reign has been greatly blessed, and I attribute this to His protection. Father Treasure has been earning merit for me as my proxy during the past year, but his time here has now expired and I am taking him back with me to Peking. He will become a full Colonel in the Valiants and will continue to be Second-in-Command of the Palace Guards.'

Trinket knelt beside the other two and kowtowed.

'You, Chalju: I want you to be my proxy for the next two years—not as a monk, though, but as a lama. I am making you a Grand Lama with authority over all the lamas here on the Wutai Mountains. You are to select a thousand men of the Valiant Regiment to be lamas here with you in your own lamasery. This is all to be secret, you understand. If you play your part well, I shall make you a Military Governor at the end of the two years.'

Chalju had been somewhat dismayed at the prospect of becoming a lama, but the comparative autonomy and rich pickings that went with a Military Governorship would more than compensate. He cheered up immediately.

'Now you, Dolong, are to take care of these captured lamas,' Kang Xi continued. 'I want you to take them back with you to Peking and get them settled there somewhere where they can be kept under strict surveillance. You are then to inform His Holiness the Dalai Lama that I long for our Empire to enjoy the benefits of the Tantric doctrine, which I acknowledge to be the most perfect vehicle of Buddhist truth, and have therefore invited these lamas to Peking, where they will be able to worship after their fashion and promote their doctrine among my people. When, after seventy or eighty years, the Truth expounded by them has penetrated throughout our Empire, I shall send them back to Tibet.'

A White Apparition

At dawn next day, Kang Xi having announced that he wanted to worship at the Pure Coolness Monastery, they proceeded there without delay. As they drew near the monastery, they saw discarded weapons lying about everywhere in the trampled grass and there were patches of still-wet blood on the grass and smears of blood on the rocks and stones. Evidently the 'disarming' of the lamas had been a rather more sanguinary business than they had been led to suppose.

After offering incense at the altars of the Buddha and the Boddhisattva Manjusri, Kang Xi wanted to see the little temple where his father and his father's two companions had lived and meditated. Nothing remained of it now but charred beams and a pile of blackened rubble. The Young Emperor reflected with a shudder that, but for the previous night's timely rescue, his father's remains would have been underneath the débris. He turned to Songgotu and gave orders for two thousand taels to be donated to the monastery immediately for the rebuilding of the temple.

Returning to the main hall inside the monastery, he asked to see and speak for a while with the thirty-six Shaolin monks who had taken part in his father's rescue. They had no idea, of course, that the distinguished youth talking to them was their Sovereign, much less that the monk they had rescued was his father the Old Emperor, whom, like everyone else, they believed dead; but it was obvious to them that this young man was a person of great consequence, an Imperial Prince, perhaps, or a *beileh*—one of the lesser princes. When he formally requested permission to stay in the monastery for a few days (being reluctant to leave so soon the place where his father had so recently been), they were glad when their little Abbot welcomed him on their behalf.

It was actually just when Trinket was in the middle of extending this welcome to Kang Xi that a shower of dust and plaster descended on them from the ceiling. Looking up they saw a large hole that had been made in it and a white shape moving above the hole. Moments later legs appeared through the hole and a creature came hurtling downwards. It was a monk dressed in a white habit and carrying a long sword.

'Vengeance for the Ming Emperor!' cried the monk, in a high, reedy voice, and made a lunge at the Emperor. Fortunately Kang Xi stepped back in time and escaped being hurt. Court protocol prohibited the carrying of arms in the Emperor's presence, so Dolong, Chalju, Prince Kang, and the others were all of them unarmed; nevertheless a number of them sought to lay hands on the intruder. To counter them he merely flapped his enormously long left sleeve like someone cracking a whip and sent them staggering backwards. They said afterwards that it felt like encountering a hurricane.

As the monk continued to advance on the Emperor, several of the Shaolin monks made a rush at him, but, for all their skill, were disposed of in the same way. Meanwhile, Kang Xi had retreated so far that his back was against the altar and he could go no further. Just when the monk apparently had him at his mercy, Trinket, not stopping to think what he was doing, jumped in front of him and received full in his own chest the thrust that was intended for the Emperor. It hurt abominably, but the sword appeared to bend slightly and did not wound him.

After staring for a moment in astonishment, the monk seemed to make a sudden change of plan. He threw away his sword, wrapped his right arm round Trinket's body, tipped him off his balance, and rushed off, at what seemed in the circumstances like superhuman speed, out of the hall and out of the monastery, carrying him like a parcel under his arm. In no time at all they were on the mountainside and climbing higher. In spite of the uphill slope and the substantial weight he was carrying, the monk easily outstripped the thirty-six Shaolin monks who were in hue and cry behind him, and before long he had rounded a bend in the mountain and was out of sight.

CHAPTER 17

*In which Trinket
becomes acquainted with
the White Nun: they
make some Startling
Discoveries; and have
a lot of Trouble with
Lamas*

Adamantine Body

A jumble of trees and clouds passed before his eyes. As they
mounted higher and higher, Trinket's fear increased.

'This crazy monk doesn't give up easily,' he thought. 'He
couldn't kill me with his sword, so now he's decided to drop me
off a mountain.'

He shut his eyes tight when the monk at last stopped and let
go of him, then gave a great cry as he landed on his back with a
thump. It took him some moments to realize that he had fallen to
the ground from a height of approximately three feet. When he
opened his eyes he saw that the eyes of the White Monk were
studying him coldly.

'I have heard it said that some Shaolin monks can make
themselves impermeable to weapons,' the monk was saying,

'but I wouldn't have expected so young a monk as you to be able to.'

Trinket listened in amazement. It was a woman's voice. This wasn't a monk, it was a woman in her thirties, a distinguished-looking woman with a pale, refined face and a pair of very beautiful but very sad-looking eyes. From her shaved head and the two rows of little scars where the incense had burned into her scalp at the time of her initiation it was evident that she was in holy orders. The White Monk was in fact a White Nun. He felt relieved. A nun, he thought, should be much easier to deal with than a monk. But just at that moment he became once more conscious of the searing pain in his chest.

'Aiyo!'

The White Nun smiled scornfully.

'So the wonderful Shaolin secret is not so wonderful after all!'

'Reverend Mother,' said Trinket, 'I don't mind telling you: there were thirty-six of the most highly trained Shaolin monks, including the famous Eighteen Lohans, in that monastery just now, and the whole lot of them, acting together, couldn't lay a finger on you. If I'd known what I know now, I'd never have entered the Shaolin Monastery in the first place, I'd have gone to study with you.'

A faint smile passed over the White Nun's glacial features.

'What's your name? How long did you train in the Shaolin Monastery?'

Trinket wasn't quite sure in which of his many guises to present himself. The White Nun was obviously anti-Manchu and in favour of a Ming Restoration, but was she a friend of the Triads? He had better not take any chances.

'I'm the orphan boy of poor Yangzhou people,' he said. 'My father was killed by the Tartars. I was sent to the Palace when I was little to be a eunuch. My name is Laurie.'

The White Nun looked thoughtful.

'Laurie. A little eunuch called Laurie. Where have I heard that before? Wasn't there a wicked minister at the Tartar Court called Oboi who was killed by a little eunuch? What was the name of the little eunuch who killed Oboi?'

'Laurie,' said Trinket. 'It was me.'

The White Nun was not sure whether to believe him or not.

'But surely Oboi was the Champion of Manchuria? How could *you* kill him?'

Trinket sat up now and gave a somewhat embroidered but on the whole truthful account of the part he had played in Oboi's arrest and assassination.

The White Nun listened in silence. When he had done, she gave a little sigh, of relief, perhaps, or satisfaction.

'If this is true,' she said, 'those Zhuang ladies owe you a debt of gratitude.'

'Do you mean Widow Zhuang and *those* ladies?' said Trinket. 'Widow Zhuang has already thanked me. *And* she's given me a maid called Doublet. Right now Doublet will be worried sick about me.'

'How did you come to know them?' said the White Nun.

This episode, too, Trinket gave a fairly truthful account of. 'If you don't believe me, Reverend Mother,' he concluded, 'you could easily send for Doublet and ask her yourself.'

'That's not necessary,' said the White Nun. 'If you know Widow Zhuang and Doublet, that is enough for me. But tell me, how did you come to be a monk?'

Trinket knew he had better not tell her anything about the Old Emperor, so he merely said:

'The Young Emperor wanted me to be his Proxy Novice. He sent me to the Shaolin Monastery first, to be made a monk, then after that he had me transferred to the Pure Coolness Monastery. I wasn't at the Shaolin Monastery very long and I didn't have time to learn much. But even if I'd been there for years and years, I'd have been no good against someone like you.'

The White Nun's face suddenly assumed a stern expression.

'You are a Chinese. Aren't you ashamed to be treating the enemy like your own kin? You risked your life just now to save their Emperor. Only the lowest slave would behave like that.'

Trinket didn't know how to answer. He had thrown himself in front of Kang Xi instinctively, without thinking. It wasn't to curry favour or win an award. It was because Kang Xi was the only person who was really close to him, like a brother. How *could* he have stood by and let someone kill him? But he couldn't explain this to the White Nun.

'The worst people are not the Tartars who stole our Ming Empire from us,' said the White Nun. 'The worst people of all are Chinese collaborators like you who do their dirty work for them in return for rank and riches.' She paused a moment and stared hard at him. 'If I throw you now from the top of this mountain, your "adamantine body" isn't going to be much use to you, is it?'

'Of course it isn't,' said Trinket. 'But you don't need to go to all that trouble anyway. A simple blow from your hand would smash my skull in.'

'So what did you hope to gain by currying the Emperor's favour?'

'You don't understand. I wasn't greasing,' said Trinket. 'The Young Emperor really is my friend. He's good. He says he'll never raise taxes. He wants to protect the common people—isn't that what River and Lake is all about?'

The White Nun looked doubtful.

'Did he really say those things—about not raising taxes and protecting the common people?'

'Loads of times,' said Trinket. 'He's often told me that all the killing that the Tartars did when they entered the Passes was bad, very bad. He says that in the Ten Day Massacre of Yangzhou they behaved like wild animals. He's very unhappy about it. That's why he came to Wutai, to visit the temples and pray to the Buddha for forgiveness. And he says he's going to give Yangzhou three years' freedom from taxes.'

The White Nun nodded thoughtfully.

'Oboi killed a lot of the good men at Court,' said Trinket. 'The Young Emperor tried to stop him, but he wouldn't listen. That made the Young Emperor very angry, so he told me to kill Oboi. If you kill the Young Emperor, all the important stuff at Court will be taken care of by the Empress Dowager. Now she's *really* bad news. She's an Old Whore. If *she* gets control of things, it'll be the Ten Day Massacre all over again, only more of it. If you want to kill Tartars, the one you ought to kill is the Old Whore.'

The White Nun stared at him coldly.

'You are not to use language like that in my presence!'

However, she ignored his apologies and appeared to be contemplating the sky.

'So what is so bad about this Empress Dowager?' she asked presently.

This was a tricky question. Trinket couldn't possibly tell her the truth, because almost all the Empress's misdeeds were connected in some way with the Old Emperor. He decided that he would have to make something up.

'Well, for one thing she says that as this is now the Qing Empire, they ought to open up all the Ming Emperors' tombs and take out the treasure that was buried with them. Then she says that

all Chinese with the Ming Imperial surname Zhu should be executed, along with all their families, so that there's no risk of their
getting the Empire back again.'

'Wicked woman!' cried the White Nun. She hit a rock in her
rage with a force that would have broken a normal person's hand.

'I know,' said Trinket. 'I told the Young Emperor he couldn't
possibly do that.'

'How could an uneducated boy like you persuade an Emperor
to change his mind?' said the White Nun.

'I said to him, "Your Majesty, everyone has got to die some
day: even Your Majesty will die sooner or later. Now," I said, "where
did King Yama and all the Officers of the Dead and the devils who
serve them come from? They're all Chinese," I said. "If you treat the
Chinese badly in this life, what's going to happen to you in the
next, after you're dead?" "You're right, Laurie," he said. "I'm glad
you reminded me." Then he gave orders for a lot of money to be
spent on repairing the tombs of the Ming Emperors, even the tombs
of Prince Fu and Prince Lu and those other ones—I can't remember all their names now.'

The White Nun's eyes were red and she began to cry. Trinket
could see the tears rolling down her cheeks and some of them even
falling on to the grass.

'If what you say is true,' she said, 'you are not at all to blame
for serving the Tartar Emperor; in fact, you have done your country
a great service. Oh!'—she began to sob again—'if that evil woman
had had her way . . .'

Trinket watched with alarm as she stepped to the edge of the
cliff and began looking down. Fearing that she was going to make
away with herself, he shouted to try and stop her.

'Reverend Mother, Reverend Mother, you mustn't give up!
Don't do anything silly, please!'

For some reason it had become important to him that this
refined and beautiful woman, so dignified and austere in her
manner and so unlike any female he had ever in his life met before,
should remain alive. He struggled over to where she stood and
reached out for her left arm, intending to pull her back. He found
himself holding on to an empty sleeve. She had no left arm.

'What nonsense!' she said, as he stood there goggling in surprise. 'I have no intention of taking my own life.'

'You looked so sad,' said Trinket. 'I was afraid you might be
thinking about it.'

'And what if I *had* committed suicide?' said the White Nun. 'You could have gone back to your Emperor and enjoyed a prosperous and happy life.'

'No,' said Trinket. 'I didn't *choose* to be a eunuch. Anyway, the Tartars killed my father. I don't really want to treat the enemy as, you know, what you said before.'

'Kin' was not a word he was familiar with.

The White Nun nodded sympathetically.

'Well, you are a good boy at heart,' she said.

She took some money from an inside pocket and held it out to him.

'Here, take this. It should be enough to get you back to Yangzhou.'

The amount she was offering him appeared to be ten or twelve taels. He thought amusedly of the gratuities he regularly dispensed himself—two hundred or more taels at a time and never less than a hundred.

'Still,' he thought, 'she has a kind heart. That's what I must work on.'

Instead of taking the money, he threw himself on his knees, clung to her legs, and broke into noisy sobbing.

'Get up, get up!' she said. 'Whatever is the matter with you?'

'I don't want the money,' he sobbed.

'Then why are you crying?'

'I haven't got a father or a mother,' he sobbed. 'I've always wanted a mother to love me and take care of me. I think my dead mother must have been like you.'

The White Nun reddened.

'What nonsense!' she said, though not unkindly. 'People in holy orders can have no family.'

'I know,' said Trinket.

He got up again, his face all wet with tears.

'I'm planning to go to Peking,' she said reflectively. 'I suppose I could take you with me. But you're in holy orders too, aren't you?'

'No, no,' said Trinket hurriedly. 'I'm not really a monk. I'll buy some new clothes in the first town we come to and dress up as an ordinary boy.'

The White Nun nodded and they set off at once on the north descent of the mountain. She was used to travelling in silence and ignored several of Trinket's attempts at starting a conversation. There was something he said, however, about his 'adamantine body', which obviously still puzzled her. When he assured her that there was really nothing 'adamantine' about it at all and opened up his habit to show her the weapon-resistant waistcoat that he wore underneath, she seemed really pleased.

'No wonder,' she said. 'I thought it was strange that one so young should have attained so high a level of skill. Well, I must say, you are a very honest boy.'

Trinket had been called many things in his young life, but this was certainly the first time that anyone had called him honest. He was puzzled, though, when he glanced up at her to see that her eyes were full of tears. He could not know that someone in the past who had been very dear to her had possessed just such a protective waistcoat as the one he was wearing.

Coal Hill

At the foot of the north face they turned towards the east, and after walking for a few miles in that direction, came to a small market town. Trinket found a shop there where he was able to shed his monkish persona and once more indulge his taste for expensive clothes; for he still had with him the packet of money and valuables made up for him by faithful Doublet when they left the Pure Coolness Monastery in disguise. Soon he was dressed up as a young swell, able to pose as the son of a rich patron and in that capacity devote himself to caring for the material needs of the unworldly nun.

She seemed to take little interest in such mundane matters as the food she ate, yet she had a natural fastidiousness, and Trinket found that if he took trouble to buy the choicest materials—ginseng, bird's-nest, *fuling* (China-root fungus), Wood Ear mushrooms, and the like—and insist that they were properly cooked (even on occasion going into the kitchen of the inn or restaurant where they were eating to give instructions to the bewildered chef), she could be coaxed into eating a few mouthfuls more. As a devout Buddhist she could eat only vegetarian food; but Trinket had been head of the Imperial Catering Department, and the Emperor and Empress Dowager both ate vegetarian dishes on the Buddha's birthday and the Rogation Days, and other feasts and fasts of the Buddhist Church, so he knew plenty of excellent vegetarian recipes.

She liked to travel in silence, and whole days went by without her saying a word. Yet Trinket had developed so profound a respect for her that, far from finding this irksome, he made a conscious effort to avoid foul language and not speak his usual nonsense in her presence.

Eventually they arrived in Peking and Trinket found a large, high-class hostelry for them to stay in. It was unusual for a nun to stay in such a place, but Trinket had pressed ten taels into the proprietor's hand almost as soon as they entered the door and, seeing that the nun was in the company of this well-dressed and obviously rich young gentleman, the man did his very best to please. For her part the White Nun treated their staying there as the most natural thing in the world and, indeed, seemed quite unaware of her surroundings. After they had eaten, she expressed a desire to go and visit Coal Hill.

'That's where the Emperor Chong Zhen died,' said Trinket. 'We must kowtow there and say a prayer for him.'

Coal Hill (which is really five hills) is just north of the Forbidden City, across the road from it. It did not take them long to get there. Trinket pointed out the tree on the central hill on which the last Ming Emperor hanged himself. The White Nun stroked its bark with a trembling hand. He could see the tears rolling down her cheeks. Presently her silent weeping turned into loud wailing and she sank to her knees at the foot of the tree.

'She must have known him,' thought Trinket. 'She can't have been his concubine, she's not old enough. Perhaps she was a maid-of-honour, like Auntie Tao.'

After a while the wailing ceased and the White Nun recovered herself sufficiently to make several formal kowtows. Then she stood up, her tears still falling, and enfolded the tree in a half-embrace with her right arm. Suddenly a trembling seized her whole body and she fainted. Trinket rushed forward to catch her as she slipped to the ground.

'Reverend Mother, Reverend Mother!' he cried. 'Open your eyes!'

It was some time before she did so. Then, when she had recovered her composure, she said:

'Now I want to go to the Palace.'

Trinket suggested that she should go back with him to the hostelry. They could both dress up as eunuchs and he could smuggle her in quite easily. But she wouldn't hear of it.

'I shall break in,' she said. 'Who will stop me?'

'Well, yes,' said Trinket, not at all happy about the idea. 'I'm sure there's no one there who could stand up to you, but you'd have to kill an awful lot of guards. Isn't it against your vows to kill for no good reason?'

She nodded.

'You are quite right. I shall wait until it is dark. You can stay behind in the inn, in case I run into trouble.'

'No, no,' said Trinket. 'I'll go with you. I'd be too worried if you went in on your own. I know everything inside there so well, the buildings and the people. It'll be much easier if I'm with you. You only have to say where you want to go and I can take you there.'

The White Nun looked thoughtful but said nothing.

The Burning-Ground Revisited

About ten o'clock that evening Trinket and the White Nun left the hostelry and made their way to the foot of the Palace wall.

'We should get in from the north-east side,' said Trinket. 'The wall's a bit lower there. It's where the *sula* live—you know, the people who do the dirty work for the eunuchs. There won't be any guards patrolling that part.'

The White Nun followed his advice. When they reached the section of wall which Trinket judged the best place to go over, she helped him up on to it, then floated down ahead of him not far from the barrack-like quarters of the *sula*.

'Well,' said Trinket when they were both inside, 'that building there is the Hall of Joyful Old Age and that one there is the Nurturing Nature Hall. What is it you want to see?'

'Everything,' said the White Nun, and after walking swiftly in a westerly direction between the two buildings he had indicated, she hurried round the two sides of a covered gallery, through two more Palace halls, and out into the Palace gardens. Trinket noticed that, although it was dark and the buildings were all unlit, she continued to walk at the same swift pace, turning corners without hesitation and only stopping momentarily to conceal herself behind a wall or a tree when there were signs of a watchman or a patrolling guard in the near vicinity. It was obvious that she knew her way around and must at one time have had her home in the Palace.

He followed her through the gardens and through the Gate of Female Repose. Outside the Palace of Female Repose she waited for him to catch up.

'Is this still where the Empress lives?' she asked him.

'No one lives here,' said Trinket. 'There isn't an Empress. The Young Emperor hasn't married yet.'

'We'll go in and have a look,' she said.

At a touch of her hand a window-catch was broken, the casement opened, and she sailed in. Trinket scrambled in after her. Inside it was musty and there was a smell of damp. He couldn't see anything at first, but presently, in the moonlight that filtered faintly through the windows, he could make out her shape, sitting motionless on the edge of the great bed of state. It was so silent that he could hear, or thought he could hear, the falling of a tear.

'Yes, definitely,' he told himself. 'She must have been a maid-of-honour, like Auntie Tao. One of the Ming Empress's maids-of-honour.'

The White Nun had raised her head and was staring at one of the beams.

'This is where the Empress Zhou hanged herself,' she said.

'Reverend Mother,' said Trinket, 'would you like to meet my auntie?'

'Who is your aunt,' the White Nun asked curiously. 'What sort of person is she?'

'I call her my Auntie Tao,' said Trinket. 'Her real name is Tao Hongying.'

'Hongying?' said the White Nun, startled.

'I thought you might know her,' said Trinket. 'She used to work for the Emperor Chong Zhen's eldest daughter, the Princess Royal.'

'Yes, yes,' said the White Nun. 'Where is she? Fetch her here!'

Normally she was so stately and unruffled. He had never before heard her speak with urgency in her voice.

'I shan't be able to get her for you tonight,' he said.

'Why not?'

'She tried to assassinate the Empress Dowager, but she didn't succeed in killing her. Since then she's had to move about all the time hiding herself in different parts of the Palace. If I want to see her, I have to leave a secret sign somewhere and go there to see her next day. The earliest we could see her would be tomorrow night.'

'What is the sign?' the White Nun asked him.

'I have to make a little pile of stones somewhere in the burning-ground and stick a big twig in the top of it.'

'Very well,' she said. 'Let's do that now.'

This time it was Trinket who led the way.

The burning-ground was the area in which the Palace rubbish was burned. The first thing he did when they got there was to look for an odd piece of board and a bit of charred wood. He used the charred wood to draw a crude picture of a bird. Then he made a little pile of stones, stuck a bit of wood in the top of it, and propped the bird picture up against the stones.

'There's someone coming!' said the White Nun as he was finishing.

He took her hand and the two of them crouched down behind a large earthenware water-jar. There was a hurried patter of foot-steps. Someone ran into the middle of the burning-ground, stopped, looked round in each direction, caught sight of the stone-heap with a visible start, then ran over to it and picked up the picture of the bird. Just at that moment the moon came out from behind a cloud and Trinket could see that it was Aunt Tao. He rose and stepped out from behind the jar.

'Auntie!' he called softly. 'Here I am. I'm over here.'

She ran to him and enfolded him in her arms.

'Dear boy! You're back at last! I've been coming here every night, hoping to see the sign.'

'Auntie,' said Trinket, 'I've got someone here who wants to meet you.'

'Oh?' she said releasing him, a trifle suspiciously. 'Who is it?'

The White Nun stood up to her full height.

'Hongying,' she said. 'Can you still recognize me?'

Startled, for she had not realized that there was another person behind the jar, Aunt Tao retreated a few steps and drew her sword.

'Who are you?' she said.

The White Nun sighed.

'You don't recognize me, do you?'

'I can't see your face,' said Aunt Tao. She sounded shaken. 'Are you . . . is it . . .?'

The White Nun turned her face into the moonlight.

'You have changed too, Hongying,' she said sadly. 'I hardly knew you.'

'You aren't . . .?' Aunt Tao's voice was shaking. Suddenly she threw down her sword, rushed forwards, flung herself to her knees, and embraced the White Nun's legs.

'Princess,' she sobbed, 'Princess! To see you again! Oh, I could die happy this very moment!'

So was this the Princess Royal? Trinket was at first startled, but a moment later felt a fool for not having realized it sooner. Aunt Tao had told him more than once how, when the rebel general Bash-em Li captured Peking, the Ming Emperor had tried to kill his favourite daughter before taking his own life, but had only suc-ceeded in cutting off her arm. Aunt Tao was there at the time and had seen it with her own eyes, but then she had fainted, and when she came to, the Princess and the Emperor had both disappeared. Of course the White Nun was a Princess! How could a person of such dignified aloofness have been a mere maid-of-honour? *And* she only had one arm.

'So you never left the Palace?' he heard the White Nun ask Aunt Tao.

'No, I never left.'

'The boy tells me that you tried to kill the Tartar Dowager,' said the White Nun. 'You have kept faith all these years.' She was weeping now herself.

'Princess, your life is precious. *You* mustn't stay here a moment longer. I'll see you out.'

'I stopped being a Princess long ago,' said the White Nun.

'Oh no,' said Aunt Tao. 'In my heart you will always be a Princess, *always. My* Princess.'

'Is anyone now living in the Longevity Rooms?'

'The Tartar Princess,' said Aunt Tao. 'But at the moment she and her brother the Emperor and the Empress Dowager are all away somewhere. There are only a few eunuchs and Palace ladies left behind there. I'll go there and kill them for you.'

'No, no,' said the White Nun. 'There's no need to kill anyone. I only want to have a look.'

From the burning-ground to the Longevity Rooms was a maze-like walk through several gates and courtyards and past several buildings, the last of which was the repository in which tea was stored. As the three of them stood outside the building which more than twenty years earlier had been the White Nun's home, Aunt Tao, knowing nothing yet of her former mistress's almost supernatural skill in the Martial Arts, once more offered to go in first, not to kill, but at least to drive out, the women and eunuchs inside.

'That won't be necessary,' said the White Nun, stretching out

her hand and giving the doors a push. Aunt Tao watched in astonishment as the bar on the inside broke with a slight snapping sound
and the doors flew open.

The White Nun, remembering the layout of the building,
knew where the sleeping women and eunuchs were to be found.
Gliding into their quarters, she swiftly, with unerring touch, pressed
the points on each one of them that would render them unconscious till the morning. Then she went into the main bedroom and
sat down on the bed while Aunt Tao and Trinket stood to one side
and waited.

'Light the candles!' she said, after sitting for a while in silence.

When they were lit, it could be seen that the tables,
chairs, and walls were covered with whips and every kind of
weapon. The room was more like an armoury than the boudoir
of a princess.

'What became of my paintings and calligraphic scrolls?' the
White Nun asked. 'And what happened to all my books? Were they
all thrown away?'

'I am afraid so,' said Aunt Tao. 'I doubt whether the Tartar
Princess can read more than a few words, and I'm sure she knows
nothing about painting.'

'It seems that she is fond of Martial Arts,' said the White Nun.

'Yes,' said Trinket, 'but she's pretty hopeless. Even I could beat
her. She's very weird. She doesn't just like beating other people, she
likes being beaten herself.'

The White Nun flicked out her left sleeve and put out the
candles.

'Princess,' said Aunt Tao, 'with your wonderful skill you
should be able to seize the Empress Dowager and force her to hand
over her Sutras. That would enable us to sever the Tartars' Dragon
Line and break their power.'

'What Sutras?' said the White Nun. 'What is this Dragon Line
you are talking about?'

Aunt Tao explained about the eight copies of the *Sutra in Forty-
Two Sections* containing some secret which would enable the person
possessing it to dig into the ground somewhere along the invisible
Dragon Line on which the Manchus' power depended, thereby
undermining their rule. After listening in silence, the White Nun
agreed that it was important to get hold of these as soon as possible and proposed that they should return to the Palace the moment
the Empress Dowager was once more in residence. Meanwhile

Hongying should stay with them in their lodging. Trinket had five of the copies himself and knew that the Empress Dowager had only one. With a bit of luck the White Nun would kill her for refusing to come up with all eight of them and he and Kang Xi would be free at last from her wiles.

They climbed out of the Forbidden City by the way they had got in, accompanied this time by Aunt Tao. Back in the hostelry, the White Nun insisted that Aunt Tao should share her own room. The two of them lay awake all that night talking, not sleeping until it was dawn.

Tartar Empress and Tartar Princess

From that day on neither of them set foot outside the hostelry, but Trinket slipped out each day to see if the Emperor had returned yet. On the morning of the seventh day he saw several large palanquins being carried into the Palace, escorted by Prince Kang, Songgotu, Dolong, and a large contingent of the Palace Guards, and knew that the Emperor must be in one of them. This was confirmed when not long afterwards he watched a continuous stream of Princes, *Beilehs*, and Ministers of State going in to pay their respects. He hurried back to tell the White Nun.

'Excellent!' she said. 'I shall go in tonight. But now that the Tartar Emperor is back, the guards will be much more on the alert. You two had better stay here.'

Needless to say, neither Trinket nor Aunt Tao was willing to be left behind and in the end she consented to let them come with her.

They entered by the same way as before and arrived at the Hall of Maternal Tranquillity without mishap. Trinket made signs to the White Nun to show which part of the building the Empress Dowager's bedroom was in. They stole round to a courtyard at the back where the maids-in-waiting had their quarters. Only three of the windows at the rear there were faintly lit. The White Nun looked in through one of them and saw a row of ten or more maids sitting side by side on a long bench, their heads bowed down with fatigue and obviously dead to the world. Entering silently by one of these windows, it was fairly easy to step through the door-curtain into the Empress Dowager's bedroom without disturbing the maids. Four large red candles were burning on a table, but the room was empty.

'I went through all the drawers in here,' Aunt Tao whispered, 'but I couldn't find the Sutras. Aiyo! There's someone coming.'

Trinket tugged at her sleeve and slipped behind the bed-hangings. Aunt Tao and the White Nun followed his example. They heard a girl's voice speaking outside.

'Mum, I did what you told me to do. What are you going to give me?'

It was Trinket's bugbear, the Princess Ning, speaking to the Empress Dowager.

'Do you expect a reward for a little thing like that?' said the Empress Dowager. 'I never heard of such a thing!'

'*Little* thing?' said the Princess. 'I bet Emperor–brother would be furious if he knew about it.'

'What's so important about a sutra?' said the Empress Dowager. 'Since we've got back from Wutai, I want to go on reading the scriptures and praying for the Emperor's safety.'

'Oh, in that case I'll tell him,' said the Princess. 'Ma's taken your Sutra so that she can pray for your health. Long life to Your Majesty! A long, long life!'

'Tell him!' said the Empress Dowager. 'I shall simply say that I know nothing about it. No one believes the nonsense that you young people talk.'

'Mum!' said the Princess. 'How can you have the nerve? The Sutra is with you here, for all to see.'

'I shall burn it, then,' said the Empress Dowager with a laugh.

'How *mean* you are!' said the Princess. 'It's one thing not to reward me for the favour I've done you, but I don't see why you have to be so nasty to me as well.'

'You've got everything,' said the Empress Dowager. 'What could I possibly give you that you haven't got already?'

'There's one thing I haven't got,' said the Princess.

'Oh, what's that?'

'A little eunuch to play with.'

'The Palace is full of them,' said the Empress Dowager. 'You can take your pick.'

'They're all useless,' said the Princess. 'The one I want is Laurie, but he spends all his time with my brother.'

'Your brother has sent him off on business,' said the Empress Dowager. 'I don't know where, or what it is he has to do.'

'*I* do,' said the Princess. 'The guards told me. He's on Wutai.'

'Oh?' said the Empress Dowager. She was obviously startled.
'How is it we didn't see him while we were there?'

'I don't know,' said the Princess. 'I didn't find out myself until
we got back.'

The Empress Dowager appeared to be thinking.

'All right,' she said finally, 'when he gets back, I'll speak to
the Emperor about it.' From the way she spoke it sounded as if her
mind was on other things. 'You'd better go to bed now. It's getting
late.'

'Mum,' said the Princess, 'can't I stay here and sleep with
you?'

'You're not a child any more,' said the Empress Dowager.
'Why can't you sleep in your own bed?'

'I'm afraid,' said the Princess. 'My room is haunted.'

'Rubbish!' said the Empress Dowager. 'How can it be
haunted?'

'No really, Mum. The maids and eunuchs told me. The other
night some spirits came and put them all under a spell. They didn't
wake up until midday next day and they had the most terrible
nightmares.'

'Worthless slaves!' said the Empress Dowager. 'When we're
away they make these things up just to frighten themselves with.
Now go back to your own room this minute!'

White Nun meets Old Whore

When the Princess had gone, the Empress Dowager sat down at
her table, on which lay the stolen copy of the Sutra. She appeared
to be lost in thought. After a while she turned her head, catching
sight, as she did so, of a human shadow on the wall. Her first reaction was to look away in terror as she thought of the victims she
had murdered; but then she remembered that ghosts are said to cast
no shadows and looked again. She held her breath and listened.
There was no sound of breathing and her terror returned. Then, a
few moments later, she heard breathing quite close to her, from the
other side of the table. A white-robed nun was sitting there, her
large and lustrous eyes staring at her unwaveringly from a beautiful but expressionless face—whether a living person or a spirit she
could not tell.

'Who are you?' she said. 'What are you doing here?'

The White Nun at first ignored her question, then, very coldly, she said:

'Who are *you*? What are *you* doing here?'

'How dare you!' said the Empress Dowager. 'This is the Imperial Palace.'

'Quite so,' said the White Nun. 'This is the Imperial Palace. What is a creature like you doing in it?'

'I am the Empress Dowager,' said the Empress angrily. 'What are you—a witch?'

The White Nun stretched out her right hand and calmly removed the copy of the *Sutra in Forty-Two Sections* from the table.

'Put that down!' shouted the Empress Dowager and aimed a blow at her face. But the White Nun had already slipped the Sutra into her bosom and parried the blow easily with her hand.

'A professional, are you?' said the Empress Dowager. 'Very well.'

She rose from her chair and proceeded to aim a succession of four or five blows at the nun. But the nun remained seated in her chair and effortlessly brushed them aside. When seven or eight more of her attacks were similarly frustrated, the Empress Dowager reached down and extracted a gleaming stiletto from her stocking. Trinket recognized the gold-inlaid stiletto of Emei steel with which she had stabbed Old Hai. He wanted to shout out, but Aunt Tao whispered to him not to.

The scene that now followed was quite extraordinary. The Empress Dowager sprang up and down like a cat, stabbing and thrusting at the White Nun, while the White Nun, sitting bolt upright in her chair and using no more than the index finger of her right hand, remained unscathed. The violent movements of the Empress Dowager caused the candles to flicker, until one by one all four of them went out. Trinket and Aunt Tao could no longer see what was happening, but they could hear the Empress Dowager panting and a moment later they heard the White Nun speaking.

'You say you are the Empress Dowager. Where did you learn to fight like this?'

The Empress Dowager made no reply, though from the continued panting and other noises they could tell that she was endeavouring to keep up the attack. Suddenly there came the sound of four sharp slaps, then a great cry of rage and surprise, and then silence. A spark flashed out in the darkness followed by a little spurt of flame, and there was the White Nun with a lighted spill in her hand. She flicked it in the direction of the candles and, by manipulating her sleeve in a way that a conjuror might have envied, caused it to light all four candles in succession and then to return to her hand, whereupon she blew it out and put it back in an inside pocket. They could see now that the Empress Dowager was kneeling down in front of her. The White Nun must have immobilized her by pressing on a point, for she seemed unable to move. To judge from her face, which was rapidly changing colour, from red to white and from white to red again, she must have been in pain.

'Kill me quickly!' she said in a low voice. 'It's not right to torture people like this.'

'I don't understand it,' said the White Nun. 'Every move you make reeks of Snake Island. How does someone living in the seclusion of the Palace come to have contact with the Mystic Dragon Sect?'

Trinket gasped. This Reverend Mother of his seemed to know everything. He had better be careful in future what lies he told in her presence. But for the moment it was the Empress Dowager who was telling all the lies: she knew nothing at all about the Mystic Dragon Sect. All she knew of Martial Arts had been taught her by an old eunuch called Hai Dafu. She had never used these methods to harm anyone. Pressed about the significance of the Sutra she set so much store by, she insisted that she wanted it only for sentimental reasons, because of its connection with her late husband.

'You are a foolish woman,' said the White Nun. 'Since you refuse to tell me the truth, you have only yourself to blame for the consequences.'

She flicked her with the tip of her long sleeve, releasing the locked point so that she could move again.

'Thank you, Your Reverence,' said the Empress Dowager. 'You are very kind.'

'Not kind at all,' said the White Nun. 'What effect does Soft Crush have on a person?'

'The eunuch who taught me wouldn't say exactly,' said the Empress Dowager. 'All he would say was that the effects were terrible and that very few people could survive them.'

'Those last seven Soft Crush blows you aimed at me I turned back on you,' said the White Nun. 'Each will have the effect on your own body that it would have had on mine. Whatever you suffer as a consequence will be self-inflicted.'

The Empress Dowager looked as if she might faint. She had seen the effects of Soft Crush on the Donggo sisters and the baby prince. The last seven blows she had aimed at the White Nun had been delivered with all the force she could muster. Any one of them would have been enough to guarantee an agonizing death. She sank to her knees again.

'Reverend Mother, have mercy!'

The White Nun sighed.

'The damage you have done yourself is irreversible. No one else can save you.'

The Empress Dowager knocked her head on the floor.

'Tell me what I can do. There must be something. Have pity on me!'

'I could have helped you, but you have only told me lies,' said the White Nun. 'In any case, you are a Tartar. You are my mortal enemy. I have shown you enough mercy already by not killing you.'

She got up from her chair.

The Empress Dowager was trembling violently. A vision of the Donggo sisters writhing in agony on their beds was swimming before her eyes.

'I am not a Tartar,' she said. 'I'm a Chinese.'

'Don't be absurd!' said the White Nun, and began to move away.

'But I am!' said the Empress Dowager. 'I really am a Chinese. I hate the Tartars.'

The White Nun halted.

'Oh?' she said. 'Why?'

'It's . . . it's a secret. I'm not allowed to tell anyone.'

'In that case you'd better keep it to yourself.'

The Empress Dowager's terror of a cruel death now drove out all her other fears.

'I'm an impostor,' she said. 'I'm not the Empress Dowager.'

The White Nun went back to her chair and sat down again. Trinket was beginning to think that the Empress Dowager was an even better liar than himself; but presently, as her story unfolded, it appeared that she was telling the truth.

She was the daughter of Mao Wenlong, a Ming general who had fought against the Manchus on the frontier for several years. Her real name was Mao Dongzhu. When both her parents were killed, she was taken into the Palace and entered the service of the Empress, the Princess of the Borjigit clan who had become the

Emperor Shun Zhi's wife. There, after years of service, she had learned to imitate the voice and gestures of her mistress so well that in the end she was able to impersonate her.

'My face is false, too,' she said, and sitting down at her dressing-table, she soaked a tissue in some sort of liquid preparation she got from a gilded jar and rubbed it vigorously on her cheeks. After waiting a few moments, she peeled off two skin-covered pads, one from each side of her face. Even the White Nun gasped. The round, fat face of the Empress Dowager had turned into that of a gaunt-faced, hollow-eyed woman.

'It certainly is a remarkable transformation,' said the White Nun. 'But when you supplanted the Empress, couldn't her other attendants spot the difference? And what about the Emperor?'

'The Emperor was infatuated with Lady Donggo, he never went near the Empress,' said this woman who called herself Mao Dongzhu. 'As for her women and her eunuchs: when I first gained control over her, before I began impersonating her, I made her dismiss them and replace them with others, so that when I took over, the ones around me were all new. I avoided going out of my apartments as much as possible; but even when I had to, Court etiquette forbids Palace staff to look members of the Imperial family in the face when they are addressing them, so that if they ever did get to look at me, it would have been from a distance, too far away for them to tell the difference.'

So far the White Nun had seemed convinced; but now, suddenly, she thought of something.

'Just a minute. You said the Emperor didn't go near you; yet you have a daughter.'

'She isn't the Emperor's,' said Mao Dongzhu. 'Her father was a Chinese. He used to stay with me sometimes in the Palace disguised as one of my women. He . . . he . . . not long ago he fell ill and died.'

Trinket and Aunt Tao gave each other a nudge. This at least they knew to be untrue.

The White Nun shook her head.

'I don't think you're telling me *all* the truth.'

'When I've just told you a shameful secret like that, Your Reverence?' said Mao Dongzhu. 'How can you doubt me?'

'What about the real Empress Dowager?' said the White Nun. 'You say you have never killed anyone. Surely you have *her* blood on your hands?'

'She is alive and well,' said Mao Dongzhu.

This was a great surprise.

'But in that case, aren't you afraid of being found out?' said the White Nun.

By way of an answer, Mao Dongzhu went up to a carpet that covered part of the wall and pulled on a tasselled cord that hung beside it. The carpet rolled up revealing the doors of a large closet, to which she applied a little golden key. She opened the doors and there, lying down inside under a bed-cover of silk brocade, was the body of a woman. The White Nun gave a little gasp.

'Is this the Empress Dowager?'

'Have a look!' said Mao Dongzhu, bringing a candle over so that the White Nun could get a better view.

The woman's face looked ill and completely bloodless. Apart from that, though, it bore a striking resemblance to what the false Empress Dowager had looked like before she removed the skin-pads from her cheeks. The woman opened her eyes slightly, then quickly closed them again.

'I shall never tell you,' she said faintly. 'Why don't you kill me?'

'I've never killed anyone,' lied Mao Dongzhu. 'You know I wouldn't kill you.'

She closed and locked the closet and let down the carpet.

'I take it you've been keeping her shut up in here for several years,' said the White Nun.

'Yes.'

'So what is the information you want to get out of her? It can only be for the sake of what she knows that you have kept her alive so long. As soon as you have it, presumably, you will kill her.'

'I am a Buddhist,' said Mao Dongzhu. 'The Lord Buddha forbids us to take life.'

'Do you take me for a three-year-old?' said the White Nun contemptuously. 'It is extremely dangerous for you to keep her here. She has only to cry out and you would be lost.'

'I tell her that if she does so I shall kill the Emperor. She is very loyal to him.'

'Why don't you use that threat to obtain the information you want?'

'She says if I do so she will stop eating and starve herself to death.'

'Come now,' said the White Nun, 'you still haven't told me what this information is that you want to get from her.'

The answer was still some time coming, and when it did it was only partly true. It did, however, to some extent, tally with what the White Nun had already learned from Aunt Tao. The Aisingioro clan, to which the Manchu Imperial family belonged, had started out in the Long White Mountains of Liaodong. Geomancers claimed to have demonstrated that their rise to power and eventual occupation of the whole of China was thanks to the favourable *feng-shui* of their old home. Anyone who dug up the Dragon Line in this area would be able to overthrow the Manchu power. The exact position of this Dragon Line was a secret that the Old Emperor had confided to his Empress—the woman locked in the closet—as he lay dying. This was the information that Mao had all these years been trying to extract from her.

'Geomancy is a superstition,' said the White Nun. 'It was misgovernment that brought down the Ming Empire. Oppression drove the people to rebel. This much I have learned during my travels. It had nothing to do with Dragon Lines.'

'I'm sure you are much cleverer than I am,' said Mao. 'Perhaps there is nothing in this Dragon Line business. On the other hand, suppose there is? Isn't it worth a try?'

'You are right,' said the White Nun. 'Even if there is nothing in it, the Tartars themselves seem to believe it. If we could get hold of the secret, it would certainly weaken their morale. So this is what you have been trying to find out from the Empress Dowager?'

'Yes,' said Mao, 'but no matter what I say or do, I can't get the wretched woman to tell me.'

The White Nun took out the copy of the *Sutra in Forty-Two Sections* from her bosom.

'You should try asking her where the rest of these are.'

Mao Dongzhu was visibly shaken.

'So you know about that too?' she stammered.

'The secret is in the Sutras, isn't it?' said the White Nun. 'How many more of them have you got?'

Mao was by now convinced that the White Nun must be clairvoyant and that it was useless to dissimulate any longer. Falteringly she told her, quite truthfully, that she had had three copies, one given by the Old Emperor to Lady Donggo which came into her possession when Lady Donggo died, and two that had formerly belonged to Oboi.

'But an assassin got into the Palace one night,' she said. 'He stabbed me and got away with all three of them. Look!'

To prove that she was speaking the truth, she unbuttoned her upper garments, tore off her breast-binder, and pointed to an ugly scar on her breast.

'I know who stabbed you,' said the White Nun, 'but the person who stabbed you didn't take the Sutras.'

'*Really*?' said Mao. 'Well, who can have taken them, then? It's very odd.'

She was genuinely startled and confused, but the White Nun thought she was play-acting.

'I don't know what game you're playing at,' she said coldly, 'and I can't really be bothered to guess. If you are a daughter of Mao Wenlong, you must almost certainly have some connection with the Mystic Dragon Sect.'

'I . . . I . . . I've never even heard of it.'

The White Nun stared hard at her for some moments.

'I am going to tell you a way of neutralizing the effects of the Soft Crush on your system,' she said. 'Three times every day, in the morning, at noon, and again in the evening, you must stand in front of a tree and strike it eighty-one times, and while you are doing that you must recite this mantra.' (She whispered some words into her ear.)

Mao Dongzhu delightedly kowtowed her thanks.

'From now on,' said the White Nun, 'if you ever use your Inner Force to inflict Soft Crush on anyone again, your bones will instantly begin crumbling and nothing on earth then can save you. Do you understand?'

'Yes,' said Mao Dongzhu in a barely audible voice and looking very much less cheerful.

The White Nun flicked her long sleeve, touching her on the Point of Consciousness. Instantly her eyes rolled up so that only the whites of them were visible, and she fell down in a faint.

Trinket and Aunt Tao came out from behind the bed.

'Now we must go,' said the White Nun.

'Let me first have a look for those Sutras,' said Trinket. 'You can't believe half of what that woman says.'

He made a pretence of searching, then, after looking almost everywhere else, he pulled the bedclothes off the bed, revealing, in the base of the bed, the little board with the inset ring in it. Under it was the secret compartment from which he had taken the Sutras.

'Look!' he said, triumphantly. 'The Sutras will be in here.'

He removed the lid with a flourish. Of course they weren't; but, to his surprise, the cubby-hole was full of jewels, silver, and banknotes.

'This stuff isn't much use to us,' he said.

'Take it,' said the White Nun. 'When the day of Restoration dawns, we shall need all the money we can get.'

Trinket wrapped up the little hoard of treasure in a piece of brocade and handed it to her.

'That woman is full of guile,' the White Nun told Aunt Tao. 'From now on you will have to watch her very carefully. Fortunately she'll no longer be able to do you any harm.'

Aunt Tao realized sadly that she was expected to stay in the Palace and was soon to be parted once more from her beloved mistress.

After painful farewells, the White Nun led Trinket over the wall once more and back to their hostelry. There she was able to give the Sutra she had taken a careful examination. It was the copy which the Old Emperor had given to Kang Xi and which the Princess had stolen from Kang Xi at her mother's behest. On the flyleaf, in large characters, the Old Emperor had written the words *Never Raise Taxes*. She showed them to Trinket and read them out to him.

'You see. You were right about that.'

Then she read through the text, which she already knew more or less by heart, from beginning to end; but she could find nothing in it out of the ordinary. Next she exposed the pages one by one to heat, in case there should be writing in invisible ink between the lines. When this yielded no result, she laid the book down on the table and stared at it for some minutes. Suddenly a thought struck her. The thickness of the book bore no proportion to its contents, which only consisted of a few pages. She tried soaking the front cover with water. After a while she was able to peel off the outer layer of yellow silk in which it had been bound. Underneath was a double thickness of parchment sewn together on all sides with thread. When she cut the thread, she found that the two layers of parchment made a sort of envelope containing about a hundred little cut-up pieces of thinner parchment which she removed and spread out on the table. The pieces were of all shapes and sizes, but all of them had markings on them, either red-ink lines or, in black ink, bits of Manchu script.

'This is it!' said Trinket excitedly. 'This is the secret! It's a map. But this will only be part of it. You have to have all the eight copies in order to make the whole map.'

'I think you are right,' said the White Nun. She put the pieces back into their parchment envelope, wrapped it in a cloth, and put it inside her bag.

Green Girl Again

They left the city next day and set out westwards for Changping. The tomb of the last Ming Emperor, which they were making for, was in the hills outside the town. The White Nun was silent throughout the journey. They found the tomb neglected, in a wilderness of grass and weeds. The nun's restraint finally gave way. Throwing herself down on the ground, she broke into noisy weeping. Trinket, too, knelt down on the ground and kowtowed. While he was doing so, he became aware of a shimmer of greenness at his side. Turning his head he saw, with a pounding heart, that it was a green skirt. As if in a dream he heard the gentlest, most enchanting of voices murmuring something.

'I'm so glad you're here,' said the voice. 'I've been waiting here three whole days.' This was followed by a sigh, then: 'Don't be so sad!'

It was the Green Girl!

'Oh, thank you for waiting,' said Trinket, scrambling to his feet and still half in a dream. 'I don't feel sad any more when I hear your voice.'

He gazed longingly at the lovely face with its expression of gentle concern, but only for a second. Its expression changed suddenly, first to confusion and surprise, and then to a look of anger and intense hatred.

'I've been longing so much to see you . . .' he was beginning to say, when a painful kick in the belly sent him sprawling and she was on him in an instant with her little sword. She would have sliced his head off if he had not rolled over in time. In fact the sword-point only pierced the ground.

'Stop it at once!' cried the White Nun, before she could strike again.

The Green Girl dropped her sword and threw herself, weeping, upon the White Nun's bosom.

'He's a *wicked* boy, Shifu,' she sobbed. 'He does nothing but humiliate me. You ought to kill him.'

Trinket was glad to discover that the Green Girl was the White Nun's disciple.

'Perhaps if I keep in Reverend Mother's good books, she'll help me to marry her,' he thought.

He got up and began to apologize, humbling himself and saying that he was sorry, he hadn't intended to wrong her and would she please try to forgive him. His answer was a hefty kick, delivered backwards, like the kick of a horse, which had him once more lying on his back, panting and unable for some moments to move.

'Ah Kor,' said the White Nun reprovingly, 'don't be so unreasonable! You can't just go kicking people the moment you set eyes on them!'

At last Trinket knew the girl's name.

'He's humiliated me many, many times,' she protested.

Trinket agreed that she had good reason to be angry with him. 'That time in the Shaolin Monastery . . .' he began.

The White Nun pricked up her ears.

'You were in the Shaolin Monastery, Ah Kor? What on earth were you doing there? You know that women aren't allowed.'

Trinket said he was sure she had been dragged there, much against her better judgement, by the Blue Girl, and that the monks she had injured were very much to blame. The news that her protégée had not only made an unauthorized visit to the Shaolin Monastery but had actually fought and injured monks there was making the White Nun seriously incensed; but just as she was about to give expression to her displeasure, she noticed the newly healed knife-wound across the girl's neck.

'Was *that* done in the fighting?' she asked.

The Green Girl had to admit that it was self-inflicted, an attempt to erase the dishonour inflicted on her by this hateful young monk. Once more Trinket admitted his guilt. He was hopeless at Martial Arts, he protested, and had been so scared of getting hurt when she attacked him that he had flailed his arms about in a panic and in doing so had inadvertently touched her in an improper manner.

The Green Girl blushed scarlet, but there was anger in her eyes.

'You see, it was not intended,' said the White Nun, patting

her gently on the shoulder. 'I don't think you should have taken it so seriously. He's only a boy, after all. And a eunuch,' she added shyly.

Trinket pursued his advantage by saying that, to compensate the Green Girl for having been refused entry to the monastery by the discourteous monks, he had invited her in and consigned her to the care of a respectable elderly monk to instruct and entertain her.

'Children, children!' said the White Nun, shaking her head. 'Who was this old monk?'

Trinket explained that Brother Simple was the monk in charge of the Prajna Hall. The White Nun nodded. The Green Girl tried to protest against this monstrous distortion of the true facts, but the White Nun ignored her and, turning her back, began silently contemplating the tomb. Trinket pulled a face and stuck his tongue out triumphantly at the fuming girl.

The three of them sat there until sundown, the White Nun contemplating her father's tomb in mournful silence; Trinket contemplating the Green Girl, feeling he would be happy to do nothing but gaze on that ethereal countenance for the rest of his life; the Green Girl in a misery of rage, embarrassment, and shame, trying, unsuccessfully, to ignore him but conscious that she was being stared at. After sitting for well over an hour, the White Nun rose to her feet.

'It's time to go now,' she said.

That evening the three of them lodged with a family of peasants. Trinket, knowing how fastidious the White Nun was, took great pains to see that there was no grime or grease to offend her, washing the bowls and chopsticks beforehand in hot water, wiping down the tables and benches, and sweeping and dusting in the room where she and the Green Girl were to sleep until everything there was spotless. Though such a lazy boy as a rule, to the White Nun he appeared industrious and thoughtful. Until the age of fifteen she had been brought up delicately as a princess, and although consciously she no longer set store by such things, unconsciously she was flattered and pleased by his attentions.

After the evening meal, the White Nun began asking about her other disciple, the Blue Girl, or Ah Ki, as Trinket heard them call her. The Green Girl had last seen her outside the Shaolin Monastery and unkindly suggested that Trinket might have killed her. When Trinket indignantly protested that he had seen her since then in the entourage of Brigadier Ma when the latter had visited the monastery in the company of Prince Galdan and the Grand Lama Sangge and their followers (he said nothing about the beard), the White Nun was not at all pleased to learn that a disciple of hers had been associating with a staff-officer of the detestable Wu Sangui. No doubt Ah Ki had at the time only just met these people, Trinket told her. However, if they could pick up the trail of any of the three personages just mentioned, it should eventually lead them to her. And since he was the only one who knew these people by sight, he would be happy to lead the search.

The White Nun thankfully accepted his offer, much to the disgust of the Green Girl, who knew that his concern for the Blue Girl was a sham and only an excuse to be near her. She resolved to rid herself of his company at the earliest opportunity.

The search for the Blue Girl began next morning. They started off in a southerly direction, as if they were returning to the Pure Coolness Monastery. Although Sangge was not among the lamas captured or killed in the abortive attempt to kidnap the Old Emperor, it was obvious that he must have been the brains behind it and was therefore likely to be, if not still in that area, at least not very far from it.

Lamas at the Inn

In the days that followed, Trinket continued to concern himself with the welfare of his two charges. He loved the Green Girl dearly, but dared not show it in the White Nun's presence. He never got a kind word out of her, and often when the White Nun wasn't looking, she would slip a sly punch or a kick in his direction; but he did not seem to mind. In spite of the kicks and punches, it was happiness enough just to be near her.

One day in Cangzhou, where, the evening before, they had put up at a little inn, he had gone out in the early morning to buy food for a breakfast which he intended to ask the servant in the inn to cook for them. Returning in high spirits after making his purchases—two pounds of cabbage, half a pound of bean curd 'skin', and two ounces of *koumo* mushrooms—he found the Green Girl standing in the doorway. He felt in his bosom for a little packet and held it out to her, smiling broadly.

'Here, I bought these for you,' he said. 'Sugared pine nuts.

They were selling them on the street. They're really tasty. I didn't think you could get anything so good in a little town like this.'

The Green Girl tossed her head.

'Anything *you* bought would be horrible. Anyway, I don't fancy them.'

This was a lie. He knew she loved sweet things but wasn't given enough pocket money by the White Nun to buy any. In the end she did accept the packet.

'Shifu is meditating,' she said. 'I'm feeling bored. Is there anywhere nice round here we could go to—anywhere quiet where there aren't any people about?'

Trinket could hardly believe that he was hearing this. Had she really relented at last? The blood was pounding in his ears.

'Aren't you still angry with me?' he asked.

'Why should I be? Are you coming for a walk, or do I have to go off on my own?'

She began walking away as she said this.

'Of course I am,' said Trinket, putting his purchases down inside the doorway and hurrying after her.

When they reached the edge of the town, she paused to look around.

'What about making for that hill?' she said, pointing in the direction of a low, tree-covered hill a mile or so south-east of the town.

'Yes, let's go there,' he said eagerly.

There was no conversation on the way, and when they got there, there wasn't really very much to look at. Just a lot of trees. But Trinket was anxious to please her.

'It's a beautiful spot,' he said.

'It isn't,' she said. 'Just a few rocks and trees. I think it's hideous.'

'Yes, I agree,' he said.

'Then why did you say it was beautiful?'

'I suppose it's because, for me, you make anywhere seem beautiful.'

The Green Girl sniffed.

'I didn't bring you here to listen to you talking a lot of drivel. It was to get rid of you. I want you to go away. Just go away. I don't ever want to see you again.'

His face crumpled, but he showed no sign of going. When

she began threatening him and he still didn't go, she took out the short-sword that she always carried with her and began slashing at him angrily. Though a very unsatisfactory pupil, Trinket had at least learned enough from Brother Simple to be able to stand up to her swordsmanship without getting hurt; but he could not go on dodging her sword indefinitely. In the end he took out the dagger from his boot and simply sheared off two-thirds of the blade. When she went for him with what remained of it, he could not retaliate with the dagger because he knew that the lightest blow from it might kill her, so he turned and took to his heels.

'Just clear off!' she shouted, as she pursued him down the hill. 'Go away, and I won't try to kill you any more.'

But then she saw, with dismay, that he was making back for the town. She wanted to head him off, but her inner training, like Trinket's, was non-existent. The White Nun had taught her some swordsmanship, but not how to cultivate her Inner Force. In a trial of strength, long-distance running for example, she could not hope to beat him. With tears of vexation, after running and running, she saw him enter the inn doorway ahead of her. As she came panting in after him, still clutching her truncated sword, some invisible force from inside the inn caused her to stumble and fall. Her fall was broken by something soft. She turned her head and saw that she was sitting on top of Trinket.

'Help me up!' she said crossly.

'I can't,' he said. 'I can't get up any more than you can.'

'You tripped me up deliberately,' she said.

Pressing a hand down heavily on his body to raise herself, the Green Girl got slowly to her feet and peeped in at the open door. She saw the White Nun sitting on the floor, defending herself with her one hand and her long left sleeve against a group of red-robed lamas—five, as far as she could make out—ranged opposite her with their backs against the wooden partition-wall. Although five against one, they seemed afraid of her. Each time one of them darted forward to strike her, some mysterious force which seemed to radiate from her would drive him back against the wall. It was this same force which had caused Trinket to lose his balance. It now caused the Green Girl to step quickly back from the doorway. She gave Trinket a kick.

'Aren't you going to get up? Shifu is being attacked.'

Trinket pulled himself up by holding onto the door and peeped inside. He could see that the lama nearest the doorway was holding a short cutlass—the kind they call a 'monk's knife'; but much as he wanted to help, he knew it would be useless for him to go inside. In desperation he picked up a broom that was resting against the wall and poked it sideways through the doorway, hoping to put the lama with the cutlass off his stroke, or, with a bit of luck, knock him over. The instant result was that there was a little jolt, and the head of the broom came flying out through the doorway, scratching his face in its passage and leaving him clutching the broomstick without the broom.

'You're *useless*!' said the Green Girl. 'Is that the best you can do?'

The wooden partition on either side of the doorway consisted of solid panels in the lower half but open lattice-work in the upper half. Whether from poverty, parsimony, or neglect, the openwork panels of the upper half had been left unpapered, so that it was possible to get a partial view of the lamas as they moved back and forth inside. Trinket got out his dagger and, crouching down so that he would be invisible from the room, waited until the lama with the cutlass had his back against the partition, then drove the dagger swiftly into the woodwork behind his back. The wood of the partition was less than an inch thick and the dagger, which could cut metal with ease, went through it like bean curd and drove several inches into the man's body. There was a sort of gurgling grunt and he slid downwards onto the floor. Surprised and delighted by his success, Trinket crept along a little farther, still keeping his head down, and shortly found an opportunity to deal in the same way with a second lama. At his third success the two remaining lamas were so terrified by what they believed to be the White Nun's magic powers that they made a run for the door. The White Nun leapt up and dealt the nearer of them a blow from behind. Instantly he began vomiting blood and sank dying to the floor. The second one, whom she could not reach with her hand, she brought down with a flick of her long sleeve, then, descending on him and quickly pressing five Vital Points on his body, she rendered him completely paralysed, so that he lay there as motionless as the other four.

She glanced at the three bodies lying side by side at the foot of the partition. From the wet patches on their red robes where the dagger had entered their backs and the holes in the wooden panels behind them she guessed at once how they had been killed. Then she looked back at the lama lying paralysed at her feet.

'You . . .' she said sternly, 'you . . . what do you . . . ?'

She began swaying on her feet. Trinket and the Green Girl rushed to catch her as she collapsed; but even as they caught her, a stream of bright blood came gushing from her mouth. Her prolonged resistance—one seated, unarmed woman against five men— had drained her of all her inner power and this final effort had proved just too much for her failing body. They carried her over to the kang and laid her down gently, supporting her head and shoulders so that she did not choke. Her eyes were tightly closed and her breathing barely perceptible. After a few moments she brought up a lot more blood. The Green Girl was terrified but could only cry helplessly, not knowing what she could do.

The innkeeper and his serving-man had removed themselves to a safe distance as soon as the fighting began. Now that it was quiet again, they came tiptoeing back and peeped inside the door. When they saw the pools of blood and bodies all over the floor they set up a great outcry and only stopped when Trinket, holding a lama's cutlass in either hand, told them, in the coarsest possible language, that if they didn't instantly shut up he would silence them himself. When they had quietened down, he got out two silver ingots each weighing five taels from his little store of treasure and handed them to the serving-man.

'We need a big covered cart to continue our journey. One of these should be enough for the hire. The other one is for you.'

The serving-man brightened, scarcely able to believe his luck, and ran off to hire a mule-cart.

Trinket counted out forty taels.

'Now,' he said to the innkeeper, 'I must settle for our lodgings. Bad men, those lamas, weren't they, fighting each other like that? I expect you saw with your own eyes how they killed each other.'

The man looked at the money, several times what he would normally have charged, gulped, and nodded.

'There we are,' said Trinket. 'I think that should just about cover what we owe you.'

Presently the serving-man returned to announce that a large mule-cart and driver were waiting outside. Trinket took a quilt from the kang to wrap the White Nun in and he and the Green Girl carried her outside and laid her down gently inside the covered cart, nearest the driver's end.

'You stay here and look after her,' he told the Green Girl before going inside again.

He got the serving-man to help him carry the immobilized lama and lay him in the back of the cart, not forgetting to first ask for a length of rope to tie him up with in case the paralysis wore off while they were travelling. Then, before himself getting in beside the lama, he told the mule-driver to follow the main road southwards until otherwise instructed.

After they had gone about three miles, the Green Girl called out to Trinket to tell the driver to stop. Trinket saw that she was crying.

'Shifu's breathing is getting fainter and fainter,' she said. 'I'm afraid—' She was unable to finish.

Trinket moved back to look. The White Nun was barely breathing. She seemed to be very close to death.

'If only there was something we could give her,' said the Green Girl tearfully.

Trinket suddenly remembered that he was still carrying in his pocket the little bottle containing the thirty Body Strengthening Pills that the King of Korea had given to the fake Empress Dowager (and which she in turn had given to Trinket to take to the Leader and Madame Hong). He took it out and shook two of the pills on to his palm.

'These might help,' he said. 'They're supposed to work very fast.'

He somehow got them into the White Nun's mouth and the Green Girl poured a little water from her water-bottle between her lips. The effect was miraculous. Within a matter of minutes she gave a little sigh and opened her eyes.

'I've just given you two pills, Reverend Mother,' said Trinket. 'They seem to have done you some good. Let me give you another two.'

The White Nun shook her head.

'Enough—for today,' she said, speaking very faintly. 'Let me get out.'

Trinket rolled the trussed-up lama out of the way and they helped her down from the cart. She sat down cross-legged on the grass at the side of the road and closed her eyes. Realizing that she wanted to meditate in order to restore some of her inner strength, they sat, in respectful silence, at some distance away from her. The Green Girl watched her anxiously, not taking her eyes off her. Trinket for his part gazed at the Green Girl until, becoming aware of his gaze, she blushed and looked cross.

After a while they noticed that the White Nun was breathing regularly. A few moments later she opened her eyes.

'We can go now,' she said, still speaking very faintly.

'There's no hurry,' said Trinket. 'Rest a bit longer.'

'No need,' she said.

Trinket wanted to give her the little bottle with all the rest of the pills, but she refused to take it. When it became clear that no amount of persuasion would induce her to accept it, they helped her back into the cart and continued their journey.

After they had been travelling for another mile or two, the White Nun told Trinket that they should find some quiet, out-of-the-way place where they could stop and interrogate their prisoner. Trinket ordered the mule-driver to head towards a little fold in the hills, out of sight of the main road. When they were there, he got the man to help him lift the lama out of the cart and lay him on the grass at the foot of the slope, with his head a bit higher than his feet. Then he told him to unhitch the mule, take it round to the other side of the hill to graze, and not come back until he was called.

Making sure that the lama could see what he was doing, he took out his dagger, cut a branch from a nearby thicket, and proceeded to trim off the twigs and branchlets until only a stout stick remained.

'See?' he said. 'Trimmed. You want to be trimmed?'

The man's eyes had followed each movement, bulging with terror.

'Not want,' he said.

'All right,' said Trinket. 'You talk then, eh?'

'Talk,' said the lama.

'What's your name?' said Trinket. 'Name.'

'Name Hubayin,' said the lama.

Hubayin was cooperative, but the information took a long time (and about a hundred questions) to extract. It appeared that they had set out from Peking, ten of them in all, to capture the White Nun and force her to hand over a copy she held of the *Sutra in Forty-Two Sections*. (It took a while to establish this, because Hubayin was more familiar with the Tibetan title of the Sutra.) He didn't seem to know what the special importance of this copy was. He said that their leader was the Grand Lama Sangge. Trinket remembered that this was the name of the lama he had been introduced to, along with the Mongol prince Galdan and Brigadier Ma from Yunnan, when he was a monk in the Shaolin Monastery. It was pretty obvious, though Hubayin didn't know this, that Sangge must have been prompted to undertake this expedition by the false Empress Dowager, since only she would have known that the White Nun had taken a copy of the Sutra from the Palace. Hubayin knew nothing about the Blue Girl.

Trinket calculated that Sangge and four other lamas must still be at large and probably not very far away. If, as seemed likely, they went to the inn to find out what had become of the other five, it was quite possible that they might soon be on their track. This was alarming. The White Nun was certainly in no condition to face an attack by another five lamas, and he and the Green Girl would be quite unable to defend her. He climbed inside the cart and told her what he had discovered. The White Nun shook her head sadly.

'Even if I were better,' she said, 'I couldn't take on the five of them. I've heard of Sangge. Of all the Tibetan Tantrics, he is known to be the most formidable.'

Somewhat diffidently, for he was afraid she might find it beneath her dignity, he unfolded a plan of escape. It was that they should buy some clothing at the first market town they came to, disguise themselves as peasants (the White Nun could be a widowed mother travelling with her son and daughter), and ask for lodgings at some farm where they could stay until she had fully recovered her strength.

The Green Girl intensely disliked the idea of posing as Trinket's sister, but the White Nun could see the sense of the plan, only insisting that, in adopting it, she should pass herself off not as a mother of children but as an aunt travelling with her nephew and niece. That decided, Trinket called back the mule-driver who re-harnessed his mule and helped him lift Hubayin back into the cart. Then, as soon as Trinket himself was in the back, they set off once more on their journey south.

On the Road with Sir Zheng

They had not been on the road again very long when they heard the sound of hooves in the distance. It sounded as if a sizeable company of horsemen was coming up behind them, riding at speed, because the sound was growing louder by the moment.

'Damnation!' thought Trinket. 'It's the lamas. It doesn't sound like five, though: more like a dozen.'

But when the horsemen came in sight, he breathed a sigh of relief. These were not red-robed lamas but laymen in black: a person of some importance attended by twelve mounted companions. As they overtook the cart, he heard the Green Girl cry out excitedly.

'Zheng! Sir Zheng!'

The leader of the company reined in his horse and waited for the cart to catch up with him. A slatted blind in the side of the mule-cart was rolled up and the dashing Sir Zheng, an extremely handsome young man of twenty-three or so, trotted along beside the cart and leaned down to talk to the girl inside.

'Miss Chen! What a surprise! Is Miss Wang with you?'

'No.'

'Are you going to Hejianfu? If you are, we can travel together.'

'No, I'm afraid not.'

'Oh, you should. It will be lots of fun.'

'Why? What's happening in Hejianfu?'

Trinket noticed with a pang that the Green Girl's cheeks were flushed with excitement. He had never seen her like this, so happy and so animated. It was clear that she had known this young Sir Zheng for quite some time and that he occupied a high place in her affections.

'We can't go to Hejianfu,' Trinket muttered. 'We're trying to escape.'

Either his remark was inaudible or the other two ignored it.

'It's the big Rat Trap Congress,' said Zheng.

From the conversation that ensued, Trinket gathered that this was the code name for the meeting of all the different anti-Manchu groups to plan joint action against the Satrap Wu Sangui. As Master of the Green Wood Lodge, he had once heard the Helmsman discussing plans for the meeting with the other Masters. The Green Girl was eager to take part.

'Shifu, *may* we go?' she asked the White Nun pleadingly.

Trinket didn't wait for the reply.

'If those lamas catch up with us, we're done for,' he said. 'Our best plan is to hide.'

'What lamas are those?' asked Zheng, pricking up his ears.

'Sir Zheng, I want you to meet my Shifu,' said the Green Girl. 'She has been attacked by some lamas and is seriously hurt. The ones who were attacking her she killed or captured, but five of the group they belonged to are still around and they are out to get us.'

Zheng whistled to his companions to halt. The mule-driver stopped the cart and Zheng jumped off his horse and leant inside it to introduce himself. He was the grandson of Marshal Zheng, it seemed, that famous Coxinga who took Taiwan from the Dutch and held it for the Ming Court in exile. The Marshal, created Prince of Yanping by one of the Ming Pretenders, had died in the first year of Kang Xi's reign. The present Prince of Yanping and ruler of Taiwan was the Marshal's son Zheng Jing. Trinket's Shifu, the Helmsman, was the Prince's military adviser. This young Sir Zheng was the Prince's second son and younger brother of his Heir Apparent. His full name was Zheng Keshuang.

The White Nun was not nearly as impressed as the young man had hoped she would be when she heard who he was. She merely made some polite remark about his being 'of loyal stock'. He could not know, of course, that she was an Emperor's daughter, to whom his princely grandfather was merely one of her father's generals. When she went on to ask him under what teacher he had trained, he told her that he had had not one teacher but three. She was a little shocked by the disrespectful way in which he referred to the first two of his teachers, but it transpired that one of them, an army officer called Shi Lang, had surrendered to the Manchus.

'If I ever meet him again, I shall kill him,' he said, looking even more dashing as he said it.

The third one, under whom he had already been training for ten years, was a professional called Feng, also known as the Blood-less Sword because of his superior swordsmanship which enabled him to kill an opponent without drawing blood. The White Nun had heard of this paragon.

'You don't need to worry about those lamas,' he said. 'We're thirteen against their five; but even if we didn't outnumber them, my men would be more than a match for them fighting just one to one. They are the pick of our fighting-men on Taiwan.'

The White Nun wasn't so sure, but held her peace. She had already half made up her mind to travel with them. Disguise and concealment, enabling her to rest and recuperate, would no doubt have been the best course, but she was not going to dress up as an old peasant in the presence of this dashing young nobleman and his twelve companions. After a little hesitation she consented to travel in their company to Hejianfu.

Trinket cursed inwardly. The insufferable Sir Zheng was older than him, taller than him, and more good-looking and well-spoken than him. And he was the son of a prince. ('Loyal stock!' he thought. 'I haven't got any stock at all!') Worst of all, the Green Girl was fond of him. And if the White Nun knew that he, Trinket, was young Zheng's rival for her hand, she would probably kill him on the spot for even daring to think about marrying her.

Now that it was decided that they should travel together, the blind was lowered and they resumed their journey. Young Zheng continued to ride beside the mule-cart, but his companions divided themselves into two groups, six of them riding ahead of the cart, the other six bringing up the rear. They took a right turn at the next junction as they were journeying westwards now, in the direction of Hejianfu.

About midday they arrived in Fengerzhuang, one of the larger market towns of West Hebei, and decided to look for somewhere to eat. When they had found a place and had all dismounted, Trinket saw just how much taller young Zheng was than himself and how magnificently dressed. His companions, too, were big, swaggering fellows, full of arrogant self-assurance.

Inside the eating-house the Green Girl helped the White Nun to a small table and, when she had got her seated, sat down herself at one of the sides next to her. Young Sir Zheng sat at the side opposite the Green Girl. Trinket was about to sit down in the remaining seat, opposite the White Nun, when the Green Girl scowled at him and told him to sit elsewhere.

'There's plenty of room over there,' she said. 'You can't sit here. I shan't be able to get my food down if I have to sit next to you.'

Trinket blushed scarlet and, with rage in his heart, went to sit alone at a distant table.

The White Nun was shocked.

'Ah Kor,' she said, 'why are you always so rude to that boy?'

'He's horrible, Shifu,' said the Green Girl. 'There's nothing so bad that he wouldn't do it. If it weren't for you, I would kill him.'

Trinket heard all this from his table and entertained dark thoughts of waiting until Zheng and the Green Girl were married, then killing Zheng and magnanimously consenting to take the widowed Green Girl as his wife. When the food was served, Zheng's companions, who were sitting all round him, fell on it like hungry wolves. Trinket was so disgusted that he took some of the steamed buns that had been served with the meal and went outside to feed Hubayin, who was still lying trussed up in the cart. Hubayin's company seemed preferable to that of Zheng's bully-boys inside. After feeding him a few of the buns, he went in again and, from his distant table, gloomily contemplated the Green Girl and young Sir Zheng happily chattering and laughing together while the White Nun ate silently between them.

Sa-sa-satisfaction!

While he was picking without much appetite at his food and trying to think of some way in which he might widow the future Lady Zheng without her finding out that it was he who had murdered her precious husband, his thoughts were suddenly interrupted by the sounds of a party of horsemen arriving and dismounting outside. A moment later five red-robed lamas came into the eating-house. The tallest and thinnest of them he thought he recognized as the Grand Lama Sangge whom he had last seen in the Shaolin Monastery in the company of Galdan and the Brigadier. As soon as they caught sight of the White Nun, they began talking excitedly to each other in their foreign language. The one whom Trinket had identified as Sangge gave an order and the five of them sat down at a table near the door and ordered a meal. From time to time, while they were waiting, they would glance round in the direction of the White Nun with angry looks. Presently one of them got up and marched towards her table.

'Hey, you! Nun!' he said in a voice loud enough for everyone in the eating-house to hear. 'It is you kill my friends?'

Young Sir Zheng leapt to his feet.

'What do you mean by it, shouting at people like that? Have you no manners at all?'

'You are *who*?' said the lama angrily. 'I talk with nun. This not your business. You fuck off!'

In a trice four of Zheng's followers leapt up and rushed on the lama to seize him, but they were quickly disposed of. Two of them he swept aside with his right arm, one he sent flying with a mighty kick, and the fourth he smashed on the nose with his fist, so hard that the man sank bleeding and unconscious to the floor.

'Right! Get in formation!' shouted one of Zheng's eight remaining men, and all eight of them jumped up, drew out their swords, and stood shoulder to shoulder for a fight. The lamas, too, drew out their monk's knives, all except Sangge, who continued to sit at his table looking on. He and his lamas, and Trinket and the White Nun's party were now the only diners left, the others having all retreated at the earliest sign of an affray.

A small mêlée now took place in the middle of the eating-house, in which, amidst the sounds of tables being overturned, crockery being smashed, and the clash of weapons, it was for a time hard to tell what was going on. Then quite suddenly there was a cry and one of the men's swords went flying upwards and lodged itself in the ceiling. This was followed by another sword and then another. Trinket watched in astonishment as, one by one, each of young Zheng's followers was disarmed in this novel manner.

'On knees!' shouted one of the lamas. 'Surrender, or cut off heads!'

But the men had courage enough to continue. Some of them put up their fists and some of them picked up benches to defend themselves with. The four lamas went back to where Sangge was sitting and flung down their knives so that they stuck quivering in the table. Then they moved in a slow and deliberate manner towards the men. Presently there were shrieks and cries and Trinket realized with horror that the lamas were systematically breaking the men's legs. Soon all of them lay groaning and helpless on the floor amidst the overturned tables and the broken crockery. To begin with Trinket had felt rather pleased to see Zheng and his companions being humbled, but now he was really frightened and wondered whose turn it would be next. The lamas went back to their own table, however, pulled out and resheathed their knives, and sat down as if nothing had happened.

'Waiter!' Sangge shouted towards the kitchen. 'Let's have some wine! What's happened to our dinner?' (Unlike the lesser lamas accompanying him, Sangge spoke fluent Chinese.)

He called several times, but there was no response.

'Holy yak butter!' shouted one of the lamas. 'Not bring dinner, we burn house down!'

This threat brought the proprietor to the kitchen door.

'Yes, yes, Your Reverence, immediately,' he said, and turned to address the trembling waiter inside. 'Quickly, boy, quickly! Take the wine and the dishes to Their Reverences!'

Trinket looked to see how the White Nun was reacting to this sudden change of fortune. She was slowly sipping tea from her cup and appeared to be totally unaware of what was going on around her. The Green Girl, on the other hand, was ashen-faced and there was terror in her eyes. Young Sir Zheng's hue was changing from blue to white by turns. He was standing with his hand on his sword, but the hand was trembling. Though honour told him that he should fight, it seemed uncertain whether honour or fear would prevail. The sinister Sangge observed this with a mocking laugh and, getting up from his table, went over to confront him. Young Zheng jumped back a pace and held up his sword in front of him.

'Wha-wha-wha-what do you want?'

His voice was husky with fear.

'What I want has to do with this nun here and nobody else,' said Sangge. 'Who are you? Are you her disciple?'

'No,' said Zheng.

'In that case, if you know what's good for you, you'll keep your nose out of this,' said Sangge.

'I mu-must ask you for your name,' Zheng stammered. 'I shall be requiring sa-sa-sa-, sa-sa-sa—'

'What will you be requiring? Satisfaction?'

'Ye-yes.'

Sangge threw his head back and roared with laughter. When he had finished laughing, he flicked the sleeve of his robe in young Zheng's face. Zheng made a feeble pass at him with his sword, whereupon Sangge, with the greatest of ease, knocked the sword flying from his hand, seized him by the collar, and forced him down on to a bench. Then he pressed a point on the back of his neck so that he could no longer move.

'Now sit there like a good boy!' he said, and returned, laughing, to his own table to rejoin the other lamas.

The lamas had now incapacitated Zheng and all twelve of his followers, yet still not laid a finger on the White Nun. Trinket couldn't understand what they were waiting for. The fact is they were scared of her. They believed she was solely responsible for the deaths of all five of their fellows in the Cangzhou hostelry, and having caught up with her at last, were simply observing her, not quite sure what they would do next.

Now that things had finally quietened down a bit, the waiter came in with some plates of food and a jug of wine. The wine-cups were quite large ones and by the time the waiter had half-filled all of them, the jug was empty. One of the lamas banged on the table angrily.

'This all wine we get? This not enough!'

The waiter, who had been trembling to start with, hurried back to the kitchen, now almost fainting with terror. Trinket had a sudden inspiration and slipped in after him. The lamas seemed scarcely to notice his departure. Even Sangge, who had met Trinket once before at the Shaolin Monastery when he had been posing as a monk, paid no attention to this little rich boy.

In the kitchen Trinket found the waiter trying to pour wine from a wine-jar into the jug, but his hands were shaking so badly that very little was going inside it. Trinket took out a small ingot of silver and held it out to him.

'Don't be afraid!' he said. 'Look, you can take what I owe for my meal from this. The rest is for you. Let me give you a hand with that wine.'

He reached for the wine-jar, which the waiter yielded up gladly, scarcely believing that the world could contain so kind a benefactor.

'Tricky bastards, those lamas!' said Trinket. 'You never know what they'll do next. Better go and see what they're up to.'

The waiter obediently went to the kitchen door to look. While he had his back turned, Trinket took from his inside pocket a paper packet containing some of the strong opiate that he always carried with him for emergencies, and emptied the entire contents into the jug. He had just finished swishing it round to dissolve the powder when the waiter came trotting back.

'They don't seem to be doing anything,' he said. 'Just drinking.'

'Here you are, then,' said Trinket. 'Better hurry. Don't want them getting angry again and burning the place down!'

The waiter went off with the wine-jug, invoking blessings on this kind young gentleman. One of the lamas snatched the jug from him and poured out another round.

'Not enough,' he said. 'Go get more!'

Trinket watched from the kitchen as they drained their cups.

'Donkeys!' he thought. 'This is one of the oldest tricks in the book. Anyone on River and Lake could have told them to watch out for drugged wine.'

One of the lamas, a big, fat fellow, had a weakness for girls. He had been itching to get his hands on the beautiful Green Girl from the moment he set eyes on her and it was only fear of the White Nun that had held him back. Already half-drunk before imbibing the drugged wine, he now, under the influence of the drug, completely forgot about his fear and went lurching over to accost her.

'Not married, girlie?' he said with a leer and reached his fat hand out to touch the smooth skin of her cheek. The Green Girl was trembling all over but managed to get out her sword. Before she could use it, however, he had seized and twisted her wrist. The sword dropped to the ground. The lama gave a great laugh and threw his arms around her. She screamed and struggled, but he only tightened his embrace.

During these last few moments young Zheng had begun to feel the sensation returning to his limbs. Now, desperate to help the Green Girl, he clung to the edge of the nearest table and attempted to raise himself to his feet; but the fat lama saw him. Still holding the struggling girl in his right arm, he lashed out with his left fist and sent young Zheng rolling on the floor.

Trinket knew that the drug would soon take effect—in fact, he couldn't understand why it had not done so already—but seeing the fat lama kissing and nuzzling the Green Girl's cheek, he could bear to wait no longer. While the other lamas' attention was fixed on their lecherous colleague, he extracted the dagger from his boot and hid it in the long sleeve of his jacket, then, ambling over with a big grin on his face, as if to show that he found the girl's plight a joke, he jovially accosted her tormentor.

'Hey, Brother,' he said, stretching out an arm towards him and delivering what any onlooker would take to be a playful dig in the back, 'what's your game, eh?'

The incomparably sharp blade slipped through his sleeve and through the fat lama's ribs, transfixing his heart. Trinket withdrew it, chuckling, and stepped aside.

'What's the big idea, Brother? Aren't you afraid of what my Shifu's going to do to you?'

The fat lama crashed to the floor, still clutching the Green Girl in his arms. When Trinket knelt down to release her from his embrace, he somehow contrived to slip the dagger back inside his boot without any of the others noticing what he was doing. Then he prised open the arms of the dead or dying lama and helped the Green Girl to her feet.

'Ah Kor,' he said (it was the first time he had ever spoken her name), 'quickly! Come with me!'

He took the White Nun's arm with his other hand and, accompanied by the two of them, one on either side of him, made

for the door, stopping only to shout at the other lamas as they
lurched towards him:

'Stand where you are! My Shifu has the power to strike each
one of you dead. You see what she's already done to your fat
friend?'

The lamas stopped uncertainly, swaying slightly. At that very
moment there was a thump, followed, moments later, by another
thump. The drug had finally taken effect and two of the lamas had
fallen unconscious to the floor. By the time Trinket and his womenfolk had reached the door, there had been two more thumps as
two more lamas hit the ground. This left only Sangge. He tried to
stop them, but his legs seemed out of his control and his head was
swimming. Before he could reach the door, he collapsed on top of
a table, so hard that it gave way beneath him.

'Sir Zheng, Sir Zheng!' cried the Green Girl as they made their
way outside. 'Come with us, quick!'

'I'm coming,' croaked Zheng and, struggling with some difficulty to his feet, he staggered after them.

Outside the eating-house there was only Hubayin in the cart,
looking thoroughly scared: the mule-driver was nowhere to be
seen. Trinket helped the White Nun inside, and the Green Girl and
Zheng got in after her. There was no time to look for the mule-
driver, so Trinket got up on the driver's seat at the front, took up
the reins, and cracked the whip. The mule started without a second
bidding, and off they went, making for the open road.

In the Sorghum Field

After they had been bowling along at speed for about three miles,
the mule began to tire and they were forced to slacken the pace. As
ill luck would have it, it was just at that moment that they began
to hear, still faint in the distance, the sound of pursuing horsemen.

'Pity we didn't take the horses,' said Zheng. 'The lamas would
never have caught up with us then.'

'The Reverend Mother can't ride,' said Trinket. 'And anyway,
who invited you to come with us in the cart?'

No one had ever spoken to the young nobleman like this
before, but as things were, there was nothing he could do but
swallow his indignation.

'Reverend Mother,' said Trinket, 'we'll have to get out and
hide.'

He looked around. They were in the open country now, not a house or a barn in sight. To the right, however, there was a field of newly-harvested sorghum. All over the field, at intervals of ten yards or so, the tall sorghum plants, none less than eight feet high, had been laid together in tent-like stooks to dry.

'We could hide in one of those,' said Trinket.

'How can I do that?' said Zheng. 'If my people got to hear of it, I should be a laughing-stock.'

'You can stay in the cart and drive on, to draw the lamas off the scent,' said Trinket.

While he was saying this, he was helping the White Nun down from the cart. He began making his way across the field with her leaning on his arm. The Green Girl stood wavering, torn between the White Nun and Sir Zheng.

'Come on, Ah Kor!' said the White Nun.

The Green Girl followed, calling to Zheng as she went.

'Come and hide with us, *please!*'

Zheng followed the other three and crouched down with them inside one of the stooks. But no sooner had they done so than Trinket remembered the cart and went running back. It was useless to hide so near Hubayin and the cart. Both, in different ways, must be disposed of. There was nothing else for it. He took out his dagger and looked into the back of the cart, intending to dispatch the lama with one swift blow. Unfortunately, since Trinket last looked at him, Hubayin's paralysis had worn off and he had succeeded in freeing one of his arms. When Trinket bent over him with the dagger, the lama clutched his sleeve in terror.

'No good,' said Trinket. 'Sorry!' and he forced the blade down into his chest.

After one or two convulsions the lama was still, but the hand continued to clutch Trinket's sleeve. Now every second counted. There was no time for remorse. Swiftly withdrawing the dagger from the lama's chest, Trinket sliced off the hand with it, severing it neatly at the wrist; then, dashing forward to the front of the cart, he poked the dagger into the mule's backside. The wretched animal kicked up its hind legs and went dashing forwards, clattering along the road at a tremendous pace with Hubayin in the cart behind it. Trinket raced across the field, still holding the severed hand, and plunged into the stook where the other three were hiding. He wasn't quite sure what to do with the hand. Perhaps he could use it later, he thought, to play some trick on Zheng. Crouching with the others in the darkness, he got out a large handkerchief, wrapped the hand in it and stuffed it inside his gown.

Inside the rick they were huddled close together. Trinket quickly discovered that young Zheng was the person next to him and that the Green Girl was on Zheng's farther side. Determined, even in this emergency, to have some fun at his rival's expense, he suddenly let out a high-pitched squeal and claimed that Zheng had been fondling his person.

'Do you mind, Sir Zheng! That's *me* you've got hold of. Keep your dirty hands to yourself!'

Then he reached behind him and fondled the Green Girl's waist.

'Sir *Zheng*!' the Green Girl exclaimed in a very shocked voice.

When this little pantomime was repeated a few moments later, Zheng, while protesting his innocence, endeavoured to move away a little and in doing so exposed one of his legs outside the rick.

Trinket had chosen a bad moment for his horseplay, because it coincided with the arrival in the vicinity of one of their pursuers. Sangge had never entirely succumbed to the opiate. He realized that they had been drugged and had retained sufficient presence of mind to call for the help of the waiter. After several dowsings of cold water, he had sufficiently recovered to attend to the resuscitation of his followers. All of them revived after three or four buckets had been emptied over them, all, that is, except the fat lama, on whom they continued to pour water until it became obvious that he was dead.

Sangge and these three survivors, not waiting to burn down the eating-house as they had promised, threw themselves on their horses and galloped off westwards down the road that the others had taken. One of them, who had far outstripped the others, was passing the field of sorghum, looking about him as he rode, when his eye chanced to light on what looked like a human foot at the base of one of the stooks.

The lama reined in his horse and dismounted. Keeping his eye on the foot—he was sure that it had moved a little—he walked stealthily across the field until he was within reach of it. He thought he could hear voices in the stook. Then a pounce, a tug, and out came Sir Zheng, a little rumpled and still protesting his innocence, in all his finery.

'Nun in there?' said the lama, dragging Zheng to his feet.

'This is bad,' thought Trinket. 'He'll have us *all* out in a minute.'

The lama was holding the front of Zheng's jacket in both his hands and shaking him. Trinket saw in a flash that this was his only chance of saving them. Dagger in hand, he leapt out of the stook and struck. The lama felt an intense pain in his back and went down without ever knowing what had hit him.

'Now,' said Trinket to Zheng, 'we've got to hide him. Give us a hand! We haven't got much time.'

He began throwing sorghum-stalks on the fallen lama and Zheng, after a moment's hesitation, followed his example. But it was too late. Sangge and the other two lamas were already visible on the road, and from their shouts and gestures it was evident that *they* had already seen *them*. There was nothing for it but to stand where they were and try to think of a ruse.

Soon the lamas were striding towards them across the field. They stopped at some distance away from them, however. At first Trinket wondered why, but then it dawned on him. It was the lama's body they had just noticed, half concealed beneath the straw. Even the crafty Sangge must believe that the White Nun had supernatural powers. Already she had eliminated seven of their number—or so it would seem to Sangge—the last two without even raising a finger.

'You see what my Shifu's powers are like?' he called to Sangge. 'She's really very merciful, though. She's willing to forgive you and not harm you if you will only go away and leave her in peace.'

'She knows perfectly well what she must do if she wants to be left alone,' said Sangge. 'She must hand over her copy of the *Sutra in Forty-Two Sections*.'

'Oh, *that*?' said Trinket. 'She's given it to *him* to look after.'

He pointed to young Zheng.

'No, she didn't,' said Zheng. 'I haven't got it.'

Sangge's two subordinates seized hold of Zheng and began feeling him all over. Then they began tearing off his clothes, ripping each garment apart to make sure that there was nothing in the linings, until he was stark naked.

'I told you, I haven't got it,' he said and began pulling his now tattered garments back on again.

'Where have you hidden it, then?' said Trinket. 'I know she gave it to you. What have you done with it?'

One of the lamas grabbed Zheng by the arm and dealt him a hefty slap on the face.

'Where it is? You tell!'

'I've told you already,' said Zheng. 'I haven't got it. I've never had it. I don't know where it is.'

The lama hit him again, even harder, on the other side of the face.

'Tell!'

'Didn't I see you burying something behind that eating-place?' said Trinket. 'Was that it? Why don't you tell them?'

'I think the boy is telling the truth,' said Sangge. 'We had better take this man back to the town.'

'Yes, better,' said the lama, and planted another hard slap on Zheng's already swollen face.

This was more than the Green Girl could bear. On hands and knees she pushed her way out of the stook and began shouting distractedly as she clambered to her feet.

'Don't listen to that boy! He tells nothing but lies. Sir Zheng has never seen that Sutra. He knows nothing about it.'

'I was trying to save you both,' Trinket muttered. 'Don't you care about your Shifu?'

Sangge motioned to the lama who was holding Zheng to stop hitting him. He wanted him in one piece.

'I think we should all go back to look,' he said. 'We'll take the children, too.' He addressed the stook: 'You, too, nun, you had better come with us.'

Trinket noticed that he didn't go any nearer the stook, although he had guessed that she was inside it.

'Let me go in and tell her,' he said.

Sangge made no objection. When Trinket crawled in, the White Nun was waiting with outstretched hand.

'Take this,' she whispered.

She was holding a little bag. Trinket recognized it as the bag in which she had put the cut-up pieces of map extracted from the Sutra's binding. Judging that her situation was now hopeless, she had resolved to die; but before she died, she wanted to leave the precious fragments with someone she could trust. Trinket felt immensely proud that she was giving them to him and not to her own disciple.

'Tell them I won't come out,' she said. 'If I can, I shall try to think of some way of saving you all. But I won't come out. I won't show myself to those lamas.'

Trinket put the bag inside his gown and crawled out again.

'She won't come out,' said Trinket. 'She says she refuses to go with you.'

'We'll see about that,' said Sangge.

He beckoned to the other two lamas to come closer, still keeping Zheng as their prisoner, and join him in a little huddle. Trinket and the Green Girl were left standing by the stook in which the White Nun was hidden, while the lamas squatted by another stook about ten or fifteen yards away, jabbering to each other in Tibetan. Puzzled, Trinket saw them get up, tear several sheaves of dried sorghum from it, and then squat down again. He didn't remain puzzled for very long, however. Soon Sangge had produced a little flame with a tinder-box he was carrying and was lighting the end of a sheaf. He hurled it as far as he could, but it fell short of the stook in which the White Nun was hiding. It lay on the ground blazing harmlessly, though making a great deal of smoke.

'We must get her out of here,' said Trinket to the Green Girl. 'You will have to help me.'

The far side of the field was bounded by a low cliff in which there was a little cave. With a bit of luck and sufficient smoke to obscure their getaway, they might get the White Nun out of the stook before it caught fire and run with her towards this cave.

He dived inside the stook.

'Reverend Mother,' he said, 'I've found a better hiding-place.'

He half-dragged her through the far side of the stook to where the Green Girl was waiting. She took the nun's other arm, and between them they began hurrying her across the field. It was a near thing. The second sheaf of burning sorghum landed right at the foot of the stook and soon flames were shooting up from it twenty feet into the air. Fortunately, as well as flames, there was so much smoke, and the breeze blew the smoke about so capriciously, that the three of them were halfway to the cave before the lamas could see that they had got away.

But when they reached the cave, they were not much better off than they had been before. This was for two reasons. The first was that the cave turned out to be a very shallow one, little more than a deep hollow in the side of the cliff, so that even when they were inside it, they were fully visible to anyone in the field, and far from affording them protection, it merely cut off their retreat. The second was that, although their flight across the field had been largely obscured by the smoke, the lamas had seen enough to guess that the White Nun was either ill or wounded, since she seemed to move with some difficulty and to need support. She therefore no longer appeared to them as an invulnerable enemy possessed of supernatural powers but as a weak woman whom they could fairly easily overcome. They hurried across the field to the mouth of the cave. Yet some residual fear of her still remained, for they did not venture in to lay hands on her, but piled up some sorghum stalks and prepared to smoke her out.

'Reverend Mother,' said Trinket, 'I think we're going to have to give them the Sutra. After all, it's no use to anyone without the pieces of map.'

'You are right,' said the White Nun, handing it over to him. 'Do with it as you think best.'

Trinket knelt down with his back to the others, laid the Sutra on the ground in front of him, and got out the severed hand, glancing over his shoulder from time to time to see how far the lamas had got in their preparations. When he had unwrapped the hand, he took out his dagger and cut some strips of flesh from it which he laid carefully on the Sutra. By this time the lamas had lit the sorghum and it was beginning to blaze. Smoke drifted towards the cave making their eyes water and causing them to cough.

'Hey!' he called out over his shoulder. 'I've got the Sutra here. If you don't put that out, I'll throw it in the fire.'

'That will keep them busy for a while,' he thought, taking out the little phial of Decomposing Powder. He didn't know if the powder would take effect on living bodies, but he thought it was worth a try. He remembered that there had to be blood for it to start working, which is why he now shook some of it on the flesh he had sliced from the hand. He glanced out at the lamas, who were throwing flat stones and earth on the burning sorghum and stamping out the flames, then back at his handiwork. The flesh strips were sizzling slightly and oozing yellow droplets. So far so good, but he needed a little time. He got to his feet and stood with the other two to face the lamas.

'Throw out that Sutra *now*!' shouted Sangge, when the fire was thoroughly extinguished.

'My Shifu will let you have it if you'll promise to use it properly,' Trinket called back. 'It's very precious. It comes from the

Palace. There's a secret locked up inside it, and anyone who can unlock it will have the power to convert the whole world to the Buddhist faith.'

He glanced down behind him at the Sutra. The strips of flesh were fast dissolving in a pool of yellow liquid.

Sangge knew that the secret contained in the Sutra had nothing to do with the propagation of the faith; but he also knew that the copy he had already sacrificed so much to obtain had in fact been taken from the Palace, and he was sure this was the one. He was trembling with excitement to think that it was now almost within his grasp.

'Tell your Shifu, the conversion of the world is very dear to my heart,' he said.

'My Shifu read through this copy of the Sutra, but she couldn't discover the secret,' said Trinket. 'She says that if *you* are able to discover it, you must promise to share it with monks and nuns everywhere, not just be selfish and keep it to yourselves.'

'Of course,' said Sangge. 'Tell her she can set her mind at rest. I am perfectly willing to give that undertaking.'

'If *you* can't work out what the secret is,' said Trinket, 'she says you are to hand it over to the Shaolin Monastery. And if the monks of the Shaolin Monastery can't make it out, they are to hand it over to the Pure Coolness Monastery on Wutai. And if the monks on Wutai can't make it out, they are to hand it over to the Zen Wisdom Monastery in Yangzhou.'

'Certainly,' said Sangge. 'I promise to abide by all of these conditions.'

It seemed obvious to him from all this that the White Nun had no inkling of the Sutra's real value. They could make what conditions they liked! Once he had the Sutra, he would dispose of the lot of them.

Trinket glanced down once more and was delighted to see that the flesh had entirely dissolved and the yellow liquid had been absorbed into the cover of the book. He doubled up the cloth in which the hand had been wrapped to protect his own hands with while he picked it up.

'Here it comes, then—your precious Sutra!'

He lobbed it for Sangge to catch, then hurriedly threw away the cloth. But Sangge suspected a trap and allowed it to fall to the ground. It was the other two lamas who picked it up, pouncing on it, and fighting each other to hold it and have a look.

'Hey, you guys!' Trinket shouted. 'Look at you! You've got centipedes on your faces!'

The lamas instinctively brushed at their faces with their hands but could feel nothing there. Stupid brat, they thought. They took the book over to Sangge.

'Look, Father,' (they were speaking Tibetan now), 'is this the book we have been looking for?'

'Let's take it over there,' said Sangge. 'We need to have a good look to make sure they haven't given us a fake.'

They sat down with it at some distance from the cave.

'It's wet,' said Sangge. 'We'll have to be extra careful we don't tear the pages.'

He began turning them over carefully, using only the tips of his fingers. While they were all looking at the book, one of the lamas unconsciously scratched his neck and suddenly became aware that his fingers were itching. Sangge and the other lama, too, felt their fingers itching, but at first paid no attention. The itching grew more insistent, however, and when they looked, they noticed that the tips of their fingers were wet with some yellow liquid.

'Strange!' they said. 'Where's this coming from? Surely it's not from the book?'

At that point the cheeks of Sangge's two companions started itching unbearably and they began furiously scratching themselves. When Sangge looked up from the book, he saw that there were bloody scratch-marks on both men's cheeks. The itching of his own fingers was now intolerable. Then he realized what the cause was and dropped the book in horror.

'Aiyo!' he cried. 'The book is poisoned!'

The yellow liquid was dripping like blood or sweat from his fingers. He wiped them frantically on the ground. The scratch-marks on the faces of the other two were now deep red furrows. Their cheeks not only itched now but hurt as well. When they saw blood on their finger-ends and drops of greasy yellow liquid dripping from their chins, they began to howl and scream and presently threw themselves to the ground, clutching their heads and writhing in agony.

In Sangge's case it was only his fingers that were affected, but finding that the tips were no better for all his dabbing and wiping and that they continued to ooze yellow liquid, he tore off his robe, wrapped the poisoned book in it, and rushed off with it under his arm to look for water.

Trinket was relieved to see Sangge run off into the distance, but the sufferings of the other two were more than he had bargained for. A quick thrust through the ribs with his dagger would, he thought, be doing them a kindness; but just as he was about to act on this merciful impulse, the men jumped up, mad with pain, and began running round in circles. Then, as if acting on the same impulse, they rushed to the cliff and began banging their heads against it. They banged and banged until both of them were unconscious.

It was then that Trinket ran over to finish them off. But the sight that met his eyes was so terrible that for a while he stood gazing down in horror, trembling too violently to carry out his purpose. The men's faces had been completely eaten away: eyes, lips, cheeks, nose were gone, leaving only traces of red scum and a few sinews on the white bones.

Presently Zheng, who had been lurking at some distance behind the lamas, came over to look at them and was promptly sick. Then the Green Girl came to join Zheng and, though warned not to look, did so out of curiosity and screamed. Even the White Nun, who seldom betrayed any emotion, gave a shudder at what she saw. She looked from the faceless bodies of the two lamas to the body of the other dead lama across the field, now charred and blackened, beside the burnt-out stook. She thought of Hubayin and those other ones who had died in the hostelry. How many more thousands or tens of thousands must die, some of them as terribly as this, before the Ming dynasty could be restored? She wondered if that was really what she wanted.

CHAPTER 18

*In which Sir
Zheng is taught
more than One
Lesson*

Trinket becomes a Disciple—Again

For some time the White Nun remained lost in thought. When she at last looked up she was shocked to see that Trinket, who had quickly recovered from his fright, was grinning triumphantly. She was grateful to him for saving her life—and probably her honour too, for the lamas, she felt sure, were no respecters of virginity—but killing people, though sometimes, as in this case, it was unavoidable, ought never, she thought, to be a source of satisfaction.

'When you were speaking to those lamas, you referred to me as "Shifu",' she said. 'In the school of Martial Arts I belong to we study only clean methods of fighting. I am grateful to you for saving our lives, but if I were really your Shifu, I would never allow you to practise the sort of murderous, underhand methods you have been using today. I hope you're not going to keep using them in the future.'

'I won't,' said Trinket. 'It's only because I'm no good at clean methods that I've had to fall back on dirty ones.'

'You say you're no good at clean methods of fighting,' said the White Nun, 'but surely you must have learned a few things all that time you were in the Shaolin Monastery? What about that Brother Simple you were telling me about? He must have taught you a thing or two.'

'All he taught me was how to avoid being killed by Ah Kor,' said Trinket.

'Well, I suppose now you've started calling me "Shifu", we'd better make it official,' said the White Nun.

At once Trinket was on his knees kowtowing. Eight times he bumped his head on the ground, each time calling out 'Shifu!' in a loud voice.

'Now that you are my disciple, you will have to behave yourself and keep the rules,' said the White Nun with a little smile. 'The school of Martial Arts I belong to is called the Iron Sword School. It's a Taoist school. Although I am a Buddhist nun, my Shifu was a Taoist. My name in religion is "Tribulation".'

Trinket was already a disciple of the Triads' Helmsman Chen Jinnan and it was entirely against the rules that someone who already had a Shifu should, unless he had special permission to do so, acquire another. But Trinket cared nothing for such niceties. As long as he could be near the Green Girl, he didn't care how many rules he had to break.

The Green Girl saw how pleased he was looking and pulled a face. She knew very well why he was so pleased and was mortified to think that now he was a fellow-disciple she could no longer try to kill him or attempt to drive him away with kicks and blows. It seemed like the last straw when the White Nun told her that the two of them must from now on call each other 'Brother' and 'Sister'. She dared not tell him what she thought of him in front of her Shifu, but she glared at him with hate in her eyes.

'You really must try to let bygones be bygones, Ah Kor,' said the White Nun. 'Remember, the poor boy is very unfortunate. He was forced to become a eunuch. You ought to feel sorry for him. It's an advantage now of course, because it means that there's no harm in the two of you being together. But you must keep this to yourself.'

For the Green Girl this information was a solace. She had previously thought of Trinket only as an evil-minded little monk. If he was a eunuch, his former behaviour towards her now seemed less heinous. She still didn't like him, but her anger against him was somewhat assuaged.

'How are you, Sir Zheng?' she said, turning to the real object of her affection. 'Are you badly hurt?'

Zheng came limping up to them.

'Not too bad,' he said. 'I think I must have pulled a muscle in my leg.'

'Shifu,' said the Green Girl, 'what are we going to do now? Are we still going to Hejianfu?'

'I suppose we might as well go, to see what happens,' said the White Nun. 'But there's a danger that the Grand Lama Sangge might come back. I'm still not very mobile.'

'Wait here and rest, Shifu,' said Trinket, 'while I go and look for a carriage.'

But the best he could do after scouting round in the neighbourhood was an ox-cart which he bought from a farmer. The White Nun and the other two sat in the cart while Trinket trudged along beside the ox. It was a very slow way of travelling. At the first little market town they came to they abandoned it and hired a couple of carriages. Trinket now had the White Nun to himself. He managed to persuade her to take some more of the Korean medicine and by the time they arrived in Hejianfu at midday two days later she had almost recovered her strength.

The Rat Trap Congress

In Hejianfu, as soon as they were installed in an inn, young Zheng went off to inquire about the congress. He returned about two hours later looking very downcast. He had been everywhere in the town asking about the Rat Trap Congress, he said, but no one had even heard of it.

'How did *you* first hear about it, Sir Zheng?' the White Nun asked him.

'The Shen brothers, who are supposed to be organizing it, got the Triads to send news of it to my father in Taiwan inviting him to send a representative,' said Zheng. 'They said it was to be held on the fifteenth of this month. There are only four days to go. I was expecting an official welcome. At the very least I thought the brothers would be waiting for me.'

'Perhaps they have found out that the Tartars have prior knowledge of the congress, so they have had to change the date,' the White Nun suggested.

'In that case they ought to have let me know,' Zheng said crossly.

But just at that moment a waiter came in to say that there was someone outside asking for him and he hurried out to see who it was. He returned much later, all smiles. The Shen brothers had come in person to meet him, he said. They were full of apologies for not having contacted him sooner, but they had been expecting him to arrive with a large escort and had been waiting several days for him outside the town. That very night they would be throwing a big party to welcome him. He hoped that his friends, too, would attend.

The White Nun shook her head.

'No, I think it would be better if you went alone. I'd rather you didn't say anything about my being here, either.'

Zheng was disappointed.

'I can understand that Your Reverence might not like the noise and excitement of a party,' he said, 'but what about your disciples? Perhaps they could come with me.'

'No, I think not,' said the White Nun. 'I'd rather we waited here until the congress opens and then go there together.'

That night Zheng came back very much the worse for drink. Some time around midnight the twelve members of his escort, who had last been seen lying, most of them unconscious, on the floor of the Fengerzhuang eating-house, came limping into the inn, some of them with a leg or an arm in splints and one or two of them on crutches. Altogether they presented a sorry sight.

Next morning Zheng treated the White Nun, Trinket, and the Green Girl to a full and glowing account of the party he had been to. He made much of how respectfully the Shen brothers had treated him, how he had been made to sit in the place of honour throughout the banquet, how everyone had praised his family for keeping the flag of resistance flying in Taiwan, and much else touching on his own importance. The White Nun asked him about the other guests who had been present, but he seemed unable to remember a single one of their names. After several unsuccessful attempts at extracting some useful information from him, she fell silent, concluding that the intelligence of this dashing young gentleman did not quite match up to his good looks.

In the remaining days before the congress the White Nun strictly forbade her two charges to go out of doors. She feared that with so many underworld characters about in the town they might get into trouble. Young Sir Zheng, however, was out almost continuously being entertained by this or that River and Lake celebrity, so that they hardly saw him until the day of the congress.

When the great day arrived, an hour or two before they were due to set out, the White Nun dressed herself up in some clothes that Trinket had bought for her. She tied a black kerchief round her head and disguised her face by rubbing a brownish powder into it and painting on a pair of heavy, downward-sloping eyebrows. Trinket and the Green Girl dressed themselves in the simple clothes of a country boy and girl. For his part, young Sir Zheng, scorning disguise, laid aside his false pigtail and put on the magnificent court dress of a high-ranking Ming nobleman. Even the White Nun, in spite of her low opinion of him, was impressed, though the flood of nostalgia brought on by this sight caused her as much pain as pleasure. The Green Girl was enraptured. Trinket muttered under his breath that he looked like a baboon in fancy dress.

The congress was, for reasons of security, planned to take place at night, beginning at nine o'clock in the evening. Promptly at eight o'clock a large carriage provided by the Taiwanese delegation drew up at the inn and conveyed the splendid Sir Zheng and his three dowdy companions to the place where the congress was meeting. This was a small, level plain called the Locust Field, a mile or two outside the walls of Hejianfu, surrounded by hills and bordered with locust trees. Normally it was used by the townsfolk and the people from the villages round about for fairs and festivals.

In spite of the darkness they could make out the large audience that had already assembled, augmented at every moment by new arrivals. Young Sir Zheng's arrival was greeted with applause and as soon as he stepped down from the carriage he was swallowed up by a crowd of enthusiastic supporters and carried off into the middle of the field. But the White Nun and her young charges quickly made for the edge of the field, where the three of them sat down under the locust trees in a place from which they could see without being seen. Soon a full moon began to rise up into the sky and details of the assembly became more distinctly visible. Seeing so great a multitude all dedicated to the extermination of Satrap Wu, Trinket began to wonder if the Triads and the Mu faction, who were in friendly rivalry to see which of them could accomplish this aim the soonest, might not both of them be beaten by some third group from among those present.

When everyone had finally got settled, a tall, very venerable old man rose to his feet and introduced himself. The White Nun whispered that he was the father of the two Shen brothers who had been a redoubtable warrior some twenty-odd years before this time. Trinket noticed that she appeared to be quite moved and guessed that she must have met him some time in the past when she was a young girl. When, in his introductory address, he came to the object of their meeting, a chorus of voices rose up from the audience calling Wu Sangui every foul name under the sun and invoking curses on him and all his family up to the eighteenth generation of ancestors. A high, boyish voice was heard after the shouting had abated, uttering an imprecation even more frightful than those which had so far been employed. It sounded so incongruous that the whole assembly burst into a great roar of laughter. The voice was, of course, Trinket's. The Green Girl was quick to express her disgust.

Shortly after this, refreshments provided by the Shen family were distributed in the form of cold beef, wheatcakes, and wine. There was comparative silence for a spell while the assembly regaled itself. Then, fortified with the wine, they set to again, excitedly shouting out the various things they would like to do to Wu Sangui if they had him in their power. At this point Old Shen rose to his feet once more and called for silence.

'My friends,' he said in his clear, ringing voice, surprising in one of his years, 'most of us here are crude fighting men, willing to shed our blood for the cause, but having little knowledge of politics, statecraft, or strategy. We are fortunate in having with us tonight the most distinguished scholar of our age, Mr Gu Yanwu, who, ever since our beloved land was taken over by the Tartars, has devoted all his time and energy to travelling up and down the country recruiting our best brains to join with him in planning for a Restoration.' He gestured to the gaunt-faced, elderly individual standing at his side. 'Mr Gu Yanwu, my friends. I am sure you will want to make him welcome.'

This was the Gu Yanwu who, with his friends Lü Liuliang and Huang Zongxi, was rescued by the Helmsman Chen Jinnan when the boat in which they were travelling to Yangzhou was taken over by government agents at the beginning of our story. As we saw then, he was a rare example of a scholar with a wide acquaintance of all classes of people and a sympathetic understanding of them, which meant that he was able to address this largely unlettered audience without talking down to them and in such a way that they felt valued and uplifted and willing to do anything he suggested to them with as much enthusiasm as if they had thought of it themselves. Gu Yanwu could see at once that what his audience chiefly lacked was organization and a proper sense of security. Personally he did not set much store on a national movement devoted solely to the elimination of an individual, but as he could not very well tell them this, he proposed an organization which could be used to expel the Manchus and bring about a Ming Restoration after this first objective had been accomplished. What he had in mind, he told them, was a nationwide 'League for the Eradication of Traitors' or 'Eradication League'—they agreed at once that this sounded more dignified than 'Rat Trap League'—which should have branches in each of the eighteen provinces. Each provincial branch would elect its own representative, but the affiliated societies and associations who elected him would keep their existing leaders and not be in any way subordinate to him: he should be thought of as an organizer who would regularly confer with representatives from the other provinces and pass on the outcome of their deliberations to members of his own branch. Gu knew that among the fighting-men in his audience there were some very temperamental individuals who would resent any challenge to the authority they held over their own communities.

There were one or two questions from the audience. A Triad whom Trinket recognized as Butcher Qian from his own Lodge asked which branch the Triads ought to join, bearing in mind that they had members in every province. Gu suggested that each Lodge should affiliate with the branch of the province in which it was located. When this and one or two other questions had been dealt with, his proposal was adopted with enthusiastic applause, and at

Old Shen's suggestion the audience at once split up into groups and proceeded to elect representatives for each province.

'Which province do we belong to, Shifu?' Trinket asked the White Nun.

'None,' she said. 'I work on my own. I like to come and go as I please. I have no need to join any society.'

'Someone like you deserves to be head of the whole League,' said Trinket.

'In future I'd rather you didn't say things like that,' said the White Nun.

The field was now dotted with separate little crowds of voters, but there were several dozen individuals wandering about aimlessly in the spaces between them. Evidently the White Nun was not the only loner. Neither Gu Yanwu nor Old Shen made any attempt to press these independent spirits into joining a group.

After a while the results of the separate elections were declared. Among those elected were the Abbot of the Shaolin Monastery, Father Wisdom, the representative for Henan Province; the Little Countess's brother Mu Jiansheng to represent Yunnan; young Sir Zheng had been chosen for Fujian; Old Shen for Shanxi; while no fewer than three provinces were to be represented by Lodge Masters of the Triad Society. When the newly elected representatives assembled, it was found that only thirteen of them were present, the rest having been elected in their absence. After conferring together for some minutes they decided to co-opt two Honorary Presidents to act as their military advisers. Gu Yanwu was invited to become one of them; the other one was to be the Triads' Helmsman, Chen Jinnan, who was not present at the meeting.

The different groups were still discussing plans for the assassination of Wu Sangui when the White Nun and her charges slipped from the field and made their way back to the inn.

Sir Zheng is taken down a Peg or Two

Early next morning they hired a carriage and began the eastward journey to Peking. The White Nun was still wearing her disguise. She knew that the roads would now be full of River and Lake figures of one sort or another making their way back home. Some of them might have known her in the past and she did not want to be recognized.

Trinket was happy to be leaving Zheng behind, a fact which the Green Girl was quick to notice. When she reproached him about it, he teased her by pretending that he had run into Zheng in the street that morning when he went out to hire a carriage, laughing and talking with four very good-looking girls.

'He told me to give you and Shifu his regards.'

'Oh?' said the Green Girl. 'Why didn't you tell me before? What else did he say?'

'He said the girls are Martial Arts enthusiasts. He's promised to take them back to Taiwan with him to see the sights.'

The Green Girl suppressed a sob.

After travelling until about midday, they stopped at a noodle shop beside the road to break their fast. As they were about to start on their noodles, a group of horsemen rode up and dismounted outside.

'Chicken, beef, and noodles!' one of them shouted as they entered the shop.

Trinket recognized them as they came inside and sat down. They were all Triad friends from his own Lodge: Brother Xu (the Eight-Armed Ape), Butcher Qian, Big Beaver, old Brother Li, the taciturn Brother Feng, Gao Yanchao, Brother Fan, and the Taoist Father Obscurus. He had recognized Butcher Qian at the meeting the night before, but hadn't seen any of the others. He decided that it would be best not to make his presence known to them. If they got talking, it would soon emerge that he had acquired a new Shifu, which would be sure to upset them. He kept his head down and avoided looking in their direction.

No sooner were the Triads settled than another party of horsemen was heard arriving and issuing identical orders to the proprietor.

'Chicken, beef, and noodles for all of us. And be quick about it! We're in a hurry!'

The Green Girl brightened instantly as they came clumping in.

'Sir Zheng!'

'Miss Chen! Your Reverence!' cried young Sir Zheng as he hurried over to their table in response to her call. 'I looked for you everywhere this morning, but I couldn't find you.'

The restaurant was a small one, and while Zheng stood by their table talking, his followers were looking for somewhere to sit.

'Hey, you, old fellow! Why don't you lot squeeze up together and let us have this table?' one of them shouted rudely to Brother Xu.

'Damnation!' said Father Obscurus, always quick to take offence. 'Who the hell does he think he is?'

Brother Li, who remembered seeing Zheng in his princely Ming costume the night before, leant over and whispered to him:

'They're our folk—the Taiwan lot. Better not quarrel with them. We can let them have this table.'

Brother Xu, Big Beaver, Brother Gao, and Brother Fan got up and went to sit with Brother Feng.

Meanwhile, Zheng had seated himself next to Trinket and the Green Girl at the White Nun's table.

'What a liar you are!' the Green Girl hissed to Trinket. 'I knew you'd made that up about the four girls.'

'All right, all right,' said Trinket. 'I know you can't eat comfortably if I'm sitting next to you. I'll go somewhere else.'

He picked up his bowl and chopsticks and went over to squeeze himself in beside Brother Xu.

'Brother Xu, it's me,' he whispered. 'Can you tell the others? I don't want to be recognized.'

Brother Xu gave a little start, and for a moment his eyes lit up with pleasure; beyond that, though, he gave no sign of recognition and turned back at once to his noodles.

'The Master's here,' he muttered from the corner of his mouth. 'Pass it round.'

Soon all the Triads knew that the Master of Green Wood Lodge was in their midst. They were delighted to have him with them, but not one of them so much as glanced in his direction.

Meanwhile young Sir Zheng was in great form, holding forth to the White Nun and the enraptured Green Girl in a voice that could be heard all over the restaurant.

'At the meeting last night they chose me to be the representative for the Fujian branch. We were up all night discussing—you know—the big job. I didn't get back to the inn until after dawn, and by that time you'd already gone. I'm awfully glad I've managed to catch up with you.'

'I must congratulate you on your election, Sir Zheng,' said the White Nun politely, 'but surely these secret matters ought not to be mentioned in public?'

'Oh, there's no one here that matters,' said Zheng loudly.

'These rustics wouldn't know what I was talking about even if they were listening.'

The Triads had disguised themselves as peasants. All of them were bare-footed and one or two had brought rakes or hoes with them which they had propped up against the wall.

'Loud-mouthed turtle-head!' said Trinket. His head was bent over his noodles and he was speaking in a low voice, just loud enough to be heard by the others at his table. 'You should have heard the things he was saying about us Triads back in Hejianfu: how one of our Masters used to empty the piss-pot for his grandfather; how our old Master Yin wasn't much of a fighter so it wasn't surprising he got killed; how he's always the boss over the Helmsman when there are meetings—a whole lot of stuff like that. And I've heard him telling people what some of our passwords are.'

These were all lies, of course, but seemed of a piece with Zheng's overbearing manner and his apparent readiness to relay information about last night's meeting to an unknown woman. Big Beaver was with difficulty restrained from banging on the table.

'I think he needs to be taught a lesson,' said Trinket. 'Brother Feng, could you do it, do you think? Don't hurt him seriously; just show him a thing or two. So that he doesn't get roughed up too badly, I'll come over after a bit and pretend to rescue him. You'll have to let me win.'

Brother Feng nodded.

Now that the Triads were looking for a fight, they didn't have long to wait for provocation. Two of Zheng's followers had still not found seats, and one of them, spotting a place vacated by Butcher Qian, who a moment before had got up and left the room, came up behind the Eight-Armed Ape and tapped him on the shoulder.

'Look, there's still room there. You could give us another table.'

Brother Xu jumped up in a rage.

'I've had just about enough of this. We've already given you a table. If there's one thing I can't stand it's young toffs pushing poorer people around.'

He turned his head and spat, seemingly at random, into the air; but in fact it was a well-aimed gob, landing, with great precision, on the back of young Sir Zheng's neck.

'Muddy-footed oaf!' Zheng shouted angrily as he took his

handkerchief out and wiped it off. 'These creatures have no respect for anything or anyone. That fellow wants a good thrashing!'

One of his followers aimed a blow at Brother Xu with his fist. Brother Xu put on a great performance, falling over and rolling about on the floor almost before he was hit.

'Oh! Oh!' he hollered. 'He's killing me!'

Zheng and the Green Girl laughed out loud.

Brother Feng rose purposefully to his feet.

'What are you laughing at? What's so funny?'

'I suppose I can laugh if I like,' said Zheng angrily. 'What's it to you anyway?'

Brother Feng reached out and dealt him a resounding slap on the face.

Recovering from his surprise, Zheng fell on him with both his fists; but Brother Feng, dodging from side to side, retreated backwards through the restaurant and out of the door, with Zheng still bearing down on him. Outside he continued to duck and weave, punching and kicking, but rarely making contact with Sir Zheng or sustaining more than a light touch from Zheng's blows.

The other Triads were anxious that their identity should not become known, since by laying hands on Zheng they were in effect breaking their allegiance to the Society's most senior patron.

'Keep it up!' Brother Li shouted to Brother Feng. 'It's for the honour of the Sitting Ox Mountain boys. Don't let yourself be beaten by a stuck-up pretty boy in fancy dress!'

'The Sitting Ox Mountain boys are in luck today,' said Brother Xu, catching on to the idea. 'We don't even have to go looking for business, it's fallen straight into our laps. He'll fetch a good ransom, this one, if we nobble him. His father will give a million to get him back.'

Now that it appeared that these bare-footed ruffians were not farmers but brigands from the neighbouring hills, Zheng's followers took out their swords and prepared to cut them down; but they would have been no match for the Triads even if they had not still been suffering from the effects of their recent brush with the lamas. Within a couple of minutes they had been disarmed and herded into a corner, where a couple of Triads with swords could keep them in order.

Both to avert suspicion and to avoid inflicting serious injury on his adversary, Brother Feng gave a convincing impression of clumsiness, several times stumbling and once or twice nearly trip-ping over. Zheng, on the other hand, anxious to make a good impres-sion on his girlfriend, was showing off all his skills. The Green Girl was sure that her hero would give the clumsy brigand a trouncing and cheered him on enthusiastically. When the White Nun told her that the 'brigand' was the better fighter of the two and only playing with his opponent, she was incredulous. As if to prove the White Nun's point, Brother Feng suddenly changed his tactic. There was a loud sound of tearing fabric and Zheng found to his surprise that his splendid embroidered jacket had been almost ripped in two. This was followed by another tearing noise and then another, until the young man's fine clothes were in ribbons and his body was scarcely decent. Brother Feng then seized him by the wrists, pulled him towards him, gripped him round the lower part of the body, gave a heave-ho, and threw him up sideways into the air.

'Catch!' he shouted to Father Obscurus, who was standing at no great distance away.

Father Obscurus caught him and threw him to Brother Gao, Brother Gao threw him to Big Beaver, and two or three other Triads spread themselves out in a circle in order to join in the game. Trinket watched them, laughing, until a sharp rap on the back of the head from the Green Girl's knuckles put an end to his laughter. She began to upbraid him, and by the time their bickering had ended the Triads' ballgame was over. They had tied Zheng's hands behind his back and were loading him on to a horse.

'Hey!' one of them shouted. 'You folk had better hurry up with that ransom. We'll be giving him three hundred of the best every day until we get the money. The longer you delay, the more he gets beaten.'

'You hear that?' said the Green Girl tearfully, impulsively seizing Trinket by the hand. 'Just travelling to Taiwan and back to get the money from his father will take more than a month. He'll never stand up to so much beating.'

'What will you do if I save him?' said Trinket. 'Will you marry me?'

'Why start that nonsense again?' said the Green Girl. 'There's nothing you can do anyway.'

She began crying even louder.

'As a matter of fact, there is,' said Trinket. 'But I'll only save him on one condition.'

The Green Girl stopped crying, uncertain whether to believe him or not.

'What condition?'

'You must stop being nasty to me.'

'All right,' she said. 'Only hurry!'

Trinket stepped forward.

'Sitting Ox Mountain boys,' he said, 'I'd like a word with you.'

'Certainly, little brother,' said Gao Yanchao. 'What do you want to ask?'

'Why do you need this money?'

'There are a lot of us up there on the mountain,' said Brother Gao, 'and we've run out of supplies. We need this million to set ourselves up again.'

'No problem,' said Trinket. 'I'll lend it to you.'

Brother Gao laughed.

'Easily said, little brother, but how do I know I can trust you? Who are you, anyway?'

'Trinket Wei,' said Trinket.

'Aiyo!' said Brother Gao in mock surprise. 'Little White Dragon! The hero who killed the Manchu Champion.' He clasped his hands and made a profound bow. 'Honoured to make your acquaintance.'

Trinket bowed in return.

'The honour is mine.'

'We'll release the young man, of course, since he's with you,' said Brother Gao. 'Forget about the money.'

Brother Xu was meanwhile fishing a large ingot of silver from an inside pocket. He presented it respectfully to Trinket with both his hands.

'Just in case you should run out of cash on your journey, Mr Wei, would you do us the honour to accept this little present?'

'That's very kind of you,' said Trinket, graciously receiving the ingot and handing it to the Green Girl. She took it from him round-eyed, her mouth agape with wonder. Never would she have thought it possible that this evil little monk whom she so despised and detested could be a person of such great consequence that even fierce bandits deferred to him. But the farce was not yet over.

'One moment!' said Brother Feng dramatically. 'Can we be

sure that you really are who you claim to be? Can you give us some proof?'

'Certainly,' said Trinket. 'What sort of proof do you want?'

'Well,' said Brother Feng, 'if it's not too presumptuous to ask, could you demonstrate one or two of your techniques? The Manchu Champion's killer is sure to be a great expert in the Martial Arts. If you really are the famous Trinket Wei, though, I must ask you to go easy with me. I don't want to get hurt.'

'I'm not all that good,' said Trinket modestly. He was laughing inwardly to think that Brother Feng, normally not so much a man of few words as a man of no words at all, could, when he was play-acting, become so voluble.

Brother Feng took up a defensive stance. Trinket, having taken up a stance facing him, darted his left hand forwards as if about to poke him with his finger, simultaneously performing a complicated circling movement with the palm of his right hand which ended in a downward chop. In pretending to defend himself, Brother Feng very nearly succeeded in falling over backwards. The attack that Trinket had used was a Prajna Hand technique taught him by old Brother Simple.

'That's a "Praj . . . Prajjer" something-or-other, isn't it?' said Brother Feng. 'Brilliant!'

Trinket followed with one or two more Prajna Hand techniques which were found equally impressive.

As a matter of fact, the Triads were genuinely surprised, not only that he knew about these techniques, but that he could execute them so stylishly. He was a quick learner and had picked up quite a few things during his Shaolin stay, which of course they knew nothing about. But his knowledge was superficial. As he was too lazy to practise anything, he had never built up either the muscular strength or the inner power to make proper use of it. If he had been fighting seriously, these fancy flourishes he was demonstrating would have proved totally ineffective.

Brother Feng and the Triads now professed themselves wholly convinced that Trinket was indeed the heroic slayer of the evil Manchu Regent. Young Sir Zheng was handed over, and after an exchange of courtesies and an invitation to Trinket to visit them on Sitting Ox Mountain whenever he liked, the Triads mounted their horses and rode away.

The Green Girl was now seeing Trinket in a new light.

'I seem to have misjudged him,' she thought. 'All those times

I beat him or got the better of him, he must have been deliberately letting me do it.'

The wretched, tattered Sir Zheng was obliged to thank Trinket for coming to his rescue.

Sir Zheng eats Humble Pie

They were now able to resume their journey. Towards evening they put in at a large inn in the county town of Xianxian in Hebei. The White Nun called Trinket to her when the Green Girl was out of the room to question him about the morning's happenings. She had not been taken in by the little pantomime he had put on with the Triads and guessed that they were friends of his.

No, he told her, they weren't his friends.

'If they're not your friends,' she said, 'why did they pretend to let you do as you liked with them? They are obviously highly skilled fighters whom you could not possibly have stood up to if they had been really trying.'

'Probably they were offended by Sir Zheng's uppity way of behaving,' said Trinket. 'I think they only wanted to teach him a lesson. I don't think they really wanted to hurt anyone.'

This explanation seemed to satisfy her, for she did not pursue her questioning. Trinket decided to go out and buy something nice for her supper. Outside he nearly ran into Zheng and the Green Girl who appeared to have left the inn just a little before he did. They were sauntering along very affectionately, shoulder to shoulder. Trinket experienced a pang of jealousy.

'Why are you following us?' the Green Girl asked when she became aware that he was shadowing them.

'I'm not,' he said. 'I've come out to buy vegetables for Shifu's supper.'

'Oh, come on, Sir Zheng,' she said. 'We'll walk in *that* direction.' She pointed towards some high ground beyond the west wall of the town.

When Trinket returned to the inn from his shopping, Zheng and the Green Girl were still not back. He was gloomily imagining the romantic tête-à-tête they were no doubt enjoying when someone came up behind him, threw his arms round him, and addressed him laughingly.

'Trinket, old fellow! What are you doing here of all places?'

He turned his head round to look. It was Dolong, Intendant

of the Palace Guards, his nominal Chief. There were a number of other Guards officers with him, all of them, like Dolong himself, dressed in privates' uniforms. It transpired that all of them except Dolong had been sent to look for Trinket by the Emperor, who had been anxiously awaiting news of his favourite ever since the mysterious figure in white ran off with him from the Pure Coolness Monastery. Dolong had decided to join them, partly out of affection for his young friend and partly, as he put it, 'to get outside for a bit'.

It seemed that they had found out about the Rat Trap Congress and two of their number had infiltrated it in disguise. They knew about the newly founded League. They even had the names of several of the regional representatives. They knew that the representative for Yunnan was the Little Countess's elder brother, Young Count Mu, and that young Sir Zheng, or 'Zheng Keshuang, the son of the rebel leader in Taiwan' as they called him, was the representative for Fujian. Trinket inquired nervously whether they would be able to recognize these representatives if they saw them again.

'No,' said Dolong. 'It was too dark for our fellows to see them properly. We only know their names.'

'I've got a favour to ask,' said Trinket.

'Fire away, Colonel!' said the guards. 'Any little job you want doing we shall be only too pleased to carry out for you.'

He had been extremely generous with them in the past and they knew that anything they did for him would be rewarded.

Trinket explained that a certain young lady in whom he had taken an interest was being led astray by a slippery and most undesirable young man. Could they, without harming the girl, find some means of discouraging the young man? Short of crippling or permanently injuring him, of course. Without naming names, he gave them as good a description as he could of Sir Zheng and the Green Girl and an indication of the general direction in which he had seen them going. Dolong and his companions were both indignant on Trinket's behalf and tickled at the prospect of what looked like being a bit of fun. While Trinket went to give the vegetables he had purchased to the cook and instruct him about the dishes he wanted prepared from them, the men went off, laughing and joking, to look for the errant pair.

When Trinket had finished giving his instructions to the cook, not forgetting to reinforce them with a generous tip, he ambled off into the west part of the town to see how the men were getting on with their errand.

He had not gone very far when the sounds of a fray—shouting, curses, and the clash of weapons—reached him from some way ahead. Hurrying in the direction of the sounds, he soon came to where the streets ended in an open space beneath the circumference wall of the town. There, with their backs to the wall, a group of seven or eight swordsmen were defending themselves valiantly against at least twice their number of Manchu soldiers, whom Trinket instantly recognized as the Palace Guards who had parted from him only a quarter of an hour before. The soldiers had surrounded the swordsmen in a half-circle from which, outnumbered as they were, they had little chance of escaping.

Just as Trinket was congratulating himself on the prompt performance of his errand, he noticed among the spectators of this fray two figures standing hand in hand on top of the wall. It was young Sir Zheng and the Green Girl. Something had gone seriously wrong. He looked again at the embattled swordsmen. The two in the middle, a young man and a girl, he now recognized with dismay as the Little Countess and her brother Mu Jiansheng, the Young Count Mu. One of those fighting alongside them was Shaker Wu, whom a year or two earlier he had helped to escape from the Palace. This was the Yunnan delegation on its way back from the congress.

Fortunately Dolong, too, was among the spectators. He had a sword in his hand, but must, at the last moment, have decided that brawling in the street was unbecoming in a person of his rank. Trinket edged up to him and whispered urgently in his ear.

'You've got the wrong couple. The two on the wall are the ones I meant.'

Then he moved away again.

Dolong shouted to his companions:

'Hey! Fellows! This isn't the one we lent the money to. Let him and his friends go free!'

Instantly the guards disengaged and fell back, allowing the imprisoned Yunnanese to depart. Young Count Mu had been assuming that he must have been recognized and denounced to the authorities and that the Manchu soldiers had come to arrest him. He was relieved to find that the only reason they had approached him was that they had mistaken him for a defaulting debtor; and as his little party was greatly outnumbered by the Manchus, he judged it best to get away as quickly as possible while the going was good. The little group hurried off without saying a word, making for the nearest town gate, and were very soon out of sight.

There was a flight of stone steps not far from where Trinket was standing which led up to the top of the wall. He climbed up to join the two others.

'Who were those people?' he asked the Green Girl. 'What were they fighting about?'

'I don't know,' she said. 'The soldiers said something about owing them money.'

'Hadn't we better get back before Shifu starts worrying?' he asked her.

'You go first,' she said. 'I'll follow you later.'

While they were talking, several of the guards were climbing up the steps.

'That's the man!' one of them shouted, pointing at young Sir Zheng. 'That's the one we lent the money to.'

'That ten thousand taels we lent you in the Hejianfu brothel the other night,' said another of them, 'we want it back.'

'Don't talk such nonsense!' said Zheng angrily. 'I've never set foot in any Hejianfu brothel. How could I possibly owe you money?'

'What do you mean, you never set foot in it?' said another of the guards. 'I saw you with my own eyes. You were sitting there with a tart on each knee, hugging and kissing.'

The Green Girl remembered the scene she had witnessed in the brothel in Tantoupu and her eyes filled with tears. Nevertheless when one of the more aggressive of the 'creditors' began punching and slapping Zheng, demanding to know whether or not he was going to 'cough up', she rushed to his defence, only to be sent reeling back by Dolong.

'Why does a nice young lady like you want to be going out with a randy little whore-licker like him?' he asked her, and restrained her from dashing once more to the rescue.

A number of the guards were standing round Zheng now, kicking and thumping him. He was bleeding profusely from his nose. Since she was unable to get to him, the Green Girl called out to them pleadingly.

'Please don't hit him any more! Can't we talk it over instead?'

'Tell him to give us back our money and we'll stop hitting him,' said one of the men.

'I think we should cut his ears off first,' said another of them and unsheathed a formidable knife.

The Green Girl seized Trinket's hand imploringly.

'What shall we do?' she sobbed. 'What shall we do?'

'I've got ten thousand taels; the question is whether we ought to give him the money if it's only for paying back what he spent in the whore-house,' said Trinket self-righteously.

'But didn't you hear? They're going to cut off his ears.' She called to the men. 'Do stop hitting him! He'll pay you back the money.' She turned to Zheng. 'Brother Wei has got the money. If you ask him, I'm sure he'll lend it to you and you can pay the soldiers back. You will lend it, won't you?' she said, tugging Trinket's hand.

Zheng, though raging inwardly, was obliged to eat humble pie again and beg Trinket for the money, which he then promptly handed over to the nearest guard. The men weren't quite sure what they should do now. Trinket had said nothing about taking money, only that the young man should be 'discouraged'. Trinket realized why they were hesitating.

'Lousy soldiers!' he shouted. 'You've got your money, what more do you want? Why don't you share it out among yourselves and bugger off?'

This was just what they wanted to hear and they began to drift away, discussing the correct way of dividing up the spoils. Dolong, however, when he saw the Green Girl at once rush over to tend to the bleeding and battered Sir Zheng, felt that the task Trinket had given them had not yet been properly completed. He strode over and took the unfortunate Zheng by the scruff of the neck.

'Now see here young man,' he said, emphasizing his words with an occasional shake, 'in future leave this young woman alone. A respectable, well-bred young lady like her has got her reputation to think of. She doesn't want a dirty, sneaking little pimp like you hanging around her. From now on if I catch you anywhere near her, I'll wring your head off.'

He put his great hands round Zheng's neck as if to demonstrate. Zheng's pale face turned purple and there seemed every likelihood that the big man would choke him to death.

'Leave him alone!' cried Trinket. 'Surely you're not going to kill him now you've got the money?'

He attacked Dolong with both his fists. The form of attack he used, a Two Dragon Snatch, was designed to strike an opponent on the temples, but because of the disparity in their heights— Dolong was a great giant of a man and Trinket still a rather short fourteen-year-old—the blows landed on his ribs just below the armpits. With a roar of counterfeit rage Dolong released the half-choked Zheng and kicked out at Trinket, deliberately missing him and demolishing a small jujube tree that was growing out of a crack in the wall. Seeing his great strength, the Green Girl cried out in alarm.

'Brother Wei, don't fight him! Let's go back to the inn!'

Trinket suddenly felt indescribably happy.

'She really cares for me,' he thought. 'At last she cares for me!'

He began to execute all the showiest figures he could remember of the ones he had been taught by Brother Simple and the old eunuch Hai Dafu. Neither he nor Dolong were doing more than barely touching each other, but the show they put on was impressive. At one point, as Dolong lurched sideways to avoid a blow, he dislodged an unstable piece of battlement which dropped off and disappeared in a cloud of dust. A moment later Trinket aimed a blow at his belly. Still play-acting, Dolong cried out as if in pain and his legs were seen to buckle under him. When Trinket followed this up with a kick, he toppled over and fell from the side of the wall.

For a few seconds he clung on to the parapet with his fingers, then his grip slackened and he fell once more, ending up spread-eagled on his back on the ground below. Trinket, not sure that this last part of the performance was intended, leant over and looked down at him in some concern, wondering if he might inadvertently have killed his friend or at the very least broken his back. But as he gazed down, the recumbent figure on the ground below suddenly raised its head a fraction, opened its eyes, and winked, at the same time giving a little wave with its hand. A second later it lay there spread-eagled and inert as before and to all appearances dead.

Trinket could feel the Green Girl tugging at his hand.

'Quickly, quickly!' she said. She already had Sir Zheng by the other hand. The three of them made a dash for the steps. As the soldiers seemed preoccupied with their unconscious leader, they were able to run back to the inn without further mishap. Seeing the Green Girl flushed and out of breath, the White Nun asked what had happened.

'Sir Zheng was set upon by a gang of Tartar soldiers,' said the Green Girl. 'Fortunately—' she seemed reluctant to go on, 'fortunately Brother Wei was able to knock out their leader.'

'I think in future it would be better if you stayed with me quietly in the inn,' said the White Nun severely. 'All this wandering about outside is just asking for trouble.'

The Green Girl hung her head and said nothing. Trinket noticed that shortly after this she hurried off to Zheng's room to see if he was all right. His companions had already attended to his injuries and put him to bed so there was nothing for her to do and she came away looking rather disconsolate. Trinket glumly reflected that, in spite of all he had done, her every thought was still only of the detestable Sir Zheng. For all his precocious cleverness, Trinket still knew very little about love.

Instructions for a Third Lesson

That night, while everyone in the hostelry was sleeping, Trinket was woken up by a gentle tapping on the window of his room. He sat up, still half asleep, and listened. Someone was calling softly to him from the other side of the window.

'Mr Wei! Mr Wei!'

The voice was familiar. After a moment or two he recognized it as that of Shaker Wu, the grizzled retainer of Young Count Mu whom he had once helped to escape from the Palace and whom he had seen that morning with his back to the town wall, fighting side by side with his master and the Little Countess when they and the other members of the Yunnan delegation were set upon in error by the Manchu guards. He jumped out of bed and went to open the window.

'Mr Wu!'

Shaker Wu jumped lightly into the bedroom and enfolded Trinket in a tight embrace. Then, having first closed the window carefully behind him, he took Trinket by the hand, led him over to the bed, and sat down shoulder to shoulder with him on the side of it.

'I asked some of your Triad people at the big meeting in Hejianfu where you were,' he said, 'but they wouldn't tell me.'

'I was at the meeting myself,' said Trinket, 'in disguise. They weren't being unfriendly: they didn't know I was there.'

'You saved my life again this morning, Mr Wei,' said Shaker. 'I don't know what would have happened to us when those Tartar soldiers attacked if you hadn't intervened. Young Count Mu was *very* grateful. At the time, we had to get away as best we could, but we couldn't have left the area without thanking you.'

'Oh, that's all right,' said Trinket. 'We're all friends, aren't we? Can't you stop calling me Mr Wei, though? Can't we just be brothers?'

'All right,' said Shaker. 'Provided you'll stop calling me Mr Wu. Tell me, brother, where are you making for?'

'That's rather a long story,' said Trinket. 'Right at the moment, I'm thinking about getting married.'

'Congratulations! Who's the lucky girl?' said Shaker, expecting to be told that it was Fang Yi.

'Her family name is Chen,' said Trinket. 'I'm having a bit of trouble, though.'

'Oh? How's that?'

'She's got another boyfriend,' said Trinket. 'He's bad news. He's trying to get her away from me. But that's not the worst of it. The worst of it is that he's a traitor. He gives secret information to the Tartars. It's because of him that you were attacked by those Tartar soldiers this morning.'

'Little swine!' said Shaker angrily. 'What's the matter with him? Is he tired of living?'

'You'd never guess who he is,' said Trinket. 'He's from Taiwan: the Prince of Yanping's second son. You know about this agreement that whoever takes out the Satrap first should be leader of the Resistance? Well, he's not prepared to play fair like the rest of us. He reckoned he could get you Yunnan folk knocked out of the competition by setting the Tartars on to you. Luckily the Tartars don't know what your master looks like, so I was able to persuade them that they'd got the wrong man.'

Shaker's head was beginning to shake at an alarming rate.

'So that's why we were attacked! Tamardy! What a dirty little rat! Leave him to me, brother. I'll teach him a lesson he won't forget in a hurry. Where can I find him? How shall I know who he is?'

'He's travelling with us,' said Trinket. 'The young man with a black eye. He could certainly do with a lesson. Don't overdo it, though. After all, Prince Yanping is our boss: we don't want to upset him. The best thing would be if you were to knock him about a bit and then let me come to the rescue.'

Having settled this important piece of business, Trinket went on to ask Shaker what had happened to him after he and the others were captured by members of the Mystic Dragon Sect. Shaker told him that the Mystic Dragons had themselves been made prisoner by a group of women who appeared to be the sole inhabitants of the haunted house and who had then proceeded to set himself and his companions free, but that another lot of Mystic Dragons had arrived on the scene and released the first lot. In the ensuing darkness and confusion they had somehow all got separated and next morning they could see no sign of Trinket and the two girls. The only resident of the house they could get hold of was a deaf old woman from whom they could extract little sense, and though he and old Xu had spent nearly a fortnight searching the whole area for some clue that might suggest what had happened to them, lack of success had forced them in the end to give up. Trinket felt thankful that Shaker and the other two men had not fallen into the hands of the sinister Leader of the Mystic Dragon Sect and been forced to become his puppets. He decided not to tell him about the two girls.

'Well, brother, I'd better be going now,' said Shaker. 'Take care of yourself! And don't forget, there are lots of other nice girls in the world. Don't worry too much about this young lady of yours.'

Trinket sighed and said nothing.

Shaker opened the window and vaulted out.

Little Flower

Next day Trinket, the White Nun, and the Green Girl, accompanied as before by young Zheng and his retainers, resumed their journey to the north. As they drove through the town gate, the White Nun rather pointedly asked Zheng where he was bound for.

'Taiwan,' he said. 'I'll escort you for just another stage of your journey, and then I'll take my leave.'

They travelled on uneventfully through the day; but the White Nun was growing fatigued with so much travel, and in the late afternoon they decided to break their journey at an inn they could see a little way ahead of them and make an early start next day. Just as they were approaching the inn, a small group of mounted peasants who had for some time been trailing along behind them made a sudden dash forward and overtook them.

'That's the one! That's him!' cried the rough-looking farmer at their head, pointing to young Sir Zheng.

Trinket could see at a glance that the farmer was Shaker Wu. The other members of the group surrounded the carriage and blocked the way ahead.

'Dirty bastard! What were you up to in Li Family Village last night?' said Shaker Wu. 'Did you think you could get away with it?'

'What on earth are you talking about, my good man?' said Zheng angrily. 'I've never in my life been near your Li Family Village. You're obviously mistaking me for someone else.'

'Filthy liar!' said a younger peasant, whom Trinket identified as Shaker's much-tattooed disciple Ao Biao, the Blue Tiger. 'You spent half the night in our Little Flower's bed. That's him, sister, isn't it?'

The 'Little Flower' he addressed was a big-boned young peasant woman, of hideous aspect but gaudily dressed in what must have been her best clothes, and with a patterned kerchief about her head. Trinket imagined they must have hired her and wondered why they couldn't have picked someone slightly less ill-favoured.

'That's him, that's him!' said Little Flower. 'After all his promises, I let him have his way with me. Oh, I'm so ashamed! Waa-aa-aah!'

She broke into a sort of quavering yell that was evidently meant to simulate weeping.

'What did he say, then, Little Flower?' said Shaker. 'Never fear! Don't be ashamed!'

'He said his father was a great prince in Taiwan,' said Little Flower. She fished a large silver ingot from her bosom. 'He gave me this. He said there were mountains of silver where this came from. He said he would make me . . . he would make me . . . Waah!'

She resumed her wailing.

While she had been speaking, a little cry of anguish, probably audible to none but Trinket, had escaped the Green Girl. The idea that her handsome Sir Zheng could have bestowed his favours on this coarse, lumpish, buck-toothed peasant girl had seemed so preposterous that she had at first assumed this to be a case of mistaken identity. But when she heard this same ignorant peasant girl mention Prince Yanping and Taiwan, it seemed obvious that it was from Zheng's own lips alone that she could have heard about them. The doubts raised by the guards' charges the day before now seemed confirmed.

'There's only one way to mend this,' said Ao Biao. 'The young gentleman will have to marry my sister, for I'm sure no one else will have her now that she's been ruined.'

Like the Green Girl, Sir Zheng's retainers were now convinced that the peasant girl really had been seduced by their master. They had been impressed by the size of the ingot. No peasant girl, they reasoned, could possibly earn so substantial a sum except by prostituting her person.

'Your sister's had her payment,' said one of them. 'Now just clear the road and let us pass.'

'Our Little Flower is an honest girl,' said Shaker Wu. 'The young man promised her marriage—isn't that so, Little Flower?'

'Yes,' said Little Flower in her raucous, hooting voice. 'He said the silver was a betrothal present.'

Zheng was now growing desperate. Ever since he had set foot on the mainland he had encountered nothing but trouble. The importunacy of these stupid yokels was the last straw. He raised his riding-crop and struck Ao Biao on the head. Ao Biao gave a yell, slipped from his saddle, and lay motionless on the ground. Little Flower dismounted and knelt beside him.

'He's dead,' she said. 'Murderer!'

'Murderer! Murderer!' cried the other peasants.

Observing the agility with which Little Flower cocked up her leg and hopped down from her horse, it suddenly dawned on Trinket that 'she' was a man—probably one of Young Count Mu's followers with whom he was not yet acquainted. He could not have been a very good-looking man: it was small wonder he made so ill-favoured a young woman. But Zheng was too concerned about his predicament to have an eye for such particulars. As the son of the Manchu government's most dangerous enemy and with an enormous price on his head, the last thing he wanted was a confrontation with the local bureaucracy. He decided to make a getaway.

'Break out!' he cried to his retainers, digging his heels into his mount so that it reared. 'Let's get away from these clowns!'

In a trice the group of peasants transformed themselves into accomplished fighters. The dead brother leapt up from the ground and dragged Sir Zheng from his horse, Little Flower flung her arms

round her betrothed in what looked more like a wrestler's lock than
a womanly embrace, and the others set about unhorsing the retainers and temporarily incapacitating them with skilful thrusts in particularly painful places. One of them produced a length of rope
from somewhere and proceeded to rope the riderless horses
together; then, once more mounting their own horses, with young
Sir Zheng still clasped in the iron grip of his future bride and with
the retainers' horses clattering along behind them, they rode off in
great good humour, promising themselves a boozy wedding party
ahead.

'Shifu, Shifu!' cried the Green Girl, running up to the
carriage. 'They've taken away Sir Zheng. What are we going to
do?'

The White Nun had all this time been lying down resting in
the carriage. She had heard the shouting and racket but seen
nothing of what was going on. Had she done so, she would have
known at once that these were no peasants who had carried off Sir
Zheng but seasoned warriors. She shook her head.

'Young Sir Zheng's conduct leaves very much to be desired,'
she said disapprovingly. 'I'm sure these countrymen intend him no
serious injury. It will certainly do him no harm to be taught a
lesson.'

The retainers had now struggled to their feet and were
running down the road after the horsemen, though with little hope
of ever catching up with them or even discovering where they were
going. This left only Trinket and the Green Girl beside the carriage.
There was nothing for it but to go on to the inn, stable the mule,
and get the White Nun settled in a room.

By now it was already dusk, but Trinket knew that the Green
Girl was bound to make some sort of attempt to find out what had
become of Zheng, and when the lamps had been lit and the White
Nun had partaken of a simple meal, he went out to the stable and
concealed himself in a pile of straw, reasoning that if she wanted
to go off to look for Zheng, she would need a horse, and that in
her anxiety to save him she would not hesitate to 'borrow' someone
else's mount. His guess proved correct, for he had not been lying
more than ten minutes or so in the darkness of the stable, when
the stable door was pushed softly open and a slight, girlish figure
glided inside. She gave a start and a little gasp when Trinket jumped
out of the straw.

'What are you doing here?'

'Waiting for horse thieves,' he said drily. 'There are a lot of them around in this part of the country.'

'Brother Wei,' she said, 'please help me. We must do something to rescue him.'

'Rescue him?' said Trinket teasingly. 'He's not in any danger. This is his wedding day. He's probably feeling very happy.'

She began to cry.

'Trinket,' she said pleadingly (he couldn't recollect that she had ever called him by his real name before), 'please help me get him back.'

Trinket relented.

'All right,' he said. 'What will my reward be if I do?'

She nearly said, 'Anything you like', but remembered that he would almost certainly revive the usual nonsense about wanting to marry her and said nothing.

'Come on!' he said.

They untied two of the horses and led them out of their stalls and through the yard, as quietly as they could. Fortunately no one seemed to have noticed, and when they got on to the road outside, they mounted and began riding along it in the direction they had come from earlier in the day. After they had been riding for some time, they came upon a group of men, one or two of them holding lanterns, sitting on the ground beside the road just before its junction with a narrow lane. It was the retainers, who had evidently given up the chase. Under the dark trees behind them they could make out the shapes of horses.

'Where is Sir Zheng?' said the Green Girl, reining in her horse.

Recognizing her voice, the retainers jumped to their feet. In the light of the lanterns it could be seen that all of them had a dejected, beaten look.

'Down there,' said one of them, pointing down the lane. 'In that temple.'

'What's he doing there?'

'The countrymen wanted him to go there to get married,' said the man. 'He didn't want to go, but they made him.'

'There weren't very many of them,' said the Green Girl crossly. 'What's the matter with you? Couldn't you have stopped them?'

'Those countrymen—they seem to be trained fighters,' said
the man sheepishly.

'Suppose they are,' said the Green Girl, 'how could you just
stand by and let your master be carried off like that? Very well. At
least you can take us there.'

'They said if we gave them any more trouble they would kill
us all,' said one of the retainers, a somewhat older man. 'They left
us our horses. They said as far as they were concerned we could
go back home if we liked, but if we tried to follow them, they
would kill us.'

'Really!' said the Green Girl. 'I thought good bodyguards were
prepared to die for their masters.'

'Yes, miss,' said the man. 'All the same, I think it would be
best if you left your horses here. We don't want to give them
warning of our coming.'

The Green Girl sniffed contemptuously, but dismounted
all the same. Trinket followed her example and the two of
them tethered their horses to a tree, a little way apart from the
others. The retainers put their lanterns down and led them down
the lane.

After a few hundred yards, the lane passed through a grove
of tall trees, then through a graveyard. At this point the retainers
refused resolutely to advance a step further and Trinket and the
Green Girl had to go on alone. Beyond the graveyard was a sizeable building, too big for a house, which they assumed must be the
temple. Light was streaming from one side of it. A sudden sound
of drums and cymbals broke out from it as they approached. The
Green Girl clutched Trinket's sleeve and together the two of them
crept round the building until they came to a gateway. Entering this
gateway, they moved stealthily across a small courtyard to a
window of the building from which the light and sound were
coming.

The scene which met their eyes when they peered inside must
have been planned to coincide with their arrival. A somewhat
battered-looking Sir Zheng was standing on a mat, shoulder to
shoulder with his gawky bride, whose head was now enveloped in
a red silk cloth beneath which only her neck was visible. Someone
had thoughtfully stuck red wedding favours in his hat. Shaker Wu,
acting as Master of Ceremonies, stood a little distance away from
them to call out the commands. The other 'peasants' stood ready
at hand to enforce his commands if necessary, though from the look

of things Zheng had already been so manhandled that he had decided to go through with whatever was asked of him without any further resistance.

'Bride and groom, first kowtow to heaven!' Shaker sang out in a clarion voice.

The incongruous pair turned to face the door of the hall, knelt down on the mat, and kowtowed.

'Bride and groom, stand!'

They stood up.

'Bride and groom, second kowtow to earth!'

They about-turned, knelt down, and kowtowed towards the inner side of the hall.

'Bride and groom, stand!'

Up they got again.

'Bride and groom, third kowtow to each other!'

They turned to face each other and kowtowed as before.

'Again!'

'Isn't that enough?' said Zheng plaintively, rising to his knees.

'Oh, no,' said Shaker. 'In these parts it's the custom to do it fifty times.'

'This is intolerable!' cried the Green Girl, and before Trinket could stop her, she had leapt through the window and was charging into the middle of the hall, brandishing her sword.

'Let him go at once, you stupid peasants, or I'll kill each one of you!'

Shaker laughed.

'If you've come to drink the bride's health, young lady, there's no need for the sword.'

The Green Girl ignored him and, presumably because he was standing nearest to Sir Zheng, struck out at Ao Biao in a rage. It was a savage blow: Ao Biao was obliged to pick up a long bench to defend himself, but so fiercely did she press down on him that he was forced to retreat.

'She's a spunky little fighter,' said Shaker admiringly and stepped in to take Ao Biao's place. Shaker was a more experienced fighter than Ao Biao, and though the Green Girl fought skilfully and Zheng leapt to his feet to help her, Zheng was quickly overpowered and it was now her turn to retreat.

'Brother Wei,' she called out, 'come and help me!'

'I'm doing my best, sister, I'm doing my best,' Trinket shouted back at her.

From the racket outside the window it sounded as if he was struggling with a formidable opponent.

'I'll handle this,' said Shaker, winking at his younger companions. Two of them quickly took over the Green Girl while Shaker, shouting 'Who's that out there?', ran out of the door. He had difficulty in not laughing out loud when, in the darkness outside, he made out the figure of Trinket, perched on a low window-ledge, single-handedly attacking the window-frame with his fists and feet.

'Aiyo!' Trinket shouted for the benefit of the Green Girl inside. 'These countrymen are trained fighters. Aiyo!'

He jumped down and ran across the courtyard with Shaker following.

'Thanks, brother,' he said, when he and Shaker were in the doorway of the temple, out of earshot of the rest. 'I like the way you've chosen to rid me of that pest. Can I ask you another favour now?'

'Anything, brother.'

'Now that you're in the business of marrying people, could you find some way of marrying me to that girl?'

Shaker suddenly looked grave.

'I don't like having to say this to you, brother, but though I don't mind a bit of fun like what we've had just now, we fighting men are not in the business of pimping for each other. I'm sorry you asked me this.'

'No, no, you don't understand,' said Trinket. 'I really, truly, want to marry this girl. I love her! I want to live with her and look after her for the rest of my life. I've wanted to for a long time. The only snag is, she's set her heart on this scumbag you've just been sorting out for me.'

Shaker brightened up again.

'Oh well, that's different. I'll have to think of some way of bringing this off. I think perhaps to start with I'd better pretend to make you my prisoner.'

He undid Trinket's belt and tied his hands behind his back with it, then, taking him by the collar, marched him back into the temple hall, where the Green Girl, now disarmed, was standing a prisoner between the two young men.

'Let the lass go,' said Shaker. 'I like her spirit. She'd make a good match for my younger brother. What do you say to it, lads? Shall we have another wedding?'

There were enthusiastic cries of assent, but the Green Girl was horrified.

'No!' she said, 'no! I'd rather die than be married to one of you.'

'Very well,' said Shaker magnanimously. 'If you won't marry my brother, what about marrying this young fellow here?' He gave Trinket a push. 'I reckon the two of you would make a good match. Both of you are good little fighters. Both of you have got plenty of spirit.'

'No!' said the Green Girl very firmly. 'I don't want to marry him.'

'I'm beginning to lose patience with you, young woman,' said Shaker threateningly. 'Tie her up!'

The young men quickly did his bidding.

'Please don't hurt her,' said Trinket. 'If all you want is a wedding, I don't mind being married instead of her. Haven't you got a sister or a daughter I could marry?'

'I haven't got a sister,' said Shaker, 'and my daughter is only three years old. What about you young fellows?' he said, addressing the other men.

'I haven't got any sisters,' said one.

'Nor I,' said another.

'My sister's already married with eight children,' said another. 'Her husband's a sick man, mind you. You could marry her when he dies.'

'We can't wait that long,' said Shaker. 'We want a wedding now.'

'We want a wedding now,' echoed the others.

'I'm sorry, sister,' said Trinket. 'It looks as if you'll have to marry me.'

'I am *not* marrying you,' said the Green Girl determinedly.

'Now I really have lost patience,' said Shaker. 'If we're not going to have a wedding, neither of you is any use to us. We might as well top the pair of you.'

'Cut off their noses!' said one of the younger men bloodthirstily.

'Cut off his too,' said another of them, pointing to Zheng. 'I can't see he'll be much use to our Flower, except to give a name to her child.'

'Is that what you want?' Shaker asked the Green Girl.

'No!' she cried in a half-scream. She had turned deathly pale.

'There's nothing for it, sister,' said Trinket. 'We'll just have to go through with this.'

'That's more like it,' said Shaker, undoing Trinket's bonds. 'They've both agreed now. Set the girl free again.'

As soon as they released her, she fetched Ao Biao a tremendous punch in the chest, but it didn't seem to concern him unduly. While another of the men held a cutlass to her neck, he plucked the red cloth from the head of the pseudo bride and draped it over hers. At this, the din of drums and cymbals broke out again, and the Green Girl, resigned now to humouring the eccentric wishes of these yokels with an outward show of compliance, allowed herself to be put through the same performance with Trinket that Zheng had shortly before been forced to undergo with the hideous Flower.

'Bride and groom,' said Shaker, when the little ceremony was over, 'I think you owe me a kowtow now as the matchmaker.'

The Green Girl's answer to this was a kick in the stomach. It doubled him up, but after getting his wind back he merely laughed.

'The bride is a dangerous young woman,' he said.

Just at that moment sounds of whistling and running feet could be heard from every direction outside. It was clear that the temple was surrounded by a considerable body of men.

Manzi, goowah tooloo!

'Sst!' said Shaker. 'Put out the lights!'

Instantly all candles in the hall, except for a little one on the altar which they somehow missed, were extinguished. Trinket seized the Green Girl's hand.

'Come on, wife, quick! We must hide.'

The Green Girl tried to disengage her hand.

'Don't call me that!' she hissed. 'That wasn't a real wedding. It doesn't count.'

'Of course it counts,' said Trinket. 'Once you've done all that kowtowing, there's no undoing it.'

A chorus of inhuman yells and cries outside caused her to draw closer to him. No longer resisting, she ran hand in hand with him to the shrine at the back of the hall and crouched down with him behind the altar. Suddenly the hall was lit up again with the light of blazing torches as a throng of some thirty or forty yelling warriors burst inside. They were the strangest-looking creatures imaginable, naked except for the animal skins round their waists and their feathered head-dresses, their faces and bodies patterned all over with warpaint. Wild Manzi! What were these savage tribes-men from the forests of Yunnan and the Burmese border doing in North China? The Green Girl cowered against Trinket's body, so close that he could feel her trembling.

The crowd of savages halted, and a big man who appeared to be their leader looked round imperiously.

'Chinee man—bad!' he said. 'All kill! *Goowah tooloo abaslee!*'

'*Goowah tooloo abaslee!*' the other savages shouted menacingly.

Shaker Wu had lived all his life in Yunnan and had picked up a few words of the Yee language spoken by many of the aborigi-nal tribesmen in that area, but had no idea what language these painted savages were speaking.

'We Chinee man good man,' he ventured in his pidgin Yee. 'Not kill!'

The Manzi chief shook his head uncomprehendingly.

'Chinee man—bad. All kill!' he insisted. 'All kill! *Goowah tooloo abaslee!*'

'*Goowah tooloo abaslee!*' shouted the other Manzi, and instantly set upon the members of the wedding party, including the unfor-tunate Sir Zheng, who to them was a 'Chinee man' like the rest.

The weapons these primitives wielded were by no means primitive and their fighting methods too were sophisticated. The Chinese fought back valiantly, but they were so greatly outnum-bered that, after a few minutes, they had all, with one exception, been disarmed; two of them, Ao Biao and one one, were wounded. The exception was Shaker Wu, with whom the Manzi leader was engaged in single combat. Shaker fought on desperately, aware that his opponent was more than a match for him but hoping against hope that he might somehow manage to overcome him and force the other Manzi to release his friends. While he was parrying a downward stroke aimed at his head, the shock made by the impact of the two blades temporarily paralysed his arm. As ill luck would have it, it was just at that moment that another of the tribesmen aimed a sweeping blow at his legs. He skipped aside to avoid it, but in that split second the Manzi chief was able to change the direction of his sword so that it ended up with the blade pressing against his neck. There was nothing for it but to drop his own sword and surrender. The tribesmen had already trussed up the others with leather thongs, so now it was his turn to be bound. He was made to sit on the floor with the rest while several of the tribesmen went round each corner of the building with their torches to see if anyone was hiding.

Trinket could see no point in waiting to be discovered. Holding the Green Girl tightly by the hand, he made a desperate dash for the door; but the two of them did not get very far. The Manzi leader darted forward, stretched out his arm, and caught the Green Girl by the collar from behind, while three other tribesmen fell upon Trinket and held him fast.

'Manzi man good. Not kill. *Goowah tooloo!*' cried Trinket hopefully.

This produced a quite unexpected result. The Manzi leader turned his head and stared at him intently. Then his expression changed. Letting go of the Green Girl, he advanced on Trinket with arms outspread and gathered him up like someone picking up a child.

'*Heehoo aboo killee wondong!*' he shouted, and began walking towards the door with Trinket cradled in his arms.

Though frightened out of his wits, Trinket managed to shout a last message to the Green Girl before the two of them disappeared into the darkness outside.

'I think this painted ape is going to kill me, Ah Kor. You'll be a widow. Don't marry that other man, please!'

The Manzi leader trotted with him across the courtyard before putting him down.

'Laurie Goong-goong,' he said, in faultless Chinese, 'whatever are you doing here?'

'You know me, Manzi-man?' said Trinket. It would be hard to say which was greater, his relief or his surprise.

'I'm Yang Yizhi,' said the Manzi, 'the Satrap's man, Yang Yizhi. You know, the one you helped win at gambling at Prince Kang's. I'm not surprised you didn't recognize me.' He laughed.

Trinket laughed too; but before he could say anything, Yang took him by the arm and suggested in a low voice that they should move to somewhere farther away from where there would be no risk of their being overheard.

When Yang was satisfied that they were far enough away to speak freely, he explained to Trinket that the Satrap, having received information from his agents that a big underworld congress was to be held in Hejianfu for the express purpose of planning some mischief against him, had sent him with other members of his bodyguard to infiltrate the congress and find out more about it. They had identified some of their old enemies from the Mu Family who were attending the congress and had been shadowing them ever since. This evening they had finally decided to strike, but because of the embarrassment it would cause the Satrap if it became known that his followers had engaged in armed violence so far outside his own jurisdiction and so near to the Capital, they had disguised themselves in this highly colourful manner so that there could be no possibility of their being identified. The Mu Family had already tried to make trouble for the Satrap by impersonating his followers in a raid on the Palace—he was deeply grateful to Laurie Goong-goong for having cleared his name on that occasion—and he was anxious that no embarrassment of that sort should occur again.

'The Emperor knew about the congress, too,' said Trinket, rapidly improvising a role for himself that would be acceptable to his friend. 'Like you, I was sent to spy on it and report back. I knew the Mu gang were your master's most dangerous enemies, and I knew the Emperor was worried about your master's safety, so after the congress was over I decided to keep an eye on them and I've stuck with them ever since. They think I'm a friend. That's how I come to be with them now. What about you? What are you planning to do with them now that they're your prisoners?'

'Take them back to Yunnan and make them talk,' said Yang grimly.

'Hm.'

'Perhaps you think that's not such a good idea?'

'Oh no,' said Trinket. 'It's just that their leader's still at large, of course—Mu Jiansheng—"the Young Count" as they call him—and old Liu Something-or-other, his adviser. And that old man you were fighting just now—he's a pretty tough customer. Do you think you can make him talk?'

'Shaker Wu?' said Yang. 'He's a bloody good fighter. No, perhaps you're right. We did have Mu Jiansheng in our sights as far as Xianxian, by the way, but then somehow or other we lost track of him. What do you think we ought to do?'

'The thing is,' said Trinket; 'I've been trying to persuade this Shaker to take me to Young Count Mu and he's more or less agreed. I'd been planning to wait until I knew where the Young Count was and then get the Emperor's men to round them all up. Catch the whole lot at one go.'

'That way's much better,' said Yang. 'In that case I'll have to think of some way of releasing you all. Hm. I can't let on that you and I are friends. Not in this gear, anyway.'

'Couldn't I go on pretending that I can speak the *goowah tooloo* stuff? We could talk away in the *tooloo tooloo* for a bit, then you could pretend that you've decided we're all pals and just go away— without any killee Chinee?'

'That sounds all right. The others will probably understand what I'm up to if I give them a wink or two. Let's go back, then.'

'Wait,' said Trinket, 'there's just one thing I ought to tell you. That girl in there is my wife. The idiot with the black eye and the red bobbles on his hat has been making trouble between us. He's a bloody nuisance! If you could find an excuse for taking him away with you when you go, you'd be doing me a very good turn. I don't mean hurt him or anything. Just get him out of the way.'

Yang couldn't quite understand what a young eunuch was doing with a wife; nevertheless, he readily agreed to do the best he could, and the two of them walked back to the hall, exchanging meaningless gibberish with each other as they came within earshot of the rest.

The fact that Trinket apparently knew the language of these tribesmen inspired Shaker and the other captives with hope. But when they saw the Manzi leader pointing at various of their number and Trinket nodding vigorously or shaking his head, they wondered anxiously what was being said. Eventually the jabbering stopped and Trinket turned to them and spoke to them in Chinese.

'I think they're going to let us go,' he said. 'The trouble is, they want to take one person with them, I can't quite make out why. I think it must be something to do with their religion.'

The leader went over to the Green Girl and made her stand up. He touched her several times and spoke a few words in his own language.

'No!' said Trinket. 'No! My wife. Me. Wife.'

'Wife?'

Evidently neither of them knew the word for this in the other's language.

'Tell him Ah Kor, tell him,' said Trinket, desperately.

The Green Girl pointed to herself and then to Trinket.

'ME—HIS—WIFE.'

The leader shook his head again uncomprehendingly.

Trinket put his arms round the Green Girl and hugged her.

'My wife, you silly painted baboon!'

'Ah! Wifee. Ha ha ha!'

The painted baboon seemed to think this a huge joke. He pointed to Zheng, who was by far the best-dressed person present and certainly, apart from his black eye, the handsomest male.

'Son?'

'No,' said Trinket, shaking his head emphatically. 'Not son.'

'Aah!'

The big man pointed again at Zheng and then gestured to two of the tribesmen to pick him up. They did so, each holding him under one arm as if he were a log. Then, at a command from the leader, with a few hoots and whistles, the whole troop of them departed as suddenly as they had come. Trinket stood in the doorway until the sounds of their departure had faded, then, hurrying inside again, he relit the candles and set about freeing the captives from their bonds. He did this as quickly as possible by cutting through the leather thongs with his dagger.

'Those savages were tidy fighters,' said Shaker. 'Good job the bridegroom could talk their lingo, or we'd all have been goners.'

'How are we going to rescue Sir Zheng?' said the Green Girl.

The false bride, who all this while had been silent, began to wail.

'The savages have taken my man. I'm sure they're going to eat him. They'll boil him and eat him, I'm sure they will.'

Shaker clasped his hands and bowed to Trinket respectfully.

'You're a hero, young man. May I know your name?'

'Wei,' said Trinket.

'I haven't yet given you a wedding present, Mr Wei,' said Shaker. He fished two minute silver ingots from an inside pocket and ceremoniously offered them to Trinket with both his hands.

'Thank you,' said Trinket, receiving them with equal ceremony.

'It wasn't a real wedding,' said the Green Girl. 'We aren't really married.'

'Of course you are,' said Shaker. 'You kowtowed to heaven and earth. You said "Me his wife" to that painted savage only a moment ago. Anyway, we must be off now. We'll leave you two newly-weds in peace.'

With a bow and a hand-clasp apiece he and his companions trooped out of the temple and vanished into the night. There was a sound of galloping, so their horses must all the time have been tethered somewhere outside.

Alone now with Trinket in the silent, empty hall, where the only movements were made by the flickering light of the candles, the Green Girl felt suddenly frightened. At the same time a wave of shame and revulsion swept over her when she thought of the words she had been forced to utter. She stamped her foot and simultaneously burst into tears.

'It's all your fault,' she cried. 'You're horrible.'

'You wouldn't say I was horrible if I rescued Sir Zheng,' said Trinket.

'Would you?' she said, suddenly brightening. 'Do you think you could?'

She looked so beautiful when she said this, that Trinket's heart was melted.

'Come on!' he said. 'Let's get out of here.'

The Bloodless Sword

There was no moon that night but, when their eyes were accustomed to it, enough starlight to see their way in the dark. There was no sign of the retainers in the cemetery or the little wood, and the two of them had to walk all the way to the main road before they found them, clustered together with a few lanterns in their midst, exactly where they had left them earlier on, their horses still tethered to the trees behind them.

'Here's Miss Chen back,' one of them called out as they approached. 'No Sir Zheng. I wonder what's happened to him.'

A tall, thin figure slipped out from their midst, moving with a speed and suddenness that made Trinket jump.

'Where is Sir Zheng?' he demanded, in a high, unpleasant voice.

He had his back to the light, so Trinket couldn't see his face, though he had thrust it forward so aggressively that it was only a few inches from his own.

'He—he was carried off by a troop of Manzi tribesmen,' said Trinket. 'We're afraid they may be going to eat him.'

'Manzi tribesmen?' said the man scornfully. 'What would Manzi tribesmen be doing in the North China Plain?'

'We don't know,' said the Green Girl. 'But they really were. Do please let's try to rescue him.'

'How long ago did this happen?'

'Not very long,' said the Green Girl. 'We started walking quite soon after they left.'

'Which way did they go?'

'Hard to say. I'm surprised you didn't hear them.'

The thin man thought for a moment.

'They must have cut across the fields to meet the road further south.'

Without another word, he jumped on his horse and galloped off into the darkness.

'Who's *he?*' the Green Girl asked one of the men.

'Sir Zheng's Shifu,' said the older retainer who had spoken to them earlier. 'His name is Feng Xifan. The Bloodless Sword. He's a world champion. He'll get Sir Zheng back all right, don't you worry.'

'Why ever didn't you send him to the temple?' the Green Girl asked him.

'He only arrived a few minutes before you did. We sent a carrier pigeon to Hejianfu yesterday asking him to come and join us.'

'So this Feng Shifu was in Hejianfu,' said Trinket. 'How come we didn't see him at the congress?'

The men looked at each other sheepishly and did not answer. Trinket guessed that his presence there had been a secret. It was beginning to look as if one half of the people at the congress had gone there for the purpose of spying on the other half.

Trinket and the Green Girl were by now exhausted. Trinket borrowed a saddle-blanket to lie down on, but the Green Girl was too worried about Sir Zheng to rest and would only sit down on a corner of it while they waited. Trinket dozed off fitfully from time to time, and when the sound of hooves and the excited cries of the retainers welcoming Feng and Zheng's return suddenly jolted him into full wakefulness, he had no idea whether he had been lying there for one hour or two hours or half the night.

'Still in one piece, then?' he asked as Zheng dismounted. 'No bite-marks?'

Zheng stared at him stonily, unaware that he was supposed to have been eaten.

'Who is this boy?' asked Feng.

'Miss Chen's brother-in-arms,' Zheng told him.

'Humph.'

Trinket had a better view of the man now. He had a yellow, cadaverous face with a little forked beard and eyes like narrow slits. He looked more like someone in an advanced stage of tuberculosis than a famous fighting man.

'Did you kill the Manzi leader?' Trinket asked him.

'They weren't Manzi,' he said curtly. 'Bogus.'

'But they were speaking the Manzi language.'

'Bogus,' said Feng again, and turned from Trinket to address Zheng, not deigning to waste words on a mere boy.

'Sir Zheng, you must be tired,' he said. 'Before we do anything else, I suggest that we go to that temple, so that you can rest a bit.'

'I think we had better hurry back,' said the Green Girl. 'If Shifu wakes up and finds that we aren't there, she will be worried.'

'Yes, we ought to be getting back,' Trinket agreed.

The Green Girl looked pleadingly at Zheng, obviously hoping that he would go with them.

'I think perhaps we ought to go straight to the inn and have something to eat,' he said, in answer to her unspoken entreaty. 'We can have a good sleep after we have eaten.'

The horses were untethered, and when everyone had mounted, they set off at a brisk walking pace along the road to the inn. Riding along beside Sir Zheng, Trinket had to listen to a lot of boasting about his Shifu, Feng Xifan, but gathered that this military paragon had not succeeded in harming Yang Yizhi.

To Peking

It was dawn when they got to the inn and the White Nun was already up. She had guessed that the Green Girl would try to drag Trinket off to rescue Zheng and had not been unduly concerned when she found that the two of them were missing. As soon as Zheng had finished introducing his Shifu, she told him that she had important business to attend to and was resolved to leave with her disciples straight away. He was very much taken aback.

'But Your Reverence, I was so looking forward to spending some more time in your company,' he protested. 'I have time on my hands at the moment. Couldn't I travel with you a little longer?'

The White Nun shook her head.

'Travelling with people in holy orders has disadvantages for both sides,' she said; and after a very perfunctory leave-taking, she hustled her two charges into the carriage, issued a brief order to the coachman, and drove away. While Zheng stood open-mouthed at the roadside watching them go, the Green Girl looked out at him with tear-filled eyes.

'Where are we going, Shifu?' Trinket asked.

'Peking,' said the White Nun. After a pause she added:

'If that young man tries to follow us, I forbid either of you to speak to him. If I catch either of you doing so, I shall strike him down.'

'But why?' said the Green Girl, startled by the extraordinary severity of the threat.

'Because I say so,' said the White Nun. 'I like peace and quiet. I don't like people round me chattering all the time.'

All this was music to Trinket's ears. Dear Shifu! He resolved in future to pray to the Buddha for her health every single day of his life! Impulsively he bent down and kissed her hand.

'Don't do that!' she cried, snatching it away; but there was a tiny smile lurking at the corners of her mouth. It was more than twenty years since anyone had kissed her hand. This further example of the nun's favouritism added to the bitterness the Green Girl already felt at being separated from her beloved Zheng. A big tear rolled down her cheek.

Now that the three of them were travelling on their own, the journey was uneventful. They reached Peking within a few days and found a quiet hostelry in the East City. As soon as they were settled, the White Nun called Trinket into her room and barred the door.

'Trinket,' she said when they were alone together, 'can you guess why we are here?'

'I suppose it's to do with those Sutras,' he said.

'Exactly. I can't see much good coming of that congress we went to. Killing Wu Sangui will not get rid of the Tartars. But if we had all the Sutras and then issued a call for a patriotic rising, there is just a chance that we might drive the Tartars out. A Ming Restoration is still a possibility. I need another month, though, to nurse back my inner strength before I can go to the Palace and look for the other seven.'

'I could go first,' said Trinket. 'You never know, I might pick up some clues.'

She nodded.

'You are an intelligent boy. It would be wonderful if you could.'

Trinket was so touched that he nearly blurted out that five of the missing Sutras were already in his hands; but then he thought of Kang Xi and what a good friend he had been to him. Depriving a best friend of his Empire was not the sort of thing that any of his favourite heroes would have done. She saw his hesitation but attributed it to fear of failure.

'Don't worry if you can't find out anything useful,' she said. 'Man proposes, Heaven disposes. We can only do our best. It's a very difficult task and I shan't at all blame you if you don't succeed. By the way,' she added, as she unbarred the door to let him out, 'you won't say anything about this to Ah Kor, will you?'

'Funny!' he thought, as he went off to his own room. 'Ah Kor is so beautiful and so lovable, but Shifu doesn't seem to like her as much as she likes me.'

The Emperor receives a Revelation

Early next morning Trinket entered the Palace and appeared before the Emperor. Although Kang Xi knew by now that he was alive and well, having recently had news of him from Dolong, he was none the less delighted to have him back, eager to know how he had escaped from the clutches of the 'evil nun', as he had learnt to call his would-be assassin. He was also anxious to discover if Trinket knew on whose behalf she had tried to assassinate him. Needless to say, Trinket was ready with a story. It was the Satrap, Wu Sangui, that she was working for, Trinket told him. While he was still her captive, she had been visited by someone called Yang Yizhi, also working for the Satrap, and he had been able to overhear the two of them talking together. It appeared that the nun had lost all her family during the Manchu invasion. The Satrap had shown some kindness to her and she had gladly undertaken the murderous mission he sent her on as a means of avenging their deaths. Yang had told her that he, too, had received kindness from the Satrap. The Satrap had done something for his father, and for a long time he had been his devoted follower. But then he had discovered that the Satrap was plotting against the Emperor and hoping to become

Emperor himself. Yang had by this time come to realize that the young Manchu Emperor was a wise and benevolent ruler and that the Chinese people were much better off under him than they would be under the cruel and capricious Satrap. After this the two of them, Yang and the nun, had had a long and earnest discussion, some of which he had not been able to hear, but the upshot was that they both decided that in future, if there was any further attempt on the Emperor's life, they would not only do nothing to support it but would actually prevent it by killing the assassin.

Trinket made up this entire rigmarole up in the hope that, if Yang Yizhi or the White Nun ever fell into the hands of the Manchu authorities, there was a reasonable chance that they would survive. Kang Xi had nodded several times throughout this recital and now remarked that these sounded like sensible people and that if this Yang Yizhi were ever to leave the Satrap and offer his services to the Court, he would personally see to it that he was rewarded with suitable employment and rank.

Trinket went on to say that, from what he had heard, the Satrap appeared to be plotting joint action with the Zhengs of Taiwan. The possibility that his all but autonomous vassal in the West might one day join forces with his most powerful enemy in the East had for some time past been giving the Young Emperor nightmares, and Trinket's fabrication produced an explosion of anger and a whole stream of 'tamardy's'. But when Trinket suggested that on the Zheng side Zheng Keshuang and his Shifu Feng were the most dangerous ones, whereas Chen Jinnan, their military counsellor, was somewhat of Yang Yizhi's persuasion—a good man who had become aware that the young Manchu Emperor was a wise and benevolent ruler and who might one day be persuaded to defect—the Emperor was not impressed. He knew all about Feng Xifan. He even knew that his *nom de guerre* was the Bloodless Sword. But he also knew about the Helmsman, in his view a far more dangerous enemy, and dismissed Trinket's estimate of him as that of an ill-informed boy whose judgement was not to be trusted. Trinket thought it wisest not to pursue the subject. A silence followed during which Kang Xi paced to and fro in the study, his hands clasped behind his back. Suddenly he stopped and turned to face Trinket again.

'Laurie, tell me something. Would you be prepared to go to Yunnan for me?'

Trinket was startled. This was rather more than he had bargained for.

'You mean to find out what Wu Sangui is up to?'

Kang Xi nodded.

'I know this is dangerous, but you are young. I don't think Wu would feel threatened by you. Anyway, you've got this man Yang there to look after you.'

'I'm not afraid of the danger,' said Trinket. 'It's the thought of leaving you. After all, I've only just got back.'

Kang Xi nodded.

'I know. I feel the same way as you do. But an Emperor can't always do as he likes. If I could do as I liked, I'd go with you to Yunnan. I'd take hold of Wu by the beard while you held his arms behind him, and I'd say, "Tamardy, Wu Sangui! Do you surrender?"'

Trinket laughed.

'All right,' he said. 'When I get to Yunnan, I'll try to think of some way of persuading him to come to Peking. Then the two of us can deal with him here!'

'I doubt you'd be able to. He's too crafty,' said Kang Xi, laughing. He paused a moment. 'I tell you what, though. I think I know what would get him here. I'll marry Princess Ning to his son. He'll have to come then.'

'But that's doing him a favour, isn't it?' said Trinket.

'Not at all. It's that vile woman's daughter I'm thinking about. When the time comes and Wu and his family are executed for treason, she'll lose her head too, along with all the rest.'

Only a short while ago, Trinket reflected, Princess Ning had been the Emperor's favourite sister. Now he hated her. It was because of her mother, the false Empress Dowager, who had killed Kang Xi's own mother and brought about the mental collapse of his father.

'As for that vile woman who murdered my mother,' said Kang Xi, pursuing the same vengeful line of thought, 'we'll say that the Princess came to a bad end because her mother didn't bring her up properly. She can't be executed, but she'll be forced to take her own life.'

Trinket judged that the time was now ripe for some revelations.

'She's not who you think she is,' he said.

'What do you mean?' said Kang Xi, puzzled.

'She's not really the Empress Dowager.'

'Not the Empress Dowager? I don't understand you.'

Kang Xi listened open-mouthed while Trinket told him that a maid-of-honour, acting on his behalf, had discovered that the person whom Kang Xi now called 'that vile woman' was an impostor who was keeping the real Empress Dowager a prisoner. The maid-of-honour story was a sudden inspiration. He couldn't very well tell Kang Xi about Aunt Tao and the White Nun.

'Where is this maid-of-honour?' Kang Xi asked him. His voice was shaking and there were beads of sweat on his brow.

'At the bottom of a well,' said Trinket. 'I didn't like to do it, but it seemed to me that this was something that mustn't be allowed to go further.'

Kang Xi was silent a moment, then nodded.

'You did right, though I'm sorry for her. Have her body taken out of the well as soon as possible and given a decent burial. And see to it that something is done for her parents.'

He got up and took two swords down from the wall, one of which he handed to Trinket.

'We must deal with this business straight away,' he said, '— just the two of us. We don't want any of the women or eunuchs to know about it.'

The Young Emperor, having learned all he knew of Martial Arts from the false Empress Dowager, felt sure she would prove a dangerous enemy. Trinket didn't let on that in actual fact her brush with the White Nun had left her practically harmless. It was agreed, therefore, that as soon as they entered the Hall of Maternal Tranquillity, Trinket should seize hold of her and Kang Xi immobilize her by cutting off one of her arms, after which he could question her at leisure.

'Shouldn't we have some guards with us?' said Trinket. 'She's a very dangerous woman. I wouldn't like to think what would happen to Your Majesty if she managed to slip out of my grasp.'

After thinking a bit, Kang Xi nodded.

'I suppose you're right. But if we do take guards with us, they'll have to be killed afterwards, to make sure that nobody hears about this.'

He summoned eight of his guards to accompany them to the Hall of Maternal Tranquillity. When they arrived, he stationed them in the garden outside the Hall with orders to wait there until they were called. As he and Trinket entered the building, the ladies-in-waiting and eunuchs knelt in silent rows to greet them. Kang Xi ordered them to wait outside in the garden and under no circumstances to come inside. The women and eunuchs tremblingly obeyed.

'Let me go in first,' said Trinket. 'The Emperor is too important a person to take risks.'

Knowing that the false Empress Dowager was powerless against him, Trinket could afford to be heroic, but Kang Xi's knuckles were white as he grasped his sword. He need not have worried, for when they entered the bedchamber there was no one there, and the plan they had made had instantly to be abandoned.

Then they noticed that the bed-curtains had been drawn. The Empress Dowager was inside resting. She must have heard them enter, for her voice addressed them quaveringly from behind the curtains.

'It's a long time since Your Majesty has been to see me. How have you been keeping?'

'I was told that you hadn't been too well lately,' said Kang Xi. 'I thought I'd come over to see how you were.' He turned to Trinket. 'Draw back the curtains so that I can have a look at Her Majesty.'

'No, don't!' said the false Empress Dowager. 'It's only a cold I've got, but I have to be careful of draughts.'

Trinket made signs indicating that he would ignore this request, throw back the curtains and seize her, and that the Emperor must be ready as he did so to strike at her with his sword; but just at that moment Kang Xi experienced a sudden loss of nerve.

'I know she's done all those terrible things,' he thought, 'but suppose Laurie's wrong about her being an impostor? However wicked she is, I can't raise my hand against the Empress Dowager.'

He shook his head and gestured to Trinket to step aside.

'I'm not happy about this cold,' he said. 'I want to see if you've got a fever or not.'

As he said this he stepped forward boldly and threw back the bed-curtains. The woman who looked up at him was gaunt and hollow-eyed.

'I shouldn't have doubted Laurie,' he thought. 'This isn't the Empress Dowager: it is an impostor. She wasn't expecting a visit, so she hasn't bothered to put her disguise on.'

'You've lost weight,' he said.

'I haven't been eating well,' she said. 'Ever since we got back from Wutai, I can only pick at my food.'

Kang Xi's mind was working quickly.

'Look, look!' he shouted excitedly. 'There's a big rat behind that carpet.'

He pointed to the hanging carpet that concealed the closet in which Trinket said they had found the real Empress Dowager.

'There are no rats in here,' said the false Empress Dowager; but Trinket had already rushed over and rolled up the carpet by tugging on the tasselled cord.

'Rat or no rat,' said Kang Xi, 'I'm sure I heard something in there. Better open it, Laurie, and have a look.'

Trinket tried the fastening, but it was locked.

'What sort of game are you two playing at?' said the false Empress Dowager testily. 'You can see I'm not well. I'm not in the mood for all this horseplay in my bedroom.'

'Game? That's it!' said Kang Xi gaily. 'It's Princess Ning again. We were playing hide-and-seek and I couldn't find her. I bet she's hiding in that closet. Can you tell us where we can find the key?'

'I've told you, I'm not in the mood for this foolery,' said the false Empress Dowager. 'Now please just get out of here and leave me in peace.'

'It could be an assassin,' said Kang Xi excitedly. 'Better force the lock, Laurie.'

Trinket's metal-slicing dagger made quick work of the lock, but when he looked inside the closet he found only the bedding that the captive Empress Dowager had been lying in.

'She must have killed her,' he thought.

Rummaging among the bedclothes for some sign of their former occupant, he thought he saw the corner of a book. Sure enough, when he lifted the bedclothes up, there underneath was a copy of the now familiar *Sutra in Forty-Two Sections*. He covered it up again hastily and glanced round to see if Kang Xi had noticed. But Kang Xi was staring fixedly at a hump in the coverlet of the false Empress Dowager's bed—an extremely large hump that could not possibly be part of her anatomy.

Kang Xi at once assumed that the hump must be the real Empress Dowager. He had better act quickly, he thought, before the false one decided to kill her—if she had not done so already.

'Why!' he cried, striving as best he could to give an impression of boyish glee, 'you've had the Princess there with you all the time, hidden inside your bed! Laurie, come here and pull her out!'

Trinket rushed over and plunged a hand beneath the covers. But what it made contact with, to his considerable astonishment, was not the real Empress Dowager but a man's hairy leg which presently shot out from under the covers and kicked him hard in the chest. As he reeled backwards with a cry of pain, an extraordinary, comical figure bounced out of the bed. It was a naked man, but his body was so extremely fat and his legs so extremely short that he looked more like a huge ball of flesh than a human being. He gathered up the false Empress Dowager, bedclothes and all, in his stumpy arms and shot out of the bedchamber, running, in spite of his burden and his dwarfish legs, at what seemed like superhuman speed. Three of the eight guards outside the building were knocked flying by him as he passed; the other five pursued, but he was over the garden wall in a trice and out of sight. Kang Xi, who had followed, called to them to come back and wait outside as before.

Trinket meantime, having recovered from the first shock of the blow, had had time to go back to the closet, retrieve the Sutra from underneath the bedding, and hide it inside his gown.

Kang Xi re-entered the bedchamber.

'So what do you make of that?'

'It looked like a monster,' said Trinket, 'A spook of some sort.'

'No, no, it was a man,' said Kang Xi. 'Didn't you see? Very short and fat, but it was a man all right. It must have been her lover.'

Trinket grinned, but Kang Xi looked serious.

'Where's the real Empress, then?'

'There's a secret compartment in the bed,' said Trinket.

He threw off the bedclothes and removed the lid of the receptacle in which the false Empress Dowager had kept her treasures, but this time the only thing in it was the gold-inlaid Emei stiletto which had been Hai Dafu's undoing. He thought for a bit.

'We could try taking the bottom of the bed out.'

Kang Xi helped him lift out the boards which made up the base of the bed. It was, as it turned out, an inspired guess, for there underneath, lying on a narrow mattress with only a thin coverlet over her, was the body of a woman. There could only have been a few inches between the bed-boards and her face.

'Light a candle,' said Kang Xi. (It was too dark inside the bed to make out who she was.)

What they saw when Trinket brought a lighted candle to shine on her were the rounded features that the false Empress Dowager in her disguise had tried to imitate. They helped her up into a sitting position. The woman opened her eyes but then quickly closed them again, dazzled by the light.

'Who . . .' she said faintly, 'who . . . ?'

'This is His Majesty the Emperor,' said Trinket. 'He has come to rescue Your Majesty.'

'The Emperor?' said the woman, then gave a great sobbing cry and threw her arms round Kang Xi's neck.

Trinket tactfully drew away from them. Still holding the candle, he went slowly and deliberately round the large bedchamber, looking in every corner to make absolutely certain that there was no other living soul there but themselves, then, placing the candle on the table, he slipped noiselessly from the room, closing the door behind him as he went.

'I guess they've got plenty to say to each other,' he thought. 'They won't want me hanging around.'

Outside, the eight guards were still standing stiffly to attention where the Emperor had left them. Behind them in rows stood the eunuchs and ladies-in-waiting, all of them with fear in their faces. Trinket walked some distance into the garden and then beckoned to them to join him.

'Now, listen,' he said, when they had gathered round. 'The Emperor has been playing hide-and-seek with Her Highness the Princess Ning. Just for a laugh the Princess disguised herself as—as a human meat-ball. I expect you all saw her just now, running away in her disguise.'

'Oh yes,' said one of the guards who was quicker on the uptake than the others. 'She's a great one for dressing up, is Princess Ning. She could make herself look like anything.'

'Well, I just thought I'd better warn you,' said Trinket: 'His Majesty doesn't much like the idea of people getting to know about these pranks of theirs. It makes him look a bit silly. So if you feel like talking to anyone about what you've just seen, remember it'll probably cost you your head. You get my drift?'

'We won't say a word,' they chorused fervently, guards, eunuchs, and women speaking almost with one voice.

Trinket nodded.

'Good.' He turned to the three injured guards. 'So what happened to you lot?'

'Weapons training, sir,' said one of them. 'We were practising together and it got a bit out of hand.'

'Grandmother's!' said Trinket. 'They're your own mates, not the enemy. In future you'll have to be a bit more careful.'

'Yes, sir,' they said. 'Definitely, sir.'

'Right then,' said Trinket. 'You can each draw twenty taels sick pay to mend your heads.'

'Thank you, sir. Thank you, Colonel,' said the men gratefully. Like all the others present, they knew that witnesses of an Imperial scandal were normally silenced by being summarily executed and that Trinket was doing his best to save them.

'Now listen, all of you,' said Trinket, 'remember what I said. If you want to keep a head on your shoulders, not a word of this hide-and-seek business to anyone. If you think there's a danger of your talking about it in your sleep, better cut your tongue out. And while we're about it, you'd better give me your names.'

They did so, one after the other, first the guards, then the ladies-in-waiting, and then the eunuchs.

'Good,' said Trinket. 'From now on, then, if I hear so much as a word of this anywhere, you're all of you for the chop—the whole lot of you.'

As he was about to leave them, they fell on their knees and kowtowed.

'Thank you, Goong-goong,' they said, 'thank you. You've saved our lives.'

'Nonsense,' said Trinket. 'It's the Emperor you've got to thank.'

He went back to the building and sat on the steps outside the door. He must have been sitting there for all of half an hour when he heard Kang Xi's voice calling him to come in. Entering the bedchamber, he found Kang Xi and the Empress Dowager sitting side by side on the edge of the bed and holding hands. He went straight up to them and kowtowed.

'Congratulations, Your Majesties. Your Majesty, I've told the thirty-five people outside who saw Princess Ning in her disguise that if a word of this hide-and-seek business gets about, the whole lot of them will lose their heads. I think I've frightened them so much that there won't be much danger of their talking. What do you think, Your Majesty? Do you want them silenced? If so, it would be better to do it straight away.'

Kang Xi seemed to be hesitating, but the Empress Dowager quickly intervened.

'My dear, this is such a happy occasion, we mustn't spoil it by taking people's lives.'

'You're right,' said Kang Xi. 'A service of thanksgiving to the Buddha is what we should be thinking about right now.'

'And this boy,' said the Empress Dowager, 'we owe him so much. He too must be thanked.'

'Nothing to thank me for, Your Majesty,' said Trinket modestly. 'I blame myself for not having found out sooner what was going on and saved Your Majesty some suffering.'

The Empress Dowager, at the thought of her sufferings, began to cry.

'He is a very good boy,' she said to Kang Xi. 'You must do something special for him, to show our appreciation.'

'Well now, Laurie, what's it going to be?' said Kang Xi. 'I've already given you about as much promotion as I can. I think we'll have to make you a viscount. That means you're a member of the aristocracy now: Lord Wei.'

Trinket knelt and kowtowed to each of them in turn, first the Empress Dowager, then the Emperor.

'Thank you, Your Majesty. Thank you Your Majesty.'

Kang Xi dismissed him with a friendly wave of the hand.

'Viscount,' Trinket thought as he left the Hall of Maternal Tranquillity. 'What good will that do me? Don't suppose there's any money in it.'

Fatty's Sutra

When he got back to his own room, he took out the *Sutra in Forty-Two Sections* from inside the front of his gown to have a look at it. The silk-covered binding of this copy was blue with a scarlet border. He remembered hearing Aunt Tao say that her teacher was attempting to steal a copy of the Sutra from the Chief Clansman of the Bordered Blue Banner when he was mortally wounded by a leading member of the Mystic Dragon Sect. This must have been the copy.

Trinket knew that the false Empress Dowager, or Mao Dongzhu as he must now learn to call her, was a member of the Sect and it seemed likely that this fat lover of hers was also a member. He couldn't imagine what the history of the Sutra could have been during the intervening years since Aunt Tao's teacher made his unsuccessful attempt to steal it, but it seemed likely that the Mao lady's pumpkin-shaped lover had come by it quite recently and had called in to see her on his way back to Snake Island to share his triumph with her and spend a few nights with her in bed. Presumably she had turned the unfortunate Empress Dowager out of her closet to make him a hiding-place, which is why he had found the Sutra there under the bedding.

'It's going to be a bit awkward if the two of them go to Snake Island now and tell the Master what's happened,' he thought. 'I'd better send him this copy, perhaps with one or two of the others, to keep him happy—after taking the bits of map out of the cover, of course. They won't be much use to him without the pieces, but we don't know anything about that, do we? Maybe he doesn't either. If he does, he hasn't said anything to me about it.

'On the other hand, suppose Fatty comes back here for the Sutra? Could be dangerous. I'd better tell Dolong to double the guards.'

His chest was hurting and he could no longer think very clearly. He decided that he had had enough excitement for one day, so, with those two resolutions in mind for acting on in the morning, he went to bed and fell asleep almost instantly.

CHAPTER 19

In which Trinket the Viscount travels to
Yunnan as an Imperial Marriage Envoy

The Helmsman and the Bloodless Sword

A couple of days later, Trinket slipped out to see the Triads, and found them in a state of great excitement.

'We're expecting a visit from the Helmsman,' Brother Li told him. 'He was already in Tianjin when we last heard from him. He should reach Peking some time today.'

'That's wonderful!' said Trinket, remembering, with a sinking heart, that he had done no training. The Triads bustled about, preparing for their hero's arrival. Some went out to buy wine, some slaughtered and dressed chickens for a meal. Towards evening, Trinket took Brother Gao aside and asked him for some tools.

When, somewhat mystified, Brother Gao supplied him with what he had specified, a chopper and a chisel, Trinket explained why he wanted them. He had had a dream, he said, in which the dead friend whose ashes he had encoffined on an earlier visit had mentioned a few things of sentimental value that he would like to have with him. Today he had brought the things that his friend had asked for and needed the tools to open the coffin with so that he could put them inside. Brother Gao accepted this as a perfectly natural explanation and was not at all surprised when the Lodge Master, on entering the outhouse where the coffin was, shut and bolted the door after him in order to be alone with the dead.

Noting with satisfaction that there was a thick layer of dust on the coffin—which showed that it had not been disturbed—Trinket set about prising open the lid, using the chisel as a lever and the blade of the chopper as a wedge. Having got the lid off, he took out the oilskin packet containing the five Sutras that he had deposited there before departing on the first of his expeditions to Wutai. He was just about to replace the lid when he heard Brother Gao call out:

'Who's that?'

This was followed by a shout:

'Where's Chen Jinnan?'

Trinket couldn't place the voice, though it sounded vaguely familiar.

'Who are you?' he heard Brother Gao asking.

'Don't worry, we'll get him out, wherever he's hiding!' said another voice that Trinket instantly recognized. It was the sneering, supercilious voice of Zheng Keshuang, his hated rival. He realized now that the first voice must have been that of Zheng's teacher, Feng, the Bloodless Sword, last seen when he rescued Zheng from the pseudo-tribesmen. There was a clash of swords, a muffled cry from Brother Gao, and the thudding sound of someone falling to the floor.

'He's probably hiding in there.'

It was Zheng's voice again. Trinket barely had time to jump inside the coffin and pull the lid down when there was a crash and a splintering sound as the barred door was forced violently inwards. In the darkness he could see a seam of light where, because of the projecting nails, the lid didn't quite meet the edge of the coffin. He wondered if the intruders would notice that it wasn't properly shut. As he lay there fearfully, each moment expecting to be discovered, he heard another voice, that of his Shifu, speaking from somewhere outside.

'Were you looking for me, Sir Zheng? What was it you wanted to ask me?'

A moment later there was a loud cry of pain followed by a clash of weapons.

'Feng Xifan,' cried the Helmsman, 'that was a cowardly blow. What reason had you to lie in wait for me?'

'I have orders to arrest you,' said Feng.

'We can no longer tolerate your insolent behaviour,' said Zheng, his voice trembling with rage.

'Little dog-turd!' muttered Trinket inside the coffin.

'I certainly intended no disrespect to you, sir,' said the Helmsman with a deference that Trinket found unbearable. 'I left Tianjin the moment I heard you were planning a visit and was travelling through the night to get here. I am deeply sorry that I was not in time to welcome you.'

'I am here on the mainland as my father's representative. Are you aware of that?' said Zheng.

'Yes, sir,' said the Helmsman meekly.

'Yet ever since I arrived I have met with nothing but insults and humiliations from your Triad rabble,' Zheng continued.

'They are ignorant men,' said the Helmsman. 'Could they perhaps have been unaware who you were?'

'Insolent man, do you presume to question what I am telling you?' said Zheng. 'The commission I hold from my father gives me full discretionary powers. Do you know what that means?'

'I do,' said the Helmsman. 'You may act as you think fit without reporting back to him.'

'And as long as I am on the mainland my orders are to be obeyed by everyone—including you.'

'Yes, Sir Zheng.'

'Very good. Then cut off your right arm!'

'But why?' asked the Helmsman in astonishment.

'Because you are a rebel and a traitor,' said Zheng. 'The contempt you have shown my person proves your disloyalty to my father. You no longer regard yourself as his subject. You have built up this network on the mainland to be independent of Taiwan. Admit it, you are planning a kingdom of your own!'

The Helmsman was aghast.

'Such an idea has never entered my mind.'

'At the Congress in Hejianfu I was chosen to be the representative for Fujian,' said Zheng. 'Do you know how many provinces were given to your Triads?'

The Helmsman said nothing. Zheng's voice rose to a shout.

'Three. And they made you an Honorary President. You are totally without loyalty towards the Zhengs of Taiwan. You place yourself above them.'

'The Triad Society was founded on the orders of your grandfather the Marshal,' said the Helmsman. 'Its aim is the expulsion of the Tartars and the restoration of the Ming Imperial house. Everything we do is faithfully reported to His Highness in Taiwan and nothing undertaken without his approval. Let me return to Taiwan to face trial. If His Highness finds me disloyal and orders my execution I shall submit willingly to his judgement.'

This seemed, temporarily, to silence Zheng. It was his sinister teacher who answered.

'Bogus. How can we trust you to go back to Taiwan? If we let you go now, you'll probably go straight off to the Tartars to betray Sir Zheng, so that you can set up your standard here alone.'

'Feng Xifan,' said the Helmsman angrily, 'was it on His Highness's orders that you made that cowardly attack on me just now? You have poisoned Sir Zheng's mind against me. It's people like you, sowing dissension in our ranks with their lies and intrigues, who ruin our chances of success. You may be the world's greatest swordsman, Feng Xifan, but I defy you!'

'He defies us all,' shouted Zheng. 'Arrest the traitor!'

Once more there was a clash of swords. It sounded as if Zheng was joining in, for he heard an anguished cry from the Helmsman entreating him not to:

'Stand back, Sir Zheng, I beg you! I can't fight you!'

'Can't you, indeed!' Zheng shouted back at him.

Trinket raised the coffin-lid a little and peeped out. The Helmsman was holding his sword in his left hand. His right arm, dripping with blood from the deep wound that Feng had inflicted on him as he entered, hung useless at his side. Already disadvantaged by fighting left-handed, he was nevertheless contriving, for the time being at any rate, to parry the swift cut and thrust of the master-swordsman Feng Xifan; but since, from a mistaken sense of loyalty, he had decided not to defend himself against Zheng— merely swerving and dodging from the repeated swipes that the cowardly young man was aiming at him but never countering them with his sword—it seemed doubtful that he would be able to hold out much longer. Trinket couldn't understand why the Triads didn't come running to his aid. Surely the noise being made must have been heard by now in the next building?

Just at that moment, as the Helmsman raised his sword to parry a particularly violent thrust from Feng, their two blades locked, exposing the Helmsman's side and enabling Zheng to take a swinging blow at it. The Helmsman tried to twist his body out of the way, but Zheng's sword caught him on the left leg, slicing deeply into the flesh. As he cried out in pain, their swords unlocked and Feng drew his own sword back, then, lunging forwards, drove the point of it forcefully into the Helmsman's right shoulder. Bleeding now from three wounds, the Helmsman could barely defend himself any longer and was retreating step by step towards the door. Fearing that he might escape, Feng leapt into the doorway and blocked his exit.

'Oh no you don't! You're not getting away from us now.'

Trinket wanted to save his Shifu from what now looked like certain death, but what could he do? If only Feng Xifan had been nearer the coffin, he might have been able to stab him from behind, but he was beyond his reach. All he could think of was to find some way of distracting his attention. Raising his voice to its highest pitch, he uttered two shrill little squawks.

'Eek, eek!'

The three men turned in astonishment and gazed towards the coffin.

'What was that?' cried Zheng in alarm. But Feng merely shook his head and returned to the attack.

'Eek, eek, eek!' squawked Trinket desperately from the coffin; and as Zheng stared at it in horror, pale and shaking with fright, the lid rose and a cloud of white powder flew out of it. Quickly it spread through the room, causing the three men to choke and cough, and blinding and burning their eyes.

Before the corpse is put into a coffin, it is usual to cover the bottom with a sprinkling of lime. Brother Gao, meticulous in his preparations, had not neglected this detail when getting things ready for the obsequies of Trinket's imaginary friend, and Trinket had found a generous layer of it already there when the coffin was delivered. It had taken him only a few seconds to scrape up a full handful of it and toss it into the room.

Feng Xifan, confident that the source of the eerie squawks and the powdered lime was no ghost but a person of flesh and blood, leapt towards the coffin, still keeping his eyes closed, and stabbed into it with his sword. As he did so he felt an agonizing pain between the ribs of his left side and knew that he had fallen into a trap. It was, of course, Trinket, who had jumped out of the coffin and dealt what he hoped was a fatal blow with his dagger before rushing for the doorway, scattering more lime as he went. Feng opened his eyes but hastily closed them again, blinded afresh by the lime. Clutching with his left hand the bleeding wound in his chest, he lurched blindly towards the wall, hitting it finally with his left shoulder. Then, sword in hand, he slid his way towards the doorway, keeping his shoulder to the wall.

Trinket saw him coming from outside the door and was for a moment at a loss to know what he should do. Then, with a sudden flash of inspiration, he drove his dagger a couple of inches into the door-jamb so that it projected horizontally at about the height of his head. Drawing back a little behind the wall, careful to keep his head at the same height as the dagger, he called out in his squeaky ghost-voice:

'Here I am!'

At once Feng's sword flashed out, but only to bisect itself on the dagger's adamantine blade. The end half flew into the air and fell to the ground, striking Feng's head on the way. Wounded and tricked once more, with a cry of pain and rage, he rushed through the door and across the garden, leaving a trail of blood behind him. Peering through the doorway, Trinket saw Zheng and the Helmsman standing apart with their backs towards each other, eyes tightly closed and waving their swords about in front of them. Now that Feng Xifan was out of the way, he felt able to deal with Zheng. But first he must reassure his Shifu.

'Shifu,' he called out, 'it's all right now. I've dealt with the Bloodless Sword. He's just run off, covered all over in blood.'

The Helmsman ceased waving his sword.

'Who's that?'

'It's me,' said Trinket, 'your disciple—Trinket.' He turned and shouted over his shoulder to imaginary allies. 'Brother Zhang, Brother Li, Brother Wang, I'm glad you've come. If this Zheng person doesn't drop his sword now and surrender, just cut him down!'

This put Zheng in a panic. He began calling out for Feng, but when there was no reply, he quickly dropped his sword.

'Kneel down!' said Trinket.

Zheng tremblingly obeyed.

'Now,' said Trinket, going over and holding the blade of his dagger to Zheng's throat, 'stand up!'

Zheng stood up.

'Turn right! Three steps forward!' This brought Zheng to the side of the coffin.

'Now get in!'

Zheng, too scared to protest, stepped into the coffin and mechanically lay down in it, whereupon Trinket, laughing out loud as he did so, banged down the lid.

'Shifu,' he said, going up to the Helmsman and taking him by the hand, 'we must go now and see about your eyes.'

A little way outside the outhouse they came upon Brother Gao, lying inert beside a bed of flowers. They thought he was dead until he spoke:

'I'm all right, Master. I've just had my points closed, that's all. See to the Helmsman first, that's what matters. I can wait.'

The Helmsman nevertheless bent down and applied the appropriate pressures to his upper back and waist to release him from his paralysis. As soon as he could move and was on his feet again, he inquired what was the matter with the Helmsman's eyes.

'Lime,' said the Helmsman curtly.

'You'll have to wash them with cooking-oil,' said Brother Gao. 'You mustn't, whatever you do, use water. Come with me, sir. I'll see to it.'

Seeing that his Shifu was in competent hands, Trinket temporarily excused himself and ran back into the outhouse. He could hear that his prisoner had been trying to raise the lid. The nails, when he slammed it down, could not have penetrated very deeply. With the back of the chopper he banged six or seven of them in.

'You can rest quiet now, Sir Zheng,' he said. 'Forget about the ten thousand taels you owe me: I'll make you a present of them!'

Picking up the oilskin packet in which the Sutras were wrapped, he walked back, still laughing, across the little garden and up into the hall. He found the floor there strewn with bodies. Butcher Qian, Father Obscurus, and the rest were lying about in all directions, immobile but alive. Brother Gao had already washed the Helmsman's eyes with oil and was now binding up his wounds. As soon as he had finished, the Helmsman set about unlocking the pressure points of the recumbent Triads. On their feet once more, they began exclaiming indignantly against Feng's treachery, expressing the hope, when they learnt what had happened in the outhouse, that the lime had blinded him permanently. The Helmsman, however, whose own eyes were red and swollen and continuously running with tears, gravely ordered Butcher Qian and Brother Gao to find Sir Zheng and attend to his eyes, too. Having done so, they were to invite him into the hall.

As they hurried off to do his bidding, Trinket gave a little cry and appeared to faint. Early in his career his use of lime as a weapon had earned him a beating. He had a strong presentiment that, in the Triads' code of honour, nailing your defeated foe in a coffin might have even more painful consequences. The others carried him to a chair and were crowding round him solicitously when Gao and Qian returned and told them that Zheng was nowhere to be seen.

The Helmsman frowned.

'But isn't he in the coffin?'

The two men exchanged puzzled glances. They had observed a coffin, but could not see how anyone could have got inside it.

'We'll go and have a look,' said the Helmsman.

They trooped over in a little knot behind him, Trinket hanging back in the rear. All over the floor of the outhouse there was blood and lime. The Helmsman's face darkened as his eye lit on the coffin.

'Trinket, did you nail Sir Zheng in that coffin?' he asked angrily.

'No,' said Trinket, 'I didn't do it. He must have done it himself. He probably thought if you found him he would be killed.'

'Nonsense!' said the Helmsman. 'Get that lid off at once, before he suffocates!'

Butcher Qian and Brother Gao set to at once with chopper and chisel and soon had the lid off the coffin. Needless to say, there was a man lying inside it.

'Sir Zheng!' said the Helmsman, and made haste to raise up the reclining figure. A cry escaped the others as he did so, and the Helmsman himself, looking into the man's face, released the body and jumped back in horror. It was Brother Guan—Big Beaver.

They raised him up again. When they felt the body, it was still warm, but he was quite definitely dead. Father Obscurus knelt down and undid Big Beaver's jacket and his shirt. There was a seal-mark on his chest, a blood-red hand.

'Feng Xifan,' he said. 'All members of the Kunlun School use that mark. Cruel devil! Wasn't it enough to rescue Sir Zheng? Why did he need to kill Big Beaver as well?'

Scarface, Big Beaver's son-in-law, began to wail. The other Triads broke out in curses. The Helmsman alone remained morosely silent.

'The Marshal was always so good to me,' he said presently with a sigh, 'and I have always done my utmost to repay him by giving loyal service to his successors. Up to now I have met with nothing but courtesy and consideration from his son, the Prince. The Prince knows I am loyal. I can't believe he would want me killed.'

'His eight sons are all at each other's throats to get the succession,' said Father Obscurus. 'This Sir Zheng is only one of them. If he can do this to you here on the mainland, who knows what damage he might do to you, with a dangerous rat like Feng to help him, when he gets back to Taiwan? Whatever you say about the Prince, blood, as we all know, is thicker than water.'

'An honourable man must do what he has to do regardless of how others traduce or revile him,' said the Helmsman with another sigh. 'Still, I never imagined that anything like this might happen. Good heavens! If it hadn't been for the resourcefulness of young Trinket here, we might all of us have been murdered. But poor Guan!' he added, remembering that one of them *had* been murdered.

Trinket wasn't sure what 'resourcefulness' was, but the Helmsman's words sounded like praise and he was relieved not to be reprimanded. Before his Shifu could have time to reflect on the dishonourable means that had been used to rescue him, he made haste to change the subject.

'We've been making such a racket here today,' he said, 'I'm sure the neighbours must have heard. Hadn't we better move our headquarters somewhere else?'

'You are absolutely right,' said the Helmsman. 'If my mind were in a more settled state, I should have suggested it myself.'

A grave was hurriedly dug in the garden for Big Beaver and as soon as they had finished burying him and had knelt and kowtowed at the graveside and bidden him a tearful farewell, they set about getting their things together for a move of house. The dangerous nature of their work necessitated frequent changes of domicile, so they were used to removals and able to take this latest one in their stride. Pretending that he was needed at the Palace,

Trinket took his leave of the Helmsman and left the Triads to their packing.

More Talk of Sutras

Back in his room at the Palace, having first carefully barred the door, Trinket unwrapped the five copies of the Sutra he had retrieved from the coffin, added the bordered blue copy he had taken from the fat man's hiding-place in the false Empress Dowager's bedroom, and set about unstitching the covers of all six and extracting the cut-up pieces of parchment that were hidden inside them. Carefully sweeping the little mound of pieces into the bag in which the pieces from the poisoned Sutra had been kept, he began the task of sewing the covers up again. He found sewing tedious: indeed, he was only halfway through the first cover when he began to tire of it and suddenly thought of Doublet, whose nimble fingers would have had this job finished in no time—poor Doublet, who was probably still languishing in her lodgings beneath the Shaolin Monastery where he had left her so many weeks ago, and who was probably wondering what on earth had become of him! He must find some means of sending for her at the earliest opportunity. After a few more stitches he was so sick of the whole business that he threw the book down in disgust and went to bed.

First thing next morning he waited on Kang Xi in the Upper Library and was informed that his appointment as Marriage Envoy charged with the duty of escorting Her Highness the Princess Ning to Yunnan was to be announced in Court next day. After telling him this, Kang Xi dropped his voice and assumed a more confidential tone.

'There's something very important, besides this marriage business, that I want you to do for me when you get to Yunnan. I've just been talking about this to the Empress Dowager. It seems that the vile woman who was impersonating her was trying to discover the secret of the Dragon Line which controls the destiny of the Manchus. Her intention, or that of the people she was working for, was to break the line by digging into it in order to undermine our power. The secret is somehow hidden inside the eight copies of a book, the *Sutra in Forty-Two Sections*.'

Trinket, who had probably known about this a great longer than the Emperor and who, at that very moment, had got six of the eight copies in his room, expressed amazement. Feeling himself on dangerous ground, he thought it safer to behave formally, as a loyal subject rather than as a friend.

'Should Your Majesty be telling me this?' he asked, with feigned anxiety. 'The fewer people know, the more chance there is of the secret staying a secret.'

'Good for you, Trinket!' said Kang Xi. 'You are learning fast. But I think I can trust *you*. If I can't trust you, I don't know who I can trust.'

Trinket felt a pang of remorse. He disguised his confusion by dropping to his knees and kowtowing.

'I won't betray your trust, I promise, Your Majesty,' he said. 'I would rather cut my tongue out than give away any secret of yours.'

And for the moment at any rate, he really meant it.

'I know,' said Kang Xi kindly, at the same time motioning to him to get up. 'That's why I'm telling you this. Now then, these eight copies of the Sutra are bound in the colours of the Eight Banners: the four plain ones, yellow, white, red, and blue, and the four bordered ones, yellow, white, and blue with red borders, and red with a white border. When the power of the Manchus was first established in China, the Regent Dorgon gave one copy to the Head of each of the Banners. This was a safety measure: the secret is divided up between the eight copies, so unless you can get all eight together, there is no means of knowing it. Three copies were kept in the Imperial Household: the plain white, the plain yellow, and the bordered yellow. You yourself have seen all three of them. Two of them you found among Oboi's things when his estate was confiscated. You were ordered to hand them in to that evil woman.'

'I wish I hadn't,' said Trinket

'If you hadn't done, you would have been in serious trouble,' said Kang Xi. 'At that time I myself didn't know that she was an impostor.'

'How did Oboi come to have two copies?' said Trinket.

'One of them was his as Head of the Bordered Yellow Banner. The other, the plain white one, belonged to his co-Regent, Suksaha. When Oboi had Suksaha executed on trumped-up charges, he took over his copy of the Sutra along with all the rest of his estate. The plain yellow one was my father's. He took it with him to Wutai when he became a monk. You brought it back to give me, remember, with a message from him inside it, after your first visit to the monastery. I used to keep it here on my desk but recently I found that it had gone missing. There's only one person I can think of who could have taken it.'

'Princess—?' Trinket began, but thought he had better not say it.

Kang Xi nodded. 'Princess Ning.'

'But that means that the Old Whore—I'm sorry, I mean that bad woman has got three of the eight copies.'

(One of the three, the plain yellow one, he had himself destroyed by impregnating it with poison and throwing it to the lamas, but before that it had for a while been in the false Empress Dowager's possession.)

'I'm afraid the *Old Whore*,' said Kang Xi as if he rather enjoyed calling her that, 'has got more than just three. The Head Bannerman who held the bordered white copy had to forfeit it because of some misdemeanour and my father gave it to the Empress Donggo. When the Old Whore murdered the Empress Donggo she would almost certainly have got hold of her copy of the Sutra. And the traitor Colonel Rui, who was her accomplice, is suspected of having stolen the copy belonging to Hochabo, the Head of the Bordered Red Banner, shortly before he disappeared; so it is highly probable that she has got that one, too. That makes five. I've been calling the remaining copies in. Prince Kang holds the plain red one. I've already asked him for it and he should be sending it shortly.'

'Poor old Kang!' thought Trinket, who had seen Prince Kang's skinny bodyguard, Qi Yuankai, stealing it from the Prince's private chapel, and had then taken it himself.

'As for Oshokha, the Head of the Bordered Blue Banner, he's an old fool,' Kang Xi continued. 'When I asked him for his copy, he said he had lost it. I had him arrested and sent to the Tianlao prison. He's being questioned there right now.'

'Poor old Oshokha!' thought Trinket. He knew about the Tianlao prison and he knew what 'questioning' meant. The bordered blue copy was the one stolen by the false Empress Dowager's fat lover which he had found in the closet and added to his collection. No amount of torture would reveal its whereabouts to Oshokha's interrogators.

'That only leaves the plain blue copy,' said Kang Xi. 'Fudeng, the Head of the Plain Blue Banner, is only a boy. When we asked

him for his copy, he said he had never had one. His father died
fighting in Yunnan and his estate, after he died, was administered
by Wu Sangui. Fudeng says all he ever got from Wu Sangui was a
seal, a few regimental banners, and a sum of money. It's obvious
that Wu Sangui must have kept back the Sutra for himself.'

'Suppose—' Trinket hesitated.

'Yes?'

'Suppose the Old Whore is working for Wu Sangui.'

'Precisely. We don't know, of course, but if that were so,
Wu Sangui would end up with six of the eight copies. That is
why it is so important that you should find some means of locat-
ing the plain blue copy when you are in Yunnan and getting it back
to me. If I can just lay my hands on those two copies, the plain red
and the plain blue, the secret is safe. We can forget about the
others.'

He fell silent and began pacing to and fro, frowning. Evidently
he was deep in thought. Trinket, wondering what he could be
thinking of, would have been surprised to learn that the young
Emperor was trying to decide just how much he ought to tell
this little urchin he had befriended and to whom up to now he
had confided all his secrets. For just as there were things Trinket
knew about the copies of the Sutra that he hadn't told the Emperor,
so there were things the Emperor knew that he hadn't yet told
Trinket.

What Kang Xi knew and Trinket didn't was that this talk of a
fateful Dragon Line was nothing more than a blind. The map,
whose cut-up pieces were divided up and concealed inside the eight
copies of the Sutra, was a map showing not Dragon Lines but the
location of a vast underground treasury in which all the loot—the
bullion, the art treasures, the jewellery, and precious stones—
amassed in the course of the Manchu conquest of China had been
deposited. In the long talk that Kang Xi had had with his father,
sitting alone with him in the temple hall of the Golden Pavilion
Monastery, Kang Xi had learned that the Regent Dorgon had
hidden this treasure there as an insurance against future failure. The
Manchus were greatly outnumbered by the Chinese they had conquered. If, through weakness or misfortune, they should ever be
driven out, the stored-up riches would enable them to begin a new
life in their old homeland. But the Regent knew about human greed
and ambition. Although, as a precaution, he had divided the frag-

mented pieces of map up between the Heads of the Eight Banners, there was always the possibility that a greedy or ambitious Head Bannerman might somehow get possession of all eight copies and seize the treasure for himself. Hence the fiction about the Dragon Line whose severance would bring about the universal destruction of the Manchus. Only the Emperor was to know the secret of the treasure. Shun Zhi had told it to the Empress Dowager before he withdrew from the world, instructing her to pass it on to his little son when he came of age. It was this duty that had sustained her throughout the dreadful years of her confinement, though, as it turned out, Kang Xi had heard the secret from Shun Zhi himself before she was rescued.

'My son,' Shun Zhi had said, 'the Chinese are many and we are few. We must rule them with justice and kindness and seek to win their hearts. If we cannot do so and they rebel against us, we must go back to where we came from. The treasure there will sustain us.'

Kang Xi loved and respected his gentle father, but he did not share his opinions. He could see that Manchu rule was becoming consolidated; moreover, he was a clever, ambitious youth and looked forward to a long and prosperous reign in which he would weld the two races into a single people. To have one's eye constantly on the possibility of escape, of running away from the difficulties and living comfortably elsewhere, would be demoralizing. He resolved to remove the possibility of anyone, himself included, being able to find the treasure by destroying one or two of the eight copies of the Sutra which were the key to its whereabouts. He also resolved not to say anything to Trinket about the treasure.

'I believe I could trust him now,' he thought. 'But who knows what he will turn out to be like when he is older?'

Having reached that decision, he ceased his pacing up and down and chatted with him for a few minutes before giving him the informal nod that allowed him to leave.

Prince Kang

As Trinket left the Upper Library, a guard stepped up and informed him that Prince Kang was waiting for him in the mess-room of the Palace Guards. It was unprecedented for a Prince of the Blood to wait on a eunuch in the Palace, but Trinket had no difficulty in guessing the reason why he was being treated with such exaggerated politeness. The Prince was sitting slumped in a chair, frowning distractedly and twiddling nervously with a teacup, but he jumped up, all smiles, as soon as Trinket walked into the mess.

'Your Highness,' said Trinket, 'you really shouldn't do this. If you want to see me, you only have to send for me.'

'You are so busy these days, dear boy,' said the Prince, 'I wasn't sure I could get you. I have hired some excellent players that I particularly want you to see. Could you possibly find time to come round now for a meal?'

Trinket having expressed himself entirely at the Prince's disposal, the Prince took him by the hand and led him to the Palace gate where two horses were being held in readiness for them to mount.

An elaborate meal awaited them at the Prince's residence, but there was no sign of any players. The Prince pressed dish after dish on his solitary guest, showering him meanwhile with compliments—on his courage, his resourcefulness, the extraordinarily valuable service he gave the Emperor, and so on and so forth—while Trinket, laughing inwardly, wondered when, if ever, he would come to the point. At last, when the meal was over, the Prince invited him into his private study and it all came out.

The Prince was in trouble, real trouble. When the dynasty was founded, he explained, the Heads of the Eight Banners had each been given a copy of a Sutra bound in the colour of his own banner. As Head of the Plain Red Banner, he was supposed to be looking after the plain red one, but now the Emperor had asked for it back and the wretched thing had been stolen. If the Emperor found out he hadn't got it, he was as good as dead. Poor old Oshokha had lost his copy and now he was in the Tianlao prison being given the works. The Prince, as he mentioned it, could almost feel his own flesh being torn.

'Save me, brother!' he said, almost tearfully, dropping on one knee—to the great consternation of Trinket, who knelt on both his own before raising the Prince up to his feet.

'You know I'd do anything for you,' said Trinket. 'I'd even give you my head.'

He proceeded to suggest one or two ways, none of them practicable, in which he might help. The least helpful was his sugges-

tion that the Emperor should be told that he, Trinket, had borrowed
the Sutra and lost it. (It was common knowledge that he couldn't
read.) It became clear, when the Prince had, as tactfully as he could,
disposed of all these proposals, that he had some scheme of his
own in mind, but it took a great deal of persuading to get him to
say what it was.

When finally he did so, it appeared that he wanted Trinket to
steal a copy of the Sutra either from the Emperor himself or from
the Empress Dowager. He had gathered a number of skilled
workmen together who would, as soon as they could set eyes on
the Sutra, work day and night to produce a perfect copy. This would
then be bound in the appropriate cover and presented to the
Emperor. The stolen copy would, of course, be smuggled back to
wherever it had come from.

To the Prince's delight Trinket had no objection to stealing
from the Emperor. He even seemed eager to begin.

'The sooner I get to work on this the better,' he said, and rose
to go.

The Prince insisted on seeing him out as far as the roadway
outside, urging him, again and again, to be careful.

Back in his room in the Palace, Trinket took out his little collection of Sutras and surveyed them. Any of them would do to lend
to the Prince except for the plain red one—the one that the Prince
said had gone missing. He decided to select the one with the bordered white cover which he had already started sewing. Having
completed, with much difficulty and a good deal of cursing, the
stitching together of the two layers of parchment, he pasted the silk
onto them and weighted it down to dry.

First thing next morning he stood at the Prince's gate with
the 'stolen' Sutra concealed beneath his gown. The Prince
came bounding out to meet him as soon as his arrival was
announced.

'Any luck?'

When Trinket nodded, the Prince was so overjoyed that he
picked him up in his arms and carried him all the way to his study,
to the astonishment and no little amusement of the guards and
attendants who saw him as he passed.

'It will take your workmen days to make a copy of this Sutra,'
said Trinket. 'Why don't you just change this cover for a red one
and hand it in straight away? You can put the bordered white cover
on your workmen's copy when it's ready. With a bit of luck—pro-

vided they can finish within a week or so—the Emperor will never find out that it's been missing.'

The Prince had secretly been intending to do this anyway, but was none the less touched by his young friend's thoughtfulness. It was true: if he had delayed handing in the Sutra for a week or two—by pretending that he was ill or had had an accident—the Emperor would very likely have smelt a rat and might well have discovered that the copy was a fake. When Trinket left to hurry back to the Palace, the Prince's eyes were quite moist with gratitude as he wrung the hands of his little saviour, his heart too full for words.

Doctor Lu and Fat Dhuta, Again

Alone in his room in the Palace he once more surveyed his little hoard. It was high time, he decided, that he sent a couple of these Sutras to the Leader of the Mystic Dragon Sect, but which two was it to be? Of the five now left, three were ones he had taken from the false Empress Dowager's bedroom: the plain white and bordered yellow ones from the secret compartment in her bed and the bordered blue one from the closet in which her balloon-like lover had been hiding. He couldn't send any of them, because she was probably back on Snake Island by now and would realize as soon as she saw them that he was playing a double game. It would have to be the two red ones, the plain red one which had once been Prince Kang's and the bordered red one which he had removed from the dead body of Lieutenant-Colonel Rui. After stitching up the covers and sticking down the silk, he took them with him to the lodgings where, during all these past months, Fat Dhuta and Doctor Lu had been staying while waiting for instructions from him.

Needless to say they were delighted to see him—even more so when they heard that he had succeeded in getting hold of two copies of the Sutra. Trinket charged Doctor Lu with the task of delivering them to the Leader.

'When you see him,' he said, 'tell him I've found out that Wu Sangui knows where the other six copies are and that I'm going to Yunnan to see what more I can find out about them. It's going to be a dangerous mission, but for the Leader and Madame Hong I'd lay my life down if necessary. Long Life to the Leader! Blessings be on Him!'

'Long Life to the Leader! Blessings be on Him!' the other two echoed dutifully.

'If he gives you the Leopard Pill Antidote,' said Trinket, 'make sure you send someone reliable with them.'

Doctor Lu told himself that this young White Dragon Marshal, who had already, while still only a boy, achieved so much, might well turn out to be the Leader's successor. He determined to waste no time in getting into his good books.

'I wouldn't dream of sending them,' he said. 'If he gives me the Pills, I shall bring them to you myself. And the Dhuta and I will see to it that you have your dose before we do.'

Being himself a master in the art of flattery, Trinket knew that he was being flattered, but was gratified none the less. While the doctor began preparing for his departure, he told Fat Dhuta that he wanted him to accompany him to Yunnan. After discussing arrangements for getting him into his retinue, he hurried back to the Palace. This all happened in the early morning of the day after he took the copy to Prince Kang.

The Reluctant Bride

Shortly after he got back to the Palace, his appointment as Marriage Envoy to the Satrap's court in Yunnan was formally announced and the title of Viscount publicly conferred on him. Honorary titles were at the same time conferred *in absentia* on the Satrap's son, Wu Yingxiong, as future brother-in-law of the Emperor. After the investiture, while he was in the Upper Library chatting informally with the Emperor, the Princess Ning was announced. No sooner was the announcement made than she came rushing in and threw herself weeping on the Emperor's neck.

'I don't want to go to Yunnan!' she sobbed. 'I don't want to be married! Please, Emperor–brother, have the Edict cancelled! And tell Her Majesty to stop refusing to see me!'

Kang Xi had always had a soft spot for this tomboyish princess. It was only recently, since he found out that she wasn't really his half-sister but the daughter of his mother's murderess, that he had begun to dislike her. Seeing her now so distressed, and knowing only too well the cause for the real Empress Dowager's refusal to see her impostor's love-child, he began to melt.

'I can't do that,' he said. 'An Edict can't be cancelled. Anyway, every girl has to get married some time or other; and I've chosen a very good husband for you. Tell her, Laurie, you've met Wu Yingxiong: he's a very handsome young man, isn't he?'

Trinket began singing the young man's praises and gave so droll an account of the Peking maidens fighting each other in the streets for a sight of him that she burst out laughing.

'Emperor-brother,' she said, 'if I go to Yunnan, you must let me keep Laurie to make me laugh.'

'Well, he can stay on a bit, perhaps,' said Kang Xi. 'By the way,' his face now assumed a sterner expression, 'a Sutra has gone missing from my desk. I suppose you haven't any idea who could have taken it?'

'Oh, I did,' said the Princess gaily. 'Mother said she wanted it for saying prayers for your safety or something, so I took it for her. Don't worry,' she said forlornly, when she saw his frown: 'I shan't be able to take your books from you when I'm far away in Yunnan.'

She was so guileless and so appealing that Kang Xi began to feel quite sorry that he was banishing her.

'You must always let me know if there is anything you want when you are living there,' he said. 'Not that it's very likely there will be,' he added, half to himself. 'Wu Sangui's court is probably richer than mine.'

Viscount Wei at Home

Shortly after midday Prince Kang saw Trinket in the Palace. He was looking very happy.

'I've handed in the Sutra,' he told Trinket. 'The Emperor was very pleased. He even praised me.'

'I'm glad,' said Trinket.

'As you'll soon be off to Yunnan, I've organized a little party for you,' said the Prince. 'Partly it's to congratulate you on the viscountcy and partly it's a way of saying goodbye.'

They left the Palace hand in hand. This time, however, Trinket found himself being taken not to the Prince's residence but to a little mansion in the East City. Though tiny compared with the Prince's residence, everything about it, both gardens and buildings, was exquisite.

'What do you think of this place?' asked the Prince.

'It's beautiful,' said Trinket. 'Who does it belong to? One of your wives?' (He didn't like to say 'your mistress'.)

The Prince just smiled and said nothing.

In the main reception hall a number of distinguished guests were waiting. As Trinket entered, all of them crowded forwards to congratulate him on his elevation, Songgotu and Dolong among the foremost.

'We're here to celebrate your appointment,' said the Prince, 'so I suppose by rights we ought to put you in the place of honour; however, as you're the host, I'm afraid we can't.'

'What do you mean?' said Trinket.

'This is your residence, Lord Wei,' said Prince Kang, laughing. 'You can't sleep in the Palace any longer now that we know you're not a eunuch. The coachmen, the cooks, the manservants, and maidservants here are all yours. I've tried to get everything ready for you in time, but it's been rather a rush. If you find anything missing, just send round to my place and let me know.'

Trinket knew that the Prince felt grateful to him, but hadn't expected the reward to be of such magnificence.

'But . . .' he stammered, 'but . . . You can't possibly give me all this!'

'Of course I can!' said the Prince. 'Didn't I tell you long ago: we are brothers! Now, everybody,' he cried to the assembled guests, 'no one gets out of here tonight until he is drunk!'

'Grandmother's!' thought Trinket hours later, as he drifted hazily sleepwards in his sumptuous bedroom, where everything his bleary eyes lit on seemed to be made of gold or silver or something precious. 'What a wonderful whore-house this would make!'

Music to Trinket's Ears

Next day Trinket went to see the White Nun to tell her that he was being sent to Yunnan. At once she proposed to accompany him on the journey. When it became clear that she would be bringing the Green Girl with her, Trinket felt that this was very much better than being made a viscount. From the White Nun's lodgings he went on to the new headquarters of the Triads.

The Helmsman, when he heard about Trinket's mission, at once saw this as an opportunity for tricking or goading the Satrap into rebellion. They could then stand by and watch the Satrap's forces and the Imperial forces destroy each other or wear each other out. He would have liked to go along with Trinket, he said, in order to help put this plan into operation, but Sir Zheng and his evil mentor, Feng the Bloodless Sword, were back in Taiwan now and Sir Zheng's father the Prince, in response to the slanders they were no doubt pouring into his ear, would probably be sending someone to the mainland soon to investigate. Let the other Triads accompany Trinket to Yunnan. He would stay on alone to face whatever charges were being made against him.

Trinket was uneasy about this. He suspected that the same precious pair would be sent over to carry out the 'investigation' and use it as a pretext for making a second, perhaps successful, attempt to carry out their murderous design. But the Helmsman patted him kindly on the shoulder and assured him that he was able to look after himself. He also took Trinket's pulse and looked at his tongue to see if he had fully recovered from the poison administered by Old Hai. His frown suggested that he was discontented with what he found. He told Trinket to put off doing his kungfu exercises until his body was completely free of it. This, needless to say, was music to Trinket's ears.

Princess Ning: Her Pain and Her Pleasure

A few days later, preparations having finally been completed, the Princess, with her retinue of eunuchs and female attendants and a large military escort made up of soldiers of the Valiant Regiment and members of the Palace Guards under the command of the Marriage Envoy, Lord Wei (as Trinket was now to be called), took leave of the Emperor and started off on the long journey to Yunnan. Disguised as waiting-women, the White Nun and the Green Girl had little difficulty in finding a place among the more menial of Princess Ning's attendants, where there would be little likelihood of their coming into contact with her, while Fat Dhuta and the Triads of the Green Wood Lodge, dressed in the uniform of the Valiants, were passed off by Trinket as orderlies forming a sort of personal bodyguard.

Riding at the head of the glittering cavalcade as it wound its way from the city and out into the countryside, Trinket, perched high on the back of Jade Flower, the magnificent grey that Prince Kang had presented to him on their first meeting, experienced a rare feeling of elation.

To the officials in the towns they passed through on their way, an Imperial Marriage Envoy escorting a Princess of the Blood was a personage only slightly less exalted than the Emperor. Everywhere he was received with smiles and flattery; at every stopping-place the same civic welcome, the same lavish entertainment awaited him.

At Zhengzhou the local magistrate had arranged for them to be housed in the gardens of a local millionaire. When the welcoming banquet was over, the Princess invited Trinket to come and sit for a while with her in the pavilion where she was lodged. She had been trying to get him on his own with her ever since they started their journey, but remembering the torments she had inflicted on him when she had got him alone with her in the past, he had so far been careful to take Butcher Qian and Brother Gao with him whenever he went to call on her, refusing, however much she stormed or cajoled, to dismiss them. On this occasion they were standing one on each side of him behind his chair, while the Princess sat in another chair with a female attendant on either side fanning her with a long-handled fan. The room they were sitting in was a lounge-like reception room giving on to the Princess's bedroom.

It was the height of summer and very hot. The Princess was wearing the thinnest of dresses, but her face was flushed and there was a fringe of tiny sweat-beads on her upper lip. It occurred to Trinket that she was very pretty. She smiled at him mockingly.

'Are you very hot, Laurie?' she asked.

'Not too bad,' he said, though he was dripping with sweat and feeling wretchedly uncomfortable in his formal clothes.

A female attendant entered carrying a large, polychrome jar containing some sort of liquid.

'Iced sour-plum drink, Your Highness,' she announced. 'It's a present from Prefect Meng. He thought it might help you to keep cool in this dreadful heat.'

'Let me try some,' said the Princess.

A little bowlful was ladled out and handed to her, together with a porcelain spoon. She dipped the spoon in it and tasted. The fragrant scent of the drink and the tinkling sound of the little pieces of ice made the mouths of Trinket and his companions water almost painfully.

'How clever of them to have ice in a place like Zhengzhou!' said the Princess. 'This is so refreshing. You must all of you have some!'

Three more bowlfuls were ladled out and handed to Trinket, Qian, and Gao. They thanked her and sipped. The cool drink was indescribably delicious. They drained the bowls eagerly and the Princess insisted that they should each of them have one more.

'From tomorrow onwards,' she said, 'now that the weather is so hot, we ought to travel no more than twelve miles a day. We should start off very, very early and stop to rest as soon as the sun gets up.'

'Your Highness is very thoughtful,' said Trinket. 'I'm sure we're all very grateful. But it's going to make it a very long journey.'

'Who cares!' said the Princess, gaily. 'If I'm not worried, why should you be? Let Wu Yingxiong wait a bit—it'll do him good!'

Trinket wanted to reply, but a sudden dizziness overcame him and his body began swaying a little. On either side of him, in rapid succession, first Butcher Qian and then Brother Gao keeled over and fell to the floor. A moment later Trinket himself was sliding into unconsciousness.

How long he remained this way he could only guess. His return to consciousness was precipitated by what he thought was a heavy shower of rain but was in fact the Princess emptying a pail of water over him. The first thing he became aware of was that he was cold and wet all over; the second, that he could not move because his hands and feet were tied. A little giggle caused him to open his eyes. Only then did he discover that he was lying stark naked in the Princess's bedroom while the Princess herself stood over him, amusedly surveying her handiwork.

'Where are the other two?' he asked.

'Oh, I've cut their heads off,' she said lightly. 'I was sick of their always hanging around when you came to see me.'

He didn't know whether to believe her or not.

'I suppose the drink was drugged,' he said.

'Oh, how clever of you to guess!' She laughed sarcastically.

She began to torment him then. This time it was even worse than the martyrdom she had subjected him to that first time in her room in the Palace. The reason, he discovered when he began to remonstrate with her, was her distress at the fact that her mother recently seemed to have turned against her and was refusing to see her (she still had no idea, apparently, that the Empress Dowager was now a different person); she believed that this, together with the fact that she was being banished into distant matrimonial exile, was all Trinket's doing. Nothing he said could persuade her to the contrary. She silenced his protests by stuffing one of his socks into his mouth and laying into him with a horsewhip.

Tiring at last of beating him, she threw down the whip.

'It would be better to burn you,' she said. 'I think I shall need some oil. I'll be back in a minute.'

She went out of the bedroom, presumably to look for oil. Trinket decided that she really must be mad and that this time he stood little chance of coming out of his ordeal alive. As he lay there, in agony of both mind and body, he heard female voices outside the bedroom window.

'Now get in there at once and save him!'

'I can't. He hasn't got any clothes on.'

It was the White Nun and the girl it pleased him to call his wife.

'Oh, you stupid girl!' he thought. 'Are you going to stand by and see your husband burned?'

Just at that moment the Princess came back into the bedroom carrying a little bottle. Having poured some oil from it onto his chest, she took one of the lighted candles from the dressing-table and was approaching him with it intending to set him on fire when there was a brief commotion outside the window.

'Quick! Now! I command it!'

The Green Girl came flying into the room (half pushed, half thrown by the White Nun), knocked the candlestick flying that the startled Princess had raised to strike her with, and after a brief struggle succeeded—almost effortlessly, for the Princess was in no way her match—in throwing her to the floor, one shoulder and one of her knees dislocated; then, with burning cheeks, hardly daring to look at what she was doing, she hastily severed the bonds that tied Trinket's hands and feet before rushing to the window and scrambling out again.

As the Princess lay, cursing but helpless beside him, Trinket painfully sat up and removed the smelly sock from his mouth.

'Horrible, stinking little bitch!' he said. 'It's time you tasted a bit of your own medicine.'

He silenced her curses with the sock, ripped her dress off, and began beating and beating her with the whip. He didn't keep it up for very long though, partly because the violent action was making his own weals more painful, but more than that because the strange, exultant look in her eyes disgusted him. In spite of the dreadful pain she must be in, she was almost enjoying herself. He took the sock out again.

'Dear Laurie, Prince Laurie,' she pleaded, 'you can go on beating me if you like, but please first put my joints back!'

This was the voice she had used when she was playing with him in the Palace, pretending to be his slave. His anger subsided somewhat and he set about trying to do as she asked. Because of his lack of experience, his clumsy efforts must have caused her agony, yet though she gasped and winced at each attempt, she somehow forbore to cry out. When he finally succeeded in getting her joints back in place, he was straddling her body and bending over her, his bare flesh touching her own. He was old enough now to be aroused and the fact of his arousal was becoming more than a little obvious.

'We'd better get dressed,' he said huskily. 'If we hang around like this, I shall begin treating you like a wife.'

'But I want to be treated like a wife,' said the Princess, clinging on to him, and Trinket, unprotesting, yielded himself to something he had known about and heard people talk about and even witnessed from his earliest childhood but whose unimaginable, intoxicating delight he had never dreamed of. He had already reached the height of bliss and was lying inert beside her when he heard the voice of the Green Girl calling outside.

'Laurie, where are you? Are you all right?'

Trinket sat up, pushing the Princess away from him.

'I'm in here,' he called back.

'Why are you still there?' she said angrily. 'What are you doing in there?'

A moment later her head appeared at the window, only to be withdrawn again with a little shriek.

'Who is that girl?' asked the Princess.

'She's my—my wife,' said Trinket.

'But I'm your wife,' said the Princess, pulling him down again and sealing his lips with a kiss. She kept him there with her for the rest of the night.

At dawn next morning, having found out where she had put his clothes, he crept silently from the room and asked the eunuchs outside what had become of his two companions. He learned that they were both unharmed but were lying still bound in an adjoining room. Too ashamed to go in and face them, he asked the eunuchs to release them and slunk back to his own room in another part of the garden to get some sleep.

He didn't see the White Nun until after noon. When he did,

he was so ashamed that he couldn't look her in the eye and he could sense that he was blushing. In spite of his fears, however, she didn't strike him dead or even upbraid him but merely remarked that the Princess was her mother's daughter and inquired after his hurts.

'If it hadn't been for you and Sister Kor,' said Trinket gratefully, 'I think she would have killed me.'

He could feel the Green Girl's eyes boring into him. They were full of hatred and indignation. Her cheeks were aflame.

'I . . . she . . . the Princess drugged me,' he stammered. 'I had to wait for the effects to wear off before I could get away.'

The White Nun blamed herself for not having given him lessons in self-defence. She offered to begin training him at once, but Trinket excused himself on the grounds that his head ached and he was still suffering from the effects of his beating.

Prince Laurie and the Willing Slave

Slowly, by short stages, their progress to the south-west continued. Each evening the Princess would send for Trinket to come to her secretly and spend the night with her. Since that first night together she had dropped her fierce ways and become gentle and docile. Trinket was the Marriage Envoy by day, but every night he became Prince Laurie and the Princess his willing slave. The bliss they had first experienced in each other's company quickly became indispensable to them. For a while Trinket went in fear and trembling that the White Nun or the Triads might find out, but soon his nights with her had become an eagerly awaited routine and he began to wish that the journey could go on for ever. The Princess's eunuchs and women were too afraid of her to talk, and Trinket was so generous with his money that most of them were in any case only too happy that a liaison which enriched them should continue.

When they reached Changsha, Doctor Lu arrived with the Leopard Embryo Antidote Pills and a message from the Leader of the Mystic Dragon Sect. The Leader was delighted with his White Dragon Marshal and urged him to keep up the good work. A brilliant future awaited him if he could obtain all six of the remaining Sutras.

'A Long Life to the Leader! Blessings be on Him!' Fat Dhuta and the doctor dutifully intoned.

'And blessings, too, on the White Dragon Marshal!' they added.

'Blessings?' thought Trinket. 'Well, I suppose I'm not doing too badly for the moment!'

The Satrap

They crossed the border of Guizhou Province and were entering the Satrap's territory. A detachment from the garrison at Luodian was waiting for them there and escorted them all the way to the Yunnan frontier. There they were met by Wu Yingxiong, who, since protocol forbade him to see or even address his future bride, addressed himself solely to Trinket, thanking him effusively for his services as Marriage Envoy and thenceforth riding with him when they were on the march.

Wu Yingxiong's arrival was the occasion of the first quarrel between Trinket and the Princess since they had become lovers. She sulked and stormed and threatened to accuse him to the Satrap of having raped her if he didn't soon think of some way of procuring her betrothed's premature demise. In the end Trinket lost patience with her and dealt her a resounding slap on the face. This produced nothing more than a giggle, but at least had the effect of restoring her good humour.

On the outskirts of Kunming, the Satrap's capital, they were greeted with the sound of trumpets while an officer rode up to them and announced that 'the Emperor's humble servant, Wu Sangui, Satrap of the West,' was approaching to 'pay his respects to her Royal Highness the Princess Ning'. Troop upon troop of cavalry in shining armour and glittering accoutrements now rode up, dismounted from their horses, which were of a tall, Western breed, and formed themselves into two facing ranks at some considerable distance apart. Through this human avenue, while the sound of trumpets was replaced by the gentler music of pipes and strings, two or three hundred boys made their way, dressed all in red and carrying silken banners, after whom, with slow, ponderous steps, strode a general who, Trinket at once guessed, must be the notorious Wu Sangui. He was a big, heavy man with a somewhat purplish complexion. In spite of his grey hairs, he still held himself very upright and looked about him with a proud, imperious air. Trinket deliberately allowed him to kneel and make his kowtow before pronouncing, on behalf of the invisible Princess, the formula that absolved a person of his age and rank from making an obeisance.

Rising to his feet again, the Satrap appeared to have been in no way put out by this incivility.

'So this is the famous Lord Wei who arrested Oboi!' he said, laughing jovially. 'My son and I are both very much beholden to you. We hope you will make yourself at home here. We'd like you to behave as if you were one of the family.'

Trinket was struck by the strong Yangzhou accent in which these words were spoken. He exaggerated his own accent in replying.

'Your Highness is very kind.'

'So you're from Yangzhou?' said Wu Sangui. 'I'm from Yangzhou too, you know. I spent much of my life in Liaodong, north of the Wall, but I was born and bred in Yangzhou—the Gaoyou district of Yangzhou. Even more reason for you to feel one of the family!'

'So you're a Gaoyou pickled egg, are you?' thought Trinket. 'Rotten luck for Yangzhou, producing a turtle-head traitor like you!'

They rode side by side into the city, where excited crowds lined the streets to watch the Imperial Princess go by. Everywhere there were flags and lanterns and decorated arches. The deafening sound of drums and cymbals was punctuated by the crackle of exploding firecrackers.

It was not in the city, however, that the Princess and her escort were to be lodged, but in a complex of buildings in the An Fu Gardens a little to the west of it. Before the Manchu conquest this had been the residence of the ducal Mu Family to which the Little Countess belonged. Wu Sangui's own residence, where he conducted Trinket after installing the Princess in the An Fu Gardens, was also outside the city. The buildings, set amidst acres of garden on the slopes of Mount Wu Hua, had been the Imperial seat of the unfortunate Yong Li, the Ming Prince who, with the support of the Mu Family, had set himself up as Emperor after the suicide of the last Ming Emperor in Peking. They were of great magnificence, having been constantly improved and augmented by Wu Sangui since the beginning of his satrapy.

A banquet had been prepared in Trinket's honour to which almost all the persons of consequence in Kunming, both soldiers and civilians, had been invited. Trinket, of course, sat next to Wu Sangui in the place of honour. After the third round of drinks,

Trinket turned beamingly to his host and addressed him in a voice which must have been audible to a great many of the guests.

'You know, Highness, when I was in Peking people were always saying that you were planning to rebel—'

The Satrap choked and his face underwent several changes of colour. The generals and high-ranking mandarins to left and right of him turned pale.

'—But I can see now that it was all nonsense,' Trinket continued.

The Satrap regained a little of his composure.

'Your lordship is too intelligent to believe all the lies that envious people tell about me,' he said.

'No, I don't believe them,' said Trinket. 'I say to myself: What would the Satrap want to rebel for? The only reason he could possibly have for rebelling would be if he wanted to become Emperor. But why should *you* want to become Emperor when you're so much better off here? Everything here, the buildings, the gardens, the furniture, the way people dress, the food—I know about that because I used to be in charge of the Palace catering— is better than in Peking. Why should you want to change it for something worse?'

A total silence had descended on the hall. Conversation, eating and drinking had all ceased. The diners sat staring, open-mouthed, wondering what this appalling boy, who had somehow become the Emperor's favourite, would say next. The Satrap inter-preted the words he had just spoken as an implied criticism of his extravagance.

'I know the importance His Majesty attaches to thrift,' he said, 'and I greatly admire him for it. But you must understand that we do not always live as luxuriously as this. It is in honour of the Princess that we have put on this show. Once the wedding is over, we shall be making big economies.'

'Oh, I don't think you should,' said Trinket. 'What's the use of being a Satrap if you can't lash out a bit? If you've got too much money, I could always help you spend it!'

The assembled diners heaved a great sigh of relief. So that's what all this was about! He wanted to be bribed! The tension resolved itself in smiles, the buzz of conversation rose again, eating and drinking continued, and when the banquet ended, the guests went off in great good humour, calculating how much they should give.

After the banquet it was the Satrap's son, Wu Yingxiong, who saw Trinket back to the An Fu Gardens. Before taking leave of Trinket, he handed him a brocade-covered box.

'This is a little money to be getting on with if you have any minor expenses while you are here. Before you leave my father will, of course, think of a more fitting way of thanking you for your trouble.'

Trinket opened the box as soon as he had gone. It contained ten wads of forty five-hundred-tael banknotes each : two hundred thousand taels in all.

'If this is just for pocket money,' he thought, 'I wonder what I could screw them for if I needed a lot. Two million?'

Next day there was a military review at which Trinket stood side by side with the Satrap on the reviewing stand while regiment after regiment paraded in front of them and executed various manœuvres. Trinket knew next to nothing about military matters but took it on himself to remark that the picked troops of the Emperor's own regiment, the Valiants, of which he himself was Colonel, were no match for these. At that moment a cannon was fired and he disgraced himself by turning pale and falling back into a chair. The Satrap was beginning to view this Imperial Envoy— and consequently the Imperial Master he represented—with contempt.

When the reviewing was over, Trinket produced the Edict he had brought with him from Kang Xi. The Satrap found that he had to read it himself, since Trinket was unable to. He did so in a fine parade-ground voice while the soldiers knelt to hear it. The Edict praised the Satrap in flowery language and concluded by awarding promotion to all the officers and men of his army. After facing northwards to kowtow, he led the troops in giving three cheers for the Emperor. The disciplined roar that went up from the ranks below nearly caused Trinket to disgrace himself again. This time, fortunately, he managed to stay on his feet.

From the parade-ground they went to the Satrap's palace to discuss the date of the wedding. The Satrap suggested the fourth of the following month as an auspicious day, but Trinket objected that it was too soon. Though the Satrap thought he was fishing for more bribes, his real reason for objecting was that once the Princess was married, his nights as Prince Laurie would be over. After some discussion, they settled for the sixteenth.

News from the Black Hole

Back at the An Fu Gardens a small crowd of Yunnanese officers and mandarins were waiting for Trinket with their 'presents'. Having thanked them somewhat perfunctorily and seen them off, he began to wonder why so far he had seen nothing of the one person in Yunnan he had been looking forward to meeting: his old friend Yang Yizhi.

Since Trinket and Yang Yizhi had first got to know each other when Yang was a member of the bodyguard that accompanied Wu Yingxiong to Peking, it was to Wu Yingxiong that Trinket now sent, requesting him to arrange for Yang to pay him a visit. Instead of Yang Yizhi, however, it was Wu himself who turned up.

Unfortunately, he said, Yang was away on business. When pressed for details, he answered evasively. When had Yang left? Recently. When would he be back? Not for a long time. Where had he gone to? Er, er, to Tibet. What important business had taken him to Tibet? Oh, nothing special. Trinket felt sure that the Satrap and his son knew of his friendship with Yang. It seemed extraordinary that they should have sent him away just before he was due to arrive. Sensing something fishy, he summoned his officer friends, Zhao Qixian and Zhang Kangnian, as soon as Wu had gone and asked them to find out what they could about Yang Yizhi by fraternizing with their counterparts in the Satrap's bodyguard.

That night, when Zhao and Zhang came back to report their findings, he was playing dice with some of their fellow-officers, having walked out on the Princess after another quarrel. (Its cause was her discovery that the wedding-date had been fixed.) Excusing himself, he retired with them to another room, where they told him that, while drinking and gambling with the Satrap's officers, they had learned that Yang had not in fact gone to Tibet but had been arrested and thrown into prison for some offence. One of the officers had volunteered that he was being held in the Black Hole, a notorious prison some two miles south-west of the Satrap's palace, but the others had said no, that was nonsense, the man was drunk. At that point they had thought it best to ask no more questions for fear of exciting suspicion. Trinket thanked them, and, leaving them to take his place at the gaming-table, went off to confer with the Triads.

The Triads welcomed what they saw as an opportunity for some action.

'Leave it to us, Master!' said Brother Li. 'We'll rescue your friend Yang for you! Even if we don't succeed, the Old Traitor will think we are acting on the Emperor's wishes, and either he'll be too scared to do anything or he'll rebel, which is what we want him to do.'

Trinket didn't see how they could get back to Peking alive if the two provinces they had first to get through on their way back were in rebellion; however, he thought it best to say nothing, leaving that problem to be faced when it arose. After discussion it was decided that they would set off first thing next morning for the Black Hole, wearing uniforms of the Satrap's own guards as disguise, while the Master entertained the Little Traitor, both to keep him occupied and so that he could be held as a hostage in the event of things going wrong.

Trinket waited until noon next day before inviting Wu Yingxiong. The invitation was ostensibly to discuss the wedding, but when Wu arrived with his bodyguard at the An Fu Gardens, a splendid reception was waiting for him. Instead of discussing business, he and Trinket sat feasting and watching plays, while Trinket's soldiers kept an eye on his bodyguard. At one point, when they were watching a noisy 'military' piece and the frenzy of action on the stage had reached its height, Trinket felt someone plucking at his sleeve. When he turned to look, it was Brother Gao, dressed as one of the Satrap's guards. As if in response to Trinket's unspoken question, he nodded and then quietly slipped away. Trinket rose to his feet.

'Just go on watching, Your Grace,' he said. 'I've got to go outside a minute to have a piss.'

'Take your time, my lord, I shall be all right on my own,' said Wu Yingxiong; but what he was thinking as he smiled politely was: 'Crude little guttersnipe!'

Trinket hurried to a room behind the hall where the Triads were waiting for him.

'Excellent!' he said. 'I hope no one got hurt. Did you manage to rescue him?'

The men remained grimly silent. He looked round at their faces. Something must be wrong.

'That Wu Sangui is a savage!' said Brother Gao passionately. He and Brother Xu went out and presently returned carrying a bloodstained carpet between them in which lay a man. They set him down gently on the floor and opened out the carpet. The body was covered, leaving only the head exposed. It was Yang Yizhi. His face was completely drained of colour and his eyes were tightly closed. Trinket approached and bent over him.

'Yang, my friend! Brother!' he said. 'You'll be all right now. We've rescued you.'

The head moved, almost imperceptibly. It was impossible to tell whether or not he had heard. Very gently Brother Xu drew back the cover. What Trinket then saw made him recoil in horror. If Butcher Qian hadn't caught him, he would have fallen to the floor. Yang's hands had been severed at the wrist and his legs cut off at the knee.

'They cut out his tongue, too,' said Brother Xu, 'and put out both his eyes.'

Trinket began crying. Suddenly his grief turned to anger. He took out his dagger.

'Monster!' he cried. 'Cruel fucking monster! I'll cut him up into pieces!'

He would have rushed back into the hall if Brother Feng had not restrained him.

'Easy now!' said that man of few words. 'Think before you act!'

Trinket calmed down a little, though still crying bitterly.

'Why did he do this to him?' he said. 'It can't just be because he and I are friends.'

'We've brought someone along with us who might know the answer to that,' said Brother Xu.

He went out and came back a few moments later, dragging a pale, fat man dressed in the robes of a seventh-grade mandarin and dumped him down on the floor, where he remained, cowering abjectly on all fours.

'This, Master, is someone you've heard of but not met. This is Lu Yifeng.'

'Ah, Mr Lu,' said Trinket, 'I heard about the fuss you made in Peking and how your master the Satrap's Heir rewarded you by breaking both your legs. What on earth are you doing here?'

He kicked him in the mouth by way of encouragement, dislodging three of his teeth.

'He's Governor of the Black Hole prison now,' said Brother

Xu. 'Just fancy! Making things a bit difficult for us he was. Said he wanted to see something in writing before he would hand over his prisoner. We thought it would be easiest to bring him along with us.'

'I've got to go back now, or the Little Traitor will get suspicious,' said Trinket. 'See if you can make him talk. If he gives you any trouble, just cut his hands and feet off!'

'I'll talk, I'll talk,' said the wretched man, spitting out blood and teeth.

Trinket dried his eyes and tried to compose himself a bit before going back to the hall. To his surprise he found it in total silence, the actors he had last seen performing acrobatics standing motionless and mute upon the stage. Wu Yingxiong had made them wait for Lord Wei's return.

'Sorry I was so long,' said Trinket. 'The Princess called me in to see her. She'd heard that I was entertaining you and she wanted to hear all about you—your taste in clothes, what you like to eat, that type of stuff. It was quite hard to get away from her.'

Young Wu was delighted.

'Oh, that's all right,' he said. 'It was worth the wait!'

When the interrupted play had ended he took his leave. As soon as he had gone, Trinket hurried back to rejoin the Triads, but they were nowhere to be seen. It was not till late that night that they turned up again, this time with another prisoner. Brother Xu explained. During the working-over they had subjected him to, Lu Yifeng had indeed revealed the reason why Yang had fallen foul of the Satrap. For some time now the Satrap had been in frequent contact with the Mongol Prince Galdan. Messages and gifts were constantly being exchanged between them and recently a Mongol envoy by the name of Hatiemo had arrived in Kunming and had talks with the Satrap lasting several days. Lu genuinely seemed not to know what they were about, but Yang evidently did and had infuriated the Satrap by remonstrating with him. The Satrap had no doubt been afraid that Yang, through his friendship with Trinket, might leak the information to the Emperor and had punished him in this ghastly way as a warning to his fellow-officers.

Trinket remembered Galdan from his visit to the Shaolin Monastery in the company of the sinister Grand Lama Sangge and the Blue Girl in her ridiculous disguise. He went to take a peep at this prisoner who was Galdan's envoy: a crafty-looking man with shifty eyes and a brownish beard.

'Take him to have a look at my friend Yang,' he said.

Two of them led him off between them. When they brought him back a couple of minutes later, he was pale and shaking.

'I don't like lies,' said Trinket. 'That man you've just seen told too many lies. I had to punish him, every time he lied. How many lies do you think he told? How many bits and pieces is he missing?'

'Seven,' said the man huskily after a little silence.

'The Satrap doesn't like lies either,' said Trinket. 'He always says that the best way to find out if a person has been lying is to wait a while and then ask him to repeat what he told you. If it's different the second time round, you know he's lying. He's got this idea that Mongols are fibbers, so he's asked me to try the test on you.'

Hatiemo's face assumed an expression of injured pride.

'The sons of Genghiz Khan are honest men,' he said angrily. 'We tell no lies.'

'I'm glad to hear it,' said Trinket. 'Now, do you know who I am?'

The crafty expression returned. Hatiemo looked about him. He was in a sort of palace. The Triads, who appeared to be in Trinket's service, were dressed in the Satrap's uniforms. Trinket himself was wearing the hat with a ruby button and a peacock's feather in it that distinguished an officer of the First Grade, and the yellow jacket normally only awarded to persons in high standing at Court. Such high rank in one so young could only be due to the status of his father. Undoubtedly this must be a younger son of the Satrap. He bowed respectfully.

'Forgive me, my lord, for not recognizing a son of His Highness.'

'Oh, that's all right,' said Trinket. 'It's clever of you to have guessed. I'm not surprised Prince Galdan chose you for his envoy. How is the Prince, by the way? It's quite a long time now since I last saw him.'

The Mongol brightened.

'You know His Highness, then?'

'He's a very good friend of mine,' said Trinket. 'Does he still see much of the Reverend Sangge? And that young lady who always dresses in blue—what's her name now—Ah Ki?'

'You know about them, too?'

Hatiemo was now totally convinced that he was speaking to a younger brother of the Little Traitor. He became quite expansive when Trinket insisted on pressing four five-hundred-tael banknotes on him, 'to have a little fun before you leave Kunming' as Trinket put it.

'You mustn't mind being grilled,' he told Hatiemo. 'My father's a bit peculiar in this way. In any case, this is a very important business and he wants to get everything crystal clear.'

'I don't mind at all,' said Hatiemo. 'He is right to be careful.'

It was in this way that Trinket managed, step by step, to extract every detail of Wu Sangui's plans while pretending that he knew about them already. There was to be a rising of the Three Satraps: Wu Sangui in the West, Geng Jingzhong and Shang Kexi in the East. In return for large territorial concessions, three foreign powers, Mongolia, Tibet, and Russia, would simultaneously invade China in support of the rebels. At sea they would be supported by the Leader of the Mystic Dragon Sect, who (it transpired) was in Russian pay. Hatiemo called the Russians 'Losha', the name that the Chinese gave to the man-eating demons of Buddhist mythology. It was calculated that the Manchu bowmen and pikemen would be helpless against the Russians' firearms. After the Manchus had been defeated, the Living Buddha of Tibet would take over Sichuan; Inner Mongolia, Suiyuan, Chahar, and Jehol would go to the Mongols; everything north of Shanhaiguan (most of Manchuria) would be occupied by the Russians; and the Leader of the Mystic Dragon Sect would get the offshore islands, including Taiwan and Hainan. Wu Sangui would become Emperor of all China except for Sichuan and the above-mentioned outlying parts of the Empire, while the other two Satraps, having served their purpose, would be quietly eliminated.

Trinket's knowledge of geography was minimal, but he understood enough of what he was being told to feel sorry for the Young Emperor. What worried him most was the thought of the Russian firearms. His heart still quaked when he remembered the man-made thunder of the cannon they had fired at the military review. Though he said 'Excellent, excellent!' he must have looked unhappy, for Hatiemo sensed that something about these plans must be worrying him and begged him to say what it was. Did he think too much territory was being conceded? Trinket didn't know how to answer this, but then he remembered what Father Obscurus had said about the struggle for succession between Zheng Keshuang and his brothers that was going on in Taiwan.

'What does it matter to me how much land my father has,' he said bitterly. 'When the time comes, it will all go to my brother.'

Hatiemo was familiar with succession struggles among the Mongol princes.

'Don't be so sure of that, sir,' he said with a smile. 'You have Prince Galdan's friendship, and I promise my own humble support. Who knows what the future may bring?'

'One of these days,' said Trinket, 'when I'm powerful, I'll remember to reward you. Look, I've got to go now and report all this to my father. Just make yourself comfortable here until I come back.' He lowered his voice. 'Don't, whatever you do, let anyone else know about our talk. If my brother got to hear of it he'd kill me.'

Rejoining the Triads, he told two of them, Brother Feng and Brother Xu, to keep a strict watch on Hatiemo and stop him straying while he went with the rest of them to look at Yang.

Yang's body had moved since they left him. It now lay obliquely, half off the carpet. There were some bloody marks beside it that looked like writing. Brother Gao thought they were the characters for 'Wu' and 'rebel'. When they touched him they found that he was dead: before he died, he must have made this supreme effort to warn his friends by writing the characters in blood with one of his stumps. Although from the Triads' point of view he was a devoted servant of their most hated enemy, they knew him for a brave man and a trusty friend. Several of them were in tears, and one of them observed bitterly that this was how the Great Traitor rewarded those who were loyal to him.

Their feelings against the Satrap became even more embittered when they learned about his grandiose plans.

'Selling his country to foreigners is getting to be a habit,' said Father Obscurus. 'If those Russians with their firearms come here, we are all of us done for.'

'Firearms are terrible things,' agreed Brother Li. 'We shall have to find a kungfu that will enable us to stand up to them.'

'Not possible,' said Father Obscurus. 'Here, look at this!'

He bared his torso for them to see. There was a dreadful round, puckered scar the size of a teacup on one side of his chest and a ten-inch-long, seam-like scar over his left shoulder. Then he told Trinket the story of how he had got them.

His family had been frontiersmen who traded in furs—mostly in sables and silver fox. Once when he was a lad he had gone out with his father and uncle and cousins on one of their expeditions to buy furs. Returning with their purchases, they had encountered a party of Russians armed with guns. The Russians had shot them all, including their three-man escort, and taken their furs and money. He alone had escaped, though badly wounded, by feigning dead. Finding himself, when he finally made his way back to civilization, with neither family nor livelihood, he had become a Taoist. Twenty years later he still had nightmares about the Russians.

Trinket's main concern now was to warn the Emperor, but he could hardly say this to the Triads. In any case, there was the even more pressing problem of the one dead man and two live prisoners who had somehow to be disposed of before the Satrap discovered what had been going on. To the Triads' astonishment, he proposed to solve two-thirds of the problem by sending Yang's body and Lu Yifeng back to the prison. Somewhat reluctantly Brother Gao went to fetch Lu Yifeng. Once more the wretched man, now much the worse for wear, was dumped on the floor in front of Trinket.

'Ah, our old friend Mr Lu!' said Trinket brightly. 'I'm afraid we've given you rather a bad time!'

'No,' Lu Yifeng mumbled fearfully. 'Not at all.'

'Now, Mr Lu,' said Trinket, 'you've done us an excellent turn by telling us the Satrap's secrets, and as one good turn deserves another, I give you my word of honour that we won't tell him or anyone else that you've been so helpful. Of course—ha ha ha!—if you want to tell him yourself, that's up to you.'

'I wouldn't dare,' said Lu Yifeng, speaking with difficulty through his broken teeth, 'I swear I wouldn't.'

'Good. Then see Mr Lu back to the prison, will you?' said Trinket to the Triads. 'And take the dead prisoner back too. We don't want Mr Lu getting into trouble because his prisoner's missing.'

The Triads were unhappy about this and obeyed him reluctantly. Trinket for his part felt sure that Lu was too scared to report his kidnapping.

The Satrap's Study

A week later, when they were still nervously expecting a reaction from the Satrap, Trinket told them that, to set their minds at rest, he would go in person to the Satrap and sound him out to see if he knew about it.

'Suppose he detains you,' said Brother Xu. 'What do we do then?'

'We're all in his power here,' said Trinket. 'He could lock the lot of us up if he felt like it. It won't make any difference if I go or not.'

He prepared for a formal visit, selecting members both of the Valiants and of the Palace Guards for his escort. The Satrap, warned of his coming, was waiting for him outside the gate of his palace. He received the young Envoy with jovial affability, taking him by the hand to lead him inside.

'My dear Lord Wei, you don't need to call on me,' he said. 'Just send for my son if there's anything you want. Make use of him!'

'I can't possibly do that,' said Trinket. 'I'm far too junior.'

'Junior?' said the Satrap, laughing. 'Why, one of these days you might be my successor.'

Trinket looked startled. What, he wondered, was the old fox playing at?

'I think Your Highness is joking.'

'Not at all,' said the Satrap. 'The Emperor thinks highly of you. Anything is possible. How old are you now—fifteen? sixteen? Already you are a Colonel in the Palace Guards, an Imperial Envoy, a Viscount. A few years from now you'll be an Earl, then a Marquess, then a Duke. The next step after that makes you a Highness. You could easily be Satrap here in twenty years' time.'

'No, no,' said Trinket. 'I know you're definitely wrong there. You see, before I left Peking the Emperor said, "Trinket, I want to be quite sure of the Satrap's loyalty. I'm marrying my sister to his son, and if I can be quite certain of their loyalty, I'm thinking of giving the Satrapy to the family in per . . . per . . ."'

'Perpetuity?'

'That's it.'

The Satrap beamed.

'Did he really say that? So do you think I am loyal to the Emperor?'

'If you aren't, I can't think who is,' said Trinket.

'Come with me,' said the Satrap. 'Let me show you my study.'

The 'study' was conspicuously devoid of books. It was more

like an armoury, its walls hung everywhere with weapons, including a number of firearms—mementoes, presumably, of the Satrap's numerous campaigns. There was one book, however. On the corner of a table that served the Satrap as a desk Trinket's sharp eyes discerned a copy of the familiar *Sutra in Forty-Two Sections*, this one with a plain blue cover. His busy brain at once set to work to think of a plan for getting his hands on it. To play for time while he was thinking, he began asking questions about the furnishings of the room. There was, for example, an armchair covered with a black and white striped fur. It was the skin of a rare white tiger, shot with his own hands by the Satrap in the course of his campaigns north of the Wall. This supplied conversation for several minutes. The carved pictures on a large screen proved an even more fertile topic.

Just as the Satrap, wondering what the purpose of this visit could be, was beginning to grow impatient, Trinket thought of a plan.

'Your Highness,' he said, speaking in a low voice and looking very solemn, 'I have a Secret Instruction for you from the Emperor.'

The Satrap jumped to his feet and stood respectfully to attention.

'Perhaps I shouldn't tell you today,' said Trinket, as if having second thoughts. 'It's a very, very important matter. It's something the Emperor wants you to do, but he said he wasn't sure he could trust you with it. He said I was to sound you out first and make absolutely certain of your loyalty before I told you what it was. I think I'd better leave it till tomorrow.'

'I'll wait on you at the An Fu Gardens tomorrow, then,' said the Satrap.

'No,' said Trinket, 'there are too many ears there. It had better be here. I'll come here tomorrow. At the same time.'

The Satrap despised the youthful Emperor as a hare-brained boy and wondered what the nature of this 'important' task could be that he wanted him to perform. He had an even greater contempt for this young Envoy whom he now showed out of the palace with every show of deference. At the same time he felt rather pleased. It was clear that they trusted him.

Outfoxing the Fox

When Trinket arrived at the appointed time next day, the Satrap showed him straight into his study. Trinket came to the point at once.

'This Secret Instruction thing I've got to tell you about,' he said, '. . . it's so important and so secret, the Emperor says it's best you don't mention it even in your most secret documents.'

'I understand,' said the Satrap. 'It will go no further than this room.'

Trinket leant over and whispered in his ear.

'Shang Kexi and Geng Jingzhong are planning to rebel.'

The Satrap changed colour.

'Surely not? Can this be true?' His voice was shaking.

'Afraid so,' said Trinket. 'At first the Emperor didn't want to believe it, but the evidence is so strong he's had no choice. They haven't actually rebelled yet, so he doesn't want to begin moving Imperial troops against them in case it puts them on their guard. What he wants you to do is to move your troops towards the Guangxi-Guangdong border—you could do this without their sus-pecting anything—and then you can strike quickly as soon as there's any sign of a rising. He says Shang's an old fool and Geng's a young idiot. With your experience and the crack troops under your command you could probably capture the two of them and deliver them to the Court in chains without a single Imperial soldier having to be moved.'

The Satrap smiled. This Secret Instruction would enable him to move troops in preparation for the rising he himself was planning without the scatterbrained boy-Emperor suspecting anything.

'As guardians of the frontier, my armies are as well equipped and well trained as the Imperial forces,' he said. 'You can assure His Majesty that we will discharge our duty with unswerving devotion as soon as he gives the word.'

The idea of a Secret Instruction was Trinket's, but he was inca-pable of inventing one on his own. He had had to consult the Triads about it the night before. It was Tertius, the most intelligent member of the Green Wood Lodge, who had suggested getting Wu Sangui to move troops against his fellow satraps. The troop movements would be interpreted by the Emperor to mean that Wu Sangui was rebelling. For once the old fox was being outfoxed.

Having dealt with the Secret Instruction, Trinket turned his attention to more important matters. He pointed to one of the firearms on the wall.

'Highness,' he said, 'is that what they call a firearm?'

'Yes,' said the Satrap, 'it's a Russian musket—a souvenir of one of my campaigns on the North-East Frontier. A very fine weapon.'

'Highness,' said Trinket, 'I've never fired a firearm. Do you think I could have a go?'

'Of course you can,' said the Satrap, smiling indulgently. 'But that musket is a field weapon for use in battle—a bit clumsy for you to begin with. Let me find you something a bit more handy.'

He went to a cupboard that stood against the wall, pulled out a drawer in it and took out a redwood case containing a brace of pistols, each about a foot long. While he had his back turned, Trinket, who was standing at one end of the Satrap's desk, abstracted a copy of the *Sutra in Forty-Two Sections* from the capacious inside pocket of his yellow jacket and exchanged it for the copy on the desk. This manœuvre was executed with such speed and finesse that he had the Satrap's copy in his pocket and his jacket buttoned up again several seconds before the Satrap turned towards him holding the case of pistols.

The copy he had substituted for the one on the Satrap's desk was the bordered blue one he had taken from the false Empress Dowager's closet. The night before this visit he had removed the red border from it so that it exactly resembled the Satrap's plain blue one.

The Satrap took out one of the pistols, rammed some black powder and three little iron bullets down the muzzle with a little ramrod, lit the fuse-like 'match' with fire from a tinder-box, and handed the weapon to Trinket. Propelling him towards an open window, he instructed him how to aim the pistol and fire. Trinket took aim at a rockery in the garden outside and pulled the trigger. There was a deafening bang and a burst of hot air seemed to sear his face. The jolt to his arm caused him to drop the pistol and stagger backwards, his head enveloped in a cloud of acrid smoke. The Satrap roared with laughter.

'Powerful things, firearms, aren't they!'

'Tamardy!' said Trinket. 'These Western things are diabolical!'

'Look!' said the Satrap, pointing to the rockery. A substantial piece had been blown off the corner of it.

'If it had been a man, it'd be a goner,' said Trinket, stooping to pick up the pistol and replacing it beside its fellow in the case.

Just at that moment one of the Satrap's guards came running in and had to be reassured that nothing untoward had happened.

The Satrap took up the case of pistols and held it out to Trinket.

'Here, take these little fellows to amuse yourself with!'

'Oh no, I couldn't,' said Trinket. 'You'll be needing these for your own defence.'

The Satrap pushed the box into his hands.

'Come on, you're a friend of the family now. What's mine is yours.'

'But these are valuable foreign things,' said Trinket. 'You may not be able to replace them.' ('Bet you will though,' he thought.)

'I wouldn't offer them to you if they weren't hard to get,' said the Satrap. 'Go on, take them!'

Trinket thanked him profusely.

'You may have saved my life,' he said. 'In future, if anyone goes for me, I shall shoot him with one of these.'

'I don't know about that,' said the Satrap. 'These foreign firearms are very powerful things, but they take a long time to fire. A good archer can shoot half a dozen arrows in the time it takes to fire a musket. If the foreign devils could make a firearm that shot as fast as a bowman, that would be another matter.'

Trinket thanked him some more before taking his leave.

Disposing of a Corpse

When he got back to his lodging in the An Fu Gardens, Trinket locked himself in his room, took out the Satrap's copy of the Sutra and unstitched the cover. He shook out the cut-up pieces of parchment from inside the cover, then fetched the bag containing the cut-up pieces from the seven other copies of the Sutra, and emptied it on top of them. Here now in this little pile was the Tartars' great secret! It made his head ache to think of the time and effort it would take to piece them all together to make the map; still, just to have them all in one pile at last was a triumph. It would have been even better if there had been someone else there he could share his triumph with and show off a bit to; all the same, he could not help feeling pleased. Leaning back in the chair and cocking a leg over his knee he began singing softly to himself—one of his favourites from those far-off days in the brothel.

A cup of wine I've poured you here,
Now tell me where you're from, my dear.
Yangzhou.

There's four and twenty bridges there
And on the bridges girls beyond compare.
Tell me . . .

His singing was interrupted by three knocks on the door. This was followed, after a little pause, by two more knocks, then by another three: the Triads' code. Quickly sweeping the parchment pieces into the bag and stowing it away, he went to open the door. Brother Xu and Brother Gao were standing there looking grim. They followed him inside.

'Is something the matter?' he asked.

'We've just been told that the Traitor's guards are looking everywhere for a Mongol. Obviously it's Hatiemo. From what we can make out, they suspect us of holding him. What are we to do, Master?'

'Tie him up and hide him under my bed,' said Trinket. 'They wouldn't dare to search my room.'

'Not when you're here,' said Brother Xu. 'But they might when you're off somewhere else.'

'Not if you tell them they can't,' said Trinket. 'They're not going to fight you about it.'

Just at that moment Butcher Qian burst in.

'The Traitor's going to set this place on fire!'

'What?' cried the other three in unison.

'I've been going round these Gardens lately keeping an eye on things in case the Old Traitor tries any funny business. Today I noticed a lot of movement in that little wood on the west side of the Gardens, and I got suspicious. When I went to look I found they'd been stacking a whole lot of kerosene and saltpetre and sulphur there. Just the sort of things you'd need for starting a big fire.'

'Tamardy!' said Trinket. 'He's not planning to burn the Princess, surely?'

'I doubt it,' said Butcher Qian. 'Much more likely he suspects we've got Hatiemo here. He can't very well ask to search the place or accuse us of kidnapping him, so he's planning to start a fire. Then he can send a horde of his people in here to put it out. That will give them the excuse to hunt anywhere they like.'

'That sounds like the sort of thing the old fox *would* think of,' said Trinket. 'So what shall we do about it?'

Butcher Qian drew a finger across his throat.

'Kill the man they're looking for and get rid of his corpse.'

'Hm,' said Trinket. 'The trouble is, this Hatty guy is the best proof we have that the Old Traitor is planning to rebel. If we can, we ought to smuggle him back to Peking so that the Young Emperor can question him.'

'Well, there are two things, then, that we've got to work out,' said Butcher Qian. 'The first is, what are we going to do about this fire. The second is, how are we going to get Hatiemo out of the Traitor's territory, bearing in mind that Yunnan and Guizhou provinces are going to be full of people looking out for him. Even getting him out of Kunming isn't going to be all that easy.'

'What about one of your China-root pigs?' said Trinket, grinning.

'Might do to get him out of Kunming,' said Butcher Qian, 'but I doubt you'd get him over the frontier that way. Smuggling him out in a coffin wouldn't do, either. That old trick's been played so many times, they'd be sure to catch on.'

'All right,' said Trinket, 'here's another way to do it. Shave his beard off, rub a bit of flour or something on his face, and dress him up as a guard. I'll choose a little detachment of the guards to go back to Peking with a whatyoucallit from the Princess to the Emperor and the Empress Dowager reporting the date of her wedding. We can stick old Hatty in the middle—after you've closed his dumb points to stop him using his voice—and make him march with the rest. The Traitor's men at the border aren't going to ask members of the Palace Guards to answer a roll-call—they wouldn't have the nerve.'

This plan met with the admiring approval of the other three.

Trinket thought for a bit.

'There must be whore-houses in Kunming.'

'Of course there are,' said Butcher Qian. 'Plenty of them.'

'Do you think we could get Father Obscurus to go to a whore-housew'

Butcher Qian shook his head.

'No way, Taoists aren't allowed to. I'll go with you if you fancy a visit.'

'I'm sure you would,' said Trinket, 'but you don't look right. Father Obscurus is just about the same shape and height as Hatty.'

'I'm sure Father Obscurus would be willing to go if he knew it was in the interests of the Society,' said Brother Gao.

This made them all laugh.

'Get him to dress up in Hatty's clothing,' said Trinket. 'And he mustn't forget his bits and pieces—the things in his pockets and so on. The rest of you dress up as officers of the Satrap. Choose a big, smart whore-house to visit and act very drunk and disorderly. Quarrel over the girls. In the rumpus you, Brother Qian, most unfortunately, will stab Father Obscurus to death.'

For a moment Butcher Qian looked startled, then realizing that Trinket was planning to fake Hatiemo's death, he entered into the spirit of the thing.

'I wonder if Father Obscurus knows a few words of Mongol. I can do a good imitation Mongol if we've got to quarrel. You'll need a body to put in his place, of course.'

'That's another job for you,' said Trinket. 'Somewhere in Kunming you've got to find a corpse about the same size as Hatty and have it ready somewhere outside the whorehouse. So when you've "killed" Father Obscurus, you chase all the whores out of the whore-house—if they haven't run out already—and Father Obscurus comes to life again and changes clothes with the corpse.'

'Yes,' said Brother Gao eagerly, 'and we'll have to mess up the corpse's face a bit so that it's not recognizable. And put Hatiemo's beard that we've cut off under the bed where we leave the corpse, so that when they find it they'll think that the murderer was trying to make Hatiemo unrecognizable.'

'Brilliant!' said Trinket. 'Brother Gao always thinks of everything.'

He laughed.

'This is going to be great fun,' he said. 'I wish I could go with you! Excellent kungfu!'

RUSSIA

Altai Mts.

Lake Balkash

Dzungars

Urumqi

Tashkent

Tian Mts.

Turfan

Hami

Samarkand

CHINESE TURKESTAN

Kashgar

Dunhuang

Yarkand

GANSU

Kunlun Mts.

KASHMIR

Kokonor

QINGHAI

TIBET

Himalayas

Lhasa

INDIA

Bhutan

YUNNAN

BURMA

**CHINA IN THE
SEVENTEENTH
CENTURY**

SIAM